NEW

GW00676532

New Writing 8 is the eighth volume of an annual anthology which promotes the best in contemporary literature. It brings together some of our most formidable talent, placing new names alongside more established ones, and includes poetry, essays, short stories and extracts from novels in progress. Distinctive, innovative and entertaining, it is essential reading for all those interested in British writing today. *New Writing 8* is published by Vintage, in association with the British Council.

Tibor Fischer was born in 1959. His first novel, *Under the Frog*, was shortlisted for the Booker Prize in 1993. *The Thought Gang* appeared in 1994 and *The Collector Collector* in 1997. He is presenter of 'Books Abroad' on BBC Radio 3.

Lawrence Norfolk was born in 1963. He is the author of two novels, *Lemprière's Dictionary* (1991) and *The Pope's Rhinoceros* (1996). He lives in London.

Also available from Vintage

New Writing 4
ed. A. S. Byatt and Alan Hollinghurst

New Writing 5
ed. Christopher Hope and Peter Porter

New Writing 6
ed. A. S. Byatt and Peter Porter

New Writing 7
ed. Carmen Callil and Craig Raine

PREFACE

New Writing 8 is the eighth volume of an annual anthology founded in 1992 to provide an outlet for new short stories, work in progress, poetry and essays by established and new writers working in Britain or in the English language. The book is designed primarily as a forum for British writers, and the main object is to present a multi-faceted picture of modern Britain; contributions from English-language writers of non-British nationality will occasionally be accepted if they contribute to this aim. It was designed by the British Council's Literature Department to respond to the strong interest in the newest British writing overseas, where access to fresh developments is often difficult. It is hoped that, over the years, and under changing editors, it will provide a stimulating, varied and reasonably reliable guide to the cultural and especially the literary scene in Britain during the 1990s.

New Writing 9, edited by John Fowles and A. L. Kennedy, will appear in March 2000. Though some work is commissioned, submissions of unpublished material for consideration (stories, poetry, essays and extracts from forthcoming works of fiction) are welcome. Two copies of submissions should be sent: they should be double-spaced, with page numbers (*no* staples), and accompanied by a stamped addressed envelope for the return of the material, if it cannot be used. They should be sent to *New Writing*, Literature Department, The British Council, 11 Portland Place, London W1N 4EJ. The deadline for *New Writing 9* is 30 April 1999.

CONTENTS

vii

CONTENTS

CONTENTS

ix

INTRODUCTION

THE MAKERS OF anthologies and their contributors are at each other's mercies. The latter can only offer their work, and the former can only accept or reject from whatever arrives in the mail. So haphazard a process means that books of this sort are more subject than most to the vagaries of chance.

Given the volume of submissions, any editing beyond selection and basic proof-reading was a practical impossibility. We read an ever-increasing flow of manuscripts over a one-year period, and we both read everything. The novelty of it soon wore off and yet, at some level and from whatever depth of weariness, we retained a capacity to be surprised and excited. No one had read these pages before and with the good, the bad, and the mad coming at us so promiscuously we never knew what might turn up next.

Our initial reaction to the submissions placed before us was, however, disappointment. Competent but mediocre writing is somehow more depressing than the frankly atrocious. This dispelled the myth that there existed in some unspecified 'out there' a vast reserve of undiscovered talent. Our problem, we thought, would be finding enough pages that we could bear to print.

Predictably, we soon enough faced the opposite problem. The full submission formed a manuscript pile which reached shoulder-height; a little over six hundred pieces in all. 'Editing', we discovered, is an unfunny business. We disagreed frequently, argued inevitably, conceded grudgingly and commiserated mawkishly. The third member of our troika, Harriet Harvey Wood, policed these shenanigans with unflappable calm, and continued to send us packages of manuscripts. Her accompanying letters expanded the term 'terse' until it encompassed a range of meanings stretching from 'outraged' to 'speechless with mirth'. Only the terms of our remit prevented us from including them but they, and their author, should be saved for the nation.

The anthology before you is something over five hundred pages long. It could have been eight hundred, but no more, for after that came a precipitous drop in quality. Writing, we discovered, is a 'sheep and goats' business. There were those who could, and there were those who palpably could not, and there was very little in the vast middle ground between these two camps. This came as a shock, but it made our work easier – until we whittled the pieces we liked down to the aforementioned eight hundred pages. The disagreements began there.

Nothing in the pages that follow has our grudging assent. We were surprised, delighted, piqued, and occasionally baffled by the material we both liked. And yet we had to choose. Procrustes took great pleasure in cutting up his guests to fit his bed. We did not. Those whom we wished – but were unable – to include have our apologies, particularly the unpublished writers amongst them. We are left with a lingering sense that apologies are no substitute for deserved inclusion.

The brief for *New Writing* is to provide a 'snapshot' of what has been happening in British literature over a one-year period. We took that brief at its word and sought to include work from both margins of the literary spectrum, namely experimental and mass-market writing. The former is normally admired in theory and ignored in practice; the latter is read avidly and yet denigrated by critics who are impotent in the face of its appeal to ordinary readers. The habitual exclusion of either or both from venues of this kind rests on a complacent stigmatisation of familiar forms as 'too easy' and unfamiliar ones as 'too difficult'. The Balkanisation of British literature is a problem of perception rather than reality.

The picture we have taken is diverse, but still coherent. We recognised the amount and degree of formal experimentation, within and without the habitual forms of poetry and prose. Amongst fiction-writers, the trend for shock tactics seems to have run its course and been replaced by a greater depth of inquiry: the truly penetrating critique is better accomplished by the pen than the chainsaw. In poetry, the ironic and allusive predominated over the declamatory, and the fabular trumped the straightforwardly descriptive. The scope and quality of the essays indicated to us both a revival within the genre, and a paucity of venues other than *New Writing* in which to publish them. Most of all though, and across the board, we were struck by a new imaginative mobility.

The British literary consciousness has always been a versatile instrument, but a firmly rooted one too. When Shakespeare sent one of his 'Two Gentlemen of Verona' to Milan by sea instead of land, he inaugurated a venerable tradition of British writers whose works have ventured abroad and got things wrong. However, the greater error has been the subsequent charge of insularity grafted on to such mistakes. On the evidence we have seen, that misperception is no longer tenable. Whether British-based writers have been reading what the Empire has written back (in Salman Rushdie's phrase) and have found it within themselves to do some writing back on their own account, or have simply discovered the joys of mass air transit and taken their cosmopolitan imaginations on extended holiday, we do not know and would not presume to guess. But British writing today appears as effective when treating of Algiers or Ulan Bator as it always has been when dissecting the *mores* of the Shire Counties or the All Saints Road.

Indeed, the balance may have tipped. The landscapes and mindscapes peculiar to Scotland, Northern Ireland and Wales were all represented amongst the submissions. The attention devoted to England, particularly rural and industrial England, seemed scant. This casts a revealing sidelight on the formulaic accusations of parochialism trotted out whenever a newspaper column or tenured professorship needs filling. If anything, the reverse is the case: a little more parochialism would not go amiss. Certain parishes appear to lack poets, although London, as ever, has a glut.

If Britain has lately become more launch-pad than terrain in its own right it is because its writers have actively chosen to seek out new challenges: a sign of writerly confidence. In turn, the diversity of what they have surveyed and logged speaks well of this country as a cultural entrepôt, a place of flux and reflux, differently but intricately connected to both Europe and the United States, historically and more problematically to the Indian subcontinent and Africa. Plenty of grist still passes through this mill called Britain.

And, therefore, it is still a place where writers can do business. 'The culture of denigration' was a much-touted tag five or six years ago. Whether or not Britain's critical climate has grown more or less poisonous since then, today's writers seem either to shrug it off or thrive on it. Readers go their own way in any case. Their taste for diversity, difficulty and the downright strange has done more to form literary tastes in this country, and thence the literatures which feed them, than any professional pundit. They will not be lectured: not by critics, or academics, or writers, or even by the editors of anthologies. So enough.

Tibor Fischer
Lawrence Norfolk

Patricia Duncker

STALKER

I KNOW THAT I am being watched. I think that women always do know when a man is watching them. Even if they aren't sure who he is. I can feel his eyes appraising my figure, following the swirl of my skirt. I feel the heat of his glance on my arched instep, delicate, visible beneath the leather thongs of my sandals. I take off my sandals to sunbathe, but even then a pale line reinscribes their shape upon my feet. He is fascinated by my feet. I hug my knees, gazing at my unpainted toes. They are sunburnt, charming, quite straight, a fine down of hair on the first joint of my big toes. All the hair on my body is a fine, pale blonde. I have always worn sensible, comfortable clothes, which reveal my body neverthe-less. I am nearly forty, but my waist is as slender as it was when I was eighteen. I want everyone to see that. I have never been pregnant. And I have never wanted to be. My body still belongs to me.

Sometimes I wish that he would reveal himself. Today, as I walked back from the hotel pool across the uneven blue mosaic towards our rooms, I could feel his gaze upon me. His desire warmed the nape of my neck. I felt the hairs rise slightly with the ferocity of his stare. The water was still on my back, my thighs. I turned, clutching my towel defensively across my breasts. I saw no one. But women always do know when a man is watching them. I know he was there.

I have begun to interrogate the face of each man at dinner. Is it you? Or you? Or you?

I do not always travel with my husband. Sometimes he is

1

away for months over the summer and I hardly see him. This year he has earned a sabbatical and his latest dig is being sponsored by the government. So here he is on this island, early in the year, with his young team of underpaid archaeologists, all anxious to work with the famous professor. They scrape earnestly away at a crumbling wall or along the crudely bevelled edge of a barely visible trench. They stake out lines of string. They carry buckets of earth carefully around the site and sift through them for abandoned trinkets, fragments of pottery and bone. Over the central pit they have rigged up a corrugated iron shed, which creates a huge sharp square of shade. And there he sits, the great professor, the famous specialist who knows how to interpret layers of pebbles and sand, with his bifocals balanced among his freckles, peering into a flat slab of crumbling earth.

This sloping site is especially interesting. It has been inhabited for millennia. My husband knows how to read the layers of time embedded in the earth. In this place the foundations have been reworked and realigned by other hands, five thousand years ago.

'Who lived here?' I ask, stroking the smooth, internal curve of a stone dish, which has been found. My husband begins a little lecture on pre-ceramic cultures. This site is clearly neolithic. For here are the neolithic walls, built in strange interlocking circles. I stand on the packed, dug earth and survey the pitted scene. My husband's colleague in Athens has sent back a number of uncalibrated Carbon 14 dates, which all range from 5800 BC to 5500 BC, the aceramic Neolithic. I find their lives unimaginable. Who was the woman who touched this dish? Did she own it? Was it her mother's? Did she make it? Did she mix grain with her dark hands? I imagine her dark colouring, like Lindsay, with her dramatic black hair and big gestures, dominating the stage in the school play. My husband never knew Lindsay then, but he has seen her in the photograph, the official school photograph.

'What can they have hoped for? Did they have ambitions? Did they dream?'

I know that I am being whimsical. I look out down the rocky white slopes to the coast. This view from the site is magnificent and appears in all the tourist brochures, huge sheer white cliffs and the tideless seas, thick blue water which, near the shore, becomes transparent, aquamarine, clear, bold colours from a child's paintbox. The earth is speckled with tiny white flowers, for it is still cool in the mornings, with a thick, traceable dew, even so early in the year.

My husband finds me charming. He is smiling. He always smiles when I am self-indulgent, infantile, whenever I produce a little flurry of clichés. I confirm his right to patronise my sex.

'Oh, I expect that they were much like us. Except that they had to work harder to eat. This village may seem a long way from the coast now. But the sea would have come further inland then. Look down into the valley. See the poplars? There's a riverside settlement there. Much smaller than this, probably because it was in a less defensible position. These people were almost certainly fishermen. Traders too, perhaps.'

Like all teachers, my husband is given to excessive explanation. He begins to tell me of the 1977 dig, sponsored by the Centre de Recherche Scientifique. They had no idea that the site was so extensive. My husband has sent urgent fax messages to all the relevant scholars. We expect the French to arrive any day. My husband is not an expert on the neolithic period. He has stumbled across this ancient site by accident. My husband is an expert on the early Greeks. He is looking for the undiscovered marvels of the temple of Zeus.

The temple of Zeus. We have written records which describe the place. There is the poet's ecstatic cry, upon seeing the distant line of the white cliffs.

Adrift in the winedark sea, our enemies far behind
us,
What joy consumes our hearts to view the temple of
Zeus,

Its noble pillars of Scythian marble, glittering high on
*   the sheer cliffs*
Of our native land...

My husband says that the poets are often accurate geographi-
cally. And that the heroic deeds they record as myths are
often histories, history as hyperbole, but history nevertheless.
The battles took place, the heroes were slaughtered, seven
garlanded bullocks were offered up to Zeus in thanks and
praise. After all, my husband says, Christianity is based not
on myth, but history. And we have Pliny and Tacitus to prove
it. But my husband has no time for religion. He regards that
kind of history as wish-fulfilment. I see no difference between
the resurrection of Christ and the transformations of Zeus.
But I say nothing.

For he comes here, year after year, scratching the dry,
white and orange earth, revealing the agora, the baths, the
granaries, the gymnasium with its fine smooth slabs, the
fallen pillars in the temple of Apollo, the traces of forgotten
offerings cast into the great pit within the holy precinct. It
should be here, sited here, in close proximity to the temple
complex, here stands the temple of Zeus. He initiates a new
dig in a sector on the slopes above the cliffs and unfortunately
uncovers the amphitheatre, which makes him famous. His
name is now associated with this site and this island for ever.
He publishes papers: 'The Amphitheatre at Hierokitia, a
preliminary report', in the *Acts of the International Archaeological Society* (1986), and the big book, four years later,
*Hierokitia: Early Greek Settlement in the Eastern Mediterra-
nean*, Yale University Press, 1990, with 142 black and white
illustrations, 6 maps and extensive appendices. As a result the
site is included in the World Heritage List of UNESCO and
overrun with tourists.

But my husband's desire is unfulfilled. His terrible, life-long
desire: to touch the noble pillars of Scythian marble, to stand
where the robed priests stood, their sacrificial knives gleaming and purified, before the altar in the temple of Zeus.

I stretch out under the sheets with my legs apart and my damp sex tingling. He is not in the room. He is not standing outside the shutters, his eyes glittering in the slit cracks, like a common voyeur. But I wish he was there. I don't want to see him clearly, but I long for his huge weight on my stomach, his face against my throat. Even with my eyes tight shut, or if he comes to me in darkness – for it is my desire that he should come to me – I shall feel his consuming glare drying the sweat between my breasts and the damp heat in the creased line at the top of my thighs. I squirm slightly against the sheets. I doze. I dream.

It is unusual for me to desire a man's touch with such intensity. When I was a schoolgirl I was in love with Lindsay, the most beautiful girl in my form. I adored the length of her arms, her swimmer's shoulders, flecked with drops as she surged into the 200-metres butterfly, and I sat cheering from the tiered benches by the school pool. You can't see it in the school photograph, which I have on top of my chest of drawers at home, but we are holding hands. We are smiling brightly at the school photographer, standing on chairs at the back, just behind our form teacher, in our blue cotton dresses with the wide dark sash, holding hands. Lindsay was head girl in the sixth. She won all the prizes. The English Composition prize, the Latin Essay prize, the 400-metres freestyle, the Poetry Recitation Medal, competing against candidates from three other high schools in the north Oxford area, and the Debating Society Award for Public Speaking. She never had any boyfriends and she was still a virgin at eighteen.

My romance with Lindsay went on for years. All those long revision sessions for our O-level exams, when we were children, when we lay among the clover and orange hawk-weed on the damp school meadows, and tested each other on our quotes from *Julius Caesar*, when we were devotedly in love. And all those hours in the music room, supposedly practising our Grade Four performances, but sneaking every opportunity to kiss one another's fingers, ears, lips. She once left a little love bite on the crest of my left shoulder-blade, under the line of my dress, where it would never be seen.

My love for Lindsay is all wrapped up with the smell of chips in newspapers, which we bought on the way home, with the huge swaying chestnuts and beech trees in the school grounds, held to the earth like marquees, tethered by daisies, where we walked in one another's arms. Everybody knew that we were best friends. Boys never asked us out because neither one would go anywhere without the other. Our parents said that our passion was a phase, which would pass. And so we remained inseparable. We hated family holidays, the depressions on the beach and the haunting of the Poste Restante in romantic expectation of the daily letter. I was the pretty one, short blonde hair cut to just below my ear and dark eyebrows, threatening to meet in the middle, which Lindsay wouldn't let me pluck. I pluck them now.

Lindsay was the clever one, games girl, prize girl, head girl, the effortless achiever with wide shoulders and long legs, black hair, the tall one with academic parents and three brothers, the one born with all the advantages. When she stood up to speak, everybody listened. And I was the girl she chose. I was her best friend.

But you know how it is. We were sent off to different universities, despite extensive machinations on the UCCA forms and lies told to parents. I went to Cambridge, read Archaeology and Anthropology and met Macmillan, the Junior Research Fellow, whom I eventually married. Lindsay went to Sussex and set herself up in a classy flat with wrought-iron balconies. She met another woman, with whom, so she told me, she had 'gone all the way'. How can you 'go all the way' with another woman? This was the most treacherous betrayal. Would I have minded so much if she had found another man? I shall never know. Lindsay never chose men. And so I sulked for an entire term and refused to return her cards, letters, flowers, calls.

Macmillan talked me round. He said you shouldn't drop your old friends when you get engaged. After all, marriage is only part of your life. The most important part perhaps, but not the only part. And so we all met up in a smart restaurant in Soho, which none of us could afford. I introduced her to Macmillan and the other woman didn't come. So it was Lindsay's turn to sulk.

But how beautiful she looked, still lean and tall, but fuller in the face, wearing a tight black top, the outline of her nipples visible inside her elastic sports bra when she took off her jacket. My thighs were glued together with wet hope all through the consumption of the carrot and coriander soup, topped with a thick swirl of cream. Macmillan delivered his first lecture on early Greek settlement in the Eastern Mediterranean, an elegant summary of current research and the latest finds. Lindsay was abstract and polite. I noticed that she wore little make-up and that her nails were cut short. I squeezed her fingers when we parted, promising to see one another very soon, but arranging no dates. She didn't return the knowing intimacy of my squeeze. That was when I knew that the affair between us was over.

I turn over onto my stomach. A faint sea breeze shakes the white curtains: fine, industrial lace, machine tooled, the curling swirls of a man pursuing a woman, satyr and nymph, his goat's legs, natty and grotesque, her backward glance, egging him on. I close my eyes so tightly that they burn. How was it for you, Lindsay? All the world's eyes upon you, night after night. Did you like the world's eyes? Who was watching you? Who was planning, with such intelligence, such vindictive precision, your very public death?

Lindsay de la Tour, her mother's maiden name, chosen in a feminist fit of patriarchal rejection, and then officially adopted as the professional *nom de guerre* for the stylish lesbian presenter of *Europe Wide*, 10.30 on weekday nights, the nation's heart-throb, the dream girl of the *Guardian* weekend features, winner of all the glittering prizes. It was chic to be a dyke the way she did it, with that drop-dead lipstick and those tight, tight tops. She was every man's fantasy of the unobtainable ball-breaker, the short-cropped butch with the long fingers and sportsman's thighs. She was the lovely lady who made politicians wriggle with discomfort, spoke French to the Euro-men, flirted with the lady mayor of Strasbourg, while asking her a lot of embarrassing questions about budgets and corruption, the newsgirl who beat Paxman's viewing ratings, let no one off the hook.

'Didn't you once know that girl at school, darling? Isn't she the one we once met at the Soho restaurant?'

Yes. I knew her. We were best friends. Now she belongs to everyone. Now everyone can admire her wide swimmer's shoulders, her ability to corner her prey in a debate, her radical candour. She doesn't care if people talk. Yes, she's a gay icon, a lesbian figurehead carved on the prow of every politically sensitive project, her picture always on the cover of *Diva*. She's a success. She has all the necessary qualities. She is slim, handsome, self-assured, desirable to all men, all women, but hands off. She's untouchable. And she talks posh.

So who was watching her, following her, evading the guards, the porters, the locked doors?

Why ask who watched? Millions watched her every night. Why ask who? It could have been one of four million, or more.

But how it happened made the nation pause. I cut out all the reports and photocopied them carefully, because the newspapers eventually turn brown and dissolve. I carefully noted the police number we should ring if we had seen anything, knew anything, had any leads. I made up a little brown folder, an anonymous file of information. I became the detective, piecing all the elements together. But even I cannot know who he was, the man who watched her.

She lived alone in a west London maisonette. The press were discreet, the exact address was never revealed. She had a driver and there was a security guard permanently on duty in the building, which was under constant video surveillance. She never travelled on public transport. She wore dark glasses and scarves when she went shopping, like a fifties film star. But she was so tall, so graceful, people often guessed. Are you, by any chance . . . ? And she always smiled.

The first sign was a small piece in the *Sunday Times* in an article about a man arrested for stalking Princess Diana. He used to wait outside the gym where she worked out. He never made threats or left messages. He simply watched. He didn't seem to care if the police hassled or threatened him. He just stood, in the streets, in the crowds, at airports, behind rubber plants and giant ferns. He paid for his tickets, but never appeared to go home. He was an ordinary chap whose bedsitter was coated in colour images of his adored Princess. She broke down in tears under the unblinking gaze and took out an injunction against him. But there it was, among the also-rans, all the other famous women who are stalked by men, with a dazzling colour picture.

> *Lindsay de la Tour, the glamorous lesbian presenter of the late-night politics programme,* Europe Wide, *has reported a persistent male presence haunting her street and following her movements. Police have been unable to identify or apprehend the man.*

I cut out this tiny detail. It was my first clue.

But the news of her death, a year later, splayed across every tabloid, on the front page of the quality broadsheets, the second item on the evening news, took me entirely by surprise.

Her body was absent. There were no pictures. Only distant shots of her front door, sealed off by yards of yellow tape, archival footage of her finest hours on *Europe Wide*, images of shocked colleagues, crushing their jealousy at her success and *schadenfreude* at her fate, pushing forward to tell the camera when they had last seen her and how happy she had looked. And there was the briefest of glimpses of the woman I had most desired to see, her lover, Helena Swann, chief executive of a major company, whose shoulder-pads drooped with grief. I devoured the press. The police described the event as a 'brutal sexual murder'. But they would give no details, for fear of copy-cat murders. It had been like this with the Yorkshire Ripper. We heard whispers of a screwdriver, but not what he did with it. Not until the trial. We had to wait until it was all over to find out what should have frightened us. I videoed the news for weeks as the story gradually faded, and watched her vanished face, freezing for ever in blurred newsreel.

The police said that they were looking for a big man, a strong man, a violent, obsessive, perverted psychopath, the kind you might meet any day, who had left neither blood nor fingerprints on her body nor on any object in her maisonette. Lindsay de la Tour was a well-known lesbian. This was almost certainly a factor in the case. They were looking for a man who had been capable of breaking down the door with some tremendous engine. The reinforced steel bar supporting the frame had buckled and given way. Then came the other odd detail, the detail which stifled my hesitations, unleashed my characteristic decisiveness and drove me into action. *The police were quite certain that she knew who her killer was.*

All her colleagues and friends were being questioned. The police begged the press to respect her family's desire for a private funeral. However, the memorial service, a Christian occasion, public and sanctimonious, which she would have loathed, held at St Martin-in-the-Fields, overflowed into Trafalgar Square. Her murder was intensively discussed, with all the details breathlessly withheld. How vulnerable they are, these glossy stars of the small screen, always in the public eye, objects of fantasy, targets of desire. Her abandoned doorway was strewn with pink bouquets. She was lavishly and salaciously mourned.

I was alone in the house that summer. Macmillan was away, lecturing in California. After his amazing discovery of the lost amphitheatre at Hierokitia, he was head-hunted for an Oxford Chair in Classical Archaeology and became as well known as Barry Cunliffe, a handsome chap who once dug up a villa at Fishbourne. Macmillan was then obliged to go on numerous lecture tours armed with a carousel of slides and diagrams suitable for overhead projectors. He was offered grants, endowments, subsidies and visiting fellowships. He came home from the Archaeological Unit to consume his supper and be endlessly praised. When he was away I fed my cats, watered the plants and dedicated myself to an intense regime of books and gardening. It was an exceedingly pleasant existence.

I have no children to occupy my time, and I have never wanted any. I hated the little part-time, underpaid jobs and extra-mural teaching, all the paraphernalia which kept the Oxford wives alive. So when Lindsay was murdered I had the leisure to speculate and to collect information. It was so easy to find out everything I wanted to know. You see, I had been Lindsay's best friend. I waited until she had been buried five days. Then I turned up in tears on her mother's doorstep.

They lived in Chipping Norton, just outside Oxford, up a leafy driveway with mossy white gates and a croquet pitch that accumulated puddles. Here was the house where I had played idle childhood games with Lindsay. Here was the tree with her swing, a huge rubber tyre, now decrepit and shredded. Here was the sloping lawn her mother had begged us to mow in decorous even lines, mounted upon a huge green diesel chariot, which sent forth a delicious jet of damp sawn-off green flecks into an inflated bag like a Hoover, billowing out behind us. Here was the next generation of untrampled marigolds and sweet peas. And here was her mother, shrivelled and old.

I stood sobbing on the doorstep. It was very effective.

Her mother drew me into the dark, rich spaces and clutched my hands.

'She was such a beautiful girl,' her mother whispered sadly.

And she had still been beautiful when they were summoned, as next of kin, to identify the body. They had seen her face, it was hers yet. And the police had spared them the photographs. But what had been done to her would become common knowledge at the inquest. Their solicitor would insist on reporting restrictions. Maniacs and murderers abroad in west London should not be actively encouraged. And the shame, the shame. Of course they had hoped that Lindsay would meet the right man, think again, it was natural enough at school, but after that, to persist! And look at you, my dear, so happily married to that nice professor.

11

But this, but this. She had put herself at risk. Too late. Too late.

I dared not outstay the usual length of such visits.

My next move was clear. I took advantage of my husband's absence. I went straight to the police.

They investigated my identity. They rang Lindsay's parents, who were pathetically grateful. Whatever she knows. Tell them. Tell them. The smallest thing may help. My speech was wonderfully prepared.

'You must not disclose my name. I am a married woman and my husband knows nothing about this. He doesn't know that I have come to see you. He must never know. You must assure me of your absolute discretion. I was one of Lindsay's lovers. I was her closest friend. I will tell you whatever I can that may help you to find the man who killed her.

'You say you are certain that she knew her killer. I may be able to tell you what he would have been to her. But first you must tell me exactly how she was killed. I am not afraid to hear. However painful, however horrible the truth may be.

'She would have been killed in a bizarre, strange, theatrical way. And that would make sense. You see, when we were younger we used to play games. Sexual games. We understood so little about sex. We used to fantasise, make up stories, act them out. It was always only a game. But sometimes our small theatre of sex unleashed strange things. We were strangers to ourselves. Lindsay made up frightening tales. In her dreams she tamed monsters, hideous creatures who desired her. She was always Perseus to my Andromeda. I was helpless, the victim bound to the rubber tyre, or to the bent beech tree branch in the garden. Lindsay played all the active roles. All I had to do was let fly piercing screams. She was the monster and the hero, the saviour and the aggressor. She became horrible, slavering, then valiant and chivalric. She menaced and tormented so that she could comfort and protect. It was all a game. We made masks, robes, shields and swords with real metal blades. But she never played the victim. That was not one of her roles.

'If the man who was watching her came at last into her

presence undesired then he had already overstepped the letter of his script.

'There was always a script. Lindsay always wrote the script.

'No man had ever touched her. She said that the first man would be the only one, the last one, her rapist, her killer, her unwritten partner, the man who watched.'

Ms de la Tour died from massive internal bleeding. She had been violently penetrated, both anally and in the vagina, by some kind of gigantic blunt instrument which ruptured her uterus and the wall of her colon. Her genitals and her anus had been savagely ripped open and torn. The lower part of her body was covered in sperm, clearly the product of at least half a dozen ejaculations. We are still awaiting the laboratory analysis which has revealed certain anomalies. Inexplicably, her upper body was covered in garlands of flowers which she had clearly been wearing when the attack took place. They were not placed upon the victim's body afterwards, like a perverted memorial, as was first supposed.

Then she died exactly as she had imagined she would.
Who is the man?
She was waiting for him. He was watching her.
The police lean forwards and the tape whirls.
Her stalker?
'Women always know when a man is watching them. Even when they aren't sure who he is. Lindsay knew he was there. Maybe she liked to feel this man's eyes lingering on her buttocks and thighs. She was a performer, a presenter. Millions of men watched her every night. Why is it so exciting to feel that you are being watched?'

I have given the police something to think about, but no hard information. Lindsay's murder revealed to me something about my character I had not known before. I am an astonishingly unforgiving woman. I think this is one of my strongest qualities. For I have had my revenge.

I laid flowers on Lindsay's grave. I visited her parents. I began to do a little research on Lindsay's last lover, the beautiful managerial executive with the crisp linen suits, the suitably tear-stained face and the prominent wedding-rings. Then my husband returned from California and I had to put the project on ice, carefully secreted away in a locked drawer. My husband has all the middle-class virtues. He never pries into my affairs. I mentioned Lindsay's death. And he replied vaguely that it was a terrible thing. How terrible to know someone to whom this had happened. But we said no more about it. And the case, to my certain knowledge, was never resolved.

Here on this island, comfortable as a cat on warm flagstones, I think of Lindsay's murder, seven years ago, and feel the aesthetic satisfaction of symmetry. My husband returns, sweaty and pleased, at the end of the day. The French archaeologists have arrived and will be joining us for supper. Dress up, my darling, I want you to impress them. A pretty, charming wife of a certain age, well read, intelligent, with a slender waist, is an academic asset. I wear simple classic suits in pale colours, no jewellery and a single gold chain around my ankle, so fine it can scarcely be seen. That is my only concession. I descend the stairs. I sit down. I smile at the French, who rearrange themselves around me, like courting lizards. And we order our aperitifs. I am the only woman present.

And then, suddenly, he is there. I feel the ferocity of his glare upon my naked shoulder-blades, the frail nape of my neck. I dare not look round. His stare moves across my back, down to the neat curves of my arse, tucked into the light wicker frame of my chair. I am sitting naked, undressed by his consuming gaze. I sit a little straighter, bend gently towards the distinguished French professor on my right. I feel my stalker's eyes, warm upon my back. His hands are covered in dark, animal hair, like a werewolf. I murmur, nod to his attentiveness, terribly excited.

All the men around the table sense my excitement. They take it as a compliment to themselves. They watch my responses to everything they say. They entertain me, they please me, they seek out the erotic glitter in my half-smile, my lowered lids, my charged sex.

My husband is delighted. Dinner is going swimmingly well, ushering in a new era of Anglo-French archaeological cooperation.

But, equally suddenly, I know when he has gone. I droop, like an exhausted butterfly at the end of summer, her wings tattered and frail. All the electric life fades from within me. I go out like the glow-worm at the break of day.

'Will you excuse me, gentlemen? I am rather tired. And I'm sure that you have serious matters to negotiate.'

They all rise as I step carefully away, through the marble bar with the fountain of Venus, covered in shells, into the overblown baroque of the old hotel. I pause at the desk to collect our key, peering at the blank green screen of the computer. Is he here? Or there? My clothes feel limp and creased, my back aches. But my stalker will have been satisfied by my performance. He will have appreciated the inward force with which I held myself, the curve of my neck, the arch of my instep, the fine line of my slender waist, braced to greet and receive his exacting desires.

There is something uncanny about the seagulls here. They are gigantic, with an unnaturally large wing-span, hooked yellow bills and colossal webbed feet. They are not tame, and yet they approach human beings with confident aggression. I lie sunbathing in the mornings for an hour by the pool. The gulls waddle close to my lounger, their heads jerking quickly towards me, then away, then back again. They rifle the dustbins, great beating wings thudding in the warm air. I see the cook, ineffective in his opposition, dashing out, armed with a broomstick and a living torrent of high-pitched Greek.

The gulls are scavengers, pillaging the waste tips like gangsters, flying solo, shrieking warnings at one another. Yet they appear to act together, like organised squadrons of bombers, persistent heavy wings battering my balcony, once my husband has gone, departing in the grey-blue cool of the early dawn. I am a little afraid of these birds.

It took me a year to find the woman who had been Lindsay's last lover, the woman she had been seeing just before she was killed, to make certain of her identity and to meditate upon my approach. All I had was the blurred photograph in the paper of her wet, twisted face. She was another woman dressed in power and success, but the grief was real enough. One thing was clear. If I can find her, she will talk to me.

I have no close woman friends. I am a woman who prefers the company of men. Women bore me, with their cloying emotional confidences, their self-indulgent assumption that I will sympathise with their great griefs and endless pain. All the Oxford wives I meet have but three topics of conversation: their greying husbands, their appalling children and their inevitable disappointments, past and present. I will forever associate coffee cups with this long women's whinge of doom. Their second-rate college was the one their headmistress had especially recommended. She went there herself, but well before the war. The Senior Tutor there had always had it in for them, all of them, personally. And the old hag's motives can only have been jealousy and revenge upon them, for being beautiful, clever and young. They were forced to abandon their research project, which would have made them famous, to become their husband's belittled assistant. They were always just too late or too old to apply for a grant, a scholarship, an award. They were bound to have won it, yes, certain, even given the competition, had they only filled in the application forms. But the resentments fizzle on and on. Their work was published under someone else's name, they were given an interview, but their age was held against them.

The whining voice is always the same. And someone else is always to blame that they are second class, second choice, second rate, second best. Their view of the world is yellow, angry and embittered. From their comfortable, well-fitted pine kitchens and William Morris-patterned sofas, they measure out the density of their disappointments. Envy is usually envisaged as pale green, but I see these yellow women in their kitchens, nurturing the fear of cancer in their drooping breasts, and pluming up their frustrations, yellow and glittering.

I will not be thwarted. I will have what I want.

I discovered her e-mail address on the Internet: helena. swann@leaderproducts.net.uk, and I sent her a very enigmatic message.

Return – Path: macmillan@ox. ac. uk
Delivery-date:
Date:
From: macmillan@ox. ac. uk
To: helena. swann@leaderproducts. net.uk
Subject: Lindsay de la Tour

dear helena i am one of lindsay's lovers i must talk to you for her sake use the return path asap sem.

For several days there was no reply. Then an urgent message in block capitals.

SEM NO IDEA WHO YOU ARE IF GENUINE RING 0171. 485. 6823 X2718 HELENA

I left the message gleaming, triumphant upon my husband's pale blue screen, and picked up the telephone. Her voice, so full of fear, was immediately reassured by my middle-class softness.

Yes. At school. We were best friends.
I'm married. My husband knows.
I'm married too. It doesn't bother him.

The relief in her voice clutters the line.
The inquest. It was awful.
It's over a year ago now.
I know. It doesn't go away.
Did you love her very much?
A deep, sharp breath.
Didn't you? How couldn't you?
Time to lie.
I still do.
She exhales.
I do too.
We pause, adding one another up.
We must meet.
Next week?
Are you ever in London?
I'll come.
Can I ask you something?
Ask.
Are you afraid?
Afraid?
That he's still there.
He is still there.
But you don't think – ?
What?
That it's personal. That we're next?
Yes. Sometimes. (Pause) Do you live with your husband?
Yes.
Does he know you're afraid?
No. I can't speak about it.
(Pause)
We'll meet. We must meet.
Come then.
I will.
Sem.
Yes.
I'm being watched.
She bursts out, in an explosion of hysterical sobs.

But all is well under control when we meet, in her hushed offices, twelve floors up, with a view of the Houses of Parliament, crisp as a model cut out from the back of the Bran Flakes Fruit and Fibre packet. We face one another and I see a great open sewer of terror in the back of her eyes. She is the chief executive of Leader Products and so her days consist of meetings, where fantastic sums are mooted and discussed, sales conferences, presentations and expensive meals. She spends her days making important decisions.

She met Lindsay at the gym. Please understand how it is. When your stress levels pass a certain limit of tolerance it's unwise to slow down. You need to work off the adrenalin somehow. I work out. On the weights. On the bike. I see her, sweat-band sodden, cycling nowhere in a mechanical frenzy. Suddenly, her chilly manner cracks. She is telling me the truth. I met her in the pool. She had the most wonderful wide swimmer's shoulders. She was strong as a man. I fell in love with her at once. When she took off her goggles I knew who she was.

The phone rings. Helena turns away, murmuring interrogatives. I flick through the prototype brochures on the glass table. She is considering new slogans and new designs.

- LEADER – soft as a swan's feather
- A wide range of products
- Feminine hygiene and household necessities
- Try our new range of sanitary towels with added security wings for all-day comfort
- HIS & HERS – Baby's Brand New Nappies – Xtra Strong – Fully Disposable especially moulded and shaped for Baby Boys and Baby Girls
- The new Move into Lavatory Paper: Soft, White, Fresh, Environmentally Friendly, Fully Recycled . . .

Why do I find the idea of recycled lavatory paper so especially disgusting? That's all they appear to recycle. Perhaps the nappies and sanitary towels were beyond redemption? Helena Swann terminates her call with a row of commands and returns to her executive settee. I smile brightly up into her perfect mask of understated paint.

'You seem to deal in nothing but excreta.'

And she has the decency to smile, suddenly anxious to know why I have sought her out, why am I here, sitting imperturbable amongst her cool green suites and glass tables, my feet sunk into her kelims from Kazakhstan.

'How do you know you're being watched?'

She crumbles a little before me.

'I may be hysterical. Some days I'm certain. I've never seen him. I sense a shadow. Just on the edge of my vision. It's so odd. I sense a big man, huge. But I can't see him directly. It happens irregularly. Sometimes, in a restaurant, or on the tube, I feel someone's eyes upon me. Not just a casual glance, but a really intense stare. I look around. No one is there. Or I see no one. But the odd thing is that even when I can't see him, even when I'm looking, looking everywhere, I still feel that I'm being watched. How can I tell the police that I know someone is there, but that I've never seen him?'

'Could it be someone you know?'

'Oh no. I'm sure of that. I work mostly with men. Some of them fancy me. One or two have tried it on. You get used to that. My husband is very trusting. There never was anybody else other than Lindsay. And think of my position. They wouldn't dare. Anyway, none of them are as big as this man.'

'How can you be so certain?'

She raises her hands helplessly.

'He just is. I know it. It's the size of the space he vacates.'

'The police say that Lindsay knew her attacker.'

Helena becomes white and silent before me. At the same moment I notice that her hair is not really blonde. It is dyed.

'I know.'

'Do you know how she died?'

'I was at the inquest. They said she was expecting him.'

'Why?'

'Oh, she was dressed, you know, she was dressed in a way that suggested she knew someone was coming. The table was

20

laid for two. She had cooked an elaborate meal. She expected him.'

'Or someone else? Not her stalker, not the intruder? Helena, the pictures of her front door were on television. The steel frame had buckled. The locks were fractured and split.'

'Then you don't know the truth. The door was broken down *from the inside*. She had let him in.'

We both stare at the diagram of a fresh white sanitary towel, soft as a swan's feather, bizarre upon the clear glass table.

Who is Helena? I am powerfully drawn to this woman, with her doubleness, her power and fragility, her arrogance and insecurity, her certainty that she is being watched, her fatal name. I see us both, the widows, the bereaved, sitting silent in the mirror. I watch the differences. She is taller than I am, wonderfully, carefully put together. She is built for show, the front-of-house woman who deals with trouble and complaints. I admire her uncreased surfaces and velvet slits. I measure out the long curve of her neck, the smooth line of her jaw. Yes, she is younger than I. As she gets up to fetch me a cold glass of orange, I see the one element of her body that makes her female, tender, touchable, and which suggests raw flesh. I see the geometric rounded globes of her arse, swaying gently inside a smooth sheath of Yves Saint Laurent.

As she puts the glass into my hand I close my fingers around hers and look up.

'Don't be afraid,' I say.

All the muscles of her mouth tighten in disbelief.

The hotel receptionist has abandoned his post behind the computer in excitement. He rushed out on to the terrace, calling my name. Your husband is on the telephone. Come at once. Come at once. I take my time. Rearrange my silk sarong which I tuck carefully into my bikini, and then stroll barefoot across the marble tiles. Macmillan is on the mobile. He has paid a fortune to make it work on the island, so that he can ring me at all hours. I can hear the echo and crackle down the line.

'Darling, we've found something. At long last I think we've found something for definite. Come up and see. Come at once.'

He is a tiny child, calling Mummy on his new toy, to tell her what he has dug up at the bottom of the garden. Macmillan is one of the reasons I have never desired to give birth to children.

But I too have an uncanny presentiment that the search is over. I dress carefully, coat my nose in Factor 25, so that I look like an Australian fast bowler, and put on a hat. My nose turns puce and bumpy in the slightest sun. And if I am not careful it swells, lurid and pickled, so that I look a little like the Elephant Man. I am always very careful here, even this early in the year, before the sun cuts its teeth on the tourists.

I take the Land Rover and drive up the long white gravel trail to the site on the cliffs. The site office is abandoned. They are all massed around a flat square of pasture, usually covered in bobbing goats with bells around their necks and a mad shepherd who harangues them. I like this old man, hideous as Thersites, with his toothless mouth, unintelligible dialect and foul-smelling, tattered clothes. He wanders up to me, demanding Coca-Cola. I give him money and he patters off, cackling. He is there now, leaning on his stick, his goats strewn over the slopes, resentful of the green wire fences, the extending barriers of the archaeological empire, stretching out like a flexible tentacle around the rocks and trees, financed by the Ministry of Culture and Historical Monuments. Here is a pair of cypress trees, one baggy and fat, the other rigid and penile, both stealthy, their shallow roots fingering the treasures beneath them.

Macmillan is in his element, standing over two of his diggers, who are now balanced on planks which spread their weight, bending carefully over the emerging fragility of a mosaic pavement. The white dirt is being removed with fine brushes. The tesserae are filthy, obscure, the patterns unreadable, each tiny square lifting its sightless colours to the sun once more, after thousands of years.

Everyone is very excited. They watch each scraping movement in a breathless hush.

One of the Frenchmen who dined with us last night holds me steady on the loose pile of dug earth with a courteous, protective arm, and tells me that the pavement will be *magnifique*, Roman of course, but *magnifique* all the same.

I peer down at the unrevealed mass of white earth. This means that we will be here for months, measuring, speculating, pondering this secret slope above the cliffs, digging an experimental trench, here, here, and here again, taking dozens of photographs. We will be here when the first summer tourists come, spewed forth from the bellies of chartered planes, squeaking infants and bony teenagers, sixteen going on thirty-five, with dyed black hair and unearthly pallid faces, make-up which resembles bruising, and ripped skirts revealing their buttocks. We will be here for the evening dances in the hotel dining room, with music from the forties and fifties that brings on indigestion. We will be here for the unspeakably embarrassing native dancing, which everyone applauds, puzzled. Here come the florid and elderly, courting heart attacks, dancing as if they were twenty-five years old, with nothing to lose. The hotel rustles up monsters: Elvis Presley lookalikes, magic acts, Greek men in white shirts balancing wine glasses on their heads and kissing fat, middle-aged women, who sit there, shrieking, smirking, loving it. I will not stay at the hotel.

Macmillan stands radiant before me. Years of research and dreaming are at last turning to tesserae and columns beneath his feet.

'This is it, Sem. I know it. This is it.'

I embrace his enthusiasm, a little bored.

'I must book one of the beach cottages, dear. For the start of the season. The hotel pool will shortly become unbearable.'

23

Macmillan doesn't understand. He imagines that everyone will be flocking up the cliffs to view the site.

'Yes, yes. We'll have to think of something to satisfy the tourists.'

But not everyone bent on quick sex, hard drugs and strong sensations dreams of an archaeological solution. Nevertheless, over the weeks that follow, a steady stream of fascinated visitors comes to view the emerging pavement. The perimeter of the site is now staked out. Huge mounds of white earth are thickening on the waste tip. An army of wheelbarrows move to and fro. The television cameras arrive and depart at regular intervals. Once more, Macmillan's wise face and imaginative Greek become well known on local television. From time to time he addresses the world and we are obliged to set up a computer link with his colleagues in America so that they can keep pace with his discoveries.

There are three guided tours every day. My husband's students, glittering with victory and satisfaction, explain the excavation and its significance. Their explanations keep changing as the dig proceeds.

Welcome to Hierokitia and to the House of Zeus. We have been able to date this house precisely. It was built at the end of the second century AD. *The mosaic before you is the first major discovery in this complex of buildings, which we now believe extends towards the east, to the very edge of the cliffs. We are almost certain that these buildings, which we are at present excavating, were constructed on the site of much older structures. Some evidence for this has already been uncovered. Now that the bedding of the mosaic has been studied it is evident that it was laid using the methods most commonly employed in the ancient world. First, the ground is levelled and beaten hard. On this surface the builders laid the* statumen. *This is a conglomerate of rough stones and coarse mortar. On top of this they laid another layer, the* rudus, *which is made of crushed stone or gravel and pottery fragments, mixed with lime. We* have found a good deal of rough, shattered pieces of pottery under the pavement, some of it painted. The last surface is the nucleus, a very fine plaster laid on top of the two previous layers. While this is still wet the tesserae are laid into it and flattened down. So it's a bit like fresco painting. The artist has to work quite rapidly on a wet surface. Very few of these figure mosaics are original designs. Whoever had ordered the mosaic would choose the figures he wished to have upon his floors. A mosaic workshop would copy the themes from design books. Sometimes the designer got it wrong and quite inappropriate figures would be incorporated into the chosen mythic scene. No, I don't know if the boss got his money back. Sometimes he mightn't notice.

Well, in this case we can see that the pavement was probably copied from an earlier pavement in a different building. The composition doesn't quite fit the available space. Look, the figure of the woman and the bird are quite central, but the tree with the perched owl is truncated, pushed against the hexagonal pattern around the rim. And here, the basin with the willow – it looks a bit like a willow, doesn't it, but of course we can't be sure – is pushed to the left, creating a slightly unbalanced space between the woman's left elbow and the fountain's edge. This kind of basin was not ornamental, but placed in the temple precincts for purification purposes. You had to wash carefully before you approached the god.

Look carefully at the tesserae. They are all cut from local stones, except for the highly coloured ones, like the deep blue, which are made of glass. In this period there were massive workshops dealing with mosaic floors. So all the background filling and even the geometric borders were probably made and put in place by apprentices and ordinary builders. Only the central figures, in this case the woman and the god in disguise, would have been finished by the master craftsman.

Now we know that these houses all followed a similar

pattern: the atrium *forms the centre of the building. The remains of a handsome colonnaded portico can be seen here, and here. The solid curved blocks on the left mark the site of the base. Yes, they are very well preserved. We haven't found any of the columns intact yet, but the island was struck by a major earthquake in the fourth century and the house may have been abandoned after that. The colonnade extended on all four sides of the* atrium, *rather like a cloister. All the roofs sloped inwards towards the centre of the building so that the rainwater could be collected in the* impluvium – *that's the little pond in the centre. This water was then carried underground in lead piping and stored in vast cisterns.*

The main rooms of the house would be grouped around the atrium. *So who knows what we'll find when we begin to dig to the north and the east of the site. That's the excitement of archaeology. You never know what treasure will appear, hidden in earth. But yes, it's mostly old tyres. No, I've never been on a dig before where we've found something as unexpected and as beautiful as this. We dug up a medieval skeleton once, back in Wiltshire, and had to wait for the police to come and check that it wasn't really rather recent.*

Follow me. But do be careful on those rough stones and try to keep inside the taped path. We dug an experimental trench here two weeks ago and some astonishing finds were uncovered.

Finds? Well, they're mostly objects. An amphora, that's one of these large vases, containing a mass of silver coins. They were Ptolemaic tetradrachms. Some dated back to 204 BC. *More importantly, we discovered that this pavement was constructed on the foundations of a much earlier Roman house from the Flavian period. We could date the remains quite precisely. It was quite usual to build on the foundations of much older buildings. We still do, don't we? And that's often how things get preserved. The Romans used to recycle cut stone. I worked on a dig back in England where we discovered an entire Roman wall incorporated into a medieval barn. We had prisoners with us, from the local jail, who were doing a bit of digging, and it was one of them who noticed. No, I don't think he was a murderer. I think he was inside for fraud.*

But the pit you can just see over there, beyond the gorse bushes, contains some of the most fascinating pieces of information about Hierokitia that we have yet discovered. It all fits together like a jigsaw. We'll have to wait for Professor Macmillan's research papers to get the full story. But I can tell you this: that part of the house was probably the site of the old kitchens. They wouldn't have elaborate pavements. Just beaten earth floors, like some of the poorer houses on the island. So we dug through and came to the remains of earlier structures, no doubt part of the earlier houses. But that part of the site overlooking the sea is very special. We discovered a sanctuary, cut into the bedrock of the island. It was quite grand once, a big space cut back into the rock. The principal find, which was dug out by Professor Macmillan himself, was the ivory carving on the handle of a knife of a boy emerging from a slit, like a wound, as if he was being born. I think that we would have made the connection even if the inscription around the base hadn't been perfectly clear.

ΔIONYCOC

It looks like that. Can everyone see? The triangle is a D and the C shapes are capital S. Yes, the carving represents the birth of Dionysos. He was born out of Zeus's thigh. His mother was one of the temple virgins. You can read the story in Ovid. The maiden wished to see her royal lover, not at night and in disguise, but as he really was. Zeus appeared to her as a thunderbolt and she was burned to pieces, but the child of their union was snatched from her womb and carried to term in the body of the god. Dionysos is a love-child, the god of wine and ecstasy. It is quite possible that the makers of the pavement knew that the sanctuary had once been here and created a pavement whose theme paid homage to the loves of the god. Taken together with the literary evidence in Homer we believe that we may well have found the ancient lost site of the temple of Zeus.

No, I'm afraid that we can't go down into the pit. The sides aren't terribly safe. And anyway, there's not much to see if you don't know what you're looking for.

And so beneath this house and this beautiful pavement there may well be an extensive temple complex of significant dimensions and cultural importance, which will transform our understanding of early Greek settlement in this part of the Eastern Mediterranean.

Does anyone have any questions?

I arrange to move into the beach house. It is some distance from the town, built on the edge of a little cluster of apartments, attached to another hotel with a less glamorous approach through a grove of bananas. All the folded trees are brown and shrivelled, the golden hoards of bananas are encased in bright blue plastic sacks. Even here they have frost in winter. The cleaning maid is called Athena. She tells me that there were three days of frost this year, shortly after Christmas. We stare at the bananas, which now look like an optimistic folly, so far north of the tropics. Athena opens the shutters leading onto the terrace. The steps are cut into the rocks, decorated with pebbles, and they fall away down to the sea. There is a rough stone beach, a tiny semicircle without sand, and a mass of white rocks, flecked with long streaks of orange, dropping into the water, this eerie, transparent mass of lapping blue. There is something sinister about a tideless sea that stays clean. I prefer the hotel pool. I look down and decide that I do not like this clean, living water, which is unpolluted, ominous with the smell of fresh sacrifice.

We now have a telephone and a fax machine in the beach

house. The computer is permanently alight with a large coloured slogan: PLEASE DO NOT SWITCH ME OFF, in English and in Greek, each word interrupted by Corinthian columns, and a motif of repeating black figure vases. A large map of the site is stuck across one wall of the sitting room. The students come here in the evenings, make thick, sweet coffee and leave a coating of white dust on the furniture. Macmillan sits exhausted, indulgent and happy amongst them. At night he lies peaceful beside me, snoring contentedly under a light summer duvet. Every day appears to confirm his initial hypothesis: that the rich man's house, built on the cliffs, covers the original site of the temple of Zeus. The shape of the sanctuary is now emerging. Yes, it was once a complex of buildings constructed on a magnificent scale, a place whose grandeur and fame was reported abroad, a landmark three thousand years ago, in the unreachable past. Macmillan sleeps content, the fluttering of doves a peaceful rumour in his ears.

I am alone on the terrace in the morning sun, reading. The telephone rings.

'Yes?'

Silence.

'Hello?'

Silence.

'Who's there, please?'

Silence.

Silence, and again silence.

I slam down the phone, my fingers tingling. After weeks of neglect he is back. My stalker is at hand, watching, waiting. For this is how it always begins. Five years ago a woman began to receive his silent calls. She knew who it was. She rang the police, hysterical.

But who is this man you say is stalking you?

He's there. There. Out there.

But madam, you yourself say you've never seen him.

I was the only person who believed her.

29

Helena Swann lived in a large house in Islington, in an early nineteenth-century row with flat façades, dominated by barristers and politicians. There was a locked barrier at the end of the street with a large sign:

NO ENTRY   PRIVATE ROAD

The wealthy climbed out of their air-conditioned BMWs to open the barrier and cruise through, nevertheless leaving their car alarms winking, the solitary red eyes alight in the half dark.

Helena Swann had a large London garden with an ornamental pond and an area dedicated to wild flowers. Here she cultivated her flag irises and marsh gladioli amidst her feverfew daisies, hairy St John's wort and water plantains. She walked in her wild garden, constructed with care, a carefully propagated mass of pink, yellow and white, with a trim little cluster of lady's mantle and stinking hellebore. When she came home in the early summer Helena Swann always changed into old clothes: jeans and an old checked shirt that had once belonged to her husband, and she walked out into her garden, unarmed with gardening equipment, to observe, caress and uproot with her bare hands, moving from place to place, apparently at random, bending to peer and meddle in the damp whiskers of cool green.

Helena Swann was particularly attentive to her pond. There were no goldfish, which eat everything, but there was an alternative mass of seething life: whirligig beetles, pondskaters racing at random among the lilies, waterboat-men sculling purposefully along on their backs, then plunging out of sight as if in obedience to an inaudible command of dive, dive, dive. And here is a mutant squad of tadpoles in the grip of inevitable metamorphosis. Helena Swann knelt at the damp edge to recuperate the shells of damsel-fly larvae hidden in the green. The original creature is hideous, a brown monster, a water beetle with foul antennae and grasping legs. They crawl, disgusting, down into the mud. But the thin fluorescent elegance of the damsel-fly, bursting into a resurrection of loveliness, abandons its monstrous beginnings, and flies free. Helena Swann collects every abandoned carapace she finds and places them on a saucer in her kitchen, a grotesque collection of abandoned corpses.

Helena Swann walks in her garden in the cool of the day. She feels safe, comforted. She never saw her attacker.

The police were unable to reconstruct exactly what had happened. The woman had not screamed. She had been found by her husband, hours later, half-naked and unconscious, sprawled among her cultivated foxgloves. There had been one great blow to the back of her neck and she had been brutally raped, several times, in her cunt and in her arse. No one had heard or seen anything. And there was one peculiar fact about her case which puzzled the investigators. Her lower body was covered with duckweed and starwort, a long trail of slimy green maidenhair was coiled around her bare left foot and her remaining clothes were soaking wet. A strange trail of weed led to the edge. Whoever her assailant was, he had apparently crawled out of the pond.

The police came to interview me. I was already on file. They suspected that it was the same man who had killed Lindsay de la Tour eighteen months before. They knew that I had visited Lindsay's parents and that I had sought out Helena Swann in her floating offices, high above the Thames. Let me tell you everything I know. I had said I would do anything to help. But now I tell them nothing, nothing.

Helena Swann survived the attack long enough to ring me from the hospital. She sounded perfectly lucid, uncannily clear, her voice urgent.

'Sem? Listen to me. There's something I didn't tell you. I couldn't tell you. I was too ashamed. About the night Lindsay was killed. I didn't tell the police either. I should have told the police. She wasn't waiting for him. But she was waiting for someone. We were breaking up. She had another lover. Her first name is Diana. I don't know her last name. But she works for the Chase Manhattan Bank in the City. Lindsay said she was a brilliant broker, buyer, whatever. She sells All Gold Securities. Something like that. She traded in some shares for me. Before I knew about her affair with Lindsay. They said that they hadn't wanted to hurt me.'

There is a pause on the line.

'Yes. I'm still listening.'

'She was waiting for Diana. Not me. Nor the man who killed her.'

But my mind is already elsewhere. I am asking myself the obvious question. If she wasn't waiting for this man, why did she let him in? She could not have mistaken the huge form of her stalker for her woman lover. Unless she just opened the door without looking down the staircase and he walked straight in. But there was a security guard on the property. There were security lights covering every side of the house which triggered the cameras. The guard saw no one that night. Or so he says. The surveillance cameras revealed nothing, just so many kilometres of blank tape. The lights were never activated. How could so gigantic a man have passed by if no one saw him? Unless he was some kind of shape-shifter.

I say nothing to Helena Swann.

'Sem. The phone calls stopped. When the phone calls stopped I knew that he was coming, closer and closer.'

'Helena. Go back to bed and rest. Be calm. Get some rest.'

'Sem. Go to the police. Tell the police.'

'What can they do?'

There is a terrible silence. Then her voice comes again, fainter, fading away.

'Then warn Diana. Find her. Warn her.'

Sometime between twelve-thirty and three in the morning, Helena Swann was murdered in her private room at the Royal Free Hospital, Hampstead. Her neck had been snapped by some kind of blunt mechanical instrument, shaped like a clamp. There must have been an enormous struggle, for her duvet was ripped apart and the room was filled with clouds of feathers. No one saw or heard anything. Or so they say.

I sound extraordinary, even to myself. You don't know me. I knew Lindsay. I was her best friend at school. I believe you're in danger. I can't tell you what he looks like or who he is. But I believe you're next.

Most women live with a certain amount of fear. But they usually fear the wrong people, the wrong places, the wrong evolution of events. Most women will never meet the sex beast in the dark, no matter how assiduously they pace the deserted streets, picking their way through the abandoned newspapers. Most women will know their attacker well. He is their neighbour, their uncle, their cousin, the priest they trusted, their father, their brother, their husband. Most women submit to sexual outrages far short of rape, and yet they rightly feel that they have been violated. Rape is the penetration of the vagina by the penis, without the consent of the woman, when the man knows that she does not consent, or does not care whether she consents or not (see Section 1, Sexual Offences Act, 1956). But have you ever been forced to lift your skirt before a gaggle of sneering boys? Have you ever had your knickers ripped with a penknife, so that they could get a better look? Have you ever had the neck of a Coke bottle rammed up your arse, while the man who has his knees on your back curses your stinking pussy? Well, it wasn't rape, your Honour. We were only having a bit of fun.

But another question bothers me. I am not, and never will be, the stalker's victim? Why? Why? Why had Helena Swann known this, as surely as I do?

There is something impersonal and intensely intimate about this man's violence. His victims are the chosen ones. They are women in the public world. Women who earn men's wages, women who take decisions, women who take risks. But the stalker is not just teaching the overreachers a lesson. He is establishing a connection with each woman first. He waits until he is acknowledged. And then he steps, invisible, over the threshold.

I sit watching late-night television while Macmillan is on the phone to America. I observe that the serial killer has become something of a Hollywood hero. I peer at the speckled screen. She has locked all the windows, all the doors. She is eight floors up. But here he comes: riding the lift shaft, or scaling the sheer metallic surfaces with miraculous, magnetic grappling irons. Technology smiles down upon the serial killer and unveils all her secrets with an open hand. Scream, my darling. Scream all you like. No one will hear you scream.

I decide that I will ring this unknown woman. I am the only one who has followed the case and understood all the evidence.

Oddly enough, she is harder to touch than Helena Swann. I run into security mechanisms, blocking my inquiries.

Who's calling, please?

Please state the nature of your business.

May I ask the reason for your call?

I'm afraid she's not available, may I help you?

Hold the line please, I'll transfer you to Personnel.

Pardon me, but are you a member of her family?

I cannot proceed without explanations. So I pose as a client with something to sell. And the doors open, the telephone rings and she answers, giving her name so briskly that I am taken aback.

'Diana Harrison. All Gold Securities. How can I help you?'

She is American. I am surprised. I did not expect an American. Behind her, like the backdrop sound on a film, I hear telephones incessantly ringing, a great roar of noise, voices unintelligible, talking rapidly.

'Hello? Hello?' Impatient.

'I knew Lindsay.' I simply make the statement. My voice is sharp and firm.

'Who is this?'

'Have you been receiving silent calls?'

'Listen, sweetheart. I don't know who the hell you are, but if this is a joke I'll have this call traced and you prosecuted for harassment.'

'No joke. I was Lindsay's best friend. I was the last person to speak to Helena Swann. Please listen to me.'

'OK. Just a minute.'

34

A door thuds shut somewhere. The noise is cut suddenly in half. I hear a man's voice saying 'I want everyone at their desks by 3.30 am on Budget Day. I mean it.' The man's voice is suddenly conversational. 'Well, if the Chancellor abolishes the claw-back on Advance Corporation Tax completely, British share prices should fall by ten per cent.'

'Have you been receiving silent calls?'

'Honey, if you've got nothing better to say then hang up. I'm busy.'

'Look. I beg you. If you get silent calls then ring 1471 and if the caller's number is withheld, then ring me. My name is Sem. 01865.722865. Did you get that?'

Mechanically, she repeats my number, but now doubt fractures her aggression.

'Yeah. OK.'

Behind her, the man's voice continues.

'Yeah. I know him. He's the city planner who invented the ring of steel which is supposed to keep the IRA out and stop them killing us all. Well, he's offered to fish some newt tadpoles out of his pond for me. He's a really nice guy.'

She slams down the phone. I imagine the rest.

1.4.7.1.
YOU-WERE-CALLED-AT-TEN-FORTY-THREE-
HOURS-TODAY-AND-THE-CALLER-WITHHELD-
THEIR-NUMBER-PLEASE-HANG-UP.

'Geoff! Trace that call. I don't care how long it takes. Find out who is ringing me up.'

But she never rings me. The police do. She was found dead at twelve o'clock on the following morning, by the woman who came to clean her flat. She lay by the telephone, naked, rigid and white, with her blank eyes open and staring, as if she were an abandoned classical statue. She had died of asphyxiation. The killer was perverted beyond comprehension. They found traces of semen in her vagina and in her mouth. And both her cunt and her gullet had been stuffed with priceless gold coins. The extracted gold was now being identified, dated, valued. The staff in the British Museum coin department touch this fantastic hoard with white latex fingers, amazed, wondering. The woman had been paid with rich pickings.

There was one telephone number scrawled on the writing pad. Mine.

The police came to Oxford to visit me.

'We can find a very clear sequence of events and circumstances linking these three cases, Mrs Macmillan. And all the links we have bring us back to you. Do you have any explanation for this?'

But I have no idea how she knew my number. I have never heard of this woman. I know nothing, nothing. How can you ask me to explain? I am still terrified by the deaths of Lindsay de la Tour and Helena Swann. How do you know I'm not next? Oh, oh, it could be my turn next. I burst into tears.

Macmillan defends me magnificently, and sees the police off the premises. I slip away to bed, and lie there, thinking.

Women's lives are the dark continent, not our sexual selves. You can peer at our bodies, legs splayed open, whenever you like. Our bodies present a deceptively simple text. But our desires, so often unuttered, are fluid, protean, inconstant. We cannot be measured. We cannot be assessed. Our inner lives are the hidden spaces. Sometimes all within is a murky coiling void, a black carnival of inchoate shapes and values. But sometimes there is a clear line of purpose, sharp and gleaming like a railway, an invisible singing, jutting out into infinity. No one knows what shapes our inner lives. That is our own business.

Look at the woman who gave birth to you. Look at the woman with whom you live. Does she sit sucking Prozac, nibbling chocolate, eyes fixed upon the television? Is she out of the door by 6.45, well on the way to glory, leaving the washing machine set to full throttle, something for tonight fished out of the freezer and resting in the fridge. Is she waving you off with a fingertips kiss, still warm from the bed, hastily wrapped in her dressing gown? Do you know what she is going to do for the rest of the day? Did she tell you? And do you believe her? Was she still asleep when you left? Does she love her children more than you? Are you one of her children? Has she walked through miles of dust to find you? Is she still squatting in the back yard, reading? Is she minding the shop? Was she gone, one Friday night, with no excuses or advance explanations, without leaving a note? Did she take all the money in the joint account, all that was left in the kitchen drawer and all her grandmother's cutlery? Did she send you the divorce papers by e-mail? Do you still love her? Do you understand why?

Women never tell the truth. They are too canny and too firmly bent on survival. Do you hear her saying, 'Oh yes, I love my husband.' I'm very happily married. I like my job. I'd do more hours if I could. My children are my greatest joy. Oh yes, I'm very lucky. I love my husband and my children. Yes, yes, yes. Or does she confront you with a lengthy catalogue of self-hatred and doomed fortunes? I do not love my own sex. But let me praise a woman's cunning. She is a master of negotiation and betrayal. She says her piece and withdraws. Here is defensible space. And I will ward off all comers with my giant structures of deceit.

I contemplate adultery with hard, steady eyes. I have never been unfaithful to my husband because I am not particularly interested in men. No man has ever given me his full attention. What they like to do is contemplate the effect they are having upon me, as I sit, radiant and gleaming before them, listening to their conversation. They fill up their chairs, very pleased with themselves.

But now someone is giving me his full attention. Attention is a kind of passion. I am being watched.

I know that I am being watched. I think that women always do know when a man is watching them. Even if they aren't sure who he is. He is fascinated by my feet and wrists. His desire warms the nape of my neck. I feel the soft hair rise slightly under the ferocity of his gaze.

I visit the site in the late afternoons, when the stones are still hot beneath my feet. The site is low to the eye. From a distance, there is nothing to see. The priceless ruins of the lost city lie abandoned in little piles. Only two columns still stand, erect on the far side of the market place. Here we study the infinite mystery of foundations. I pad softly through the white dust. The last two tourist cars, their pink plates thick with dust, pull away from the car park. The sun is no longer vertical over the perspiring archaeologists, who squat like white dwarfs along the crossed lines of their trenches, or sweat it out half-naked under their green tarpaulins, their mouths pink and obscene, washed clean by fresh water.

Here I stand on the brink of the sanctuary. The emerging shape in the white rock is a crude, uneven square. This is the house of the god. I duck past the huge succulents, great spiky lobes of conglomerate cacti, dripping white juice from their accidental slits. He was here, and here, and here.

There is nothing to see, just the white earth, peeled back. I avoid my husband and creep away.

The air does not cool as the evening advances. There is water in my mouth as I gulp the damp heat, salt in the trickle of sweat between my breasts. Far out over the sea, towards the south-west, the sky blackens. I am overcome with nausea in the shower and retch violently into the basin. A yellow spiral of sick forms around the plughole. I retreat to the bed and lie down. The first wind stirs the white curtains.

Why am I being treated differently? Why have you waited for me to give you a sign? You aren't afraid of him. You've come back. You've chosen him. You sought him out. Tracked him down. You forced him to notice you. You looked up.

I feel his presence now, achingly close, hot between my thighs. It is my desire that he should come to me. I lie with my legs apart, stroking my sex. I pull the hood back from my pink mound and thrust my fingers inside myself. I want him to come. I am quite unafraid. I get up, dim the lights, unlock the doors.

Then I hear a voice calling from the terrace.

I rush out, half clothed, and see a strange, tall boy standing at the bottom of the steps. He is Greek, barely sixteen. A giant motor bike leans behind him, balanced on a slender silver peg. His handsome, blank face scarcely registers my presence. His hair is an unusual reddish blond. He stands, arrogant and uncaring, in the leaden luminous air, grotesquely overdressed in black leather. His English is barely intelligible.

'I've got a message for you from the boss. He says he wants to see you. Get ready. I'll come back.'

When he turns around I see the shape of a chalice, etched in gold, glittering between his shoulders. He mounts the bike, which swells into life, and is gone.

Macmillan spends the evening in a panic-stricken rush of activity as the stormy light thickens. The team are stretching tarpaulins over the gouged earth, hastily hammering tent pegs into the unyielding rocky soil, weighing down plastic with stones, packing up the drawings and tools, setting out the buckets in a fireman's row to catch the coming rain. The wind is rising, rising. And we hear the first mutters of thunder, far away in the hills.

But suddenly it is upon us, all around us, with the first lurid bolt of electric fire, revealing the fabulous pavement of the half-naked woman and the swan plucking at her robes, in a white, illuminated flash. The makeshift shelters quiver in the gusts and the roofs buckle beneath the giant breath of hot wind.

Then the rain begins.

The blue plastic sacks shielding the bananas bulge and sag beneath the weight of grey, driving rain. The night floods in.

I stand on the steps in a white silk dress, which reveals my breasts and blows against my thighs. The sea shifts beneath me, evil in its caress. I look out. And there, coming towards me, through the banana plantations, out of the boiling dark, is the single silver disc of light from a black motor bike.

Philip Hensher

ELEKTRA

THERE IS AN oddly festive atmosphere between the eight of them; unaccountable, since the room – a disused office – has the brown-edged light which windowless rooms always have, and seems grubby to Anna, though it is, in fact, perfectly clean. The three men, two of whom have not spoken and will not speak, are similarly dressed, each in a dark grey suit, with a white shirt and dark tie. Care, on the other hand, has been taken to make the clothes of the five women not just similar, but identical. This in itself is not unusual; the five women are police officers, and used to wearing uniforms. But these clothes are not their uniforms. They consist of an ugly blue dress and a knitted cardigan. Anna feels she must look conspicuously unaccustomed to these uncomfortable clothes. She looks at the others. They do not; she probably does not. The clothes have successfully turned them all into high-security prisoners.

In any case the real high-security prisoner – somewhere in the building, behind probably no more than half a dozen locked doors – has had only a week to get used to the uniform.

The man in charge of the operation looks again at his watch. He is, like them, either nervous or excited. It is not clear what could go wrong, but things have gone wrong before, and must not again, The telephone rings and he picks it up. He does not speak. The voice at the end can be heard to say a few things. The man says 'Yes', and puts the telephone down.

'The witness is in place,' he says. 'It is fully understood what is to be done by the participants.'

Having no leader, the women say nothing. Anna tries to look alert, keen, capable. Until she joined the police force, and for almost a year afterwards, she was an enthusiastic amateur actress; she enjoyed the evenings with a group of people, pretending with her lines to have relations with people she did not know, entering into the imagined lives of people who probably never existed, and making them real. She liked, in rehearsals and during them, to sit around with the other amateur actors, and pretend for a while to be a real bohemian, to complain about trivial things, about the play and the director and be late for things. She never thought she would act professionally, although years ago at school people had sometimes said perhaps she should. She had never wanted to. She had always wanted to be a police officer. And now, she thinks irrelevantly, she could be an actress too, just for the afternoon.

The man in charge doesn't seem to take their silence as meaning that they understand and remember what they have been told. He lives, in fact, in an apartment block next to the one Anna now lives in. In the months she has lived there, in a quiet part of Zweibrücken, she sees him getting into his car, at much the same time as her, a minimum of three times a week. He does not acknowledge her, although he knows who she is, and speaks to her when they are in the station together. Anna has mentioned it to her husband, Peter; he was interested mainly in who the man was that she was talking about. She described him as if he were a suspect – muddy blond hair, average height, inclining to plumpness – until Peter said, teasingly, 'No distinguishing features,' and they forgot about it.

In any case he is going to explain once more what their task is this morning.

'Instructions from the top are that the prisoner has repeatedly attempted to refuse to take part in an identity parade,' he starts. 'Refusal has not been granted. The prisoner will be placed second in the parade. Each of you will go in separately. The conduct of the prisoner will be observed carefully by each of you. Each of you will go in three times in the same sequence.'

He pauses, and looks at one of the other two men. Anna is obscurely irritated by the words, 'Refusal has not been granted', but she cannot think of the proper way to say what he means.

'It is understood that the prisoner will attempt to protest in the course of the identity parade. Legal advice has been received that protestation may be taken by the witness as identifying the prisoner over and above the witness's memory of the prisoner's appearance. It is therefore necessary that protest be anticipated and enacted by the participating lady officers.'

'Is it known,' Anna says, irritated by almost everything this man says, 'what form the protest is likely to take?'

The man looks from side to side. Each of the other men moves his head almost imperceptibly.

'Not in precise detail,' he says. 'It is presumed that physical resistance will take place. It may be that the prisoner will attempt verbally to identify herself in an attempt to invalidate the identification procedure.'

'In which case – '

'In which case it will be necessary for the participating lady officers likewise to identify themselves.'

'To identify ourselves?' says one of the other women, obviously not understanding. 'As police officers?'

'Naturally not,' he goes on. 'As Ulrike Meinhof.'

The prisoner is already in the large cell which serves as anteroom to the identification room when the five women enter. Ulrike Meinhof looks very unlike her photograph in the newspapers. There, she looked defiant, healthy, well-cared-for, even – Anna thinks with a tinge of amusement – even rich. In the flesh, she is pale, her skin sallow, with a rash or even spots; perhaps from a poor diet, from lack of exercise. Well, Anna thinks, she's not likely to get much of that for a few years. Her hair is dry and unkempt, like a dog's. She is surprisingly thin. She, too, is wearing the ugly blue dress and knitted cardigan. She looks up as they come in, perhaps in surprise at seeing people dressed identically to her. Of course, she has seen no other prisoners since her arrest. She quickly looks down again, unwilling even to look at police officers.

Also in the cell are six women prison officers. Two of them are holding Ulrike Meinhof tightly, although there is little imaginable way that she could escape. Still, things have gone wrong in the past, and things could go wrong again. It is not known how, precisely. It is merely known that it is possible.

The cell, though large, is now almost uncomfortably crowded. One of the warders looks at the five pretend prisoners, then at Ulrike Meinhof.

'Her hair,' she says. It is true. Ulrike Meinhof's hair has not been brushed for many days, and is in a mess. The five other participants, however, have neatly cared-for hair. She stands out. We need a hairbrush for her.

'I refuse,' Ulrike Meinhof says.

'We need a hairbrush,' the warder says. Another warder goes out.

'I refuse to permit my hair to be touched,' Ulrike Meinhof says. 'The forcible brushing of my hair constitutes assault. Specific regulation must be made to allow such an act of abuse.'

'I thought you didn't recognise regulations,' the warder says as the other returns with a hairbrush.

'You live by your own rules,' Ulrike Meinhof says. 'It's all shit.'

'Language, madam,' the warder says ironically, as she starts to brush the hair. 'Hold her head.' Her hair is obviously knotted and unkempt; the hairbrush sticks at once. She pulls a little, and then, so as not to hurt more than necessary, she lays the flat of her hand against the root and tugs. She need not have troubled; as soon as she took the hairbrush, Ulrike Meinhof started to scream. An oddly feminine, panicky scream, high-pitched and, in the bare cell, deafening. It must be painful, to have your hair brushed like that, Anna thinks, but the screaming has nothing to do with pain, and continues after the brush is taken out. She remembers her mother in their small flat, how she liked to brush her daughter's hair; the quiet pain she endured as she pulled on the scalp, the exquisite feeling of drained cleanliness, of new blood in the head when it was finished.

The warder takes two or three minutes over it, though the noise is unpleasant. She puts the brush down, and abruptly Ulrike Meinhof stops screaming. She looks up, balefully.

'My lawyer should be here,' she says finally.

'Your lawyer is in the identification hall,' the warder says. 'We are ready now.'

Anna has been married for only a few months now. She and her husband both work hard. They want to get on. Often, they do not see each other for long stretches of the week; when one is awake, the other is asleep. They sometimes eat together; they speak every day on the telephone, speaking ordinarily about ordinary things. Sometimes, holding the telephone receiver in the police station, Anna feels a wave of love and smiling tenderness come over her so strongly that she has to close her eyes, so that Peter, who cannot see her, will not hear a change in her voice. Sometimes he wants to go on talking to her, when there is nothing to say, and she is reassured that it is not only she who feels this about him, but he who, looking at her, is submerged by her love for him, as she is in his love for her.

Only at the weekends do they have time together; they like to visit the public parks and semi-urban castles where they walked before they were married. They do not find a routine in their trips, but each time a new pleasure, an old pleasure revitalised. Their weekly trips to the same six or seven places are like the pleasure she takes in his body; it is utterly familiar, and yet she looks at the hair on his body and realises she could never know every single hair on it, never count them, never exhaust what there is to know about his flesh, the dark smiling eyes in his dear round face, his love for her.

Their routine Sunday morning is to sit over breakfast, a meal which never seems to stop, just to pause for half an hour before he gets up and makes more to eat, pours more juice or slices some more cheese or ham. He likes to sit in his dressing gown; she likes to dress. Mostly he gives way, and puts on some clothes, though she would never ask him to; sometimes he rebels, grinning at her without justifying himself, without comment on his unshaven face and well-worn, too-small green dressing gown. That is nice too. They read the papers to each other. He is interested in what she is doing today; they have read a great deal about Ulrike Meinhof and her killings, her planted bombs and her aims to overthrow society with her associates. It seems quite strange, quite distant, but frightening in an immediate way, like a remote thunderstorm approaching at an incalculable speed, unstoppably. It is something they read a lot about, and talk a lot about. They do not quite understand it.

'It says that a man arrived at the flat of Joachim B., a teacher in Wuppertal,' Peter reads, 'and asked him if he would be prepared to shelter "comrades in the struggle" for a time.'

'Was he a friend of the teacher, the man who turned up?'

'No,' Peter says. 'It says he did not recognise him.'

'What did the Joachim say?' Anna says.

'He said he would,' Peter goes on. 'But then he talked to his wife, and she thought there was something strange about the request.'

'Well, there was,' Anna says. 'If a complete stranger arrives and rings our doorbell, and asks if some more complete strangers could come and stay with us for some time, well, what would you say?'

'Or even not complete strangers,' Peter says, because the week before, his brother had asked if he could come and stay, and, with no reason at all, Peter had said that it wasn't convenient.

Anna smiles; they, too, are conspirators. 'What happened?'

'His wife told the police, without the teacher knowing, and they turned up and lay in wait for the Baader–Meinhof people. But they never came. And the teacher is in prison under suspicion of knowing more than he says. You wouldn't do that, would you?'

'Tell the police?'

'You are the police.'

'Read me my horoscope.'

There are six of them now, identical, waiting to be ushered into the room. In the hall is a witness who saw a woman in Hamburg who might have been Ulrike Meinhof. They have not been told whether this witness is crucial or trivial in the case. The identification will proceed, anyway. Ulrike Meinhof is second in the line. The door is opened.

The first policewoman to go in resists her guards, trying to pull away from them and moaning slightly. Anna observes her; she is very unconvincing. Ulrike Meinhof follows, and she is also unconvincing; she has been standing sullenly, silently in the wings, as it were, and as soon as they start to lead her forward, she begins to struggle and to shout, as if enacting a part.

'I am the Meinhof,' she shouts. 'I am the Meinhof. *Das soll eine Gegenüberstellung sein?* Is this supposed to be an identification? I am the Meinhof!'

She attempts to turn her face away from the witnesses, while shouting her name. She is struggling, although it is not clear why. She cannot escape. She turns her head, pulling at the guards who are making an ungainly progress across the room, like a three-legged race. As she does so, she looks up, away from the witnesses, and for a tenth of a second her gaze sweeps over Anna, standing next in line in the wings; and for a second, Anna seems to see all the things the Meinhof has seen, all the suffering and cruelty and violence she has seen in society, all the suffering and cruelty and violence she put into society, and what, for a tenth of a second, she sees in the eyes of the terrorist is terror; the terror of a animal in a cage who does not understand its captors, thinks that restraint is cruelty, that its restrictions are deliberate torture. They stumble on, awkwardly, the group; she twists so much that

one of the officers almost falls to the ground, bringing the
others with her.

Anna is next. She starts shouting 'No', before the Meinhof
is out of the hall. She invents a line; 'I am the Meinhof' is too
banal, and has been used before. 'Don't you see,' she shouts
as she goes into the hall, struggling convincingly, 'don't you
see it's me you're supposed to look at? It's me, you swine!'

On the whole she is quite pleased with herself. The other
three do not do so well, not trusting themselves to shout
convincingly; they merely struggle and turn their heads.

On the second time round, they all seem to relax a little.
Anna recognises the ease which settles over actors after the
interval. They all start shouting this time; Ulrike Meinhof
tries to make what is perhaps a joke, shouting *Und hier ist
nochmals die Meinhof*, here comes the Meinhof again.' They
let themselves be dragged across, they refuse to walk and are
carried. The Meinhof's antics seem quite moderate, compared to theirs. Anna, who this time is first, tries 'It's all a
sham. It's me. It's me, it's me.' And then a line comes to her,
like a prompter whispering through the din and struggling.
She shouts, 'Can't you see, it's all a performance?' She tries to
hit one of her guards; she notes the surprise and flash of fear
on the guard's face. She will remember the sign that she has
been real to him.

Afterwards, Ulrike Meinhof is taken off to the cells, and
they go back to the office of the man in charge. He has a
bottle of schnapps, and they have an unexpected but
necessary drink. They do not, quite, toast each other. He does
not congratulate them; they were, after all, doing their duty.
But, before doing anything else, he sits down and fills out a
form quickly, while they stand with their glasses, and speaks
as he writes, as if dictating to himself.

'In the opinion of the undersigned,' he says, breathing
heavily as he writes, 'it was impossible for the witnesses and
the officers in the hall to deduce from the behaviour of the
women paraded the identity of the prisoner.'

They all understand that this is his way of saying that they
did well. He offers them more schnapps.

'Do you have a hobby?' he says to the nearest of the policewomen.

'I like playing tennis,' she says. 'At the weekend.'

'Ah, tennis,' he says. 'A funny thing, tennis. I've never tried to play tennis, not for years. I've always been convinced that I'd be no good at it if I tried. I don't know why. I just think that. I don't think I'd be very good at tennis, maybe it's something to do with the temperament.'

They do not quite know what to say.

'I like to collect things,' he says. 'I have five collections of different small things. Well, I say they're small, but together they take up a lot of room in my flat. I don't know why I started, really, but they just grew and grew, and now I find a lot of relaxation in it. It's relaxing, really, going round, finding an example you haven't got, something you'd never seen before. One day, I suppose, one of my collections is going to be complete, and then I don't know what I'll do. My wife often says that. She says, You, if you ever finish with your collecting, I don't know what you'll do with yourself.'

Anna is thinking about Ulrike Meinhof. She knows what she did; she read it in the newspapers, every day, every week, something else. Something every day, something every day; and, quite abruptly, like a light being switched on, she knows why. It is because she is unhappy. It is because she wants things to come to an end, not start again, that she is killing everyone, that she wants to kill all men, every father she can find, starting with her own. And when all the fathers are gone, that will be nice, she thinks; she will sit down on a rock and look around at the nothing that is left and plan a society which is no longer there to be planned. Because there is no end to the fathers, just fathers begetting fathers begetting fathers, and there is nothing but an end to the Meinhof; an end which anyone, once they begin, in a cold hall behind the locked doors of a police station, to act out her life, could see, just as the Meinhof, struggling, identifying herself to stop herself being identified, can see her own end, and struggles against it.

Peter is already in bed when she gets home. He works at

odd times, starting at six in the morning. He is usually in bed by nine o'clock. Anna stands at the bedroom door, looking at his dear face in the half-light from the hall, beyond happiness, beyond worry or fear, in sleep. The novel he is reading and likes to read in bed has slipped from his hand and lies abandoned on the bedspread; he will roll on to it and wake up. She leaves the light on in the hall – she likes to sleep with a little light filtering through – and quickly undresses. She puts the book on the bedside chair, and gets into bed with her husband. She moves against him; he does not move or resist. She eases herself back against his body. On his side, his knee bent, it is as if he is waiting for her, for her to fit herself into his body. Right now, though she does not know it, she is pregnant. Their lives are new, and they will always be like that, for decades to come, for generations. They have been married for four months; they have not owned a single item of their furniture for longer than that. They barely have to trust each other. Their hands touch. One sleeps. The other, for a few more moments, before joining her husband, is still awake. *For her brother*, she thinks, with an amusement she cannot, for the moment, quite explain; *for the sake of imaginary brothers*. Her eyes are shut.

A. S. Byatt

BRIEF LIVES

An extract from work in progress

I MADE MY decision, abruptly, in the middle of one of Gareth Butcher's famous theoretical seminars. He was quoting Empedocles, in his plangent, airy voice. 'Here sprang up many faces without necks, arms wandered without shoulders, unattached, and eyes strayed alone, in need of foreheads.' He frequently quoted Empedocles, usually this passage. We were discussing, not for the first time, Lacan's theory of *morcellement*, the dismemberment of the imagined body. There were twelve postgraduates, including myself, and Professor Ormerod Goode. It was a sunny day and the windows were very dirty. I was looking at the windows, and I thought, I'm not going to go on with this any more. Just like that. It was May 8th, 1990. I know that, because my mother had been buried the week before, and I'd missed the seminar on *Frankenstein*.

I don't think my mother's death had anything to do with my decision, though as I set it down, I see it might be construed that way. It's odd that I can't remember what text we were supposed to be studying on that last day. We'd been doing a lot of not-too-long texts written by women. And also quite a lot of Freud – we'd deconstructed the Wolf Man, and Dora. The fact that I can't remember, though a little humiliating, is symptomatic of the 'reasons' for my abrupt decision. All the seminars, in fact, had a fatal family likeness. They were repetitive in the extreme. We found the same clefts and crevices, transgressions and disintegrations, lures and deceptions beneath, no matter what surface we were scrying.

I thought, next we will go on to the phantasmagoria of Bosch, and, in his incantatory way, he obliged. I went on looking at the filthy window above his head, and I thought, I must have *things*. I know a dirty window is an ancient, well-worn trope for intellectual dissatisfaction and scholarly blindness. The thing is, that the thing was also there. A real, very dirty window, shutting out the sun. A *thing*.

I was sitting next to Ormerod Goode. Ormerod Goode and Gareth Butcher were joint Heads of Department that year, and Goode, for reasons never made explicit, made it his business to be present at Butcher's seminars. This attention was not reciprocated, possibly because Goode was an Anglo-Saxon and Ancient Norse expert, specialising in place-names. Gareth Butcher did not like dead languages, and was not proficient in living ones. He read his Foucault and Lacan in translation, like his Heraclitus and his Empedocles. Ormerod Goode contributed little to the seminars, beyond corrections of factual inaccuracies which he noticed even when he appeared to be asleep. No one cared much for these interventions. Inaccuracies can be subsumed as an inevitable part of postmodern uncertainty, or play, one or the other or both.

I liked sitting next to Goode – most of the other students didn't – because he made inscrutable notes in ancient runes. Also he drew elaborate patterns of carved, interlaced plants and creatures – Celtic, Viking, I didn't know – occasionally improper or obscene, always intricate. I liked the runes because I have always liked codes and secret languages, and more simply, because I grew up on Tolkien. I suppose if the truth were told, I should have to confess that I ended up as a postgraduate student of literature because of an infantile obsession with Gandalf's Middle Earth. I did like poetry too, and I did – in self-defence – always know Tolkien's poems weren't the real thing. I remember discovering T. S. Eliot. And then, Donne and Marvell. Long ago and far away. I don't know, to this day, if Ormerod Goode loved or despised Tolkien. Tolkien's people are sexless and Goode's precisely shadowed graffiti were anything but. *Plaisir, consommation, jouissance.* Glee. He was – no doubt still is – a monumentally *larger* man. He has a round bald cranium, round gold glasses round round, darkly brown eyes, a round, soft mouth, several chins, a round belly carried comfortably on pillars of legs between columnar arms. I think of him, always, as orotund Ormerod Goode, adding more Os to his plethora, and a nice complex synaesthetic metaphor – an accurate one – to my idea of him. Anyway, there I was, next to him, when I made my decision, and when I took my eyes away from the dirty glass there was his BB pencil hovering lazily, tracing a figleaf, a vine, a thigh, hair, fingers, round shiny fruit.

I found myself walking away beside him, down the corridor, when it was over. I felt a need to confirm my decision by telling someone about it. He walked with a rapid sailing motion, lightly for such a big man. I had almost to run to keep up with him. I should perhaps say, now, that I am a very small man. 'Small but perfectly formed' my father would say, several times a day, before his disappearance. He himself was not much bigger. The family name is Nanson; my full name is Phineas Gilbert Nanson – I sign myself always Phineas G. Nanson. When I discovered – in a Latin class when I was thirteen – that *nanus* was the Latin for dwarf, cognate with the French *nain*, I felt a *frisson* of excited recognition. I was a little person, the child of a little person, I had a name in a system, *Nanson*. I have never felt anything other than pleasure in my small, delicate frame. Its only disadvantage is the number of cushions I need to see over the dashboard when driving. I am adept and nimble on ladders. But keeping up with Ormerod Goode's lazy pace was a problem. I said, into his wake, 'I have just made an important decision.'

He stopped. His moon-face considered mine, thoughtfully.

'I have decided to give it all up. I've decided I don't want to be a postmodern literary theorist.'

'We should drink to that,' said Ormerod Goode. 'Come into my office.'

His office, like the rest of our run-down department, had

dirty windows, and a dusty, no-coloured carpet. It also had two high green leather wing-chairs, a mahogany desk, and a tray of spotless glasses which he must have washed himself. He produced a bottle of malt whisky from a bookcase. He poured us each a generous glass, and enquired what had led to this decision, and was it as sudden as it appeared. I replied that it had seemed sudden, at least, had surprised me, but that it appeared to be quite firm. 'You may be wise,' said Ormerod Goode. 'Since it was a bolt from the blue, I take it you have no ideas about what you will do with the open life that now lies before you?'

I wondered whether to tell him about the dirty glass. I said, 'I felt an urgent need for a life full of *things*.' I was pleased with the safe, solid Anglo-Saxon word. I had avoided the trap of talking about 'reality' and 'unreality' for I knew very well that postmodernist literary theory could be described as a reality. People lived in it. I did however, fatally, add the Latin-derived word, less exact, redundant even, to my precise one. 'I need a life full of *things*,' I said. 'Full of facts.'

'Facts,' said Ormerod Goode. 'Facts.' He meditated. 'The richness,' he said, 'the surprise, the shining *solidity* of a world full of facts. Every established fact – taking its place in a constellation of glittering facts like planets in an empty heaven, declaring *here* is matter, and *there* is vacancy – every established fact illuminates the world. True scholarship once aspired to add its modest light to that illumination. To clear a few cobwebs. No more.'

His round eyes glowed behind his round lenses. I found myself counting the Os in his pronouncements, as though they were coded clues to a new amplitude. The Glen Morangie slid like smooth flame down my throat. I said that a long time ago I had been in love with poetry, but that now I needed things, facts. '*Verbum caro factum est*,' said Ormerod Goode, opaquely. 'The art of biography is a despised art because it is an art of things, of facts, of arranged facts. By far the greatest work of scholarship in my time, to my knowledge, is Scholes Destry-Scholes's *magnum opus* about Sir

Elmer Bole. But nobody knows it. It is not considered. And yet the ingenuity, the passion.'

I remarked, perhaps brashly, that I had always considered biography a bastard form, a dilettante pursuit. Tales told by those incapable of true invention, simple stories for those incapable of true critical insight. Distractions constructed by amateurs for lady readers who would never grapple with *The Waves* or *The Years* but liked to feel they had an intimate acquaintance with the Woolfs and with Bloomsbury, from daring talk of semen on skirts to sordid sexual interference with nervous girls. A gossipy form, I said to Ormerod Goode, encouraged by Glen Morangie and nervous emptiness of spirit. There was some truth in that view, he conceded, rising smoothly from his wing-chair and strolling over to his bookcase. But I should consider, said Ormerod Goode, two things.

Gossip, on the one hand, is an essential part of human communication not to be ignored. And on the other, a great biography is a noble thing. Consider, he said, the fact that no human individual resembles another. We are not clones, we are not haplodiploid beings. From egg to eventual decay, each of us is unique. What can be nobler, he reiterated, or more exacting, than to explore, to constitute, to open, a whole man, a whole opus, to us? What resources – scientific, intellectual, psychological, historical, linguistic and geographic – does a man – or a woman – not need, who would hope to do justice to such a task? I know, I know, he said, that most biographies are arid or sugary parodies of what is wanted. And the true masterpiece – such as Destry-Scholes's *magnum opus* – is not always recognised when it is made, for biographical readers have tastes corrupted both by gossip and by too much literary or political ideology. Now you are about to reconstitute yourself, he said, to move off towards a *vita nuova*, you could do worse than devote a day or two to these volumes.

I was somewhat distracted by counting the Os – which included the oo sounds represented by 'Us' – in Ormerod Goode's words. In the late afternoon gloom he was like some demonic owl hooting *de profundis*. The sonorous Os were a code, somehow, for something truly portentous. I shook myself, I was more than a little slewed.

So I nodded solemnly, and accepted the loan of the three volumes, still in their original paper wrappers, protected by transparent film. They filled the next two or three giddy days when, having decided what I was *not* going to do and be, I had to make a new life.

Volume I, *A Singular Youth*, had a frequently reproduced print of a view of King's College, Cambridge, on the cover.

Volume II, *The Voyager*, had a rather faded old photograph of the Bosphorus.

Volume III, *Vicarage and Harem*, had a brown picture of some stiff little children throwing and catching a ball under some gnarled old apple trees.

It was all very uninspiring. It was like a publishing version of the neighbour who insists on showing you his holiday snaps, splashes of water long smoothed out, ice-creams long digested and excreted. I flicked through the pages of old photographs reproduced in little clutches in the middle of each book. Scholes Destry-Scholes had been sparing with visual aids, or maybe they had not been considered important in the late 1950s and early '60s. There was a photograph of Sir Prosper Bole, MP, looking like God the Father, and one of the three buttoned-up and staring Beeching sisters with scraped-back hair – 'Fanny is on the right'. I assumed Fanny was Bole's mother. There was a very bad drawing of a youth at Cambridge, resting his head on his hand. 'Elmer (Em) drawn by Johnny Hawthorne during their Lakeland jaunt.' There was a map of Somaliland and a map of the Silk Road, and a picture of a ship ('The trusty *Hippolyta*') listing dangerously. Volume II had a lot more maps – Turkey, Russia, the Crimea – a *cliché* of the Charge of the Light Brigade, another of the Covered Bazaar in Constantinople, a photograph of a bust of Florence Nightingale, a ridiculous picture of Lord and Lady Stratford de Redcliffe in fancy dress as Queen Anne grandees receiving Sultan Abdulmecid, and what I took to be Sir Elmer's wedding photographs. He appeared, in a grainy way, to have been darkly handsome, very whiskered, tall and unbending. His wife, who also appeared in a miniature silhouette, in an oval frame ('Miss Evangeline Solway at 17 years of age'), appeared to have a sweet small face and a diminutive frame. Volume III was even less rewarding. There were a lot of photographs of frontispieces of Victorian poetry books, and fairy stories. A lot more maps, vicarage snapshots and more conventional views of the Bosphorus. They all had that brownish, faded look. I looked on the back flap, then, for information about the author himself. I think most readers do this, get their bearings visually before starting on the real work. I know a man who wrote a dissertation on author-photos on the back of novels, literary and popular. There was no photograph of Scholes Destry-Scholes. The biographical note was minimal.

> *Scholes Destry-Scholes was born in Pontefract, Yorkshire, in 1925.* He is working on further volumes of this *Life*.

Volumes II and III added critical encomiums for the previous volumes to this meagre description.

And so I began reading, in a mood at once a grey-brown smoky penumbra, induced by the illustrations, and full of jagged shafts of bright lightning on purplish vacancy, induced by my own uncertain future. Odd lines of Scholes's description of Bole's life have become for me needle-like mnemonics, recalling alternate pure elation and pure panic, purely *my own*, as Bole prepares to fail his Little Go, or sneaks out to stow away on a vessel bound for the Horn of Africa. Most of these mnemonics are associated with Volume I. For it has to be said that as I progressed, the reading became compulsive, the mental dominance of both Bole and Destry-Scholes more and more complete. I do not pretend to have discovered even a quarter of the riches of that great book on that first gulping and greedy reading. Destry-Scholes had, among all the others, the primitive virtue of telling a rattling good yarn, and I was hooked. And he had that other primitive virtue, the capacity to make up a world in every corner of which his reader would wish to linger, to look, to learn.

'There were giants in those days.' Bole used that phrase frequently – in his speculative work on the Hittites, in his history of the Ottomans, in his work on Cromwell. Bole himself crammed more action into one life than would be available to three or four puny moderns – and I include, amongst action, periods of boredom in a consular office in Khartoum, periods of studious seclusion in Pommeroy Vicarage in Suffolk, working on his translations, romances and poems. He travelled long distances, on sea and land – and along rivers, exploring the Danube as a student and the Nile as a middle-aged grandee. He went to Madagascar and wrote on lemurs. He travelled the Silk Road from Samarkand. He spent years in Constantinople, the city which, perhaps more than any human being, was the love of his life. He conducted secret negotiations in Moscow and St Petersburg, in Cairo and Isfahan. He was – and this is soberly attested – a master of disguise, could pass himself off as an Arab, a Turk or a Russian, not to mention his command of Prussian *moeurs* and Viennese dialect. He fought in the Crimea, and gave moral and practical support to Florence Nightingale, whom he had known as a young woman, frustrated by family expectations in the days when his great friend Richard Monckton Milnes (Lord Houghton) had wanted to marry her. He was part of Monckton Milnes's dubious circle of Parisian sexual sensationalists, as Destry-Scholes proved conclusively with some fine work in the archives of Fred Hankey and the Goncourts in Paris. He had known everyone – Carlyle, Clough, Palmerston, George Henry Lewes and George Eliot, Richard Watson Dixon, Swinburne, Richard Burton . . . And yet, beside this incessant journeying, political activity, soldiering and dining out he had found time to write enough books to fill a library. Nowhere had been visited without a record of his travels, which would include an account of the geography and climate, the flora and fauna, the history, political and military, the government, the beliefs, the art and architecture, the oddities and distractions of places as diverse as the Sudan and Austria-Hungary, Finland and Madagascar, Venice, Provence and, always returning, Byzantium, Constantinople, Islambul, Stamboul. He wrote histories – one of the great days of Byzantium, one of its fall, one of the Ottoman rulers, one of the reign of William the Silent, as well as his more technical works on Cromwell's New Model Army and military organisation under Louis XIV. If he had done nothing else – as Destry-Scholes points out – he would be remembered as a great translator. His collections of Hungarian, Finnish and Turkish fairy tales are still current in reprinted forms. His loose translation of the early eighteenth-century divan poetry of the great Tulip Period 'boon companion', Nedim, once rivalled Fitzgerald's *Omar Khayyám* in popularity, with its haunting rhythms and hedonist chants. He translated the Arab chivalric romance, *The History of Antar*, all thirty-three volumes, as well as several erotic oriental works for the furtive presses of Fred Hankey and Monckton Milnes.

The most exciting of these translations – Destry-Scholes certainly thought so, and conveys the excitement – was his version of the travels of the seventeenth-century Turkish traveller, Evliya Chelebi. Elmer Boles's translation included those passages expurgated by the Ritter Joseph von Hammer, the first Western translator, who had felt it proper to omit, for instance, Evliya's initiation into 'all the profligacies of the royal pages, the relation of which, in more than one place, leaves a stain upon his writings'. Bole had also followed Evliya through bath-houses where the Ritter had stopped at the door. Evliya Chelebi had, it appears, had a vision of the Prophet, in his twenty-first year, in which, stammering as he was, blinded by glory, he had asked, not as he meant to, for the intercession of the Prophet (*shifaa't*) but for travelling (*siya'hat*). Travelling had been granted, in abundance. Elmer Bole, undertaking his dangerous journeys disguised as a Turkish bookseller, had used Evliya's other name, Siyyah, the Traveller, and Evliya's dream-stammering, written in Arabic, transliterated according to William Jones's system, appeared on the front pages both of Bole's account of his Syrian escapade, and of Destry-Scholes's second volume, *The Voyager*. I was delighted, as humans are delighted when facts slot together, when I saw the significance of these lines.

Bole wrote many romances of his own, all popular in their day, all now forgotten. *A Humble Maid at Acre*, *Rose of Sharon*, *The Scimitar*, *The Golden Cage of Princes*, *A Princess among Slaves* are a few of the titles. He also wrote verse, also now forgotten. A verse-novel, *Bajazeth*, collections of lyrics – *Shulamith*, *How Beautiful are Thy Feet*, *A Spring Shut Up*, *The Orchard Walls*. The lyrics are conventional, and the novels are wooden, melodramatic and stilted. This judgement has its importance, beyond the unmournable disappearance of the romances, because it has a bearing on what is generally (in this, as in everything I say, of course, I follow Destry-Scholes) acknowledged to be Elmer Bole's literary masterpiece.

This was his translation, if it was a translation, of Evliya's account of his travels through Europe, his exploration of 'the seven climates', setting off from Vienna, where he had been secretary to Kara Muhammad Pasha's embassy in 1664, travelling through Germany and the Netherlands, as far as Dunkirk, through Holland, Denmark and Sweden, returning through Poland, via Krakow and Danzig, to the Crimea, after a journey of three and a half years. This European exploration was well attested, and constantly referred to by Evliya in his accounts of his Middle Eastern travels. The problem was that no manuscript existed, and experts, including the Ritter von Hammer who had searched sale-rooms and bazaars, had come to believe that he never wrote the European volume being, as the Ritter puts it, 'probably prevented by death when he had completed his fourth volume'.

Elmer Bole, however, claimed to have found the manuscript of Evliya's fifth volume, wrapped as packing round a seventeenth-century Dutch painting of tulips, in an obscure curiosity shop deep in the Bazaar. He had compared it to that manuscript of Eusebius which was in use as a cover for a milk-pitcher. Scholars, including, especially, Scholes Destry-

Scholes, had made exhaustive attempts to rediscover this lost manuscript, in Istanbul, in London, in the libraries to which Scholes's papers had been bit by bit dispersed, in the attics and dusty ottomans of Nether Applewick Vicarage. It had never come to light, and many scholars, both Anglophone and Turkish, had concluded that it had never existed, that the *Journey Through Seven Climates* was an historical novel, a pastiche, by Bole himself.

Destry-Scholes came down, cautiously, arguing every inch of his conclusions, on the other side. His argument, a delicious example of 1950s pre-theoretical intuitive criticism, derives in part from the extraordinary deadness and badness of Bole's acknowledged fictions. They are vague, verbose and grandiose. Bole's Evliya, like the earlier Evliya, is precise, enumerative, recording buildings, customs, climates with scrupulous (and occasionally tedious) exactness. He notices things about the personal cleanliness (or lack of it) in Germany, about the concealed ostentation of rich Dutch burghers, the behaviour of women servants in Stockholm and Krakow – things which, as Destry-Scholes points out with effortless comparative cultural knowledge, would have been those things a Turk in those days, far from home, would have noticed. The account is full of lively action, dangers from pirates and footpads, amorous encounters with mysterious strangers, conversations with connoisseurs and savants, discussions of the price of tulips and the marketing of new strains from the Orient, comparisons of Turkish and Dutch tastes in these precious bulbs (the Dutch prefer closed cups, the Turks pointed petals turned outwards). How, asks Destry-Scholes, could Bole have known all this well enough to *inhabit it imaginatively* with such concrete detail, such delightfully provocative *lacunae*. He remarks on the fact that Bole's translation is written, not in high Victorian English but in a good approximation of seventeeth-century prose, the prose of Aubrey and Burton, Walton and Bunyan. When I have one of my frequent fits of wishing to disagree with Destry-Scholes, I tell myself that his 'voice', this put-on vocabulary, this imaginative identification were perhaps in themselves enough to transmute Bole the banal follower of Scott and Lytton into Bole the inventor of Evliya Chelebi. But it is hard to disagree with Destry-Scholes for long. He knows what he is talking about. It was his belief that Evliya's manuscript was given to the young Nedim, who may have taken it on his own travels. I am getting ahead of myself. I have not got to Nedim.

Another possible argument for Bole's authorship – also, it has to be said, carefully considered by Destry-Scholes – is his capacity to soak up knowledge, to make himself an expert on matters of historical or linguistic or aesthetic scholarship. His knowledge of Ottoman court ceremonies, of religious toler-ance and intolerance under successive rulers of the Sublime Porte, his study of the weaponry of Cromwell's forces, his investigations into British military hygiene are remarkable – as of course, in another vein, is his study of pornographic Roman jars, or his famous collection of *phalloi*, from many cultures. He read, and wrote, as the great Victorian scholars did, as though a year could contain a hundred years of reading, thought and investigation. I have often wondered what has happened to my own generation, that we seem to absorb so pitifully little. I have strange dreams of waking to find that the television and the telephone have been unin-vented – would those things, in themselves, make the difference? Would it be desirable?

Like Destry-Scholes, I was most drawn to Bole's mono-graphs on Byzantine mosaics and on Turkish ceramic tiles, especially those elegant and brilliant tiles from Iznik, with the dark flame-red (tulips, carnations) whose secret has been lost. Where did he find time to travel to Ravenna and Bulgaria, to spend so long staring, I ask myself (and Scholes asked himself, before me). Scholes permits himself to express surprise that Bole did not rediscover, or claim to rediscover, the chemistry of the Iznik red. He certainly haunted potteries, in Iznik and in Staffordshire, discussing glazes with the Wedgwoods. One of the most beautiful things I have ever read is Bole's account of the creation of light in the mosaics of Hadrian's Villa, Ravenna and Santa Sophia, the rippling fields of splendour created by the loose setting of blue glass tesserae at various angles to catch the light, the introduction into these fields of light of metallic tesserae (first gold, then silver), the effect of candlelight and polished marble to make soft, fluid, liquid light . . .

I say, the most beautiful thing I have read is Bole's account, and so it is, I stand by that. But it is displayed and completed by Destry-Scholes's account both of Bole's research (into the colour and composition of the beds of red glass on which the gold was set, into vessels of layered glass, with leaves of gold foil sandwiched between them) and of Christ in the church of the Chora in Istanbul, covered in plaster and unknown in the days of Bole's study. Destry-Scholes writes as though he were looking with Bole's eyes, describing in Bole's measured yet urgent paragraphs. Yet he introduces, tactfully, integrally, modern knowledge, modern debates, about perspective, about movement and stasis, which do not supersede or nullify Bole's thought, but carry it on.

Destry-Scholes believed that Bole's life was shaped by the ease with which he learned languages. He had the usual British schooling, for his time, in Latin and Greek, and could compose poems in either, with facility. Destry-Scholes says that these classical poems are better than his English effusions. My own Latin, I regret to say, although good enough to make a rough translation of the sense of his poem on Galla Placidia's mausoleum, is nowhere near good enough to assess its aesthetic qualities. I have taught myself to read the Greek alphabet, and therefore to recognise certain recurrent key Greek concepts from Plato and Aristotle. But I have to rely entirely on Destry-Scholes for his judgements of these works. (I do speak and write good French, and reasonable German, and have always made a point of studying critical theory written in those languages in the words in which it was written and, indeed, *thought*. This linguistic interest of my own, this delight in linguistic parallels and differences, encouraged me to accept the justice of Destry-Scholes's interpretation of Bole's very different intellectual 'set'. I know, in my small way, the pleasures of grammatical exploration, the seductions of different articulations and rhythms.) Bole went on in a purely scholarly way to acquire classical Arabic, which led him to Turkish, and to the Finno-Ugric language complex.

Destry-Scholes believed his travels were to a certain extent dictated by romantic visions opened up by the acquisition of these tongues. Even Russian he appears to have learned as an exercise in a new alphabet, although he travelled several times to St Petersberg and out towards Mongolia. He is on record as saying that his time spent disguised as a Russian student of religious history was undertaken initially out of pleasure in keeping up the rhythms of the speech. Destry-Scholes appears to have learned Bole's languages. He is able to comment knowledgeably – to quote – in Russian, Hungarian, Turkish, Arabic, as well as the usual Romance languages and German. It is part of the complex pleasure of his text that he is able to convey the complex pleasure of linguistic fluency from insider knowledge, so to speak. And if he had not been able to read Turkish manuscripts, he would never have made his most dramatic discoveries.

It occurs to me that I have just written a summary – one of many possible summaries – of Destry-Scholes's three volumes, from the point of view of my own initial interest in them, which was that of a man in need of facts – of things – of facts. I have listed facts, and facts about Bole's interest in other facts. That was the richness and strangeness I found in the text, and I am being true to my first excited understanding. Destry-Scholes found his bright idea in his understanding of the fundamental importance of linguistic forms in Bole's life. I found mine, I could say, provisionally, in Destry-Scholes's resourceful marshalling and arranging of *facts*. Nevertheless the facts I have listed are hardly of the kind which attract the British chattering classes to the endless consumption of biographies. I have hardly mentioned Bole's personal life. His loves, hatreds, rivalries and friendships are what these readers would look for, skipping his (and Destry-

Scholes's) speculations about Byzantine *ekphrasis* or Lord Raglan's inadequacies in the field.

The wooden hagiography, written at his widow's behest by Thomas Pittifield, observes the Victorian conventions of respecting privacy and not speaking ill of the dead. Destry-Scholes wrote at the beginning of what I would call the first wave of Freudian biography. By the first wave, I mean those biographies which made the assumption, explicit or implicit, that the direction of a subject's libido (more particularly the unconscious and unacknowledged direction) is the single most important thing about his, or her, life. The second wave of psychoanalytic biography entails elaborate unmaskings of contrary and hidden senses and motivations, so that often the 'real' story appears to be the exact opposite of the 'apparent' story, a loving father must be an abusive rapist, an object of detestation and contempt must be a secret object of desire, and so on. Two tales for one. If Destry-Scholes considered a Freudian life of Bole, he rejected the idea quite deliberately – I am sure of this, because of the tact with which he introduces a Freudian reading where it *is* appropriate, in Bole's aversion to self-mortifying clergymen, for instance, or in his failure ever to mention, anywhere, his maiden (unmarried, at least) aunt Theodora, who lived with the family from his birth until his final rupture with them, at the time of his marriage – which Pittifield ascribes to a quarrel over financial settlements.

No, Destry-Scholes recounts Elmer Bole's personal life exactly as far as it can be known, and no further. His own magnificent *coup* in this area was provoked, rather beautifully, by a coded metaphor in Bole's field journals from the Crimea, a metaphor which he later discovered, in abundance, to abound in the lyrical poems. This metaphor is one of apples. Bole was peculiarly fond of the contrast between red apples and green apples. Destry-Scholes has an elegant statistical table showing the incidence, in Bole's published and unpublished works, of references to green apples, red apples, and the two together (the most frequent). In his account of his deciphering of this riddle Destry-Scholes permits himself to depart from his usual detached narrative tone (he was fortunate enough to live before the idea of 'objectivity' was deconstructed) and take on the note of personal involvement and excitement of Symonds's *Quest for Corvo* (the analogy is Destry-Scholes's own).

The 'red apple' was, of course, the Ottoman image for the Other, the Kingdom to be conquered, Rome, or later, Vienna. High Byzantine Christian officials were also represented with red apples in their hands, as a sign of office. So for some time, Destry-Scholes believed that the red apple represented some desired promotion for Bole, and the green the bitterness of disappointment. It was only when ferreting through the Turkish correspondence of a Pasha who was a friend of Bole, in whose *yali* on the Bosphorus he was believed to have stayed, that Destry-Scholes found the clue to the riddle.

The red apple was a Turkish lady, Yildiz, the pasha's sister, who had a dashing reputation. The green apple was Bole's childhood sweetheart, Evangeline Solway, daughter of an impoverished evangelical clergyman. Destry-Scholes established that Bole had married both, in the same year, and had in the same year established two households, one in an old red-painted wooden house on the shore of the Bosphorus, and one in the little Old Vicarage at Nether Applewick. Yildiz, the red apple, had borne three sons, called after Turkish poets Nedim, Fuzûlî and Bâkî, and Evangeline had borne three daughters, Rose, Lily, and Violet who became the Principal of an Oxford women's college. Destry-Scholes points out that although Bole's associations with the red apple are of rich sweetness, warmth, fullness and ripeness, his associations with the green apple are not negative, but speak of tartness that makes the mouth water, of unexpected sharpness that makes sweetness sweeter, of firmness which is better than softness, and so on. He also quotes letters (found by himself) from Evangeline to her intimate friend, Polly Fisher, describing the advantages of her husband's long absences, in terms of a lessening of the terror of pregnancy, and an increase in delight on his return. 'For we have tales to tell each other, whose mysteries would fade with daily intimacy, and to him returning from the sordid and teeming East, my little life of green grass and clean sheets has freshness, a paradisal quality, he says, which is constantly renewed by absence.'

Destry-Scholes invokes *The Quest for Corvo* again, when, after his meticulous description of Bole's disappearance and the British reaction to it, he discusses Nedim's hypothetical arrival at the vicarage three years later, as a young man of about twenty-five years. As Destry-Scholes rightly says, decorum forbids any account of an event of which there is absolutely no record. You cannot, he says, introduce phrases like 'what must the sorrowful widow have thought, seeing the handsome dark stranger carrying his small valise through the apple trees?' We know neither that Nedim forewarned her, nor that he did not. We do not know for certain that Nedim revealed his parentage to his stepmother and half-sisters though, Destry-Scholes says cautiously, we must suppose that he did, or why did he come? We know, from Rose's letters, that he stayed in the vicarage for a year, and we know, from the Goncourts' journal (another brilliant *trouvaille* by Destry-Scholes) that when Nedim took up his post at the Sorbonne, as Professor of Finno-Ugric languages, Rose went with him, as we know that she was with him during his travels in Finland, which are described in the French account of his journey found in an antiquarian bookshop in Oslo by Destry-Scholes.

It is difficult to recall the state of febrile excitement I was in over my own release from a life of theoretical pedagogy. I *did* nothing about my new future. I sat in my little flat, or walked about in bare feet, and occasionally completely naked, to mark my new state, but this brought me no nearer any sort of future. Perhaps because my own life was a fluid vacuum, I became obsessed with the glittery fullness of the life of Elmer Bole. Compared to the busy systems, the cross-referred abstractions, of the life I had renounced, the three volumes loomed in my mind as an almost impossible achievement of contact with the concrete world (always eschew the word 'real' is an imperative I *have* carried over from my past), of arrangement of things and events for delight and instruction.

On each re-reading I transferred more of my attention from the myriad-minded Bole to his discreet historian. It was a surprise that Bole knew the morphology of Mediterranean solitary bees, the recurring motifs of Turkish fairy tales, the deficiencies of the supply-lines of the British Army. It was, on reflection, even more of a surprise that Scholes Destry-Scholes knew all that Bole knew, had tracked down his sources and corrected his errors, where necessary (they were frequent). Not only that, Scholes Destry-Scholes was able to satisfy the reader's (that is, *my*) curiosity in that he knew more of Bole's subjects than Bole did, or could. He had the benefit of Paul Underwood's exemplary revelations at the Church of the Chora. He had read the secret military telegrams – including those about Bole's activities – which Bole had no access to.

It is true that the force, the energy, the first fierce gaze of desire, the first triumphant uncovering or acquisition were Bole's. He was a free agent, Destry-Scholes followed in his footsteps. (I found myself in my wilder moments of naked abandon chanting 'King Wenceslas' to myself on hot summer evenings, a can of beer in one hand, *The Voyager* in the other. 'Mark my footsteps, good my Page, Tread thou in them boldly. Thou shalt find the winter's rage, Freeze thy blood less coldly'.) Destry-Scholes's work was a miracle of meta-morphosis. Bole was always Bole. Even his Burtonian versions of seventeenth-century Turkish had a Bolean ring, so to speak. But Destry-Scholes was subtle. He could write like a connoisseur of faience, like a brisk strategic analyst, like John Addington Symonds or even like George Eliot, where it was appropriate – some of his accounts of Evangeline's attitudes to Bole's curious mystical beliefs could have come out of *Daniel Deronda*.

He could write, as I have suggested, like a good literary critic, pointing out salient words and echoes of other texts. He could describe alien cultures in a supremely tactful and intriguing paragraph – his own account of the Turkish *hamam*, the bath-house, is not, as far as I can ascertain, derived from Bole but from other sources, or from personal knowledge.

Or from personal knowledge. This faceless writer constructed this edifice of styles, of facts, and even wrote in the first person where it seemed to him appropriate to do so. Sometimes it seemed as though he thought he was doing journeyman-work, making a record, simply. Sometimes there appeared to be a glimpse of pride in his own mastery, his art, you might even say. I had a vision of him sitting over a desk in lamplight, deftly twisting a Rubik cube into shape. Or, in a more complex vision, selecting the tesserae, blue, green, ivory, white glass, gold and silver, laying them at different angles on their bed of colour to reflect the light in different ways.

The project may have come to me in a dream. I am not being fanciful, simply precise. I woke one morning and thought 'It would be interesting to find out about Scholes Destry-Scholes.' I had a vague memory of a dream of pursuit through dappled green and gold underwater caverns. Of rising to the surface and of seeing a pattern of glass balls, fishermen's floats, on the surface of the sea, blue, green, transparent.

'I could write a biography,' I said to myself, possibly even aloud, 'of Scholes Destry-Scholes.' Only a biography seemed an appropriate form for the great biographer. I never had any doubt about that. I had discovered the superiority of the form. I would write one myself.

I made an appointment to discuss this idea with Ormerod Goode. He gave me dark, syrupy sherry on this occasion, Oloroso. I was offered no choice, though the half-full bottle of the spirituous Glen Morangie stood amongst the clean glasses. I had brought the three volumes to return to him, and explained my project. He smiled mildly, and said I could keep them until I had contrived to procure copies of my own, which could easily be done from good second-hand book-shops. He said that it might be possible to contrive to hold my postgraduate scholarship, if I were to change subjects and transfer to Goode himself as supervisor. This – although it lacked the drama of renunciation – seemed a prudent course of action. He asked about the dissertation I was about to abandon – had abandoned. Its title was 'Personae of female desire in the novels of Ronald Firbank, E. M. Forster and Somerset Maugham'. I sometimes thought it should have been 'Female personae of desire in the novels of Firbank, Forster and Maugham' and could not make up my mind as to whether this changed the whole meaning completely, or made no difference at all. I did not discuss it with Goode, who simply nodded solemnly when I told him, and remarked that there was certainly no one else in the department who would be interested in a biographical study of Scholes Destry-Scholes.

'You must understand,' he said, 'that I have no particular competence in the field either. I am a philologist, a taxono-mist of place-names. I met the man, but it cannot be said I knew him.'

'You met him,' I said, swallowing my excitement. 'What was he like?'

'I hardly remember. Blondish. Medium-sized. I have a bad memory for faces. He came to give a lecture in 1959 on the Art of Biography. Only about half a dozen students attended, and myself. I was deputed to manage the slide-projector. I invited him to a drink, but he wouldn't stay. Of course, when I heard the lecture I hadn't read the biography, didn't realise it was out of the ordinary, or I'd have pressed him harder, perhaps. I had a problem I wanted to get back to, I remember, I was waiting for him to go away. He probably noticed that.'

We looked at each other. I sipped the unctuous sherry. He said, 'Come to think of it, I can give you your first research document. He left his notes. Well, a carbon copy of the notes of his lecture. I put it in a drawer, meaning to send it to him, and didn't. It was only a carbon, I expect he had the top copy. I'll hunt it out.'

His filing-cabinet was orderly. He handed me the desiccated, yellow paper, with the faint blue carbon traces of typing. Three foolscap sheets. 'The Art of Biography'. The full-stops had made little holes, like pinpricks. I put it in my bag, with the returned returned biography. I said.

'How do you suggest I set about finding out about his life?'

'Oh, the usual ways, I suppose. Go to Somerset House, look up his birth and death. Advertise in the *TLS* and other places for information. Contact his publishers. Publishers change every three or four months these days, but you may find someone who remembered him, or some letters in an archive. That's the way to begin. I've no idea if he was married or anything. That's for you to discover. All I know for certain is how he died. Or probably died.'

He poured more sherry.

'Probably died?'

'He drowned. He drowned off the coast of the Lofoten Islands. Or at least an empty boat was found, floating.'

I didn't know where the Lofoten Islands were. I vaguely assumed they must be not far from the Dardanelles, the Bosphorus, the haunts of Bole.

'The Lofoten Islands, you know, off the north-west coast of Norway. He may have had an idea of taking a look at the Maelstrøm. There was a small item in the press – I noticed, because by then I had read the book, I had an interest. The Norwegians said they had warned him, when he set out, about the dangerous currents. He was on a solitary walking holiday, the press said. I was a bit surprised. It's my stamping-ground, I thought, not his, full of nice linguistic tit-bits and old legends. He was never found, but then, he wouldn't have been.'

My imagination wouldn't form an image of the Lofoten Islands.

'You'll have to find out what he was doing there, too,' said Goode, cheerfully. 'Detective work. What fun.'

I went home, quite excited. It seemed to me I was about to embark on new ways of working, new kinds of thought. I would talk to people who, like Goode, remembered the man, remembered facts and events, and with any luck, remembered more, and better. I would hunt down Destry-Scholes, I told myself, I would ferret out his secrets, I would penetrate his surface compartments and lay bare his true motives. I then thought, how very nasty all these metaphors were, and one at least of them contained another word ('penetrate') I had vowed forever to eschew.

Moreover, the clichéd metaphors weren't accurate. I didn't want to hunt or penetrate Destry-Scholes. I wanted, more simply, to get to know him, to meet him, maybe to make a kind of a friend of him. A collaborator, a colleague. I saw immediately that 'getting to know' Destry-Scholes was a much harder, more anxious task than hunting or penetrating him would have been. It required another skill, which carried with it yet another word I most vehemently avoided – 'identify'. I hate marking essays by female students who say plaintively that they can't identify with Mrs Dalloway or Gwendolen Harleth. It is even worse when they claim that they *do* 'identify with' Sue Bridehead, or Tess (it is almost always Hardy). What on earth does 'identify' mean? Sees imaginatively, out of the eyes of? It is a disgusting *skinned* phrase.

Destry-Scholes certainly never 'identified with' Elmer Bole, though I think it is clear from his writings that most of the time he liked him, or liked him well enough. Bole didn't annoy him, morally or intellectually, even when he betrayed friends, even when he wrote badly. Or else he was a supremely tolerant man (Destry-Scholes, I mean). It occurred to me that it was a delicious, delicate tact, being, so to speak, the third in line, organising my own attention to the attention of a man intent on discovering the whole truth about yet a third man.

I was brashly confident in those early days. I wrote off to the publisher of the biography, Holme and Holly, which had been subsumed in an American conglomerate, which had been bought by a German conglomerate. I addressed my letter To Whom It May Concern. I wrote, and paid for, an advertisement in the *TLS* – 'letters, information, manuscripts, anything helpful for a biographical study of Scholes Destry-Scholes, biographer of Sir Elmer Bole.' I went to Somerset House and made my own first discovery. Scholes had indeed been born in Pontefract, on July 4th, 1925; but his given name had been not Scholes Destry-Scholes, but Percival Destry-Scholes. His parents were Robert Walter and Julia Ann Destry, née Scholes. It had to be the same man. Two men cannot be born in the same small town on the same day with Destry and Scholes in their names. He must have given up the Percival for reasons of his own, and doubled the Scholes for other reasons – did he love that side of his family better? I know about not liking one's given name. My mother must have thought Phineas was an inspiration – I remember her saying, when I was a little boy, and cried because I was bullied for being odd, that I would grow up to be glad to be unusual, to have something remarkable about me, if only a name. I think Percival – or any diminutive, Percy, Perce – would have been worse than Phineas for a little boy in a provincial Yorkshire town. I wondered, in a moment of random inspiration, if he had chosen his name because its rhythm matched that of Ford Madox Ford, who had remade himself as an Englishman, after the First World War.

Of course, I immediately read, and re-read, and annotated Destry-Scholes's notes on 'The Art of Biography'. A large part of these three pages was, unfortunately, simply typed-out quotations from Elmer Bole, including the famous references to the red and green apples, with the terse instruction, 'explain and discuss'. He appeared to have conceived his lecture as a primer – and to a certain extent a theoretical inquiry – for aspiring biographers. This in a sense included me, although, of course, the lecture was delivered many years before my birth. I found it hard to put aside my ingrained habits of suspicion and contentiousness, even before the simple, reasonable tone of the document, which said many things I had already thought, might indeed have been written by the friend and colleague I was looking for. I could not throw off a 1990s need to think a 1950s critic both naïve and disingenuous. He wrote:

ABOUT FACTS

First find your facts.
Select your facts. (What to include, what to omit.)
Arrange your facts.
Consider missing facts.
Explain your facts. How much, and what, will you
*   explain, and why?*
This leads to the vexed question of speculation. Does it
*   have any place, and if it does, on what basis.*

He had also written:

A HYPOTHETICAL ILLUSTRATION

We may say 'He travelled by train from Edinburgh to London.' We know that, because we have the ticket, let us say, as well as knowing where he dined in London and whom he visited in Edinburgh. We do not have to adduce the railway ticket. A biography is not an examination script.

We may also say 'He would have seen, from the train, Durham Cathedral where he was married.' But we do not know. He might have been looking the other way. He might have been asleep. He might have been reading The Times *– or* War and Peace, *or the* Inferno, *or the* Beano. *He might have looked out of the window on the other side of the train and witnessed a murder he was not sure was a murder, and never reported.*

If he were a character in a novel, the novelist would have a right to choose between The Times, War and Peace, *the* Inferno *and the* Beano, *and would choose for his own reasons, and would inevitably be right. Though if he did not explain the* Beano, *he might lose a little credibility, unless he were a surrealist.*

A biographer must never claim knowledge of that which he does not know. Whereof we cannot know, thereof must we be silent. You will find that this requirement gives both form and beauty to a good biography. Perhaps contrary to your expectations.

On another page, he had written:

VALUES

A life assumes the value of an individual. Whether you see that individual as unique *or as a* type *depends on your view of the world and of biography; you will do well to consider this before setting pen to paper. (There are many possible positions to take up.)*

You may believe in objectivity and neutrality. You may ask 'Why not just publish a dossier with explanatory footnotes?' Why not indeed. It is not a bad idea. But you are probably bitten by the urge [change this silly metaphor, SD–S] to construct a complete narrative. You may be an historian or a novelist manqué, *or that* rara avis, *a true biographer. An artist-biographer, we may nervously and tentatively claim.*

An artistic narrative in our time might analyse the leitmotifs of a life, as a musical critic analyses the underlying form of a Wagnerian opus. A good biographer will do well to be lucidly aware of the theoretical presuppositions he is making use of, in such an analysis. In our time, the prevailing sets are Freudian, or Marxist, or vaguely liberal-humane. The Freudian belief in the repetition-compulsion, for example, can lead to some elegant discoveries of leitmotifs. *The Marxist belief that ideology constructs the self has other seductions. We are not now likely to adopt mental 'sets' of national pride, or hero-worship, though both of these are ancient propensities, like ancestor-worship, from which none of us is free. We cannot predict, of course, future sets of beliefs which will make our own – so natural to us – look naïve or old-fashioned.*

I was particularly moved by Destry-Scholes's note to himself about the metaphor. I was delighted by his choice of adjective – 'silly', the straightforward, *right* adjective for that metaphor – as I was delighted by his preoccupation with silly metaphors. There was an affinity between us. It would reveal itself in other ways, I was sure.

Whilst I was waiting for answers to my letter and advertisement, I thought I would walk in Destry-Scholes's traces, at least in the place where I myself was most at home, the British Library. I asked, jokingly, at the issue desk if it was known where he had sat, or when he had come, but such records are not kept. It is known where Karl Marx sat, because he never moved away from his singular place. I had the silly idea that if I were to move round the whole reading room from Row A to Row Z, and to sit once in every seat, I would necessarily have sat where Destry-Scholes had sat. I had no idea of the shape of his bottom (I imagined it thin) or of the cut of his trousers (I imagined them speckled tweed). I found it necessary to have *some* image, however provisional.

I proceeded in an orderly way, ordering all the books in the extensive bibliographies of Destry-Scholes's three volumes. I read the three volumes themselves again and again, mostly at home in bed, noting new riches and felicities of interpretation at each reading. I also embarked on a course of scholarly study of my own, giving myself a competence in Byzantine art, Ottoman history, folklore motifs, nineteenth-century pornography, the history of the small-arm, and the study of Middle Eastern Hymenoptera – this turned out to be the area of Bole's gentleman-amateur expertise which excited me the most. I was a keen bug-collector and bird-watcher as a boy. I knew the names and species of most British butterflies. I spent a pleasant few days sitting along rows EE and FF in the library, studying bee books, ancient and modern.

During a lunch-time stroll in the little Bloomsbury streets surrounding the library, my eyes was caught by the image of the Bosphorus I knew so well, in a tray of bargain books. I acquired, that day, both *A Singular Youth* and *The Voyager* in copies which had belonged to someone called Yasmin Solomons ('Yasmin from Woody, with love on your birthday, May 23rd, 1968'). The shopkeeper rummaged for a long time in boxes and shelves but could not come up with *Vicarage and Harem*. This meant that, at least in the case of the first two parts, I could now interleave and annotate Destry-Scholes's record of Bole, with my own record of Destry-Scholes.

I wanted both to read everything Destry-Scholes had read, and to go beyond him, to know more, not only those things I could know simply because I came later, when more work had been done; I wanted to notice things he had missed. I was full of pointless pride when I was able to insert, in *The Voyager*, next to Destry-Scholes's reproduction of Bole's drawing of the reproductive organs of *Bombus locorum*, a neat copy of my own of the expert, Chris O'Toole's recent drawings of the huge penis, knobbed and hairy, concealed inside the modest folds of the male organ, its presence unsuspected by Bole, and not indicated by Destry-Scholes.

But this pleasurable pride was, to use Destry-Scholes's word, silly, because he could not have known Chris O'Toole. The true delight was to track him through the maze of his and

Bole's reading, and come unexpectedly on a trace of his presence, or even of a mistake he had made. Correcting his errors (unlike Bole's, they were *rarissimae*, shining little jewels hardly observable in moss – the analogy is from beetle–hunting) – correcting his errors gave me a peculiar thrill of achievement, of doing something solidly scholarly, adding to the sum of facts. But the thrill was just as great when, three-quarters of the way through a book I believed Destry-Scholes should have read, and had not, I would come upon his tracks – a quotation he had used from a critic or a soldier, or, often enough, a sentence he had included in his own work, lifted whole or loosely rewritten.

Postmodernist ideas about intertextuality and quotation of quotation have complicated the simplistic ideas about plagiarism which were in force in Destry-Scholes's day. I myself think that these lifted sentences, in their new contexts, are almost the purest and most beautiful parts of the transmission of scholarship. I began a collection of them, intending, when my time came, to redeploy them with a difference, catching different light at a different angle. That metaphor is from mosaic-making. One of the things I learned in these weeks of research was that the great makers constantly raided previous works – whether in pebble, or marble, or glass, or silver and gold – for tesserae which they rewrought into new images. I learned also that Byzantium was a primary source for the blue glass which is the glory of Chartres and Saint-Denis. The French, according to Theophilus, were skilled at making panes of blue glass from ancient vessels, such as Roman scent-bottles. They also recycled ancient mosaic cubes, making transparent what had been a brilliant reflective surface.

At this time I had a recurrent dream of a man trapped in a glass bottle, itself roughly formed in the shape of a man. Sometimes it was blue, sometimes green, sometimes clear with a yellowish cast and flaws in the glass. This man was and was not myself. I was also the observer of the events of the dream. Sometimes he was cramped by the bottle, sometimes a small creature scurrying at the base of a sheer glass cylinder. I mention this, because it seems to fit, but I do not offer any interpretation of it. I have done with psycho-analytic criticism.

It took me longer than it should have done, moving along D and G and even H as I found vacancies where I had not sat before, to realise that I was acquiring only second- or third-hand facts. I was not discovering Destry-Scholes, beyond his own discoveries. No answer came to my letter or to my advertisement. I realised I did not have much idea about how to look for any more facts. I decided that I would do something Destry-Scholes himself claimed often to have done. I would visit the house where he was born. It was, after all, the only place where I knew he had been – apart, of course, from Bole's birthplace, London home, Nether Applewick Vicarage, Bosphorus *yali* and other brief resting-places. Pontefract was the place to start. It was the place where Destry-Scholes was Destry-Scholes, as opposed to the biographer of Bole.

I would have liked to go to the Bosphorus, but it was financially out of the question.

Pontefract is a small town in Yorkshire with nothing much to recommend it, except a very large, largely ruined castle, where Richard II died. It must once have commanded a confluence of important roads and rivers but now is famous only for a kind of liquorice coin called a Pontefract cake. I do not like liquorice, and wondered whether Destry-Scholes did. He might have felt a local pride in the local product. Or not. I went there on a coach, changing at York to a local bus.

I had the address of the house from which his birth had been registered; it was on the way out of the town, in the direction of a village called East Hardwick. I walked there, looking at shop fronts, bus stops, pubs, supposing I might feel his presence, and registering, accurately and honourably, that I felt nothing. His parents' names were what I thought of as 'posh'. Robert Walter and Julia Ann – especially Julia – were not working-class names. I had expected number 8, Askham

Way, to be a substantial house, a house with an orchard, or anyway a big garden, where an imaginative boy might play, a house with gables and dormer windows. When I found 8 Askham Way, it was a red box in a row of red brick boxes, all attached to each other.

They had little strips of front garden, and, for the most part, little wrought-iron garden gates with latches. They had tiled roofs and identical fronts – a thin door, with a high knob and a dull metal letterbox, beside a cramped bay window with leaded lights. Above the door were little porthole windows, and two square upper-storey windows, also leaded, with catches, not sashes. There was a laburnum tree in flower next to the gate of number 8, which had a well-kept lawn, and a border of Californian poppies. I do not know how long-lived laburnum trees are. I stood there, trying to think what to think. Askham Way is simply this row of red brick boxes set back from a main road. There is a new and shiny Texaco garage on the other side, which certainly does not date back to 1925. Nor do the street lamps, which are concrete and ugly. The house resembles, quite a lot, the square red brick box in which I was born in a suburb of Nottingham. I tried not to think of this. I don't like the place where I was born, and don't go there. Destry-Scholes's childhood is nothing at all to do with mine. The sky was blue with a few aeroplanes' exhaust trails, also things not to be seen in 1925. A woman came past me, carrying a brown imitation-leather bag of shopping (bread and bananas sticking out) and wearing a bright green beret. She asked if I needed help

I said I was looking for a man who used to live there. Who was born there, in the late twenties I said, trying to make it less remote. She said she had only been there five months and couldn't help, and the people she had bought it from hadn't been there long, either. She smiled, and went down the path, and into the house, and shut the door.

I went on looking at the red box, trying to think what to think. I felt a feeling I used to have going into our own red box – that such boxes are the only *real* homes *real* people live in – everything else is just images and fantasies. And that they were traps, with their narrow doors, and boxy stairs, and busily divided-up little windows. Or like beehives, repeating similar cells.

I noticed that the woman was looking at me out of an upstairs window. She drew the curtains with a swish. After a moment, she appeared at the other upstairs window, looked at me again, and swished those curtains, too. She may have done that every evening. Or not.

I felt like a voyeur. I also felt like a failure. I could have said something different and she might have asked me to tea and told me about the Pontefract of the past. (It was quite improbable that she knew anything about the Pontefract of the past.) I could have knocked at the meagre door of every house in that meagre row, asking if there was anyone there old enough to remember. But I wasn't going to. I was beginning to feel trapped by this ordinary place. I set off back to Pontefract, and the bus station. I could have walked round the castle, but I didn't. It was just a castle. He had been born into that box, that was certain, but anything he might have felt as a boy, patrolling moats and dungeons, came under his own heading of Speculation, and was a little disgusting.

Thinking about the impossibility of the castle made me see that I had, in some sense, registered the red box. I knew it. I had been there, even if I had not gone in.

Action of some kind was becoming necessary. I began to wonder if it had been foolish to address my letter 'To Whom It May Concern'. I decided to use the telephone. One amongst my many disadvantages as a biographical researcher is a horror of initiating phone calls. The switchboard lady at the mega-publishers was kind but unhelpful. Holme and Holly had been subsumed into Deodar Books which had been swallowed by Hachs and Shaw. At Hachs and Shaw I was passed from voice-mail to voice-mail, forced to listen to the Rolling Stones and Ella Fitzgerald and a mournful snippet of plainsong. Finally I got an elderly female voice who said, as though I was a silly boy, 'But you want the *Archivist*.' I said I didn't know there was one, and what was the extension? The archive had been sold to the University of Lincoln, said the voice. You want *their* Archivist. She had a moment's kindness. 'Her name is Betty Middleton.'

I wrote to Betty Middleton, and continued my progress round the Reading Room. Rows L, M, N. Persian and Turkish ghazals, prayer book revisions, the siege of Vienna. Lady Mary Wortley Montagu, on a whim. Destry-Scholes had taken several of her *minor* sentences, and reset them. Betty Middleton answered. All that could be found were a few typed letters. Did I want copies? She was afraid they were not very exciting, she added, sounding like a human being.

When they came, I experienced a moment of pure discouragement. There were only about a dozen. Of these, three said: 'I return the proofs herewith, as requested. I have not made any substantial changes. Yours sincerely S. Destry-Scholes.' Two more pointed out minor errors in the accounting of royalties, and one asked, baldly, whether the royalties were overdue, or whether there were none, and the publishers had not seen fit to inform the author, as the contract required them to. One said: 'I shall be very happy to meet you for lunch, on Thursday next, at the time and in the place you suggest.' One – the only one of any conceivable interest – asked if Mr Holly knew any source of finance for authors wishing to undertake journeys for research purposes. 'I have, as you know, already had a British Academy grant for my Istanbul trip. I should like to be able to take a look at the Maelstrøm. I wonder if you can help?'

There was no copy of any reponse to these letters. They were all written on the same typewriter, and headed Jolly Corner Hotel, Gower Street. I went, of course, to look at this hotel, which was still there, another version of the blank façade in a repeating series, this time grey, and to my untutored eye, Georgian. I summoned up my courage, went in, and asked if anyone would know anything about an author who appeared to have lived there in the early 1950s. The owners were Pakistani and friendly. They had been there five months. They didn't have any of the records of the previous owners. 'It was a little dingy, you know, quite a bit of a sad sort of a place. We are modernising, and cleaning it up. We are trying to make it jolly, though we are seriously considering changing the name.'

I wrote to the Archivist and asked if any of the answers to these messages had been preserved. She wrote back, still amiably, saying no, and that there was a note saying Aloysius Holly always replied in his own hand, on carefully selected postcards. I could see the royalty statements if I liked.

There was one more thing, she said – a packet that had been nagging her because it had been lying loose *under* the hanging folders in the cabinet. It did appear to contain a bundle of sheets (?37 to be precise) typed on what she was convinced was the same typewriter, on foolscap sheets of blue carbon. The material appeared to be biographical. There was even a mention of the Maelstrøm. She would be quite glad, she said, if I were able to identify the fragments positively as belonging to the Destry-Scholes archive, since she had no idea where else to put them. It would, she said, give the archive a little more body, so to speak. Would I like photocopies? She was afraid she would have to charge 5p per page.

I was excited by the idea of foolscap sheets of blue carbon, for I knew, as she did not, that the 'Art of Biography' notes had been made in that form. I wrote back, saying I would like to have the 37pp, and enclosing a cheque.

Ian McIntyre

THE GOD OF HIS IDOLATRY

*An extract from a biography of David Garrick to be
published autumn 1999 by Penguin*

SOME TIME IN 1767, the Mayor and Corporation of
Stratford-upon-Avon decided to demolish their old Town
Hall and build a new one. It was to be a modest affair, built
of Cotswold stone. On the north face the design provided for
a large ornamental niche, looking down on Sheep Street – just
the place for a statue of the town's most famous son.

The wordy agreement with the contractors demonstrated
that there was no intention of squandering the townspeople's
money. Wherever possible, salvaged materials were to be
used: 'Good Doors for the two Water Closets to be made out
of the old Doors.' A price of £678 was initially agreed, but
the Council decided that its own contribution should be
limited to £200. The task of raising the balance fell to the
town clerk, William Hunt.

It proved uphill work. There was a possibility that building
would have to be halted; and if there were insufficient funds
to complete the fabric, there would certainly not be enough to
decorate the interior – or fill that niche on the north face.

Then a man called Francis Wheler had an idea of brilliant
simplicity. Wheler was Steward of the Stratford Court of
Records. He was also a shrewd observer of human nature,
and having cleared his idea with the Corporation, he
addressed a letter to David Garrick. He began with a brief
description of the new building; then, with an elegance that
would have excited the admiration of Izaac Walton, Wheler
sent his fly hissing over the water:

*It would be a Reflection on the Town of Stratford to
have any publick Building erected Here without some
Ornamental Memorial of their immortal Townsman,
And the Corporation would be happy in receiving from
your hands some Statue Bust or Picture of him to be
placed within this Building, they would be equally
pleased to have some Picture of yourself that the
Memory of both may be perpetuated together in that
place wch gave him birth & where he still lives in the
mind of every Inhabitant –*

If that had been strictly true, the inhabitants might have
prodded the Corporation to celebrate the bicentenary of their
immortal Townsman's birth three years previously. No
matter; Wheler reeled in his line and cast a second time:

*The Corporation of Stratford ever desirous of Express-
ing their Gratitude to all who do honour & Justice to
the Memory of Shakespeare, & highly sensible that no
person in any Age hath Excelled you therein would
think themselves much honoured if you would become
one of their Body ... And to render the Freedom of
such a place the more acceptable to you the Corporation
propose to send it in a Box made of that very Mulberry
tree planted by Shakespears [sic] own hand ...*

Hook, line and sinker, naturally. The Corporation commissioned a casket, and Garrick approached Thomas Gainsborough to paint a portrait of Shakespeare, suggesting that he
might use as a model the familiar Martin Droeshout
engraving with the high forehead from the first Folio.

Gainsborough expressed his coolness to the idea with
characteristic forthrightness:

*Damn the original picture of him, with your leave; for I
think a stupider face I never beheld ...*
    *I intend, with your approbation, my dear friend, to
take the form from his pictures and statues, just enough*

84

to preserve his likeness past the doubt of all blockheads *at first sight, and supply a* soul *from his works: it is impossible that such a mind and ray of heaven could shine with such a face and pair of eyes as the picture has* . . .

Garrick then suggested he should inspect the bust over his tomb in Stratford, but this proved equally unfruitful: 'God damn it,' Gainsborough replied, 'Shakespeare's bust is a silly smiling thing, and I have not sense enough to make him more sensible in the picture, and so I tell ye, you shall not see it.' And no more he did, because Garrick settled instead for an unremarkable painting by Benjamin Wilson.

'Some Statue Bust or Picture.' Stratford was plainly soliciting a sculpture or a painting – one or the other. But what if Garrick were to offer them both? Thriftily, he turned to the sculptor John Cheere, the partner of his better-known brother Sir Henry. Henry, a pupil of Scheemaker, had done the statue of Shakespeare erected in Westminster Abbey in 1741 and a later version for Lord Pembroke at Wilton. The Cheeres had a flourishing practice in funerary monuments; more to the point, their workyard at Hyde Park Corner churned out copies of well-known statues in lead, and it was the Wilton Shakespeare which served as the model for Garrick's gift to Stratford.

Having responded thus generously to the Corporation's overtures, Garrick felt justified in suggesting that the expense of his own portrait might reasonably be borne by Stratford. He returned to Gainsborough and asked him to rework a portrait painted two years previously. Garrick looks pretty pleased with himself – possibly because, like so many of Gainsborough's subjects, he has been flatteringly elongated. Hat in hand, he leans nonchalantly against a bust of Shakespeare, rather like a drunk propping up a lamp-post. One arm is draped in a casually proprietary way round the top of the plinth; the bard might *just* be saying something to him out of the corner of his mouth.

Exactly when the idea of some sort of Shakespearean celebration at Stratford first occurred to Garrick is not clear. Henry Angelo records in his memoirs that he had often heard his father Domenico say that Garrick 'had long contemplated some public act of devotion as it were, to his favourite saint.' His thoughts certainly crystallised rapidly during the negotiations about the freedom: when he filed Wheler's first letter, he endorsed it, 'The Steward of Stratford's letter to me which produc'd yᵉ Jubilee.'

On his first visit – it was now the summer of 1769 – the new burgess was greeted by the pealing of church bells and entertained at the White Lion. Addressing the company after dinner, he outlined his ideas 'with much perspicuity, to the perfect approval of the meeting.' Garrick's way with words disguised the fact that those ideas were still extremely sketchy, but once Hunt had walked him round the town, his fertile mind was soon racing. A site must be found for 'the Great Booth,' a structure to serve as the main venue for formal dinners and indoor entertainments. Where could a display of fireworks best be mounted? What use could be made of the River Avon?

Some things moved forward with remarkable speed. Garrick had marked down a meadow, on the far side of the river, as a promising site for the fireworks. The view from the town, however, would be obstructed by trees, and Garrick asked Hunt to see if they could be felled. The land belonged to the Duke of Dorset, then High Steward of Stratford; on July 14th, a gang of workmen appeared, and by nightfall Banstead Mead had been cleared of well over a hundred willow trees.

Back in London Garrick gave his mind to the Jubilee to the exclusion of all else. He had already polished off the words of the dedication ode which he proposed to declaim to music: 'Dʳ Arne works like a dragon at it – he is all fire, & flame about it,' he told Hunt. As summer wore on, however, reports reached Garrick that not everyone in Stratford was as well-disposed as his Grace of Dorset, and he quizzed Hunt anxiously:

I heard Yesterday to my Surprize, that the Country People did not seem to relish our Jubilee, that they looked upon it to be popish & that we sh^d raise ye Devil, & w^t not – I suppose this may be a joke, – but after all my trouble, pains labour & Expence for their Service, & ye honor of ye County, I shall think it very hard, if I am not to be receiv'd kindly by them –

By mid-August Garrick was exhausted. 'I have really half kill'd Myself wth this business,' he told Hunt, '& if I Escape Madness, or fevers I shall be very happy.' On a more cheerful note, he had a secret to impart: 'I will whisper a word in y^r Ear. I am told that his Majesty wishes to hear the Ode, & I shall tomorrow make an Offer of performing it before him, at his Palace privately –' The offer was graciously accepted, and Garrick announced that the reading had met with 'much approbation'; he had been with the King and Queen for three and a quarter hours.

Garrick had also been churning out great numbers of ballads, glees and roundelays, but getting these set did not prove easy. He had a particularly difficult time with Charles Dibdin. The young singer and composer, twenty-four at the time, was convinced that Garrick had no ear for music. Years later, in his memoirs, he relived his exasperation:

I set and reset songs to it till my patience was exhausted, which were received or rejected just as ignorance or caprice prevailed ... He really had not an idea of how to write for music, and I frequently ventured at hinting alterations, as to measure, for the advantage of what he wrote ... Matters went on in this train, till at last I was so palpably insulted that I declared I would not go to Stratford.

Slowly – very slowly – the Rotunda was taking shape, although when Garrick's friend Joseph Cradock rode over to Stratford at the end of August he was appalled. The workmen were short of tools, and some building materials had still not arrived. 'Take care,' said the acquaintance who showed him round, 'that you do not cut your shoes from the broken lamps; they were intended for the illumination of this building; but, if they ever left Drury-lane in safety, you see they are all here shivered to pieces.'

Garrick became worried as the Jubilee approached at reports of profiteering by the townspeople, and wrote to Hunt in some agitation:

> *The exorbitant price that some of yᵉ People ask, will Effect the whole Jubilee, and rise up a mortal Sin against us – such imposition may serve yᵉ Ends of a few selfish people, but the Town will suffer for it hereafter, & we for the present –*

The press was having a field day. No need in 1769, with Stratford to write about, for the silly season to be brought forward. Garrick was reported to have despatched Robert Baddeley, celebrated for his portrayal of the Lord Mayor in *Richard III*, to give the Mayor of Stratford lessons in etiquette; a fat landlady in the town was said to have been injured falling from a hay-loft while practising the balcony scene from *Romeo and Juliet* . . .

Garrick left London five days before the grand opening. Stratford had been filling up for a week past. The *London Chronicle* reported that there were upward of forty carriages at the White Lion, and 'they were obliged to turn several great families away.' It was not just the quality who were flooding in, however:

> *Hairdressers? – a world; though when one sees what numbers of bushel-heads there are in town every day, it is not to be wondered where they find employment . . . Wenches! never was any paradise so plentifully and beautifully inhabited as here at this time . . .*

Stratford-mania spilled from the editorial columns into the advertisements:

For the STRATFORD JUBILEE

*To those who would appear really elegant there, or
elsewhere, the Albion Dentifrice is recommended, as
without a sweet Breath and clean Mouth (which no
cloying Odours of perfumed Essence will give) there can
be no communicative Satisfaction . . .*

Someone who was becoming thoughtful about communicative satisfaction – more precisely the lack of it – was
Charles Dibdin. He had made his gesture. He had flounced
out, and, rather spitefully, had taken with him the unset
words of the dawn serenade with which Garrick had hoped
to start the first day's proceedings. Now the young composer
was having second thoughts, and the desire to hear his music
publicly performed grew by the hour; rapidly he set the words
for guitars and flutes.

Then he rushed off to Stratford, scoured the taverns and
lodging-houses for musicians and rehearsed them through the
night. Soon after five the next morning, wearing masks and
got up as grimy-faced yokels, they made their way to
Garrick's lodgings:

> *Let beauty with the sun arise,*
> *To* SHAKESPEARE *tribute pay,*
> *With heavenly smiles and speaking eyes,*
> *Give grace and lustre to the day . . .*

Most of the town was in fact already wide awake; at first
light, there had been a triple discharge of seventeen cannon
and twelve mortars. This was followed by the ringing of
church bells; a musical detachment from the Warwickshire
Militia was also on duty, parading the streets to the fife and
drum.

Shortly after eight, Garrick arrived at the Town Hall to
check the preparations for breakfast. He was attired in his

velvet Jubilee suit, trimmed with gold and lined with taffeta. The colour shifted in the light from mole to amber; he wore a long waistcoat with thirteen gold buttons and a rather special pair of white gloves – said to be the very ones worn on the stage by Shakespeare himself.

Breakfast was followed by Thomas Arne's oratorio *Judith*, conducted in the collegiate church by the composer. One visitor arrived late, but made a gratifyingly arresting entry just as the elegant audience was beginning to leave:

> *I was exceedingly dirty; my hair hung wet about my ears; my black suit and the postillion's grey duffle above it, several inches too short every way, made a very strange appearance. I could observe people getting together and whispering about me, for the church was full of well-dressed people. At last Mr. Garrick observed me. We first made an attitude to each other and then cordially shook hands. I gave him a line I had written to let him know I was incognito, as I wished to appear in the Corsican dress for the first time they should know me. Many of those who had stared, seeing that I was intimate with the steward of the Jubilee, came up and asked who I was. He answered, 'A clergyman in disguise.'*

James Boswell had arrived in town. He had recently achieved some celebrity. His account of his adventures in Corsica, and his friendship with the rebel general Paoli, was already in a third edition.

He had not originally intended to go to Stratford. Having recently become engaged to his cousin, he had travelled to London for treatment of his old venereal complaint; once there, however, he found himself 'within the whirlpool of curiosity, which could not fail to carry me down.' It was also a splendid opportunity to publicise his book – and himself. His Corsican patriot's uniform was unfortunately in Edinburgh, but in three days he had assembled a reasonable replica, complete with pistol, stiletto, long musket and a grenadier's cap embroidered in gold with *Viva la Libertà*. The connection with Shakespeare was not immediately obvious, but that did not bother 'Corsican' Boswell.

Seven hundred guests sat down to dinner at the Rotunda that afternoon. The fare included 'all the rarities the season could afford.' Service was slow, but the wine was good; Lord Grosvenor proposed a full bumper to the Steward's health 'for his Care and Attention,' and Garrick responded with a toast to the Bard of Avon. A highlight of the singing which followed was Garrick's lyric 'Sweet Willy O.' This had an unsettling effect on Boswell: 'I rose and went near the orchestra,' he wrote, 'and looked steadfastly at that beautiful, insinuating creature Mrs Baddeley of Drury Lane.'*

An army of stage-hands and assistants had little more than two hours to prepare for that evening's Ball – minuets until midnight, and then cotillions and country dances until the small hours. Three short hours later, the cannon boomed out again and the church bells rang. There had been occasional drizzle the day before, but now the English autumn declared itself in earnest; the cobbled streets were awash and the Avon, already high after a wet summer, was rising ominously.

Local wiseacres had theories. Some pointed to the effect of the morning cannonades on swollen rain clouds. Others blamed the comet which had been observed for some nights past – 'of a livid blue Colour, situate to the Right of the Pleiades, a little below Taurus.' Darker reasons were also adduced – it was a sign of divine displeasure at the town's lapse into pagan idolatry. Out and about in the streets, young Henry Angelo encountered an elderly dowager who sounds like a character from one of Garrick's farces: 'What an *absurd* climate!' she exclaimed.

---

* Sophia Baddeley, then in her mid-twenties, was the daughter of George II's serjeant-trumpeter. She had eloped at the age of eighteen with the actor Robert Baddeley, from whom she was now estranged. She was equally celebrated for her exceptional beauty and the looseness of her morals.

Garrick's day had begun badly. He had a cold, which had affected his voice, but there was worse:

The man who was to shave him, perhaps not quite sober, absolutely cut him from the corner of his mouth to his chin ... the ladies were engaged in applying constant stiptics to stop the bleeding.

Then Garrick set off to salvage what he could of the day's events. He was deeply reluctant to abandon the pageant. Apart from the fireworks, it was the element in the festival most calculated to appeal to the sceptical townsfolk – no tickets were required. Lacy, however, his Drury Lane partner, hostile to the scheme from the start, was adamant:

Who the devil, Davy, would venture upon the procession under such a lowering aspect? Sir, all the ostrich feathers will be spoiled, and the property will be damnified five thousand pounds.

The procession was abandoned. Garrick sent an urgent order to the printer for 500 quarto handbills – the Ode would be performed in the amphitheatre at noon.

The audience that assembled there was not in the best of moods. The roof of the hastily completed Rotunda was beginning to leak. When the cannons boomed and Garrick took his place in front of Arne and the hundred-strong orchestra and chorus, it seemed to the correspondent of *Lloyd's Evening Post* that he looked 'a little confused or intimidated.' Not for long, however. There was a brief overture. Garrick bowed to the company, and received in return 'a very respectful Clap of unanimous Applause.' Then, quietly, he launched into the first recitative:

> *To what blest genius of the isle,*
> *Shall Gratitude her tribute pay,*
> *Decree the festive day,*
> *Erect the statue, and devote the pile? ...*

'Tis he! 'tis he!
'The god of our idolatry!'

He took his audience by surprise. To most of them recitative
meant 'that which is in general the most languid and
neglected Part of a musical Performance.' Here the words
were *spoken*, and they were spoken by the most famous and
most brilliantly controlled voice in England.

For the rest of the performance Garrick held the audience
in the palm of his hand. The Ode does not withstand
particularly rigorous scrutiny as poetry – it is, in truth,
something of a hodge-podge, echoes of Shakespeare, Milton
and the oratorios of Handel cheek by jowl with common-
place phrases like 'tuneful numbers' and 'our humble strains.'
The performance was all, however, and it was frequently
interrupted by 'turbulent applause.'

Towards the end, there was a sequence where Garrick sang
the praises of the Avon, setting it higher than the Thames, the
Cam and the Isis. This was followed by the sixth air. The
words are appalling rubbish, but the ravishing Mrs Baddeley
sang them so enchantingly that an encore was called for:

. . . Flow on, silver Avon; in song ever flow,
Be the swans on thy bosom still whiter than snow,
Ever full be thy stream, like his fame may it spread,
And the turf ever hallow'd which pillow'd his head.

At this point Garrick ventured an audacious *coup de théâtre*.
The doors of the Rotunda were thrown open. Very little of
the ever-hallowed turf was to be seen; the meadow had been
churned into mud, and the silver Avon – rather a dirty brown
by now – was swirling alarmingly close to the audience.
Nobody giggled. The spell was unbroken. At that moment
the magic of Garrick's Steward's wand was every bit as
powerful as Prospero's.

As he made his bow, there was a rush of admirers to the
orchestra rail, many of them 'illustrious for rank and literary
talent.' The enthusiasm of the audience was too much for the

fabric of the Rotunda. A number of benches gave way under the strain, and people were thrown to the floor. In some places the walls buckled: 'had it not been for a peculiar Interposition of Providence, Lord Carlisle, who was very much hurt by the fall of a Door, must inevitably have been destroyed.'

The performance had overrun. With dinner to serve at four, the cooks and waiters were becoming restive. When the guests were readmitted, they feasted on a huge turtle. When alive, it had weighed 327 pounds – 'which with a number of other Dainties, and rich Wines,' wrote Victor, the Drury Lane treasurer, 'was only a proper Entertainment for the splendid Company assembled there.' Not everyone agreed. 'We, indeed, had something which was called turtle,' wrote one correspondent, 'and something which went under the denomination of claret; but if it had not been for the dignity of the appellations, we might as well have been regaled upon neck of beef, and Southampton port.'

Outside, on the far bank of the river, Domenico Angelo was contemplating the collapse of his dreams. He had volunteered to look after the fireworks; his son Harry never forgot how wholeheartedly he had thrown himself into the preparations:

> *I think I yet see my father, looking another* Marlborough – *great as that hero, ordering the lines and circumvallations before Lisle or Tournay, as he stood, directing his engineers, in the fabricating of* rockets, crackers, catherine-wheels, *and* squibs . . .

In the meadow, a huge transparent screen had been erected. The design on the central arch showed Shakespeare being led by Time to Immortality, flanked on either side by Tragedy and Comedy. The townspeople had braved the rain in impressive numbers, and lined the river bank. All manner of pyrotechnic marvels had been promised – Diamond Pieces of Stars and Fountains, Porcupine's Quills, Tourbillons, Pyramids of Chinese Fires.

'The fireworks were in dudgeon with the waterworks. The rockets would not ascend for fear of catching cold, and the surly crackers went out at a single pop.' Henry Angelo managed to make it sound amusing in his memoirs, but his father was not amused on the night. The touch-papers were sodden and matches fizzled out the moment they were struck. Little more than half way through the programme, Angelo conceded defeat.

One last item remained on the day's programme – the Masquerade. The Rotunda was now surrounded not just by mud but by great expanses of water. An over-long speech of welcome by Garrick went down like a lead balloon, and it took some time for anything resembling a party spirit to develop.

Lady Pembroke and two other celebrated beauties ran about cackling hideously as the witches from *Macbeth*; when, to great applause, they unmasked, 'the contrast between the Deformity of the feigned, and the Beauty of the real Appearance was universally admired.' There were Shepherd-esses, Pierrots, Chinese Mandarins, Foxhunters and High-landers:

> *One gentleman had no other disguise than a pair of horns, publickly owning himself for a cuckold ... and wearing the badges of his dignity erect. Some indeed said, this character ought not to be admitted, lest it should be deemed a reflection on the worthy corpora-tion.*

At one point a fight broke out between one of the several Devils present and a parson called Cook from Worcestershire who had come as a chimney-sweep – both wished to dance with the same lady. Later in the evening, Cook was accosted by the lively and extremely pretty Lady Craven, already at nineteen well-known in London society for her forward ways. 'Well, Mr Sweep,' she demanded, 'why don't you come and sweep my Chimney?' To which Cook, with some presence of mind, replied, 'Why, an' please your Ladyship, the last time I swept it I burnt my Brush.'*

The dancing continued till dawn. 'All zealous friends endeavoured to keep up the spirit of it as long as they could,' wrote Cradock, 'till they were at last informed that the Avon was rising so very fast, that no delay could be admitted.' Descriptions of the scenes that followed suggest a painting by Breughel. Some of the dancers decided that the only thing for it was to wade through the flood, and an unfortunate few found themselves wallowing in concealed ditches. Several gallants – they included the Devil who had done battle with Parson Cook – offered to carry ladies to safety pick-a-back. One helpless female was not what she seemed, however. Halfway to firm ground, 'the Rudeness of the Wind occasion'd the Discovery of a Pair of Buckskin Breeches underneath her outer Garments.' The impostor was promptly dumped, and the Devil waded on alone, holding his tail clear of the water.

The Jubilee was now clearly holed below the water-line. On the third morning Garrick took grim stock of the situation, cancelled the pageant a second time and quietly shelved a projected second performance of the Ode. In spite of the state of the course at Shottery, it was decided that the race for the Jubilee Cup should go ahead. All five entries ran, if that is what horses do when they are knee-deep in water – the race, Lady Archer was heard to say, 'should have been between Pegasuses.' The winner was a groom called Pratt, riding his own horse, Whirligig. He received a silver cup worth £50 engraved with Shakespeare's arms. Afterwards, he declared that he would never part with it, though 'he knew very little about *Plays*, or Master SHAKESPEARE.'

The rain finally stopped, and that evening Angelo salved his pride by letting off the handful of serviceable fireworks

* The Countess of Craven (1750–1828), wife of the sixth Earl, later left her husband (by whom she had six children) and travelled extensively abroad. She lived with, and subsequently married, the Margrave of Anspach. She published an account of her travels, and several of her plays were performed on the London stage.

that remained to him. The Rotunda was unusable, but at the request of several determined ladies, a small company assembled one last time at the Town Hall. 'Mrs Garrick danced a Minuet beyond description gracefully, and joined in the Country Dances, which ended at Four, and put an end to the Jubilee.'*

An end to the Jubilee, but the beginning of a national and international cult. This curious festival – at which not a single work of Shakespeare's was performed – marked the birth of Bardolatry, even though more than a hundred and thirty years would pass before George Bernard Shaw coined the actual word.† The Rotunda was the first location of that flourishing multinational concern which we know today as the Shakespeare industry. Nowadays it has plant on both sides of the Atlantic – from London's Barbican to the festival theatres at Stratford, Ontario, from the splendid Folger Shakespeare Library in Washington DC to the mock-Tudor McDonald's on Waterside.

The man who started it all got back to his house at Hampton on September 11th. He was dispirited, angry and exhausted. The new season at Drury Lane was due to begin in five days' time.

---

* St James's Chronicle, 9–12 September 1769.
† Shaw first used the word in the preface to his Plays for Puritans in 1901.

Don Paterson

PROVERBS

after Antonio Machado

You see an eye
because it sees you

∾

Seek him in the mirror,
your fellow traveller.

∾

Your Narcissus
begins to fade
as he *becomes* the glass.

∾

Always today, always

∾

The Sun in Aries; my window
open to the cold air . . . listen:
the dusk has awoken the river

∾

And deeper down . . . listen:
the water in the living rock
of my own heart

∾

A surprise – the smell
of ripe lemons
in the rose-leaves

∾

Now spring has arrived,
don't chew on the wax –
get out of the hive!

∾

In my solitude
I have seen things
that are not true.

∾

Water, thirst, sun, shadow – they're all good things.
There's a honey from the flowerless fields
as well as from the rosemary flowers.

∾

At the side of the road
there's a stone fountain
and a small earthen jug –
glug – that no one steals.

∾

So . . . what's meant
by the spring, the jug
and the water?

∾

. . . but I've seen men drink
from ditches;
ah, the caprices
of the parched mind . . .

∾

Singers: best
to leave the cheering
to the rest.

∾

Singers, wake up:
the echoes have stopped

∾

It's not the true
I the poet's after:
it's the *you*

∾

. . . But that *you* in my song
doesn't mean you, pal;
no – that's me.

∾

What the wise
forget to say
is that today's
always today

∾

Christ taught: love your brother
as yourself, but don't forget –
you're one thing, he's another.

∾

He spoke another truth:
find the you that isn't yours
and *can't* be.

∾

So many lies
from the man
who can't fantasise

∾

You told a half-truth?
Now you'll be twice a liar
if you tell the other half.

∾

All things in good time –
like the river, the lover,
the cup must be full
before it runs over

∾

After the life and the dream
comes what matters most:
the awakening

∾

His thin voice trembles when he sings;
he thinks they don't know art –
it's not his song they hiss at, though:
they're hissing at his heart

∾

Have you heard the latest?
cogito ergo non sum.
In your dreams . . .

∾

Two gypsies:
'Where're you taking us?'
'A detour on the shortcut.'

∾

Hey – let's divide the work, so
the bad guys dip the arrows,
the good guys flex the bow . . .

∾

To keep the wind working,
he sewed the dead leaves back again

∾

Bees, singers, remember:
it's not the honey you're
sipping at – it's the *flower*.

∾

Light your poem from two angles:
one for the straight reading,
one for the sidelong

∾

Not the sunrise
but the waking bell

∾

Among figs I am soft as a fig,
among rocks, hard as rock;
in other words . . . useless.

∾

Your truth? No, *the* truth.
Come on, we'll look for it.
Yours . . . please, keep it.

∾

Guadalquivir!
I've seen you in Cazorla,
clear water bubbling
under a green pine;
and today, dying in Sanlúcar.
As you slow with salt and mud
and the sea draws near,
do you thrill with the blood
of your first spring
as I do mine?

∾

Take an old man's word:
not his advice

102

∾

But Art? . . . pure play,
which is to say, pure life,
which is to say, pure fire –
we'll see it, one day.

Matthew Sweeney

DO NOT THROW STONES AT THIS SIGN

Do not throw stones at this sign
which stands here, in a stony field
a stone's throw from the sea
whose beach is a mess of pebbles
since the sand was stolen for building,
and the few people who dawdle there,
rods in hand, catch nothing,
not even a shoe – might as well
bombard the waves with golfballs,
or wade in and hold their breath,
or bend, as they do, and grab a handful
of pebbles to throw at the sign,
and each time they hit it they cheer
and chalk up another beer, especially
the man who thought up the sign,
who got his paintbrush and wrote
'Do Not Throw Stones At This Sign'
on a piece of driftwood which he stuck
in this useless field, then, laughing,
danced his way to the house of beer.

ROADKILL

Scrape the cat off the road,
take it home and fillet out the flesh,
throw it in the marinade
where the deer you wrecked your bumper on
a week before Xmas, sits
in chunks, alongside slivers of fox,
a boned, de-spined hedgehog,

the legs and breasts of a slow hare –
all in a bath of red wine
with onion slices and garlic,
and an ounce of juniper berries.
That cat was the last ingredient
you didn't know you needed
and had better keep secret.
After a day, strain the marinade
and cook the meat all morning
in the wine and blood.
Serve in bowls, with bread.

Jeffrey Archer

SOMETHING FOR NOTHING

JAKE BEGAN TO dial the number slowly, as he did every evening at six o'clock since his father had passed away. For the next fifteen minutes he settled back to listen to what his mother had done that day.

His mother led such a sober orderly life that she rarely had anything of interest to tell him, least of all on Saturday. She had coffee every morning with her oldest friend, Mollie Preston, and some days that would last until lunch. On Mondays, Wednesdays and Fridays she played bridge with the Taylors across the road; on Tuesdays and Thursdays she visited her sister, Nancy – which at least that gave her something to grumble about, when he rang on those particular evenings.

On Saturdays she rested from the rigours of the week. Her only strenuous activity was to purchase the bulk of the Sunday edition of the *Times* just after lunch (a strange New York tradition), which at least gave her the chance to tell her son what stories he should select from its three hundred pages the following morning.

Each evening's conversation would consist of a few appropriate phrases according to the day. Monday, Wednesday, Friday, how did the bridge go, how much did you win/lose? Tuesday, Thursday, how is Aunt Nancy? – really, that bad. Saturday, anything interesting in the *Times* that I should be looking out for tomorrow?

Observant readers will be aware that there are seven days in any given week and will now be wanting to know about

Sunday. On Sunday Jake's mother always came to lunch with the family so her son didn't need to call her.

Jake dialled the last digit of his mother's number and waited for her to pick up the phone. He prepared himself to learn what would be in tomorrow's New York *Times*. It usually took two or three rings before she answered the phone, the amount of time required for her to walk from her chair by the fire to the phone on the other side of the room. When the tone continued past four, five, six or even seven rings, Jake began to wonder if she was out. But that was surely not possible. She was never out at six, winter or summer. She kept to a routine that would have brought a smile to the lips of a marine sergeant.

Then came the click, and he was about to say 'Hi, Mom, it's Jake', when he heard a voice that was certainly not his mother's, and was already in mid-conversation. Realising he'd got a crossed line, he was going to put the phone down when he heard the voice say,

'There'll be one hundred thousand dollars in it for you, all you have to do is turn up and collect it. It's been left in an envelope for you at Billy's.'

'So where's Billy's?' said a new voice.

'On the corner of Oak Street and Randall. They'll be expecting you around eight.'

Jake tried not to breathe in or out as he wrote down on the pad by the phone. Oak and Randall.

'But how will they know the envelope is for me?' asked the second voice.

'You simply ask for a copy of the New York *Times* and hand over a hundred dollar bill. He'll then produce an envelope, which he will slip inside the paper. He'll also give you a quarter change, as if you'd handed him a dollar. That way if there's anyone else in the shop they won't become suspicious. And remember, don't open the envelope until you're in a safe place, there are a lot of people who would like to get their hands on $100,000, and whatever you do, don't contact me again, because if you do, it won't be a pay-off you can expect to get this time.' The line went dead.

When Jake heard the purring sound he replaced the phone on the hook, having forgotten that he was supposed to be ringing his mother.

He sat down and considered what to do next . . . if anything. Ellen had taken the kids to a movie, as she did every Saturday, and they weren't expected back until nine. His uncooked dinner would be waiting in the microwave with a note to tell him how many minutes it should be switched on for. He always added one minute.

Jake found himself flicking through the New York tele-phone directory A–F. He turned over the pages until he reached *Bi, Bil, Bill, Billy, Billy's*. And there it was on 1127 Oak Street. He closed the directory and walked through to his den where he continued to play out the game. On the bookshelf behind his desk he searched for his gazette of New York. He found it wedged in between a volume of Schwarz-kopf's memoirs and *How To Lose Twenty Pounds When You're Over Forty*.

He turned to the index in the back and quickly turned to the right page. He began checking the numbers on the side and the letters across the bottom before he placed his finger on the correct square. It would take him at least thirty to forty minutes to travel over to the West Side. He glanced at his watch. It was 6.14. What was he thinking? He had no intention of going anywhere. To start with, he didn't have a hundred dollars.

Jake took out his wallet from the inside pocket of his jacket, and leafed through some small notes. Thirty-seven dollars. He walked through to the kitchen to check Ellen's petty cash box. It was locked, and he couldn't remember where she hid the key. He took a screwdriver from the drawer below the hob and forced open the box to discover another twenty-two dollars. He paced around the kitchen trying to think. And then he remembered.

He left the kitchen and went up to his daughter's room. Suzie's Snoopy money box was on her dressing table. He picked it up and walked over to the bed where he turned the box upside down, shaking all the coins out on to the bed. Suzie had saved seven dollars and seventy-five cents. He sat on the end of his daughter's bed, desperately trying to concentrate, and then recalled the fifty dollars he always kept folded in his driving licence for emergencies. He put all the money on the bed and began to add it up. It came to one hundred and sixteen dollars and seventy-five cents.

Jake checked his watch. It was 6.23. He would go and take a look – no more, he told himself.

He collected the money, removed his old overcoat from the hall cupboard, and left the apartment, checking as he did that all three locks on the front door were securely bolted. He pressed the elevator button, but there was no sound. Out of order again, Jake thought, so began jogging down the stairs. Across the street was a bar where he often had a drink, whenever Ellen took the children to the movies.

The barman smiled as Jake came in. 'The usual?' he asked, somewhat surprised to see Jake wearing a heavy overcoat when he only lived across the road. 'No, thanks,' said Jake, 'I just wondered if you had a hundred dollar note in the till,' he added, trying to sound casual.

'Not sure if I do,' the barman replied, making it sound as if it was not a request he was asked that often. Rummaging around in a stack of notes, he turned back to Jake. 'You're in luck. Just the one.'

Jake handed over the fifty, a twenty, two tens, a five, five ones and received in exchange a one hundred dollar bill. Folding the note carefully in four, he slipped it into his driving licence, which he returned to the inside pocket of his jacket. He left the bar and walked out on to the street without saying goodbye.

He ambled slowly across two blocks, until he came to a bus stop that would take him to the West Side. Perhaps he would be too late, and then the problem would take care of itself, he thought, as a bus drew into the kerb. Jake climbed the steps and pushed two dollars into the plastic box, before taking a seat near the back, still uncertain what he planned to do when he reached the West Side.

Jake became so deep in thought about the phone conversation he had overheard, that he travelled one stop too far, and had to walk almost a mile back up town before he reached Oak Street. He began to check the numbers on the door. It had to be be at least another three or four blocks before Oak Street crossed Randall.

As he covered each block he found his pace slowing with every step, but suddenly there it was on the next corner, half way up a lamp-post, a white and green sign – Randall Street. His eyes returned to the ground, then quickly checked all four corners, almost missing the sign above the newsagent that read 'Billy's', because the cream letters were so faded. He stared, and then checked his watch again. It was 7.43. He began to walk round the block, fearing that anyone who saw him standing there might think it suspicious.

He strolled back up the North Side and watched as one or two people went in and out of Billy's. He came to a halt on the corner opposite the shop. A moment later, when the light on the other side started flashing 'Walk', he found himself being pushed across by the other pedestrians.

He checked his watch yet again. Nine minutes to eight. He walked slowly past the door of Billy's and spotted a man behind the counter stacking papers. He wore a black T-shirt and jeans. He must have been around forty, a shade under six foot, with shoulders that could only have ended up that way by spending several hours a day in a gym.

A customer brushed past Jake as he stood in the doorway of Billy's. He ordered a packet of Marlboros, and passed over a note to the man behind the counter. While the shopkeeper was handing him his change, Jake stepped into the shop, and pretended to take an interest in the magazine rack.

As the customer turned to leave, Jake slipped his hand into the inside pocket of his jacket. He then took out his driving licence, and touched the edge of the one hundred dollar bill. As the Marlboro man walked out on to the pavement Jake put his driving licence back into his inside pocket, leaving the hundred dollars in the palm of his hand. The man behind the counter stood waiting impassively while Jake slowly unfolded the bill. 'A copy of the New York *Times*,' Jake heard himself saying, as he placed the one hundred dollar bill on the counter.

The man in the black T-shirt glanced at the note and checked his watch. He seemed to hesitate for a moment before placing his right hand under the counter. Jake tensed at the movement, until he saw a long thin envelope emerge which the man proceeded to slip into heavy folds of the newspaper's business section. He then handed the paper over to Jake, his face still impassive. He took the one hundred dollar bill, rang up seventy-five cents on the register, and gave Jake a quarter change. Jake turned and walked quickly out of the shop, nearly knocking over a small man who looked equally nervous.

Jake almost ran down Oak Street, glancing back over his shoulder several times to see if anyone was following him. Checking again, he spotted a yellow cab driving towards him and quickly hailed it. The East Side, he said, jumping into the cab.

As the driver eased back into the traffic, Jake slid the envelope out from between the mass of papers and transferred it to an inside pocket. He could hear his heart beating. For the next fifteen minutes he could barely take his eyes from the back window.

Seeing a subway coming up on the right, he ordered the driver to pull into the kerb. Jake handed over ten dollars, jumped out of the taxi and dashed into the subway, emerging a few moments later on the far side of the road. He then hailed another taxi going in the opposite direction. This time he gave the driver his home address, pleased with his little subterfuge, which he'd seen carried out by Michael Douglas in Movie of the Week.

Nervously Jake touched his inside pocket to be sure the envelope was still in place. He no longer bothered to look out of the rear window, confident that no one could now be following him. He was tempted to look inside the envelope, but the voice on the phone had warned against anyone observing its contents. There would be time enough to do that, once he was back in the safety of his apartment. He checked his watch, 8.21. Ellen and the children wouldn't be back from the movies yet.

'Another fifty yards on the left,' Jake told the driver, happy to be back on familiar territory. He cast one final glance through the rear window as the taxi drew in to the kerb near his block. In the road behind him was a pantechnicon and the blue bus that took him to work every weekday morning. Jake put his hand into his pocket, and paid off the driver with the quarters and dimes taken from his daughter's Snoopy box. He then jumped out of the taxi and ran into the building.

He rushed across the hall and banged the elevator button with the palm of his hand. It still wasn't functioning. He cursed and began to run up the seven flights of stairs to his apartment. Breathless, he unbolted the three locks of the front door, and once inside, slammed it behind him, resting against it while he got his breath back.

He was pulling the envelope out of his inside pocket when the phone began to ring. His first thought was that they had traced him, and wanted their money back. He stared at the phone, picked up the receiver nervously, and listened.

'Hello, Jake, is that you?'

'Yes, Mom,' and then he remembered.

'You didn't call at six,' she said.

'I'm sorry, Mom. I did but . . .' He decided against telling her what had happened.

'I've been trying to get you for the past hour. Have you been out or something?'

'Just across the road for a drink. I sometimes do whenever Ellen takes the children to the movies.'

He placed the envelope next to the phone, desperate to be rid of her, but aware that nothing would stop her going through the Saturday routine.

'Anything interesting in the *Times*, Mom?' he heard himself saying, rather too quickly.

'Clinton looks unlikely to be impeached, but he's bought a new meaning to "fag end of an administration". I can't think why I voted for him in the first place.'

'I did tell you not to at the time,' he said, giving the standard reply. Jake picked up the envelope and squeezed it, testing what a hundred thousand dollars felt like.

'Anything else of interest, Mom?' he threw in.

'Fascinating insight piece, in the style section, about widows of seventy still having the sex drive. Now their husbands are safely in their graves it seems they're popping Viagra and getting back into the old routine. One of them is quoted as saying, "I'm not so much making up for lost time, as attempting to catch up with him."'

As he continued to listen, Jake began to ease open the envelope at the top right-hand corner.

'I'd try it myself,' his mother was saying, 'but I can't afford the necessary facelift that seems to be part of the deal.'

'Mom, I think I can hear Ellen and the children at the front door. I'd better say goodbye. We'll see you at lunch tomorrow.'

'But I haven't told you about the fascinating piece in the business section.'

Sliding his little finger into the top right-hand corner Jake began slowly to tear open the envelope.

'I'm listening.'

'It's a story about the latest scam. I don't know what they'll think of next.'

The envelope was half open. Jake itched to continue.

'It seems that a highly sophisticated gang have found a way of tapping into your phone, while you're dialling another number.'

Another inch and he could tip the contents out on to the table.

'So when you dial you think you've got a crossed line.'

Jake dropped the envelope onto the table and listened more carefully.

'They then set you up by making you believe you are listening to a real conversation between two people.'

Sweat began to appear on Jake's forehead, as he stared down at the half-opened envelope.

JEFFREY ARCHER

'During the conversation you are led to expect that, if you travel to the other side of the city and hand over a hundred dollar note, you will receive in exchange an envelope containing one hundred thousand dollars.'

Jake felt sick at the thought of how easily he had parted with his hundred dollars, and how skilfully they had induced him do so.

'They're using tobacconists, newsagents, even small delicatessens to carry out the scam,' continued his mother. 'And in fact it's them who end up clearing one hundred thousand a week.'

'But what's in the envelope?' demanded Jake.

'Now that's where they are really clever,' said his mother. 'Because they enclose a small booklet in the envelope giving advice on how to make a hundred thousand dollars, so they're not even breaking the law. You've got to hand it to them,' she added.

I already have, Mom, Jake wanted to say, but he just slammed the phone down and stared at the envelope, as the front door bell began to ring. Ellen and the kids must be back from the movie and she had, once again, left her keys behind.

The bell rang again.

'OK, I'm coming, I'm coming,' shouted Jake. He seized the envelope, determined to leave no trace of its embarrassing existence. As the front door bell rang a third time, he ran into the kitchen, opened the incinerator and threw the envelope in. He pressed a button and heard the whirring sound, as the bell rang again. This time Ellen was keeping her finger on the button. Jake ran to the door.

He threw open the door to greet his wife only to find three massive men standing in the hallway. The one wearing a black T-shirt and crumpled jeans jumped forward and held a knife to his throat, propelling him back, while the other two threw him on to the floor. The door slammed closed.

'Where's the envelope?' the man shouted, holding the knife to Jake's throat.

'What envelope?' protested Jake. 'It was all a con.'

'Don't play games with us,' shouted the second. 'We want our hundred thousand dollars.'

'But there was only a book inside. I threw it into the incinerator. Listen, you can hear for yourself.'

The one in the black T-shirt cocked his head, while the other two remained silent. There was a distant sound of the incinerator coming to the end of its duty.

'Then you're going to have to go the same way,' said the man holding the knife.

He was just about to cut Jake's throat when the phone and the front door bell both began ringing at once.

Mordecai Richler

PEDDLER'S DIARY

VAUDEVILLE ISN'T DEAD. But the traditional song-and-dance men, jugglers, animal acts and stand-up comics have been displaced by jet-lagged authors, a far less entertaining bunch, who will read from their works in bookshops on the circuit, wherever at least eight potential customers can be found. On a typical week in Los Angeles, the *Los Angeles Times Book Review* (October 29, 1997) lists no less than eighty peddlers reading in various locations. These include Peter J. Harris, author of *The Vampire Who Drinks Gospel Music*; Mollie Katzen, who has written *Mollie Katzen's Vegetable Heaven*; Terry Berland, who will discuss his very own *Breaking Into Commercials*; Jared Diamond, author of *Why Sex Is Fun*; and a highly suspect 'writers' workshop for teenage girls' in Beyond Baroque, out there on Venice Boulevard. To be fair, the same week there are also some better-known scribblers working the territory: John Berger, James Ellory, Judith Rossner, Arundhati Roy and Will Self.

September 16, 1997. Montreal. A day before starting out on a cross-Canada book promotion tour, the omens are bad. Striding down Crescent Street, late in the afternoon, bound for my favoured watering hole, I am stopped by a gentleman from Vancouver.

'Aren't you Mordecai Richler?'

'Yes.'

'Let me shake your hand. I've read everything you've written. I think you're wonderful.'

'Well, thank you.'

'Now let me ask you a question. What do you do for a living?'

Then there is a letter from a college in Hamilton, Ontario, inviting me to speak: 'Your book, *The Apprenticeship of Duddy Kravitz*, has long been a fixture in our English classes. Students are amazed to discover that you are still alive.'

September 17. Toronto. In town to deliver the Donner Foundation lecture, I first submit to lunch with Ms. Jan Wong, a *Globe and Mail* columnist. 'How tall are you?' she asks.

Five foot eight, I say, startled.

'And how tall is your wife?'

'Why do you want to know?'

'I need to describe you.'

Pursuing her literary inquiries, she asks if our children are getting a Jewish education. Married to a Jew herself, she allows, with a self-satisfied smile, 'We have a seder every Friday night.'

'That must be a Jewish-Chinese custom. We manage it only once a year. On Passover.'

Finally, she is annoyed with me. 'You're not living up to your reputation. You didn't have much to drink. I think it's because you're trying to impress me.'

There's a six-page fax waiting for me back in my hotel room. It's from Knopf Canada. A list of interviews, readings and book signings I'm to do cross-Canada. I've been wary of morning show TV interviewers ever since one of those relentlessly cheerful young women squeezed me in for a couple of minutes between a cooking demonstration and a chat with a spiritual healer. Brandishing my novel, she demanded, 'Is this a true story or did you just make it up out of your head?'

Publication wasn't always such an ordeal. When I was a young writer, rooted in London, I would deliver my manuscript to my publisher, who would immediately remind me of the unearned advance on my previous effort. When my novel came out nine months later I would sit at home waiting for cherished friends to phone and read aloud my worst review, just in case I had missed it. Those, those were the days when novelists could be condescending about travelling salesmen, men who lugged their sample cases from town to town, but we have long since joined the club. Last time out in New York, I was driven in a limo from bookshop to bookshop, popping in to sign copies of my novel, preceded and followed by other writers in other limos signing theirs. Bookshops can return unsold copies of a book to the publishers, but they can't refund those that are autographed. So the publisher's flack who accompanies authors on these excursions usually says something like, 'I'll chat up the sales staff and while they aren't looking, you sign as many goddamn copies as possible.'

Bruce Jay Friedman once told me that he had gone to do a signing in a Boston bookshop only a day after his new novel had earned a rave review in the *Boston Globe*. Nobody turned up. 'What would have happened,' he asked the bookseller, 'if my novel had been panned yesterday?'

I have had a somewhat similar experience. Maybe ten years ago I was invited to Montreal's annual Salon des Livres to sit with the translator of a new French-language edition of *The Apprenticeship of Duddy Kravitz*, our table stacked high with books. Our moment arrived after a voice booming out of a loudspeaker announced to the milling crowd that we were now available for signings at Booth Number 12. Ten minutes passed and nobody came. Finally a man stopped at our table. He pulled out a cigarette and asked, 'Got a light?'

September 18. Toronto. My marching orders from Knopf read: '12.30 pm. The *Globe and Mail* (national) with Liz Renzetti. At Avalon Restaurant (private booth where you can smoke etc. . . .)' *Private booth? Etc.?* What's expected of me, I wonder?

'3 pm. 1 hr. *Eye Weekly* magazine (local) with Robyn Gillam (woman).'

Now that I am an ageing pro (man), somebody who has been around the block (national) possibly once too often, I don't make rookie mistakes. I will, for instance, no longer do radio or TV call-in shows. Once, at a late-night call-in show in Chicago, I sat round a table with two other writers. We watched, astonished, as the technician in the control booth rapped on his glass window and held up a message for our host. 'Remember, Dave,' it read, 'this is a night of the full moon.'

When my turn to sell came, I went on, as required, about the torments of my difficult craft. How Hell is a blank sheet of paper, and so forth and so on. Then a listener addressed a question to me: 'All that's well and good, Mort, but I live on the North Side, and I want to know how come there was no garbage collection this week?'

And now I've been out there peddling for only a few days and I am already weary of the most frequently asked questions:

'Why did you write your novel in the first person?'

'Why not?'

'Do you use a computer, Mr Richler?'

'No, every morning I slip into my Armani silk dressing gown and monogrammed velvet slippers by Dior, and begin to write with my goose quill pen.'

September 25. Fly to London with my wife for British publication of *Barney's Version*. Good news and bad news. Splendid reviews in both the *Daily Telegraph* and *Sunday Times*, but Melvyn Bragg has cancelled my appearance on BBC radio's 'Start the Week' and John Walsh, of the *Independent*, no longer wants to take me to lunch at The Ivy, as I have already been interviewed by Mark Steyn, in Montreal, for the *Daily Telegraph*.

London is still in mourning for Princess Diana, whose death proved a bonanza for British newspapers, which increased their press run by twenty per cent, and for florists as well. A friend of mine, stopping at a kiosk to buy flowers for his wife a few days after Diana's death, was told, 'Sorry, sir, but there's a fifty per cent surcharge this week.'

October 1. Manchester. My publisher, Chatto and Windus, has arranged for me to do a reading at Waterstone's bookshop, but this also happens to be Rosh Hashanah, so many of my people have cancelled. Militant feminist Andrea

Dworkin is reading in another room at Waterstone's. An incurable romantic, Ms. Dworkin has written: 'Intercourse remains a means, or the means, of physiologically making a woman inferior: communicating to her, cell by cell, her own inferior status ... pushing and thrusting until she gives in.' On the other hand, she doesn't believe that all men are rapists, which is awfully decent of her.

The *Sunday Independent* has launched a campaign to decriminalise pot, its initiative backed by more than 100 heavy-hitters in business, the arts, science and politics. They include authors Harold Pinter, Martin Amis, Auberon Waugh and Fay Weldon, film directors Mike Leigh and Peter Greenaway, numerous doctors and psychiatrists with the most impressive credentials, as well as the Marquess of Bath and the Marchioness of Worcester. But it strikes me that at least one supporter of the initiative is vulnerable to a conflict of interest charge. He is the Revd R. H. A. Scott, MA Oxon., who is currently serving four years in the slammer for growing cannabis.

My own feelings are mixed. I also favour decriminalising pot, but I fear if this campaign were successful in North America it could ruin the economy of Florida, and could oblige many an underpaid Montreal gendarme to live off his salary. It could also undermine the work ethic of muggers here, there and everywhere.

London, in early October, is still balmy, sidewalk cafés flourishing, but I do notice one change. Strolling down the King's Road, I see an increasing number of bald-headed women. I'm not sure whether this is the new fashion, however ill-advised, or if the women have been treated for head-lice. In either case, I am not impressed.

October 5. Montreal. Time to check out a week's mail. A professor at an Ontario university is writing a paper on minor novelists and wants me to answer 26 questions. An eyeglass museum in Tennessee would like a pair of my old spectacles. An invitation to lecture, beginning, 'We are a non-profit society ...' I read no further. A query from Knopf's publicist in Calgary inviting me to appear on a CBC radio show called 'Mountain Top Music':

'This interview is a personal profile of Mr Richler. They have requested the followed information:

1. His five favourite pieces of music
2. The title and author of his favourite book
3. Where he would like to spend his last days on earth (this can be anywhere, a mountain top, an island, at home etc.).'

October 6. Toronto again. More TV, radio and press interviews, followed by an evening reading at the University of Toronto's Convocation Hall. Afterwards, at the book-signing, I am confronted by a hostile young woman: 'I read your last novel, *Solomon Gursky Was Here*. It took me two years. WHAT A STRUGGLE!'

October 8. Ottawa. Reading and signing at the National Public Library. A man asks me to inscribe a copy of my novel 'to Judith', and requests that I add a personal message. 'Think of something witty,' he says.

I protest that I don't know Judith, so I can't add a personal message.

'I doubt that she'll have time to finish it anyway,' he says, grabbing the book. 'She's suffering from terminal cancer.'

October 18. Victoria, Vancouver Island. Midway through my reading, at the Open Space Gallery, the microphone begins to leak music from a local rock station. First time I perform with a back-up group. Among those waiting to have a book signed, there is a pretty young girl. 'My mother enjoys your work,' she says. Somebody else tells me, 'My husband was in your class at Baron Byng High. He couldn't come tonight. Heart attack. One minute he was reading the *Globe and Mail* at the breakfast table, and the next he keeled over.' I don't recognise the name, but I say I remember him well.

October 19. Vancouver. Last time I was here, locals were complaining about the influx of Chinese from Hong Kong, and how they had inflated real estate prices. Now the same people are fulminating because so many of the Chinese are leaving, worried that they could soon be taxed on their overseas earnings. Real estate prices are collapsing. My minder says, 'The parents return to Hong Kong, and leave their teenage kids behind in those big houses, just in case. They're usually left with a clothes allowance of $40,000. White kids hit them for protection money during school lunch hours.'

Interview with a woman from the *Western Jewish Bulletin*. She wants to know, speaking frankly, is it true that I'm an anti-Semite?

Item: A story, possibly apocryphal, told to me by a Hollywood film director. Years ago, Daniel Fuchs, a gifted novelist and short story writer, was hired to work on a screenplay in Hollywood with his idol, William Faulkner. Faulkner, a sensible man, did not suffer Hollywood easily. He was drunk most of the time. Following a difficult couple of weeks, the sensitive Fuchs said, 'Mr Faulkner, this collaboration is not working.'

Faulkner agreed that was the case.

'It's not working,' said Fuchs, 'because you're an anti-Semite.'

'Yes,' said Faulkner, 'but I don't like gentiles either.'

October 21. Florence has to fly home and my flight takes me to Calgary on a cloudless day. The mountains, as always, are spectacular. Last time I was in Calgary, I stopped somebody and asked him if he could direct me to the main street. 'We haven't got one,' he said.

October 22. At Calgary airport, bound for Winnipeg, I cannot find a copy of my novel in the bookshop. I ask the teenager behind the counter, 'Have you got a copy of *Barney's Version*?'

'Jeez. They went so fast, we haven't got any left. But I could order you one from our other shop.'

'I don't need one. I wrote it. Now why don't you reorder?'

'Not a bad idea.'

At my book-signing at the McNally Robinson bookstore, in Winnipeg, a young woman says, 'My father used to live just upstairs from you on Jeanne Mance Street.'

'I remember him well,' I say, but I never lived on Jeanne Mance Street.

October 23. Montreal. Home at last. But, late in January, I will have to set out again, this time on my American book-peddling tour. Last time out, I remember staggering off a plane in Seattle, having already been overnight in six other cities. The minder who met me eyed me suspiciously. 'Have you been drinking?' she asked.

'*Certainly not*. But I wouldn't mind if we stopped somewhere before my first interview.'

'We can't do that. Your first interviewer is a Mormon.'

'They all are.'

'I said Mormon, not moron.'

'Whoops. Sorry about that.'

Back in the early fifties, in London, I used to drink occasionally with Louis MacNeice in a pub round the corner from the BBC. He told me that he had once been to lecture in Montreal. Two nice club ladies met him at the airport. 'I'd like to stop for a drink first,' said MacNeice.

'Oh, you mustn't worry, Mr MacNeice. We'll be serving tea at the hall.'

'I mean a drink drink,' he said.

So they stopped at the Ritz-Carlton Hotel, he told me, and waited for him in the car outside: 'You'll find what you want in there.'

So it goes.

Naeem Murr

SIDNEY'S STORY

Extract from a novel in progress

'I HAVE A friend who's a kind of cat burglar. He breaks into houses. However, he doesn't steal, and his victims never even know – not consciously at least – that he's been. At night (so he told me), to enter a strange house is like entering the sleep of its inhabitants. It's as if he were inside them, a figure in their dreams. He's extremely adept, and is always pushing the limits of his invasion. Sometimes he even engages people in conversation in their sleep. Children especially are susceptible to this, and in these night-time conversations, he will reveal to them things he has discovered about their parents, the contents of secret letters bundled in old handbags behind cupboards.

'He would also leave traces of himself – a photograph, for example, in the family album. One day, leafing through, they will say, "Who on earth is that?" He would even bring an instamatic camera with him to take pictures of himself in their own home, holding a glass of wine ("Wasn't that Charlotte's dreary boyfriend?" "No, no, he was your mother's friend, the one who was studying to be an accountant"). Or he would add letters, written on artificially aged paper, to the letters of their past, weaving in personal details that he'd discovered to give them an unmistakable ring of truth: "Dear Mum and Dad: I hate it here. Can't I just come home at the weekends? Dad, is your eye better? I know they steam up, but it's really essential to wear safety glasses in the court. And, Mum, when are you going in for your operation? Remember to keep the gallstones. Roland's mum had a necklace made out of hers. Anyway, my poor invalids, look after yourselves. All my love, Paul." And years later, on some nostalgic night, they read the letter and think, "Oh my God, did we have a son? Did we forget our son?"

'And, remarkably, there was almost no house without its secrets, love letters hidden beneath a piano, certain fetishistic objects, and one time in the home of the most ordinary of suburban couples he discovered . . . Ah, but that's a story for some future night. For tonight another discovery, one that he swears to me is absolutely true.

'One winter night, about two years ago, our friend, let us call him – ?'

'Sidney?' Hecta suggested with a show of innocence.

'Call him Billy,' Juliet said, frowning at Hecta.

'All right. Well, one night, Billy went to Mortlake, a part of London he was, as yet, unfamiliar with. It's a little run down, as you know, and in his reconnoitring he set his eyes upon a large, rather decrepit, two-storey detached house. It attracted him because of its complete isolation in a street made otherwise derelict by its proximity to the Mortlake Sewage Works, which spoiled the view and filled the air with a noxious odour. Just as he was surveying, from a distance, the high fence surrounding the house, a car came out of the gate and went off down the road. Taking his chance, Billy broke into the house.

'The house was old and vast, with high ceilings. He went straight upstairs. On the second floor all the rooms were damp and completely empty, with no sign that they were used at all. Then, opening one of the walk-in closets, Billy discovered the inhabitant's bedroom. The large closet contained a mattress, a Bible on a pedestal table, and an enormous silver bowl containing dozens of photographs of people, photographs which had been cut into tiny pieces and all mixed together. Billy made a mental note to add his own fragmented photo at the first opportunity. He liked this house. It reeked of secrets.

'He then made his way downstairs into the living room, which contained only one armchair beside a still glowing fire, and a gramophone. A record sat on the turntable, and replacing the needle, he wound the handle. A drowned voice, made even more remote by the record's quality – it had obviously been played countless times – sang that old sailor's song:

> *So I'll drink to the wind that blows*
> *And I'll drink to the ship that goes*
> *And I'll drink to the lass,*
> *Yes, I'll drink to the lass,*
> *The lass who loved a sailor.*

There was not another record anywhere to be found.

'The hollow, creaturely meagreness of the whole house sent a shiver even down Billy's spine. He went into the kitchen. A door there led out to the back, but it was Chubb-locked, with no keys in sight. Now our friend could smell something even beneath the stench of the sewer works. On the floor in the kitchen lay an oriental rug, which seemed an incongruously ornate piece of furnishing. Shifting this aside with his foot, he found beneath it a cellar hatch, which he pulled up. It was then that a putrid smell struck him with its full force, almost causing him to retch.

'Wooden stairs led straight down into the frigid depths of a deep stone cellar. After covering his mouth and nose with a handkerchief, he took a few steps down; then, carefully balancing the rug on top of the hatch, closed it over him. Using the small torch he always carried, he located the light switch and turned it on . . .

'And there they were, sitting up against the walls, at least thirty of them. The corpses.

'You would have to know Billy to understand that it did not so much shock as thrill him to have discovered this, to be here in this most secret of places. The bodies ran the gamut of decomposition, and one – a timid-looking woman of perhaps forty – appeared as if she might just be sleeping. For the sake of security, he switched off the light and used only his torch. Though his instincts told him he should leave and return when he'd learned a little more about the occupant's habits, he couldn't resist going down and walking the full length of the bodies, exhilarated to be among those thirty mortal sins. But his instincts had been right, and when the headlights flooded into the high, opaque, barred windows of the cellar, it was too late.

'A moment later, he heard the man running up the front stairs and entering the door. Above him, the floorboards creaked. Then the man went out of the door again, back to the car. He heard the crunch of the man's feet on the gravel driveway, then the slamming of the car boot. A few minutes later, the man was back in the house, the front door shuddering shut. The creaks, for some reason, were now much louder. Billy followed this man's movement across the floor of the living room into the kitchen. Then came a thud, as if the man had dropped something heavy. Billy had no doubt now that the man was coming into the cellar. He looked around him, but there was nowhere to hide. All he could think to do was to push himself between two of the corpses, pulling the stiff, livid hand of one into his lap, and resting the head of the other against his neck, so as slightly to cover his face. He let his mouth gape, his eyes staring. He became one of the dead.

'Finally, the cellar hatch was pulled open. By means of a net and string, the man lowered a body into this silent, cold hell. Through that hole it came, like a cocooned insect. A moment later the man himself descended and gently unwrapped the body from the netting. Billy saw the man lick his own fingers and wipe away some marks on the corpse's face with maternal solicitude. The man then sat the corpse up carefully at the end of the row beside the timid-looking woman. It was a teenage boy with a downy moustache and an expression of amazement.

' "Right, Gareth," the killer said. "Now you must forgive me, but names were never my forte. I never forget a face," he declared with real conviction, "but names can be a real trial to me, though I will remember if I don't get too flustered. Well, now. That's Rupert." He pointed across the cellar to the first corpse. "And that's Shelly; David; Sarah – no, Sandra, not Sarah; and that's Laura – though I insisted on calling her Lara for years and she was too polite ever to correct me; then Bethany, with her gorgeous red hair, if she'll forgive me being so bold; Andrew, who was a doorman at the Tivoli, you know – opened doors for the likes of Minister Seeley." And so on along the line until he came to a corpse he didn't know, the corpse of our friend, Billy. The killer, after a moment's astonished silence, came right up to Billy. Our friend was lucky that his skin was always cold and that, by the long practice of his occupation, he could remain extremely still. The man hunkered down before him. Billy could hear him reiterate to himself in a whisper, "Shelly, David, Sandra . . ." as if he might remember Billy's name as part of the rhythm of the sequence. He then gently pushed aside the head that was half covering Billy's face, took hold of our friend's jaw and raised it to examine his features. Thus our friend had no choice but to look, however abstractedly, into the fatty, sad, opaquely blue eyes of death.

' "I always remember a face," the man said, obviously perplexed. "Perhaps not the name, but always the face." He then clucked to himself in sad disappointment. "Well, well, must be getting old." And with a resigned sigh, he let Billy's head slump back.

'He then carried on with the names of those beyond our friend: "Rick; Zoe; Shelly – I call her Shelly Two, because we already have a Shelly you see. . ."

'Finally, the killer, taking his place at the centre of the room and gesturing towards the new corpse said, "And this, everyone, is Gareth – can cope with Gary, but not Gaz, if I remember correctly. Now, I'll leave you all to get acquainted." With that he climbed back up into the house.

'For two days our friend remained in that cellar, never quite feeling it safe enough to escape, not hearing the man leave, only, periodically, the creak of the floorboards above him. A few times in those days, the killer came down into the cellar to converse with the corpses. He talked to them as if they were actually responding to him. Then, on the third night, our friend heard the man's car leave the driveway. And though so stiff from the cold that he was barely able to move, he escaped from the house . . .'

'Oooooh,' Sybil shivered out, 'I think my willies have packed for the coast.'

'There's a coda,' Sidney said, lifting a finger.

'A few months later, Billy went to the wedding reception of a relation of his. At one point, his attention was taken by a couple whispering heatedly at a table. As he drew closer in an attempt to overhear what they were saying, he was startled by a tap on his shoulder. It was the groom, together with another man.

' "Billy," his cousin said, "I want to introduce you to Father Hopkins."

'So Billy's eyes met once more the fatty, sad, opaquely blue eyes of Death.

'Father Hopkins broke into a smile.

'They all talked desultorily for a few moments, and then, of course, Billy made his excuses – even rather rudely, as you could imagine, visibly embarrassing his cousin.

'But as he walked away, the priest called after him: "I say, my friend." And when Billy turned, the priest asked: "What was your name again?"

' "Billy."

' "Yes, Billy, of course," he said, as if it were a name he'd been trying to remember for a long time. "Yes, yes. You see, I'm terrible with names, *terrible*, but I never, *never* forget a face . . ." '

Once more applause erupted as Sidney put the candle back on to the table and then returned to his place in the darkness.

No one picked up the candle for a long time.

Finally, Dagmar said. 'Juliet, come on, you tell us a story.'

'I can only think of a true story,' she said.

'Well, we've only heard true stories,' Dagmar protested.

'I know. But this is a *true*, true story.'

'Excellent, then the evening is moving up through avatars of truth, as it should.'

'Well, if I tell it,' Juliet said somewhat reluctantly, 'it's important for you to know that this is only one story among millions of such stories I've heard from the refugees I try to find positions for among my friends. You can hardly believe what happens to people when order breaks down. This is a story told to me by a Ludlow woman who escaped from Manchester. You all know how they were slaughtered, how they were considered less than human.'

Vanessa, who'd been knitting furiously all this time, suddenly looked up, giving Juliet an incredulous, almost angry look. Juliet met her eyes, shook her head gently, and some secret understanding seemed to pass between them.

Jeff Noon

OBLIVION GIRLS

WITH THE MOON a bloated shimmer, and all the lights of the city made poison-blur by slow rain that falls on council estate, sports ground, leisure centre, convenience store. Without pity, falling on the sodium-lit motorway that stretches over the scene. One of the flyover's offshoots juts out into nowhere; a waiting, expectant half-built road, hanging its frozen tongue over dark air like a swallowing. Maybe the council ran out of money, of love, of caring, of desire, of planning permission, of concrete. The kids around here call it Oblivion Drop. Some of them have pulled down the edge-barrier; listen now, the rolling echo of the bladers as they speed along nightsilver towards the world's sudden emptiness.

Teetering . . .

And then pulling back last second, hard braking, cracking sparks, too far away from takeoff to be a genuine Queen of the Blade. It's a girl thing, this teasing of the edge. A way to prove, perhaps; leaping with the blade's motors turned off. Or else a hunger dream, still not satisfied. But then one of them makes it, chances the flight, or else just leaves the pull-back too many goddamn nanoseconds too late. Whatever the reasons, there she sails . . .

Moon-golden.

The girl-in-motion to the night's hovering clutches. But turn now to the others, the others still bound by the fear. One of these losing girls turns her blade back on, makes it safe. She glides around, away from the failure; too much gravity in

131

her heart. She moves to the easy-drop, resets her blade now to elevator mode. The coward's mode, they call it. Floating downwards, hummingbird slow, she glimpses the little display panel in the blade carefully making amends; a fluttering of the numbers. The various equations of weight, mass, deceleration. Halfway down she hears the other girls cheering, meaning somebody just made a good landing. There's a new oblivion girl tonight; but it's not her, not this sunkenhearted kid with too much glue on her boots.

And that's all that matters.

The girl's bladename is Tipsy; Tipsy Sleepwalker. She can't remember how many times she's failed the edge. Fifteen years old, nearly sixteen, living on the nearby estate, with her mum, and a brother, no dad. Her mum is out for the night, thinking her daughter in bed by now. And, reaching the ground at last, becoming earthed, maybe that bed wouldn't be such a bad place, after all. Get some dreaming done, before school in the morning. In dreams, you should see that girl fly, you really should. So, another reset; blade to normal weight, and she turns for home.

Something stops her.

Underneath the flyover, encased in wire, a basketball court echoes to the sound of running feet. All is darkness as she approaches the fence. Black sky made of motorway, suddenly, perched high above on stalks, keeping the rain off. Creeping sodium overspill, ragged at the edges when cars zoom overhead. Tipsy presses her face against the wire, searching for the noises. The court belongs to the nearby college of science, and it's way past official closing time. A small globe of orange light moves through the air in random patterns. Blackness dances beneath. Somebody screams; the ball jerks to one side, as though on a string.

Shockball. Two teams, six players in each. The ball hardly exists, more a bundle of energy. It burns with a harsh electric charge every so often, according to a random mechanism. A game invented by students at the college, and highly illegal. Like the hoverblade she rides upon, like just about anything worthwhile around here, you have to buy your fun off the science students, or else steal the danger. Because what use is fun without danger? That's why the charge on the shockball can be adjusted. But never turned off. Sometimes they set the charge so high, players get burned. Of course, it's a nothing game compared to nightblading, but you do hear rumours told in whispers of players getting killed by the shock. It's a boy thing, and that draws Tipsy forward.

Out of nowhere, a mighty surge of light fills the court with shape. Jesus, they've broken the code on the power-box. Floodlights in bloom, four of them, one at each corner; a sick and yellow etching of the game in progress.

A cheer goes up, the ball is passed with dazzle now. They have half an hour, perhaps, before they get kicked off court. All to play for. Older kids, and nowhere near being students, not ever. Estate trash, like herself. Tipsy floats her blade a little higher, to see the game better. It's so beautiful, the way the floodlights bloom shadow-flowers around each player, four petals for each. The ball flashes orange again, a sizzle of flesh, a piercing cry from the pitch. Another player has the glow before it touches ground. And off, weaving the gameplay, making a pass. But something's happening, nothing to do with the game. A circle is forming. One player stands at the centre of this attention, and far from where the ball now drops to the ground, refused, ignored. Only now, separated as he is, does Tipsy recognise this lonely figure: it's her brother, Charlie. Somebody laughs at him; someone else curses. Tipsy floats higher still, to see what the problem is.

And when she does see, when she finally notices what all the other players are backing away from, well, she almost falls off her board, and that would be a first in a long time. Because all the players are shadow-blossomed; but Charlie, he hasn't got any flower, no bloom to him, no dark petals, none at all.

The changes: hiding away, days off work, avoiding bright lights, taking his meals in his room. Tipsy had seen the strangeness in her brother, coding it down to a broken love.

133

Now she knows different. The night of the shockball game, back at the house, she follows him into his bedroom. The room is dark, the curtains clenched across the window. And when she reaches for the light switch . . .

'No.'

And realises, with a shock; this is the first word she'd heard from him, in ages. So, leaving the darkness in soft, gentle place, she comes close, sits on the bed with him.

'No. Don't touch me.'

'Charlie, it's all right.'

Making contact; the skin is quite cold, with a grainy quality.

'Don't touch me. Get away from me.'

Tipsy moves along the bed. She's near the window now; the curtains are held together by clothes pegs, six of them.

'Oh Charlie . . . please.'

The words from her lips, whispered. Whispered like the touch of him. Like the sound of her name, barely returned. A shiver in the dark.

And then the turning on of a bedside lamp. The brother flinching from the sudden sharpness of it, the spilt acid of the light. The sister turning the anglepoise to shine a crazy moon on the stripy wallpaper, and then bringing her hand into the lightpath, making that small eclipse of the young. The bedroom cinema: the rabbit and the howling dog; the flapping bird and the elephant. Tipsy makes the walls alive. And then the brother bringing his own hand, slowly, into play. Only the faintest animal shapes dance from his fingers, like a disappearing species on the surface of the moon.

Charlie's shadow, draining away.

'It's getting worse, Tips.'

'When did it start?'

'I don't know. How can I know?'

'You don't feel anything, pain I mean?'

'Pain? No. Only . . .'

'Yes?'

'It's like I'm getting emptier, somehow. Can that happen?'

'It's not possible. It can't be possible.'

'Oh God, Tips, what's happening to me?'

'The doctor's –'

'Doctors?'

'Mum –'

'No. No . . .'

And the sister says no more, because the brother is crying now. Great sobs that she feels like a second heart, growing calmer only when she clicks off the light.

The simple turning off of a bedside lamp.

Strangeness is bad news, on these little estates. When Charlie gets into work the next day, driven by a sister's kindness, the garage lads won't even look at him, won't even talk to him, most of them. And that's bad enough, but suddenly the tools seem too heavy for his grip. A spanner slips through his fingers, making a scratch down somebody's precious little car. And the laughter then . . . and the names they call him. The Blank. Charlie's a blank!

Strangeness, treated like disease.

'You what?' says Tipsy that night, when he finally unlocks his door to her.

'Packed it in. Had to.'

'Charlie, Mum'll go mad.'

He shrugs. 'Don't care.'

'Charlie, you're disappearing, and you –'

'I am not disappearing. I'm evaporating.'

'You're what? Jesus!'

'I'll show you.'

He drags her along to the bathroom, where he steps straight on to the scales. Now Charlie is a big guy for seventeen, just shy of six feet tall, with a good, strong physique, a natural-born garage hand. He pushes the needle around, that evening, the distance of a skinny nine-year-old no-hoper. 'I've always wanted to lose weight,' he says, looking deep into the bathroom mirror, letting his fingers sink into soft skin.

'Oh, that's all right then,' says Tipsy. 'Wait, where are you going?'

'Out.' He picks up the shockball, in its protective bag.

'But Charlie . . .'

Of course, Tipsy follows him, keeping the distance on her blade. When she floats up to the basketball court, he's already playing, just by himself, throwing the ball against the wire again and again. The court is in twilight, bleached of colour. Every so often the shockball flashes orange, burning, but Charlie never makes a sound. Sometimes he holds the ball for too long, surely on purpose, waiting for the shock to come. Like this is the only thing he can feel any more.

Gradually, the other players arrive. But they won't enter the court; instead, they stand around outside the netting, looking in. All the kids are silent, as Charlie takes shock after shock. Tipsy doesn't know what to do, how to break the rhythm. Night falls, completely. Above her head, she can hear the blader girls teasing the drop, but all that seems a thousand miles away. By her side, one of the lads is messing with the power-box. A cut and splice of the wires, and the floodlights bleed the air clean. Still, the boy on court plays on. Shadowless, uncaring of the looks, uncaring of the sizzle and the blaze and the skinflame. The kids around the court watch this punishment, all in the same deep silence; and then, as gradual as they came, one by one, walking away.

Until only one remains.

Tipsy looks at this last kid, the same one who had turned the lights on. She knows him by reputation; William Lobo. His cage of a face holds something brutal in place, only by the sheerest willpower. Without a sound, he watches. Without a sound, five minutes. Then he walks towards the gate, enters. Tipsy follows, bladeshod, thinking her brother in danger. Instead . . .

Lobo catches the shockball, mid-flight, makes a feinting run. Charlie gives chase, intercepting a bounce-back, making his own run. A game of expert play. Tipsy floats closer, already guessing: that Lobo's shadow is grey and wasted, compared to her own, and the petals dance weakly there, as though fuelled by a dying, faraway star. Another sufferer. And then Charlie himself comes towards her, holding his hand high for her to see, as the fierce light seeps into it, and through.

So that Tipsy can see her brother's bones, inside the skin.

That was it for Tipsy. She could only think the whole world was going mad. The next evening, after school, she goes to see the doctor. When he asks her what the matter is, Tipsy replies:

'Nothing, with me. It's my brother.'

'I can hardly examine him, if –'

'He won't come.' Her voice rising now. 'It's serious. He's seriously ill, and he won't do anything about it.'

'The symptoms?'

'Symptoms?'

'Come on, Tipsy.'

Now the doctor knows Tipsy, he knows her brother; he's treated them both since they were babies. Healthy kids, on the whole, especially the girl. But he's never seen her like this before, so wild, so fixated. Maybe she's the sufferer? And when he eventually gets her to describe her brother's symptoms, well, maybe she's on drugs or something.

'What's wrong with you?' the girl demands. 'Don't you believe me? It's not just him, you know? There's two of them now. Two of them. Maybe more. Maybe loads more! What will you do about it?'

By the way he was looking at her, she knew his thoughts.

And how mad was she, anyway?

When she gets back home, Charlie, as usual, is locked in his room. But things are different. Tipsy can hear voices from inside. Light is seeping from under the door, which hasn't been seen for weeks now. And all her demands for entry, ignored. 'Charlie!' she shouts, 'If you don't let me in, I'm telling Mum, tonight, soon as she gets home. I am!'

The door is opened, slowly. Her brother's there, along with William Lobo, and one other, a girl. She's slightly older than they are, perhaps nineteen, twenty. Tipsy has never seen her before.

'Who's this?'

'Tipsy, meet Gina.'

'Gina? Where's she from?'

'The college.'

'The college! Since when do you hang around with student girls? Oh. She's one of . . .'

The overhead light is shining bright, also, the bedside lamp. Like they just don't care any more what they are, what they aren't.

'Gina knows why,' says Charlie.

'It's a good thing,' adds William, 'us losing it.'

'What does he mean?' Tipsy asks her brother. 'What's good about it?'

'Gina knows why,' repeats Charlie. 'It's an experiment.'

'She's further gone, ain't she?' says William.

Tipsy looks at the college girl. She's wearing a raincoat, which she now undoes, slithers out of. With the bedside lamp behind her, it's like looking into a misty pool. A pool of shimmer, red and blue in stripes, the same as Charlie's wallpaper. The girl's body is merging with the room, so that when she moves, as she does now, towards Tipsy, the whole world seems to shift, drunken, unglued. Tipsy falls backwards, shocked, against the wall.

'Jesus!'

And she's out of there, blade-high and nightbird fast, even at ground-level. It takes her ten minutes only to get to the police station. And twenty minutes of hovering outside, going nowhere. Because who will believe her?

It starts to rain.

So Tipsy's just floating, static, getting wet. Only one inch off the ground, but the transport, the beloved hoverblade, something's wrong with it. Playing up. She can't get the drift of it, as though the rules have been changed. Stepping off, she lets it settle to the ground, the tiny digits of the weight display returning to zero. She picks it up, turns it over. Lifted up like this, a blade is just a piece of plastic, a few switches, the display panel, the hand-painted design. Nothing much, and nothing much to open up. She will have to take it in, to be retuned.

It kind of hits her then, quite softly. Creeping up, the way the moon gathers now, rain-painted over the city. There's nothing wrong with the board, nothing at all. It's herself that's gone wrong. She climbs back on board, noting where the digits settle. There's not enough numbers showing. Which can only mean . . .

She's losing weight.

There's a streetlamp nearby. Gliding to it, she holds her hand up in front of her face. It seems solid enough, yet. Then she places the hand flat in the light's beam, to study the shadow cast on the pavement. Crouching down, she brings her hand closer to the ground, closer still.

A young girl on a street corner, trying to measure her fade.

As Tipsy approaches the flyover, she can see the bladegirls on the Oblivion Drop, some of them getting ready to chance the flight. Underneath the structure, two boys are playing shockball, a girl watching them. Her brother, and his new friends.

Tipsy gets to the easy-lift point, flicks into elevator mode, rises up slowly, slowly, using her skills to compensate for the weight-loss. When she gets to the top, the other girls turn to look at her, some of them laughing. Because they know what's happening to her brother, and they know she will never make the leap anyway, you can only fail so many times.

Tipsy ignores them. Calmly now, she sets the blade to empty. Naked flight. The motors fade to zero. And then, she just speeds.

I mean, she just speeds.

The other girls have to get out of her way, so fast she glides. So fast, so bladed, so far out on the edge of herself. And then, suddenly. The world empties beneath her . . .

And golden.

Becoming projectile to the moon's dominion.

Becoming information: the precise curvature of the wind; the calculated heft, just so, of the body's motion; the exact weight of the rain in her face. Vapourware.

Going for the download.

Just a skinny girl-kid sailing the ozone on a piece of goddamn plastic, powered by electro-pixies for all she knows. A mere breath of a girl, making it happen. Seemingly still, seemingly fixed in the sky and the rain. Destination: Manchester; that small patch of it down there, the welcoming circle of grass, beyond, beyond, beyond. Objective: to make it down clean, missing the road and the traffic and the copcars and all the twisted shit of a twisted life, and the tarmac slam of a bad landing.

Slicking the thermals.

Tipsy Sleepwalker gives a whoop, the shout whipped away, the air unwheeled. The whole of the city stretched out for her arrival. A college of science, the ghostly limb of a motorway, a basketball court, a nondescript housing estate. Some kids, some students. A game of shockball. And a young girl, floating in space. Descending now . . .

Descending . . .

Oblivion girl. Knife-frozen.

One of God's print-outs.

Christopher Emery

THE CHURCH OF CHRIST PSYCHOPATH

In the Third Church of Christ Psychopath
no ruined mothers may pray for dust. Occasionally,
unelected Elders order random executions of executives,
that priests on weekdays covertly choose as saints.
And large-scale whippings often ensue on traditional
Nights of Holy Disaffection. Such nights being wholly
  charged
with miraculous bouts of ritual boasting from the grave.
On Tuesdays, steel crosses are recycled in each parish
for the conversions of the famished poor; whom we adore
as divine atrocious food, all gristle and lice. And obese
flagellants repose on the designated benches, staring at
a prostrate sea, their incandescent robes signifying still
neglected island martyrs; stalwarts of the recent purges,
for whom most pray for dunkings in the Hermeneutic
Lake of Blood. And idealistic Wednesday pogroms
in season still flourish, where, through the provinces,
bishops in shabby wigs ride pigs through the streets,
stopping only to piss on the lewd exiles of the Faith.
Everyone takes time to share God's lesson of venomous
absence with the sad pathetic Council of the Damned.
And all the while, itinerant priests continue calling on tall
houses in the city, lecturing insomniac Magistrates
and Councillors on the indecency of science
and the amnesty of lies.

Iain Sinclair

ANGELS OF CHANCE

'Anything I can do, boss?' he asked.
'Watch this movie for me,' I said.
James Crumley

A crimson mouth smirks in his frosty forehead,
Steady increment of metropolitan desire; she sucks
the wrong stone, censoring her first best thought.
'That's what comes of working six months
in a bookstore on Madison Avenue.' Pavements
ill-suited to licensed heels, she spikes
the lazy voyeur's sporting eye. 'The eye altering
alters all.' 'Now,' she cries, 'now I understand.'
Sheer nakedness deposed as she lectures the chilling
stiff, not forgetting to flip her stitched collar, to wink
at the blind doorman. 'Night, Charlie.' 'Night, Miss
Moonbeam.' A radon icepick filched from
the scuppers of a Nantucket whaler spoils the line
of her pocket, uptown in an illegitimate trenchcoat,
bestowing custom on the yellowest cab in the universe.

WHY I DON'T LIKE POETS

They are too privileged and always
celebrate death with posies and nosegays
unweeping effusions, owl tables
sour milk in dishonest kitchens, misremembered
sunlight, harp strings, flat rib-
notes; all drink until the liver creases and
craves SILENCE; and then it hurts, nothing's true

142

they've rehearsed that Buddhist breath-cloth,
tinkling bells, the light
that won't behave; the sea, they speak
of that, think they belong, thin feet
too late, amen and shut your mouth for God's sake,
one pure crystal instant of truth, then rush
if you must to your black notebook, record
the nosebleeds and the rusty gold; poetry is
impolite, too much previous, too many
awkward, chastened voices . . .

Billy Childish

A Sad Donkey and a Fat Man Smiling

Speaking as a man who doesn't eat cheese
and who paddled into 2nd place in the
Kent Schools under-18s Slalom 1975.
(Three entrants only)

Speaking as a man who doesn't own a television set
doesn't read daily papers
and the radio remains clicked to off.

Speaking as a man with twelve fillings,
four verrucas
and one O level (Art grade A) Walderslade Secondary
School for Boys 1976.

Speaking as an artist of dubious merit
and the writer of lewd verses.

Speaking as a man who carved The Reclining Admiral
and Van Gogh Without a Moustache.
Apprentice stone mason
Her Majesty's Dockyard Chatham 1976.

Speaking as a man who caught Paul Weller's plectrum
thrown into the audience at Battersea Town Hall,
Jubilee Week 1977. (Support group The Boys)

Speaking as a man who tried to run down Johnny Rotten
on the pavement outside the Roebuck Public House, Kings
   Road
London 1978. (Drunk in charge of a push bike)

Speaking as a man who wore second-hand clothes
up until he was 33.

Speaking as a man with eyes the shape of little fishes,
the hands of my father and somebody else's legs,
I see that truth only comes staggering up the mountain
   side
like a sad donkey teetering under the weight of a fat man
   smiling.

Lana Citron

THE SCORE BOARD

AUGUST ON THE Costa Flesh the sun high and the heat sweltering. Five lads staggered off a bus plane, claimed their baggage and hailed a cab. The driver spoke pidgin English.

Tweet tweet, welcome, welcome English pigs and off he drove at high Spanish speed.

Arnold sat in the back, his face half out the window. Thoughts of aeroplane food rushing through his head, a sweating piece of shiny turkey, near-frozen bread, nuts and beer, gin, vodka, wine, and suppressing a wet belch he groaned.

'Stop the car . . . I . . .' Projectile vomit flew.

'Scaam,' muttered the driver. He slammed his foot down on the accelerator, there was no point in taking the tourist route.

'Scum yourself,' echoed Tony from the back. He had studied Spanish GSE, was damned if he was going to let some wog treat him like that.

'Yeah, you tell him,' said Gary.

Jacko, sitting in the front turned to the driver and told him to relax. 'We'll sort you out mate, OK.'

Martin squashed in the middle leant forward. 'Yeah we'll see you right.'

Arnold chucked again. Missed the window and the smell began to circulate. The driver banged the steering wheel. 'Fuckeen' SCaaaM.'

Jacko felt obliged, delved into his pocket and took out a

crisp peseta note. 'That should shut you up. They're worse than at home lads, eh.'

Arnold had slumped over Martin, who was doing his best to mop up the mess with a Kleenex.

'Great stuff, Arnold,' said Gary.

'Start as you mean to go on wot,' laughed Tony.

Jacko was rubbing his hands together. 'It's going to be great guys. I can feel it in my waters. Two weeks of sun, sand, sangria . . .' and suddenly Arnold burst into song.

A cunting we will go
A cunting we will go
Hey ho the merry o
A cunting we will go.

They never made it to their apartment. A pub reminiscent of home tripped them up and by the time they were out of it, their legs had packed in, so they crawled till their arms gave way and flaked out on sun-loungers.

'At least we beat the Jerries.'

Gary rang Tony and put the idea to him.

'What you up to for the holidays?'

'Hadn't thought about it.'

'Fancy an all lads?'

'You're on mate, you're on.'

So down the local the seed was sown. Drawn around the table were Tony, Gary, Jacko, Martin and Arnold.

Gary and Tony were best mates. They had grown up together, met Jacko sometime in their teens, when they'd been nicking cars and having gang fights. Jacko introduced Martin, who worked in the same building as himself. Last and most certainly least was Arnold. Arnold was roped in as it was always good to have someone to take the piss out of on a group holiday. Fairly new in town, he was dead chuffed at having been asked. It was a sign of acceptance and for the first time he felt like he belonged.

The only obstacle blocking the way was getting their women to go along with the escapade. Fortunately, this proved easier than anticipated. Once one agreed, the others followed suit in domino fashion.

Tony told his missus he was off on holiday. 'She was to give him no lip, right.'

Gary didn't think it worth mentioning to Molly. He never said anything to Molly and besides he didn't 'need some fuckin' burd' telling him what to do.

Jacko told his Susan that as Tony's missus had given him the all clear and Gary's too, 'wouldn't it do her the world of good to have him out of her hair for a couple of weeks?'

Martin had the toughest time and had to promise to bring Denise and the kids away at Christmas, as well as upping her weekly allowance by a tenner. Arnold had no one, so he rang his mother.

'Have a good time, son.'

'I will, Ma, I will, and I'll bring you back sommit nice.'

They raided the local travel agent and spent the whole day deciding on their options. Gary's brother recommended Costa Flesh.

'I guarantee you, none of yous will come back disappointed.' His opinion was trusted and Costa Flesh was booked.

Costa Flesh, one of many resorts lining the coast of the tiny island of Poranao, was free of crippled widows dressed in black sitting on front porches. Constructed during a pregnant pause in the 1970s, it was not a place to spend time admiring the architecture. It was modern and high rise with everything heaped up along the coast. The beach was wide and sandy, the promenade full of dog shit and the pier stunted. The native population had all but expired and in peak season it resembled one great big melting pot of Viking descendants. The brochure shouted its praise unreservedly:

'Almost as good as Blighty with the sun, a real home from

home.' Let go, urged the brochure, everything within staggering distance. And so it was. The only identifiable thing about Costa Flesh was the smell of spunk and spew.

No one scored the first night. First nights were for acclimatising. Sniffing out the merchandise. Getting your ball bearings.

The next morning the lads woke with their tongues stuck to the roofs of their mouths, found the apartment, claimed a bed and laid down the ground rules.

'No minges in the apartment, right.' said Gary.

Arnold, confused, asked why.

'Cos they'll know where you're staying,' explained Tony, adopting the tone of speaking to a moron.

Arnold wasn't getting it at all.

'See, Arnold, the aim is quantity, you don't want some hole fallin' for you, be at you the whole time, discretion is the name of the game, right lads?'

'Too right, Jacko, too right,' agreed Martin.

They each laid fifty quid on the table. A sheet of paper immaculately ruled was produced and pinned to the wall. This was Martin's *pièce de résistance*. Everyone had their own row, columns listed various activities and at the bottom was a scoring table. Winner takes all, the point system as follows:

> *Straight sex with rubber equals* 10 *points*
> *without rubber* 20 *(add* 10 *if you dump inside her)*
> *from behind* 25
> *heavy petting* 5
> *blow job* 15
> *if she swallows* 30
> *under age* 50
> *anal* 85
> *two at a time* 120
> *virgin* 180

Cans raised and may the best man win.

May the best man win.

All prepared and rarin' to go, they donned the love gear, paid respects to their Adonis-like physiques, then started spouting lines from gangster movies. It was imperative to be equipped with decent transport, and the first thing they did was rent motorbikes. It ensured easy access into all the nooks and crannies. Gave the girls a bit of a thrill, vibrations for 'getting the gees gooey' was, in the words of Arnold, a top priority. On their marks, they were set and going to have a holiday of a lifetime.

They all managed to get laid on the second night. It was touch and go to begin with, but they drank themselves confident and went for the dregs of the resort. One could always tell when women were gagging for it. They stood out a mile, usually cos they were dogs or chronically overweight, and aching for a good shag. Foreign girls were rated tops. Easier to impress, you could rely on body language and they weren't aware of classification by accent. Foreigners liked sex, had fewer hang-ups. English girls knew exactly what they were getting.

Arnold's first encounter was with an English rose. She was pig ugly, her body loose and flabby.

'Me friends have fucked off,' she screeched in a high pitch that whistled down his ear. Here was a lady who knew what she wanted and wasn't afraid to ask. 'Fancy a shag?'

Swept off the ground, Arnold felt lucky. He was a shy lad from up north whose heart had been wrenched from his chest by his last girl, a nice lass he'd planned to settle down with.

'Set me heart on a house, got up a sizeable deposit an' everythin' an' she looked like a dolly an' she broke me heart.' And he drank away the money.

He was only nineteen. The guts of a year had passed since he'd left home and come south.

Arnold was softer, younger than the rest. Urbanity hadn't quite got its claws into him. He landed a job in the post-room of a big city firm and fell in with Martin. He lodged with a couple out in suburbia and trained it to work every day. He wasn't exactly God's gift to women and the guys liked to take the mick.

'We'll make a man of you yet, Arnold. Don't you worry.'

'Call that a cock,' said the cow. Arnold was too gone to be put off. Hadn't she wanted him, hadn't she pulled him out of the bar and down to the beach?

'I hate gettin' sand up me gee, what.' She was lard lovely, sticking her fat fingers inside his underpants, pushing her hanging tits in his face.

Fat bitch, and he thought of Gary.

'Never let them know you can't get better, you're the one in control, bitches like a bit of domination, none of your sensitive crap.'

She pulled her knickers to one side and squatted down on top of him. He could feel nothing. She was as wide as the Grand Canyon and he was riding the wave of blubber. To his great dismay he shrivelled. His cock went limp and he began to panic. He continued banging away, even in this state, he knew he couldn't afford to lose face, and pretended to come. What the heck, she was so far gone she wouldn't know the difference. She got up and, without looking at him, slumped back up the beach, to the bar.

Arnold wiped his prick, smelt his fingers and thought of the points he had scored.

He confided in Martin about the slag.

'It was right 'orrible.'

Martin consoled him.

'Won't get much worse, mate.'

They sat on the beach in their sunglasses and glossy trunks, listening to House music on a portable tape deck. Arnold's skin had begun to blister badly although Factor 15 had been liberally smeared.

'This is heaven Arnold.'

'Paradise.'

'Make you think.'

'Yeah . . . about what?'

'What the fuck I'm doing.'

'What do you mean?'

'I'd love to pack it in and stay out here.'

'But you've a great job and a missus and kiddies.'

'It means fuck all Arnold.'

Martin hadn't had such a laugh for ages. Being with the lads was the best. The girls were great and he felt like he was winning, like he was young. The other night he'd struck the jackpot with Geena.

He looked at the girl whose mouth encased his cock. He was pushing it in deep, hitting it off the back of her throat. She must have been about twenty and she wasn't bad. Fuck it, she was ten out of ten. Her skin was lightly tanned, blonde hairs standing up on her arms. They had met by the poolside, she was sitting alone, reading a novel, obviously available. The lads had been watching her, each one fancied his chances. Straws were picked, a dare was set, Martin got lucky.

Martin loved football, he had been the top scorer at his school, had a few trials for some clubs and practised hard. He could have made something of himself but the road was wet and the night was dark. His motorcycle skidded, a car swerved out in front of him and his kneecap shattered. Denise his girlfriend stood by him. They had met after a winning match. Denise was a ride and precious with it. Her reputation preceded her and she was considered 'one of the untouchables', the girls you didn't dare shag without intention. So they married and soon after Martin got a permanent position in the big city company. The job was bollocks but the pay was fine. In a few more years Martin would be in control of the whole post-room – not bad for a man of twenty-six. He still played footie but only on the weekend to keep in shape. His chosen mate hadn't fared so well. Denise began to lose it after her third kid. He didn't like to admit it but she was beginning to resemble her mother. Denise's parents were fairly comfortable, they'd always thought their daughter could have done a little better for herself. They had paid for the wedding, helped buy the house, minded the kids, and gave Denise and Martin all the advice they needed without having to be asked. Martin did well marrying Denise and he wasn't allowed to forget it.

Martin held the girl's cheeks in his hands and whispered, 'You're beautiful, God you're fucking beautiful.' He took his cock from her mouth and came all over her face. He stiffened just thinking about it.

'I'm goin' for a swim, Arnold.' Arnold had the stereo on his lap and was fiddling with the volume. He felt like he was in page three paradise. Legs, arms, tits, ass an' – oh hokey hokey pokey. He'd never seen such available flesh. His dick had been in a semi-permanent state for the last four days.

'For fuck's sake.' Some geezer kicked sand in his face.

'Good to see you too, mate.' Gary stood above him, lifted his sunglasses. 'You got a great view here.'

Arnold thought of Gary as the one in charge, leader of the pack, and Gary thought so too. He wasn't the sort of person to do things by half measures. He always took what he wanted. If he'd been born on the other side of the fence he would have been called a philandering bounder, but most people referred to him as that 'bastard'.

'What happened to Trish?' Arnold asked. Gary had bumped into a girl he knew from home.

'She's in a state of recovery.'

Arnold laughed.

'Are you comin' for a bevvey?'

Martin stood by his towel and cursed Arnold. Hadn't the fool only gone and left his belongings unguarded.

'Hello, Martin.' Geena stood before him in a crotcheted bikini. He could see the outline of her pubic hair in the shade of the knots.

'Hi.'

'Hi.'

The day after the night before and they felt a bit awkward. They talked for a while. They walked for a while. Then Martin said fancy a drink and they both blushed. Into Bar Sol they sauntered and spotted Arnold spotting them.

Too late.

'Martin, we're over here.'

The thing with Gary was he didn't like being outdone. A hole is a hole is a hole and one man's meat is another man's . . .

Gary had a lot of charm. He was very seductive, looked like a tameable bastard, the bit of rough every woman dreams of. He made women feel dirty when they were with him; women loved to feel dirty.

'So you're from Bavaria then, Geena.'

Martin got a round in and Gary got going.

He asked if Bavaria was the land of the sausage and she laughed. He told her she reminded him of one of those black and white classic movie actresses, the one who'd been in Casablanca, Ingrid Bergman.

He held her gaze and touched her face lightly.

Due to nerves Martin got too drunk too quickly. She wasn't looking at him enough and he was staring at her continually. He went for a piss and when he came back she had gone. So had Gary.

In his late teens Gary had done a bit of modelling. The money was unreal but the lads took the mick, said he was a ponce. He did catalogue stuff and the odd catwalk, pretty boring after a while. Most of the guys he met were bent backwards and he loathed the sight of them. One of them made a pass.

It was a spring collection, linen suits and lots of long hair. This queer was a bit too clever, as he came poncing down the catwalk he pinched Gary's arse. And as he ponced back up the catwalk, the bum bandit blew Gary a kiss. Gary waited for the fag to twirl. He waited for the queen to come skipping by. The pretty-eyed boy fluttered his eyelashes, pursed his lips and Gary took him behind the curtain. Smashed him up so bad the guy was in hospital for three weeks. Gary was brought to court and the judge sympathised, said poofs were bad for society so don't get caught next time. Modelling gave Gary up.

The apartment was Spartan, there were two small box rooms, a bathroom and kitchen-cum-lounge. The larger of the rooms was shared by Gary and Tony. Jacko shared the smaller with Martin, and Arnold was on his own, on the sofa. The scoreboard was filling up steadily, Gary racing ahead followed closely by Tony. Jacko was making steady progress but Arnold was way behind. Tony said it was because he was trying too hard. Since the first night Arnold had only got one more hole and that was because Tony gave it to him. Martin had lapsed a little too. He never did say anything to Gary but he was well pissed off at not having had a second chance with Geena. He hadn't seen her since, reckoned she must have gone home. Gary turned to him one night when they were playing on the arcades.

'You shouldn't have given her a second thought, mate.'
'Fuck you, Gary, she was class.'
'She was a tight-arsed git.'

One afternoon they decided to take off on their scooters and ride down along the coast. They happened upon a more upmarket replica of their own resort with an original village to boot. Gary and Jacko decided this was the place to do some shopping and went to the *banco* to cash some cheques. There wasn't much on offer; tacky souvenirs, overpriced and breakable, and T-shirts with well-worn slogans. A platinum blonde caught their eye.

'Awright, boys,' She had three-inch heels on tanned tight legs, a G-string bikini and man-made breasts barely covered by a cut-off T-shirt. She was playing with a kitten.

'Just admiring your pussy,' said Gary.
'Ohh, steady on.'

'Can I give it a stroke?'

'Naughty!'

'We're up for the day.'

'I bet you boys are.' She pursed her lips and raised an eyebrow.

Cindy's ambition was to become a holiday rep. She said she spent most of her time hanging out at this really wicked club, she said she was a trained dancer.

'Do you want to come then?'

'Ever ready.'

'Ohh, hark at him.'

She said there wasn't another like it on the island.

'I think it'll be right up your alley, boys.'

'Rather up yours.'

'Go away with you,' and they left shortly after.

Jacko said why pay for it when you can get it for free.

The lads talked it over. Martin thought it would be an experience, Arnold thought when in Rome . . . and Tony was all on for it.

'I'm sick of playing with amateurs, time for the professionals.'

'No points for whores though,' said Jacko.

'Fuck that, look at the slags you've had, they were giving it away.'

'Yeah, rougher than dog's, what,' said Gary, getting his oar in.

Arnold thought back to the withered English rose, she couldn't have charged if she'd wanted to.

'Fellas, fellas,' Martin intervened, 'the point was getting as many normal girls without paying for it.'

Tony wasn't convinced.

'You're such a stickler, Jacko, what difference does it make?'

'Plenty.' Jacko was getting annoyed.

'As I say, a hole is a hole,' quipped Gary.

A rook was storming. Tony, pissed at Jacko's attitude, demanded a vote be taken.

'Look, none of us are watching over each other's shoulders, anyone could be cheating.'

'Don't look at me,' declared Arnold, so they did.

'The game is over unless you play by the rules.'

'Fuck you, Jacko.'

'Fuck you, Tony.' Jacko was adamant.

Gary shouted, 'What are we arguing about cunts for, we're meant to be on holiday.'

Jacko left to his own devices decided to mount his mean machine and take to the road, ride up the coast for a while.

Head of security at a dump of a city company, Jacko spent his time pacing back and forth and checking people over. He was straight down the line, and if a job was worth doing, it was worth doing well. He'd had hopes of being in the army but didn't make it. Then he tried the fire brigade, then the police. He drifted from job to job, had been in a bit of trouble, assault and such like. Probably why they held it against him. He was too headstrong, all that discipline, couldn't take orders. For the last couple of years, he'd been at the security lark. It was fine for the time being.

At the age of twenty-eight Jacko had one kid he never saw and three step-kids. The first one came as a result of playing truant from school. She was fifteen and pregnant, he was sixteen and felt obliged. They married, divorced and lost touch. His Susan had come a few years later. She cornered him in the local, she'd just got a job there. Susan was a brassy lady, older than him and had come with a ready-made family. They had a laugh together, she was a good woman, drank like a fish, could drink him under the table and gave as good as she got.

In the distance Jacko made out a small crowd of people huddled around a bonfire. He was glad now he'd stocked up on cans, there was no point in crashing a party empty-handed. He rode down on to the sand to take a better look. There were a fair few youngsters dancing to hippie music, getting smashed and smoking pot. He spotted a few girls with braces on their teeth and guessed he was on to the freshest flesh this side of the ocean. He was going to have to be on his best behaviour.

'You don't mind, do you?' Jacko said to one of the lads and offered the bloke a can as a gesture of friendship.

'Cheers, I'm Geoff.'

'Jacko.'

Geoff was Irish and having the crack.

'Me too,' said Jacko, 'me too.'

Siobhan stood close to the flames, too close. She was very tipsy, swaying and wobblin' and 'Be careful,' Jacko caught her arms, 'you could have burnt yourself, love.'

'Can I've a beer?'

'Of course you can, gorgeous.'

'Jacko,' he said introducing himself.

'Jacko, are you Irish?'

'No.'

She seemed a little disappointed.

'Well, tell a lie, there is a bit of me that's Irish but it's only a small bit.'

Siobhan was romantic, she said. 'I want to walk by the shore and look at the stars.'

Jacko knew he could have her, just had to get her well oiled first and she looked fresh, Jesus did she look fresh.

The lads were gob-smacked.

'I don't fuckin believe you.'

'Cross my heart.' Jacko relishing his moment of glory.

'Yah lucky bastard.'

'How the fuck did you manage that?'

Jacko danced around the room.

'See, I haven't lost the touch, wha'.'

'Fourteen, you say.'

'Yeah, took my time, got her all pliable, said she wanted to see some stars. Lay on the sand, kissed her up a little, felt her

up a little, put her hand on me cock, told her, darlin' that's all
for you . . .'

'I can't,' she said.

'What do you mean you can't? You want to, don't you?'
'Yeah but . . .'

'Doing the old No means Yes thing.' The guys nodded their
heads at this one, happened to them all before.

'It was like I dunno, I fucking had her, guys.'

The lads clapped him on the back. Jacko was victorious.

'How was your night?'

The club turned out to be a massage parlour, the kind on
most London high streets. A place for wankers with tired
arms. They queued, they came, they left.

The best thing about package holidays is the knowledge that
a fresh batch of people are continuously on the way. This
kept the lads on their toes and they danced a merry dance
round several nubile lovelies. The days sped by and before
they knew it, their last night of freedom was upon them. They
aimed to go out with a bang.

Tony had befriended a crowd of clubbers from Leeds a
couple of days earlier. They had been heading for Ibiza but
got shafted by a tour operator. Graham, a DJ, knew his stuff,
had the best sound system on the island or so he said. They
were having a party and it was going to be mad. If it was
going to be mad then the lads were going.

Martin and Jacko leant against the counter in the kitchen,
laughing about the big city company. Someone had rolled a
joint and passed it to them.

'Wicked spliff, man,' and they shouted their respect. Tony
came over, said he could get them some E's if they were into
it. They were. The place was cookin' with strobes, visuals,
bottled water, poppers, E, whiz, tequila, the works. The lads
got off their faces and started to blend in. Martin took a tab
and went on a bad trip. Jacko took an E and went into

hysterics. Arnold didn't give a fuck if he scored or not. He just wanted to move, to dance, to move. Gary and Tony pulled two Asian babes, Surita and Ritasu, masquerading as twins. The result being the lads filled almost all columns on the scoreboard plus they could verify it. This happened in the room given over to Love and the Essence of Purity.

Tony, a bit of an amateur photographer, was mad into gadgets and things technical. He'd spent a lot of time taking shots of the obvious beauty spots Costa Flesh had on offer, got in a bit of video work too. Gary was in a sandwich, Tony pressed record and dived in.

Tony was a dabbler, a little bit of this, a little bit of that, thumb in every pie. He lived with missus and sprog, cos there was always a hot meal on the table waiting for him if he got in. Missus was pathetic, the only thing she had going for her was the money she brought in, the sprog was worse, whining and whinging all the time. Truth be told he couldn't stomach either of them.

Tony made sure he stood, didn't want the camera identifying him. Gary looked great on camera, this was going to be good. He liked looking, always got off on it. There was a small packet to be made from the visuals he collected.

'Gar, do you want to play a game?'

Tony asked Surita if she had any more friends who'd like to join. She'd one called John. A very pretty John.

Arnold was dancing in the middle of the room when the most gorgeous woman he had ever seen strolled over to him. She moved provocatively beside him, swaying her hips slowly, running her nails up and down his arms.

Arnold felt wicked, the drugs were working. He smiled at the vision before him, slipped his hand around her waist and drooled.

'How about it . . .'

Arnold tried to spot the others, they'd never believe what he had just pulled. They started to make love by the poolside. Arnold taking it slowly, she was something else, he never had lassies like this, she was different. He wanted to savour every moment. They kissed for ages.

'I want to please you,' she whispered pushing his head towards her groin.

Arnold the gentleman bypassed her crotch, he was going to start right at the beginning. She moaned, she groaned, she mooed with pleasure. He wanted her, all of her from the tips of her toes, to her calves, her knees, along her thighs, further ... further ... onward ... until ... until he came to her ... cock and then he threw up.

Gary and Tony jumped from the bushes, clapping and howling.

'Fuck's sakes!'

Jacko was in hysterics and Arnold was awarded ten points for being so perverted. Tony had the whole thing on video. Pretty John settled for twenty quid and a couple of E's. Arnold was in shock. The lads said it was a laugh, just a joke.

'Ah, Arno, you took it like a man.'

'Don't be so serious, Arno, we all make mistakes.'

'They meant no harm, Arnold,' Martin said. 'Forget it, it happens to the best of us.'

Two weeks of sowing wild oats had come to an end. The scoreboard was full and the lads shagged out. Gary came first, followed by Jacko and Tony in joint second. Martin came a respectable third and Arnold had a lot to learn.

As they boarded the plane, clutching their bags of duty-free, they hailed their manhood and pledged never to tell the women, but Martin was beginning to itch. Tony said not to worry.

'Fuck it, if she gets it, blame her.' Martin wasn't convinced so he bought her a nice bottle of perfume from the sexy air hostess.

'I wanna sign up,' said Jacko. She knew what he was alluding to. The thing was these guys thought they were original, entertained the thought they might have a chance with her, that in some obscure way they were paying her a compliment.

'Pardon me, sir?'

'To the mile high club.' Through a thick layer of make-up she was seething.

'Scum,' she thought. 'Fucking scum.'

Emily Perkins

THE THIRD GIRL

Extract from a novel in progress

THERE ARE THESE three teenage girls, walking along a sunlit road.

The road is wide and open to the light. Low, scrubby plants line it on either side. Way beyond these are stripes of the clouds that lie along the horizons to the east and west. An aeroplane glints like a speck of glitter in the smooth blue sky, too far away to hear.

This is a road they have walked along all their seventeen-year-old lives. They don't even notice it any more.

Chicky says to Rachel: You coming round our place for tea tonight?

Julia looks straight ahead. She can see a rock in the middle of their path. With every step they take she counts how much bigger it's getting. By an eighth, by a fifth, by a third. Now shown actual size. As they pass she doesn't kick it.

Rachel has jerked her head towards Julia and raised her eyebrows at Chicky.

Chicky says: You have to go home don't you? to Julia.

Julia says, Yeah.

All right then, answers Rachel. Sure.

Early summer and the grass isn't dry yet on the front lawns. In suburban homes radio alarms buzz into life. The sleepers do not groan and flail for the snooze button, they do not clutch their knees to their chests and pull blankets tight under their chins, slipping back into the shadows of their dreams.

163

This early summer morning the radio's demands are obeyed. Sheets are flung back and feet barely touch the floor as the newly wakened rush to their bedroom windows. With a breath they draw the blinds, tiptoe, peer, and there it is, the early summer sun, soft and loving like a wish, warming the rooftops, the gardens, the pebblestone paths of their town. Everything is warmed to life by its glow. Dogs stretch back from their front legs in a salute. The morning papers lie warming on front steps or in letterboxes. Coffee bubbles on stovetops, water sluices over soapy bodies, gushing from shower rosettes at a gentle temperature. In the park the old man finishes his tai chi with his face turned towards the sun, closed eyes caught in its intensifying heat. In this weather anyone who wants to can share the belief that their lives are good, that this town is the perfect place to spend their days and years, here in peace with their good, normal neighbours. This is the weather of tourist brochures, of civic pride, of living the dream. It is weather to make you forget that bad things can happen.

Mary smiles as Julia's pale face enters the kitchen. 'Morning,' she shouts in her daughter's left ear.

'Mum. Spare it.'

Last night the kids had celebrated the end of exams. The final one was English, so all the seniors were at school together for the first time since study break began. Most of the boys had brought beers.

After three hours of scratching silence the students had pushed out of square, low-ceilinged classrooms. They swarmed down strip-lit hallways, dumping pencil cases, note paper and cheating copies into rubbish bins. Kids slapped hands and punched each other on the arm. A couple of girls burst into tears. One of the sporty guys hoisted a tape deck on to his shoulder. Guitar rock blasted from the speakers as students ran down faded lineoleum steps, out into the daylight, across the asphalt quad, around the side of B block, down the slope to the bottom field.

Here the pack split into loose groups, some walking, some still running over the grass towards the chickenwire fence with huge, jagged holes in it. The urgency of a minute ago was gone; the pace took on a leisurely, easy feel. Julia had been conscious of her arms and legs moving through the air, blood warm in her veins. Chicky and Rachel were either side of her. Other girls and a couple of boys walked with them, satellites. The sporty guys ahead turned and shouted, 'Bridge! Bridge! Bridge!' Their girlfriends, in a group of their own, twisted their heads on swan-like angles and giggled at one another. Behind them, the nerdy kids hung back, unsure if for once the bridge would become neutral territory, if the end of school heralded a new, egalitarian regime, or if, following the crowd down there, they would get the shit kicked out of them.

Habit prevailed. They stayed in their allotted corner of the bottom field while the jocks, the pretty girls, the regular squares, the drama gang, the student magazine team, the class clowns, and Julia, Rachel and Chicky clambered through the fence, skidded down the shingle bank and crossed the disused railway lines to the cracked concrete, graffiti-stained bridge. The geeks and losers, from the field, could hear more anthemic rock pulsing up towards them on the afternoon air. They could hear laughter and shrieking sounds and one or two of them caught, longingly, the scents of cannabis and cigarette smoke, of sweat and sex and beer.

Another thing the rejects – the fat boys, the pigeon-chested swots – might have picked up on the wind, but didn't – a failing of the senses – was the slow smell, rising in warm waves from the kids at the bridge, of dawning alarm.

'I hope your hangover's gone by tonight,' Mary says now to Julia, placing the coffee jug and an empty cup on the table in front of her.

'I'm not hungover.'

'Right. You hear that, Martin?' Julia's dad has wandered in from the back garden. He has what looks like a walkie-talkie in his hand. 'Julia's not hungover.'

Martin looks in their direction. 'Do we have any double-A batteries?' he says, on his way to the front door.

'So. Are you sure you don't want to go to the salon this afternoon?'

'Nah.' All the other girls'll be doing that big hair for the leaver's ball tonight. 'They'll be booked up.'

'OK.'

Julia glances up as Mary is putting her lipstick on in the stainless steel reflection from the cooker. 'Mum?'

'Mn?'

'We'll be going from Chicky's, OK. So I might not see you.'

Mary drops the lipstick into her pocket and squeezes her daughter's shoulder. 'Oh yeah,' she says, 'I'll see you.'

They sat on the floor of Chicky's flat, which was really a converted wash-house six feet away from her parents' back door. Chicky was going to wear high-heeled sandals so she had cotton wool stuffed between her toes and was trying to paint the nails the colour of fresh blood. Julia and Rachel took turns with the hand mirror, the mascara, eye-liner and a dirty pot of rouge. A bottle of pink Chardon was passed from mouth to mouth. They did lipstick and Chicky rolled a joint.

'Is Johnno going?' Rachel asked the question.

Chicky shrugged. 'Dunno.'

'Did he really cry?'

'Yup. Only cos I was the first girl to dump him. Thinks he's such a stud.'

'Yeah.'

'That'll be the worst thing if I fail. No way am I going back. Do another year with those retards. Johnno's dad won't let him leave until he's passed, and I bet you he hasn't. He'll be like, twenty before he gets out of that place.'

The school hall was decked out with red and yellow lights and strips of red foil that milk-bottle tops had been cut out of, hanging from ceiling to floor along the walls. On hessian boards just inside the two sets of double doors, photographs of the leaving year – sports teams, fêted couples, guys goofing off in the quad – were pinned amongst cartoons of teachers and end-of-term messages. *Mr Andrews we'll miss you. Lewis takes it up the xxxx* was scribbled over with ineffectual 2H pencil. *Brandi u r the 1 4 me from ???* Someone had tried to raise the tone, in cursive script: *Come, dear children, let us away; Down and away below.* Then *Year Six 4 eva.* And underneath a photograph of the school's – in fact the town's – only publicly acknowledged homosexual, Bryce Ellmann, who has spent the last three years fielding taunts and random violence, were scrawled the words *Gay + Gay = AIDS.*

'Jesus,' said Julia as she pulled the picture of Bryce away from its drawing pins and shoved it in her bag. 'Get me away from here.'

The band were taking their first break as the girls pushed their way into the hall. Chicky led them to a corner and drew a water bottle filled with white rum out of her large coat pocket. They passed it between them. Julia's mouth felt clacky from the sweet drinks and the dope they'd smoked. There was a sugary sensation in her jaw and in her knees. She laughed. They all laughed. Around them stood their class-mates: girls in short dresses, tugging nail-bitten hands at their knicker-skimming hems; Charlene Quigley hoisting her cleav-age up by the spaghetti straps; boys self-conscious in chinos and check shirts. Leroy Karr wore his scarred denim jacket and jeans as usual. And there was Johnno, his arm hooked around Tarin Verschoor's neck, leaning in to give her a long meaty kiss while shuffling as close to Chicky as he could manage.

And the band slouched back on to the stage, long grey raincoats over stovepipe jeans. Three of them were ex-students who lived in the city now and occasionally toured the far-flung towns, filling a garage or a working men's club or a school hall like this one with their serious stares, petulant lyrics and frequent guitar solos. They thrashed out number after number and the kids danced. There was none of the previous day's relief or exhilaration in the air, only an almost aggressive flatness. Students filed out to be sick in the rockery outside the principal's office. Illicit cigarettes were smoked openly; the girl's toilets were bottle-necked with queues for diet pills and hash. At one point the hall emptied – a rumour had flown round that there was a knife fight in the car park – but gradually everyone traipsed back in, disappointed.

While she danced, Julia watched the guy playing bass guitar. She remembered him being a senior when she'd first started at the school. His boyish, appley face hadn't changed very much. She remembered the first time she and Rachel had dared to go down to the bridge. He'd been there with his friends and as the girls lay on the rough gravel, their bare knees bent up towards the sun, they had overheard the older boys talking. He was funny, the bass player, he was telling jokes about leprosy and herpes – what do you call twenty lepers in a swimming pool? soup – and she and Rachel had to turn their faces away because they were laughing, silently, so hard it made their noses redden and their eyes water. He just kept going and the day was hot and the gravel cut into Julia's elbows. Behind her the concrete bridge stood grey and scrawled with painted codes, declarations of love and hate, and the boy sang to the tune of *Yesterday*, *leprosy – I'm not half the man I used to be – bits are falling off all over me* . . . trying not to laugh out loud, trying not to betray herself. She had a crush on him from that day on, until he left at the end of the year and disappeared into the city.

There were no requests for encores. As the band packed up most of the kids headed home, some still suffering the humiliation of parents in waiting cars. The 'supervising' teachers ventured warily into the hall to check for debris and breakages. Chicky was outside having a stand-up row with Tarin Verschoor while Johnno sat in the driver's seat of his customised Beetle, throwing up on to the asphalt under his open door. Rachel and Julia reached them just as Chicky struck Tarin's sunburnt shoulder hard with the flat of her hand. It was a familiar gesture: they knew where it would lead.

'Come on, Chick,' said Rachel.

'And he told me you've got a sloppy box,' said Tarin, just before the back of Chicky's hand collided with her jaw.

'That tiny dick couldn't feel a wormhole,' Chicky shouted from waist-level, where Tarin was holding her head by a fistful of hair.

Julia wiped her hands over her eyes, remembering too late that she was wearing mascara. From the car, Johnno groaned and heaved again.

'Come on, Chick,' Rachel insisted, about to step in. The two girls were doing a stomping dance on each other's toes. Tarin, in court shoes, had the advantage. The hydraulic, reinforced-glass doors to the hall foyer swung open on to the scene. Out walked the band, a whisky bottle poking up from a mackintosh pocket, an instrument case in one hand, a cigarette behind the drummer's ear, a mic stand under somebody's arm. They saw the fighting girls and stopped.

'Hey, ladies,' said the singer, 'what's all this?'

Chicky couldn't reply. She had a mouthful of Tarin's forearm and her hand pressed hard up against Tarin's face. Tarin's free arm flailed at Chicky's back. She screamed for Johnno to intervene. Johnno spat on the ground.

'Fucking help me,' said Rachel to the guys from the band. 'Get them off each other.'

Julia looked at the bass guitarist.

Later, they're in a converted storage shed down the bottom of an empty field. The walls are lined with empty bottles and scraps of tinfoil. It's dark, with an orange lava-flow candle in the middle of the floor giving off a brown sort of light. The only object in the room is a wire-wove camp bed with a foam mattress: all the shelves that might have been filled with boxes and cans of weedkiller are empty. On one wall the stencil outlines of various tools are painted, vacant. A hammer, a jigsaw, a knife. Chicky and the drummer are out the front of the shed, leaning against its rotting planks, kissing. At either end of the camp stretcher, Rachel and the singer sit with shoulders rolled forward and heads lolling in sleep. The guitarist is splayed in the corner by the door, gazing out through it at the moon or the black and white long-grass or Chicky and the drummer. In the centre of the room, by the candle, Julia sits cross-legged facing the bass player, who has one knee pulled up towards his chest and one leg extended in front of him, running at an angle close to the line of Julia's thigh. But not touching.

They have been in the singer's car, a wide low-slung number with a bench seat in front. Outside the school hall, the singer released Chicky's hand from its grip on Tarin's face and dragged her away by the wrist. The other band members and Rachel and Julia followed. The singer only told Chicky to shut up after the third time she had twisted her head nearly 180 degrees on her neck and shouted *Fucking bitch I hope you rot in fucking hell* to Tarin. After that she was quiet. They were all quiet for most of the time they were in the car, the silence broken maybe by the drummer's soft laughter as the singer skidded the car into a patch or, once they were on the outskirts of the town, swung over the uncambered road in lurching curves. Flung up against each other in the back, the girls and the guitarist didn't laugh.

Now, in the musty gloom of the shed, the bass player says to Julia, 'So, you getting out straight away?'

'I don't know,' she answers, picking at a thumbnail. 'I've got a holiday job, at this shop, then. I've got to wait for results. Find out about university and that.'

'Well, are you thick?'

She giggles.

'Think seriously before you answer.'

'No,' she says. 'I'm not thick. I don't think.'

He opens another beer and passes it to her. 'A whole summer in this fucking cul-de-sac. What are you going to do?'

She shrugs. 'What are you doing?'

'We're heading tomorrow. For the coast. Take a week or so

to get there, a couple more gigs. Then bumming on the beach with all the other wasters.'

If only, Julia thinks, swallowing some tepid beer, he would ask her to go. And if only she was the sort of girl, brave enough, who would. She could be free, living out of a car with her apple-cheeked boyfriend, swimming and selling watermelons and listening to him play the guitar. But then – he's leaning back on his elbows now, and he seems to be closer than last time she looked up – she imagines older girls hanging around, scary and relaxed, and how would they buy food, and what if they got arrested, and if they slept in the car what would they use for a bathroom? Then the bass guitarist sits up, shifts forwards on to his knees, leans his altarboy's face into hers and kisses her. She makes a decision. She'll go.

After an hour or so of kissing, and hands under each other's clothes, he still hasn't asked her. Rachel and the singer have slanted towards each other until their shoulders are providing a mutual support. Chicky comes in from outside, without the drummer.

'Let's go,' she says, slumping down on Rachel's side of the triangle she's making with the singer. The springless bed buckles. Rachel flops at the waist and swings round to lean on Chicky, who puts an arm around her and strokes her hair. 'You,' she says to the bass player. 'Drive us.'

All the slow crawl home he doesn't ask her. It's under-standable: he is concentrating on staying in the middle of the road, and more than once a bird flies out of the dark bushes and across the half-light of the path ahead, making him fumble for the brakes and clumsily accelerate again, letting the steering fend for itself as he does. 'Can't work my feet and my hands at the same time,' he laughs, and Julia gazes out the window from the suicide seat and wonders if she needs to worry about the rest of her life at all. The sky is getting paler, a furry blue that bleaches out the stars and blackens the surrounding trees. As they grate over an old cattle-stop Chicky grunts. Julia turns to see her friends slack-mouthed in sleep, bodies flung deep into the gravity of the back seat as if they've been shot. Chicky's solid thighs are spread, and in the other corner, Rachel's hair has tumbled prettily across her face. The drunken choirboy is keeping his eyes on the road.

She tells him to pull up at the corner of her street. He switches off the engine and they sit for a moment, the only sounds the rhythmic breathing of the girls behind them.

'So what time are you leaving?' Julia asks, her voice quiet.

'I'll go back and chuck the guys in the car, then I guess straight away.'

'Oh right.' She puts her hand on the door handle. He reaches out to touch the back of her neck, pulling her into a kiss. After a few minutes they hear Chicky's voice:

'Excuse me, guys. Do you mind?' Julia turns to her friend, nostrils flared and jaw jutting in annoyance. Chicky returns her stony glare with a widening of her own eyes, and a shrug. The guitarist has swivelled back to face the windscreen, hands in his lap.

'OK.' Julia opens her door. 'See you,' she says to him.

'See you,' he says.

'Are you going to drop us home?' asks Chicky.

Rachel yawns and stretches awake. 'Unh?' she says.

'No,' the guitarist says. 'I'm going back now.'

'Righto.' Chicky hops out and pulls Rachel on to the sidewalk with her. 'We'll come in for breakfast,' she tells Julia.

The car coughs into life. Julia leans down towards the passenger seat window. 'Bye.'

'Bye,' he says, not looking at her, at the same time as he steps on the accelerator.

Julia holds a hand up in farewell. He's gone.

'Come on,' says Chicky. 'I'm starving.'

Rachel yawns again.

Though they're trying to be quiet it's impossible not to wake Mary because she's been sleeping in the living room on the couch.

'Hey,' she says a second after the front door's closed. 'In here.'

The three of them crowd into the doorway. Mary sits up, her face puffy. 'Good time?'

'Yeah,' say the girls.

She presses her palms to her eyes, then to her cheeks and then her mouth. 'Hungry?'

The kitchen is filled with light grey light. A sound of birds comes from the garden. They make cereal, scrambled eggs, toast and coffee. Mary gets her camera from the living room.

'I wanted a picture,' she smiles. 'You guys look terrible.'

'Mum.'

'Come on.'

They squeeze up at the breakfast bar: Chicky – rosy-cheeked, shoulders sliced into by the thin straps of her dress, a red mark on her neck that threatens to become a bruise; Rachel in the middle, dishevelled hair and her usual soft, slightly startled smile; and straight-browed Julia, looking at the lens with a level stare, enjoying the feeling of Rachel's arm around her waist, but dreaming of escape.

The shutter clicks. They all relax, back to their plates.

'Where have you been?'

'Some place. The guys from the band.'

'The guys from the band. I hope you were careful.'

'Mum.'

'Well I do.'

'They were dicks,' says Chicky, her mouth full of eggs. She swallows. 'The drummer asked me to go away with them. Spend the summer on the beach, in a car.' She snorts. 'As if.'

Rachel Cusk

FOUR GIRLS

'MY WIFE,' SAID the Sicilian hotelier, in explanation of his good English, 'comes from Banbury, in Oxfordshire. Do you know it?'

'I don't think I've ever been there.'

'I lived there with her for twenty-five years. We have four grown-up children.'

His white pyjamas were gravely luminous in the gloomy interior of the lobby; the white of tombs in churches, of sheets in a narrow alley in the shade. A patient seam of blue blazed beyond the still-shuttered windows. It was early, but the surprise of the day was already waiting outside.

'Do you see her often?'

'She comes to Catania every year for a fortnight. As a matter of fact, she is staying here at the moment, in the hotel. I'm sure she would love to meet you. She is asleep just now, in that room at the end there, but perhaps later, when she wakes up . . . ?'

'Yes, of course, I'd be delighted. Do you ever come back to England?'

'I haven't been to England for many years,' said the hotelier sonorously. 'I have the hotel, of course. I get visitors all through the year and it is difficult for me to leave. And England has changed so much! My wife always tells me so. The last time I visited London I hardly recognised it. The atmosphere, too, seemed to have changed. It felt very violent to me. Perhaps I am just old.'

'What about your children? Where are they?'

'My sons are both rich bankers.' He cackled delightedly, one hand on his narrow chest. 'They got out while the going was good! One lives in Switzerland and the other in France. My daughters have married Italians. And they all come and stay with me here.'

'You've certainly got plenty of room.'

'That's right. That's right. And what about you? You live in London, with all the other – what is the expression – all the other young things.'

'Yes, I do.' His description of her propelled her up momentarily above her own life, like the spring of a diving board. 'But I've been thinking of going somewhere else. I don't like London very much.'

It was what she had to do, to show her unhappiness; to provide, by no matter what clumsy subterfuge, a quick, vital glimpse of it, like the signal of a spy, before it became once more impossible for her to communicate.

'*Really?*' He raised his eyebrows in concern. 'So you are going to live all alone in the countryside? Or abroad. Ah!' He raised his eyebrows again. 'Here is your friend. How are you today?'

'Morning!' Matthew's hair was wet and slicked back flat against his head. He held out his hand and the hotelier shook it. 'Well, we slept *very* well,' he said, with a rueful, laugh, 'too well probably. This is a great place you've got here. It's amazingly quiet.'

'Good.' The hotelier bowed slightly.

There was a pause, filled with the echo of Matthew's arrival. His eyes darted about the lobby, inquiring and affronted.

'Are you ready to go?'

'She's been ready for hours,' said the hotelier jovially. 'To fill the time she has been submitting very charmingly to my conversation. So!' He looked at them both. 'Today you are going to be tourists. You have your maps, your books, your training shoes. Is it a good book, that one? Does it mention the Villa Romani?'

'That's what I was talking about last night,' said Anna.

'What was that?' said Matthew, opening the book and half-proffering it to the hotelier. 'The Villa Romani?'

'It says,' said Anna. 'Right at the end. I know where it is.'

'We've got it, we've got it,' said Matthew. 'Villa Romani. So it's worth going to see, is it?'

'Oh certainly. Although I think you can only go there by car,' said the hotelier. 'I don't know. I'm afraid I can't remember. It has been a long time.'

'But it's worth seeing, is it?'

'The mosaics are unequalled. The Romans built it as a hunting lodge, I believe. They had just begun excavation when I saw it. It was not for tourists, but now – who knows? They might have arranged something. It was a very important find. There is nothing else like it in Sicily. But perhaps you can't get there.'

'Hang on, let's see. Ah – yes. It says here you can get a bus about two-thirds of the way.' Matthew looked up from the book. 'We can always hitch from there.'

'Why not hire a car?' The hotelier shrugged. It seemed that he might tell them not to hitch; might advise against it, for Anna's sake. They would never, of course, hire a car; but like a half-hearted dissident she found consolation in mere agreement. 'It's a lovely drive through the mountains.'

He smiled, as if at some greater and entirely ordinary view he had of their life which they themselves did not have. It could have been the polite, denying smile the able-bodied give to the disabled; but to her it felt preliminary and real, like the first, investigative beam of a torch directed into some dark, susceptible cavity.

Outside, the pavement was crowded with the determined traffic of commuters. Ranks of well-dressed men and women moved alongside a honking river of cars and buses and the air bloomed with their sophisticated smells, of perfume and styled hair and pressed clothes and leather. It was a wide street, a broad, straight boulevard like the floor of a ravine that ran through the centre of the city. At one end of it, in the distance, the volcano sat benign and silent in the sunshine. At the other it pooled into the junction of the main square. It was rush-hour, and the city was preoccupied. It functioned around the tourists, ordering the frenzy of arrival and departure, of coffee and newspapers and money changing swift, practised hands, like a busy adult around children marooned by their own helplessness. Matthew rooted himself, looked left and right, and unfolded the map.

'It's so silly,' he said. 'The bus station's miles from the centre. Look, it's all the way over here. It doesn't look like a very nice walk, either. You have to go along this big road.'

He was absorbed, screwing up his eyes against the sun, his mouth ragged with concentration. His bearing seemed to bristle with challenges to unspoken judgements. She felt interrogated, though it was she who was watching.

'Can't we get a taxi?'

'Actually, maybe there's a better route. We could go through the park, I suppose. What do you think?'

'What's wrong with a taxi?'

He didn't reply. She wondered whether a response was inching through him with the silent intent of a clot through a vein.

'Right. OK.' He began folding the map. 'I've got it.'

He walked off abruptly, looking to either side of him. Anna stayed still, her heart rising like a fist in her throat. She had wanted him to show himself, but now that she had provoked him she felt blameless and fatigued, as if his behaviour were an inexplicable imposition. She waited, momentarily buoyant with rebellion, then sinking into a state of strange, impermissible absorption. All around her she could hear the urgent tap of heels on the pavement. The air moved with the bustle of bodies. Eventually she looked up and saw him standing with his arms folded fifty yards or so ahead of her. She walked towards him, and when she was within a few feet of him he set off again.

'I want some breakfast,' she said.

He walked on, stopping when he reached the corner. He unfolded the map again, and after glancing at it turned left and disappeared. She stopped. Now that he was out of sight she found herself assuming a bewildered attitude. She was aware that this attitude was self-conscious: it lay to one side of her, just as the unfamiliar detail of the city, whose interest, she now saw, could be squandered, lay to the other. She looked around anxiously. After some minutes she began to walk slowly towards the corner, and turning it almost collided with him coming back the other way.

'Where did you go?' he said. 'I've just spent the last ten minutes looking for you.'

'No you haven't,' she said.

'You just disappeared! What's wrong with you?'

'I want some breakfast,' she said. 'I'm hungry.'

'Why do we always have to stop just because you want something?'

'Normal people have breakfast. We're supposed to be on holiday.'

'Look.' An expression of fury passed over his face, as if some untamed anger lived there of which an occasional glimpse could be caught. 'We're going to miss the bus. If you want to spend all day in some café, then that's up to you. You'd better make up your mind, because I want to go.'

They set off along another broad, straight road whose features were screened by a portcullis of shade. Young, slim trees were planted at regular intervals along it. There were fewer people here, and the identity of the city receded slightly. Anna felt a stirring of accommodation. As if by a methodical shift of weight, her opposition to Matthew, to their garb, their pairing, their plans, was reversed. She took his hand, and their arms swung between them like a pendulum. Their control of the situation, the familiarity they brought to what was strange, functioned again unimpaired. Anna delighted in everything that minutes earlier had seemed unbearable. The walk, after all, was satisfying, and they had avoided not merely the expense but the betrayal – of themselves, of the boundaries of their agreement, beyond which lay a cold and uninhabitable chaos – of a taxi.

Some time later they reached the bus station, a curving, desolate prairie of concrete studded with glass shelters, which lay sprawled in the rough, habitual heat of the city's perimeter. Modern blue buses with tinted windows moved like barges across the flat glare.

'There it is!' shouted Matthew, breaking into a run. Anna ran behind him. 'I'll go and get the tickets and you tell him to wait,' he called over his shoulder, veering off.

She watched him go, heading for a low modern building some distance away. She saw the back of his head, indifferent and vulnerable, his pumping calves beneath long, old-fashioned shorts, his billowing T-shirt dancing with a crazy, momentary joy around his torso as he ran. The bus crouched fuming to her left. She approached it, unsure of what she was expected to do. A worm of anger unfurled in her stomach. Like the first twinge of pain after an illness that had been thought cured, the feeling seemed more real to her than the contentment in which she had momentarily, but never entirely confidently, revelled. The door of the bus was open. She stood by it aimlessly, looking at the driver. He was wearing sunglasses, but he lifted his head towards her inquisitively. She nodded in the direction of the ticket office. He nodded briefly back, and sat back in his seat. Gazing off to one side, Anna felt her frame pulse with gratification at the casualness of the exchange, the confirmation it appeared to provide of her distinctness, her private way of doing things.

'Well done,' panted Matthew as they clambered up the rubber-clad steps. 'That was close. Apparently it was two hours until the next one.'

The doors closed behind them, and Anna felt a brief shock of disloyalty as they passed the driver. The bus was uncrowded and they sat together. Matthew had the small rucksack on his lap and they both rooted around inside it for things. Anna read the guidebook as the bus hissed and swayed. She read about the places they planned to visit later, going through them like a memory in reverse, ingesting details not of their sights and highlights, but of hotels, restaurants and bars, finding in each brief description some fleeting refuge, some human assurance, like a trail of stepping-stones across a river, of the fact that there was a way through.

Matthew was leaning avidly towards the window, as if miming the act of looking. She saw in his posture an elaborate reprimand for her reading rather than looking at the view. Every now and again he would give a slight gasp and then a whistling sigh, jamming around in his seat to look back at some rejected marvel.

'Look at that,' he said finally. They were out of the city, sailing in long curves around empty green and brown hills. A pale, solitary castle was lodged above them in a crown of morning mist. As if to warn her of his command, and perhaps evade the question of whether or not he could enforce it, he turned around and bent, squinting at her page. 'I can't believe you're reading about gay nightclubs in Palermo,' he said, nervously sardonic. 'One of these days you'll probably end up reading about something while we're actually doing it.'

His voice got louder as a laugh tried to unfold itself in his throat. She pitied him for the suppressed laugh and laughed herself to console him, leaning forward and resting her elbows on his thigh so that she could look out of the window. Down below, at the roadside, a scattered trail of people carrying spades and sacks moved slowly. Each of them seemed to meet her eye as the bus swept past, their faces upturned and caught in imploring snapshots, like people abandoned at a quayside. She leapt briefly into their lives, submerging herself again and again in each instant. The bus had filled up. People stood in the aisle. She had no idea suddenly where they were all going, and she felt a sense of common enterprise, of contingency and readiness for risk. Matthew put his hand on her back and began to stroke.

An intense, flat heat lay over the town where the bus stopped. Everyone got off. The other passengers welled briefly around them and then trickled away down the gullies of narrow streets until they were alone on the pavement. Anna waited while Matthew looked at the map, the open rucksack held in her hands.

'Right,' he said. 'We want to get back down on the main road.'

'What's wrong with here? There are cars coming along here.'

She was conscious of having responded automatically, as if they were the two parts of some ingeniously self-defeating mechanism. Deliberately she pointed herself somewhere else, randomly, with the grinding of a telescope on a rusty axis. She examined the view, feeling the dry, barbaric heat, interrogating the brown vista of the crumbling town, its weathered surfaces, the jigsaw of its roofs, the private meanderings of its roads and alleys. It resisted the futility of her acquaintance, forcing her back on Matthew.

'Well, they won't be going our way, will they?' he said. 'We need to be on this road, look –' he invited her into the map with a guiding finger, as if instructing her in his responsibility, 'so that we can get here, and then there's just this bit up here.' His finger rose up a tributary. 'We can probably walk that, actually. It'll be lovely. The problem's going to be getting down to the main road without going all the way back round. It should be just down there.'

He turned and leaned over a low wall behind them. A flank of dry scrubland sloped steeply out of sight.

'Yeah, it should be down there at the bottom. I wonder if there's a path down. Look, we can walk all the way round if you want.'

'No, we might as well go this way if it's quicker.'

They climbed over the wall and began to descend through rubble and the sharp, dry claws of bushes. There was no sign of a path. Old tin cans and plastic bags littered the slope. Their shoes quickly grew brown with dust, and the sun pounded on their unprotected heads and shoulders. The road came into view far below, with tiny cars beetling along it. At the bottom of the slope there was a dry ditch and then a concrete wall separated it from the road.

'All right?' shouted Matthew from ahead, sliding a foot or two down on a scree of dirt and small rocks.

'Yeah,' called Anna. She was being robust about the walk, partly to justify her going along with it, and partly from a sense that she could store it up, along with countless other unvoiced injustices, like a prisoner patiently hoarding things whose uses, though currently unclear, might one day contribute to an escape.

They paused at the ditch at the bottom. Anna's legs were cross-hatched with scratches and one of her shoes was torn. The rucksack was covered in dust. Matthew's eyebrows and hair were powdered light brown.

'Oh for God's sake!' she cried suddenly, bending over and plucking at the tear in her shoe.

'What is it now?' barked Matthew.

'Why do we always have to do things like this? Why can't we do anything properly?'

'You wanted to!' he shouted, drawing closer. 'I asked you if you wanted to go the other way and you said no!'

'I didn't know it was going to be like this!'

'Well, nor did I! Why don't you try finding the way yourself, instead of just complaining all the time?' He threw the map at her and it half-unfolded in the air, flapping crookedly and striking the side of her face. She cried out, clapping a hand over her eye. Her gesture, though not a response to pain, provided her with a temporary respite, like sleep.

'Anna! Anna!'

He bounded over to her, and her other hand went up automatically to shield the other half of her face. He braced one arm around her shoulders and with the other tried to wrench away her hand. She was surprised at the violence of his pulling. It was clear to her that behind the shield of concern he desired, was attempting even, to injure her; that his concern was not, in fact, real, was one of the many masks in which they clad unnamed, untutored emotions in order to stage an imitation of love. The realisation was chastening. She had never, from the loftiness of her dissatisfaction, doubted that he at least was rooted in sincerity; but now she saw that it was perhaps merely that he was less willing to tell her how far from her he secretly wandered.

'Let me look, let me look,' he said agitatedly.

An unexpected gush of tears salted the darkness behind her

fingers. She could feel the sun on her head, boring through the confusion of the unfamiliar slope and the sound of the forgotten road nearby. There was nothing wrong with her eye, but she kept her hands where they were while he tugged at her wrists. She pressed her face harder into the dark slime of tears, and her shoulders heaved. The gestures were unexpectedly feeble. It would take more than that to power the walk back up the slope, the bus alone back to Catania, a flight after that. She sensed some ugly conspiracy between the two of them, something which suggested she had somehow forsaken her own righteousness.

'Come on,' said Matthew presently, loosening his grip.

They struggled across the ditch and then over the wall to the roadside. Anna felt the throb of self-pity still suspended in her chest, but with every passing minute of silence the feeling grew smaller and denser and deeper, until it was lodged like a piece of shrapnel behind her ribs. Matthew went to the edge of the road and stuck out his thumb. A black saloon car with tinted windows pulled over, its ample indicator leisurely flashing.

'That was quick,' said Anna as they ran towards it. 'People are so nice here.'

A spurt of gratitude for the kindness pricked at her still-swimming eyes. The argument with Matthew had, she felt, left her helpless before the heat, the terrain, the alien language. The generosity, the gentleness of strangers seemed to constitute not a rescue from her circumstances but an unbearable acknowledgement of their difficulty; an acknowledgement which, like that of a kind confessor, contained within its pity an acceptance of what she herself would not accept.

'*Grazie, grazie*,' said Matthew, opening the back door and leaning in.

She got in after him. The car was chilly with air conditioning. The black leather seats were cold and slippery. A man and woman, both wearing sunglasses, sat in the front. They turned anxiously around in their seats, nodding protectively at the tourists. The man said something to the woman with an expression of concern, his hand on her knee, and they both nodded again. Anna saw that they were distressed to have found the young couple on the roadside; distressed not at their proximity to some real or perceived danger, but at their lack of arrangements, a void into which their own well-arranged contentment naturally overflowed. Next to Matthew sat a small, dark girl of eight or nine in a wedding dress. Her face was tranquil, but her brown hands clutched at the gauzy white veil on her lap. With a rasp of leather the father wrenched further around in his seat and said something to her, grasping her hand with his own.

'*Alla chiesa?*' said Anna, suddenly working it out as the car pulled back on to the road.

The parents cheerfully cried out their assent, laughing with delight at her words.

'She's on her way to her first communion,' Anna explained to Matthew.

'Ah!' he said loudly, nodding eagerly. They nodded back.

Anna looked at the roadside, its heat and dirt suppressed by the tinted window, the humiliation of their crawl down the bank whisked away like something left-over and unsavoury by the swift, silent car. Presently Matthew leaned forward with his map and opened it up between the man and the woman. The man acknowledged the distraction with brisk turns of his head between windscreen and map. The woman removed her sunglasses and leaned over it, the red, glossy talon of her fingernail next to Matthew's hand on the page. She said something to her husband and they both nodded again.

'Villa Romani,' said Matthew.

'*Si, si,*' they replied, lightly but to Anna's ears with some indecipherable nuance. The nuance, she realised after a while, was of relaxation. They were not dismissing the Villa Romani. They might go, or have been, to it at some time; but the importance, the desperation, the mad scramble and tortuous route were Anna and Matthew's own, as were their dusty trainers, their sunburnt limbs, their rucksack with its drama of straps, their tourists' clothes. The woman shifted in her seat, crossing her legs, and Anna felt the faint breeze of her, deep with perfume. The man's skin was clean and pungent. The little girl emanated nothing but air, her dress hopeful white, her soft hands folded over the veil in her lap.

Sometime later the car left the main road and began to ascend a smaller, steeper road heavily forested to either side. Anna realised that they were being taken all the way to the Villa Romani, and that this was the road Matthew had imagined they would walk. She looked at it through the window, from the security of the strangers' decision. It was a long way. She saw them walking, and saw too how Matthew would have preferred it, how he did not want the luck of their lift. A feeling of homesickness passed over her at the thought of the journey's end and her ejection from the momentary, painful consolation of the strangers' world.

'We can walk down at least,' said Matthew when they'd got out, looking with dramatic longing back down the road, where the black car receded and then disappeared around a bend. 'It's a shame, though. It would have been lovely to walk up here.'

'I thought it was really nice of them,' said Anna. 'They went out of their way, and they must have been in a hurry.'

'She was gorgeous, that little girl,' said Matthew.

They stood in the shade of pine trees at a crumbling gateway. A narrow, rocky path wound beyond it through a glimpse of dim, penumbral gardens. Matthew did up the rucksack and put it on his back. They set off down the path, which passed through damp, shaggy lawns screened from the sun by the overhang of vast evergreens. The sound of running water played in the silence. Presently they arrived at a second gateway, set in a high stone wall. On the other side of it was a courtyard with a fountain at the centre. There were people here, clearly tourists, sitting meditatively in the shade on slabs of pale, eroded stone. On the floor of the courtyard was the stain of a faded mosaic. They walked slowly, reverently, through the courtyard. An old woman in a black veil was sitting in the shade at the end. Next to her was a large wicker basket and a dish of coins.

'Wait a second,' said Matthew.

He approached the woman, who drew back the white cloth from the top of her basket. Matthew held up four fingers. Anna looked away. Seconds later he was back, with a bulging paper napkin. He opened it, and there were four small cakes.

'There you go,' he said, holding it out to her. 'Breakfast.'

She took one and bit it. Its top was brown and sweet with caramelised sugar. Inside was pale yellow custard.

'Glad we waited?' he said.

'Let's go in,' she said.

'Hang on a second, let me finish my breakfast. This looks great.' He looked around, chewing, and then swallowed. 'OK. Is there somewhere I can put this?' He held up the crumpled napkin in his fist.

They passed between two stone pillars and up a narrow flight of steel steps, and found themselves standing in the body of the ruin on a raised corridor of scaffolding. Above them was a glass roof. Some feet below were the mosaic floors.

'God, they've really sorted this out, haven't they?' said Matthew. 'You get a much better view from up here. This is incredible.'

'It's amazing,' agreed Anna.

'I see, I see.' Matthew had the book open. 'This whole room is one big hunting scene. Look, it tells the story of the hunt from one end to the other.'

Anna drew away from him and leaned thoughtfully on the metal railing, signalling her readiness for the mosaic as one would signal readiness for a kiss; her bearing poised for some flattering, tragic communion, some historical caress, the intimate welcome she, in her loyalty to her vision of her own doom, had come to expect from the sad, sisterly throng of the past. The floor writhed with bodies, animal and human, bristling with spears and gushing blood, as flat and bright as if time had rolled heedlessly over it, leaving faces contorted with brutal, frozen pleasure, the instant of warring limbs stamped on by the violent boot of years. For a moment she felt herself falling over an unseen precipice of isolation as she looked down; as if in her rush to make her own, private acquaintance with the world, to meet it first, alone, she had overestimated its kindness and safety. Matthew was reading passages aloud from the guidebook, moving methodically along the walkway.

'Can't we just look at it?' she said. 'Can't we just enjoy it in silence?'

He continued to read aloud in a quieter voice, as if to himself. Her heart pounded with daring and fury, and with thoughts of where it might lead her. She decided then that if he continued to read aloud, she would leave. Her body felt contained, streamlined, as if forged by the heat of anger into a weapon or an instrument of flight, something that wanted to respond to the trigger of his voice. Presently she turned around and walked off.

For a few seconds the feeling powered her along the walkway, until she veered off doubtfully into a smaller room to one side. She leaned on the cold, steel pole that bordered the walkway. Below her were four girls. They stood in a row, almost naked, and they seemed to be dancing. They danced in emptiness, flat and paper-thin as if they had slipped to the floor unnoticed and been forgotten. Their slender, contoured limbs were held in graceful poses, their hair expectantly arranged, their red smiles hopeful. They danced in a cracked yellow nothingness, young and lovely and full of the fatal delight that kept them prisoner there, clothed only in two strips each of red and blue; waiting for life that would never be given them, for joy that pressed helplessly as if at a screen of glass, for their long, long moment of readiness to end, when they could run into the arms of the world and forget the terrible discipline, the lonely pleasure, of their dance.

'I can't believe you keep walking off,' said Matthew behind her. 'This is supposed to be our honeymoon, and all you can do is act like you don't want to be here. It's not very nice for me, is it? You might as well just enjoy it. It's not so bad, being here. Oh, I've seen a picture of this before. This one's famous. Apparently it commemorates a female sports tournament.

Look, that one's holding weights, and that one's holding a kind of racket thing. I didn't know the Romans wore bikinis.'

She clung to his voice as if to the bars of a small safe cage, looking at the girls whose tender faces gazed back at her in stony, silent hope.

Clare Naylor

AMERICA

'I'LL GET MYSELF some cowboy boots. Or maybe just a cowboy.'

Lucy thought that the black suitcase on wheels named Executive wasn't really the thing for a roadtrip from Los Angeles. She wondered what was. Something brown and hide as a Californian roadsweeper's neck. Perhaps she'd pick up the perfect holdall patched with colour on the Mexican border. She'd bring it back and take it on trains and tubes and to weekends away as if it were a polished silver trophy until the day she saw one just like it stuffed with scrunched up *Daily Mirrors* in Camden market. Lucy didn't think cowboys were her type. She didn't really think that cowboys were Mimi's type. Even though Mimi's type was known for its diversity. Mimi was planning to meet up with a man with the same name as a large American bank in New York where he kept two apartments.

'That's fine but just don't go off, will you?' Lucy said to Mimi. She didn't want to be left eating the continental breakfast alone in some Holiday Inn in Bumblefuck, Arizona.

She imagined that they'd be going through Arizona though it wasn't exactly on her map. All she'd been able to find was a *World Atlas for Young People*. It showed you the American flag and had coloured-in pictures of Navajo Indians next to a dissected America. Texas was freckled with little blue oil rigs and the east coast boasted many a yellow cob of corn. She wondered what she'd eat. The locals would turn all that corn into little tacos and nachos and cheerios. Maybe she should take a packet of All-Bran with her.

Mimi was packing only cheesecloth shirts and pearl nail-polish. This was the tradition of the American Road Trip. Nobody ever rode in a Buick with nude toe-nails. She was also thinking of putting a gun in the glove compartment next to the Aitoids Curiously Strong Mints that were the only British thing Americans seemed to know about. Well, those and Diana. Even the Nigerian cab driver who drove her to Bloomingdales on a foul February afternoon had met Diana. Lucy didn't know how she felt about the gun. She'd never actually seen one. Thought it might be heavier than you'd imagine. Mimi said they could blow away any sick and twisted Texans with it. Lucy knew that having one didn't necessarily make you safer. Your attacker was bound to abuse steroids and would tower over you and wrest the gun from your grasp before you'd fully wrestled with the idea that though you'd never voluntarily killed a spider and could certainly never squeeze the life out of something furry you were about to shoot a human being. Lucy would rather they just bought some Mace in a canister the size of your forearm. Then with a thrill of illegality she'd carry it in her bag in Clapham and tell friends she picked it up in New Orleans where she felt a bit unsafe.

Neither had she driven on the right hand side of the road before. She worried about overtaking. Maybe she should practise in Safeway's car park after dark. Trouble was Safeway was now open all night so there was always bound to be someone who'd run out of tinned tomatoes coming in or out. Almost everything was open all night nowadays. More and more like America. Thank God. She was fed up with living in a country where you couldn't buy new trainers on a Sunday. But with Safeway and being able to get lawnmowers on the Internet it was beginning to feel a bit like civilisation.

Her mother, though, wasn't really sure why she was going to the States. 'Strange things happen on the roads there, you know. You should watch that film with the two girls with the red hair.' Lucy already had. She'd not been terribly interested in the part with the husband – if you married a man with a moustache you deserved all you got. But she had thought that holding up petrol stations and stealing teeny bottles of Jack Daniels seemed cool. And she'd identified with the one who worked in the diner. Working on the cold meats counter in a south London supermarket was probably the equivalent on the other side of the Atlantic. Mimi called it the Pond, but as Lucy had only been to New York the once when she'd won her Weekend of a Lifetime, Pond felt a bit like a very large gobstopper in her mouth. Though she had started to say hey instead of hello. Sometimes she'd try it out on callers to the flat.

'Hey.'

'Hello? Hello? Lucy.' Then she'd have to concede and say, 'Hi. Yes, this is Lucy.' Everything except vowels was elongated in England. Lucy longed for the shortest route. She longed to date. She was fed up with English men and their protractedness. The drawn-out struggle not to relinquish their independence. They always would in the end though, her magazines assured her. You'd meet him in a pub with a slug on the sign on Saturday night and he'd amble to a phonebox sometime on Wednesday. Lucy wanted a man with a sense of immediacy and a thin grey mobile phone. Brett. Brad. Ted. In chinos from the Gap or even better a pink shirt with a polo pony over his hairless left nipple.

She was hoping to find him in LA at the beginning of her trip and then she'd leave him behind sore-hearted as she filled up with gas and wore denim hotpants all the way to Boston. She'd call him from New York by which time he'd be so beside himself without his English rose that he'd invite her to live in his maisonette in the Canyon. Fifteen minutes from Rodeo Drive. But Mimi said forget it, men in LA prefer lap dancing to real sex. They were only interested in manicures and actresses. It was Catch-22. You needed to be in Hollywood before you became an actress. Lucy had been Blanche Dubois in *Streetcar* in her sixth form. There'd actually been two Blanches and only one Marlon for them to

191

desire. The Blanches came in wearing ever shorter skirts for half a term until Marlon got expelled for sniffing Tippex thinner one Thursday lunchtime. Lucy could definitely be an actress. Her nose was much tinier than Sandra Bullock's and she'd managed to fool the Indian woman in the launderette with her Southern drawl on quite a few occasions.

This year was the hottest summer on record. But they always said that. Lucy would be glad to get to America and be revived by cans of Dr Pepper. To escape the radio news telling you every morning you woke that this was going to be the hottest day so far this year. The driest since the summer of standpipes and The Drifters. And just never enough rain. Even the slurping vortex of the water dispenser in the staff room at work had dribbled to a halt. Steaming condensation instead of a mountain spring. Yesterday they'd all gone home after lunch as the air-conditioning had choked to death and regulations were regulations. A supermarket without air-conditioning was an outbreak of E-coli waiting to happen. The staff took off their bakery hairnets and gingham overalls and spilled out into the street in shirtsleeves wondering what you did with a weekday afternoon. Lucy had caught the 345 to Clapham Junction and bought a couple of Soleros to take to Sarah's house. Sarah's flatmates were being gently resuscitated by corporate fans in the city so they watched Children's ITV.

'I'm a tot. You're a tot. Teeny Tot and Tiny,' the set churned out. They went to sit on the front wall and kicked their shoes off.

'I saw this programme on Death Valley. People just keel over with the boredom and heat,' Sarah said, licking a raspberry dribble from between her fingers. 'You should come to Ibiza with us instead.'

'You're kidding. I'm going to fall in love and get a job there. GCSEs are really highly respected.'

'Yeah, well.' Sarah pushed her lolly stick down a crack in the wall.

'Mimi might be able to find me something in PR.' Lucy looked down at her hastily fake-tanned legs and the bits she'd missed on her feet. 'It's all about your nails. Do your nails right and you can go anywhere.' They went inside and covered the kitchen table in nail dust and strands of rubbery cuticle.

It was on the Weekend of a Lifetime trip that Lucy had met Mimi. The limousine had arrived at Newark and Mimi had emerged from the back. The closest Lucy had ever got to Oscar night glamour. She was the representative of the travel agency and had once given a blow job to one of the Brat Pack before his big break. She took Lucy to Saks Fifth Avenue to buy hair accessories and they had dry roasted peanuts and Martinis with green olives in the Rainbow Room. They hit it off instantly and Mimi took Lucy to her gym on a guest pass. This hadn't been part of the Weekend of a Lifetime package.

The day Mimi called and asked Lucy if she wanted to join her on the drive across America Lucy put the garlic sausage and thin sliced turkey breast on to the wrong salvers. They'd take three weeks and the southern route. Mimi was actually moving house. The male drought in LA had begun to depress her. If it didn't work out with the man with two apartments in New York she'd go to Boston and rent a brownstone near the Harvard Business School. She'd put Lucy on her car insurance for the trip.

'Actually I may emigrate,' Lucy had told the manageress of her supermarket.

'Then you know I can't keep your position open. I'll put a card in the window tomorrow.' The manageress had taken her granddaughter to Florida once. Before last summer's spate of tourist killings. Lucy had woken up once or twice in the middle of the night and imagined her face grainy and tragic on the front of the newspapers. Cut short in Nashville. Someone with a stud through her nose would take her place on cold meats. But mostly she didn't worry. Because she only had to watch *Friends* to know that she could be great and fall in love. There was more to her than slicing pressed pork. She'd rent an apartment and fill it with candles and cushions.

Enrol at salsa classes and be taken to downtown pizza parlours by her slithery-hipped instructor. Before she married an attorney.

'Would you like to sample the special offer Dutch Edam, sir?' Lucy smiled at the man called Tommy wearing clothes by the same label. You didn't often get visiting Americans in Clapham.

'You know what? I want something different. What have you got for me that's different –' he thumbed his glasses up his nose and looked at her Lucy Here to Help plastic badge. 'Lucy?'

'Well, sir, we have this whipped soft cheese from Alpine goats.' She eased her gloved hand over the top of some blocks of Sage Derby 'Or there's some fine Jarlsberg here.'

'Fat-free?' It didn't look that way to Tommy. To Tommy it looked like cholesterol city.

'Actually no. But there is a ninety-eight per cent Brie here.' Lucy wiped her hand on her apron as she waited for the man to decide. He insisted on trying a sample on a triangle of cracker. She had to ask her boss to open a packet of cream crackers specially. Then he wondered whether the renin in it would play merry hell with his sinuses.

'You're from the East Coast, aren't you?' she asked coyly. He nodded, unimpressed by her global aptitude.

'Boston.' Well, she couldn't say she was surprised. On her roadtrip she'd discovered that all the men in Boston were like this. Especially the ones with cell-phones. She'd spent some time working in a deli there. Five weeks, actually. Cash in hand. Singles would come in on Thursday nights and complain that they ate so much cinnamon babka they were gaining weight, but even when she made herself sound like Helena Bonham-Carter and said, 'You don't look like you need to worry about *that*' with a tiny chuckle and even if they had smiled back, they would still opt for low-fat bagels and not ask her on a date.

At heart they were protracted too. And though she had hated to admit it, perhaps just a little too health-conscious.

Tim Liardet

DISTILLER'S UNSTABLE DAUGHTER
EXPLAINS HER ABSENCE
FROM THE CLASS

The men have come out of the ground again.
I have to tell you the successful distiller
of spirits has a seventh tall daughter.

Listen. They call me from under the street.
They lean on shovels, down under the awning
in the hole in the pavement, exposing the bright wires.

They wear hard hats, and though not magicians
will restore to me my visibility –
green eye, breast, gangling leg, painted toe-nail.

Yes, they ease me back into view. And I, slipping
in and out of my most perfect of minds –
monster of my yellow psychiatrist – step down

into the sunlight. The sex is clean and necessary.
The orange awning, warmed from the inside, contains
the closest approximation of day.

Now that I can be seen, I am lethal. See –
my *vividness*. But will my six sisters and mother
and distillery-owning father deep into their storm

have the eyes, the twenty/twenty vision
against the old glaucoma, the eclipsed pupil?
Now there is a question for the red optometrist.

SANTA PELTED WITH EGGS

Not battery eggs,
you understand,
but *Free Range*,

as if to make
of the Egging a
yolkier insult,

more addled mucus
than water,
more *snot*:

and there he was,
clung-to in the float
by the clotted,

tremendous sneeze,
plus bits, appalled
out of his remit

of *yo ho ho*
to reaction
less festive;

children never thought
Santa capable
of such expletives –

keep eggs,
he implied, for
the brilliant sins

of our doubtful
stout rotarian, not
your stainless Santa:

on he went,
dripping, dripping
with the birth fluids
of an unborn bird.

Simon Armitage

ALL FOR ONE

Why is it my life won't leave me alone?
All day it sits on the arm of the chair
plucking grey hairs like thoughts out of my skull,
flicking my ear with a Duralon comb.

Evenings when I need to work, get things done;
nine o'clock, my life stands with its coat on
in the hall. Fuck it. We drive to the pub,
it drinks, so yours truly has to drive home.

I leave at sunrise in the four-wheel drive –
my life rides shotgun on the running board,
taps on the window of my log-cabin,
wants to find people and go night-clubbing.

Social call – my life has to tag along.
Hangs off at first, plays it cool, smiles its smile;
next minute – launches into song. Then what:
only cops off with the belle of the belle

of the ball – that's all. Main man. Life and soul.
Makes hand-shadows on the living-room wall.
Recites *Albert and the Lion*, in French,
stood on its head drinking a yard of ale.

Next morning over Anadin and toast
my life weeps crocodile tears of remorse
on to the tablecloth. *Can't we be close?*
I look my life square in the face and scream:

life, find your own family and friends to love;
life, open your own high-interest account;
offer yourself the exploding cigar;
put whoopee-cushions under your own arse.

It's a joke. I flounce out through the front door;
my life in its slippers and dressing gown
runs to the garden and catches my sleeve,
says what it's said a hundred times before.

From distance it must look like a strange sight:
two men of identical shape, at odds
at first, then joined by an outstretched arm, one
leading the other back to his own home.

Julian Barnes

A Short History of Hairdressing

I

THAT FIRST TIME, after they moved, his mother had come with him. Presumably to examine the barber. As if the phrase 'short, back and sides, with a little bit off the top' might mean something different in this new suburb. He'd doubted it. Everything else seemed the same: the torture chair, the surgical smells, the strop and the folded razor – folded not in safety but in threat. Most of all, the torturer-in-chief was the same, a loony with big hands who pushed your head down till your windpipe nearly snapped, who prodded your ear with a bamboo finger. 'General inspection, madam?' he said greasily when he'd finished. His mother had shaken off the effects of her magazine and stood up. 'Very nice,' she said vaguely, leaning over him, smelling of stuff. 'I'll send him by himself next time.' Outside, she had rubbed his cheek, looked at him with idle eyes, and murmured, 'You poor shorn lamb.'

Now he was on his own. As he walked past the estate agent's, the sports shop and the half-timbered bank, he practised saying, 'Short back and sides with a little bit off the top.' He said it urgently, without the commas; you had to get the words just right, like a prayer. There was one and threepence in his pocket; he stuffed his handkerchief in tighter to keep the coins safe. He didn't like not being allowed to be afraid. It was simpler at the dentist's: your mother always came with you, the dentist always hurt you, but afterwards he gave you a boiled sweet for being a good boy, and then back in the waiting-room you pretended in front of the other patients that you were made of stern stuff.

Your parents were proud of you. 'Been in the wars, old chap?' his father would ask. Pain let you into the world of grown-up phrases. The dentist would say, 'Tell your father you're fit for overseas. He'll understand.' So he'd go home and Dad would say, 'Been in the wars, old chap?' and he'd answer, 'Mr Gordon says I'm fit for overseas.'

He felt almost important going in, with the adult spring of the door against his hand. But the barber merely nodded, pointed with his comb to the line of high-backed chairs, and resumed his standing crouch over a white-haired geezer. Gregory sat down. His chair creaked. Already he wanted to pee. There was a bin of magazines next to him, which he didn't dare explore. He gazed at the hamster nests of hair on the floor.

When his turn came, the barber slipped a thick rubber cushion on to the seat. The gesture looked insulting: he'd been in long trousers now for ten and a half months. But that was typical: you were never sure of the rules, never sure if they tortured everyone the same way, or if it was just you. Like now: the barber was trying to strangle him with the sheet, pulling it tight round his neck, then shoving a cloth down his collar with thick carroty fingers. 'And what can we do for you today, young man?' The tone implied that such an ignominious and deceitful worm as he obviously was might have strayed into the premises for any number of different reasons.

After a pause, Gregory said, 'I'd like a haircut, please.'

'Well, I'd say you'd come to the right place, wouldn't you?' The barber tapped him on the crown with his comb; not painfully, but not lightly either.

'Short-back-and-sides-with-a-little-bit-off-the-top-please.'

'Now we're motoring,' said the barber.

They would only Do Boys at certain times of the week. There was a notice saying No Boys On Saturday Mornings. Saturday afternoons they were closed anyway, so it might just as well read No Boys On Saturdays. Boys had to go when men didn't want to. At least, not men with jobs. He went at times when the other customers were pensioners. There were three barbers, all of middle age, in white coats, dividing their time between the young and the old. They greased up to these throat-clearing old geezers, made mysterious conversation with them, put on a show of being keen on their work. The old geezers wore coats and scarves even in summer, and gave tips as they left. Gregory would watch the transaction out of the corner of his eye. One man giving another man money, a secret half-handshake with both pretending the exchange wasn't being made.

Boys didn't tip. Perhaps that was why barbers hated boys. They paid less and they didn't tip. They also didn't keep still. Or at least, their mothers told them to keep still and they kept still, but even so the barber would bash their heads with a palm as solid as the flat of a hatchet and mutter, 'Keep *still*.' There were stories of boys who'd had the tops of their ears sliced off because they hadn't kept still. Razors were called cut-throats. All barbers were loonies.

'Wolf Cub, are we?' It took a while for Gregory to realise that he was being addressed. Then he didn't know whether to keep his head down or look up in the mirror at the barber. Eventually he kept his head down and said, 'No.'

'Boy Scout already?'

'No.'

'Crusader?'

Gregory didn't know what that meant. He started to lift his head, but the barber rapped his crown with the comb. 'Keep *still*, I said.' Gregory was so scared of the loony that he was unable to answer, which the barber took as a negative. 'Very fine organisation, the Crusaders. You give it a thought.'

Gregory thought of being chopped up by curved Saracen swords, of being staked out in the desert and eaten alive by ants and vultures. Meanwhile, he submitted to the cold smoothness of the scissors – always cold even when they weren't. Eyes tight shut, he endured the tickly torment of hair falling on his face. He sat there, still not looking, convinced that the barber should have stopped cutting ages ago, except that he was such a loony he was going to carry on cutting and cutting until Gregory was bald. Still to come was the stropping of the razor, which meant that your throat was going to be cut; the dry, scrapy feel of the blade next to your ears and on the back of your neck; the fly-whisk shoved into your eyes and nose to get the hair off.

Those were the bits that made you wince every time. But there was also something creepier about the place. He suspected it was rude. Things you didn't know about, or weren't meant to know about, usually turned out to be rude. Like the barber's pole. That was obviously rude. The previous place just had an old bit of painted wood with colours twirling round it. The one here worked by electricity, and moved round all the time. That was ruder, he thought. Then there was the binful of magazines. He was sure some of them were rude. Everything was rude if you wanted it to be, this was the great truth about life which he'd only just discovered. Not that he minded. Gregory liked rude things.

Without moving his head, he looked in the next-door mirror at a pensioner two seats away. He'd been yakking away in one of those loud voices old geezers always had. Now the barber was bent over him with a small pair of round-headed scissors, cutting hairs out of his eyebrows. This was disgusting. It wasn't even rude. Then he did the same with his nostrils; then his ears. Snipping great twigs out of his lugholes. Absolutely disgusting. Finally, the barber started brushing powder into the back of the geezer's neck. What was that for?

Now the torturer-in-chief had the clippers out. That was another bit Gregory didn't like. Sometimes they used hand-clippers, like tin-openers, squeak grind squeak grind round the top of his skull till his brains were opened up. But these were the buzzer-clippers, which were even worse, because you could get electrocuted from them. He'd imagined it hundreds of times. The barber buzzes away, doesn't notice what he's doing, hates you anyway because you're a Boy, cuts a wodge off your ear, the blood pours all over the clippers, they get a short-circuit and you're electrocuted on the spot. Must have happened millions of times. And the barber always survived because he wore rubber-soled shoes.

At school they swam naked. Mr Lofthouse wore a pouch-thing so they couldn't see his whanger. The boys took off all their clothes, had a shower for lice or verrucas or something, or being smelly in the case of Wood, then jumped into the pool. You leaped up high and landed with the water hitting your balls. That was rude, so you didn't let the master see you doing it. The water made your balls all tight, which made your willy stick out more, and afterwards they all towelled themselves dry and looked at one another, though without looking, sideways, like in the mirror at the barber's. Everyone in the class was the same age, but some were still bald down there; some, like Gregory, had a sort of bar of hair across the top but nothing on their balls; and some, like Hopkinson and Shapiro, were as hairy as men, and a darker colour already, brownish, like Dad's when he'd peeped round the side of a stand-up. At least he had *some* hair, not like Bristowe and Hall and Wood. But how did Hopkinson and Shapiro get like that? Everyone else had willies; Hopkinson and Shapiro already had whangers.

He wanted to pee. He couldn't. He mustn't think about peeing. He could hold out till he got home. The Crusaders fought the Saracens and delivered the Holy Land from the infidel. Like Infidel Castro, sir? That was one of Wood's jokes. They wore crosses on their surcoats. Chainmail must have been hot in Israel. He must stop thinking that he could win a gold medal in a peeing-high-against-a-wall competition.

'Local?' said the barber suddenly. Gregory looked at him properly in the mirror for the first time. Red face, little moustache, glasses, yellowy hair the colour of a school ruler. *Quis custodiet ipsos custodes*, they'd been taught. So who barbers barbers? You could tell this one was a perve as well as a loony. Everyone knew there were millions of perves out there. The swimming master was a perve. After the lesson, when they were shivering in their towels with their balls all tight and their willies plus two whangers sticking out, Mr Lofthouse would walk the length of the poolside, climb on to the springboard, pause till he had their full attention, with his huge muscles and tattoo and arms out and pouch with strings round his buttocks, then take a deep breath, dive in and glide underwater the length of the pool. Twenty-five yards underwater. Then he'd touch and surface and they'd all applaud – not that they really meant it – but he'd ignore them and practise different strokes. He was a perve. Most of the masters were probably perves. There was one who wore a wedding-ring. That proved he was.

And so was this one. 'Do you live locally?' he was saying again. Gregory wasn't falling for that. He'd be coming round to sign him up for the Scouts or the Crusaders. Then he'd be asking Mum if he could take Gregory camping in the woods – except there'd only be one tent, and he'd tell Gregory stories about bears, and even though they'd done geography and he knew bears died out in Britain at about the time of the Crusades, he'd half-believe it if the perve told him there was a bear.

'Not for long,' Gregory replied. That wasn't too clever, he knew at once. They'd only just moved here. The barber would say sneery things to him when he kept on coming in, for years and years and years. Gregory flicked a glance up at the mirror, but the perve wasn't giving anything away. He was doing an absent-minded last snip. Then he dug into Gregory's collar with his carrot fingers and shook it to make sure as much hair as possible fell down inside his shirt. 'Think about the Crusaders,' he said, as he started pulling out the sheet. 'It might suit you.'

Gregory saw himself reborn from beneath the shroud, unchanged except that his ears now stuck out more. He started to slide forward on the rubber cushion. The comb snapped against his crown, harder now that he had less hair.

'Not so fast, young fellow-me-lad.' The barber ambled down the length of the narrow shop and came back with an oval mirror like a tray. He dipped it to show the back of Gregory's head. Gregory looked into the first mirror, into the second mirror, and out the other side. That wasn't the back of his head. It didn't look like that. It didn't match the front. He felt himself blush. He wanted to pee. The perve was showing him the back of someone else's head. Black magic. Gregory stared and stared, his colour getting brighter, staring at the back of someone else's head, all shaved and sculpted, until he realised that the only way to get home was to play the perve's game, so he took a final glance at the alien skull, looked boldly higher up the mirror at the barber's indifferent spectacles, and said, quietly, 'Yes.'

II

The hairdresser looked down with polite contempt and ran a speculative comb through Gregory's hair: as if, deep down in the undergrowth, there might be some long-lost parting, like a medieval pilgrim trail. A dismissive flip of the comb made the bulk of his hair flap foward over his eyes and down to his chin. From behind the sudden curtain, he thought, Fuck you, Jim. He was only here because Allie wasn't cutting his hair any more. Well, for the moment, anyway. He thought of her now with passionate memory: him in the bath, her washing his hair, then cutting it while he sat there. He'd pull out the plug and she'd hose the bits of cut hair off him with the shower attachment, flirting with the spray, and when he stood up, as often as not she'd suck his cock, there and then, just like that, picking off the last bits of cut hair as she did so. Yeah.

'Any particular . . . place . . . sir?' The guy was feigning defeat in his search for a parting.

'Just take it straight back.' Gregory jerked his head revengefully, so that his hair flew back over the top of his head and back where it belonged. He reached out of the wanky nylon robe-thing and finger-combed his hair back into place, then gave it a fluff. Just like it had been when he walked in.

'Any particular . . . length . . . sir?'

'Three inches below the collar. Take the sides up to the bone, just there.' Gregory tapped the line with his middle fingers.

'And would you be requiring a shave while we're about it?'

Fucking cheek. *This* is what a shave looks like nowadays. Only lawyers and engineers and foresters delved into their little sponge bags every morning and hacked away at the stubble like Calvinists. Gregory turned sideways-on to the mirror and squinted back at himself. 'That's the way she likes it,' he said lightly.

'Married, are we, then?'

Watch it, fucker. Don't mess with me. Don't try that complicity stuff. Unless it's just that you're queer. Not that I've got anything against the condition. I'm pro-choice.

'Or are you saving up for that particular torment?'

Gregory didn't bother to reply.

'Twenty-seven years myself,' said the guy as he made his first snips. 'Has its ups and downs like everything else.'

Gregory grunted in an approximately expressive way, like you did at the dentist's when your mouth was full of hardware and the geezer insisted on telling you a joke.

'Two kids. Well, one's grown up now. The girl's still at home. She'll be up and away before you can turn round. They all fly the coop in the end.'

Gregory looked in the mirror but the fellow wasn't making eye contact, just head down and snipping away. Maybe he wasn't so bad. Apart from being a bore. And, of course, terminally malformed in his psychology by decades of complicity in the exploitative master–servant nexus.

'But perhaps you're not the marrying kind, sir.'

Now hang *on*. Who's accusing who of being queer? He'd always loathed hairdressers, and this one was no exception. Fucking provincial Mister two-point-four children, pay the mortgage, wash the car and put it back in the garage. Nice little allotment down by the railway, pug-faced wife hanging out the washing on one of those metal carousel-things, yeah, yeah, see it all. Probably does a bit of refereeing on Saturday afternoons in some crap league. No, not even a referee, just a *linesman*.

Gregory became aware that the fellow was pausing, as if he

expected an answer. He expected an answer? What rights did he have in the matter? OK, let's get this guy sorted out.

'Marriage is the only adventure open to the cowardly.'

'Yes, well, I'm sure you're a cleverer man than me, sir,' replied the hairdresser, in a tone that wasn't obviously deferential. 'What with being at the university.'

Gregory merely grunted again.

'Of course, I'm no judge, but it always seems to me that universities teach the students to despise more things than they have a right to. It's our money they're using after all. I'm just glad my boy went to the tech. Hasn't done him any harm. He's earning good money now.'

Yeah, yeah, enough to support the next two-point-four children and have a slightly bigger washing machine and a slightly less puggy wife. Well, that was for some. Bloody England. Still, all that was going to be swept away. And this kind of place would be the first to go, stuffy old master-and-servant establishments, all stilted conversation, class-consciousness and tipping. Gregory didn't believe in tipping. He thought it a reinforcement of the deferential society, equally demeaning for tipper and tippee. It degraded social relations. Anyway, he couldn't afford it. And on top of that, he was fucked if he was going to tip a topiarist who accused him of being a shirt-lifter.

These geezers were on the way out. There were places up in London designed by architects, where they played the latest hits on a funky speaker system. Cost a fortune, apparently, but it was better than *this*. No wonder the place was empty. A cracked bakelite radio on a high shelf was playing tea-dance stuff. They ought to sell trusses and surgical corsets and support hose. Corner the market in prostheses. Wooden legs, steel hooks for severed wrists. Wigs, of course. Why didn't hairdressers sell wigs as well? After all, dentists sold false teeth.

How old was this guy? Gregory looked at him: bony, with haunted eyes, hair cut absurdly short and Brylcreemed flat. Two hundred? Hundred and forty? Gregory tried to work it out. Married twenty-seven years. So: fifty? Forty-five if he got her in the club as soon as he whipped it out. If he'd ever been that adventurous. Hair grey already. Probably his pubic hair was grey as well. Did pubic hair go grey?

The hairdresser finished the hedge-trimming stage, dropped the scissors insultingly into a glass of disinfectant, and took out another, stubbier pair. Snip, snip. Hair, skin, flesh, blood, all so fucking close. Barber-surgeons, that's what they'd been in the old days, when surgery had meant butchery. The red stripe round the traditional barber's pole denoted the strip of cloth wound round your arm when the barber bled you. His shop-sign featured a bowl as well, the bowl which caught the blood. Now they'd dropped all that, and declined into hairdressers. Tenders of allotments, stabbing the earth instead of the extended forearm.

He still couldn't work out why Allie had broken it up. Said he was too possessive, said she couldn't breathe, being with him was like being married. That was a laugh, he'd replied: being with her was like being with someone who was going out with half a dozen other blokes at the same time. That's just what I mean, she said. I love you, he'd said, with sudden desperation. It was the first time he'd said it to anyone, and he knew he'd got it wrong. You were meant to say it when you felt strong, not weak. If you loved me, you'd understand me, she replied. Well, fuck off and breathe, then, he'd said. It was just a row, just a stupid sodding row, that was all. Didn't mean anything. Except it meant they'd broken up.

'Anything on the hair, sir?'

'What?'

'Anything on the hair?'

'No. Never mess with nature.'

The hairdresser sighed, as if messing with nature was what he'd spent the last twenty minutes doing, and that in Gregory's case this all too necessary piece of interference had ended in defeat.

The weekend ahead. New haircut, clean shirt. Two parties. Communal purchase of a pipkin of beer tonight. Get stonking drunk and see what happens: that's my idea of not messing with nature. Ouch. No. Allie. Allie, Allie, Allie. Bind my arm.

I hold out my wrists to you, Allie. Wherever you please. Non-medical purposes, but plunge it in. Go on, if you need to. Loose my blood.

'What was that you said just now about marriage?'

'Eh? Oh, the only adventure open to the cowardly.'

'Well, if you don't mind my making a point, sir, marriage has always been very kind to me. But I'm sure you're a cleverer man than me, what with being at the university.'

'I was quoting,' said Gregory. 'But I can reassure you that the authority in question was a cleverer man than either of us.'

'So clever he didn't believe in God, I expect?'

Yes, *that* clever, Gregory wanted to say, just *exactly that* clever. But something held him back. He was only brave enough to deny God when among fellow sceptics.

'And, if I may ask, sir, was he the marrying kind?'

Huh. Gregory thought about it. There hadn't been a Madame, had there? Strictly mistresses, he was sure.

'No, I don't think he was the marrying kind, as you put it.'

'Then perhaps, sir, not an expert?'

In the old days, Gregory reflected, barber-shops had been places of ill repute, where idle fellows gathered to exchange the latest news, where lute and viol were played for the entertainment of customers. Now all this was coming back, at least in London. Places full of gossip and music, run by stylists who got their names in the social pages. There were girls in black sweaters who washed your hair first. Wow. Not having to wash your hair before you went out to have it cut. Just saunter in with a hi-sign and settle down with a magazine.

The expert on marriage brought a mirror and showed twin views of his handiwork to Gregory. Pretty neat job, he had to admit, short at the sides, long at the back. Not like some of the blokes in college, who just grew their hair in every direction at the same time, bogbrush beards, Olde Englishe muttonchops, greasy waterfalls down the back, you name it. No, mess with nature just a little bit, that was his real motto. The constant tug between nature and civilisation is what

keeps us on our toes. Though of course, that did rather beg
the question of how you defined nature and how you defined
civilisation. It wasn't simply the choice between the life of a
beast and that of a bourgeois. It was about . . . well, all sorts
of things. He had an acute pang for Allie. Bleed me, then bind
me up. If he got her back, he'd be less possessive. Except he'd
thought of it as just being close, being a couple. She'd liked it
at first. Well, she hadn't objected.

He realised that the hairdresser was still holding up the
mirror.

'Yes,' he said idly.

The mirror was put down on its face and the wanky nylon
robe unwound. A brush swooshed back and forth across his
collar. It made him think of a soft-wristed jazz drummer.
Swoosh, swoosh. There was lots of life ahead, wasn't there?

The shop was empty, and there was still a glutinous whine
from the radio, but even so it was a lowered voice close to his
ear which suggested, 'Something for the weekend, sir?'

He wanted to say, Yeah, train ticket to London, appointment with Vidal Sassoon, packet of barbecue sausages, crate
of ale, a few herbal cigarettes, music to numb the mind, and a
woman who truly likes me. Instead, he lowered his own voice
and replied 'Packet of Fetherlite, please.'

Complicit at last with the hairdresser, he walked out into
the bright day calling for the weekend to begin.

III

Before setting off, he went into the bathroom, eased the
shaving-mirror out on its extending arm, flipped it over to the
make-up side, and took his nail-scissors from his sponge-bag.
First he trimmed out a few long mattressy eyebrow hairs,
then turned slightly so that anything sprouting from his ears
would catch the light, and made a snip or two. Faintly
depressed, he pushed up his nose and examined the tunnel
openings. Nothing of extravagant length; not for the
moment. Dampening a corner of his flannel, he scrubbed

away behind his ears, bob-sleighed the cartilaginous channels, and gave a final prod into the waxy grottoes. When he looked at his reflection, his ears were bright pink from the pressure, as if he were a frightened boy or a student afraid to kiss.

What was the name for the accretion of stuff that whitened your damp flannel? Ear-crust, he called it. Perhaps doctors had a technical term for it. Were there fungal infections behind the ear, the aural equivalent of athlete's foot? Not very likely: the location was too dry. So maybe ear-crust would do; and maybe everyone had a private name for it, so that no common term was required.

Strange that no one had come up with a new name for the hedge-trimmers and topiarists. First barbers, then hairdressers. Yet when did they last 'dress' hair? 'Stylists'? Fake-posh. 'Crimpers'? Jokey. So was the phrase he used nowadays with Allie. 'Just off to the Barnet Shop,' he'd annouce. Barnet. Barnet Fair. Hair.

'Er, three o'clock with Kelly.'

An indigo fingernail stumbled down a row of pencilled capitals. 'Yes. Gregory?'

He nodded. The first time he'd booked over the phone and they'd asked his name he'd replied, 'Cartwright.' There was a pause, so he'd said 'Mr Cartwright,' before realising what the pause had been about. Now he saw himself upside down in the ledger: GREGGORY.

'Kelly be with you in a minute. Let's get you washed.'

He still, after all these years, couldn't slide easily into the posture. Maybe his spine was going. Eyes half closed, feeling for the lip of the bowl. Like doing the backstroke and not knowing where the end of the pool is. And then you lay there, with cold porcelain holding your neck and exposing your throat. Upside down, waiting for the guillotine blade.

A fat girl with uninterested hands made the usual conversation with him – 'That too hot?' 'Been on holiday?' 'You want conditioner?' – while half-heartedly attempting with scooped hand to keep the water out of his ears. He had, over the years, settled into a half-amused passivity at the Barnet Shop. The first time one of these red-faced trainees had asked 'You want conditioner?' he'd answered, 'What do you think?', believing that her superior view of his scalp made her the better judge of his requirements. Stolid logic suggested that something called 'conditioner' could only improve the condition of your hair; on the other hand, why pose the question if there wasn't a valid choice of answer? But requests for advice only tended to confuse, drawing the cautious answer, 'It's up to you.' So he contented himself with saying 'Yes' or 'Not today, thank you', according to whim. Also according to whether or not the girl was good at keeping water out of his ears.

She watchfully half-led him back to the chair, as if drippingness were close to blindness. 'You want a tea, a coffee?'

'Nothing, thanks.'

It wasn't exactly lutes and viols and the assembly of idle fellows exchanging the latest news. But there was stonkingly loud music, a choice of beverage, and a range of magazines. He normally picked something like *Marie Claire*, the sort of women's magazine it was OK for a man to be seen reading.

'Hi, Gregory, how are things?'

'Fine. Yourself?'

'Can't complain.'

'Kelly, like the new hair.'

'Yeah. Got bored, you know.'

'Like it. Looks good, falls well. You like it?'

'Not sure.'

'No, it's a winner.'

She smiled. He could do this stuff, customer banter, meant and half-meant. It had only taken him about twenty-five years to get the right tone.

'So what are we doing today?'

He looked up at her in the mirror, a tall girl with a sharp bob he didn't really like; he thought it made her face too angular. But what did he know? He was indifferent to his own hair, and went to Kelly not for whatever skills she deployed but for her restful presence.

When he didn't reply immediately, she said, 'Shall we splash out and do exactly the same as last time?'

214

'Good idea.' He smiled. The same as last time, and next time, and the time beyond that.

He wasn't sure he actually enjoyed being here. The salon had the mixed-ward atmosphere of a jolly outpatients' department where no one had anything serious. Still, he could handle it; social apprehensions were now long gone. The small triumphs of maturity. 'So, Gregory Cartwright, give us an account of your life so far?' 'Well, I've stopped being afraid of religion and barbers.' He'd never joined the Crusaders, whatever they had been; he'd evaded the hot-eyed evangelisers at school and university; now he knew what to do when the doorbell rang on a Sunday morning.

'That'll be God,' he'd say to Allie, 'I'll do it.' And there on the step would be a spruce, polite couple, one of them often black, sometimes with a winning child in tow, and offering an uncontentious opener such as, 'We're just going from house to house asking people if they're worried about the state of the world.' The trick was to avoid both the true Yes and the smug No, because then they had a landing-line across to you. So he would give them a householderish smile and cut to the chase: 'Religion?' And before they in turn could decide whether Yes or No was the correct response to his brutal intuition, he would end the encounter with a brisk, 'Better luck next door.'

Actually, he quite liked having his hair washed; mostly. But the rest of it was mere process. He took only mild pleasure in the bodily contact which was all part of things nowadays. Kelly would lean an unaware hip against his upper arm, or there'd be a brush from another part of her body; and she was never exactly overdressed. Way back when, he'd have thought it was all for him, and feel relieved that a draped sheet covered his lap. Today it didn't stir his mind out of *Marie Claire*.

Kelly was telling him how she'd applied for a job in Miami. On the cruise liners. You went out for five days, a week, ten days, then had shore leave to spend the money you'd earned. She had a girl-friend out there at the moment. Sounded like fun.

'Exciting,' he said. 'When are you off?' He thought: Miami's violent, isn't it? Shootings. Cubans. Vice. Lee Harvey Oswald. Will she be safe? And what about sexual harassment on the cruise ships? She was a nice-looking girl. Sorry, *Marie Claire*, I mean woman. But girl in a way, because she provoked these semi-parental thoughts in someone like him: one who stayed at home, went to work, and had his hair cut. His life, he admitted, had been one long cowardly adventure.

'How old are you?'

'Twenty-*seven*,' said Kelly, as if such an age were at the ultimate extremity of youth. Without immediate action her life would be compromised for ever; a couple more weeks and she would turn into that old biddy in rollers on the other side of the salon.

'I've a daughter almost your age. Well, she's twenty-five. I mean, we've another one as well. There's two of them.' He didn't seem to be saying it right.

'So how long you been married then?' Kelly asked in quasi-mathematical astonishment.

Gregory looked up at her in the mirror. 'Twenty-eight years.' She gave a larky smile at the idea that anyone could have been married for the enormous length of time that she had been alive.

'The elder one's left home, of course,' he said. 'But we've still got Jenny with us.'

'Nice,' said Kelly, but he could see she was bored now. Bored with him, specifically. Just another ageing geezer with thinning hair he'd soon have to comb more carefully. Give me Miami; and soon.

He was afraid of sex. That was the truth. He didn't really know any more what it was for. He enjoyed it when it happened. He imagined, in the years ahead, that there would be gradually less of it, and then, at some point, none at all. But this wasn't what made him afraid. Nor was it anything to do with the daunting specificity with which they wrote about it in magazines. In his younger days they'd had their own daunting specificities. It had all seemed quite clear and bold, back then, when he stood up in the bath and Allie took his cock in her mouth. All that stuff had been self-evident, and imperative in its truth. Now he wondered if he hadn't always got it wrong. He didn't know what sex was for. He didn't think anyone else did either, but that didn't make the situation any better. He wanted to howl. He wanted to howl into the mirror and watch himself howl back.

Kelly's hip was against his bicep, not the edge of her hip either, but the inner curve of it. At least he knew the answer to one of his youthful questions: yes, pubic hair does go grey.

He wasn't worried about the tip. He had a twenty-pound note. Seventeen for the cut, one for the girl who'd washed him and two for Kelly. And just in case they put the price up, he always remembered to bring an extra pound. He was that sort of person, he realised. The man with the back-up pound coin in his pocket.

Now Kelly had finished cutting and stood directly behind him. Her breasts appeared on either side of his head. She took each of his sideburns between thumb and finger, then looked away. This was a trick of hers. Everyone's face is a bit lop-sided, she'd told him, so if you judge by eye you can end up making a mistake. She measured by feel, turning away towards the cash-desk and the street. Towards Miami.

Satisfied, she reached for the drier and finger-flicked a soufflé effect which would last until the evening. By now she was on automatic, probably wondering if she had time to pop outside for a cigarette before the next damp head was guided to her. So she would always forget, and fetch the mirror.

It had been an audacity on his part, some years back. Revolt against the tyranny of the bloody mirror. This side, that side. In forty years and more of going to the barber's, the hairdresser's and the Barnet Shop, he had always assented meekly, whether he recognised the back of his head or not. He would smile and nod, and seeing the nod reproduced in canted glass, would verbalise it into 'Very nice' or 'Much neater' or 'Just the job' or 'Thank you'. If they had clipped a swastika into his nape he would probably have pretended to approve. Then, one day, he thought, No, I don't want to see

217

the back. If the front's OK, the back will be too. That wasn't pretentious, was it? No, it was logical. He was rather proud of his initiative. Of course Kelly always forgot, but that didn't matter. In fact, it was better in a way, since it meant that his timid victory was repeated every time. Now, as she came towards him, her mind in Miami, the mirror dangling, he could raise a hand, offer the indulgent smile he used every couple of months, and say,

'No.'

David Malouf

WHEN THE WRITER SPEAKS*

THE REAL ENEMY of writing is talk. There is something about the facility of talk, the ease with which ideas clothe themselves in the first available words, that is antithetical to the way a writer's mind works when he is engaged in the slower and, one wants to say, deeper business of writing. And of course once the words have come in one form it is more difficult to discover them in another. The voice of easy speaking has already occupied the space that needs to be filled by that quieter, more interior, less sociable voice that belongs to solitude and to waiting – to waiting patiently for the writing itself to speak. That is why writers are so unwilling to talk about work in progress. They are afraid of speaking too soon and from the wrong place, with the wrong voice; of resolving too quickly, in talk, the tension whose energies they will need to draw on later, in solitary struggle and against the resistance of what has not yet been articulated. The writer needs both to trust words and to be wary of them. A writer, as Thomas Mann tells us, is someone who finds writing difficult.

Silence: that is the natural state from which writing proceeds; a state in which the voice in our head, which only very reluctantly ceases to argue and assert, to hold forth on what it knows or to mull over old occasions and slights and controversies, falls still at last and allows that other, smaller voice to be heard that knows nothing of 'issues', has no

---

* This is the transcript of a talk given at the UK PEN International Writers Day on March 28th, 1998

opinions or convictions, is curious, doubtful, and interested in *everything*, eager to live inside each thing and to discover and recreate, so far as language allows, the life that is in it.

Of course the writer I have been evoking is what we loosely call the imaginative writer, the poet, the teller of tales whose business, as he would see it, is with discovery; not the articulating [or illustration] of some previously-held view but the groping through words towards something only vaguely grasped and which he will recognise only when words have set it down on the page.

There is, of course, another kind of writing, and if I make a distinction between the two it is not to create a hierarchy but to suggest that they are products of different states of consciousness.

This other form of writing does belong to the world of moral or social or political issues; to argument, opinion, judgement. It is the product of a consciousness that is very active and alert and it needs these qualities to do what it must do, to challenge, question, turn received ideas on their heads, and the more it knows, and the more, at the very moment of writing, it can draw on what it knows, the richer the writing will be, the more focused, the more wide-ranging and convincing.

This argumentative or expository sort of writing is too varied to have a single name. It would have to be a very loose term indeed that would contain say, Milton's *Areopagitica* and the pamphlets on divorce, Johnson's *Lives of the Poets*, Tom Paine and Burke, Thoreau's 'On Civil Disobedience', Hazlitt and Emerson's essays, Shaw's musical criticism under the name of Cornetto di Basso, or such contemporary examples as the work of Janet Malcolm and Julian Barnes's pieces for the *New Yorker*. The point of distinction, as I say, is not quality but the different attitudes of mind out of which the two forms of writing are produced: the one active and supremely self-conscious, focused in reason but open to the spirit of play, the other, in the Keatsian sense, [deeply] passive, where the less conscious you are of what you already know, the more of previous knowledge, and the attitudes and opinions that come with it, has fallen out of your head, the more responsive you will be to what the writing itself is about to discover, the readier you will be to get on with the real business of attending – in both senses – on what you are about to be told.

The novel, which for the past hundred and fifty years or so has been the major literary form in our culture, is an interesting case because it is mixed.

In earlier novels, Hugo's *Notre Dame* for instance, or *Moby Dick*, the two forms of writing are kept distinct. The essayistic chapters that interrupt and expand the narrative in *Notre Dame* are brilliantly argumentative, full of dazzlingly original speculations on the relationship between language and architecture – for instance, the idea in the chapter called 'Ceci Tuera Celà' that the printing-press killed architecture – or on the social changes behind different architectural styles. But however playful and imaginative they may be, however full of poetic flare, these chapters belong to a different mode, a different form of thinking, from the bold language-act by which Hugo appropriates a neglected and half-ruined building and raises it out of the realm of stone into that of language, makes of it a verbal artifact, a text that is literally written all over with multilingual graffiti, or from the descent into the unconscious, into the world of folk-tale and dream or nightmare, that creates Quasimodo as a living extension of the cathedral, one of its gargoyles made flesh. And we might make the same distinction between the various parts of *Moby Dick*, where the essays on every aspect of whaling, precise, poetic, self-consciously playful, sceptical and even subversive in the manner of the Encyclopaedists, belong to a different world of invention from that of Ahab and the others, which dives down deep into a Romantic form of poetic thinking that is continuous with dreaming and demands a different and more 'poetic', that is allusive and reverberative, language.

A century later this essayistic quality gets integrated into the main narrative, and Thomas Mann, for instance, goes to considerable lengths to insist that the philosophical arguments and political exchanges in *The Magic Mountain* are as much a product of the poetic spirit as the complex imagery of disease that makes the rest of the book so clearly a work of the imagination.

Mann recognises a crisis here. What he has to say about the novel reflects on his own position in the earlier part of this century but points to something generally true that we need to take account of. The novel, he tells us, 'because of its analytical spirit, its consciousness, its innate critical attitudes, can no longer remain undisturbed and sweetly oblivious of the world'.

That 'no longer' suggests that the situation is new, and in some ways it is. Mann is speaking of an age in which the novelist too, as he sees it, 'can no longer remain undisturbed and sweetly oblivious of the world'.

Mann had not always taken this line. Before he began the long investigation of his social and aesthetic attitudes that he called *Reflections of an Unpolitical Man*, which kept him occupied for three whole years from September 1915 till the end of the war, he would have taken it for granted that his purely imaginative work, *Death in Venice*, say, or *Tristan*, stood apart from his political writings and that 'to think and judge humanly is to think and judge unpolitically'. But the events of those years, and the writing of the book, changed him. When he began he was a conservative nationalist, an anti-democratic in the tradition of Schopenhauer and Nietzsche. Too much the writer, that is too eager to live in contraries and contradictions, too ironical, too aware of the need to qualify, to be a true polemicist – the writer is by nature and in his nature as writer always in at least two minds on every issue – Mann found himself, as he emerged from his three-year ordeal and transformation, no longer on one side of the political line but on the other, a social democrat no less, and a committed supporter of the new republic. By the mid-thirties he could claim that he did not 'rank the socio-political sphere lower that that of the inner life'.

This business of the writer discovering, as he writes, what

222

he really thinks, which may run counter to what he believes he thinks, comes close to the heart of what I want to say.

This is when the writer speaks: out of his activity as a writer rather than as a good citizen or as a holder of this or that set of views. What he finds himself saying then may surprise and even shock him – and the writing will please him most perhaps when it does. It will be his assurance that a real act of writing has occurred. But it can happen only if he is prepared to go lax and empty. To give up what he *thinks* he knows and allows some other faculty to take over. Hugo may have been the earliest writer to recognise this phenomenon and put it into words. 'All great writers,' he tells us, 'create two *oeuvres*, one deliberate, the other involuntary.' And again: 'As a person, one is sometimes a stranger to what one writes as a poet.'

Hugo's first proposition is wonderfully illustrated in his great contemporary Balzac.

Balzac was by conviction a conservative. Catholic and Royalist, he speaks with contempt, even as late as the revolutionary year of 1848, in his preface to his last-published book, *The Peasants*, of 'the democratic vertigo to which so many blind writers succumb'. He must have depised the woolly liberalism and drum-banging about Progress, and the sentimentality about peasants and workers (Balzac actually knew his peasants) that is at the damp centre of Hugo's writing.

But what the books themselves dramatise is not a right-wing view, or any view at all in that sense, but radical insights into a phenomenon that Balzac found more fascinating than any other and which he approaches with the excited detachment of the naturalist who has discovered another form of Nature: in this case, nineteenth-century entrepreneurial capitalism, the way it corrupts private and public values, divides families, hardens the heart and makes of the mind an instrument that can be deadly in its excessiveness and blind determination. The drive to success, the beating down of others in order to win, that is what animates Balzac's characters, and as a writer the living *in* the phenomenon, as he observes and recreates it, is what animates him. Even sex here is either something to be manipulated and traded, or money-making becomes the expression of sexual energy in another form. The Market, whose working for Balzac is like the mysterious working of the universe, is a machine in which all his characters are caught, a [visible and] contemporary version of what older writers, and writers like Hugo, call God or Fate.

It is as if these novels were written by the left hand of a man whose convictions they entirely violate. Even religion is not sacred. In one of the finest comic scenes he ever wrote, Madame Marneffe in *Cousin Bette* does a devastating imitation of poor Madame Hulot's virtuous piety as she pleads for mercy from her seducer Crevel, and the malicious delight Balzac takes in it, the energy it generates in him, is impersonal; it has nothing to do with his own loyalties and allows nothing to the fact that Madame Hulot is genuinely virtuous and also helpless. He enters with delight into his creation, Madame Marneffe. Carried away by the situation itself and what it offers, he exploits her comic inventiveness with a savagery that even Diderot, at his most anti-clerical, does not match.

What we see here is that exuberant joy in the pheno-menon itself, for its own sake and outside moral judgement, that is the true characteristic of the artist: a delight in God's creation but also in his own. To enter, in a spirit of joyful play, even into what is reprehensible – that is the artist's way, which is why satirists so often get into trouble for loving too clearly what they excoriate. But what else should they do? Delight in the thing itself, the getting inside it, the taking into yourself of its energy, the giving of your own energy to the free expression of it, the letting it go on its own course – that is what constitutes the artist's interest in things, in the *otherness* of things. Outside the work he might take a stand; but in so far as he does it inside the work, even if it is on the side of the angels, by so much the less is he an artist. The work as a delighting of the spirit in *what is* has nothing to do with consciousness-raising or progress or right religion or right thinking. Chaucer may make a deathbed renunciation of his works on the grounds of their immorality, their impiety, and poor Isaac Babel in the Lubianka his on the grounds of political incorrectness, but the works, in all their lively incorrectness, shine clear.

Of course one can argue that there are more important things than art. There are. But they are not what concern the writer while he is writing. If he wants to put his work at the service of a cause, that's his choice. Time will make its own judgement, both on the cause and his attachment to it.

When the writer speaks then, when he most truly speaks, is when he allows the writing to speak. But given Mann's statement that the novel, and by implication the novelist too, 'can no longer remain undisturbed and sweetly oblivious of the world', when should the writer speak up, speak out *in propria persona*, as a citizen, but also, unavoidably in his case, as one who comes invested with whatever 'authority' the writing itself has won for him?

Some writers, on some occasions, have always done so: Voltaire for example, when he took up the case of Calas, Zola when, in *J'accuse*, he spoke out in the Dreyfus affair, most of all Hugo who set himself up in his attack on Louis Napoleon in *Napoléon le Petit* as the embodiment of an alternative France, the president in exile of a republic of the spirit that was the *true* France – and it is worth noting perhaps that all three cases are French.

Hugo was also the first writer after Voltaire to have a universal celebrity, almost separate from his fame as a writer, but growing out of it, [who] that gave his name on any petition, in any cause, real currency, from Mexico to Vietnam. His is the earliest example of a phenomenon that has now become general; in which writers, in a world where virtually everything has been subsumed into the culture of advertising, are asked increasingly, like those fake housewives who used to promote the virtues of washing-powder on TV, to endorse anything that needs for its selling that little extra push, from one another's books to every sort of appeal for funds or the support of this or that political party, but also, to move too quickly from the trivial to the deadly serious, in protest against the horrors that, despite old Hugo's optimism, show no signs of going away; and here it is appropriate to pay tribute to the work PEN and its members have done, over the century, against the silencing – in all senses of the word – of writers in every part of the world and under every kind of repressive regime.

Thomas Mann is perhaps the most significant example in our century of a writer drawn out of his role as pure writer into that of public adversary; driven to speak up, out of what he called the 'spiritual confusion' of his time, for reason, justice, humanity, but most of all for that humane culture without which these cannot be sustained.

One of Mann's most moving statements is one he made in 1931 in answer to a question from young people about how, in a period of intense political struggle, one could go on writing. We do it, Mann answered, 'because we believe in play and its dignity. We believe in secrets, in the human secret of art.' What makes the statement so moving is that it speaks up for what is deeply personal, for what was closest to Mann's heart, and to the centre of his private world, at a moment when he is already moving, or being moved, on to the public stage, as the figurehead of the 'other Germany', much as Hugo had been of the 'other France'.

It was a role he accepted very unwillingly and after a good deal of vacillation. He knew in advance what it would cost him. Speaking in a diary entry of 1933 of the defection to the Nazis of the grand old man of German letters, Gerhart Hauptmann, he writes: 'I hate this idol whom I helped to magnify, and who magnificently regrets a martyrdom that I also feel I was not born for, but which I am driven to embrace for the sake of intellectual integrity.'

What tormented Mann was the fear that this role that had been forced upon him by an accident of history might also have driven him out of what he had always seen as his natural course: the one that large-handed Nature had offered him, like Goethe, as one of her favoured sons. In a diary entry of March 1934, he writes: 'The inner rejection of martyrdom, the feeling that it is not appropriate for me, continues to be strong. Just now it has been re-awakened, and was confirmed and reinforced, when Lion quoted a remark made by Gottfried Benn a long time ago, "Do you know Thomas Mann's house in Munich? There is truly something Goethean about it" – The fact that I was driven away from that existence is a serious flaw in the destined pattern of my life, one which I am attempting to accommodate to – in vain, it appears; and the impossibility of setting it right, and re-establishing that existence, impresses itself upon me, no matter how I look at it, and gnaws at my heart.'

What these private diary entries reveal is how unnatural it is for the artist to enter the world of political action and to speak there rather than in his own place on the stillness of the page. Mann is deeply torn; his reactions, from day to day, are contradictory; he wants to save himself from all this. But he does speak out at last, but being Mann, is also aware of the irony of his position, of the unpolitical man's having become after all, as he puts it, 'an itinerant preacher for democracy – a role whose comic element was always plain'.

But irony does not diminish in any way either the energy he expended in his fight against Nazism, or his courage. It cost him many years of exile and his natural audience, the one that over more than thirty years he had made his own, and the right to publish in his homeland. It is only because he was such an indefatigable worker and had such a strong sense of his own destiny as writer, because he needed so much to hang on to his 'secrets', to the 'dignity of play', that it did not cost him as well the greatest of his works. The Goethe book, *Lotte in Weimar*, and the four Joseph novels, are not only a marvellous expression of culture as he understood it – and all the more since they were made in defiance of the absolute challenge to it – but a tribute as well to his powers of dedication and belief. It is they, with their essential lightness, their freedom from taint, rather than his political activities, that stand as a counterweight to the brutalities of the period and a rejection of their final importance and power.

Mann, as I say, had always written articles on social and

political matters; however much he protested the fact, he was at home with controversy. He also saw himself, in a very German way, as 'representative' – the idea has no equivalent in our literary culture, where no writer has ever presented himself, I think, as the personification of the language, [and] the living embodiment, for his time, of all that can best be said in it. Mann had always been in the public eye. He orchestrated his reputation, enjoyed his fame, and enjoyed even more when it came, from America of course, his celebrity; and it was his celebrity that had to be exploited when he came to fulfil his role as the good German, since its main target, however deeply he may have felt it, [and however painfully,] was political opinion in the United States. I say this not to diminish the part he played but to suggest how many-sided it was, and the ways in which the use of it, the usefulness of it, was not always in his control.

Given the way Mann saw things, he could have done nothing else; but there were others and they acted differently. One of them was the poet Gottfried Benn, the same poet we have just seen Mann referring to his diary.

Another unpolitical man, Benn was the leading poet of pre-Nazi Germany, an expressionist, a Francophile, insistent always that poetry existed in its own world, free of the socio-political. But in a famous broadcast of 1933 he supported the election of the Nazis, and as vice-president of the writers' wing of the Prussian Academy drafted the declaration all German writers were asked to make giving their unconditional support, with a simple yes or no, to the new regime. Incidentally, the answer Mann gave was deliberately ambiguous, and it was to be another three years before he made his final break with his homeland. Benn meanwhile, within the year in fact, had seen his error, and while Mann was still being published in Germany, was expelled from all his official positions and forbidden to work professionally in either medicine (he was a skin specialist) or literature.

Early on in the regime he had written a letter of challenge to the *émigrés*, especially those, like Mann, who were not Jewish. Now he did not leave Germany and join them but went into what he called an inner emigration: silence. He joined the army, put himself at the service of German soldiers on the Eastern Front, practised his art only for himself, and did not publish again until 1948. His interior exile was lived with only himself as witness; and of course he was choosing to share with his fellow Germans an experience he felt he could not walk away from because they could not. As a writer he would live through whatever they had to live through.

In the writer's way of being always in two minds, I find it hard to choose between these two very different ways of responding to an impossible situation: the one an acting up to an international audience, an endless speaking out and making himself available for comment, of a man who wanted nothing more than to be allowed to get on with his own writing, but who recognised a solemn duty; in Benn's case an acceptance, out of view of all witnesses but himself, of a silence he could only hope would be temporary, and a dedication, in the meantime, to the physical suffering of men whose life and fate, inside the historical moment, he felt it was his fate to share.

Like a good many writers, I suspect, who have spent their whole lives on the light side of history, I am haunted by the lives of those who have found themselves in darker places and in darker times: by that no doubt terrifying phone-call from Stalin, for example, that left Pasternak unable to find the few words of praise for a fellow poet that might have saved Mandelstam from deportation to Siberia and an anonymous death; by the situation Camus found himself in at the height of the Algerian war; by the different paths taken, in the Nazi period, by Mann and Benn.

Of course all choices are important, every situation puts *something* in jeopardy; but on the whole the ones we who are fortunate enough to live in stable societies have to make are not matters of life and death, [either to the society we live in or to our work,] though from a cultural point of view they may be quite serious enough. At a time when everything, including even what we used to call history, has become spectacle, an extension of the media, we might have to resist the recruiting of our support, which means our name and whatever may have accrued to it in the way of 'recognition value', in any but the most serious causes. The expression of opinion, which is a slippery enough commodity anyway, as just another form of self-presentation in the vast space that is offered by twenty-four hours a day of empty airwaves, is a temptation to talk, and trivial talk, that is, as I said at the beginning, the real enemy of the writer, and the more tempting because it flatters with the assurance of public importance, and because [energy], real or merely whipped up, can seem, in the over-heated world of the media, such a reassurance of *presence*.

The writer is most present in the writing itself; which is a product [, as I said earlier,] of silence. We are luckiest, as writers, if the society we live in allows us the privilege of silence – but one that is chosen, not enforced.

Salman Rushdie

THE FIREBIRD'S NEST

*Now I am ready to tell how bodies are changed
Into different bodies.*

Ovid, *The Metamorphoses*,
translated by Ted Hughes

IT IS A hot place, flat and sere. The rains have failed so often
that now they say instead, the drought succeeded. They are
plainsmen, livestock farmers, but their cattle are deserting
them. The cattle, staggering, migrate south and east in search
of water, and rattle as they walk. Their skulls, horned mile-
posts, line the route of their vain exodus. There is water to
the west, but it is salt. Soon even these marshes will have
given up the ghost. Tumbleweed blows across the leached
grey flats. There are cracks big enough to swallow a man.

An apt enough way for a farmer to die: to be eaten by his
land.

Women do not die in that way. Women catch fire, and
burn.

Within living memory, a thick forest stood here, Mr Maharaj
tells his American bride as the limousine drives towards his
palace. A rare breed of tiger lived in the forest, white as salt,
wiry, small. And songbirds! A dozen dozen varieties; their
very nests were built of music. Half a century ago, his father
riding through the forest would hum along with their arias,
could hear the tigers joining in the choruses. But now his
father is dead, the tigers are extinct, and the birds have all
gone, except one, which never sings a note, and, in the
absence of trees, makes its nest in a secret place that has not

231

been revealed. The firebird, he whispers, and his bride, a child of a big city, a foreigner, no virgin, laughs at such exotic melodramatics, tossing her long bright hair; which is yellow, like a flame.

There are no princes now. The government abolished them decades ago. The very idea of princes has become, in our modern country, a fiction, something from the time of feudalism, of fairy-tale. Their titles, their privileges have been stripped from them. They have no power over us. In this place, the prince has become plain Mr Maharaj. He is a complex man. His palace in the city has become a casino, but he heads a commission that seeks to extirpate the public corruption that is the country's bane. In his youth he was a mighty sportsman, but since his retirement he has had no time for games. He heads an ecological institute, studying, and seeking remedies for, the drought; but at his country residence, at the great fortress-palace to which this limousine is taking him, cascades of precious water flow ceaselessly, for no other purpose than display. His library of ancient texts is the wonder of the province, yet he also controls the local satellite franchises, and profits from every new dish. The details of his finances, like those of his many rumoured romances, are obscure.

Here is a quarry. The limousine halts. There are men with pickaxes and women bearing earth in metal bowls upon their heads. When they see Mr Maharaj they make gestures of respect, they genuflect, they bow. The American bride, watching, intuits that she has passed into a place in which that which was abolished is the truth, and it is the government, far away in the capital, that is the fiction in which nobody believes. Here Mr Maharaj is still the prince, and she, his new princess. As though she had entered a fable, as though she were no more than words crawling along a dry page, or as though she were becoming that page itself, that surface on which her story would be written, and across which there blew a hot and merciless wind, turning her body to papyrus, her skin to parchment, her soul to paper.

It is so hot. She shivers.

It is no quarry. It is a reservoir. Farmers, driven from their land by drought, have been employed by Mr Maharaj to dig this water-hole against the day when the rains return. In this way he can give them some employment, he tells his bride, and more than employment: hope. She shakes her head, seeing that this great hollow is already full; of bitter irony. Briny, brackish, no use to man or cow.

The women in the reservoir of irony are dressed in the colours of fire. Only the foolish, blinded by language's conventions, think of fire as red, or gold. Fire is blue at its melancholy rim, green in its envious heart. It may burn white, or even, in its greatest rages, black.

Yesterday, the men with pickaxes tell Mr Maharaj, a woman in a red and gold sari, a fool, ignited in the amphitheatre of the dry water-hole. The men stood along the high rim of the reservoir, watching her burn, shouldering arms in a kind of salute; recognising, in the wisdom of their manhood, the inevitability of women's fate. The women, their women, screamed.

When the woman finished burning there was nothing there. Not a scrap of flesh, not a bone. She burned as paper burns, flying up to the sky and being blown into nothing by the wind.

The combustibility of women is a source of resigned wonder to the men hereabouts. They just burn too easily, what's to be done about it? Turn your back and they're alight. Perhaps it is a difference between the sexes, the men say. Men are earth, solid, enduring, but the ladies are capricious, unstable, they are not long for this world, they go off in a puff of smoke without leaving so much as a note of explanation. And in this heat, if they should spend too long in the sun! We tell them to stay indoors, not to expose themselves to danger, but you know how women are. It is their fate, their nature.

Even the demure ones have fiery hearts; perhaps the demure ones most of all, Mr Maharaj murmurs to his wife in the limousine. She is a woman of modern outlook and does not like it, she tells him, when he speaks this way, herding her sex into these crude corrals, these easy generalisations, even in jest. He inclines his head in amused apology. A firebrand, he says. I see I must mend my ways.

See that you do, she commands, and nestles comfortably under his arm. His grey beard brushes her brow.

Gossip burns ahead of her. She is rich, as rich as the old, obese Nizam of ——, who was weighed in jewels on his birthdays and so was able to increase taxes simply by putting on weight. His subjects would quake as they saw his banquets, his mighty halvas, his towering jellies, his kulfi Himalayas, for they knew that the endless avalanche of delicacies sliding down the Nizam's gullet meant that the food on their own tables would be sparse and plain; as he wept with exhausted repletion so their children would weep with hunger, his gluttony would be their famine. Yes, filthy rich, the gossip sizzles, her American father claims descent from the deposed royal family of an Eastern European state, and each year he flies the *élite* employees of his commercial empire by private aircraft to his lost kingdom, where by the banks of the River of Time itself he stages a four-day golf tournament, and then, laughing, contemptuous, godlike, fires the champion, destroys his life for the hubris of aspiring to glory, abandons him by the shores of Time's River, into whose tumultuous, deadly waters the champion finally dives, and is lost, like hope, like a ball.

She is rich; she is a fertile land; she will bring sons, and rain.

No, she is poor, the gossip flashes, her father hanged himself when she was born, her mother was a whore, she also is a creature of wilderness and rocky ground, the drought is in her body, like a curse, she is barren, and has come in the hope of stealing brown babies from their homes and nursing them with bottles, since her own breasts are dry.

Mr Maharaj has searched the world for its treasures and brought back a magic jewel whose light will change their lives. Mr Maharaj has fallen into iniquity and brought Despair into his palace, has succumbed to yellow-haired doom.

So she is becoming a story the people tell, and argue over. Travelling towards the palace, she too is aware of entering a story, a group of stories about women such as herself, fair and yellow, and the dark men they loved. She was warned by friends at home, in her tall city. Do not go with him, they cautioned her. If you sleep with him, he will not respect you. He does not think of women like you as wives. Your otherness excites him, your freedom. He will break your heart.

Though he calls her his bride, she is not his wife. So far, she feels no fear.

A ruined gateway stands in the wilderness, an entrance to nowhere. A single tree, the last of all the local trees to fall, lies rotting beside it, the exposed roots grabbing at air like a dead giant's hand. A wedding party passes, and the limousine slows. She sees that the turbaned groom, on his way to meet his wife, is not young and eager, but wispy-haired, old and parched; she imagines a tale of undying love, long denied by circumstance, overcoming adversity at last. Somewhere an elderly sweetheart awaits her wizened amour. They have loved each other always, she imagines, and now near their stories' conclusion they have found this happy ending. By accident she speaks these words aloud. Mr Maharaj smiles, and shakes his head. The bridegroom's bride is young, a virgin from a distant village.

Why would a pretty young girl wish to marry an old fool?

Mr Maharaj shrugs. The old fellow will have settled for a small dowry, he replies, and if one has many daughters such factors have much weight. As for the oldster, he adds, in a long life there may be more than a single dowry. These things add up.

Flutes and horns blow raucous music in her direction. A drum crumps like cannon-fire. Transsexual dancers heckle her through the window. Ohé, America, they screech, arré, howdy-podner, say what? OK, you take care now, I'm-a-yankee-doodle-dandy! Ooh, baby, wah-wah, maximum cool, Miss America, shake that thing! She feels a sudden panic. Drive faster, she cries, and the driver accelerates. Dust explodes around the wedding party, hiding it from view. Mr Maharaj is solicitude personified, but she is angry with herself. Excuse me, she mutters. It's nothing. The heat.

('America'. Once upon a time in 'America', they had shared an Indian lunch three hundred feet above street-level, at a table with a view of the vernal lushness of the park, feasting their eyes upon an opulence of vegetation which now, as she remembers it in this desiccated landscape, feels obscene. My country is just like yours, he'd said, flirting. Big, turbulent and full of gods. We speak our kind of bad English and you speak yours. And before you became Romans, when you were just colonials, our masters were the same. You defeated them before we did. So now you have more money than we do. Otherwise, we're the same. On your street corners the same bustle of differences, the same litter, the same every-thing-at-onceness. She guessed immediately what he was telling her: that he came from a place unlike anything she had ever experienced, whose languages she would struggle to master, whose codes she might never break, and whose immensity and mystery would provoke and fulfil her greatest passion and her deepest need.

Because she was an American, he spoke to her of money. The old protectionist legislation, the outdated socialism that had hobbled the economy for so long, had been repealed and there were fortunes to be made if you had the ideas. Even a prince had to be on the ball, one step ahead of the game. He was bursting with projects, and she had a reputation in financial circles as a person who could bring together capital and ideas, who could conjure up, for her favoured projects, the monetary nourishment they required.

A 'rainmaker'.

She took him to the opera, was aroused, as always, by the power of great matters sung of in words she could not understand, whose meaning had to be inferred from the performers' deeds. Then she took him home and seduced him. It was her city, her stage, and she was confident, and young. As they began to make love, she guessed that she was about to leave behind everything she knew, all the roots of her self. Her lovemaking became ferocious, as if his body were a locked gateway to the unknown, and she must batter it down.

Not everything will be wonderful, he warned her. There is a terrible drought.)

His palace, unfortunately, is abominable. It crumbles, stinks. In her room, the curtains are tattered, the bed precarious, the pictures on the wall pornographic representations of arabesque couplings at some petty princeling's court. No way of knowing if these are her husband's ancestors or a job-lot purchased from a persuasive pedlar. Loud music plays in ill-lit corridors, but she cannot find its source. Shadows scurry from her sight. He installs her, vanishes, without an explanation. She is left to make herself at home.

That night, she sleeps alone. A ceiling fan stirs the hot, syrupy air. It simmers, like a soup. She cannot stop thinking of 'home': its nocturnal sirens, its cooling machinery. Its reification of the real. Amid that surplus of structures, of content, it is not easy for the phantasmagoric to gain the upper hand. Our entertainment is full of monsters, of the fabulous, because outside the darkened cinemas, beyond the pages of the books, away from the gothic decibels of the music, the quotidian is inescapable, omnipotent. We dream of other dimensions, of paranoid subtexts, of underworlds, because when we awake the actual holds us in its great thingy grasp and we cannot see beyond the material, the event horizon. Whereas here, caught in the empty bubbling of dry air, afraid of roaches, all your frontiers may crumble; are crumbling. The possibility of the terrible is renewed.

She has never found it easy to weep, but her body convulses. She cries dry tears, and sleeps. When she awakes there is the sound of a drum, and dancers.

In a courtyard, the women and girls are gathered, young and old. The drummer beats out a rhythm and the ladies respond in unison. Their knees bent outward, their splay-fingered hands semaphoring at the ends of peremptory arms, their necks making impossible, lateral shifts, eyes ablaze, they advance across cool stone like a syncopated army. (It is still early, and the courtyard is in shadow; the sun has not yet lent the stone its fire.) At the dancers' head, tallest of them all, fiercely erect, showing them how, is Mr Maharaj's sister, over sixty years old, but still the greatest dancer in the state. Miss Maharaj has seen the newcomer, but makes no acknowledgement. She is the mistress of the dance. Movement is all.

When it's finished, they face each other, Mr Maharaj's women: the sister, the American.

What are you doing?

A dance against the firebird. A propitiatory dance, to ward it off.

The firebird. (She thinks of Stravinsky, of Lincoln Center.)

Miss Maharaj inclines her head. The bird which never sings, she says. Whose nest is secret; whose malevolent wings brush women's bodies, and we burn.

But surely there is no such bird. It's just an old wives' tale.

Here there are no old wives' tales. Alas, there are no old wives.

Enter Mr Maharaj! Turbaned, with an embroidered cloth

flung about his broad shoulders, how handsome, how manly, how winsomely apologetic! She finds herself behaving petulantly, like a woman from another age. He woos and cajoles. He went to prepare her welcome. He hopes she will approve.

What is it?

Wait and see.

In the semi-desert beyond his stinking palace, Mr Maharaj has prepared an extravaganza. By moonlight, beneath hot stars, on great carpets from Isfahan and Shiraz, a gathering of dignitaries and nobles welcomes her, the finest musicians play their mournful, haunting flutes, their ecstatic strings, and sing the most ancient and freshest love-songs ever heard; the most succulent delicacies of the region are offered for her delight. She is already famous in the neighbourhood, a great celebrity. I invited your husband to visit us, the governor of an adjacent state guffaws, but I told him, if you don't bring your beautiful lady, don't bother to show up. A neighbouring ex-prince offers to show her the art treasures locked in his palace vaults. I take them out for nobody, he says, except Mrs Onassis, of course. For you, I will spread them in my garden, as I did for Jackie O.

While the moonlight lasts, there are camel-races and horse-races, dancing and song. Fireworks burst over their heads. She leans against Mr Maharaj, his absence long forgiven, and whispers, you have made a magic kingdom for me, or (she teases him) is this how you relax every night?

She feels him stiffen, smells the bitterness leaking from his words. It is you who have made this happen, he replies. In this ruined place you have conjured this illusion. The camels, the horses, even the edibles have been brought from far away. We impoverish ourselves to make you happy. How can you imagine that we are able to live like this? We protect the last fragments of what we had, and now, to please you, we plunge deeper into debt. We dream only of survival; this Arabian night is an American dream.

I asked for nothing, she said. This conspicuous consumption is not my fault. Your accusation, your diatribe, is offensive.

He has had too much to drink, and it has made him truthful. It is our obeisance, he tells us, at the feet of power. Rainmaker, bring us rain.

Money, you mean.

What else? Is there anything else?

I thought there was love, she says.

The full moon has never looked more beautiful. No music has ever sounded lovelier. No night has ever felt so cruel. She says: I have something to tell you.

She is pregnant. She dreams of burning bridges, of burning boats. She dreams of a movie she has always loved, in which a man returns to his ancestral village, and somehow slips through time, to the time of his father's youth. When he tries to flee the village, and returns to the railway station, the tracks have disappeared. There is no way home. This is where the film ends.

When she awakes from her dream, in her sweltering room, the sheets are soaked and there is a woman sitting at her bedside. She gathers a wet sheet around her nakedness. Miss Maharaj smiles, shrugs. You have a strong body, she says. Younger, but in other ways not so unlike mine.

I would have left him. Now I just don't know.

Miss Maharaj shakes her head. In the village they say it will be a boy, she explains, and then the drought will break. Just superstition. But he can't let you leave. And afterwards, if you go, he'll keep the child.

We'll see about that! she blasts. When she is agitated her tones become nasal, unattractive even to herself. In her mind's eye the story is closing around her, the story in which she is trapped, and in which she must, if she can, find the path of action: preferably of right action, but if not, then of wrong. What cannot be tolerated is inertia. She will not fall into some tame and heat-dazed swoon. Romance has led her into errors enough. Now she will use her head.

Slowly, as the weeks unfold, she begins to see. He does not own the casino in his palace in the city, has signed a foolish contract, letting it to a consortium of alarming men. The rent they pay him is absurd, and it is stipulated in the small print that on certain high days each year he must hang around the gaming-tables, grinning ingratiatingly at the guests, lending a tone. The satellite-dish franchises are more lucrative, but this greedy old wreck of a country residence needs to eat off far richer platters if it's to be properly fed.

This rural palace is ageless: perhaps six hundred years. Most of it lacks electricity, windows, furniture. Cold in the cold season, hot in the heat, and if the rains should come, many of its staterooms would flood. All they have here is water, their inexhaustible palace spring. At the back of the palace, past the ruined zones where the bats hold sway, she picks her way through accumulated guano and sees a line form before dawn. The villagers, rendered indigent by the drought, come under cover of darkness, hiding their humiliation, filling their supplicant pitchers. Behind the line of the thirsty there stands, like a haunting, the high black shadow of a crenellated wall. A village woman with a few unaccountable words of English explains that this charred fortress was, in former days, the larger part of the prince's residence. Great treasures were lost when it burned; also, lives.

When did this happen?

In before time.

She begins to understand his bitterness. Another princess, Miss Maharaj tells her, a dowager even more destitute than we, recently ended her life by drinking fire. She crushed her heirloom diamonds in a cup and gulped them down.

So Mr Maharaj, visiting America, had turned himself into an illusion of sophistication and innovation, had won her with a desperate performance. He has learned to talk like a modern man but in truth is helpless in the face of the present. The drought, his unworldliness, the decision of history to turn away her face, these things are his undoing. In Greece, the athlete who won the Olympic race became a person of high rank in his home state. Mr Maharaj, however, rots, as does his house. Her own room begins to look like luxury's acme. Glass in the windows, the slow-turning electric fan. A telephone with, sometimes, a dialling tone. A socket for her laptop's power line, the intermittent possibility of forging a modem link with that other planet, her earlier life.

He has not taken her to his own room because he is ashamed of it.

Sensing the life growing inside her, she wants to forgive its father; to help him out of the past, into the flowing, metamorphic present which has been her real life. She will do what she can do. She is 'America', and brings the rain.

Again and again she awakes, sweating, naked, with Miss Maharaj murmuring at her side. Yes, a fine body, it could have been a dancer's. It will burn well.

Don't touch me! (She is alarmed.)

All brides in these parts are brought from far afield. And once the men have spent their dowries, then the firebird comes.

Don't threaten me! (Perplexed.)

Do you know how many brides he has had?

Terrified, raging, bewildered, she confronts him. Is it true? Is that why your sister has never married, why she gathers under her roof, to protect them, all the spinsters of the village, young and old? That interminable dance class of lifetime virgins, too frightened to take a husband?

Is it true you burn your brides?

Ah, my mad sister has been whispering to you, he laughs. She came to your room at night, she caressed your body, she spoke of water and fire, of women's beauty and the secret, lethal nature of men. She told you about the magic bird, I suppose. The bird of death.

No, she remembers, carefully. The one who first named the firebird was you.

Mr Maharaj in a fury brings her to his sister's dance class. Seeing him, the dancers stumble, their bell-braceleted feet lose the rhythm and come jangling to a halt. Why are you here, he asks them, raging. Tell my bride why you have come. Are you refugees or students? Sir, students. Are you here because you are afraid? Oh, please, sir, we are not afraid. His inquisition is relentless, bellowing, and all the while his eyes never leave his sister's. Miss Maharaj stands tall and silent.

The last question is for her. How many brides have I had? How many do you say? They are locked in each other's power, brother and sister, each other's eternal prisoner, outside history, beyond time. Miss Maharaj is the first to drop her eyes. She is the first, she says.

It's over. He turns to face his bride, and spreads his arms. You heard it with your own ears. Let's have no more of fables.

The heat is maddening. Skeletal bullocks die on the brown lawn. Some days, there are mustard-yellow clouds filling the sky, hanging over the evaporating marshes to the west. Even this hideous yellow rain would be welcome, but it does not fall.

Everyone has bad breath. All exhale serpents, dead cats, insects, fogs. Everyone's perspiration is thick, and stinks.

In spite of all her resolutions, the heat hypnotises her. The child grows. Miss Maharaj's dancers grow careless about closing doors and windows. They are to be glimpsed, here and there, painting one another's bodies in hot colours and wild designs, making love, sleeping with limbs entwined. Mr Maharaj does not come to her, will not, while she is 'carrying'. But each night, Miss Maharaj comes. Since her brother's descent upon her dance class, Miss Maharaj has barely spoken. At night she asks only to sit at the bedside, sometimes, almost primly, to touch. This, Mr Maharaj's American bride allows.

Her health fails. She begins to sweat, to shiver with fever. Her shit is like thin mud. Only the palace spring saves her from dehydration and swift death. Miss Maharaj nurses her, brings her salt. The only physician hereabouts is an old fellow, out of touch, useless. Both women know the baby is at risk.

During these long, sick nights, quietly, absently, the sexagenarian dancer talks.

Something frightful has happened here. Some irreversible transformation. Without our noticing its beginnings, so that we did not resist until it was too late, until the new way of things was fixed, there has occurred a terrible, terminal rupture between our men and women. When men say they fear the absence of rain, when women say we fear the presence of fire, this is what we mean. Something has been unleashed in us. It's too late to tame it now.

Once upon a time there was a great prince here. The last prince, one could say. Everything about him was gigantic, mythological. The most handsome prince in the world, he married the most beautiful bride, a legendary dancer and temptress, and they had two children, a girl and a boy. As he aged, his strength ebbed, his eye dimmed, but she, the dancer, refused to fade. At the age of fifty she had the look of a young woman of twenty-one. As the prince's force faded, as that glamour which had been the heart of his power ceased to work its magic, so his jealousy increased . . .

(Miss Maharaj shrugged, moved quickly to the story's end.)

The fortress burned. They both died. He had suspected his wife of taking lovers but there had been none. The children, who had been left in the care of servants, lived. The daughter became a dancer and the son a sportsman, and so on. And the villagers said that the old prince, consumed by rage, had been transformed into a giant bird, a bird composed entirely of flames, and that was the bird that burned the princess, and returns, these days, to turn other women to ashes at her husband's cruel command.

And you, asks the ill woman on the bed. What do you say?

Do not condescend to us in your heart, Miss Maharaj replies. Do not mistake the abnormal for the untrue. We are caught in metaphors. They transfigure us, and reveal the meaning of our lives.

The illness recedes and the baby seems also to be well. The return of health is like a curtain being lifted. She is thinking like herself again. She will keep the child, but will no longer be trapped in this place of fantasies with a man she finds she does not know. She will go to the city, fly back to America, and after the child is born, what will be, will be. A quick divorce, of course. She has no desire to prevent the father from seeing his child. Extremely free access, including trips East, will be granted. She wants that, wants the child to know both cultures. Enough! Time to behave like an adult. She may even continue to advise Mr Maharaj on his financial needs. Why not? It's her job. She tells Miss Maharaj her decision, and the old dancer winces, as if from a blow.

In the dead of night, the American is awakened by a hubbub in the palace, in its corridors and courtyard. She dresses, goes outside. An impromptu armada of motor vehicles has assembled: a rusty bus, several motor-scooters, a newish Japanese people-carrier, an open truck, a Jeep in camouflage. Miss Maharaj's women are piling into the vehicles, angry, singing. They have taken weapons, the domestic weapons that came to hand, sticks, garden implements, kitchen knives. At their head, revving the Jeep, shouting impatiently at her troops, is Miss Maharaj.

What's going on?

None of your business. You don't believe in fairies. You're going home.

I'm coming with you.

Miss Maharaj treats the Jeep roughly, driving it at speed over broken ground, without lights. The motley convoy jolts along behind. They drive by the light of a molten full moon.

Ahead of them stands a ruined stone arch, an entrance to nothing, beside a fallen tree. The armada halts, turns on its lights. The dance class pours through the archway, as if it were the only possible entrance to the open waste ground beyond, the portal to another world. When she, the American, does likewise, she has that feeling again: of passing through an invisible membrane, a looking glass, into another kind of truth; into fiction.

A tableau, illuminated by the lights of motor vehicles. Remember the old bridegroom, on his way to meet his young, imported bride? Here he is again, guilty, murderous, and his young wife, uncomprehending, at his side.

In the background, silhouetted, are the figures of male villagers.

Facing the unhappy couple is Mr Maharaj.

The women burst shrieking upon the charmless scene, then come raggedly to a halt, intimidated by Mr Maharaj's presence. The sister faces the brother. Somebody has left their lights flashing. The siblings' faces glow white, yellow, red in the headlights. They speak in a language the American cannot understand, it is an opera without surtitles, she must infer what they are saying from their actions, from their thoughts made deeds, and so, as clearly as if she comprehended every syllable, she hears Miss Maharaj command her brother, what started between our parents stops now, and his response, a response that has no meaning in the world beyond the ruined archway, which he speaks as his body turns to fire, as the wings burst out of him, as his eyes blaze; his words hang in the air as the firebird's breath scorches Miss Maharaj, burns her to a cinder, and then turns upon the dotard's shrieking bride.

I am the firebird's nest.

Something loosens within the American as she sees Miss Maharaj burn, some shackle is broken, some limit of possibility passed. Unleashed, she crashes upon Mr Maharaj like a wave, and the angry dancers pour behind her, seething, irresistible. They feel the frontiers of their bodies burst and the waters pour out, the immense crushing weight of their rain, drowning the firebird and its nest, flowing over the drought-hardened land that no longer knows how to absorb the flood which bears away the old dotard and his murderous fellows, cleansing the region of its horrors, of its archaic tragedies, of its men.

The flood waters ebb, like anger. The women become themselves again, and the universe too resumes its familiar shape. The women huddle patiently under the old stone arch, listening for helicopters, waiting to be rescued from the deluge of themselves, freed from fear. As for the American, her own shape will continue to change. Mr Maharaj's child will be born, not here but in her own country, to which she will soon return. Increasing, she caresses her swelling womb. The new life growing within her will be both fire and rain.

Pauline Melville

THE PROCURESS

FOR THE FIRST time in exactly ten months, Sylvia Jarvis turned the key in her front door and pushed the wooden handle to enter. The apartment greeted her with a mild fustiness as if it had been holding on to a secret until her return and was now prepared to share it with her and her alone. The door of the first floor flat in Mecklenburgh Square opened straight on to the high-ceilinged drawing room. Dust had settled on the furniture but a glance around confirmed that everything was in its usual place. French windows reached almost to the floor and the shutters were partially open just as she had left them allowing two parallelograms of light to rest on the pale blue Chinese rug. Mrs Jarvis placed her bag on the small nest of tables and sank with relief into the familiar armchair piled with green velvet cushions.

It had been a widely acknowledged fact that whoever entered Mrs Jarvis's London flat, regardless of class or background, felt at home there. The furnishings were simple but elegant. She frequently changed the bowl of pot-pourri mixtures on the mantelpiece so that the scents in the room varied from faint orange to jasmine or lily of the valley but never lavender which is the call to death. The rosewood coffee table supported a carved, wooden dish holding curios – marble eggs, tiny porcelain fruits and a miniature turtle itself made of burnished tortoiseshell. Many of these ornaments were gifts from grateful clients. Nothing was glaringly expensive but all had the feeling of being chosen with special care.

She used to serve tea in wide bone-china cups that let the amber liquid cool too quickly and she encouraged her visitors to help themselves to milk from a tiny jug. Mrs Jarvis would sit where she was sitting now, with her back to the french windows. In warm weather she opened these windows and let the room fill with soft breezes. When she felt that something had been achieved, she would allow herself to smoke a Turkish cigarette with one of her visitors.

No one ever saw Mrs Jarvis dishevelled or untidy, even when they called on her at some ungodly hour in the morning. Then she would pad over the wooden floor in her tiny Japanese slippers, having pulled a wrap around her shoulders. Her black hair, worn in a roll at the nape of the neck, would be in its bedtime plait halfway down her back, but she always remained reassuringly composed, cheerful and considerate.

Whoever came usually sat in the chair opposite hers and more often than not appeared to be distraught and agitated, sometimes even rigid with tension. Mrs Jarvis, on the other hand, whose widow's peak framed oval symmetrical features, was the picture of relaxation. Her hands were either clasped in her lap, her head on one side, or she would cup her dimpled chin in her hand, resting the elbow on the arm of the chair, with her ankles crossed. Somehow her limbs always seemed to complete a circle which made her seem more than ever self-contained. Gradually, people would relax and succumb to her composure. Sylvia listened to her callers with a seriousness that was not too grave and did not prevent her from bursting into infectious laughter every now and then in a way they usually found comforting.

Another fact acknowledged by all who knew her was that it was possible to tell Sylvia Jarvis absolutely anything.

It was while her husband was alive that she first acquired a reputation as a hostess. There was a special charm to dinner parties at the Jarvis household. People struck up acquaint-anceships that rooted and grew into long-standing friend-ships. Young men fell in love with younger or sometimes older women. A scientist might suddenly find the mathematical solution to his own problem as he listened to a painter talk about colour coding. Recent widowers who had adored their wives became smitten with women who had given up all hope of finding a suitable partner. Blushing students found their tongue for the first time and made heartfelt speeches that were greeted with smiles and raised glasses. Women who had never dreamed of such a thing found themselves catching the eyes of other women and allowing their lives to open up passionately in unexpected directions.

And all this took place under the lively gaze of Sylvia Jarvis as she ladled out button mushrooms from the silver dish that had belonged to her husband's mother or tempted her guests with venison in orange sauce as she stood behind them, the steam from the food curling up under her nose, her eyes sparkling with delight in the pleasure of her guests. Occasionally she tilted the conversation towards someone who was remaining too silent or brought two shy people together through some line of interest common to them both.

It was a gift she had been blessed with since childhood. Neighbouring parents had often begged to 'borrow' Sylvia because their own children did not seem to quarrel and fight so much when she was there. And once there, she invented wonderful games so that parents could relax and doze off, hearing only mysterious whispers and giggles from other parts of the house.

Her father was a doctor and at the age of nineteen through some instinct for the symmetry of patterns, she herself married a doctor. Richard Jarvis was thirty-two at the time of the marriage. He smoked heavily despite having specialised in cardiology. She loved his bushy eyebrows and the smoky smell of his clothes. He in turn fell in love with Sylvia because he found her intriguing. At nineteen she had beautifully arched black eyebrows. No one could ever decide whether her eyes were blue or grey. But what appealed to him more than anything was an expression in them that made her seem party to some sort of mischievous secret:

'Our eyebrows fell in love with each other,' he joked.

Her grace attracted him. And besides, she seemed to be complete in herself, unlike most other girls of her age who were waiting for somebody else to complete them.

All her gifts were already in place. Syvlia had shown no startling academic skills, no outstanding ability in the field of sports but she was merry and unfailingly popular. From the beginning of her married life, she charmed her husband's patients and colleagues alike. She seemed to conduct a delightful and harmless flirtation with everyone she met, even with her own two children when they eventually came along. She loved to cook. The couple began their married life in a small flat in Shepherd's Bush. Her husband was in private practice. Sometimes he told Sylvia how he would inject his elderly hypochondriacal patients with water and then charge them a fortune. The practice prospered. When their children arrived the couple moved to a large house in Notting Hill Gate, where they established a tradition of throwing expensive and popular dinner parties.

Throughout her marriage, Sylvia Jarvis was contented but vaguely aware that there was something else in life for which she was destined, but which she had not yet discovered. Married life with two children kept her fully occupied. She was not a woman given to soul-searching. And so she relaxed, confident that whatever it was would be revealed to her in the fullness of time. And if not – *tant pis*.

One morning, shortly before their fifteenth wedding anniversary, Sylvia stood next to the dining-room table which gleamed with lemon-scented polish, opening her mail. Her husband, who had recently changed his smoking habits and taken up a pipe, was standing by the mantelpiece digging into the bowl of the pipe with a small penknife as he spoke:

'I didn't think the Hobsons seemed . . .'

He gave a small snorting sound, pivoted on his heel and crashed to the floor, his head narrowly missing the metal fireguard. At the age of forty-seven he had suffered a coronary. He appeared to be looking at her slyly through half-open eyes as if he were testing her to see what she would do in the light of this unexpected event. She knew immediately that he was dead.

That afternoon when the children returned from school, she took them by the hand to their bedroom and explained gently what had happened.

'Can we have a puppy now?' asked her small daughter, twisting her foot on the ground and putting on what she imagined to be an appropriate look of sorrow. She had repeatedly pestered her father for a dog.

Her mother laughed. 'Well, I don't see why not.'

Twelve years later, when the children were off her hands, Sylvia Jarvis decided to leave the house. It was far too large for her alone. Her husband's insurance policies and the sale of the house had left her financially comfortable. She bought a flat in Mecklenburgh Square which she loved because it reminded her of an apartment in Paris where she and her husband had once spent a holiday, breakfasting every day in the faint blue haze of traffic fumes on a wrought-iron balcony that overlooked the Boulevard Raspail.

The move to Mecklenburgh Square coincided with her discovering the true nature of her gift.

Friends who had rallied round her after her husband's death still called but she no longer threw dinner parties. Instead she enjoyed long conversations on an individual basis with the same friends, several of whom came to see her. She would listen with genuine interest and concern to the stories of infidelity and unrequited love, boredom, debts, the death of a relative, hopes of promotion, rebellious children and the mad behaviour of pets. They poured out their hearts to her. Occasionally, she would offer a suggestion or some advice. Everyone who called left her apartment feeling in some way refreshed.

A few years after the move, she suffered from a detached retina in the left eye. Her vision had become cloudy, the eyelid drooping a fraction. That eye had always been a problem. It had a slight cast in it. She went to see a colleague and old friend of her husband's, a consultant at St Thomas's Hospital.

After the examination, he sat on the edge of the desk in his white coat to ask her how things were going. He was an ugly man with a small, lop-sided mouth, thick-lensed spectacles and a large misshapen nose pocked like a strawberry. Very soon the conversation turned to his own anguish. He felt that his wife and children took him for granted, that he was a source of income to them and nothing else. He felt excluded from their activities almost as though they ganged up against him. Worst of all, he felt they despised him. Every day he was conscious of time flying past and of his life being a desert. Sylvia Jarvis saw clearly the pain in the ugly man's eyes.

'Tom, you need a mistress,' she said.

He laughed and got off the table, staring down at the floor in confusion. He twisted the pencil-torch in his hand.

'That would only complicate things.' He sighed and went back to his desk. 'Now then, about your eye. We don't need to do anything for the moment but be careful . . . any blow to the head might detach the retina completely.'

That afternoon, as Sylvia Jarvis prepared summer pudding with blackcurrants and raspberries, she thought long and hard about Tom. His predicament seemed like a personal challenge to her. When the pudding was ready, she put it in the fridge. Then she went out and bought several bunches of yellow mimosa and arranged them in bowls and vases around the flat. She flicked a cream tablecloth over one of the small tables and called her friend Julie on the telephone. Julie had taken early retirement from the private school where she taught French. Now she lived on her own in Ealing.

'Julie, I've just made a delicious summer pudding. Come over and share it with me. I want to talk to you about something . . .'

It worked perfectly.

All she did was suggest that they would enjoy each other's company from time to time. The affair developed. It was

conducted discreetly. Julie found the occasional companionship congenial. Tom underwent a new liberation as he
discovered a woman to value him once more.

That was Mrs Jarvis's first success. The happy couple gave
her a lovely crystal decanter out of gratitude. She was
delighted. She replayed it over and over in her mind. She
began to think of other partnerships which she could arrange.
Similar successes followed and finally she understood her
vocation. It was to be a fixer, a love broker, a matchmaker.

Her intuition was extraordinary. She possessed some
instinct about the relationship of a person's soul to the images
which attracted it most and so she was able to divine their
deepest desires. Sometimes the knowledge imparted itself to
her in the form of an image or as a myth she had read as a
child, or the hazy memory of a painting. Sometimes it could
be a scent that gave her the clue to work on. Word got round.
Her intuition was never clouded by moral judgement.
Whatever she felt was required, she would suggest or, if
possible, arrange. Grateful friends showered her with gifts. In
many ways, she saw herself as a healer and so did those who
called on her. She began to keep a register.

Initially, she never accepted money. But after a while she
became convinced that her services were worth paying for
and she began to bank the discreetly written cheques. An
element of greed entered the proceedings. Her life speeded up
as she dealt with a legion of appointments. Neighbours heard
Sylvia Jarvis's pleasant laugh through the walls late at night.
She found that by concentrating hard, an image would float
into her mind as she talked to a client, an image of a
particular type of person to whom they would be profoundly
attracted.

She worked hard. Her success depended on subtle intro-
ductions amongst the middle and upper-middle classes. After
two years, she was making enough money for her bank
manager to give her the most cordial treatment. She discovered that she possessed an astute financial brain and positively relished settling down with her ledgers of figures. But in

the end, even if someone had no money, Sylvia Jarvis could rarely resist the temptation of trying to find them their match.

It did not take long for Sylvia to realise that not everybody's desires could be fulfilled through her own limited list of friends and acquaintances. Sometimes she could help by advising people to frequent certain places where she felt they would be likely to meet suitable partners – art galleries, theatre clubs, sports pavilions, the races, certain clubs, dance halls. But she was a perfectionist and some people had very specific needs.

And so one morning, with her usual unerring judgement, she lifted up the telephone and spoke to a woman she had met socially some years before and who was now the governor of Holloway women's prison.

'I thought I would like to do something useful. Some prison visiting. Could you arrange it for me? So what do I have to do? Wonderful. Thank you, Bridget. I'll get on to it right away.'

It was in this way that she met Janie Springer.

Janie Springer had achieved minor success as a night-club singer before ending up in jail for running a brothel. She was thirty-seven, with metallic, bleached blonde hair and a harsh but pretty face in which Sylvia Jarvis immediately recognised a combination of cunning and stupidity. Janie annoyed the other prisoners by ingratiating herself with the warders, flaunting a mink coat over her leopard-skin leotard and seeming to have an endless supply of cigarettes. Mrs Jarvis found her amusing and laughed at her stories.

When Janie Springer left jail, Mrs Jarvis kept in touch with her because she knew that Janie would go back to being a professional madam. And, quite rightly, she guessed that Janie would be able to provide unusual services for those whose passions could be assuaged in no other way.

It was Sylvia who put Freddy Noakes, her tubby solicitor, in touch with Janie. Freddie was impotent. Viagra did not work. He would rush away from his marital bed in Epsom in tears and drive all the way to London where he would collapse in an agony of frustration and hysteria in the Mecklenburgh Square flat.

Sylvia used her gift to discover what Freddie needed. She grew to understand Freddy's compelling need to be embryonic once more. She consulted with Janie. Janie said she would have to go to Amsterdam to get the equipment.

When Freddy Noakes arrived at the Earl's Court brothel, two of Janie's girls were waiting with the giant balloon. They had to blow it up with special bellows. Blown-up, it was nearly the size of the room. They managed to get him into it, allowing him to breathe through the neck of the balloon and put an airpipe in his mouth so that he could still breathe when the balloon subsided and closed over him like a second skin of fine, black rubber. Then the girls lifted Freddy Noakes into the warm bath they had run and left him in it. Every so often, one of them would go into the bathroom and put a drop of amyl nitrate in his breathing tube. Occasionally, one of them would come in and swirl the water around his genitals. He could feel the erection struggling to lift the skin of the balloon. At home with his wife, he recovered his libido – by imagining he was in the balloon again. Through Sylvia Jarvis, Freddy Noakes had found his bliss. He paid enough for her to go on a cruise in the Greek Islands which she thoroughly enjoyed.

It was only after she had sorted Freddy out that she realised the true extent of her instinct for understanding precisely the obsessions and desires of her visitors and that none of these needs had anything to do with morality. Indeed, for her, they transcended morality. In her matchmaking, she was true only to her art and no moral compunction prevented her from bringing people together just because this one might be married or that one extremely young or that yet another had previously been heterosexual. If she thought that someone would be happier with animals than people, she told them so. She prided herself on these instincts. Her flair was undeniable.

On some days, she sat in her favourite armchair with her feet coiled underneath her, looking round with satisfaction at what she had accumulated. She had become the centre of an enormous and complex web. Only on rare occasions was she disappointed at the outcome of an introduction – when the relationship did not root as strongly as she would have hoped.

There had been one spectacular failure on her part. It was with Mr Anstey who had been introduced to her by Freddy Noakes, the solicitor. He was a wealthy accountant from Wimpole Street whose bloodpressure was so shockingly high that his doctor had advised him to lie down on his office floor during his lunch-hours and listen to Beethoven symphonies or Bach sonatas to calm him. He was a well-built man, with wiry black hair and shoulders unnecessarily powerful in an accountant. When they met, she encountered in him a titanic emptiness that puzzled even her and gave rise to no corresponding images for him at all. However much she screwed up her eyes, she could only see blackness. He was a silent, burly man who stood in her flat like an awkward actor waiting for a costume fitting. She tried twice more but was baffled and could only sense the lacuna behind his eyes – although later she found that she had doodled the words 'uncommon rage' next to his name in her appointment book. He was the one person whom she felt she had singularly failed.

But Mr Anstey was the exception. With each match made, each successful introduction, each carnal fantasy well-judged and each deal struck, she experienced growing confidence in her own achievements as a businesswoman.

Every July, her daughter, Louise, came from her home in Leicestershire to stay in London for the summer holidays. Louise was pleasant, humorous and unexceptional. She had known from her childhood that she would never be able to rival her mother's charm and had set her sights slightly lower. She brought with her Sylvia's eight-year-old granddaughter, Amy. Mrs Jarvis adored her granddaughter who already showed signs of imagination. The three of them went on shopping expeditions to the July sales and took Amy to the park. They returned to Mecklenburgh Square with piles of carrier bags containing expensive bargains, delicacies from Harrods Food Hall and small treats for Amy.

It was the only time that Sylvia Jarvis deliberately cut down on her appointments, in order to enjoy their company.

'How about the zoo and tea by the Serpentine,' she would suggest, as Amy toured the flat, enthralled by all the new ornaments and gifts that had arrived since her last visit. This time she fell in love with a porcelain Chinese monkey and carried it everywhere with her.

However, when an old friend telephoned late one evening, in great distress, Sylvia Jarvis made an exception and agreed to see the friend's mother and brother.

The tetchy physicist was brought to her flat the next day by his eighty-nine-year-old mother. Dr Foreman fiddled with his teeth and barked and sneered at almost everyone who spoke to him. He preceded almost every answer with an explosive: 'Oh for God's sake.'

His ancient mother was in despair. She would have liked to see him settled in some way before she died. Sylvia could see why as he stood in her front room, occasionally muttering a vicious, derogatory comment to himself about something that had been said. His beard was meagre, his hair mousy and thin and his movements were tense and jerky.

Mrs Jarvis knew exactly what was needed and she did not hesitate.

'Amy,' she called out to her granddaughter in the next room.

The child swung the door open and held on to the door handle, peering round into the room. Her hair was caught up in a spiky pony-tail. More wisps of hair hung in front of her ears and round the curve of her neck. Her expression was full of excited anticipation. She arrived in the room like Ariel answering a summons from Prospero, ready to do her grandmother's bidding.

'Amy, I want you to take Dr Foreman for a walk in the square and show him the gardens. Then his mother and I can have a chat together. He's getting a little bored with us, I'm afraid. You will be much more fun for him. I'll give you the key to the gardens.'

One of the things that Sylvia Jarvis noted when her matchmaking instincts were operating at their best was that timing made the liaisons seem almost inevitable, as if she had only nudged open the door for fate.

As soon as they had entered what Amy called 'her magic garden', she turned her back to the bush at the entrance, took Dr Foreman's hands and smiled up at him.

'I like you,' she said, her face appealingly framed by the yellow-splodged laurel leaves.

She said it to everyone. She had discovered that this simple phrase, said with enough sincerity and a direct gaze or smile, softened the hardest of adult hearts, although children were not taken in so easily.

Two days later Dr Foreman returned on his own with a gift for Amy. Sylvia Jarvis smiled at him. The gift was a miniature model of the solar system. Amy was thrilled. He knelt awkwardly at the side of the child's bed and constructed it for her so that she could look at it last thing at night and first thing in the morning. The model was electrically operated and at the flick of a switch, the globes and spheres started to spin and move in their elliptical orbits.

Two weeks later, Janie Springer came up the stairs of the flat in Mecklenburgh Square on a spur-of-the-moment social call. With the foresight of the truly cunning, she looked through the letter-box of the front door before she knocked. At first, she was not at all clear as to what she was seeing. Then she realised that in the armchair with its back to the window, a man was seated. He had a straggly beard. Kneeling at his side was a child with long, straight hair the colour of honey. The man's head was thrown back sideways at the odd angle at which Christ's head is often depicted during the Crucifixion. Tears were streaming down his face. The child was smiling to herself with an air of satisfied authority, as if she had complete control of the situation. Lowering her eyes, Janie saw the man's flies were open and that, with her hand, the child was stroking his penis with the same concentration and careful strokes that little girls sometimes give to brushing their doll's hair. Janie Springer shut the letter-box without making a sound, paused to think how she could turn the situation to her advantage, and then tiptoed silently down the stairs.

Dr Foreman's first thought when he received the blackmail letter was that it could only have come from Mrs Jarvis. Distraught, he rushed round to the flat and pummelled on the outside door with his fist until someone let him in. It was eleven o'clock in the morning. Neighbours heard his raised voice and Mrs Jarvis's soothing tones interrupting him occasionally. Then they heard the door of the flat bang shut and the sound of footsteps hurrying down the stairs from the first floor and then the heavier slamming of the front door.

Mrs Jarvis went over to the mantelpiece and took a cigarette from the jade cigarette box. She lit it and sat down in her front room, shaken by what she had heard. Who could know about Dr Foreman and her granddaughter? She tried to recollect her conversations over the last few weeks. Had Amy told anyone? Amy had returned to her mother in Leicester, light-hearted and joyful as ever, having kissed her grandmother goodbye at the station and asked if she could come again during the next school holidays. Mrs Jarvis sat in her chair for several hours trying to puzzle the thing out. The telephone rang and she ignored it until eventually it stopped. Then she remembered a conversation with Janie Springer. Janie had asked casually about the bearded man she had passed one day on the stairs when she came to call. She must have mentioned his name to Janie. Janie would only have needed to look up the name in the telephone book to find his address.

Before Sylvia Jarvis could pick up the telephone to call Janie, the door-buzzer went. Two policemen, both with guarded, unresponsive faces, stood framed in the doorway, their backs to the curving staircase.

From then on, events moved too fast for Sylvia to control. After the police had left, she stood staring at the model universe next to Amy's bed. Dr Foreman had been found hanging at his home. A long and bitter confessional note implicated Mrs Jarvis in both blackmail and in procuring a minor for sexual purposes, her own granddaughter, in fact.

Three days later, the police returned and arrested Sylvia Jarvis. They took with them her address book.

Between the arrest and the trial, all her friends deserted her. The telephone stopped ringing. There were no callers. There had been one or two heated flurries between herself and Janie Springer. Eventually, the charges of blackmail against her were dropped but the charges of procuring remained.

After one telephone conversation with her worried daughter in Leicester, Sylvia Jarvis realised that she had a choice. Oddly enough, Louise was not utterly horrified. She had spoken to Amy and Amy had recounted what had happened, a little embarrassed but nothing more. She seemed to have suffered no ill effects. What worried Louise was the prospect of the trial. By pleading guilty Sylvia could save Amy the experience of testifying. If she involved the child, the child would almost certainly disclose a series of sexual encounters with Dr Foreman.

To Sylvia Jarvis, it did not look good either way.

Janie Springer, wallowing in spurious self-righteousness, made dramatic sworn statements that Sylvia Jarvis procured clients. She described with great prurience what she had seen through the letter-box of the Mecklenburgh Square flat. She was prepared to give the same evidence in court. Sylvia's heart sank as she imagined Janie's emotional posturing in the witness box.

Her lawyer advised her to plead guilty. She was sentenced to fifteen months' imprisonment. The tabloids blazed with stories and pictures of the procuress who procured her own granddaughter. Television programmes on child abuse were organised to coincide with the trial. Panels of TV pundits discussed the affair. And Sylvia Jarvis found herself, with a mixture of shock and fury, sitting in a green prison van with horizontally barred windows, alongside that day's haul from

the courts – two shoplifters, a fraudster and a drug offender –
heading for Holloway prison.

Six months into her sentence, Sylvia was looking out of the
window of a cell she shared with two others. The space
between the vertical bars on the window was especially
designed to prevent the women getting their heads through,
although one of her cell-mates had nearly managed it. A
huddle of women walked disconsolately round the asphalt
yard. Some of the younger ones played with a ball. She tried
to ignore the sound of screaming from the wing opposite and
the noise of abuse yelled by other women at the screamer. She
flicked with unseeing eyes through a magazine.

But it was not the noise so much as her growing
preoccupation with Janie Springer that prevented her from
reading. Janie Springer was becoming an obsession. She
imagined Janie in her leopard-skin leotard, puffing on a
cigarette in the pink boudoir of her Earl's Court flat, that
hypocritical smile on her face. She imagined her pushing a
trolley round the supermarket in her scuffed high heels and
obscenely tight skirt, the true hardness of her face showing
only when she thought no one else was looking. Every time
she thought of Janie, a volcano of hatred erupted in her chest.
For the first time in her life Sylvia Jarvis wanted to destroy
somebody. I have always introduced people to their fate, she
thought, why should I not also be able to introduce them to
their death?

The screams from the yard faded into the background as
Sylvia Jarvis concentrated on bringing an image of Janie
Springer to her mind. The picture became clear. Janie was
standing in the pink-furnished lobby of her Earl's Court
brothel grinning foolishly. Just out of shot, so to speak, Sylvia
Jarvis was aware that someone else was standing beside Janie.
She allowed her eyes to pan like a film camera to the left of
Janie's figure. She saw the arms and the broad shoulders and,
raising her eyes, finally the face. Of course. Mrs Jarvis smiled
to herself at the inevitability of it.

The face belonged to Mr Anstey, the accountant whom she had failed to satisfy when he had come to her for help.

From that moment on Sylvia Jarvis served the rest of her sentence with increasing light-heartedness. On the day of her release, she stepped through the gates feeling almost delirious with anticipation, to be greeted at the red brick entrance by her anxious daughter. They drove away from the place as quickly as possible. For a month, she stayed in Leicester with her daughter and Amy, who was as sweet as ever and waited on her grandmother hand and foot.

However, it was with relief that she returned to her own home in Mecklenburgh Square and lowered herself exhaustedly into the armchair to sit for a while in the peace of the front room which overlooked the square.

She thought hard and long over how to bring Mr Anstey and Janie Springer together. Then, with her instinct for balance, even in revenge, she decided that she too would write an anonymous letter, as Janie had to Dr Foreman. For a long time, she pondered over how she could get the letter directly to Mr Anstey without the risk of it being opened by a secretary. Then she remembered how he was obliged to lie on the floor of his office during lunch-breaks and listen to classical music in order to calm himself and recover his equilibrium. The secretaries, he had told her, always slipped out so that he could be left entirely on his own. She crossed town and went into a newsagent. At one o'clock precisely, she sent a fax to Mr Anstey.

It was unsigned and simply said:

What you need is at Flat 3, 115 Earl's Court Road between the hours of twelve and two o'clock in the afternoon.

Janie always attended to business at that time. Appointments were not made for clients until two in the afternoon, when the girls arrived. When Sylvia returned home, she absent-mindedly emptied her pot-pourri jars of orange and rose petals and filled them with lavender.

For the next few weeks, Sylvia Jarvis paid careful attention to news reports on the television. She took the trouble to go over to the Earl's Court district once a week and buy the local paper. Once she even walked past Mr Anstey's office in Wimpole Street at lunch-time where, in spite of the traffic, she could hear the faint sound of a cello concerto she did not recognise being played behind the closed windows.

She made no attempt to pick up the threads of her former life. Nearly all her former acquaintances had deserted her. She shopped in her local delicatessen and came back to her flat to make small delicious meals which she ate alone. On the whole, she felt calm and level-headed.

At the end of the third week, she saw what she had been expecting. The headline in the *Earl's Court Gazette* read:

BROTHEL BUTCHER MURDERS EX-SINGER

Janie Springer's body had been found wearing a black leather helmet and nothing else. She was placed on the floor in the front room of the brothel. Her eyes and mouth had been gouged out to match the openings in the leather helmet and a carving knife from the tiny kitchen had been used to slit her open from the sternum to her pubic mound. Traces of semen were found in the wound.

For several days after she read the report which was also featured on television, Sylvia Jarvis panicked in case she could be implicated in some way. However, months passed and the item disappeared from the news. She relaxed.

One morning, the letter-box flapped and she went to collect the mail. A thick letter in a brown envelope caught her attention. Inside were the photographs and deeds of owner-ship of a small, whitewashed house on the island of Paros in Greece. She studied the deeds curiously. They were in her name. Mr Anstey must have guessed, which alarmed her slightly but he would also know that his secret was safe with her. Nothing took long. The flat in Mecklenburgh Square was quickly sold.

Two months later, she was on a small boat with an

outboard motor, travelling through the warm evening air from Athens to Paros. The journey took several hours. As the sun sank in a riot of crimson on the horizon, the sea turned dark purple. Mrs Jarvis turned to the boatman who was next to her:

'How much longer will it take?'

'One hour,' he said, then added, 'You can smell the island from here even though you can't see it. Try.' She breathed in deeply and indeed she could smell a strong fragrance in the air.

'How lovely. What is that?'

'Lavender,' he replied.

'Ah yes. Of course,' she said. 'Lavender,' and turned her head to the sensuous massage of the evening breeze.

Lavinia Greenlaw

SPIN

The Giraffe House (1836)

A cool exaggeration, five-metre doors
made reasonable with Roman arches.
An arrangement of parts, the giraffe
carries himself off, all height, no weight.

His ancestor arrived in London at the dawn
of transcendentalism and acetylene.
Walking from the dock to Regent's Park,
he freaked at the sight of a cow in Commercial Road.

Fellow ungulates, they met in the year
of the Arc de Triomphe, *The Pickwick Papers*
and the birth of the state of Arkansas,
feats of design.

STOMP

The Elephant Pavilion (1965)

The idea is a herd in a scrum,
trumpeting out of fear or just for fun.
The Americans bombed North Vietnam.

Flower power, mini skirts, stalled effervescence.
The oxodised copper trunks
fizzing out of the concrete are only roof vents.

STOMP

Hessian, spotlights, the interior design
of the sleeping quarters is of its time, circular.
Just a skull and howdah as a reminder.

Linda Leatherbarrow

GORILLA

SOMETIMES I'M STILL for hours. The longer I sit still, the
more it pisses them off.

'He's not real, Mum. He's stuffed!'

'Course he's real. There, he moved.'

I'll slam myself at the bars in a minute and they'll scream.
Show the teeth and they'll scream again. It was sitting still
that first brought Garry over. He was a little guy, half
drowned in top hat and ringlets, pure bone wrapped up in
striped silk and perched on six-inch, hand-painted platforms.
Not that you noticed the boots. It was the eyes that got you.
Blue lightning eyes in a mud-coloured kisser.

'Wow, man,' he said. 'A monkey that meditates.'

I turned my head away slowly, turned my whole body
away, inch by inch, quiet, calm, thoughtful, went to the back
of the cage, picked up a handful of straw and shit, strolled
back to the bars then hurled the lot straight in his face.

Garry didn't blink. Debris trickled off his hat.

'I bet you can levitate too,' he said.

He slipped me a Bounty. I undid it and handed him back
the wrapper. If there's one thing I hate, it's untidiness.

Garry was the same, precise and unhurried, a creature of
routine. Most days, he went to the rose garden and hung little
silver foil packets on the bushes, tucking them in under the
blooms, then he sat down on the grass and waited for
custom. He took the money off the punters then told them
where to look.

'Check out the central bed,' he'd say. 'Yellow Rose of Sharon. Crimson Duchess.'

Usually, he dropped a little something into my drink, drizzled magic dust into my bowl.

'Stay loose, man,' he said.

Garry was the space between people, the side step into the dark.

He sat on the grass, lounging and smoking, and one by one the needy would come and go. He brought a tranny and turned the volume up so it made a room of sound, a secret space no one entered without permission.

'Come in, man,' he'd say. 'Got a light?'

He was the king of dreams but I was your nightmare. All the big stars came to see me. Everyone. They wanted that buzz. I was Kafka's beetle and God saying No! I was Harry Lime watering down penicillin. I was Hiroshima and Dr Mengele. Pop stars, royals, journalists, they all came. Oh yes, I was in the Sundays. A Life In The Day Of. Bloody nerve. All that stuff about Lomie. You don't know about Lomie? You've forgotten? Lomie was supposed to be my mate, soul mate. The public wanted a baby gorilla, something cute to ooh and aah at. Just the thought made me shudder but I didn't have a say, it was all decided.

'Lomie arrives next week,' said my keeper. 'Bet you can't wait. Twenty and still a virgin.'

I gave him one of my looks, showed him my teeth, may even have banged the bars a little, I don't remember. Put it this way, I wasn't amused.

Garry understood.

'Why get upset, man? Like sex is everything? What do they know?'

Just the same, twenty years is a long time to live on your own and I had bachelor habits, the whole pad to myself, empty space.

'No such thing as empty space, man,' said Garry. 'Not even a cage. All space comes pre-packaged, filled with dreams.'

Garry could say what he liked and I didn't mind.

We used to do the clubs together. He had an arrangement

with my keeper, a regular supply in exchange for the key. Garry needed protection and that was where I came in. Of course I was also a marker. Spot the gorilla and you were home. In Soho, we used to head down an alleyway, slide down the stairs to the basement, and knock on the door. Bang in the middle was a peep-hole with a shutter. The doorman opened it up a chink. He was built like me, long arms, barrel chest, wide as the door.

'How many are you?' he growled. 'Oh hi, Garry, how ya doing?' Then to me, 'Hi, man, nice suit.'

Before I went out with Garry, I'd spend hours getting ready, sitting in my den and combing my hair. Garry was just as fastidious about his appearance but he liked you to think his clothes were an accident.

'Why think about things, man? Just let them happen.'

I wished I had some of his cool. I was edgy, thinking about Lomie and what she might expect. It was only days before her arrival and I was beginning to lose it. The sun hurt my eyes during the day and at night I couldn't remember where I was. The clubs were all the same, dark and cobwebbed. The coloured lights spun on the ceiling but the walls were roughcast concrete, the floors stank of urine, the girls of patchouli, the steps of vomit, the doormen of Brut.

Garry fed me downers.

'When in doubt,' he said. 'Go with the paranoia. Trust me.'

I ran up the bars and swung from the ceiling.

'Forget her,' said Garry. 'Last night of freedom, right?'

We baby boomers were never logical.

I made myself presentable and waited in my den. It was nearly midnight when I heard Garry talking to my keeper.

'There you go, man,' he said. 'Be happy.'

A moment later, the back door opened and Garry smiled, all brown teeth and gaps. I used to get through twenty ice-cream cartons a day and as many sweets as I liked so I was particular about my teeth. Not Garry. Smiling was a mistake. Like a chasm opening up, the sudden drop into the dark.

We strolled through the park, cut down into Camden Town, then up West. Nights had a pattern we didn't like to vary, party-hopping in Belgravia, clubbing in St James's, run-ins with the local fuzz, run-ins with the local heavies. And girls. Always girls. They told Garry he had a cute bum, which he did, but he never took things further. Girls were good for business, decoy ducks, but Garry and I were a double act. He let them buy us a drink though. Vodka and lime was my tipple. Rum and black was Garry's. Lomie never drank anything but milk. Two pints a day. Disgusting.

Forget Lomie. She hadn't arrived yet and the night was still young. Sometime in the small hours we were back in Regent's Park, by the rose garden. Garry took a packet off a bush, sat down on the grass, opened it and rolled himself a joint.

'My grandmother was a Salishan Indian,' he said. 'A long time ago, man, when the world was young, there were only a few stars in the sky. Now, they are countless.'

Here, he paused, inhaled slowly as if he were smoking a peace pipe, narrowed his eyes and leant forward. He leant so far forward I thought he would fall on his nose.

'Each star is a campfire, man. Where the spirits can warm themselves.'

He meant people spirits. We animals were meant to stand in the cold and the dark, and watch. Garry could be a bit of a jerk at times. Most people have only four grandparents. With Garry, I lost count. In addition to the Salishan grandmother, there was also the last gypsy to be hung for horse stealing, the first woman submariner, a Chinese herbalist, a polar explorer, a Russian violinist and an African princess brought to Liverpool by white slavers. The last I could believe. Garry had a short nose, wide mouth and silky brown skin. He also had a Liverpool accent. Sometimes.

I lay back on the grass and imagined I was shopping with Garry, buying a suit in Lord John, pin stripes and a bowler hat. I bought a cane with the stars of the zodiac inlaid in ivory and a silver tobacco tin.

'Your grandmother is a Micmac Indian,' said Garry. 'And your granddaddy was white trash. You came out of the Californian dust bowl and you live in LA.'

I gave Garry a hug. All right, so three hours is a long hug

and I was seven foot wider than Garry but there was no need for him to freak.

'Far out,' he said, closing his eyes.

I looked at him lying on the grass. All over his waistcoat were hand-threaded beads. His buttonhole held an orchid. It always did. I put out my hand and touched his cheek but he didn't stir. It struck me that he might get cold so I went over to the roses, pulled off the petals and heaped them over him. I stripped most of the bushes before I got him covered. My hands are tough and I didn't notice the thorns. He looked peaceful. Like all the gaps in the storm clouds had closed up and now there was only rain. The lightning in his eyes had gone away, flashing off into the distance.

'See ya later,' I said and took myself home.

The next day my keeper announced the new rule. No Feeding The Animals. No sweets, no ice-cream. For three days, I stayed in my den, lay on the floor, moaned from time to time, and refused to move. Nothing happened. My keeper ignored me. He looked pretty rough in fact and every now and then he moaned himself. Eventually I got bored, went out into my show cage and took up the lotus position.

My keeper looked as bad as I felt. Sweat stood out on his brow, his hands shook.

'This is terrible, man,' he said.

I gave him a look.

There was a kid on the other side of the bars with a triple decker Neapolitan, an easy snatch, but my keeper didn't notice.

'Got any Valium?'

What was the matter with the guy and where was Garry? The space on the grass was empty, not so much empty as empty of Garry. A couple with a baby had put down a blanket and the girl was making daisy chains. She slipped one over the baby's head and laughed and suddenly I felt sick. There should have been music, Garry's beautiful room and the hungry stepping sideways through the sounds. There should have been Garry. I closed my eyes.

'He's not real, Mum.'

'Yes he is.'

'Don't he look like Dad?'

I threw myself at the bars, beat my chest and hollered. The little kid's ice-cream fell to the ground and he burst into tears.

'Now look what you've done,' said his mum. 'You big bully.'

The next day, Lomie arrived.

'Hello, darling,' she said.

I ignored her and waited for Garry but he never came. My head was still full of light and sounds and I groped around for my Cooper's pellets, scratching in the straw. Like, I ask you, why do they have to throw them on the floor? Lomie kept diving in, snatching them up, laughing at me and jumping away. Last thing I felt like was playing silly buggers.

With Lomie, I lost heart. Not that there's anything wrong with her, don't get me wrong. Lomie is a nice chick, if a bit of a hayseed. What got to me was the way she messed things up – banana skins, cabbage leaves. I like to stow the left-overs in my bowl but she just tosses them over her shoulder. It's little things like that that can sour a relationship. I mean she doesn't even clean her teeth. They're brown like Garry's. Every time she grins at me, I want to punch her in the face.

I did once or twice, we even had a wrestle, but I couldn't pretend to be interested. Lomie was a drag. Whenever I looked at her, I felt ashamed. Like I was letting her down. Crap. I never asked her to move in. Didn't fancy her, that was all. As I said, she's a great kid really and it wasn't her fault.

After a while they took her down to Bristol where she had a fling with Sampson, her dreamboat she called him. Leaky skiff if you ask me, all bilge and no boiler room. She came back and had her baby. I insisted on separate sleeping arrangements after that. I mean a guy has his pride. She does her thing and I do mine. Now, I never go out. I stay in my den and let Lomie entertain the crowd.

I sit with my back to them and think about Garry, think about the last time I saw him, the way he lay down after I'd hugged him, lay on the grass and looked up at the sky.

'It's all in the mind, man,' he says. 'All in the mind.'

For Guy the Gorilla 1946–1978

Alex Moseley

THE CAT FLAP

MY DAD HAD never really wanted children, he didn't think the world was fair enough or pleasant enough for them to grow up in but somehow he did have children. I'm not sure how, there has always been an abundance of storks in our village. My earliest memory was of a long yellow beak and soft white feathers that were warm and soft to the touch. Not only was I born but I had some brothers too. Can you imagine? Three kids for a man who believed the human race should just give up and call it a day. My brothers came by stork too. All at the same time. We were all the same age except I assumed I was the eldest and so hence adopted the persona. My brothers decided which of them was the eldest and which was the youngest. How they did that I don't know, that's their business.

When I was old enough to talk, my dad came into the kitchen to see how we were doing and he said to me:

'Son, I don't want to hamper your life with rules and oppressive doctrines. I firmly believe that you'd do a better job raising yourself, so you'd better get on with it and just see how it goes. You never know, it might be fun one day.'

He was a theorist, my father, and was always conducting a new experiment that would probably turn out to be nothing remarkable.

Me and my brothers did bring ourselves up. We used to walk around like a six-legged creature, looking at things and making observations of one kind or another. We were quite clever really. We saw our dad from time to time. He came into the kitchen one night (we only ever saw him in the kitchen as I don't think he really existed anywhere else apart from that small wooden room). He just stood there and looked at us for a bit. I was in the middle of preparing a quite difficult crab and lemon soufflé, I needed my concentration and could have done without absent parental observation so late in life. I was quite narked because the damn crab kept sticking his claw through the delicate but heady soufflé mix. My brother was cutting my other brother's hair, he wanted to look like Cary Grant for the season. My dad stood there grinning, seemingly pleased with his offspring. I said to him:

'Christ, Dad, I've burned the soufflé now. If you bother my culinary practices again I'll have to lock you out of the house for good.'

'OK, son, OK, don't fret,' he said in the responsibility-free way that he had. 'I was just checking that everything was present and correct.'

'Well it isn't. This was a celebratory dinner for Tractor' (We chose our own names). 'He has been accepted at Oxford to study philosophy, and crab and lemon soufflé is his favourite.'

'You shouldn't base your life on soufflé, son.'

'I know that, but it's the results that count, not the thought. I don't want him going away thinking how he could have had a good soufflé.'

'Yeah, and look what you've made me do to Tractor's hair, he looks more like Clark Gable than Cary Grant now, God dammit!'

'Clark Gable is an equally admirable icon of the silver screen, son. I'm sure most people wouldn't notice the difference.'

My father left us in peace after that. A burnt soufflé is one thing but a Cary Grant/Clark Gable image dilemma is something else. Even he realised that.

My brothers and I sat around the table that night and decided it would be best if Dad didn't distract us from what we were doing any more. I had always had a way with wood so I cut some good cherry from the edge of the village and I nailed up all the windows and doors in the kitchen. I reckoned the rest of the house was father-proof, seeing as he had only ever been seen in the kitchen. It made the kitchen quite dark but cherry is quite an amiable wood and it smelt great.

The next night we were sitting around the table again just talking and who should we see standing there, large as life, but our father. I had forgotten to nail up the catflap. It wasn't really a catflap because our cat was in fact an Irish wolfhound: we called him cat to test his loyalty, and to prove that he was loyal, he used to miaow at us. Our dad stood there grinning successfully, he'd outsmarted his sons for the first time despite their gallant efforts.

'You know, boys, I'm rather pleased with the way you guys have turned out, you could have been accountants or something. You should be grateful for my revolutionary fatherhood techniques.'

We thought about that for a few moments and then Tractor turned to him and said:

'You know, Dad . . . in a way I think we are.'

Hanif Kureishi

FOUR BLUE CHAIRS

AFTER A LUNCH of soup, bread and tomato salad, John and
Dina go out on to the street. At the bottom of the steps they
stop for a moment and he slips his arm through hers as he
always does. They have been keen to establish little regular-
ities, to confirm that they are used to doing things together.

Today the sun beats down and the city street seems
deserted, as if everyone but them has gone on holiday. At the
moment, however, they feel they are on a kind of holiday
themselves.

They would prefer to carry blankets, cushions, the radio
and numerous lotions out on to the patio. Weeds push up
between the paving stones and cats lie on the creeper at the
top of the fence as the couple lie there in the afternoons
reading, drinking fizzy lemonade and thinking over all that
has happened. Except that the store has rung to say the four
blue chairs are ready. They can't wait for them to be
delivered, but must fetch them this afternoon because Henry
is coming to supper tonight. They shopped yesterday: of the
several meals they have learned to prepare, they will have
salmon steaks, broccoli, new potatoes and three-bean salad.

Henry will be their first dinner guest. In fact he will be their
first visitor.

John and Dina have been in the rented flat two and a half
months already and most of the furniture, if not what they
would have chosen themselves, is acceptable, particularly the
bookshelves in all the rooms, which they have wiped down
with wet cloths. Dina is intending to fetch the rest of her

books and her desk, which pleases him. After that, it seems to him, there will be no going back. The wooden table in the kitchen is adequate. Three people could sit comfortably around it to eat, talk and drink. They have two brightly coloured table-cloths, which they bought in India.

They have started to put their things on the table, mixed up together. She will set something out, experimentally, and he will look at it as if to say, what's that, and she watches him; then they look at one another and an agreement is reached, or not. Their pens, for instance, are now in a shaving mug; her vase is next to it; his plaster Buddha appeared on the table this morning and was passed without demur. The picture of the cat was not passed but she won't remove it at the moment, in order to test him. There are photographs of them together, on the break they took a year ago when they were both still living with their former partners. There are photographs of his children.

But, at the moment, there is only one kitchen chair and neither of them wants to sit on the narrow seat and hard back.

John has said that Henry, whom she met once before at a dinner given by one of his friends, will take an interest in the blue chairs with the cane seats. Henry will take an interest in almost anything, if it is presented enthusiastically.

It has only been after some delicate but amiable discussion that they finally agreed to go ahead with Henry. John and Dina like to talk. Most of the time they talk. In fact she gave up her job so they could talk more. Sometimes they do it with their faces pressed together; sometimes with their backs to one another. They go to bed early so they can talk. It is part of how they enjoy one another. The one thing they don't like is disagreement. They imagine that if they start disagreeing they will never stop, and that there will be war. They have had wars and they have almost walked out on one another on several occasions. But it is the disagreements they have had before, with other people, and the fear that they will return, that seem to be making them nervous at the moment.

But they have agreed that Henry will be a good choice as a

first guest. He lives nearby and he lives alone. He loves being asked out. As he works near Carluccio's he will bring exotic cakes. There won't be any silences, difficult or otherwise.

They first saw the blue chairs four days ago. They were looking for an Indian restaurant nearby, and were discussing their ideal Indian menu, how they would choose the dall from this restaurant on King Street, and the bhuna prawn from the takeaway on the Fulham Road, and so on, when they drifted into Habitat. Maybe they were tired or just felt indolent, but in the big store they found themselves sitting in various armchairs, on the sofas, at the tables, and even lying in the deckchairs, imagining they were together in this or that place by the sea or in the mountains, occasionally looking at one another, far away across the shop, or closer, side by side, thinking in astonishment, this is him, this is her, the one I've chosen, the one I've wanted all this time, and now it has really started, everything I have wished for is today.

There seemed to be no one in the shop to mind their ruminations. They lost track of time. Then a shop assistant stepped out from behind a pillar. And the four blue wooden chairs, with the cane seats – after much sitting down, standing up and shuffling of their bottoms – were agreed on. There were other chairs they wanted, but it turned out they were not in the sale, and they had to take these cheaper ones. As they left, Dina said she preferred them. He said that if she preferred them, he did too.

Today on the way to the store she insists on buying a small frame and a postcard of a flower to go in it. She says she is intending to put this on the table.

'When Henry's there?' he asks.

'Yes.'

During the first weeks of their living together he has found himself balking at the way she does certain things, things he had not noticed during their affair, or hadn't had time to get used to. For instance the way she likes to eat sitting on the front steps in the evening. He is too old for bohemianism, but he can't keep saying no to everything and he has to sit there with pollution going into his bowl of pasta and the neighbours observing him, and men looking at her. He knows that this is part of the new life he has longed for, and at these times he feels helpless. He can't afford to have it go wrong.

The assistant in the store says he will fetch the chairs and they will be ready downstairs in a few minutes. They wait. At last two men bring the chairs out and stand them at the store exit. The couple are surprised to see that the chairs haven't come individually, or with just a little wrapping. They are in two long brown boxes, like a couple of coffins.

John has already said they can carry the chairs to the tube, and then do the same from there to the flat. It isn't far. She thought he was being flippant. She can see now that he was serious.

To show how it must be done, and indeed that it is possible, he gets a good grip on one box, kicks it at the bottom, and shoves it right out of the shop and then along the smooth floor of the shopping centre, past the sweet seller and the old women sitting on benches and the security guard.

At the exit he turns and sees her standing in the shop entrance, watching him, laughing. He thinks how lovely she is and what a good time they always have together.

She starts to follow him, pushing her box as he did his.

He continues, thinking that this is how they will do it, they will soon be at the tube station. But outside the shopping mall, on the hot pavement, the box sticks. You can't shove cardboard along on concrete; it won't go. That morning she suggested they borrow a car. He had said they wouldn't be able to park nearby. Perhaps they would get a taxi. But outside it is a one-way street, going in the wrong direction. He sees that there are no taxis. The boxes wouldn't fit in anyway.

Out there on the street, in the sun, he squats a little. He gets his arms around the box. It is as if he is hugging a tree. Making involuntary and regrettable sounds, he lifts it right up. Even if he can't see where he is going, even if his nose is pushed into the cardboard, he is carrying it, he is moving. They are still on their way.

He doesn't get far. Different parts of his body are resisting. He will ache tomorrow. He puts the box down again. In fact he almost drops it. He looks back to see that Dina is touching the corners of her eyes, as if she is crying with laughter. Truly it is a hot afternoon and it was a rotten idea to invite Henry over.

He is about to shout back at her, asking her whether she has any better ideas, but watching her, he can see that she does. She is full of better ideas about everything. If only he trusted her rather than himself, thinking he is always right, he would be better off.

She does this remarkable thing. She lifts her box on to her hip and, holding it by the cardboard flap, starts to walk with it. She walks right past him, stately and upright, like an African woman with a goat on her shoulders, as if this is the most natural thing. Off she goes towards the tube. This, clearly, is how to do it.

He does the same, the whole African woman upright stance. But after a few steps the flap of the cardboard rips. It rips right across and the box drops to the ground. He can't go on. He doesn't know what to do.

He is embarrassed now, and thinks people are looking at him and laughing. People are indeed doing this, looking at him with the box, and at the beautiful woman with the other box. And they look back at him and then at her, and they are splitting their sides, as if nothing similar has ever happened to them. He likes to think he doesn't care, that he is strong enough at his age to withstand mockery. But he sees himself, in their eyes, as a foolish little man, with the things he has wanted and hoped for futile and empty, reduced to the ridiculous shoving of this box along the street in the sun for ever.

You might be in love, but whether you can get four chairs home together is another matter.

She comes back to him and stands there. He is looking away and is furious. She says there's only one thing for it.

'All right,' he says, an impatient man trying to be patient. 'Let's get on with it.'

'Take it easy,' she says. 'Calm down.'

'I'm trying to,' he replies.

'Squat down,' she says.

'What?'

'Squat down.'

'Here?'

'Yes. Where do you think?'

He squats down with his arms out and she grips the box in the tree-hugging pose and tips it and lays it across his hands and on top of his head. Then, with this weight pushing down into his skull he attempts to stand, as Olympic weightlifters do, using their knees. But unlike those Olympic heroes he finds himself pitching forward. People in the vicinity are no longer laughing. They are alarmed and shouting warnings and scattering. He is staggering about with the box on his head, a drunken Atlas, and she is dancing around him, saying, 'Steady, steady.' Not only that, he is about to hurl the chairs into the traffic.

A man passing by sets the box down for them.

'Thank you,' says Dina.

She looks at John.

'Thank you,' says John sullenly.

He stands there breathing hard. There is sweat on his upper lip. His whole face is damp. His hair is wet and his skull itching. He is not in good shape. He could die soon, suddenly, as his father did. He reminds himself that he must enjoy himself and appreciate things while there is time.

Without looking at her, he picks up the box in the tree-hugging stance and takes it a few yards, shuffling. He puts it down and picks it up again. He covers a few more yards. She follows.

Once they are on the tube he suspects they will be all right. It is only one stop. But when they have got out of the train they find that getting the boxes along the station is almost impossible. The tree-hugging stance is getting too difficult. They carry one box between them up the stairs, and then return for the other. She is quiet now; he can see she is tiring, and bored with this idiocy.

At the entrance to the station she asks the newspaper seller if they can leave one of the boxes with him. They can carry one home together and return for the other. The man agrees.

She stands in front of John with her arms at her side and her hands stuck out like a couple of rabbit ears, into which the box is then placed. As they walk he watches her in her green sleeveless top with a collar, the sling of her bag crossing her shoulder, and the back of her long neck.

He thinks that if they have to put the box down everything will fail. But although they stop three times, she is concentrating, they both are, and they don't put the box down.

They reach the bottom of the steps. At last they stand the box upright, in the cool hall, and sigh with relief. They return for the other box. They have found a method. They carry it out efficiently.

When it is done he rubs and kisses her sore hands. She looks away.

Without speaking they pull the blue chairs with the cane seats from the boxes and throw the brown wrapping in the corner. They put the chairs round the table and look at them. They sit on them. They place themselves in this position and that. They put their feet up on them. They change the table-cloth.

'This is good,' he says.

She sits down and puts her elbows on the table, looking down at the table-cloth. She is crying. He touches her hair.

He goes to the shop for some lemonade and when he gets back she has taken off her shoes and is lying flat out on the kitchen floor.

'I'm tired now,' she says.

He makes her a drink and places it on the floor. Then he lies down beside her with his hands under his head. After a time she turns to him and strokes his arm.

'Are you OK?' he says.

She smiles at him. 'Yes.'

Soon they will open the wine and start to make supper; soon Henry will arrive and they will eat and talk.

Then they will go to bed and in the morning at breakfast time, when they put the butter and jam and marmalade out, the four blue chairs will be there, around the table of their love.

Toby Litt

TOURBUSTING

'WOULDN'T THE COOLEST thing now be to be Japanese?'

We are in Rotterdam Europe lost in thick fog together.

'A bridge over a river next to a church. Haven't we walked past this once before?'

That's me, name of Clap, dissecting the bridge–river–church interface. With me, Nippo-theorising, is Syph.

We are from Seattle. We are in a band called *okay*, lower case, italics. We are on our third European tour.

'I mean, think about it. We can't match those copycats for hipness. No way. You see, Clap, we've completely forgotten how to be ourselves. But *they* know how. They know that it's about choosing who you want to be, not being destined to be anyone in particular. And they are better at choosing than we ever were.'

'Can we sit down for a minute,' I say. 'I'm not feeling too great.'

'When the Japanese are punks, they are the greatest punks ever; when they are rockabillies, not even Elvis can touch them.'

Twenty days in.

This is it – we have reached the point of self-annihilation. So much of what comprises who one is has been left behind. Jackson Browne found a phrase for it, Running On Empty. In this non-state you can go for two days without having a single real thought. *How did I get here?* – that is the thought that most intrudes. The non-thought is always – *next, next, next*. Next gig. Next girl. Next goodbye. Aspects of it I do

285

sincerely appreciate – I love the sense of left-behindness. You never use a bar of hotel soap more than once – if at all. (And if you're really sensible, you carry your own with you: so that's not a very good example.) But if you don't like something – a magazine containing a bad review, a tape that's gone fucked in your Walkman – you just drop it. Within seconds, it is miles away. Another country. (As the lyrics to my favourite of our songs go: 'I've reached out in the dark to touch things that are a thousand miles away'.) Similarly, if you freak out some girl and she has hysterics at you, she's two towns behind before her slap even hits your face. You become impervious to pain – of a non-serious sort. Self-harm becomes a bit of a game. (Not that *okay* are great ones for stage-diving. It's not part of our image.) You eat nothing but shit. You look like a piece of shit. And you talk shit a hundred per cent of the time.

Twenty days to go.

'You see them, walking around downtown – children dressed like souvenir teddy-bears – groups of girls with their heads close together and their hands over their mouths – couples holding hands, each so cool you can't decide between them – serious young men buying huge stacks of CDs – companymen, who break into a mild sweat as they move from the pavement to the road – senior citizens in beige and fawn golfing clothing.'

I am the drummer. Syph is the lead vocalist. We have a bassist, Mono. We have a rhythm guitarist, Crabs.

Our mothers did not call us by these names – though Syph's is starting to. None of us know if she knows what it means.

'Do you remember when we were on tour in Tokyo?'

'I feel bad. I'm sitting down. You can keep walking.'

I sit down on a low concrete wall with black railings stuck in it looking out across a street of cobblestones and grey-green walls.

'Like, no one gives blowjobs like the Japanese. It's the kind of thing they probably have instruction manuals about that are a thousand years old. Like the Kama Sutra.'

'The Kama Sutra is Indian.'

I stand up, lean over the railings and puke into the hedge. 'They do ancient things with their tongues and with the roofs of their mouths.'

I hear a whining sound.

'Did you fart?' I ask.

Syph looks shocked. He can't remember.

'I don't think so,' he says. 'Was it in tune?'

I lean back over the fence and look beyond the hedge. I see a paw, an ear – black and white.

I turn back to Syph.

'I think I just puked on someone's dog.'

'Are they Japanese?' he says, and does ancient things with his tongue.

'What are we going to do?' I ask.

'We need to score.'

Syph is right – we smoked the last of the grass before the border. Syph is superstitious about carrying grass over international divides. He says it has to do with Paul McCartney. But he is quite happy about having speed in his pocket while making passport control. Which means that, until we have scored some dope in each new city, he is unbearable. And because he is likely to speed his way into getting arrested, I always go with him to try and track something down. If we are lucky, there's someone from the local fan club to help us connect. But *okay* aren't very big in Rotterdam, as we are finding out.

'I'm going to have a look at it.'

'Whatever,' says Syph, and plucks his Marlboros from his suit pocket.

Members of *okay* wear suits at all times. We play gigs in suits and we play basketball in suits. It's part of our image.

Our music is slow and formal with lyrics about love and guilt. We also sing about the sea.

We sound like the Velvet Underground on quarter-speed.

Climbing over the fence feels surprisingly easy. I haven't eaten anything in two days. Maybe I am getting the better of gravity.

I fall into the hedge, branches digging into my legs through my suit.

With a flip of my arms I roll off on to a patch of grass.

'Are you okay?' says Syph.

'Dollar,' I reply, keeping very still.

Whenever one of us uses the name of our band in a context not relating specifically to our band, that person is required to put a dollar in the stash-pot. It is a band rule.

'You didn't break your back?'

'I'm fine,' I say. I haven't opened my eyes yet. I don't feel any pain in my body.

Then a warm wetness crosses my nose and I smell a bad smell. I open my eyes into the face of the dog.

'Hi,' I say.

It continues licking.

I'm not sure if the bad smell is the smell of the dog's breath or the smell of my puke, which runs all down the dog's back.

I roll away. The dog tries to follow me, to carry on licking, but it is tied to the hedge by its lead.

'You've gone all quiet,' says Syph, then laughs. 'Is the dog Japanese?'

'Throw me your cigarettes and your lighter,' I say.

He throws them. I light up. I throw them back.

'Shit,' he says. 'That almost went down the drain.'

'Sorry,' I say.

I lie on my side on the lawn in Rotterdam Europe, looking at the dog.

It is a mongrel, black and white. It doesn't look like anything much. Except thin. It looks kind of bony and shaky. Like Syph.

Syph got the job of lead-singer mainly on the strength of his hips. To this day, he's never been able to find a pair of pants that stay up. His mother used to make him wear dungarees or suspenders. At school we called him Wall Street.

The girls always loved him. Still do.

Some nights I get seconds and some nights thirds and maybe once a tour I'll settle for fourths. But Syph always gets firsts.

We drummers have our own distinct kind of girls. They are enthusiastic long before you are successful and loyal long after you're shit.

Drummer-girls tend to have long hair and large breasts and bring their own contraceptives and leave when asked.

Lead-singer-girls, from what I've seen and heard of them, are model-like and neurotic and bring drugs and want to do really weird sex-things on you so that you never forget them.

Some nights Syph doesn't even get laid, because none of the girls in that town comes up to his high standards. But that is way rare. Syph's standards vary from town to town. Sometimes he ends up with Little Miss Rancid-and-a-half. (And I end up with her mutant grandmother.)

'It's a nice dog,' I say.

I look down at myself. There are a couple of muddy paw prints on my shirt. There is a bit of puke on my lapel.

'I think it's homeless.'

'Hey!' I hear Syph shout. 'Hey! Yeah!'

'Yeah?' I say.

'Come over here, I wanna talk to you. Yeah, come on. yeah. Hi, I'm Steve.'

It was a girl. It wasn't hard to tell.

'What's your name?'

There is a giggle.

'I'm Inge.'

'Would you like a cigarette, Inge?'

'I have to go.'

'Hey, Syph!' I shout. 'Ask her if she knows whose dog this is?'

'Who is there?' Inge asks.

She was *so* beautiful. I just knew it was going to break my heart all over again to watch Syph closing his hotel door behind them as they walked in, smiling. She was so beautiful I didn't even need to see her to know it.

'That's my drummer,' said Syph. 'He's found a dog.'

Inge says, 'A dog?'

'Yeah,' says Syph. 'Woof-woof.'

Usually the beautiful ones laugh at Syph's unfunny funny

jokes. And the more beautiful they are, the more they laugh.
And the sooner that door closes behind them.

I decide to stand up.

'Do you happen to know where we might chance upon
some blow?' Syph is now doing his comic Englishman.

When I get to my feet I find myself standing face to face
with an angel called Inge, with only a vomit-covered hedge
separating us. Inge is very slim with short-cropped white-
blonde hair. Her eyes are dream-blue. And oh her skin . . .

'I'm Inge,' she says.

Syph rises to stand slim-hipped beside her.

'I'm Brian,' I say, hating my name totally.

'Where is the dog?' she asks.

'It's down here,' I point. 'Is this a garden or something?'

'I think it is a park,' Inge says. 'I will come round.

Without turning towards Syph she starts off.

When she gets a few paces away Syph looks at me and
mouths: *mine*.

I shake my head.

'Musical differences,' I say. This is the threat anyone in the
band always makes when they take something so seriously
that they are prepared to break up the band over it.

'I saw her first,' says Syph. 'You wouldn't even have said
hi.'

'If it hadn't've been for the dog, she'd've walked off.'

'I tell you, if she goes for me I'm having her.'

Inge has found a way into the park.

'Hello,' she said, and holds out her hand to be shook.
'Brian.'

She has an angel's ankles.

'Hi,' I say.

We shake.

Then she turns her attention seriously to the dog, addressing it in Dutch or whatever language they speak in Rotterdam. She can't fail to notice the puke, but she doesn't seem to
associate it with me. I reach in my pocket and take out some
gum to chew, to get rid of the smell.

Syph climbs up on the railings, jumps the hedge and joins us.

'What does he say?' I ask. 'Does he belong to anyone? Are they coming back?'

Inge says, 'I think he was left because they did not want him.'

'Sometimes they have addresses on their collar,' says Syph.

Inge says, 'There is no address.'

She stands up.

'What were you going to do?' she asks.

I look at Syph. Inge's eyes follow mine.

'Well,' he says, 'we are actually going to score some blow. Do you know where we could find some?'

Inge turns back to me – a little shrug, eyes rolling to the heavens where she belongs.

'I was going to wait here to see if his owner came back. Then I was going to try and find a police station.'

And please can I kiss you?

'Give me your handkerchiefs,' she says.

Members of *okay* have handkerchiefs in the breast pockets of our suits at all times. It's part of our image.

'We must clean the dog.'

I hand over part of my image quite happily. Syph is flirting with the idea of refusing and of using his refusing as a way of flirting.

'Give it her,' I say.

Inge cleans most of my puke off the black and white dog with our handkerchiefs.

'Do you want them?' she asks.

Syph says, 'Nope.'

I say, 'Yep.'

Inge hands them back, and I wrap them in the handkerchief I always keep in my side pocket for real use.

'I will take you to the police station,' Inge says.

Syph looks at me with *no way* in his eyes.

'But we have to be somewhere else,' he says. 'Don't we?'

'I'll come with you,' I say.

Inge kneels down and unties the dog's lead from the branch of the hedge.

'But we need to score,' says Syph.

'See you back at the hotel,' I say.

Inge looks inquiringly at both of us.

'Come on, boy,' I say to the dog.

Inge speaks to it in the Rotterdam language.

We walk off, leaving Syph behind.

Outside the park gates we turn left into the fog.

'You are a drummer in a group?' Inge asks.

I am stunned. She's been paying more attention to Syph than she's let on. She really doesn't like him.

'Yeah. We're on tour. We're playing tonight at some club.' As I am halfway through the line, I go on with it anyway. 'Would you like to come?'

'Maybe,' she says. 'The police station is very close here.'

I hear footsteps running behind us in the fog. I don't need to look. Things have been going too well. It is Syph.

'I thought I'd lost you guys,' he says.

Inge leads us up to a doorway and into the police station.

Inge tells the policeman the story in the Rotterdam language. He then asks us to confirm a few details in English. It seems like Inge's left out any mention of the puke. I am glad of that.

We give them the name and address of our hotel.

Inge gives them her address and telephone number.

Inge and I say goodbye to the dog and watch the policeman take it off down a long white corridor.

On the foggy street outside the police station, Inge says, 'What is the name of your band?'

'It's *okay*,' I say. 'Spelt o-k-a-y.'

'Do you know where we can score?' whispers Syph.

Inge looks at him pitifully.

'Come on,' she says, and leads us off round the corner.

Unexpectedly, she stops, reaches into her rucksack and brings out a clingfilm-wrapped chunk of dope. She breaks off a corner and hands it to Syph.

'God,' he says. 'The woman of my dreams.'

Inge turns to me.

'You are a kind person,' she says, and kisses me on the cheek. 'Goodbye.'

I watch as she walks off into the fog.

Syph doesn't even look. He is sniffing the dope.

'This is really good shit,' he says. 'Let's get back to the hotel.'

That evening the lighting set-up means that I am unable to see anything of the audience – it is just a sheet of white light which applauds whenever we finish a song.

Our set-list goes: Thousand, Blissfully, Jane-Jane, Mother-hood, Sea-Song #4, Hush-hate-hum, Walls, Queen Victoria, Long Cold Lines, With Strings, Gustav Klimt and Work. We encore with Sea-Song #1 and our cover of Marquee Moon.

Syph dedicates one song to a girl we met today. Thanks. Etcetera. For services rendered.

At the end of the encores, I walk straight up to the mike and say, 'Inge, if you're here, I'll see you in the bar.'

Two Inges show up, neither of which is the right one.

Back in the dressing-room there is a drummer-girl but I brush her off.

'I'm going for a walk,' I say.

'What?' says Mono.

'A walk?' says Crabs.

'See you back at the hotel,' I say.

'Maybe,' says Syph, who has one girl sitting in his lap and one opening him a beer.

For an hour or so, I wander about trying to find my way back to the park. But the fog has gotten even thicker and everywhere looks even more the same.

I stop a cab and tell the guy to take me back to the hotel.

Inge is sitting in the lobby with the black and white dog at her feet. As I walk up, the dog I puked on recognises me and starts to strain on its lead.

'You didn't come to the gig,' I say.

'I was there,' she says. 'I left.'

'I asked you to meet me in the bar. Didn't you hear?'

'I thought you would get another girl. I wanted to see. I came to wait here.'

'What, you were testing me?'

'I don't know,' she says, smiling. 'Maybe.'

'Hi,' I say to the dog.

Someone has obviously given it a bath. And love. He licks the salty spaces between my fingers, looking up at me with wet eyes.

'Brian, meet Brian,' says Inge.

'They let you keep it?' I ask.

'I went back and told them that the story we said before was a lie. I told them that I lived with you and that you didn't want the dog, so that you made me give it to them. I told them that we had split up and that I wanted my dog back. They didn't want the problem of a dog. They gave it to me without question.'

'Do you have a boyfriend?' I ask.

'No,' she says. 'I have a dog called Brian.'

I am very close to saying woof-woof.

Just then, Syph and his two girls, both Japanese, plus Mono, Crabs and their girls, plus several other girls and a couple of boys come through the hotel doors.

'Great dope,' Syph says to Inge as he walks up.

His girls are already getting jealous. They touch him even more.

'Musical differences,' I say to the whole band. 'I'm afraid to say.'

'Nice doggie,' says Mono.

'Irreconcilable musical differences.'

'Really?' asks Crabs.

'You have dope,' asks one of Mono's girls.

'Yes,' I say. 'I think so.'
Syph says, 'No way.'
'Yoko,' says Crabs.
I smile at Inge and she smiles back.
'Let's go,' Inge says.
And I say, 'Okay.'

That last bit didn't really happen. It's just how I day-dreamed it the following afternoon on the tourbus. Cologne was next. Then Munich. Then Berlin. Nineteen days to go. What really happened was that I went back to the hotel, alone, only to find Inge not there. No sign of that dog, either. Then I went for a walk, to try and find the park or the police station. But I couldn't. I got lost again in the fog. Then I stopped a cab and told the guy to take me back to the hotel. That detail was true. Syph and the others were there in the bar with a group of girls. None of them was Japanese. But one of them I saw straight off was a drummer-girl. I think she had long hair and large breasts and brought her own contraceptives and left when asked. It's just, you meet so many and remember so few.

Elizabeth Berridge

OLD AGE IS NOT FOR CISSIES

THE COLONEL SAT in the winter garden at Beech Grove at a small cast-iron table well away from the dropping rust of the framed glass windows above his panama'd head. He had enjoyed his lunch and now dozed through advertisements in *The Lady*, left by one of the other residents, blessing his escape from refined widows willing to housekeep for gentlemen in their seventies and no hanky-panky.

This magazine was evidently required reading for elderly or middle-aged persons left alone. Cries of fear and courage and appalling loneliness seeped out through these chin-up offers. Capable, cheerful lady, family grown-up (and gone away like foxes to their earths). Own car. Good gardener, manager, cook. Willing to do light housework. South Coast preferred. He had seen similar offers in *The Times* and *Daily Telegraph* and in less reputable papers where the offers were more forthcoming and titillating. In these, women boldly advertised their charms, seeking fun, companionship and 'something more'. Men, too, sought slim blondes of between 30–40 with a liking for classical music, good conversation and 'something more'.

He was lucky to have a pension to top up his savings – and the money left him by his wife – which enabled him to live in this comfortable retirement home among reasonably congenial people. One of whom came up behind him now.

'It makes one think of Charlotte Brontë, all that brave gentility,' said Miss Lapidus, looking over his shoulder, catching him out. 'Are you thinking of leaving us, Colonel, for a willing widow?'

'Thank God, no.' Rising, he pushed forward the other heavy iron chair with its dented chintz cushion.

As always, the Colonel was glad to see Miss Lapidus. Since Christmas they had been spending more time out here, sharing the fitful sun with the geranium cuttings and houseplants that hibernated on the broad ledges. He liked her, yes. She flowed quietly into her chair, she did not chatter, she never offered to mend his socks. More than ever, she seemed to him as comfortable as well-handled silver, as full of quality as his soft pigskin wallet. Soon, when the weather grew warmer, he would ask her to come with him to Kew Gardens. He would motor her there in his Rover, which he rarely used these days – keeping it more as a gesture of independence and saving his stiff leg. He would give her tea at The Maids of Honour. Maybe he wouldn't go up to town by himself any more. That silly business the other day with the impertinent chit at the National Gallery had quite upset him. There were new young members at the Army and Navy Club, and he'd lunched alone. He had called in at the Oriental, but there was nobody who remembered him except the old hall porter. He'd stayed long enough to send his nephew's boy a line on the familiar headed writing paper, addressing an envelope with the little embossed elephant on the flap. Well, the lad might be impressed. The Colonel always collected his stationery from the clubs to which he had once belonged. He reckoned he was owed something, all the money they'd had off him in the past.

About once a month Colonel Penberthy found his way up to the National Gallery to look again at Rubens's women. The train service from Dorking to Victoria was convenient and quick. He did not regard this outing as a spree, although certain members of the staff at Beech Grove did so. 'The Colonel's off again on one of his sprees then,' the local girl who came in to help with the ironing giggled to the housekeeper. Together they would watch him; tallish, spare, his back straight, his left leg swinging awkwardly as he marched off down the drive.

'He ought to use a stick,' said the housekeeper.

I ought to have brought my cane, thought the Colonel, but that would be giving in.

The journey excited him, and in order to taste the fullness of a London day he sat on the top deck of the bus to Piccadilly, planning to walk down to Trafalgar Square. The stir of traffic and people made him blink a little faster and his heart jolt with pleasure. He felt like an animal after hibernation; tentative, hungry, receptive. The strange young people of the 1990s sat around the statue of Eros in tiers, or leaning against the protective barriers, drinking out of tins, eating hamburgers. He could smell the grease. Pity the fountain had stopped playing. None of these hefty young people in shorts or torn jeans could know what it had once been like, frolicsome on its island among buses and taxis, with Londoners criss-crossing in a hurry to avoid a soaking. Piccadilly Circus, the hub of a once-great Empire.

He looked up at Eros. That little God of Love was shooting his arrow in the wrong direction, down the Haymarket instead of up into Shaftesbury Avenue. It always irritated him, getting it wrong like that. Nobody knew their history nowadays, Lord Shaftesbury was forgotten after all his work for the abused factory children of a century ago. Wait a bit, though, words changed their meanings, and the abuse he meant was exploitation, wickedly long hours that killed childhood. You had to watch how you put things these days.

Once he had asked a thin and shaggy youth with a rolled sleeping bag on his shoulder where he was from; he had the air of a traveller. But was confounded when he'd belatedly disentangled the meaning from a thicket of contorted Midland vowels.

'Hitched up from Brum. Spare any change, mate?'

He had given the boy – for that was what he was, a boy – a handful of coins and moved on quickly. Beggars embarrassed him. Of course, the Strand was full of them, youngsters sleeping rough in doorways. Girls, too. He'd seen them on the box, wedged between the cold stone angles of office buildings. They looked as if they needed a bath and a haircut, poor young devils. But the encounter had made him feel out of touch. This wasn't his remembered London with poverty so blatantly on show. He thought of his father's London; wide clean streets fit for gentlemen to walk along to their clubs, a carnation in one's buttonhole from one of those old flower sellers. Or a sprig of white heather from a gypsy near Fortnum's, offered with a smile and a blessing for the tendered half-crown.

Was this why he had fought the war?

He walked briskly enough into Trafalgar Square. The geometric symmetry of it, unchanged, made him feel less of a *revenant*, less troubled. He looked benignly on the massed pigeons, clattering among the tourists throwing grain; at the fountains' private rain blowing in the cold wind as it had always done. He sent a comradely nod up to Nelson on his plinth, still riding high. As he passed a fringe of young men and women hanging over the balcony of the National Gallery on his way in he was briefly comforted by the thought that it took more than wars and their aftermath to cancel out enduring certainties.

Inside it was warmer. Hushed, yet full of quiet activity. There was space, but enclosed space, with ceilings out of sight, a great sweep of steps, wide corridors. As he trod over the Roman mosaic, familiar figures in muted patterns beneath his feet calmed him. What should be the first, as an entrée – the Cuyp landscapes with all those cows, the Rembrandts? Was Saskia still there as Flora, and that other woman, his mistress, hoisting up her skirts in a stream? Rembrandt buoyed him up. He felt an affinity with the unsentimental, Puckish toughness of those later self-portraits. He walked through several galleries dominated by patriarchal figures grouped around columns, congealed in the aspic of the past making statements no one now heeded. Then, at last, the Rembrandts. To his surprise the room was empty apart from the slumped figure of an elderly bearded man on a bench. The

Colonel walked over to look at the portrait on the wall near by, 'Old Man in an Armchair'.

As he stared at it, the man on the bench below shifted his position, wafting a fetid breath of musty layers of clothes and some sharp spirit. They exchanged glances, the Colonel looking back keenly at him, then up at the picture. There was no doubt about it. That old man up there sitting in the wooden armchair three hundred years ago could be a tidied up version of this tramp – tramp he must be, come in out of the cold. Hadn't Rembrandt in his lean times been known to haul a vagrant in off the street; give him a square meal, throw a rich Venetian cloak round him, sit him down and start to paint? This old man, with his empty contemplative eyes, had the same hint of ruined nobility, all but lost behind his unpruned beard. Then he put a hand up to his face, just as in the portrait.

Impulsively the Colonel pulled out a five-pound note, crushed it into the mittened hand, nodded, said, 'Well, there you are then, up there.' Gave him a wink and walked away, his leg turning painfully, feeling a fool. Probably this was the old rogue's pitch, before he was thrown out by an attendant. A clever old rogue, so blast that. Maybe he was an eccentric millionaire like that late Howard Hughes, with a Swiss bank account. Blast that too. Such encounters spiced up a dull life, and the Colonel was smiling as he came at last to Rubens.

Rubens's wonderful women never changed. He felt himself relax, expanding into happiness. He was all eyes, all response, savouring the richness of that honey-and-cream flesh. No woman he had ever known had those pink shadows in buttock or elbow, or tucked away in the body's secret places. No woman – certainly not his meagre wife – had possessed that beautiful ample flesh sitting solid, rounded and mellow and yielding and melting. He longed to draw a slow, gentle finger down the curve of that backbone, down and down . . .

'Ha,' said the Colonel aloud, letting out a long sigh. 'There's my roly-poly!'

A smothered giggle by his side stopped his tongue.

'Doing a Bloom, are you?' asked a thin elderly-looking

schoolgirl with bold black eyes. He didn't understand what she was saying or where she had come from, but his eyes blazed at her as she walked off jauntily. He watched her go, noting the skin-tight jeans that imprisoned small buttocks hard as boiled eggs. They topped concave thighs that let the light through. Yes, go away, miss. Thin squeaky bones and bitter knowing tongue. Go away at once. But his morning was spoilt.

In the winter garden Miss Lapidus watched the Colonel doze off suddenly in the heat thrown out by the glass panes. She was accustomed to these unheralded catnaps and noted how, as with many other retired professional soldiers, war and its aftermath had acted like a clever embalmer, bequeathing a look of animation yet drying him up. The flush in his cheeks, the brown scalp which gives baldness a pleasing patina, were legacies of desert commands. Seemingly alive, inwardly scoured and dried, he walked and talked stiffly about a world he had expected – and hoped – to leave. His thin eyelids flickered in dream time, his mouth pursed up to release several small explosive puffs of air.

He intrigued Francesca Lapidus, who was having trouble with her embroidery. She was completing the third square in the story of the life of a Persian beauty, Laila, for a firescreen. The lapdog Laila was holding looked more like a cat. This discrepancy bothered her, because a favourite theme of Urdu poetry was the devotion women demanded their lovers should extend to their lapdogs. However unliberated women were judged to be in the East, what Western poet had ever written lines like Hafiz to his sweetheart?

> *I hear that dogs have collars*
> *Why don't you put one round Hafiz's neck?*

How had the Colonel been as a lover? she wondered idly, unpicking the delicate stiches. All that he had said of his wife was that she was very light-boned, adding apologetically,

'Like thistledown,' as he told sympathetic listeners of her extraordinary end. 'Blown off a cliff near Beachy Head. The wind got up under her deckchair.' Had a tiny smile lurked under his moustache? 'I was in Abu Dhabi at the time.'

What sort of woman would allow herself to be blown off a cliff? And at Eastbourne of all places. No blame can be attached to me, the Colonel's attitude seemed to imply. Yes, he intrigued her.

Miss Lapidus's own life had not been unadventurous, although she never spoke of it. She had made two foolish choices, one during the war. Shared danger was a powerful aphrodisiac, she had found, and she was certainly not alone in that. Then, some time later while doing some research into Persian miniatures for a publisher, she had started a long and intermittent affair with one of the Museum experts in this field. A married man. To his chagrin, she had finished it on her fifty-eighth birthday and sometimes regretted it. Yet she had found that a celibate and uncomplicated life was more to her taste, and her fascination with Persian art remained.

A sudden flurry of hail against the glass hexagons of the conservatory woke the Colonel up, with a tiny snore he contrived to conceal. He had been dreaming about lying clean-picked in the desert and these days it took a little time to reassemble himself. Yes, he thought, watching Miss Lapidus working at her petit point; noting her pretty hands, plump and deft. We'll go to Kew. I'll ask her. And began to hum the old tune, 'Come down to Kew in lilac time . . .' but couldn't remember how it went on.

'. . . It isn't far from London,' Miss Lapidus finished, lifting her head with a smile. She laughed because love was on her mind. 'I had a proposal in Kew Gardens when I was seventeen. So romantic under the cherry trees.' She laid three strands of silk on her frame: purple, blue, green. 'But he was killed in the war, poor young man.'

The Colonel was silent. What could he say that would not upset her? Luckily the tea-bell jangled from inside the house. Miss Lapidus put away her embroidery slowly and said, as he stood by her chair,

'No, you go in, Colonel. I'll follow later.'

Alone, she waited a moment, then went upstairs to her room. Today she could not face the drawing-room for tea, did not want to see the old, expectant faces turned up to be fed. In an elegant suede boot in her wardrobe was a bottle of dry sherry. On a shelf, tucked underneath a black velvet beret (such as Rembrandt wore in one of his self-portraits – floppy on him but becoming on her), was a crystal sherry glass and a packet of Marie biscuits. They mopped up the evidence, she had found.

'Ah, thank God,' she said as she drank. Kew! In lilac time, and with the Colonel. And yet, after her second glass, sitting on the bed leafing through a book of Anne Thackeray's letters, she smiled to read, 'Who says Youth's stuff will not endure? It lasts as long as we do and is older than age.' Good for Annie Thackeray.

The next afternoon the winter garden was empty. The Colonel had spent the morning polishing his Rover. He was told that Miss Lapidus had had 'one of her heads' and gone for a walk. He felt curiously aggrieved: he would have gone with her if she'd asked him. But she hadn't. He would have put on his old tweed hat and taken up his blackthorn. Together they could have gone striding out along country lanes. He felt left out, as he had done years ago at prep school when young Fisher chose another boy to walk with him to church.

Then, as luck would have it, he spotted old Gilpin in his wheelchair, outside in the fitful sun. Apart from his being the only other man in the place, the Colonel had taken to him after overhearing an interchange between him and one of the irritating women residents.

'You don't want to sit staring into space, Mr Gilpin,' she had said strongly, rustling up with her newspaper, hoping to pick what few brains she considered he had left for the crossword.

'Why not?' Old Gilpin had swivelled an unsteady eye at her. 'I see more in space than most people.'

So now the Colonel suggested that they might take a walk together, and propelled the wheelchair away and out of the gates and along to his favourite place near by: a large overgrown churchyard where they could do some birdwatching. Old Gilpin was never without his binoculars.

Apart from the birds, he liked the churchyard. It was full of positive statements, headstones standing to attention or slewed like fainting soldiers, their legends brief and to the point. Name, age, station in life. He ignored the regrettable craven expectations; it was like asking for mercy from an enemy to waffle on about being gathered in to everlasting arms. There was one grave they always passed by, a stone table top with the legend: *A Hero of the Indian Mutiny. Aged 37. 'I hope I have done my duty.'* The Colonel envied him for dying at his peak.

Old Gilpin had his binoculars levelled.

'Great tit, if I'm not mistaken,' he said. 'Listen. He's in that tree.'

The song went on, strong and clear, matching the green striving of spring. But the Colonel grew restive.

'That bird's an idiot, Gilpin. It's all wrong. It has no reason to sing, man! He's a disappointed bachelor, all the females have been snapped up by now ... It's too late.'

Old Gilpin lowered his binoculars; the bird had flown away, chastened. Indignantly he said, 'How d'you know it isn't a lovecall that's already been answered, eh?'

'Did *you* hear any answer?'

Old Gilpin wasn't up on the mating habits of great tits. He suspected his friend of coming on this nugget of information in some newspaper article, and using it to best him.

'No, you didn't,' the Colonel went on now. 'That bird was desperate. What interests me is that Nature appears to have no inhibiting factor in a case like this. That song will now attract predators – not a mate – if it goes on with that call ...' From a distant part of the churchyard they heard the song start up again defiantly as if to mock his words, and the Colonel clapped his hands. 'Stop that, fool bird!'

He pushed the chair roughly and rapidly over the grass and along the paths, its occupant swaying from side to side, until the Colonel's temper cooled. They went soberly up the drive.

'You're laughing,' he said. 'But I'm right, you know. Sorry if I banged you about.'

Old Gilpin had to catch his breath.

'You've hit it, Penberthy. That bird could teach us old men a thing or two.'

But the Colonel was not listening. Miss Lapidus was also coming up the drive, her cheeks pink and bonny from the sharp sunny air. She greeted them cheerfully and he asked, with a new, bullying bonhomie,

'And where have you been, to look so chirpy?'

'I'm dying for a cup of tea. Let me take my things off first and I'll tell you.'

The drawing-room did not bother her today, but she chose an alcove by the bay window with just two chairs with their backs to the room. She accepted a buttered scone and said, 'I went to the Woodland Gardens to look at the Children of Israel. There weren't many people, but spreads of early daffodils out under the beech trees.'

'Aha!' He put on a good face. 'And I take it they hadn't crossed the Red Sea yet, eh?'

She did not smile, but looked evenly at him across the rim of her cup.

They had gone together once, on a crisp winter's day, to see these fabulous threatened Children of Israel, her refugees, as she fancifully called them. By the side of a straight channel of water cut from a nearby lake were several swamp cypresses whose roots rose in a long ragged column, each a foot or more above the water's edge. This strange formation had some biological purpose to do with breathing, he understood. He had taken them for tree stumps at first glance before he realised that the texture of the thin reddish bark was too supple for dead wood. They stood in groups, these blunted rudimentary figures which Miss Lapidus had insisted were families awaiting rescue: grandmothers with shawled heads, bent and clutching; young children held hard against parents' shoulders. One or two patriarchal figures gesturing, standing out, going ahead alone into the water as if watching for a deliverance that never came.

To her it was obvious: Nature copying Art. Henry Moore came to mind, for who could not respond to that stolid endurance, that curious privacy? Her companion's non-comprehension made her feel lonely. Worse, she felt she had been guilty of a misjudged enthusiasm, a flight indeed of fancy, which belittled her.

But she could not know how much they had repelled him as he gazed on this forlorn company, unspeaking.

There they stood, for all the world like irregular clumps of amputated limbs, their tops polished reddish brown like the stumps of legs and arms long after battle. He had known men with knobs where their hands had once been. He recognised the slight burnish of calloused skin on which had once been serviceable arms and elbows and knees. Knowing all this, how could he spoil a charming lady's fancy?

So he was after all grateful for not being included in her walk.

'Ah,' he said now, reading her expression, 'not all goals are within marching distance,' and gallantly offered her the last doughnut. Though just who he was supposed to be consoling he could not be sure.

Jonathan Treitel

A GREAT EXHIBITION

LITTLE BY LITTLE it was pandiculating. My sister, Augusta, always attributed its beginnings to the Great Exhibition, and I do think she could be right; that otherworldly interjection in the centre of things, how glorious it seemed to us then (we were but girls), how right and proper its pomp, the braveness of its vision, its immensities . . . Besides, every lady desires a plumper frame than the one Providence has given her; in the course of that decade it became a fashion to wear more and yet more layers of petticoats and shifts and slips, in cotton and wool and linen, not to speak of all sorts of ingenious and hefty arrays of horsehair padding; it is as if one were lugging around on one's person the contents of a whole laundry chest . . . And then, suddenly, in the summer of 1861, my sister and I chanced to be flipping about in a French magazine (*La Belle Hélène*) and there it was, the latest mode from Paris, the hoop-skirted crinoline!

'Pshaw,' my sister said, literally, as it is spelt. 'Whatever will they think of next?'

Guarded, I said, 'I do not think it so very unseemly, Gusta.'

'Not in the slightest, Friddy' (my name being Frideswide).

'Absolutely notto.'

'We really must purchase it, as ess as pee.'

'My sentiments exactly.'

To celebrate our joint decision, I inhaled vastly; then Augusta jabbed her fingers into my cheeks, causing me to deflate with a popping sound.

It would hardly have been proper for us to visit the shop

ourselves for a fitting. We instructed our maid, Annette-Marie, to retake all our measurements (adding on an optimistic inch here and there) and head over to Maison Tooley in South Audley Street to inquire about possibilities and to collect samples of fabric. My sister's absolute favourite was the ox-blood satin, she would die if she didn't have it; mine was the deepest midnight purple. And, a scant fortnight later, Maison Tooley delivered two giant packages wrapped in striped paper, but light, undense as a meringue.

Annette-Marie on her own brought them up to us in our chamber, one box on top of the other, obscuring her bosom and face. 'Shall I dress you now, mesdemoiselles?'

'Certainly not,' said Augusta.

I furnished an explanation. 'Gusta and I shall dress each other. We shall dress ourselves.'

After the maid had curtseyed and departed, my sister and I gazed down at the carpet, then at one other. Augusta was biting her lower lip, as if to suppress laughter. 'Would you like to go first, Friddy?'

'No, you, please, Gusta.'

'I assure you I –'

'Does your mother know you're out?' (This was a catch-phrase of the period, and meant nothing in particular; or rather, it could mean everything.)

'Let us do it together?'

'Very well.'

My sister and I unbuttoned each other's afternoon gowns, and we took them off. Then we removed successive undergarments – for it was of the essence of the new fashion that nothing interrupt the sway of the crinoline – until all we had on below the waist were our drawers, the base of our corset, and an abbreviated linen shift. Next we attended to the packages. We detached the sealing wax and unknotted the string. Carefully we peeled the wrapping paper. The lid came free. Now the crinolines were ours to lift up and away.

But just as I was fingering the embedded satin, Augusta addressed me sharply.

'Kneel and shut your eyes, Friddy.'

308

'But, Gusta . . .'

'Friddy. Do what I say, or I shall tickle you.'

'See if I care!'

'I shall afflict you with unspeakable torments.'

I obeyed. (Augusta is my older sister, after all.) I pretended I was in church, deep in prayer. I pressed my palms together – only to feel them being separated by my sister – for otherwise my body would present an insoluble geometrical conundrum. Next I sensed a cool flap, a brief pat of satin against my cheek, the caress of fabric skimming my arms. I was aware I was in utter darkness; then an impression of returning brightness. 'Stand up, now, Friddy . . . Open your eyes.'

At first I could scarcely interpret what I saw and felt. It was like being a traveller in the Orient or Africa, where nothing makes sense. The garment, the crinoline, stretched into the distance – it was as if I were mounted on top of a monument – yet at the same time it was so featherweight it seemed it could waft away. Distances were exaggerated – as if I were viewing the drawing room from afar: through a telescope, as it might be; I was miles away from the familiar wallpaper, the glass dome containing the stuffed birds, my sister herself . . .

'How does it feel?' she said.

'Heavens, Gusta,' I said. 'You are on the moon.'

'And where are you, Friddy?'

'On Venus, I hope,' I said, a little daringly.

My sister laughed.

I said, 'Now you must put on yours. Please, sister, quickly. For I cannot truly know how I look until I see myself in you.'

Augusta said, 'I should never look as queenly in mine as you in yours.'

'Do you think I am beautiful, Gusta? I ask only because I know you will lie to me, dearest. Will I attract a fine gentleman?'

'A fine and wealthy gentleman, Friddy.'

'All the better.'

'An aged gentleman, who will expire on the wedding night, bestowing on you an independence of ten thousand pound a year.'

'I should prefer –'

Augusta leaned back against the mantelpiece, with one foot hoisted on an andiron, and gnawed on a knitting needle as if smoking a pipe. In a deep, vulgar voice she taunted me, 'Friddy kissed me when we met / Tumbling on the bed I piss in / Time, you thief, who love to put / Sweets into your book, put this in / Say I'm smelly, say I'm sad / Say that health and wealth have missed me / Say I'm dropping dead but add / Friddy kissed me!' And she actually strode over and sought to buss my cheek, in a manly fashion – except of course that, even leaning out as far as she could, she could not reach me.

My blushes were about as crimson as they ought to be.

Augusta propped her dress on the fauteuil, with its whalebone framework extended, and by getting down on the carpet and wriggling up inside, she managed to put on her crinoline unassisted; fastening the ties at the back was the very devil.

'How do we look, Friddy? Pretty perf, no?'

Actually we looked like . . . I could not find words for it. Our dresses seemed to be expanding even as they were worn, occupying the entire room between them, pressing outwards . . . soon we would be perched on separate Alps; on separate constellations . . . I took the hankie from my sleeve and waved it.

'Goodbye, Gusta . . . Bye-bye-ee, dearest sis . . . wherever you are . . .'

Augusta blew me a kiss.

I sighed. 'I wonder when we'll be allowed to wear these in public?'

'Whenever we want. They are respectable, decent. They cover up all our unmumblables, do they not? . . . Let's take the air in them, right now!'

'Oh, no, Gusta . . .'

'Oh, yes! We can walk to church in them.'

'Today? On a Monday?'

'It is a matter of extreme urgency. We crave to ask the vicar at what hour is evensong, and whether we could assist the parish in some charitable capacity.'

'We could send Annette-Marie to find out that . . .'

'I hereby command you to accompany me, so you shan't feel you're to blame . . . And I promise to protect you, so you needn't be a fraidy-cat . . . *A propos de bottes*, why is a sailor like a mouse?'

'I don't know, Gusta, why is a sailor like a mouse?'

'Because both are afraid of the cat! . . . "Cat?" Cat-o'-nine-tails.'

'Oh, that's a good 'un. Who did you hear it off?'

'Annette-Marie.'

'And who did she hear it off?'

'The butcher's boy, I do believe.'

'And who did he hear it off?'

'I daren't think!'

Whereupon both of us burst into laughter, our crinolines rocking hugely as we giggled, although really it wasn't awfully clear what either of us might have said that was funny.

My laughter turned into coughing; and Augusta made me take a camphorated cachou; then she had one herself.

We passed through the doorway – for which we had to turn sideways, since the framing is sprung at the back. We descended the stairs – the motion was surprisingly like a normal walk, provided one didn't think about it; if one wondered where one's feet were and what they were up to, one would be sure to take a nasty fall.

We put on our bonnets, which had the queer effect of making our heads look smaller, though one'd think it would be the opposite. Our kid gloves, next. We had thoughts about umbrellas but decided against; should the heavens open while we were outside, umbrella or no umbrella, our dresses would be drenched.

George, the footman, unlatched the door. I sailed out, followed by my sister. He asked if we wanted him to get us the carriage. Augusta bade him not to bother, since we were just dropping by the church.

When he had gone, I stretched out my arm to take my sister's – only of course this was impossible. Anyway she was engaged in discreetly spitting her cachou into that conical thing the link-boys used for extinguishing their torches, before the gas light put paid to the old ways.

I stepped forward down the path, proving to myself I could.

'Which church are we going to, Gusta?'

'St Clement Dane's.'

'Why on earth are we going all the way in our crinolines past Trafalgar Square and along the Strand to St Clement Dane's?'

'Precisely, Friddy.'

How can I describe the sensation of wearing a crinoline? Truly to appreciate it, one must first imagine what it had been like in earlier days, an oppressive tonnage of undergarments suffocating the hips. Now imagine the freedom of it – the skirt trembling like a dahlia in the breeze – the coolth stealing up above our knees . . . All that stood between our legs and the weather was a flimsy pair of drawers.

To walk, it turned out, was easy. We simply operated our feet in the normal fashion, being unencumbered, and our bodies drifted along – gliding smoothly over the streets of London. Evenly down Blenheim Street. Woodstock Street. Oxford Street where the grand shops are.

'I'm swimming, Gusta.'

'I'm flying, Friddy.'

Also there was the matter of our girth. This did have to be taken into account; in general I had to trail behind my sister since the pavement was seldom wide and unpopulated enough for us to move side by side. We had to make nice allowances to fit past carts and projecting shopfronts. Kindly folk would make room for us, skipping aside, like pedestrians when an omnibus goes by. Naturally, being in the latest fashion, we were the cynosure of attention.

'That man in the grey beaver,' I whispered to my sister. 'He's looking at your ankles.'

'I shall pretend not to notice.'

'Now he's looking at mine.'

'I wonder why.'

There was nothing that could be done about it. Inevitably the crinoline swings, revealing more than the wearer had bargained for; yet we were blameless, for our dress was nothing less than decent; a lady cannot be held responsible for the Laws of Motion.

We hoped the pavement was clean enough, though we had no basis for this supposition. The sky was grey and certainly it had rained, judging by the puddles and the general gleam. A moderate degree of murk was only to be expected. If we were about to step on something untoward, we would have no way of telling.

As we advanced along Oxford Street, curiously manumitted, marvelling at the oddity of being ourselves – two ladies of reasonable birth and appearance and fortune in the capital city of the mightiest empire the world has ever known – of a sudden, by the entrance to Marshall and Snelgrove's, I felt a strange desire to laugh, much as one sometimes needs to sneeze, and my sister must have experienced the same urge, for she and I broke into absurd guffaws simultaneously. How strangers must have been puzzled by the sight of two young, innovatively costumed ladies in the throes of inexplicable amusement. At that moment a Prince of Wales wagon passed quite close (it was transporting kegs of beer) and our dresses were delicately splashed. But even this did not dampen our high spirits. We were being impelled, it seemed, by some unseen pressure or tide, towards the junction with Regent Street.

At Oxford Circus the road had been torn up, in order to build the new railway. We turned up Shaftesbury Avenue, which was not clean. A street sweeper brushed the dirt out of our way, and Augusta gave him a halfpenny. (Strictly speaking he was breaking the law; if a policeman caught him, he'd be hauled up before the magistrate. But the crinoline makes one buoyantly kind-hearted, full of pity towards the less fortunate.) As we were crossing Wardour Street, I overheard a couple of 'cits' comment on us. 'She's a blooming balloon,' one said. And his comrade remarked, 'I'll bet Hodgkins has been up in her' (Hodgkins being a then-celebrated aeronaut, much in the news for having piloted his Montgolfière from Birmingham to Wolverhampton). I reflected that Lord Shaftesbury – he after whom the Avenue was named – had been a tireless campaigner for the emancipation of slaves throughout the Empire; unless I was confusing him with Mr Wilberforce.

In Leicester Square, just as we were averting our gaze from the fallen women who are not unknown there, and bestowing a sympathetic glance on 'Toesy' Humphries the armless nosegay maker, a little mongrel, a terrier mostly, ran around Augusta's legs.

'What's the doggie doing, Friddy?'

'He's sniffing. I think he's curious.'

'I think he's licking my knee.'

'Your ker-knee, Gusta?'

'Yes. And my ker-calf and my sher-shin.'

'How different, how very different, from the home life of our own dear Queen.' (Another of those all-purpose catch-phrases then the vogue.)

The mongrel yapped and scampered away.

The crowds were making it difficult to manoeuvre down the Haymarket. A gentleman in a sulky touched his hat to us; or to Augusta at least. It was as much as we could do to rotate several times, making an effect for which the crinoline is invaluable. We flowed with the populace along the northern edge of Trafalgar Square.

It was in Hayes Alley, by St Martin-in-the-Fields, that we encountered an obstacle. A half dozen boys, younger than us, were tumbling for money. One of them, whose face was blackened with burnt cork or some similar substance, as we approached, sang, 'I wish I was in Ole Varginney / Wid Dinah and de pickaninny . . .' The other boys cartwheeled and leapfrogged about us, making it difficult for us to continue on our way. I stood close to my sister, and copied her, resting my hands in an authoritative manner on the front of my crinoline, over the decorative ribbon, in the style of a banker blessing his paunch, while gazing blandly into the middle distance, at a pigeon on the portico of the National Gallery. Then the boy started waving his limbs in a jerky dance. He commenced a new song: 'Wheel about and turn about and jump jis so / Ebry time I wheel about I jump "Jim Crow"' – appropriate motions accompanied the words. Just as he reached the 'Jim Crow' he slipped on the damp kerb, falling supine on the ground beside me and slithering along till his head was underneath my crinoline. Meanwhile the remaining urchins began an importunate chorus, 'Give us a penny . . . a farthing . . . a sovereign . . . Give us your dosh.' I was in an awkward position. I did not care to have an urchin in blackface staring up between my legs, whether or not he had done so deliberately; furthermore I had no desire to be robbed by a gang of footpads, if that was what they were and that was their intention; but in any case I was physically unable to move. At least my crinoline gave me some perspective: it seemed I was perched on top of it, looking down at the scene with wonderment and concern, as if I were already in after years, recollecting the emotion in tranquillity.

Augusta heaved me aside, and literally ran over the 'Jim Crow' boy. The urchins, momentarily shocked, gave no resistance as Augusta sallied through their ranks in the direction of the Strand, and I followed in her wake.

We paused to catch our breath at the lower end of Trafalgar Square, from where the Thames' stink can hardly not be inhaled. Augusta was flushed with the fun of the fight.

'Three cheers for us!' she said.

'Hip hip hooray!'

'Once more unto the breach, dear Friddy!'

'A Gusta's a Gusta for a' that!'

I looked tentatively around and up. The city was pewter-tone, the uniform dull brightness which is the glory of England. The sky was that indeterminate mix of clouds which indicates that possibly it will rain though probably not but there again it is the better part of valour not to bet on it. Pigeons swirled; below on the Square, near the fountain, an old woman had just caught a bird in her apron ... it was struggling ...

At this point, incautious, I stepped backwards. A foolish thing. For I had not taken into consideration the radius of my crinoline – and I heard the rip before I associated it with my own clothing; then I felt the breeze. An utter panic, as an aeronaut must suffer when, five hundred feet up, he realises the fabric of his balloon has torn.

Augusta hissed, 'Don't turn round Friddy, the tear's at least, oh, it's all the way up to the calf!' She actually laughed. 'I'm sorry, Friddy, but you're worthy of being sketched by a cartoonist for *Punch*!'

She motioned me to stand behind her. We backed into the yard in front of a public house, The Whistle.

Now I could see what had caused the damage. A 'mush faker' – a man who repairs umbrellas – had set up his stall in front of The Whistle, and had left it unattended (whether to answer the call of nature or to obtain refreshments within). A broken umbrella spoke had cut into my clothing. There was a knife on the table; its handle was rusty but the blade looked honed. Augusta moved so that I, being between her and the blank wall of The Whistle, was invisible from the road.

'Shut your eyes, Friddy.'

I didn't quite shut them. I wanted to see it happen.

In one rapid motion my elder sister plunged the knife into my belly, rather below the corset, and hooked the blade out, and pulled it along, slicing the satin fabric around the entire circumference of my hips, then vertically downwards through the rear fastenings, detaching the whalebone framework. I was (my drawers aside) naked below the waist. Surely no passer-by glimpsed me, but certainly Lord Nelson, high on his column at the midpoint of Trafalgar Square, would have had a perfect view; and even a couple of the bronze lions, couchant at the column's base, had me within sight.

At no point did I blush.

'Get down, Friddy.'

The incident had resolved itself. Dutiful, I crouched. August flipped her crinoline – so that I was within it. It seemed that little had changed: a minute ago I was wearing a crinoline and now, so to speak, the crinoline was wearing me. I steadied myself by placing my bonneted head between my sister's thighs, and clutching on to her knees.

In this manner we progressed, slowly but surely, across a stretch of damp pavement streaked with mud and fallen tobacco ash and pigeon excreta, to the kerb.

The casual observer, I suppose, would have noticed nothing amiss – a young lady of fashion dressed in an ox-blood crinoline, carrying in her arms a quantity of purple satin; a more thorough inspection might have revealed that she appeared to possess four legs.

The crinoline hailed a hackney cab. The crinoline climbed up into it (slowly, quadripedally, with every care) ... And thus the crinoline returned to our family home in South Molton Street.

What happened on subsequent adventures with our crinolines, how we paid a visit to the Orpheum in Great Titchfield Street where we saw a performance by Jack 'I can't think where I put it' Wilson and by Nerina Naiad of the Deep, how my wise sister was repelled by the bestial nature of the goings-on and vowed henceforth to live a virtuous life whereas I was seduced, becoming a *lion comique* and male impersonator myself under the stage name Martin St Martin, appearing notably in no less than one hundred and thirty-five perform-ances of *Esmeralda; or, The Carpathian She-Bandit*, how I sank through successive stages of degradation, until finally, gin soaked, a prey to base instincts and unnatural lusts, I was saved through the blood of my Redeemer, will be revealed in forthcoming chapters.

Suffice it to say, what was for myself a consequence of a ripped crinoline, a failure in a length of pleated purple satin lined with taffeta and supported on a whalebone structure, and might for someone else be the product of some other seemingly chance event – that brief and unforgettable ecstasy, when I stood all but naked in Trafalgar Square, free, while pigeons grunted and Nelson on his column gazed eternally at the empyrean, and London was aglow with blessed radiance, which seemed at the time worth everything, worth more than the rest of our petty existence put together – was in truth not so: it is a snare and a delusion, and in the end leads to nothing but the dark. This is my testimony.

Christopher Sinclair-Stevenson

BOOKS DO FURNISH A
PUBLISHING HOUSE

THE FIRST FOUR months of 1998 were witness to two strange and perhaps symptomatic events. At the instigation of its owner, Rupert Murdoch, the distinguished firm of Harper-Collins (an ungainly contraction of William Collins and the American company of Harper and Row) decided not to proceed with publication of a book on the Far East by the former Governor of Hong Kong, Chris Patten.

The reason given, and leaked to the media, was that the book was too long and too boring. Unfortunately, the editor who had originally commissioned it had already pronounced it one of the most exciting books he had ever read, it was bound to be a bestseller, etcetera. There were internal memoranda which made the same point. It soon became perfectly clear that Mr Murdoch had been influenced by his fear that the Beijing government might look less cordially on his plans for expansion in the Far East if he were to publish a book severely critical of that very government.

The commissioning editor resigned, the literary agent acting for Mr Patten took the book to another publisher, Mr Patten sued HarperCollins for breaking a contract, the Editor of *The Times* (another Rupert Murdoch property) and his media correspondent, who had failed to cover the incident, looked foolish, various writers under contract to HarperCollins gave interviews expressing degrees of horror and disgust (though only two of them returned their advances and cancelled their contracts), and a number of pundits in the trade declared that HarperCollins was finished as a serious publisher, and that no agent would in future offer them a book. The lawyers flexed their muscles and calculated their fees. A good time was had by all.

There is no obvious precedent for this extraordinary series of events. In the past, owners were less interfering (though Roy Thomson, filled with puritan fervour, once stopped one of his publishing companies from proceeding with a series of mildly dirty novels – there were no resignations), and the global political and business scene less invasive.

A few weeks after the HarperCollins imbroglio, the vast German-owned conglomerate, Bertelsmann, swallowed the vast American-owned conglomerate Random House, who had previously swallowed the rather smaller but nevertheless substantial Dutch-owned conglomerate Reed International. Bertelsmann now owned in England alone: Transworld, Corgi, Black Swan, Anchor, Bantam, Doubleday, Chatto and Windus, Jonathan Cape, Ebury Press, Century, Hutchinson, Heinemann, Secker and Warburg, Methuen, Vintage, Barrie and Jenkins, Arrow, and a great many more smaller imprints.

In 1961, when I became a publisher, things were rather different. For a start, British publishing consisted of a number of small, independent, often family-owned or -originated firms: Rupert Hart-Davis, Victor Gollancz, Faber and Faber, the Bodley Head, Hamish Hamilton, Michael Joseph, Secker and Warburg, Cassell, Collins, Chatto and Windus, John Murray, Longmans, Constable . . . In addition, there were a few energetic companies started by refugees from Central and Eastern Europe: Weidenfeld and Nicolson, André Deutsch, Paul Hamlyn.

It is salutary to analyse this list. Faber, John Murray and Constable are the only companies which can claim still to be independent. Of the others, some have vanished altogether, the rest have been gobbled up, occasionally digested, all changed out of recognition.

It would be simplistic to claim that publishing in the early 1960s was better, or even more enjoyable, but it was certainly different. The underlying reason for this state of affairs was scale. Publishing companies were small. To give a personal example, Hamish Hamilton consisted of the founder, his editorial partner, the head of production, the company secretary (the only four directors), one additional editor, a minute children's department, a similar educational department, a sales manager, a team of sales representatives, a few secretaries and a book-keeping and invoice department. There was in addition a warehouse and trade counter within a five-minute walk.

There was no publicity department, the concept of marketing would not have been understood, subsidiary rights were handled by one of the editors. There were sales agencies in all major areas overseas, mainly in what used to be called the British Empire, but also in Europe. There were, of course, no computers, no desk-top publishing, no e-mail. From this small group of people, mainly men, came about seventy-five titles a year. It took six months to have a book in the shops from the moment of delivery of the script. Few books were commissioned, few agents had any influence.

Perhaps as a consequence of the virtual invisibility of agents, perhaps because publishing was a closed shop, there was an inherent stability. Authors very rarely left their publishers, partly because they had a close relationship with their editors, who would expect to work in the same company for their entire career; and partly because there was no real inducement to move. Publishers felt almost an obligation to publish everything a writer offered. There was more time to build an author's reputation. And, of course, books sold more copies. The public library system, one of the country's greatest glories, now a dim memory, ensured that sales of 2,000 copies of any but the most specialised title could be guaranteed.

Review coverage could be guaranteed as well. Far fewer titles were published, and there were far fewer people involved in the process of publication. The most prominent publishers knew the most prominent literary editors and critics (very often, they published them as well). In an age when bookshops were either small independents or W. H. Smith (and, astonishingly to readers in the 1990s, W. H.

Smith were extremely good booksellers who felt it their duty to stock such esoterica as poetry and first novels), the influence of the sales rep was considerable. Sales reps read books, all the books on a publisher's list; so did the bookseller.

It *was* a closed shop, and, like all closed shops, it had grave inequalities and inequities. It was extremely difficult to break into the charmed circle: George Weidenfeld needed Nigel Nicolson, and André Deutsch gained considerably from the contacts which his co-director, the cartoonist Nicolas Bentley, brought him. Once you were in, it was usually a matter of picking up the telephone to the literary editor of the *Sunday Times* or to the chairman of W. H. Smith. And the authors benefited.

One case history gives a clear impression of how the system worked. Hamish Hamilton had had a huge success with L. P. Hartley's *The Go-Between*. His next books did less well (they were less good but far from negligible); some of Hartley's earlier novels and collections of short stories were reissued. Then came a sad decline in his powers. A couple more fair-to-middling novels appeared. Then a demonstrably bad one was delivered, at the same time as a collection of esays with a far-right political message. Should they be published or would it be better for the writer's reputation if they were put away in the proverbial bottom drawer? Hartley was adamant that they should be published. They were published. The reviews were less savage than they could have been (a few more well-directed telephone calls). But it was a pathetic end to a considerable career.

The story demonstrates a number of points. The author–publisher relationship was extremely strong. Publishers cared about their authors' reputations. If pressed, they would proceed with publication of a book which they knew was bad, simply because they had always published that author. Few authors had agents whom they could consult; it was the editor or no one.

Was it a better environment? Advances were lower (but

royalties were often higher). Publicity barely existed. Marketing did not exist at all. Fewer books were published but sold in larger quantities. A review by a Cyril Connolly or a Raymond Mortimer or even a Robert Pitman (the influential literary editor of the *Sunday Express*) could create a bestseller. There were almost no prizes, certainly none carrying more than a £500 cheque. The speed of production was surprisingly fast. Printers read proofs and suggested changes. The bindings of books were sewn and held together. The paperback world was dominated by Penguin, until Pan came on the scene. Novels cost seven shillings and sixpence, and biographies a guinea.

Above all, publishing companies were oligarchies at best, dictatorships at worst. This *status quo* was utterly destroyed as the 1970s and 1980s brought mergers and take-overs and the arrival of the media monsters. It was thought, for peculiar reasons, that every newspaper or television magnate should have a few publishing companies in his portfolio. Synergy was the word of the moment. Owner-editors notoriously did not understand figures. Suddenly, accountants were essential – and powerful. The purchasers needed them and the sellers thought they needed them, though often their blind faith was disappointed.

Small was certainly no longer thought to be beautiful. Size was all. The number of titles published grew year by year. Volume replaced careful selection. The library system began to crack, as the sheer weight of books coincided with drastic cuts imposed on government and local authority spending. The new owners, ignorant in the eccentric ways of publishing but eternally optimistic, recognised that margins in general publishing were disturbingly lower than in technical or academic publishing; realised soon enough that sales patterns in both fiction and non-fiction often resembled a steeplechase with far too many horses, favoured by the bookmakers and tipsters, falling at the first fence, thus making nonsense of the form-book; but still felt that they – and perhaps they alone – possessed the key which would unlock the barrier to profits combined with prestige.

Eventually, the accountants seemed less all-knowing. If they were incapable of producing satisfactory end-of-year figures, then conceivably the marketing experts could be relied on to turn dross into gold. Pay a very large advance for a book, preferably by a young, photogenic writer with no track record, give the marketing department a sizeable budget, and something very wonderful would transpire. Or at least that was the theory. Misdirection of funds usually exacerbates a weak starting position.

We return to the last years of the present millennium. Soon, there may be only a few very large publishing companies, and a few very small ones. George Steiner has stated that the written word is finished, that no one in a few years' time will actually read books. This is palpable nonsense. Books, however old-fashioned in concept and design, will never be replaced by screens, when the reader's aim is pleasure in the most convenient form rather than education.

The novel is dead. The old-style publisher's editor, reasonably intelligent, committed, preferring authors to power and words to office politics, above all long-lasting, no longer exists. The barbarians are not only at the gates, they have broken them down and sold them off to the scrap-metal dealers.

This hypothetical portmanteau quote conceals as much as it reveals. But, to adapt Mark Twain's celebrated cable, the report of the death of the English novel is an exaggeration. Battered, yes. Disregarded, often. Transmuted into strange versions, Glasgow, Belfast, India and Sri Lanka and Trinidad, certainly. But there's life in the old thing yet.

It is salutary to take a look at the list of the winners of Somerset Maugham Awards for young writers, a remarkably sound barometer of quality. In a period taken at random, between 1960 and 1985, and with a great many distinguished writers omitted, we find the following: Ted Hughes, V. S.

Naipaul, Dan Jacobson, John le Carré, Paul Bailey, Seamus Heaney, Angela Carter, Piers Paul Read, Susan Hill, Martin Amis, Ian McEwan, Julian Barnes, A. N. Wilson, William Boyd, Adam Mars-Jones, Peter Ackroyd, Alan Hollinghurst, Nicholas Shakespeare, Helen Simpson, A. L. Kennedy and Philip Hensher. And these are just the novelists and poets, or some of them. Then there are the historians and the biographers and the travel writers.

Does the heart lift? Is the novel dead? Is the book dead? Is there light at the end of the tunnel?

The answers are yes and no and no and yes. And they are confident answers. Publishing has undoubtedly altered out of all recognition during the last twenty-five years, and the process will continue. Groups will coagulate and split, new companies will appear, some of them destined to perish, a few to survive. But editors, however disregarded, will still buy books. And, above all, writers will continue to write.

One must address the question, however, of how well the book, in particular the novel, is faring as a consequence of the changes within the publishing culture in the UK. The bringing together of more and more imprints and consequently the emergence of fewer and fewer people who actually take the decisions, must mean that the novelist, in particular the first novelist, suffers. Literary agents, for reasons of cash flow or greed, tend to concentrate on those writers whom, with their first novels, they identify as money-spinners. The theory goes something like this. Persuade a publisher to pay £100,000. Publishers in other countries will jump on the bandwagon. A self-fulfilling prophecy has been established.

The theory is fallible. Often, the book is not really worth the advance. Even if it is, the advance may not be earned. Then the publisher is reluctant to buy the next book, unless for a much reduced advance. The downward spiral has commenced.

The smaller publishers (perhaps the more committed ones) cannot compete in such an overheated market. The bigger publishers feel they must be seen to compete, and to have the financial resources to back their judgement. It is an unhealthy environment for the writer who is starting out on a career. It is – less obviously – an unhealthy environment for the publishing industry. Like all speculative bubbles, it has a tendency to burst when overblown. The writers, as has been noted, are certainly there. But will there be enough publishers around in, say, five years' time to publish them? The threat is all too obvious.

Michael Foley

REGARDING THE BED

Yet another indictment – that we scarcely see much less thank
A partner who can *daily* and *simultaneously* meet
The two most common and pressing but mutually exclusive
   human needs
– At once security and adventure, support and release.

Yet a bed combines motherly warmth with the reckless *mardi
   gras* of dream
In the kind of self-effacing service we never thought to see
   again.
Devoted, loyal and supportive all the way through life,
It will bear us up to the end, our truest four-legged friend.

In this case four short bandy ornate legs
That conceal the real grey steel legs beneath
But reveal the temperament of the former owner
Who liked to hide function with scrollwork.

Suddenly it comes to me with a shudder – *this was once my
   mother's bed.*
Why did I take it when I took little else?
Some unconscious dark urge to defile and avenge?
(Proust adorned a male brothel with his dead mother's
   things.)

It certainly embodies her passion for furniture
And abiding dislike of the rectilinear
With its curves and curlicues and whorls
Its flutings and spirals and frothy headboard.

Not the bed in which she died – but where her coffin was laid

While the bourgeoisie of Derry came to pay their respects,
Returning in force for the final journey
And remarking my calm with distaste (so I've heard).

Burghers, those lacking charity can often be fair.
To Derry and provincial towns everywhere
I hereby gladly give their due. You may not be
Able to live in them – *but they'll bury you in style.*

Better a solitary city death in the four-legged friend, going out
As I've lived – book in hand. My own statue – at least for a
  while.
Till the people next door get my first and last message – the
  smell.
(I too yearn for community – it's just neighbours I hate.)

Not the bed in which she died but where she spent her last
  days
Dependent on massive oxygen cylinders in peeling black paint
Grotesquely and undisguisably functional with a brass valve
  and gauge.
Not just giving breath, they helped anchor her withering
  frame to the earth.

As the soul becomes heavy and clinging the body lightens and
  craves release.
Every buttoned-up shrunken old lady now reminds me
Of my mother's last years. Those heavy coats aren't just for
  warmth
But to keep them from blowing away in the breeze.

And, preceding the physical, the spiritual shrinkage.
While the rites of spring fade its old wrongs remain fresh
(My mother's sad tape loop of six ancient wrongs).
We bed down in old grievance like glad nesting birds.

After food, warmth and sex our great need is a whinge.
Men gathered in caves not for safety but in order to *whinge.*

328

Grim and inexorable the spiritual shrinkage. Even of strong
    spirits
Pledged to resistance. Even of spirits not large to begin with.

Farewell ye sand dunes, laneways, sofas, back seats of cars.
All our love is now made in this bed – and at conventional
    hours.
Not that I'm ungrateful – not in the least.
(Ageing lovers should kneel and say grace before sex.)

But is this the only answer to shrinkage – appreciate the less
    more?
Is there no way to keep the small thing we are whole?
For the desiccated spirit that toughens and shrivels
Can we not find restorative unguents and chrisms?

Another function of beds – to lean on when we pray.
Sweet Lord, let not my soul be cold and hard before its flesh.
Let me marvel and praise and let nothing be stone but these
    tablets of law:
Thou shalt not shrink. Thou shalt not whinge. Thou shalt not
    crave.

Michael Hofmann

FUCKING

A zero sum game, our extravagant happiness,
matched or cancelled
by the equal and opposite unhappiness of others,

but who was counting as you came walking from your car,
     not off the bus,
early for once, almost violent in your severity,

both of us low on our last, stolen day for a month,
uncertain, rather formal,
a day of headaches, peaches and carbonated water,

by the stone pond whose ice you smashed as a girl . . .
or how we wound up
jubilant, a seesaw at rest, not one foot on the floor.

SEELE IM RAUM

I could probably
just about have swung a cat
in that glory-hole –

maybe a Manx cat
or that Cheshire's gappy grin –
and for a fact I could open the door

and perhaps even the window
without raising myself
off the plumbed-in sofa

but what really hurt
was the rugby football
deflating from lack of use,

a pair of void calendars
and the pattern of my evenings
alone on the slope

overlooking the playground
the paddling pool
gradually drained of children

the bullying park attendant
crows sipping from beercans
as if they'd read Aesop,

sun gone, a nip in the air,
the grass purpling
and cold to the touch,

and later on, in near darkness,
watching a man's two boomerangs
materialize behind him

out of the gloom,
like the corners of his coffin
on leading-strings.

Liz Jensen

THE FRIENDSHIP CENTRE

THERE'S A QUOTATION my therapist likes to use in our Social Awareness Class: it's from the Bible. *Faithful are the wounds of a friend.* It means, we may forgive, but we don't forget. Be vigilant. Value this friendship. We're family. Hurt us, and you're hurting yourself.

I kept a diary at the time it all happened – just jottings. I've reconstructed it, and it's been a revelation. All the connections are exposed. You could plot it on a graph, from its homely beginnings to the final –

Let's just say, *A* happened, which led to *B*, the inevitable result of which was *C*, followed by *D*, *E* and *F*.

The alphabet of my decline.

January 19th was a normal Sunday in every respect. I dropped Harry off at his football match – he's in the under-11s team – then drove over to the Friendship Centre with Millie. Sunday's always the most crowded day, but I still managed to find a space in my favourite section of the car park, 4A, which is by the bottle bank. You can kill two birds with one stone that way. I opted for the car valeting service, then dropped Jim's suit at the dry cleaning facility, the photos at the Fotophast and Millie at the World of Adrenalin. I did the shop: night-nappies, toilet roll, kitchen paper, veg, cat food, the usual. The total bill was £31, but that was reduced to £27.50 with yesterday's Friendship vouchers. Sensing I was on a retail roll, I decided that tomorrow I'd opt for the extra five Family Size packets of crisps, so as to be eligible for the Father's Day Offer, open – exclusively – to members of the

Friendship Scheme. *To one of our most valued customers*, said the letter they sent with the Customer's Charter.

They meant me.

When I went to collect Millie from the World of Adrenalin she was snivelling. 'I wanted to ride in the trolley,' she whined, 'I wanted to come with you!' How do you explain to a child that you lose Friendship points that way?

'It's for your own sake, darling,' I coaxed. But being kind and understanding only makes things worse, in my experience: sometimes better just to slap them. I would have done, but the World of Adrenalin manageress was hovering about, mosquito-like, her HERE TO HELP badge flashing in the light like she was some kind of emergency vehicle, so I held back, and let Millie explode more tears and snot at me, which I mopped at with a Thomas the Tank Engine hanky. 'Look, sweetheart, Mummy's bought you a Lucky Bag!' I crackled the bag at her, and she grabbed it, still sniffing.

'Shall we book her in with the Family Psychologist this week or next?' the manageress inquired. 'I've checked your client card, and she's due a visit.' We settled for next Wednesday.

'Why not let her have a couple of rides on the Noddy-mobile and then treat her to an ice-cream up in the Koffee Stop?' she suggested. Millie brightened up at that, and I remember thinking: they really *are* there to help!

As I said, a normal Sunday.

The next day, I made my usual trip to the Friendship Centre. Although Mondays are generally quieter, my favourite parking space in section 4A was taken; I see now I should have taken it as an omen, but I didn't. There was a huge poster in the lobby: 45 PERCENT OF MEN DIE INTESTATE. Inevitably, that got me thinking – *yes, why not get the family paperwork in order* – so I signed up for the will-writing offer. They were only asking for ten per cent of your estate, which was reasonable enough, I reckoned, especially as you'd be dead and it wouldn't affect you personally. Then I went to the Redemption Desk to get a refund on the hamburgers I'd bought on Sunday; I'd been having second thoughts since the BSE scare. I'd only bought them because there was a 500-point Bumper Bonus on all beef products.

'Me again,' I said.

The girl looked up at me sharply. 'Fine, Mrs Coleman,' she said. Her voice had a little hint of frost in it, I thought. 'No problem.'

They say 'no problem' a lot; it's one of their mission slogans – and she was wearing a badge that declared the same thing, in capital letters – NO PROBLEM! But there *was* a problem, because when she scrolled through to my name on the computer, it made a beep.

'Anything wrong?' I asked. I began to feel nervous; I could feel my hand sweating as it clutched my patent leather purse. 'I won't lose Friendship points, will I?'

'Oh, no. Oh no, no.' But she didn't look at me when she said it. 'Just a routine procedure for our records.'

It was a relief to hear it, but I was still left with a nagging, indefinable worry. I handed over the hamburgers – they'd sort of half-defrosted – and she gave me two Friendship vouchers.

'We're here to help you!' she called after me as I wheeled my trolley off towards the neon horizon of the bakery section.

It was on the Tuesday that I started coming down with 'flu, but I still made it to the Friendship Centre for a few bits and bobs, because Tuesday's always been my bits and bobs day. A man with a clipboard – his badge said I'M YOUR FRIEND – collared me by the bottle bank as I was smashing in Jim's empties. 'Have you had your eyes tested lately, madam?'

I squinted at him. Had I dropped a bottle in the wrong-coloured hole or something? It wouldn't be the first time, and they were tending to police it more these days.

'Free sight tests at our Optical Centre,' my Friend explained. And could he interest me in an appointment for a Family Portrait?

I signed up for both – I remember thinking: *that's tomorrow and Thursday sorted* – and he handed me a couple of Friendship vouchers. When I dropped Millie off at the World of Adrenalin, the manageress gave me a courtesy car sticker. It said: HAVE YOU HUGGED YOUR CHILD TODAY? No, I thought, guiltily. I haven't hugged either of them. Haven't wanted to. They've been behaving like a couple of spoilt brats.

I'd finally remembered to bring my stool sample; it had been lurking at the back of the fridge for a week. At the Healthcare Desk they reminded me I was also due for a blood test on Thursday. Ten Friendship points if I could come before 9 am.

'Count on me,' I said.

When the girl keyed in my details, her computer made that familiar beep.

'You still haven't returned the medical questionnaire we sent you.' Her voice was polite, but there was reproach in it. 'I can't go ahead with the full Healthcare package if I don't have all the records. And according to this, you and –' she peered at the screen – 'you and *Jim* missed your last Marriage Checkup.'

I didn't bother telling her Jim had left me the previous month. He popped back twice a week to see the kids, drink some beer and pick up his dry cleaning, so I hadn't given up hope of a reconciliation. Though I must admit the Singles Evenings looked tempting.

The next day, Wednesday, the 'flu had really kicked in. I felt terrible, like something that's been badly microwaved. So after I took Harry to school, I dropped Millie at my mum's for the day and went straight to bed. It felt strange. A day didn't go by, normally, when I didn't pop over to the Friendship Centre. Silly, but it almost felt like a kind of betrayal when I finally staggered up the road to the local shops. At the Centre, there are always posters warning you about the cowboy retail outlets that spring up overnight and rip you off and then disappear, so I must admit I felt a bit uneasy as I dropped off Jim's dry cleaning at the Armenian laundry, and bought his beer at the corner shop, and some throat pastilles at the Indian chemist's.

Weird, this, but I must have transmitted my unease telepathically, because when I came home, the phone was ringing. She didn't give her name. But she was from Them.

'Just phoning to inquire whether you're happy *with* our services, Mrs Coleman? You are aware that we *do have* a tele-shopping facility, are you?' She didn't give me a chance to reply, but went on, 'Look, we'll be sending you a courtesy questionnaire which we do request you to fill in and return to us *by* the end of the week, *at* your convenience, Mrs Coleman. So if you could just pop that *in* the post for us.'

There was a pause. I was supposed to say something.

'Right,' I managed eventually. My voice was just a thin croak through the throat pastille.

'Great!' she said. She sounded like she really meant it. 'Bye, then, Mrs Coleman!'

The questionnaire arrived the next day, but for some reason – this is the difficult bit, and it's something I'm still grappling with in therapy – I didn't even open the envelope. I just left it propped against the cornflakes box. Even the thought that it might contain a couple of courtesy Friendship vouchers didn't do anything for me.

Incredible, when I look back.

I did the school run wearing just my nightie and dressing gown, then dropped Millie at Mum's. After that I just stayed at home again, doing a bit of cooking.

Having a break from it all.

I still didn't open the envelope, but I felt its presence.

'I'm Kimberley. The Customer Welfare Officer,' she said. 'From the Friendship Centre.'

My heart sank. 'You'd better come in,' I mumbled, gesturing her in. It was Monday; it had been three whole days since I'd been to the Centre, but it felt like a lifetime. We'd been living out of the freezer over the weekend.

'Kimberley' was very young, and very thin, so I hated her instantly. She followed me into the living room and sat down on the sofa, then pulled a computer printout from her briefcase.

She spread it on the coffee table.

'This is your customer service sheet, Mrs Coleman,' she explained. 'It's a computer analysis of your retail habits.' She had one of those twangy Croydon accents.

I just stared.

'They've been rather erratic lately, according to this.'

'What?'

'Your retail habits, Mrs Coleman. They've been erratic. See here?' she said, pointing to a line of numbers. 'And here?'

It meant nothing to me. 'I don't understand.'

'What it means is, you've made a series of consumer errors. Look, you can see how they convert into figures.'

She pointed at some numbers, and then looked up at me; her eyes were a delicate china blue, fringed with navy mascara lashes. I felt stupid, and hated her even more.

'I was never any good at maths,' I said. I felt resentful. 'You'll have to explain.'

She took it slowly, enunciating her words. 'We'll take it chronologically, shall we?'

I felt myself flush, and I looked down at the carpet. It was strewn with kids' toys, as usual. That was one of the reasons Jim left: you can't ask a man to live in a pigsty, he said.

Kimberley was explaining that there was the occasion – *for example* – when I could have completed my store circuit and checkout by 10 am and entitled myself to five air-miles or a free bag of hot chicken wings, but instead I'd sat staring at my doughnut in the Koffee Stop, and not taken up the two-for-the-price-of-one cappuccino offer. And how only last week, I'd delivered an out-of-date stool sample. How my children hadn't visited Snippers for their haircut in a month. How, just last week, by failing to turn up to my sight test or my Family Portrait appointments last Wednesday and Thursday, I'd reneged on my Customer-Client contract. She said all this apologetically, like it was her fault, not mine. As she finished the catalogue of my consumer errors, her voice dropped into the murmur of practised concern.

'On the basis of the evidence here, I'm afraid we will have to place you *on* the Customer Blacklist,' she finished.

A blacklist. I suddenly felt like I'd stepped in some dogshit, and I actually had to check the soles of my slippers. But they were spotless.

'I've been depressed,' I said finally. I felt guilty, but my words came out sounding wheedling and egotistical. 'I don't know why.'

She cocked her head sideways and looked at me inquiringly, like I was a child in playgroup who'd demanded her attention.

'We try to do our best *for* our customers,' she said gently. 'If there *is* anything you're not happy with, all you need do is fill in a Feedback coupon. We welcome feedback.'

'I know,' I apologised. 'It's just – I wouldn't know what to fill in on it. It's nothing in particular, you see. It's the whole thing.'

'The *whole thing*?' The Welfare Officer looked genuinely puzzled.

I was puzzled, too. I'd never felt this way before. So I surprised myself as much as her when I said: 'I think I might have to withdraw from the Friendship Scheme altogether. Just shop locally, you know. It'd be hard, but –'

She smiled patiently.

'Are you sure that would be wise?'

'Why not?'

She sighed gently. 'Look, Mrs Coleman, I'll have to be frank with you at this point. Your recent absences *have been* noticed. And our close-circuit video records indicate a lot of evidence that *over* the past month, your customer behaviour *has been* in contravention *of* our Courtesy Code.' She paused to let this sink in. 'As a consumer, Mrs Coleman, you *do have* responsibilities as well *as* rights.'

She was reaching down now, and pulling a video cassette out of her briefcase. 'D'you mind? Won't take a minute,' she said, inserting it into the machine and pressing the remote.

And there I was, in the Koffee Stop, smoking a fag in the non-smoking section. Next shot: a Safety Officer escorting me out of the building.

'We could have banned you then,' she said, 'but we like to give our clients the opportunity to develop positively when they've experienced retail burnout.'

'I remember that,' I said, squirming as I saw myself captured on the video. I looked fat and ill. I looked like a madwoman. I'd joined their Stop Smoking aerobics class the next day; it was one of their Friendly Suggestions. Another clip followed; instead of taking advantage of the twenty Friendship points offered me by choosing the multi-pak of Ribena, I was filmed opting for a single brick of orange juice at twice the cost.

'We're here to help, you know,' she said. 'We don't put those signs up just for fun.' I felt a lump forming in my throat.

When the video finished, with a clip of me fumbling about in my purse at the checkout, and failing to pick up a free Friendship magazine, she explained that my consumer errors had cost me valuable Friendship points.

'After we made the necessary deductions,' she said, 'your Friendship status was negative, I'm afraid.'

'Negative? You mean I *owed you*?'

'We don't put it quite that way. You were in deficit.'

While I was thinking about this, Kimberley picked up one of Millie's Barbie dolls from the floor and began taking off her tiny cowgirl outfit. 'Your deficit came to over five thousand Friendship points,' she said, smoothing Barbie's discarded jacket. 'The air miles you collected have gone to charity, I'm afraid, to make up some of the shortfall. That's our policy. Leukaemia Research, and Guide Dogs for the Blind.'

I watched her as she finished stripping Barbie. Silently, I handed her the miniature clothes-basket, and she selected a little red business uniform from the Executive daywear range. 'This is nice,' she murmured. When she'd finished dressing Barbie in the new outfit, she looked up. 'Oh. And of course the Redemption Desk will be put on the alert.'

That knocked me sideways. 'What d'you mean, on the alert?' Suddenly, I remembered the beep the computer had made when I'd asked for a refund for the hamburgers, and I felt my face grow pale.

'Look. You purchased a special Hygiene Toothbrush on December 9th,' she explained, plonking Barbie in the clothes-basket and applying herself once more to the printout. As she concertina'd it out in front of me, it seemed to double in length. 'Then you returned it on December 11th, claiming it was faulty.'

'And?'

'And then on the 13th, you bought a whole roast chicken which you returned the same afternoon, saying it was off.'

'So?'

'So on January 8th, you asked for a refund on the Terminator you bought for your son on Christmas Eve. You alleged that when your son undid the packaging, he found that the Terminator's right arm was malformed.'

'Yes. It was all melted-looking. What are you getting at?'

Kimberley looked down at her nails – neat and unvarnished – and then back at me.

'Some of our more disturbed customers,' she said slowly, 'develop a habit of actually damaging products themselves, and then requesting a refund.'

My heart lurched, and I felt a flush spread over me. They were actually accusing me of sabotage. *Christ!* Of seeking attention by bringing back products that I'd tampered with. A sort of retail Munchausen's Syndrome! The Welfare Officer's face was at once both bland and accusing. There were places for people like me; that was the clear message.

'No! It's not like that!' I blurted. 'How can I – ?'

How can I make you believe me? I was beginning to feel guilty and confused. A voice seemed to be singing a tuneless little aria at the back of my brain. Da-de, da-da, da-de, da-da . . .

Had I actually melted the Terminator's arm? *Had* I tinkered with the Hygiene Toothbrush, and somehow injected salmonella into the chicken?

The computer printout started to blur in front of my eyes, which seemed to be suddenly clotted with tears, giving everything a sort of Cubist look.

'God. I can't remember,' I said finally. Then, clutching at straws: 'Look. OK. Yes. Perhaps I *was* using the Redemption Desk as a place to make a cry for help.'

There was a pause, and Kimberley picked up the Barbie doll again, and the miniature hairbrush.

'We *do have* a twelve-step programme,' she offered, running the brush through Barbie's nylon hair. 'But like all programmes, it requires a commitment *from* you *as* the client. Sometimes it's hard being part *of* society. But that's life, I s'pose, isn't it, Mrs Coleman? Just look on the streets.' She shrugged, gesturing towards the window. 'You see all the outcasts. Some of *them* had Friendship cards once.' As if on cue, a sad-looking gent on crutches hobbled past with a newspaper under his arm.

Kimberley lifted Barbie up level with her own face, and the two of them gazed at me with their blue eyes.

I couldn't meet their stare, and instead I focused hard on my bitten nails, fighting back the lump that had swelled to the size of a tumour in my throat.

'I'll do my best,' I croaked.

It's normal to feel anger, Gordon says. He's my therapist. He says that everyone has a *bad child* inside them. What happened, the day after the Welfare Officer's visit, was that I let the *bad child* out to play at an inappropriate time. Instead of turning all the *bad child's anger* against myself, as I should have done, and as most women in my situation do, because that way they get to be part of the *fabric of society*, some freakish wave of *bad childness* had spilled over, and caused me to bite the very hand that fed me. He drew a sort of diagram for me on the blackboard, illustrating this. It looked like a spaceship with lots of ancillary modules.

It's normal, too, to feel this level of shame afterwards, Gordon says.

I was still feeling feverish, but I knew that I had to make it over to the Centre. Just to get back to normal. Just to clear my name, for Christ's sake, and get myself off that blacklist.

I'd always been a model customer, I reckoned.

I remembered the phrase from that letter they'd sent me when I joined the Friendship Scheme: *To one of our most valued clients.*

They owed me that second chance.

I don't remember much, even though they showed it all to me on video afterwards. It could have been a complete stranger doing all that.

This is the painful bit. My retail crisis.

I'd started my usual route round the aisles – Dry Goods, Oils and Pickles, Milk and Milk Products, Household and Electrical – but then I got stuck at Washing Powders and Fabric Conditioners. I normally buy Daz, but it wasn't there. There was just a gap where it should have been. It threw me, and I just stood there for about ten minutes, staring at all the other washing powders. The boxes seemed to stretch to infinity. I'd never associated feelings with inanimate objects before – it's a kids' book thing, a thing you see in cartoons – but suddenly, I was intensely aware that they were all beckoning at me to buy them. Their need was almost tangible. The choice seemed mind-bogglingly difficult. Infinitely delicate. A matter of supreme importance.

Other shoppers selected their washing powder and wheeled their trolleys by in a trance, but I just stood there staring at the contents of the aisle. Both rows triple-stacked. I wondered whether even God could have come up with this much variety, this subtlety of difference in packaging, quantity, quality. Biological, or non-biological? Micro or Multi-Pak?

Hand-wash for delicates, or all-purpose Family Load? It was staggering. It made me feel very small and mortal, to be faced with such – don't laugh – such *riches*.

Then, as I stared at the boxes, the bright colours began to dance, and paranoia started skittering about at the edge of my brain. *Was it a test? Had they set this up?*

It became a sudden, furious conviction.

Bastards! With the conviction, came a great sweep of anger. *How dare they not restock the Daz shelf!*

Before I knew it, my feet had uprooted themselves and I'd started ripping open boxes of washing powder, and swishing the contents across the floor. I was sort of aware that a crowd was quickly gathering, and some people were yelling at me to stop, and the security people were being called over the tannoy, but I carried on. I started spilling other stuff. Fabric conditioner. Then more washing powder. Then washing-up liquid and bleach. I couldn't seem to stop. Now I was pushing people out of my way, and trolleys were crashing about, and a woman – possibly me – was screaming in a high, shrill voice, and I was charging about in the aisle, ripping open boxes and unscrewing plastic caps and yelling that they were all a bunch of fucking bastards and they could shove their fucking Friendship up their arse.

It felt like I was *freeing things up*. That's the only way I can describe it. I've since realised it was all to do with the wrongly channelled anger that Gordon's been telling me about. But I hadn't heard of the *bad child* then, had I? All I know is that at the time, it felt – amazingly – like an act of liberation.

Then an alarm bell rang, and the sprinkler system started showering the whole store with water.

The Duty Manager, 'Dave', was a small burly man with a pock-marked face, a slippery nylon tie, and a jacket festooned with badges: DAVE, DUTY MANAGER, I'M YOUR FRIEND, and the obligatory HERE TO HELP. He had special emergency powers, he explained.

'Just follow me, will you, Mrs Coleman?' he offered, gesturing me along the moving walkway.

'Where are we going?' I asked, as we glided past the Flower Stall and the Experience Simulator.

'To the Courtroom. We hold disciplinary hearings, in cases like yours.'

The hearing was held in their small interdenominational Place of Worship, a breeze-block annexe by the toilets. I still had the smell of washing powder in my lungs; the mixture of chemicals made me weak and dizzy.

'Sit down, Mrs Coleman,' the Duty Manager said, and gestured to a low plastic sun recliner. 'Just make yourself comfy there. The others are on their way.'

Just as he said that, two people walked in; one was Kimberley, the Welfare Officer who'd come to my house and dressed the Barbie doll. Straight away I realised that she had come as my defence representative. The other was a man in a kind of hooded track-suit uniform.

'This is Ken, our Security Adviser,' said the Duty Manager.

I didn't say anything; I just fingered one of the potted plants. They had bright green leaves and little red berries. I'd seen them on sale last week.

Kimberley and the two men sat on white plastic garden chairs that still had the bar codes on. The Duty Manager shuffled his paperwork on a plastic patio table. Then he looked up at me.

'I'll come straight to the point here, Mrs Coleman,' he said. 'You've actually caused us a major chemical health hazard in there. Plus damage to produce, and an unquantifiable loss of customer loyalty.'

I picked at the potted plant; three of the red berries fell off and rolled on to the floor. I shifted on my sun recliner; I couldn't get into a position I felt dignified in. Kimberley was taking notes.

'I'm sorry,' I said. It was true. I was.

The Security Adviser shook his head. 'We hear *sorry* a lot in here,' he said. 'I'm not a psychologist or anything, but the question is, *why*, Mrs Coleman? Why?'

'She claims she had 'flu,' offered the Welfare Officer. My heart gave a thud of gratitude: she *was* going to put my case! I looked up at her, and she returned my gaze as she went on, levelly, 'But instead of taking advantage of our tele-shopping facility, she bought throat pastilles at the local Indian chemist.'

The Duty Manager sighed. 'OK, let's look at the customer service analysis.'

Kimberley took the printout from her briefcase, and the three of them scrutinised it in silence for a couple of minutes.

A whispered discussion followed, and I picked off all the red berries from the plant.

'Right, Mrs Coleman,' said the Duty Manager, finally. 'We've reached a unanimous verdict here.' I looked up, my hand full of berries. 'Mrs Coleman, I'm afraid we find you guilty.' He paused, so that I could absorb this.

Guilty. I've felt guilty all my life, I thought. At least it's out in the open now.

'We'll have to confiscate your Friendship card,' he said, 'and ban you from the Centre for a month as of today. During that period, you'll be invited to attend a Customer Re-Training programme.'

'You mean – ' I couldn't believe this yet – 'you'll let me back in? Afterwards?'

I felt small and alone. But they'd offered a shred of hope.

'Subject to conditions,' qualified the Welfare Officer.

'Thanks,' I mustered. My voice was just a whisper. 'Thanks.'

I'd squashed all the berries that were in my hand, and I just sat there on the sun recliner, with the orange juice trickling down my wrist. There were yellow seeds in it.

It's been an intensive couple of weeks. The World of Adrenalin is fostering the kids full-time till I've got myself sorted. I'm in a dormitory in the Healthcare Centre on the Upper Shopping Level, so it's home from home, really. Jim's even agreed to come for a weekend visit and join me for a courtesy Marriage Checkup.

I've learned so much here. About friendship, and the nature of relationships. It's a sort of eco-balance, when you look at it 'macrocosmically', as we've been urged to. I've learned how *organic* the whole thing is.

It wouldn't even be an overstatement to say that my whole attitude has changed. It wasn't a good attitude that I had before. I'm only grateful that I don't seem to have infected anyone else.

At my Interim Hearing in the Place of Worship, the Duty Manager decided that I'll be allowed back in early March, accompanied by my therapist, Gordon. After five supervised visits with Gordon acting as my 'shopping Buddy', I'll be allowed to enter the store alone, but I'll have a special electronic panic alarm, so I can buzz Gordon or one of his colleagues if I need to. There are quite a few wobbly customers like me, apparently, who make use of the service. It's all a bit hush-hush, they said.

Slowly, with my new Careful Spender guidelines, and the therapy, they'll help me build things up again, and re-assemble my personality into a shape I'm happier with. I'll have a physical makeover, too. I'll get to choose new underwear from their in-house lingerie line, and some nice comfy daywear at reasonable prices. Pastel ribbed polo-necks, nylon leisure slacks, some navy co-ordinates, furry slippers, that sort of thing. Vouchers again, if I do well. And then – come next pre-Christmas Season, if I'm lucky – I'll be entrusted with my very own, brand-new Friendship card.

Faithful are the wounds of a friend. I've thought about that phrase a lot. And I've learned – maybe a little late in life – that a friendship takes two.

You can't just take. You've got to give, as well.

I've taken out a loan, to cover what I owe them for all this.

Lindsey Sill

CHRISTMAS SHOPPING

1. Make list.
2. Go to Marks and Sparks, buy hat, high heels, silk knickers, velvet leggings, skirt, glasses. Put back skirt.
3. Swallow juice in a delirium.
4. Cross off glasses.
5. Try on brown leather fur-trimmed gloves. Go home.
6. Try to forget gloves.
7. Next: Next. Try on too-short skirt and one top in two sizes.
8. No more 12s? You can reserve a 12 in Basingstoke?
9. Buy skirt.
10. Hello! Christmas shopping? Isn't it ghastly?
11. Oh, you parked in mother-in-law's drive? How handy.
12. Gone into a home?
13. Ah (*knowingly*). Juggling mothers?
14. All this materialism, makes one want to sluice oneself with poetry.
15. (Just let me track down those gloves, that top.)
16. Note: boots clang more satisfactorily on stone than concrete and mine are the colour of old wet tarmac and the last trodden stages of crepitating leaves.

Emma Kay

THE DIARY OF ANNE FRANK

ANNE FRANK 1947, Macmillan, London 1995

705 objects in order of appearance, 235 pages

SCHOOL satchel, hair curlers, handkerchiefs, school books, comb, old letters, shoes, dresses, coats, underwear, stockings, 2 vests, 3 pairs of knickers, dress, skirt, jacket, summer coat, 2 pairs of stockings, lace-up shoes, woolly cap, scarf, cardboard boxes, bedclothes, film star photographs, picture postcards, paste pot and brush, copy of 'Young People's Annual', radio, curtains, drawing pins, codeine, potty, hat-box, divan, folding tea-table, letter, writing pad, cloth filled with sawdust, camp-bed, muffler, sheets, dinner-service, plates, soup plate, book about women, napkin, slice of bread, pans, family tree, a 'Joop ter Heul' book, copy of 'Midsummer Madness', exercise books, pencils, rubbers, labels, books, copy of 'Heeren Vrouwen en Knechten', copy of 'Koenen', long-sleeved dress, 3 cardigans, white sheep's wool jumper, moth biscuits, lemonade, letter, envelope, potatoes, wash-tub, fire-guard, glass preserving jar, small presents, flowers, red carnations, skirt, new skirts, copy of 'The Assault', apple, lamp, fuse wire, candles, copy of 'Eva's Youth', copy of 'The Plays of Goethe', copy of 'The Plays of Schiller', prayer book, book with drawings, Monopoly, razor, lighter, bread, 4 ration cards, 150 tins vegetables, 270 pounds dried peas and beans, coffee, cognac, pair of field glasses, wooden candlestick, large basket, St Nicholas paper, presents, doll whose skirt is a bag, book-ends, meat for preserving, sausages, sauerkraut, Gelderland sausages, apron, potatoes, eau-de-Cologne, vaseline, scraper, butter, biscuits, 2 cakes, card-index box, notebook, margarine, torch, preserved sole, kidney beans, haricot beans, ski-boots, rush sandals, dry bread, coffee substitute, spinach, lettuce, potatoes, oilcloth, flannelette sheet, corsets, brassiere, 3 vests, knickers, shaving brush, copy of 'The Mythology of Greece and Rome', sweets, little radio, grey coat, writing table, escape bag, copy of 'Henry from the Other Side', eiderdown, sheets, pillows, blankets, concertina bed, pink bed-jacket, cotton wool pads, hydrogen peroxide, soap, hairpins, curlers, black-out, rubber mat, metal pot, vacuum-cleaner, carpet, pudding, newspaper, red coat, black bedroom slippers, horn-rimmed spectacles, wine-coloured suede wedge-heeled shoes, forbidden book, newspapers, knives, potatoes, pan of water, apron, porridge, 'puppy-dog' plate, copy of a Dickens book, bolsters, book, valerian pills, pot of jam, cheese, meat and bread coupons, flowers, fur coat, grape sugar, cod liver oil, yeast tablets, calcium, fountain pen, milk, large laundry basket, bows of pink and blue carbon copy paper, large piece of brown paper, paper package, milk and honey, sugar, lozenges, compresses, wet cloths, dry cloths, hot drinks, cushion, hot-water bottles, lemon squash, thermometer, oil, sweets, syrup, brooch, cake, fondants, Christmas cake, a pound of sweet biscuits, bottle of yoghurt, bottles of beer, modern dance frock, gym shoes, copy of 'Cloudless Morn', copy of 'Cinema and Theatre', coffee, potatoes, pocket mirror, cigarettes, handkerchief, scent, fried potatoes, full cream milk, kale, barrel, negligée, endive, spinach, swede, salsify, cucumbers, tomatoes, sauer-kraut, pea soup, potatoes with dumplings, potato-chalet, turnip tops, carrots, soup, packets of julienne soup, packets of French beans, packets of kidney beans, gravy substitute, beetroot salad, liver sausage, jam, dry bread, lemon punch, pamphlets, biographies, history books, divan cushions, packing case, 2 hard brushes, jacket, chopper, tin waste-paper basket, paper, pillow, blanket, store-cupboard, chlorine, tea towel, woollen knickers, pyjamas, red jumper, black shirt, white over-socks, sports stockings, diary, diarrhoea remedy, jam pots, pieces of bread, mirror, comb, matches, ash, cigarettes, tobacco, ash tray, books, pair of pants, toilet paper, tea, chlorine, bread, lemonade, 3 bunches of narcissus, bunch of grape hyacinths, copy of 'The Emperor Charles V', copy of the Bible, copy of 'The Colonel' by Thackeray, bottle of piccalilli, packet of razor blades, jar of lemon jam, copy of 'Little Martin', plant, eggs, boiled lettuce, sewing silk, cheese, wood shavings, copy of 'Galileo Galilei', copy of 'Palestine at the Crossroads', copy of a biography of Linnaeus, nature book, copy of 'Amsterdam by the Water', gigantic box, 3 eggs, bottle of beer, bottle of yoghurt, green tie, pot of syrup, roses, carnations, 50 fancy pastries, spiced ginger- bread, portfolio, algebra book, vase, currant cake, copy of 'Hungarian Rhapsody', copy of 'Sprenger's History of Art', set of underwear, handkerchief, 2 bottles yoghurt, pot of jam, spiced gingerbread cake, 1 botany book, double bracelet, sweet peas, sweets, exercise books, copy of 'Maria Theresa', 3 slices of full cream cheese, bunch of peonies, copy of 'An Ideal Husband', 24 trays of strawberries, 6 jars, 8 pots of jam, bucket, skimmed milk, 19 pounds of green peas.

LADY CONSTANCE'S PRISONER

FE CAMPBELL, HOM Inc, Los Angeles 1993

220 objects in order of appearance, 162 pages

PADLOCKS, rocks, chain, car, straw, key, cord, leather collar, car, clothes, leash, double whisky, food, riding crop, rope, safety pin, panties, cane, mirror, bottle of Irish cream, bottle of White Lightning, car, bottle, pot of coffee, blanket, chains, shackles, key, scissors, soap, stocks, pillory, rack, thumbscrews, hoist, trapeze bar, bench, chains, shackles, straps, whip, whipping post, cage, padlocks, dress, shoes, handcuffs, cord, ankle-cuffs, silver tableware, chair, table, plate, food, whip, desk, cup of coffee, brandy, pyjamas, bedclothes, food, spoon, cord, rope, key, basket, vegetables, pot, spoon, bed, Dewar's Black Label, blanket, crayons, cameras, light, sawhorses, packing crate, noose, shirts, stool, knife, 2 glasses of Guinness, clock, car, blanket, tool bag, 2 trapeze bars, gag, riding crop, wire, blanket, Rolls Royce, cup of tea, cane, key, glass, knife, fork, chastity belt, basque, mirror, chain, padlock, tweed hat, jacket, shotgun, key, jacket, clothes, bag, bundle of bank notes, car, cup of coffee, cord, documents, suitcase, table, 2 chairs, syringe, metal band, padlock, pants, silk shirt, tray, coffee pot, cups, airline holdall, rope, chain, 2 stretchers, food, spoon, bag, steel cuffs, crop, whip, canvas, brush, white sheet, blindfold, bicycle, phone, coffee, bench, belt, straps, crop, iron collar, padlock, chain, food, drink, bucket of water, coffee, mirror, buggy whip, clothes, wooden bench, tray, coffee, cup, handcuffs, leather wristlets, steel ring, easel, canvas, hook, dress, helicopter, gun, handbag.

Nick Rogers

Destination Earth; or, Polishing the Rocket

Extract from a novel in progress

Tuesday, November 3

Morning: cogitate. Auxiliary: Slingsby storage trolley on wheels with lid.

Afternoon: cacchinate. Auxiliary: Slingsby storage on wheels without lid.

Evening: ululate. Auxiliary: 'Checklist of Essential Elements in Fiction' (p. 53, *The Fiction Writer's Handbook* by Nancy Smith. London: Judy Piatkus Ltd, 1991).

Wednesday, November 4

Morning: masturbate. Auxiliary: 'Nemesis' leather ankle-boot with feature elasticated gussets. 3-inch heel. Black.

Afternoon: masturbate. Auxiliary: 'Addict-2' sling-back court shoe. Supple leather upper. Built-in arch support. Durable non-slip sole. Heel height $2\frac{1}{2}$ inches. Beige.

Evening: Superintendent Miss Temple goes down the pub in her slippers –
   'I'm going down the pub in my slippers. Take it easy, Chopper.'

'Yeah.'

Masturbate. Auxiliary: Jacques Vaché in uniform, 1918 (plate 83, *Dada Art and Anti-Art* by Hans Richter. London: Thames and Hudson, 1965).

Thursday, November 5

Morning: DUMBBELL EXERCISES – ARMS:

> Single Arm Triceps Stretch
> Two Hands Single Dumbbell Triceps Stretch
> Single Arms Triceps Extension

Afternoon: DUMBBELL EXERCISES – UPPER BODY:

> Lateral Raise Sideways and Upwards
> One hand Swing
> Flying Exercise

Evening: The Most Reverend Root arrives at 7.00. Clench fist tightly contracting the biceps. Hold for four seconds –

'No, Reverend! You don't have to be a chicken-chested skinny weakling like what I was a few weeks ago.'

'No, Mr Harris.'

The Reverend leaves. Masturbate. Auxiliary: Barbara La Marr in casket (p. 98, *Hollywood Babylon* by Kenneth Anger. New York: Dell Publishing Co., 1981).

Friday, November 6

Depressed. Auxiliary:

> *Good Christ what is*
> *a poet if any*
> > *exists*

353

> *a man*
> *whose words will*
> > *bite*
> > > *their way*
>
> *home – being actual*
> *having the form*
> > > *of motion . . .*

William Carlos Williams

Saturday, November 7

Still depressed. Auxiliary:

> *Attacking space*
> *is what it's all*
> > > *about.*
>
> *To score*
> *a lot of*
> > *goals*
> > > *at all*
>
> *levels – you've got to*
> *attack space and*
> > > *take chances . . .*

Gary Lineker

Sunday, November 8

Morning: masturbate. Auxiliary: Genesis xxxviii, 9.

Afternoon: masturbate. Auxiliary: standard towelling briefs. 78% cotton, 22% nylon. Assorted pastels.

Evening: Superintendent Miss Temple goes down the pub without any knickers –
'I'm going down the pub without any knickers. Hang loose, Chopper.'
'Yeah.'
Masturbate. Auxiliary: Camille Paglia in conversation with Desmond Lynam. Private Tape.
Miss Temple returns from the pub half-cut –
'Ungird thy strangeness, arsehole!'
'After *The South Bank Show*?'
'Yeah, all right, Chopper.'
Midnight: fairly full penetrative sex.

Monday, November 9

Thumb up bum, mind in neutral –

seeing things: Southampton's Jimmy Gabriel in an FA Cup third round tie at the Dell; a French counter-attack at Dien Bien Phu; Cllr Michael Gammon – Conservative leader of Surrey County Council; Lizzie Siddal in the bath at Gower Street . . .
hearing voices: 'You fucking rotter!'; 'Dat lijk me ook een goed idee . . . !'; 'Dead! Sybil dead! It is not true!'; 'A single to Neasden, please.'

Tuesday, November 10

Amazing-page-turnability-quality.

Wednesday, November 11

Morning: masturbate. Auxiliary: 'The Revolt of Islam' by Percy Bysshe Shelley, Cantos 1–6.

Afternoon: masturbate. Auxiliary: 'The Revolt of Islam' by Percy Bysshe Shelley, Cantos 7–12.

Evening: masturbate. Auxiliary: 'Dick-Hungry Darlings', pp. 12–16, *Lovebirds*, No. 132.

Thursday, November 12

Morning: shoplift.

Afternoon: masturbate. Auxiliary: Electrolux 'Dolphin' remote control cleaner. 1,400-watt pulse power. Full remote control on hose handle. Electronic suction control for 400–1, 100 watts. Aluminium accessories. Neon indicator display panel. Hose-to-body-clip. 6-litre re-usable dust bags. Built-in tool storage. Cord rewind. Air freshener. Purple.

Evening: dinner with Big Nose Kate. She accuses me of pedantry.

Saturday, November 14

Morning: breakfast with Big Nose Kate. I accuse her of epiblast.

Afternoon: look it up. Epiblast, noun. The outermost layer of an embryo. Gutted.

Evening: masturbate. Auxiliary: Diagram 37 – A typical formation for away fixtures in the European Cup (p. 63, *Understanding Soccer Tactics* by Conrad Lodziak. London: Faber and Faber, 1966).

*

Thursday, April 1

Morning: receive a self-addressed envelope, postmarked Fulham. Open it –

> *Dear Mr Harris,*
>   *I'm afraid Ian Porterfield no longer works here. However, I did enjoy reading your diary – very bizarre – but I don't think it would fit in the Chelsea match programme.*
>   *Sorry.*
>   *I hope you get what you want.*
>
> Ken Bates
Chairman

Afternoon: sulk.

Evening: masturbate. Auxiliary: Figure 4.4. Diagrams of the four proposed mechanisms for the evolution of altruistic behaviour (p. 98, *Sociology and Behaviour* by David P. Barash. London: William Heinemann, 1978).

*

Between April 1993 and February 1999, Mr Harris stopped writing his log, which he kept in a little, red memo book, but proceeded to decorate Miss Temple's journal . . .

William Boyd

FANTASIA ON A FAVOURITE WALTZ

CLARA BILLROTH HANDED the baby to Frau Schäfer and the child went gladly to the old woman, its cries diminishing to gurgles and whimpers. 'Say goodbye to your mama,' Frau Schäfer said uselessly, as she did each evening, taking the baby's wrist between finger and thumb and making the tiny fingers parody a farewell wave. 'Say "Goodbye, Mama". Say it, Ullrich.' 'Please don't call him Ullrich,' Clara said, 'I don't like the name.' 'You've got to give him a name soon,' Frau Schäfer said, hurt, 'the child's nearly four months old. It's not correct. It's not Christian.' 'Oh, all right, I'll try and think of one,' Clara said and turned away, pulling her shawl around her as she went down the stairs, feeling the cold wind rush up from the tenement door to meet her. April, she thought: it still might as well be winter.

She walked briskly down Jägerstrasse towards St Pauli, a little late, her shoes pinching her feet, making her shorten her pace, making her favour the right foot over the left. The left was sore. Anneliese said that your feet were never exactly the same size, you should have a different shoe made for each foot. Anneliese and her nonsense. In what world would that be, Clara wondered? How rich would you have to be to have a different –

She saw the boy leaning against the gas lamp, holding on to it with both hands as if it were a mast and he were on the pitching deck of a ship in a stormy sea. As she drew nearer she watched him press his forehead to the cool moisture-beaded metal. The wind off the harbour was full of

358

threatening rain and the gas lamps wore their mistdrop halos like shimmering crowns in the gathering dark. The boy, she saw, was about fourteen or fifteen with long hair – reddish blond – folded on his collar. His eyes were shut and he seemed to be speaking silently to himself.

'Hey,' Clara said, watchfully, 'Are you all right?' He opened his eyes and turned to her. He was a stocky young fellow with good features, blue eyes, the thick honey-blond hair drawn off his forehead in a wave. 'Thank you,' the boy said, blinking his pale-lashed blue eyes at her. He had a distinct Hamburg accent. 'Migraine,' he said. 'You wouldn't believe the headache I have. But I'll be fine. I just have to wait until it's passed. You are kind to stop but I'll be fine.' Clara peered at him: his eyes were shadowed with the effort of talking. Sometimes she had those headaches herself, especially after little Katherine had died and then when she was pregnant with the baby boy, whatever she would call him – with 'Ullrich'. 'All right then,' she said. 'But don't let the police see you. They'll think you're drunk.' The stocky boy laughed politely and Clara went on her footsore way.

Clara arranged the front of her dress so that her bosom bulged freely over the bodice. The men liked that, it always worked. She tugged the front lower, arching her back, contemplating her reflection in the glass, turning left and right. She looked pretty tonight, she thought: the cold wind off the Elbe had brought colour to her face. She dipped her finger in the pot of rouge and added a little more to each cheek and a dab on her lips. She wanted to make a good impression on her first night; Herr Knipe would be pleased with her. She was early too, none of the other girls were there and when she came through the bar the glasses were being polished and the dance floor swept. It appeared a prosperous place, this *lokale*, not like the last one, there were even sheets on the bed. Herr Knipe seemed more generous too – keep half, my dear, he had said, and the more you work the happier I am.

In the bar the pianist had arrived and was sitting on the little raised dais, playing notes again and again as if he were tuning the piano. She walked towards him to introduce herself – it was important to befriend the musicians, then they would play your favourite melodies. The pianist heard her footsteps crossing the dance floor and turned. 'Hey,' Clara said, surprised. 'Migraine-boy. What're you doing here?' He smiled. 'I work here,' he said. 'How's the head?' Clara asked. He had the clearest blue eyes, all shadow gone from them now. 'Bearable.' He was trying not to look at her bosom, she saw. 'What's your name?' she said. He was too young to be working here, fourteen or fifteen only, she thought. 'Ah, Hannes,' he said. 'Hannes . . . Kreisler.' 'I'm Clara, Clara Billroth. Do you know any waltzes?' 'Oh yes,' said the boy Hannes, 'I know any number of waltzes.' 'Do you know this one?' Clara sang a few notes. 'It's my favourite.' Hannes frowned: 'You are not a very good singer, I'm afraid,' he said. 'Is it like this?' He turned to the piano and with his right hand picked out the tune. 'Yes,' Clara said, singing along, and then she saw him bring his left hand up to the piano and suddenly the dance hall was filled with the waltz, her waltz, her favourite waltz. She was amazed, as she always was, how they could take a simple tune, a few notes, and within seconds they were playing away – with both hands, no sheet music – as if they had known the waltz all their lives. Clara swayed to and fro to the rhythms. 'You're quite good, young Kreisler, my lad. Oh my God, look there's Herr Knipe. I'd better go.'

Four men – forty marks, twenty for her, a fair start. A fat sailor, then his little friend. Then some dances. Then a salesman from Altona who proudly showed her a daguerreotype of his wife – she hated it when they did that. Then a dark, muscly fellow – Norwegian or Swedish – who smelt of fish. Clara sniffed at her shoulder, worried that it had rubbed off on her. He had heaved and heaved, the Norseman, took his time. None of her tricks seemed to work. Took his own sweet time.

She finished her beer, pulled the sheets back up and tucked them in. She was unhooking her shawl when there was a knock at her door. It was Hannes. 'Hey, little Kreisler. Thank you for playing my waltz.' 'It's quite pretty, your waltz,' Hannes said. 'I like the tune.' 'Want some beer?' Clara said. 'No, I must go,' Hannes said, 'I came to say goodbye.' 'I'll see you tomorrow,' Clara said; she noticed he was looking at her breasts again. 'No, no, I'm going away,' he said. 'To convalesce. I'm not very well.' He smiled at her wearily. 'I can't take any more of these migraines. I think my head will explode.' Clara shrugged. 'Well, I hope they get someone as good as you on the piano.' They walked down the stairs to the rear entrance together. 'That was real class tonight, Hannes, my boy. You're a talent, you know.' Hannes chuckled politely, the sort of polite chuckle, Clara thought, that told her he knew full well just how talented he was. They paused at the door, Clara tying her shawl in a knot, pulling it over her head. 'So, hello and goodbye, Hannes Kreisler.' Then she kissed him, as a sort of goodbye present, really, and because he had been nice to her, one of her full kisses, with her tongue deep in his mouth, to give him something to remember her by, and she let him fumble and squeeze for a while at her breasts before she pushed him away with a laugh, clapped him on the shoulder and said, 'That's enough for you, my young fellow, I'm off to my bed.'

It was funny how everything could change in a year, Clara thought, as she wandered through Alster Arcade looking at the fine stores. She liked to do this before she went down to St Pauli for her evening's work. '47 had been, well, not too bad, but '48? . . . My God, not so good. If only Herr Knipe hadn't died. If only Frau Schäfer hadn't gone to live with her son in Hildesheim, if only the baby had been healthier, not so many doctors needed. Money. All she thought about was money. And everywhere there was revolution, they said, and all she could think about was money. She looked at her reflection in the plate glass window of Vogts & Co. She should put a bit more weight back on: the gentlemen didn't like skinny girls these days. She sighed and went to stand in a patch of

WILLIAM BOYD

sunlight 'to warm my tired old bones,' she told herself, with a chuckle, 'for a moment or two'.

There was a big piano store across the street, the pianos in the window lustrous and glossy, their lids up, the grained wood agleam with wax polish. The early summer warmth meant that the double doors of the shop were thrown open and she could hear over the noise of the cabs and the horse trams the demonstrator inside playing away at a waltz. Dum dee dee, dum dee dee . . . Good God in Heaven, she thought, that's my waltz.

It was little Hannes Kreisler all right, Clara saw, though not so little any more, the back was broader, the jaw squarer, the hair longer, if anything, playing away on the small stage in the centre of the great emporium, but he wasn't calling himself Hannes Kreisler, these days. The fancy copperplate on the placard that advertised the demonstrator's name (and his address for piano lessons) read 'Karl Wurth'.

Clara strolled into the shop, grateful that it was busy, thinking that with a bit of luck no one would tell her to leave for a while. A small crowd stood in a semicircle around 'Karl Wurth' listening to him play. It was her waltz, that was true, but it was different also, the tune was freer: it kept changing, changing pace and rhythm and then coming back to the original notes. She edged closer, watching Hannes play, seeing that he was reading music, there were sheets propped in front of him, concentrating, staring at the notes. The music grew faster and then finished in a kind of a gallop and a series of shuddering chords, not like a waltz at all. He slowly took his hands away from the keyboard. There was applause and Hannes looked round with his fleeting smile and gave a small dipping bow before he stood up and stepped away from the piano, taking his sheet music and removing the placard with his new name.

'Well, hey, if it isn't the famous pianist Herr Karl Wurth,' Clara said, tugging at his coat tail. He turned and recognised her at once, she saw, and that pleased her. 'Clara,' he said,

362

'what a surprise.' 'How's the nut,' Clara said reaching up and tapping his forehead. 'How's the brain-ache?' 'Much better,' Hannes said. 'I spent last summer at Winsen. Perfect. Full recovery. Do you know it?' 'Winsen? Oh, I'm never away from the place,' Clara said. 'That was my waltz you were playing. You've even written it down.' He had rolled his sheet music up into a tight baton. 'Here,' he said, handing it to her. 'It's a present.' 'How will you play it, if you give it to me?' she said. 'Oh, it needs improving. I'll do some more work. It's all up here,' he touched his head, lightly. 'So, Clara, still at Knipe's *lokale*?' he asked. 'He's dead,' Clara said, 'Tuberculosis. It all changed. I've moved – to a place on Kastanienallee. They could do with a decent pianist, I can tell you. So if you're looking for a position, I'll put in a good word.'

Hannes was about to speak but another boy appeared beside him, carrying a music case. 'And who might this charming young lady be?' the boy said. He had lively, mobile features, dark hair and a pointed chin. 'This is Clara,' Hannes said. 'An old friend. And this is my brother Fritz. Who's late.' 'My apologies,' Fritz said, and bowed to Clara. 'He – that one –' pointing at Hannes, 'is a slave driver,' he said and stepped up on to the stage and opened his case, taking out sheets of music. 'I have to leave,' Hannes said. 'I've a lesson to give.' 'We all have to earn a living,' Clara said. 'On you go. I'll look at the pianos.' They shook hands. 'What's the name of your *lokale*?' Hannes said, lowering his voice, 'Maybe I'll pass by.' She wanted to tell him but she decided not to. 'Oh no, it's not the place for you, Hannes Kreisler Karl Wurth.' 'I'll find it,' he said. 'Kastanienallee isn't so big. I probably worked in it. I worked in a lot of these places.' So she told him the name: Flügel's. What was wrong with that, she argued, he was almost a man, he was earning some money, why should she turn away the chance of earning some money herself? 'Please take this,' he said, handing her his scroll of sheet music again. 'A souvenir.' She took it from him. 'See you soon, Clara,' he said, but they both knew that was very unlikely. Still, you never could tell about a man and his appetites. 'For sure,' she said. 'Come by any time after six. We'll have a dance.'

She managed to look at the pianos for a few minutes before one of the floor managers asked her to leave. As she walked past the demonstrator's stage Fritz Wurth smiled at her and nodded goodbye. Except his name wasn't Fritz Wurth at all, she now saw as she glanced at his placard, it was Fritz Brahms. Brahms. What were they like, these boys? First Kreisler, then Wurth, now Brahms – it was all a game to them.

She rode in the omnibus down to St Pauli trying not to think of the floor manager's expression as he had asked her to leave. To distract herself she unrolled the sheet music Hannes had given her. Hannes had been kind, decent, he had remembered her. All written by hand, too, the little squiggly black scratching of the notes. How can they play from that? His brother had been polite also. She read the title slowly, her lips moving as she formed the words: 'Fantasia on a Favourite Waltz'. A souvenir. A nice gesture. She said it out loud, softly: '*Phantasie über einem beliebten Walzer*' . . . There were some decent people about in the world, not many, but a few of them. Hannes. It was a good name, that, short for Johannes . . . Yes, maybe that was what she should call the baby. Hannes Billroth.

She was still musing on the baby's new name when she arrived at Herr Flügel's *lokale*. Hannes Billroth – it had a ring to it. It was only when she took her position by the bar, and the pianist started thundering away noisily at a boring old polka that she realised she had left the music behind her in the horse tram. It made her angry at her carelessness, for a moment or two, before she asked herself what she could possibly do with such a manuscript anyway, and certainly that ape pounding away on the piano wouldn't have been able to make head or tail of it, not something so delicate and beautiful. *Phantasie über einem beliebten Walzer*. I ask you. Head or tail.

Claire Messud

LEAVING ALGIERS

Extract from a novel, The Last Life, *to be published by Picador in August 1999*

MY FATHER LOVED his homeland. When, in those last crazed weeks of June 1962, fuming buses and flatbed trucks poured into Algiers from the mountains and beyond, overflowing with white refugees and the tokens of generations, and juddered their honking, diesel-drenched way to the wild bazaar that the port had become, he stayed shuttered at home and pretended, for as long as he could, that all would be well. A mere boy of seventeen, he clung to his world: his parents had crossed the sea to France and a new beginning a year before, leaving their obstinate adolescent in the care of his grandmother. He had not wanted to leave; nor had she. They still did not want to.

Towards the end, young Alexandre scrabbled for any portents of stability, however fragile. Had de Gaulle not once promised, that famous day in Mostaganem, that Algeria was part of France and would forever remain so? And would the country's French inhabitants not hold him to that promise somehow, in spite of everything? Had the downstairs neighbours not, but eight months before, opened a restaurant in the rue Bab Azoun, and did it not spill its dance of shadows and conversation nightly on to the plaza?

These, at least, were the phrases with which he soothed the old woman. She, bed-ridden and in the final stages of her cancer, insisted that the very breeze and the bougainvillea were French and would remain so, unable to concede that the deed was done and the country lost. He monitored the radio

365

broadcasts and filtered out the reports of slaughter that punctuated the news. He played instead the swollen 78s of Debussy or Mendelssohn to which his grandmother was, even at the last, partial. The apartment was cloistered from the piercing sun, its heavy nineteenth-century furnishings (the shape of his own mother's girlhood) filmed with dust that last month when the *bonne*, Widad, no longer came by, having excused herself tearfully after eight years of service on the grounds that it was, for her and her family, no longer safe: the bodies of too many Muslims lay fly-bitten in the streets.

An odd normality did persist: neatly suited, the doctor rapped on the door morning and night to check on his deteriorating patient, measuring blood pressure and dosing morphine. And a nurse, a quiet young nun in starchy white, padded about the apartment in the afternoons, leaving Alexandre free, when he chose, to go out. Twice a week, Sundays and Thursdays, his parents telephoned from their new home, their anxiety and the crackling line one and the same, blurring them. His mother offered to come, and wanted to (it was her mother, after all, who was dying), but Alexandre put her off, and off, with the hollow assurances he would use again later in life. She, afraid and wanting to believe him, believed.

At night, in the cavernous darkness, he lay awake alone, awaiting only death and departure, both of which seemed so impossible that they shaped themselves instead as fear. He listened until the street noises started up again near dawn, jolted from near-sleep by the rumble of vehicles in the small hours, or the irregular spatter of footsteps on the pavement outside. He envisioned attack and pillage, flashing knives and walls of flame, interior pyrotechnics all the more extreme for the dulled quiet in which he, and his husk of an ancestor, spent their hours.

When she was awake, he read to her and cooked for her, although she consumed little more than clear broth and the occasional mouthful of bread. Alexandre sipped his morning coffee alone, cross-legged on the terrace, watching the movements of the city, its jerky rushes to departure, its veneer of familiar calm. Daily Algiers held fewer friends to reassure him that life would go on, and although they dripped away to France, these people were, to his purposes, as good as dead. Walking the streets he could hardly believe that only in the spring he had strolled in those same paths with his comrades, and they had batted at each other with their briefcases; that in spite of the *plastiquages* and the ubiquitous smell of burning he had been preoccupied, above all, with playing off one pretty girl against another, with going as far, sexually speaking, as was feasible without courting disaster. Everyone had been aware of what would have to be (the peace accords with the FLN had been signed in March, and that after so many long years of battle), but they had thought – no, more than thought, insisted – that they could just continue in the familiar round of their days.

Granted, that familiar round differed for some. My father had a cousin who had joined the OAS, a mere boy of twenty-one, his childhood playmate, now a terrorist flickering on the fringes, in order, as Alexandre and his friends saw it, to whip up hysteria and make matters worse. The OAS was responsible for the corpses, brown and white, or for most of them. Many secretly supported them, blasting the tattoo of 'Al-gé-rie Fran-çaise' on their car horns, or on their pots and pans; but in the flesh, their members were outlaws, and unwelcome.

As late as early June, this cousin, Jean, appeared at the apartment unannounced, after dark. His knock alarmed my father, convinced that Arab murderers beat at last upon the door, but the sight of Jean was hardly preferable. Ostensibly, the young man came to pay his respects to the dying, but in the kitchen, in a whispered hiss, he exhorted my father once more to join him, to fight to the last man, with the last bomb.

'And Grand'-mère?' asked Alexandre. 'How could I leave her?'

'And her grave?' countered his cousin. 'Will you just leave that, and this –' he gestured, 'your life, as if it were nothing? Come on, man, look at the choices.'

Failing there, Jean tried another tack: 'And the *métropole*? You think they want us there, any more than you want to go?'

Alexandre hesitated. But he said 'no' a final time, and, after allowing the young man to kiss his slumbering grandmother, hurried him out of the door and back to his desperate cell.

Inevitably, change bore down upon my father. His suspended quiet – the life of a man in his third age, not his first – crumbled. The university library burned to the ground, and with it his final hopes. Then, the following Monday, his grandmother forsook consciousness, a development which prompted young Alexandre to the highly unusual step of calling his parents. His mother sobbed into the ocean of air between them, while his father suggested the names of friends who might help – all of them, Alexandre knew, already gone.

That evening, on his round, the doctor drew my father aside. 'It's a matter of days,' he told him. 'Two, maybe three. I'll try to come by, when I can. But my wife and children are leaving on Wednesday, and I myself am due to fly out before the weekend. I've got a lot to see to before then. I can't do anything now but bear witness, and that is as well done, or better done, by the sister. She'll get the priest. You need to be making your own plans. There isn't much time left.'

'I can't leave her.'

'Do you plan to bury her here, or take her to France with you?'

The choice had not struck my father clearly before that moment: he was young, unaccustomed to the rituals of death. He had forgotten there would be a body. But once it was put to him, the answer seemed evident: 'She'll come with me, of course. For my mother, for the funeral.'

The doctor clicked his pen several times. 'Are you sure that's what you want?'

'Absolutely.' It occurred to my father that his grandmother, having made Algeria her home, would be loath to leave it even in a coffin; but he knew, too, that she was French above all, and that an Algeria no longer French, no longer Catholic, was no resting place for her.

'It might be easier, given the circumstances –'

'It is my family's wish.'

'Have you been to the port? Have you seen?'

Alexandre waved his hands in fussy dismissal.

'Have you booked passage on a ship?'

'I'll take care of it. I will.'

'Is there nobody to help you?'

'I'll manage.'

The doctor shrugged. 'I'll try to come by. I'll see what I can do.'

That night, the nurse stayed. She sat beside the old woman's bed in the puddle of light cast by the lamp, knitting, her prayer book open upon her lap. Alexandre perched opposite, in shadow. He held his grandmother's hand for a time, running his fingertips back and forth over her ridged nails: two months before, those stubby digits had peeled potatoes and tousled his hair, had written out shopping lists in the crabbed remnants of a once-elegant hand. My father eventually slept in his hard-backed chair, soothed by the nun's clacking needles and the knowledge that the wait was almost over. He slept better than he had in weeks. His grandmother, too, seemed more peaceful, her breath a shallow snore.

In the morning, instead of the doctor the priest came by, a tall man with the mournful face of an El Greco portrait. He delivered the last rites. All bone, his hairy toes unseemly in sandals, he embraced Alexandre, then spoke in hushed tones to the nurse, and departed.

The nun stayed on, and by this Alexandre knew his grandmother might die at any time. The younger woman rested for an hour on the sofa in the sitting room, her shoes neatly paired beneath her, and when she awoke, unwrinkled, she deftly plumped the cushions as though she had never lain there. Alexandre brought her coffee.

'Do you have somewhere else to be?' he asked.

'No.'

'And no plans? Aren't you planning, like the doctor, to go?'

'God doesn't care who governs this country,' she said. 'I'm not going anywhere. But you need to get home now, to your family in France. Go this morning, and arrange for it.'

369

'This *is* home,' said my father.

The nun shook her head, with a small smile.

Alexandre set off for the port. As he drew nearer, the streets grew crammed with traffic. The paved expanse by the water, inside the gates, was thick with people, milling and shouting among their packages and the abandoned furniture of the already departed. He passed beside a refrigerator, a stack of studded trunks, a battered armoire. Some families had clearly been there for days, their shirts and blouses grimed, the men's chins whiskery, the women's hair lank and unkempt. They gave off the sour stench of travel, in heat, which mingled everywhere with the fetid drift of sewage. Others, newer to the vigil, arranged their belongings into tidy pyramids and fed their children cold sausages and bread from string bags. One young mother suckled her baby, her mottled breast burst from her modest sprigged shirtwaist. A few feet away, a fat man swayed uneasily, fanning himself with a newspaper, a limp handkerchief upon his naked crown, sleeves rolled up to reveal his butcher's forearms an angry crimson from the sun. The elderly sat blank and tear-stained upon their cases, clutching at incongruous objects: a frying pan, a mantel clock. An abandoned canary twittered in its ornate cage, alone on a bollard. The children, to whom the scene was an adventure, marauding in small packs, taunting the infants and bullying the leashed dogs, so that mingled with the calls and cries of people came the variegated, desperate barks of canines big and small.

Several red-faced sailors, sloppily uniformed, pushed through the fray, their destination an office on one side of a pier. Alexandre pushed behind them, sliding in their wake. He envied them their size and their nonchalance. From the mainland, they had no attachment to the crowd. Their task was to man the ship that would ferry the refugees away; then, perhaps, they would stay in Marseilles, perhaps return for more, again and again until all the white flotsam along the shores of Algeria had been cleared. It might as well have been cattle they were transporting. They did not, as did Alexandre, see toil and marriage and death in the fraying sacks and rope-

bound boxes, or in the creviced features of the peasants and
housewives: they saw only cargo. And they knew, unlike the
haranguing, paper-waving mob clustered around the har-
bour-master's office, that when the ship pulled out of port,
they would be on it.

They strode easily into the office, but at the hand of a sailor
more gross even than they, the door was barred to all others,
my father among them. Jostled, he stood incredulous.

'But I want to book a passage,' he said loudly, to the vast
chest of the man in front of him.

'Don't we all, sonny. Wait your turn,' said a woman at his
shoulder. 'I've watched three boats go without me, and I'm
not going to miss the fourth.'

'My grandmother is dying.'

'*She* won't need a place then, will she?'

My father turned away from the woman's shrill voice. He
pushed against the swell of bodies, like everyone else.

A stout official emerged from the building, fingering a list.
He stepped on to an overturned bucket; he cleared his throat.
'This afternoon's departure is fully booked. Only those with
tickets purchased through the central office, for this ship
specifically, will be permitted to board. If, at 3 pm, any berths
have not been filled, then they will be open to those first in
line. We will take nothing more than what you can carry
when you board. We cannot accommodate furniture of any
kind. Please remain orderly. There will be two departures
tomorrow, but be advised that they, too, are fully booked.'

The crowd broke into rowdy protest.

'My grandmother – a coffin –'

The official was close enough to look my father in the eye.
'A coffin would be considered furniture. No coffins allowed.'

How amusing, in other circumstances, such a veto might
seem: 'No coffins allowed – can you imagine?' said my
mother to me, with a guilty titter. 'It's ridiculous.' But my
father was never able to make light of it.

'And me?' he asked.

'Have you a ticket?'

'No.'

'Then I suggest that either you stay here, like everybody else, and wait for standing room – which could take several days – or else go to the booking office in town and purchase a ticket.'

'For when?'

'How would I know? You can see how many people there are.' He looked at my father's crisp shirt, his neatly combed hair. 'Don't you know somebody who could help you? That would be the best way.'

Alexandre walked back through the city. His cousins, Jean excepted, were not in Algiers. His closest friends were gone, and had been for a month or more. His last girlfriend had left for a three-month English course in Kent and now, he knew, she would never return. He was reluctant to call his father and ask for help, but this he resolved – upon seeing the queue, two blocks long, outside the ticket office in town – to do. He made a detour to pass in front of his neighbour's restaurant: its open windows and bustle, he decided, would reassure him.

It could not. An array of envelopes blanketed the mat inside the door. A notice on the glass, handwritten, hasty, announced that the establishment would be closed until further notice. The tables were set, the napkins folded in their flowery cones at every plate, already wilted and forlorn. On the bar at the rear of the restaurant, Alexandre could see, with his nose pressed to the glass, bottles standing in disarray: liquor, wine, empties, jumbled up together. My father sat on the kerb, stared at his shoes, and started to cry.

Monsieur Gambetta, the neighbour in front of whose business my father crouched despondent, then happened by, a shiny, bulbous man in his late forties, jangling a great ring of keys. Theirs was, for my father, a serendipitous meeting: Gambetta was expecting a cheque and thought it just might have been delivered to his restaurant. He recognised young Alexandre, and when he learned of the boy's troubles, offered a solution. Well-connected as they were, he and his wife had secured not merely tickets, but an entire cabin for the crossing, forty-eight hours thence. There was no reason, he said, if Alexandre didn't mind sleeping on the floor, why he couldn't share the space with them.

'It's very hard,' he said, a sympathetic arm around the boy's shoulders, 'to be suffering from the death of your grandmother at such a time. We're happy to do what we can, in the face of our tragedies.'

'But Monsieur,' said Alexandre, 'my grandmother isn't dead yet. It's true, she's dying – they say it could be any moment – but she is still alive.'

'You wouldn't leave her?'

'I can't imagine – No. I think, from what the doctor has said –'

'Let's wait and see.'

'The priest came this morning.'

Both men were awkward. Alexandre did not feel he could broach the subject of the coffin. He thought about it, though: it occurred to him that perhaps it could lie on the cabin floor, and that he could sleep on top of his grandmother. But he didn't mention it.

'I'm so grateful,' he said.

'Think nothing of it. We can arrange, on the morning, when to meet. We could go to the port together, depending . . .'

'I'm so grateful. Perhaps, when we get there, my parents –'

'Think nothing of it.'

From that moment on, my father spent the hours praying for his grandmother's demise. He sat in the hard chair in the gloom, the knitting sister impassive across the sheet, and listened eagerly for the death rattle. The old woman was unlikely to open her eyes again: all she needed to do was to let go. He whispered in her ear, when the nun left the room: 'It's OK, Grand'-mere. God is waiting for you. Grand-père, too, and your sisters, and paradise. Let go, Grand'-mere.'

But his grandmother, like her fellow colonials, braved adversity, tough and recalcitrant. Her tense was the present continuous, and she clung to it with all the blind will of a mole. 'I am dying', 'she is dying', 'our country is dying': the tense lingers in a defiance incomprehensible to those for whom there remains the simple resignation of adopting the past.

Twenty-four hours passed, in which Alexandre did not sleep; nor did he eat, even when the nurse brought him soup. He was trapped, with the old woman, in the ongoing, in that chasm between past and future.

The nurse, who knew of the Gambettas' offer, reassured him: 'She will die. She will die in time. God wills it. Have faith.' But he could not believe her. He could not remember what faith might mean. Had he not had faith in de Gaulle's promise? Had he not had faith in Gambetta's restaurant?

On the evening of the next day, the nun, ever practical, sent an unwilling Alexandre to do the unthinkable: she dispatched him to the undertaker's to order his grandmother's coffin. She advised him to spare no expense: 'If you pay, they'll have it ready by morning. Pay enough, and they'll work through the night.'

'She's dying, but she isn't – How can I, when she isn't?'

'Because you must. Because she will be.'

When he returned, however, well after dark (minus his grandfather's gold watch, with which he had had to bribe the swarthy carpenter; and all the more firmly set in his plan to take the coffin to France, as the undertaker had informed him that burials were very backed up and bodies putrefying in the morgue), his grandmother was breathing still. She had barely stirred. The nun was unravelling a new skein of yarn: other than that, nothing had changed.

They sat with her, again, through the night, although several times my father, depleted, gave in to sleep, his head lolling on his chest. Each wakening start was accompanied by the hope – but no, she lived on.

At nine, on a morning fiercely hot and airless, Monsieur Gambetta came to the door. 'We're going now,' he said. 'Because of the crowd at the port. Surely you've seen them?'

'Of course.'

'Not yet?' Gambetta made an embarrassed nod towards the bedroom.

'Not yet.'

'By two, my son. You have until two, at the very latest. After that, we'll be boarding, and they won't let you on without us. Did you hear that the widow Turot's throat was cut last night? In her apartment. Not three streets from here. Hard to know who to blame. It's time, my boy. At the port, before two. We'll be as near to the gangway as we can get, in the ticket-holders' section. Courage.'

My father then pretended to pack. He paced the apartment, removing silver from drawers and pictures from walls. He took the sepia photograph of his grandparents on their wedding day from its frame and folded it in four, so that it would fit in his trouser pocket. He took his shirts from the dresser and laid them on his bed, only to put them back again. He placed three silver coffee spoons in each sock, where they were initially cool against his ankles. He removed a cushion cover needle-pointed by his grandmother from its cushion, and stuffed it, along with a single pair of underwear and a small framed watercolour of the Bay of Algiers, into a canvas sack. He took down his grandmother's photograph album, weighed it, and left it on the sofa; then returned to pluck from it an assortment of memories, trying to guess what his parents would most want, tearing the edges of some, until he had a handful to go into the bag. Every so often, he slid into his grandmother's room: the nun would look up and shake her head, and Alexandre would begin again his restless perambulation of the flat.

At 10.30, there came a hammering at the door. The coffin-maker sweated on the landing, Alexandre's watch shiny on his wrist.

'It's downstairs, on the truck. Help me carry it up – I'm by myself. Can't do it alone.'

It took the better part of half an hour to hoist the unwieldly box up three flights. Alexandre was drenched in perspiration, and had to rest at every storey. He knew little about coffins, but could tell that this one was enormous, long enough for a man of six feet, and wide.

'It's huge,' he panted, halfway up. 'So heavy.'

'You didn't tell me how tall she was. Couldn't take any

chances. And the wood I had handy was thick. There's no help for it. Better too big than too small, you know. She's got to rest in it a long time. She might as well be comfortable.'

When they at last reached the apartment, they laid the coffin, its door swung wide, on the living-room floor, alongside the sofa.

'Where's the deceased then?' asked the undertaker's man, wipiing his slick, hairless brow with his slick and hairy arm.

'She isn't – just a minute.'

My father went to the door of his grandmother's room. Her knitting to one side, the nun leaned over the old woman, cradling her head with one hand and beating at the pillow behind her with the other. As Alexandre came into the room, the nun let his grandmother's skull slip gently back into the newly blooming down. The nun, so long unruffled, seemed flushed, her smooth face pink and beaded.

'I wanted her to lie nicely. She's gone, poor dear. While you were on the stairs. She's ready to come with you now.'

'But when?'

'As I say, a minute or two ago, when you were in the stairwell. She didn't suffer. The Lord is merciful.'

There wasn't time for my father to cry, or to wonder at his elder's impeccable timing. For the promise of a standard lamp, a soup tureen and a silver candelabra, the man from the undertaker's was persuaded to shuttle Alexandre and his grandmother to the port. With the help of the sheet beneath her they made a sling, and lifted her, still warm and in her nightgown, into the living room and into the box. She lay marooned there, tiny in the space. The nun shadowed them, praying quietly.

'She'll shift around. She's not stiff enough,' said the man. 'Got anything to hold her still?'

It was Alexandre's idea to use the sofa cushions, their faded green velvet of no other use to him by then. The men stuffed them in around the body, one squashed at her feet and two flattened along her sides. Beneath her head they laid the pillow from her bed, which gave off the sickly scent of illness and her perfume.

'That'll do.'

The man let Alexandre bend to kiss the old lady one final time, allowed him to rearrange her hands (those ridged fingernails!) across her chest, and then he swung the hinged lid and fastened the shiny bolts in place.

Full, the coffin was even heavier, but to Alexandre, precious. He was careful on the descent. He didn't quite believe that his grandmother would not flinch at the bumps, and so took great pains not to scrape the box in the turns, or to let it fall. Once she was safe in the truck, the two men returned, one last time, to the apartment. The nun had packed her things, was ready to make her way back to the hospital. Alexandre took his canvas sack, throwing into it, at the last, a cardigan of his grandmother's, and the little cedar crucifix from above her bed. The man shouldered his lamp, crooked the tureen under his arm, and asked the nun to wield the candlestick. The three of them left together, without bothering to lock the door.

The nun declined a ride, preferring to stroll the stifling streets for the first time in days. She embraced my father, and blessed him. 'You've done well,' she said. 'Your parents will be proud.'

It was almost one by the time they reached the port. The truck could not advance even to the gates, so thickly massed was the ramp down to the pier. A few vendors with more interest in money than in politics had installed themselves along the seafront to cater to the departing, and they hawked fruit and ice-cream and french fries in waxed cones at inflated prices.

Unloading my great-grandmother was one thing; proceeding to the far edge of the pier reserved for ticket-holders proved another. People crushed up against them: some banged on the box; children scurried underneath it. The older men and women stepped back to let them pass, and one or two crossed themselves furtively. The undertaker's man smoked while he hauled, puffing out of the corner of his mouth, allowing the cigarette to droop and rise with his breathing. When he was done, he spat the glowing butt into the fray with an upward flick of his chin.

The sailor at the barrier was mercifully young, and had evidently not been apprised of the decree against coffins: he lifted the gate for them without question when Alexandre caught sight of Monsieur Gambetta and the latter, waving, called out. 'He's with us. Let him through.'

The ticket-holders were calm, their end of the pier comparatively uncluttered. They waited in the heat-shim-mered shadow of the sleek ship, the *El Djezair*, a vessel whose canvas-covered lifeboats dangled like baubles above its deck. The air was saltier at this end, less choked with the fumes of decay. Alexandre, the coffin-maker and their load advanced without obstruction to the Gambettas' pile of suitcases. No sooner were they unburdened than the man gave a small salute. 'Best of luck. See you over there, maybe,' he said, and was gone.

The Gambettas stood beyond surprise. Madame Gambet-ta's cherry mouth fell agape, and her fingers fluttered to her hair as if its bun might unravel from the shock.

'What's this, what's this?' spluttered Gambetta.

'My family – a funeral – she must come with me to France.'

'Quite. Oh, quite, but my boy, I don't see how –'

'I thought we could put her on the floor. I'll sleep on top of her. She won't really be in your way. It's not so far. I'm sorry, but you must understand –'

'Quite. Oh yes, of course, but I don't – well, no, I see.' Monsieur Gambetta sat back on his suitcase, his features crumpling in defeat. 'No, you're right. Naturally. We'll manage. She is, uh, properly – I mean, the box is –' He pulled at the fleshy lobe of his ear. 'It's just, it's very hot weather, you know?'

'It's a proper coffin. Very solid.'

'Yes, I can see that. It seems extremely – *big*.'

'He didn't have her measurements.'

'No, I see.'

Madame Gambetta stepped forward and spoke in a

whisper from behind her linen handkerchief. 'You're absolutely sure she won't *smell*? I'm very sensitive, I can't help it. I should be sick.'

'There's not been time. She's only just gone. And the coffin is very solid.'

'As long as she doesn't smell.'

How I pity the poor Gambettas, whose kindness was repaid with a corpse. But they were not going to abandon the boy there – how could they? – and he so young to be mixed up in such a business. He should have been flirting on the esplanade, as handsome as he was, not standing hunched and crushed before them with the burden of the dead on his shoulders.

'We're all on a hard road,' said Gambetta. 'But we're on it together.'

'And our Saviour will guide us,' said Madame, crossing herself. A moment later, when she thought my father's attention elsewhere, she rolled her eyes at her husband and hissed, '*Quel cauchemar!*' What a nightmare.

In the event, the Lord showed mercy upon the Gambettas. When the moment came to board, Monsieur was called upon to fight for my great-grandmother, and he did. 'I paid for the cabin and I can put in it anything that I choose. I could transport a horse or a washing machine if I wanted to. The space is mine. Now give this boy a hand and show some respect for the dead.'

Madame stood to one side, all sombre dignity, and shook her head. 'Imagine,' she murmured to a cluster of fellow passengers. 'The boy is bereaved and they want to rob him of a proper funeral. As if selling out our homeland weren't disgrace enough.'

A minor uproar ensued – had these people not lost everything? Could they countenance a further theft? – as a result of which the coffin was hoisted up the gangplank by two sailors, upon whose impressive musculature the great weight appeared to float. The Gambettas followed, and Alexandre, all of them laden with the *bibelots* of the Gambettas' flat in bulging leather cases.

The party crossed the deck, and stood, arrested for a time, while the deceased and her casing were manoeuvred down the narrow well to the floor below, where the Gambettas' cabin was located. There, the grey corridor was very narrow, and the coffin could only advance on its side.

'Be careful,' urged Alexandre, picturing his grandmother pressed between the velvet cushions.

'Show some respect,' admonished Gambetta again.

But when they reached the cabin door, it became immediately clear that there was not sufficient space to turn the coffin.

'We won't be able to get it in,' said the sailor in front. 'There's not room. The angle is too sharp. The corridor's too narrow. Won't go round.'

'Try, man. You haven't even tried,' said Gambetta. Madame shook her head, whether in agreement with the sailor or her husband it was not clear.

They tried. For a quarter of an hour, they tried. They tipped the coffin on its end, they pushed and scraped it; they pulled and grappled with it, their breaths spuming in the heat. Even the strong men wearied at the box's terrible weight. And the sailor was right: my great-grandmother would not, could not, share the Gambettas' cabin.

'What now?' asked my father, his limbs jellying from the prolonged emotion.

'What indeed?' asked Gambetta.

The first mate was summoned, and the the captain. The corridor, so full of people, grew stuffy, and Madame, tightly corseted, threatened to faint. Alexandre fanned her busily with the packet of family photos from his bag, which made only a little breeze.

The captain, a slight man with a prissy moustache and crooked teeth, stood unspeaking for some minutes, his arms folded across his brass-buttoned breast.

'I have a proposal,' he said at length to Monsieur Gambetta, leaning forward on his toes as if sharing a secret.

'This young man is the next of kin,' said Gambetta. 'Put your proposal to him.'

'In principle,' said the captain, turning to lean towards Alexandre, 'Coffins aren't allowed. Not at this time, when we need every square foot for passengers. They count as furniture, you see.'

'But my grandmother –'

The captain raised a hand to silence my father. 'Hear me out, young man. I appreciate your difficulty. I was going to suggest, for the dignity of all concerned, a burial at sea.'

'Well – indeed,' said Gambetta.

'How perfect,' breathed Madame, her colour returning. 'A solution.'

'I suppose – I guess – what choice do I have?' asked my father, who felt by now so unwell that he had turned his improvised fan on himself, and was beating furiously.

'None,' said the captain. 'If you wish to sail today.'

And so my great-grandmother came to rest in the mouth of the Bay of Algiers. No sooner was the ship underway (its decks a writhe of passengers, their waving arms like an infestation of worms) than the captain stood up at the stern, the coffin held aloft beside him by four solemn-faced sailors (one of them all but chinless, so that his mouth seemed inadvertently to fall open) and read through a silvery megaphone the prayers for the dead. My father stood there also, by the railing, and when he bent to kiss the coffin, his tears fell in splotches on to the rough wood.

The crowd on shore could see the funeral too, or so my father believed, because they seemed to grow still, and a hush fell over the bay in the brilliant afternoon sun. When the coffin slipped, with a muted splash, into the oily Mediterranean, and was swallowed, the ship's human cargo stood motionless and wide-eyed: mourning this reminder of the dead they left behind, and their own deaths to come, and the glinting white glory of their city, lost to them like Atlantis, wavering there on the hillside, so near, but gone for ever.

Courttia Newland

COMPLEXION DOES NOT MAKETH THE (BLACK) MAN

Alright; now here's the lesson for today . . .
Queen Latifah

BEFORE WE GET started – that is to say, before we embark on this journey towards truth, and the *real* reality of our situation here – I would like to show the less-informed readers in our midst exactly what I'm talking about, with a little tale. Don't worry, I won't deviate from my *main* topic – which, in case you haven't guessed, is our (the Black race's) absurd preoccupation with our skin colour, brought upon us by years of slavery and indoctrination by people who trained us to hate ourselves, and who took our land and our knowledge and our ancestors, and spread each of those things to the four corners of the earth . . .

(Control – that's what my English Lit lecturer used to tell me – I must control the gateway between my thoughts and my pen . . .)

So OK – now you know what this is all about. And I *realise* it's a touchy subject – a subject that Black people on road don't stop talking about, and a subject that Black people in business suits definitely *won't* talk about. But I've had enough of it – really, truly, seriously, had enough – and the reason I've had enough all stems from the story I'm gonna tell after the story – I mean the story after the first story – I mean –

Fuck it, I'll just tell the damn thing and you'll get what I mean, OK?

OK. Here goes.

A dark-skinned Black woman picks up a magazine in a doctor's waiting-room, and proceeds to flick through it idly. She's not really looking at the hairstyles (as her regular stylist

382

had attended to her several days before, and up to now the horse hair is still strong-looking and healthy-looking, and her weave is still woven thank you very much); instead, she's whiling away her time, barely glancing at the articles, and quickly skimming through the masses of interviews and book reviews.

The more the Black woman flicks through the magazine, the slower her page-turning gets. The further she gets through the magazine, the more she starts to think about the images she's seeing for each and every hair-care or make-up advertisement; bold images, on bright, colourful, glossy, sun-kissed pages, that assault her eyes and insult her pride. She looks at all the straight noses and long hair – not for the first time – and closes her eyes, as if to block out the sight of the light-coloured eyes and thin lips – not for the last time – and the White woman sitting next to her in the waiting-room wonders what's wrong as she sits there and closes her eyes tighter and tighter, the same thought going over and over in her mind, the thought that convinces her that *I do not equal beauty*, no, not even that, because the *man on road think I'm alright*; in fact, it's more like – they *do not think I equal beauty*. And somehow, to that Black girl right there in the doctor's waiting-room, in that single moment of self-doubt, *that* – or they – are much more important to her. And the White woman watches her, concerned, but unable to under-stand, as the girl lets the magazine fall to the table – and even as the woman peeps at the cover, and spies the single word – EBONY – she still doesn't get it, even though she puzzles over what was bothering the girl as she makes her way home on the bus, and the girl's desolate and hopeless face haunts the woman until she gets back to her husband, her family and her home – where she very quickly forgets the whole thing.

I will not spell out what I mean by that story – you must read and understand it yourself. This is the reality of the situation that we, as Black men and women, are living in. I will not attempt to offer a solution to this problem (at the risk of sounding like a smartarse), even though I believe I possess one; and I will not accept the point of view of anyone who uses Naomi Campbell as an argument against my example – for what we want (or what *I* want), in a Black Supermodel, is not some blue-eyed, horse-hair wearing ... *somebody*, who denies her Blackness and her working-class roots in order to elevate her ownself – but a true and fair representation of *all* – and I do mean all – aspects of the Black Diaspora. Maybe we don't see anything like this because it differs so very greatly from the world-wide view of us as a criminal people. Maybe because, like that girl from M People sings – *it's all too beautiful*. You get me?

Anyway, the more I sit here and talk, and prattle on about this complexion thing, the more I realise that you (the reader) must be agreeing with my old English Lit lecturer by now – so I'll get on to tale number two. But first of all I'd just like to say something – *for the benefit of the tape*, as they say in all those crappy American police dramas. Another one they kill in the US of A is – *you can quote me on this* – you know dem ones? Both phrases apply in the following sentence.

I love Black women whatever their complexion.

There – just to get that off my chest. And you, the reader, I know what you're thinking – if you're White, you're probably thinking; *wha' the fuck's dis guy on – has he got a complex or what, eh? I tell ya, the guy's got a chip on his shoulder the size o' the Nat West fuckin' buildin' mate!* And if you're Black you're probably thinking – *wha' the fuck's he even bringin' it up for? If he's bringin' up tings like dat, you better believe you ain' seein' my man wid no Benson complexion gully – blatant!*

But the fact of the matter is, I have to bring it up; and if you saw me you'd realise why. See – I'm what Black people would call a light, red, or even yella skinned Black man – and what White people would call 'tanned'. And man, the second story has everything to do with my love of Black women (and a little to do with my love of women period – I ain' no racist); because it was exactly that that got me into this situation I'm gonna show you about right now.

Like I said, I'm a light-skinned, hazel-eyed Black man – both my parents were Black, but they were kinda light too. My mum, a lively, beautiful, kindly woman from St Kitts, always used to say there was a White man in our bloodline – Dad would cough and rattle his copy of the *Sun* and rant about him *nah 'ave nuh White man blood ina 'im vein dem* . . . But even then, even at seven years old, I knew the score – I didn't like it very much, but I knew.

I've often found myself in a curious position because of my complexion – through college, the scales would usually tip at both ends and my skin was either completely ignored by the other students, or remarked upon in so many different ways, I just wished it wasn't an issue any more. I never found the perfect balance.

The worst thing of all were the student parties – for no matter what kind of girl I went for – no matter how stunning, intelligent, or cute they were – I always caught somebody looking at me like I was letting someone else down – and I always felt more than a little bad at the end of the night. Not overpoweringly bad; or bad enough not to sleep with my chosen girl. But bad enough to recall the snide glances and curled lips on my first quiet moment alone. Bad enough to recall the hate in the eyes of the hater.

If I left with a dark-skinned Black girl – *the White girls wouldn't talk to me because most of the darker girls in my college were into Black power an' shit, an' pro-Black meant Anti-White to them. Believe.*

If I left with a light-skinned Black girl – *the dark-skinned Black girls called me a 'wannabe' and said that light-skinned was the closest I could get to White-skinned – and that – and only that – was the reason for me wanting to roll around on my bed with her for a couple of hours.*

And if I left with a *White* girl – *Woy! If I left with a White girl – which I only dared to do once – man, I wouldn't have a friend who was Black and a girl in that college from the minute we was seen together, no fuckin' joke either . . .*

Seriously though, the one time I did it, I came to college the Monday an' when some girl called Sianna come up to me, talking about, *she saw me leavin' on Saturday*, and, *don't I have any self-respect* – I panicked man, I have to admit I panicked, cause I knew what was comin', an' I could see a whole heap of Black girls earwiggin' not far away – so I jus' said, 'Nah man, she was drunk and she was a frien' so I took her to her yard, dropped her off an' dat's it man! Dat's it!'

Sianna didn't believe me, but I insisted man – ended up swearing on my mum's life that that girl was a friend – an' I know that's cold, but what could I do; the White girl was screwing when I told her I wouldn't be able to see her any more, an' I kinda regretted it cos she weren't that bad . . . but there was some *fine* sisters in my college man, with dem kinna back-offs that jus', jus' . . .

You know what I mean.

I tried to talk to my bredrin Carlos about it, but the fucker just laughed at me man.

'Don't mek Sianna an' dem gyal twis' you up like so man,' he told me, as we got ready to go to the fateful party that was on that night. 'You're a strong, God-fearin', Black back-off worshippin', good-lookin' *nigga*!' He exploded, fiddling with the last few buttons on his crisp blue shirt.

'I agree wid you on everythin' but the nigga,' I told him lazily. Carlos was like a woman when it came to dressing. I'd been ready from time.

'No matter,' my flatmate replied. 'What I'm sayin' is, you can't afford to let dat guilt stop you from havin' a good time wid *whoever you please man*. You're a man. Live by yuh own code, not no one else's man, shit . . .'

'OK, OK,' I said, touching his fist. 'I'm gonna do dat man. I'm gonna start from tonight star.'

'I'll be watchin',' he warned.

'Anyone I choose man,' I muttered, picking up my car keys and going for the door. 'Hurry up – nigga.'

But by the time we eventually got to the party, my confidence had eroded like limestone. Scores of beautiful girls were making their way to and from the entrance – White, Black, Oriental, Asian . . . as I pulled up and parked I could feel the old worry reappearing in my veins. Carlos looked at me and shook his head, guessing why I'd gone so quiet. We got out the car.

Once inside the house (which was converted from an old shop) I didn't feel much better. Swingbeat blasted from huge black sound speakers. Crews of girls hugged the walls, dressed in bright coloured skirts and cleavage-revealing tops. D&G wearing guys smoked it up in the corners, and watched the girls dancing lustfully. I went to the bar while saying my hello's and got a drink for myself and my friend, who was eagerly talking to the first set of women he'd come across. Leaning over the bar area, I ordered two cans of Red Stripe.

The two girls behind the bar were stunning. One of them had skin which reminded me slightly of peaches .... for although she was as light-skinned as I, there was the trace of a peach-like blush in her cheeks; as warm as the red dusk of a setting sun. Her eyes were bright and chestnut brown, and her lips cast for ever in a pout that drove male students crazy. Her name was Karen.

The other bartender was a girl I'd lusted over for some time before now. With skin that was blemish-free, as smooth as satin, and as dark as the night that came after the setting sun, she had curious slanted eyes, long, long eyelashes and a body full of curves I'd long ached to touch. Her name was Zenobia.

We chatted briefly – mainly small talk about college work, for they were both in my English classes – then I went over to get the drinks to Carlos, who was in heavy conversation with a set of Spanish girls, never mind the bad looks he was getting. By the time I returned I'd made my mind up. I wasn't going to talk to anybody – just have a good time by myself, that was all.

Carlos introduced me to his new friends. A girl called Rosa – dark-haired, full-lipped and brown-eyed – caught my attention. Within minutes we were talking, laughing and dancing animatedly.

The next time I went over to get the drinks, the atmsophere behind the bar had cooled by a good few degrees.

'Uhh . . . Can I 'ave two more Red Stripes an' two rum an' Cokes please . . . An' go easy on the Coke.'

Zenobia cut her eye at me, but it was Karen who spoke her mind first.

'Sellin' it are we Paulie? After all dem talks you're always givin' about the Black race stickin' together an' all dat, it seems a bit strange to see you chattin' up a English girl.'

'She's Spanish,' I informed them.

'Pah! They were jus' as bad,' Zenobia said, while pouring more Wray & Nephew. 'They got us, the Aztecs, an' the American Indians!'

'Who said I was chattin' her up anyway?' I shot back, feeling a mite defensive. After all, my integrity as a Black man was being questioned. 'The minute a Black man starts talking' to a White girl, he gets it from everybody! Black man, White man, Black woman, White woman. I believe it stems from the intense preoccupation everybody has with the Black dick.'

They laughed at that. Luckily.

'I'm sorry, but I for one am not preoccupied wid your tings,' Karen said through her laughs.

Zenobia just shook her head.

'Go back to yuh friends man, they're waitin' for yuh,' she ordered, pointing over at Carlos and the others. Sure enough, they were all looking over.

'Alright, I'm goin', but she ain' my girl, an' dis conversation ain' over OK?'

Zenobia gave me a stomach-churning smile. 'OK.'

I went back over to the others. Carlos was staring at me, but no one said anything. The music stepped up a pace, as Hip Hop came on the set.

But I didn't feel right. Every step I took with Rosa was filled with paranoia. She must have noticed, because she started wanting to cling on to me, the more I wanted to move away from her. Every time I looked around I could see Karen and Zenobia's silhouettes, watching me dance and fraternise with 'the enemy'. Other Black girls I knew passed me by, looking me up and down with open disgust. I excused myself from Rosa, and went outside for five minutes. Some African students were smoking weed in the small back garden, so I took some blasts and talked with them about the complexities of the Black woman. Like – they wouldn't give me none themselves, but couldn't stand to see me getting some from a White woman. It just didn't make sense. One of the students said a good-looking brother like myself should have no trouble finding a good-looking sister to hook up with. Another said maybe I wasn't into good-looking sisters as much as I'd claimed. That did it. I went back inside.

When I got back Ragga had come on. Carlos was winin' up with his Spanish girl. When I looked for Rosa, she was amateurishly doing the same with one of the African students. I watched jealously for a second. Carlos spotted me, shrugged and mouthed '*Yuh too damn slow.*' I nodded and went back to the bar.

'I see White gyal fin' a nex' Mandingo fe please 'er,' Karen said snidishly. I shrugged.

'Minor man, I wasn't chirpin' her anyway. Gimme a rum an' Coke will yuh?'

'So rudebwoy, you ah lick de hard stuff now?'

I laughed. 'Jus' gimme the ting man, stop pressurin' me.'

She did as she was asked. Zenobia came out of a back room with a tray full of meat patties.

'Oh, so yuh back!' she smiled.

'Yeah man, I had to come back an' check on my Afro-Caribbean queens, mek sure dem alright, y'get me?'

'We can look after ourselves thank you,' Zenobia sniffed. 'An' I don' even like the term Afro-Caribbean – I'm Black British . . .'

There are so many different names and titles for what is essentially one people, I always manage to screw up somewhere along the line.

'Ah come on Zenobia, don't go on like dat man . . . Furthermore, when you gonna come from behind dat counter an' bus' a lickle two-step wid me, eh? You bin goin' on about the race gettin' together too y'nuh, so help me get it together man! Come nuh.'

I reached over the counter and took her hands, pulling her towards me. 'Come on Zen, all work an' no play . . .'

'Later,' she replied wrenching her hands away. 'I'll be finished in a hour, den we can dance alright?'

'I'm settin' my Timex!' I warned. She laughed, a warm, bright and lovely sound.

'You set it den!'

'I soon come!'

I made my way back into the party area. It was slow jam time; Carlos was busy crubbin' with his Spanish girl in a corner – lucky git, it was the same every time we went out. My former Spanish girl was nowhere in sight. I scanned the room and saw an Oriental girl, very pretty, standing against the wall with her friends – a couple of White girls and a Black girl. She'd been staring until I turned her way – she looked down quickly as I stared back, pretending she'd never even been looking my way. I decided to chance it.

'Fancy a dance?' I asked, my hand out, ready to take hers. She blushed and looked down, while her friends smiled in delight and coaxed her good-naturedly.

'Go on – I ain' gonna bite.'

She took the hand and I led her on to the dance area. Her hands went around my neck slowly. I could feel the dampness of them as they rested against the lump of bone at the top of my spine. She was very, very pretty. I whispered my name to her; she smiled a little and said her name was Daphne. Slowly, we started to move together.

We danced for around three or four songs. Her body felt good – small, snug and warm – against mine. Her parents were from Thailand, but she'd been brought up in Tottenham for the majority of her life. She was studying Occupational Therapy, and was really enjoying the work, though she thought it would be even better when she got a placement. I told her about my course in journalism, and my hopes that one day I could work for a decent, broadsheet Black paper. She said she understood why; there were no papers for British-born Thai people either, and she understood the way it felt to be ignored by society as a whole. It was only three or four songs, but that was the closest I'd ever felt to a complete stranger for my whole entire life.

I tried to steer the talk away from drinks, but what could I do, it was a dance wasn't it? After the third tune she looked like she was dying of thirst, so after a few minutes I went back to the bar. Zenobia's icy glare was back.

'I see you couldn't wait,' she muttered between her even white teeth. I sighed.

'What am I supposed to do, wait aroun' for you to finish, an' not dance wid no one? It's a party man, I'm supposed to be havin' fun. You're supposed to be havin' fun!'

'So how come I ain't seen you havin' fun wid no Black women, eh?' she snapped back. 'Is it because for all your big talk you ain't no different from Frank, or Chris, or Mr bloody Motivator . . .'

She broke off and stared at something. I looked around. Daphne had come to the bar.

'Is anythin' up?' she asked timidly. I shook my head, feeling embarrassed. Zenobia's eyes rested on me like the eyes of a judge about to pass sentence on a proven murderer.

'You haven't got my drink yet,' she laughed nervously, looking from my face to Zen's, to Karen's, who was hovering near the back door, eavesdropping on every word. 'I wanned a Martini an' ice . . .'

She stopped as she realised I was staring somewhere else. Anywhere where I couldn't see her. I mean, I couldn't look at her, I felt that bad. Zenobia's words had made an impact on me, and I felt small, tiny – in fact I felt like the world's smallest hypocrite. Daphne looked over the bar again, then over at Karen and Zenobia's resolute faces – and she knew who they were all right – both girls were well known for their militant attitude where the Black race was concerned – then she turned to me and said,

'OK, Paul . . . OK.'

Then she walked out of the party and left.

I went back outside after that, my mind a maze of conflicting thoughts and feelings. Was I right? Was I wrong? Even up to now, as I write this all down, I can't work out whether I did the right thing. Something tells me I'll never know.

Nothing really happened after that, beside this one thing with Zenobia. I went back inside after a few more hours, to see the party was winding down. Carlos had no doubt left with his Señorita, for there was no sign of him. I went back to the bar feeling like shit, and thought that since I'd thrown away the chance of a night with an Oriental Princess, I might as well throw caution to the wind and try my luck with a Black Queen. I stepped to the bar with a confidence born out of no regard for the consequences, and found the girls tidying up with an assortment of others. I called her name.

'Whassup?'

'I wanna chat Zen.'

'I'm busy now Paul.'

'Two seconds man, c'mon two secs.'

She looked up and must have seen the desperation on my face.

'OK . . . OK . . .'

She crossed the counter and stared at me with her hands on her hips. Damn, I can still see that body! So I said,

'Lissen Zen, it's crazy man, you know dis whole thing dat happened tonight is . . .'

'It's cool Paulie. If you don' like Black girls dat's your business guy. Plenty of Black men dat do.'

She went to turn away but I held on to her arm and pulled her gently back.

'Lemme finish man. I . . . lissen, I do like Black girls Zenobia, believe me I do. I mean . . . I like women man, beautiful women, dat's what I like. I like *you* Zenobia.'

She covered her mouth with her hand and stifled an abrupt giggle; but I heard it. I fuckin' heard it.

'I'm sorry Paulie,' she said quickly, 'I know I sound rude, but I thought you knew . . .'

'Knew what?'

'Dat I don't go out wid mixed-race guys, dat's what . . .'

'Huh?'

I was honestly shocked.

'I said, "I don't go out wid mixed-ra . . ."'

'Yeah, yeah I heard you . . .' I stood still for a second, taking this in. 'But I ain' mixed-race Zenobia. An' in dat Black Awareness meetin' las' week wasn't you sayin' we're all Black no matter . . .'

'I did – but dat has no bearin' on my sexual preference,' she told me wisely. 'You seem jus' as confused as Karen, Paul – so even though you ain' mixed-race, you seem to've bin landed wid the same burden. *Know* what you want, Paul. *Dat's* why I don't see mixed-race guys, or for dat matter, light-skinned guys. Lissen, I'll see you on Monday OK? See yuh aroun'.'

She went back to the bar. I left the party, drove home and could not sleep. I couldn't sleep for a long time. And that was that.

I saw Daphne not long after that. It was in college and I was between lessons, crossing the building. She looked fine – she was wearing those figure-hugging jeans and a baggy woollen jumper that made her look small, and kind of defenceless. I called over to her. She looked over, saw me and smiled – then remembered. She put her head down and walked away as fast as she could. I was gonna follow an' explain, but then I got to thinking – I don't blame her really. Do you?

Harry Smart

THE LATERITE ROAD

THIS IS ABOUT Africa, and therefore certain things are compulsory. There is always, for example, a boat in sections. We have Mary Kingsley to thank for this observation; 'there is *always* a boat in sections,' she says, writing in the late 1890s. Nothing since that time has happened to suggest that she was wrong. Down the Congo with the Lady Alice. On Lake Mweru with Kalawfwa. As a rule, the boat in sections is made, in sections, in Scotland. As a rule it is a Clydeside boat. It may be a steam boat, or it may be a row-boat. It may be of wood or it may be of metal. But it is a boat in sections.

And there must be a laterite road. The laterite road goes on and on. Graham Greene, for example, has laterite roads in West Africa, in *The Heart of the Matter*. Later, when he writes *A Burnt-Out Case*, which he sets in the Congo, he has laterite roads. The burnt-out case occurred in 1959 or 1960; there are references in it to riots in Leopoldville, but there is no politics there. The Belgians he portrays are, for the most part, good Catholics; or they are bad in that petty, human way which in Greene's books is indistinguishable from virtue.

And there are stumps in the Congo, the Democratic Republic, as there were in the Belgian. Hands whittled back, finger by finger, to the dull stump. Hands gone, feet gone. But these are, some of them at least, the victims of leprosy. That, at least, is what they were in Greene's book. They suffer less, in some ways, than those poor patients in whom the disease takes a different course, not mutilating, but causing agony. We must choose between mutilation and agony, it seems, although the choice is made for us, by a virus or by God. The laterite road stretches out before us. Walk it or drive it, we must face the laterite road. There is no alternative.

More recently, William Boyd's *Brazzaville Beach*, first published in 1990, follows the laterite road. Brazzaville is, of course, just across the water from Kinshasa; and the edge of Malembo Pool, though it is really just part of the river bank, is known as the beach. Brazzaville Beach, however, is not in the Congo, neither the French, nor the Belgian, nor the Democratic; it is in Angola. Boyd never says Angola straightout, but it's the only former Portuguese colony which fits the bill, and his UNAMO can only be UNITA. Unless, of course, we are in Tanzania and UNAMO is RENAMO. Tanzania is just next to the Congo, on the right-hand side, across Lake Tanganyika. We'll settle for Tangola, or Golzania, or Tangangyolia; You can add your own examples.

The laterite road reaches out from Sierra Leone, in West Africa. Sierra Leone is where Greene worked from 1941 to 1943, for the Foreign Office. He insists that his Africa novels aren't *romans à clef*; on the other hand, he acknowledges the specific places where he spent time; they gave the setting for the books, if not the characters. So the road leads us from Sierra Leone in the 1940s down to the Congo in the late '50s and early '60s, and on into Angola for the '80s. It is the archetypal colonio-post-colonial Africa road, pale and pink and dusty, just as the archetypal river is grey-green and greasy. Truth to tell, it is not even solely African; it reappears, for instance, in India, in Arundhati Roy's *The God of Small Things*. Though perhaps, via Naipaul's *A Bend in the River*, which takes us back to Africa, there is a natural connection here.

But wherever it is, it can be lovely, the laterite road, when the last light of evening falls upon it; 'the last pink light upon the laterite roads at sundown'. This is Greene's 'hour of content', as he called it earlier in the novel: 'In the evening the port became beautiful for perhaps five minutes. The laterite roads that were so clay-heavy and ugly by day became a delicate flower-like pink.'

Boyd gets his laterite in even more quickly; second paragraph. Second paragraph of the prologue: 'one day, over the laterite road that leads down to the shore, some workmen erected this sign: Brazzaville Beach.' At that stage we don't even know the name of the woman who's at the centre of the book (it's Hope Clearwater); but we know there's laterite about. There's a lot of it about.

What is laterite? It comes from the Latin – the word, that is – *later*, a brick. We have F. Buchanan Hamilton (1807) to thank for the name, which he initially applied to a ferruginous rock from India. A similar rock was found in the Futah Jallon territory of West Africa. So there we are, it's not just the coincidence of Roy, Naipaul and Greene; it's geology, a universal, it's applied physics and chemistry. It's the old-fashioned world of the syllogism, of covering-law explanations, of the major and minor premise; the world of *always*.

Laterite is the product of weathering, the breakdown of basalts, granites and shales. It is a porous, clay-like rock, rich in iron and alumina. The iron occurs as ferric hydroxide, typically in small pisolitic nodules. You can look up 'pisolitic' for yourself. When the alumina fraction is high, it is called bauxite.

When first quarried the rock is soft enough to cut with a pick. After exposure it dehydrates and hardens. 'Lateritic debris possesses the property of re-cementing into masses which resemble the primary material . . . It makes a fair building stone.'

Indeed it does, for Scobie, in *The Heart of the Matter*, observes laterite bricks. 'Father Clay was up and waiting for him in the dismal little European house which had been built among the mud huts in laterite bricks to look like a Victorian presbytery.' Pemberton gazed across at this dismal building, day after day, which is why he hanged himself. Improbably, he hanged himself from the picture rail. Just twenty-five years old, debt, Syrian traders, pimples, and the heat, and the damned flies. He couldn't cope with the flies, unlike Yusef, the Syrian trader, who comes to Scobie to discuss Pemberton's death: 'Yusef eased his great haunches on to the hard

chair and noticing that his flies were open put down a large
and hairy hand to deal with them.'

Neil Rollinson

THE PENALTY

The stadium comes to a hush;
it is so quiet you can hear a light-bulb
hum to itself in the dressing room.
You carry the ball in your hands,
your palms are sweating, you feel nauseous.
The goal-mouth rushes away.
You can just see, in the distance,
the white glow of the cross-bar,
the German keeper waving his arms.
You can hear him shouting: '*Du schafts
das nicht, du Wichser.*'
You settle the ball on its spot.
Do you place it, or blast it?
If you miss this kick you're finished,
your team-mates will sink to their knees
in the grass. You step back from the ball.
'*Du schafts das nicht,*' the keeper repeats.
You take a run. You are running all day
and night. When you get to the ball
you are weak with the effort.
You swing your leg, your foot
finds what you think is a perfect purchase,
the crowd goes wild, they rise in a wave
behind the goal. You watch the ball –
you can't believe where it goes.

THE WEATHER-MAN

Having drawn the short straw in the Christmas rota,
he sits on the icy roof of the Weather Centre
watching the sky for a solitary snowflake
that will make this Christmas a white one.
He sips hot coffee from a thermos flask,
munches his way through a bait-box of turkey rolls,
and a slice of his wife's sad cake.

At four o'clock he watches the stars
from Hampstead to Crystal Palace flicker on,
but nothing by way of a snowflake. He sees
a meteorite or two, and every so often the quiet
track of a satellite crossing the sky. He wonders
if one of them might be a spy-in-the-sky,
if maybe somewhere, on a microchip
in a Pentagon computer, there's a photograph
of himself sipping tea on a frost covered roof?
He sticks two fingers up as they pass.

He yawns and closes his eyes for a moment,
they'll be showing old re-runs of Morecambe and Wise
on the telly, the kids will be fast asleep,
dreaming of empires of Lego, his wife will be making
her lonely way through a bottle of wine. Never mind,
he'll take her away when he picks up his winnings.

He has a whole month's wages on a white Christmas;
ten to one against, the bookies say, he can't believe his
    luck.
He's done his homework, his calculations, it all seems
clear enough, the barometer is already falling.
He scans the sky; a few pale wisps of cirrus
obscure the Pleiades: the start of a frontal zone
if he's not mistaken. He screws the top

off a hip-flask and takes a sip, he thinks about
sunshine. The Bahamas will be fine this time of year;
he can smell palm trees, he can smell tiger-prawns
grilling on charcoal; he can smell snow on the breeze.

A Poem about Golf, Dave

'That looked like a slice to me, Al.'
Fred Haise to Alan B. Shepherd,
Apollo 14 Moonshot

It's great to be out before Earthrise,
knocking the balls about, it keeps me sane,
keeps my feet on the ground as they say.
When you hit a ball up here it goes for miles,
you can see it glow, bright as a bullet
over the craters. An inspiration,
the drive of a lifetime. Dave on the other hand
sits in the capsule, brooding,
looking through telescopes, shaking his head.
It's not a theme park, he'll say,
it's a sacred place. Dave's a poet.
Write a poem about Golf, Dave, I tell him.
You might see something you never imagined.
But golf is no fit subject for a poem.

I watch the Earth rise every day like a glass marble,
silent, and stupid. I gaze for hours,
watching the brown smudges of Africa,
China, Australia. At night in the metal
hum of the landing craft, I dream of the green
fairways of Ballyliffin, the palm trees of Valderama,
the salty rain of St Andrews, the whole
moon's surface covered in grass.
I'll be home soon, the weight of gravity
dulling my dreams – a metaphor, Dave!
The arc of the golf ball falling short time after time,

the missed sitters, the cuts, the tops and
slices, and anyway, at the end of the day,
you need the practice, wherever you are.

George Szirtes

COOLIDGE IN INDIGO

There are bad scenes. The film with the jagged
edge between two murders when the curtain
moves and the child stands lost and uncertain
staring at shadows, imagining the haggard
face of his mother opening her mouth wide
and the sound of a fly, the simmering
of a pan and the distant clock glimmering
like his image in the window, multiplied
as if for ever between two moments. So
into that dusk came Coolidge, its shuttered
general store and desolate garage
trailing off into dust which seemed to blow
from nameless places where nothing had mattered
for years or suffered some terminal haemorrhage.

Then Anthony got out to check the map.
Three or four men glanced over. They were poor,
the kind who lend themselves to metaphor
with nothing else to lend, caught in a trap
which had closed over them. Their mouths closed
over each other in that twilight, stranger
than cinema. Each one smelled of danger,
of damp but flammable rooms. They posed
in their dreamscape like symbols, long detached
from anywhere but the desert and the long
featureless road where station-wagons rusted.
This was a bad moment. My foot gently touched
the gas pedal. Something was clearly wrong
with the map in which we had naïvely trusted.

And then the road trailed off and hot dust threw

itself against the tight window. A road sign
pointed to towns way off the marked line.
The thin Arizona wind gathered and blew
vague traffic past us, and later we arrived
in some lit town, and later still in Scottsdale,
in time for our dinner date. The night was stale
with relief. We felt we had survived
some insignificance. Our host waited
in the lobby and we drove off to a vast
inedible dinner. The sky was indigo,
with many stars like something inflated.
Our host was counting his credit cards. At last
he found his preferred option and we could go.

TURQUOISE

1.

Good to have reached the turquoise age. Not green
not blue but something in between, this
smoky, crystalline concentration, clean
as an iceberg, astringent as the kiss
of water on iron. So your hair drifts
across the sky where everything turns grey.
So the louring cloud-mass shifts
and colour filters into day.
So, between folds of skin your sea-grey eyes
echo the green of your jumper which is turquoise.
(Wings of house flies or dragonflies or butterflies
hover briefly, freeze into flightless poise.)
Perhaps we've chosen this very spot, this *now*,
and might return if only we knew how.

2.

The balance is tipping. We feel the scales
go down. We live in a fortunate age.

403

Our teeth are still our own, our tops and tails
are in order. We need not rage
against the dying of the light. We touch
each other's skin with pleasure and trace
the lines of limbs, squeezing neither too much
nor too little. The fine bones of the face
retain a sort of tender brittleness,
their threatened beauty yields a thrill
as fingers follow eyelids or caress
the whorls of the ear with acquired skill.
But still the scales go down. Under the dress,
under the shirt and vest, it's all downhill.

3.

We watch a TV documentary
on breasts. It's so bloody American,
so pathetically anxious to carry
its terrors like trophies. One thin old woman
grimaces and waves, performs a burlesque.
Her pathos has turned comic. When we laugh
it's not quite at her. Something in the mask
parodies us, part sassy and part naff,
making uneasiness easy. In the dark
my hand slides across your thigh. I sink
my teeth into your neck. Your fingernails spark.
Electrical appliances go on the blink.
Even this gentle pressure leaves a mark,
a turquoise, purple, blackening smear of ink.

4.

Our knees are stiff, getting up is a pain.
We take care of our bowels, eat sensibly,
nothing too spicy after nine. No gain
in weight. No dope. No fags. I calmly drain
my glass of Jameson's but feel my heart
accelerate. Sheets full of cancer haunt

the chest of drawers. Minor discomforts start
long trains of thought. The mirror's gaunt
reflection follows us about the room.
Skulls in the desert open their dry mouths
to utter comic prophecies of doom.
They're desperate to confront us with home truths.
You'll turn to prose, fools! We reply in mime,
watching our shadows coupling. There's still time.

5.

Turquoise. Under the sea, in slim leaves
of current the fish are brilliant repulsive
flecks of light. The predator deceives
its prey by simulating softness, gives
only to swallow. Sharp, spiny exoskeletons
form ridges to scrape a knee on. A squid
lounges, hunched and expectant. Patterns
of weed on rock form an undulating grid.
I watch my skin grow ridges. Some organic
process throws up warts, disfigurements.
Fronds of grey at the temple. Hair less thick
than it once was. We observe events
like divers in an alien ocean. But then
oceans are (it is their nature) alien.

6.

Turquoise. It was an old woman's parasol
lying in the waiting room. Under its wings
the trapped air of the decade. Chirrupings
of dead birds. The half-dressed discarded doll
in the garage. I've seen one queuing up
at the post office counter, rubbing her hands
beside garish coloured advertising stands,
her complexion delicate as a chipped cup.
This poem's becoming elegiac, like her.
In Viennese cafés the waiters hum

whole operettas into aged ears. The words come
naturally, settling on a line of fur,
between the fingers of gloves. Time to kill
between the opening parasol and the bill.

7.

Try turquoise once more. Turkish opulence.
Think of those soft cushions and the bleak curve
of the scimitar. The pasha's residence
is where we used to live. The girls would serve
sticky confections as we lay in bed
watching light crumple across the ceiling rose.
The petals were stirring overhead,
the leaves of the window would open and close
and the air would billow through. Occasionally
we'd hear the whine of an ambulance, wake
to boys on motorbikes with their crude reveille.
Sometimes the bed itself would gently shake
beneath us. Of course this was years ago,
or never happened. It's getting hard to know.

8.

Hermione, the teacher of Greek grammar,
has her face reconstructed by computer
animation. This lends a touch of glamour
to her more prosaic status as a tutor.
("A studious and meek schoolmistress
without a trace of show or ornament"
said Petrie, another scholar.) Her tenderness
has a stern edge, that is true, but her scent
is deeply sensuous and grave, her hair
parted in the middle shows a light line
of lovely mortal skin, perfectly aware
of its mortality as part of the design.
She emerges from the photo-booth and waits
for the line of four to slip out through the gates.

9.

Death is more Woody Allen than Lord Byron.
Being there at the time is the only drag.
No one gives us a branch to hang our spare tyre on
or offers to hide our face in a paper bag.
It's a bit of a joke, this old curmudgeon drone
and sneer. A Larkinesque panicky shrug.
So Mary Magdalene turns into a crone,
and Balzac to an energetic slug.
A true Lawrentian ripeness is the goal,
but somehow the body gets so out of breath
it loses contact with the panting soul
and fails to make the seasonal Ship of Death.
And all that violet eye, and turquoise gaze
drowns in a murky swirling sea of days.

10.

The Shakespearian ending which turns round
to claim your immortality in words
performs a gesture. I like its human sound
and proud disdain. I like its afterwards
and quibbles, its hyperboles, its dumb
struggle with silence. And after all, there's truth
in its assertions. How many have come
to the sonnets, from the pimply youth
with his A levels, to the old botanist
dying on his sofa, mouthing the lines?
I cannot myself close a perfect fist
about the couplet which defines
the perfect closure, capturing desire.
I too am burning in the turquoise fire.

Isobel Dixon

AIR ON PAPER

See how the wind beyond the window heaves,
and how far the paper chain of folded blossoms swings.
This is a night of sound
in darkness, a slur of air on the night's calm face,
shaking the twig-held leaves
down to the root of the tongue.

Stirring, dark-voiced
spill of night
past the sober brim of day,
unbind and loosen, let your maimed feet go free.
Walk off the pathway of the sure
and prudent, break the stem.

See, in the light,
the scattered leavings on the grass.

My tongue is folded back
upon its hinge, calm table
neat as origami,
quiet paper string.

Dan Rhodes

BLIND

My girlfriend used my going blind as an excuse to start dressing sloppily. In the days when I could see her, she had always looked immaculate in the latest cuts of the best designer labels. Now, her high heels have been replaced by trainers, her silk stockings and short skirts by jeans, and her figure-hugging blouses and smart jackets by baggy jumpers. I haven't said anything yet, but it's getting to the point where I'm embarrassed to be seen with her as she gently holds my hand and guides me along, making sure I don't trip or bump into anything.

MILESTONES

My girlfriend left me. I found she had been seeing lots of other men all along. She was loose, and I thought the world should know. I calculated the road distances from her house to over two thousand different locations around the country, and began to carve milestones. 'Mette's open legs 263km.' That was the first one. I laid it on a verge just outside Ulfborg. After I had planted nine hundred and forty, I realised that it was not making me any happier, that I was carving them in heart-shapes, and that I missed her like nothing on earth.

Derek Robinson

SCOTTS LANDING, TENNESSEE, 1856

Extract from a novel in progress

'DOLLAR,' SAID THE man at the door. He had his foot up on
a chair, blocking the way in.

'*Dollar?*' George Taylor said. His hand with the money in
it came back like it was on springs. 'I heard three dollars.
Listen, he ain't dead already, is he? It said on that paper
that –'

'Three-dollar seats all gone. Lemme ask you somethin',
sonny,' the man said. He had not looked up from counting
his handful of money since Taylor arrived at the entrance to
the theatre. 'Where you all from?' The coins clinked like
small machinery.

'Burkesville, Kentucky.' From the side of his eye Taylor
saw Sue-Anne look up sharply at him, wondering why he had
said Burkesville and not Rock Springs. 'You just hush,' he
ordered. He was tired of telling people where Rock Springs
was. 'We're down here visitin' kin.'

'I ain't never heard of Burkesville,' the man said. 'Fact is, I
ain't but scarcely ever heard of Kane Tucky. Over to the east
somewheres, ain't it?'

'North,' Taylor said. 'Next state north.' Now more people
were behind him, pressing, impatient to get in.

'North, huh?' the man said in that same smooth, insulting
drawl. 'This here is the South, sonny. Scotts Landing,
Tennessee, is truly the South with a big Ess, yunnerstan me?'

'Yes sir,' George Taylor said. 'Take my dollar.' They were
holding up the line, and the midday sun was pitiless.

'Now the thing about the South . . .' The man found a half-

411

dollar with a dent in it, and he frowned, his thumb failing to smooth the dent. 'We got a lot of that old-fashioned courtesy, see. So when you ask me that question, *He ain't dead already?* which most folks in my position would find offensive if not downright insultin', bein' as it suggests deceit an' fraud –'

'I'm sorry,' Taylor said. 'Take the dollar, please.' The crowd was getting noisy and he was sweating all over. 'I didn't mean nothin', sir.'

'How old are you, sonny?'

'Seventeen, sir.' Again, he felt Sue-Anne's sharp glance.

'Uh-huh. No rifles allowed. No shotgun. What you got?'

George Taylor opened his coat to show the sidearm in its holster. The man nodded and took his dollar, but when George pushed Sue-Anne forward the man kept his boot on the chair. 'Not her,' he said.

'Another dollar? She won't take up no space, she can sit –'

'No children.'

Knees and hands were prodding and poking Taylor in the legs and back. 'You wait here, Sue-Anne,' he told her. 'I'll meet you here after the show.' The boot came off the chair and he was inside, in the gloom and the blessed cool, and he was trembling with rage.

The dollar seats were up in the gallery. He climbed the stairs and went through swing doors into a roar of talk and a stench of cigar-smoke. There was a space in the fifth row back, extreme left. The man he sat next to was balding, with lank black hair flopping about his ears, and a drooping moustache. His chin receded. His shoulders sloped. Everything about him looked slack, except the revolver in his lap.

Now every seat in the gallery was taken. The stalls were full. One or two boxes still had some room in them. Everywhere George looked, whiskey was being drunk out of flat pint bottles. Occasionally, singing broke out. The atmosphere in the theatre was pumped-up with expectancy, like waiting for a big horse-race or a hot revivalist preacher. On stage, the heavy scarlet curtains twitched occasionally as some hidden activity touched them.

The balding man nudged George. 'Mayor just arrived,' he said. In one of the boxes a large, handsome man was shaking hands. 'Now maybe we can get on with things.'

'I'm from out of town myself,' George said. 'Exactly what did he do?'

'Mayor didn't do nothin', which is how come he got elected, because people around here don't like interference and sure enough that's what the mayor supplied, no interference, and now he's runnin' for election again, same platform plus free bourbon, bound to win.'

'I didn't mean what did the mayor do,' George began, but a great deep-throated roar went off like an explosion of approval. A man in a black tailcoat and black trousers with a four-in-hand tie of red silk had stepped on the stage. He smiled, and nodded to the mayor. He remained close to the wings.

'Gentlemen,' he said, and that too brought a cheer. 'I know everyone here wants to be fair to his neighbour, so let me repeat: no rifles, no carbines. And please remember what happened on the last occasion, in this very theatre.' Heckling had begun. He had to shout. 'Someone got over-excited and there were one or two painful injuries. Nobody gets hurt today, OK?'

Then he was gone.

The golden tassels at the bottom of the curtain trembled. George's heart was thumping so hard that it hurt. His pistol was in his hand and he couldn't remember drawing it. 'When do we start?' he asked. The balding man was holding the long-barrelled revolver in both hands, pointing at the painted nymphs on the ceiling. 'Is there a signal?' George asked.

The curtain rose so fast it was like it fell upwards. In the centre of the stage, lashed hand, foot and elbow to a chair, sat a middle-aged negro, crying. The rocketing climb of the curtain had startled everyone into silence. George heard the negro sob. For an instant he had their total attention. George thought: *Bet nobody ever looked twice at him before this.*

A man in the mayor's box fired first, a casual, playful shot that made splinters jump a yard from the chair; and then the theatre was a storm of gunfire. For perhaps ten seconds the negro's body jumped and bounced as the bullets battered it; after that it was just so much bloody meat, tied to the chair. But the firing went on. George, stupefied by the racket, gawked at the countless streaks of flame. Nearby, a man with a gun in each hand was cheerfully blasting away, hooting and howling his enjoyment. George looked back at the stage. A thin mist of dust arose, battered out of the floor; blood had sprayed twenty feet from the chair; there were white guts spilling out of the black body; the head was smashed and mashed and knocked back until it no longer had a face. And still the shooting went on. The chair was sturdy, and it had been nailed to the floor. George saw bullets punch holes in the red-black chest and shoulders, and realised that he had not fired. He extended his right arm and aimed for the heart. The pistol's kick hurt his wrist and shoulder, but the pain was worth it. He was sure he had scored.

The curtain came down. A few incorrigible spirits put bullets through it, but everyone knew the show was over and everyone was content. As they shuffled out they made way for the doctor. Two paying customers in the stalls had been hit by ricochets or maybe wild shots.

'Worth a dollar, huh?' George Taylor said to the balding man with the drooping moustache.

'Worth a dollar to *me*. I killed that nigger, first shot.'

'I never did figure out what it was he done wrong.'

'He got born. Always a dangerous thing for a nigger to do.'

Sue-Anne was waiting in the street. 'I want to go back to Aunt Sarah's,' she said. 'It's hot, and boys keep lookin' at me and laughin'. Let's go.'

'Which boys?' George asked. He opened his coat and hooked his thumb in his holster.

'Don't be so dumb, George.' She began walking and he had to follow. Sue-Anne was only thirteen but she looked fifteen and there were times when he felt junior to her.

'Don't you want to hear about it?' he asked.

'I heard. The whole town heard. I've had enough of this place, George. Let's go back to Rock Springs.'

'Hey, it's not so bad here. You get good value for your dollar in this town. Damn good value.' She said nothing, but he was too excited to be silent. 'I plugged him clean through the heart,' he said. 'Clean through.'

Hari Kunzru

DEUS EX MACHINA

PEOPLE SAY THAT everyone has a Guardian Angel. I don't object to that. It is *the way* they say it. The way they use it as a synonym for luck, or some other chance process. I find it demeaning to be reduced to a metaphor. However, given that literal manifestation, spectacular miracles and all the rest of it have been banned since the dawn of the Age of Reason, what can I do?

Of course, the phrase 'Guardian Angel' is an example of the worst kind of folk theology. I'm not about to correct it here, since to do so to the satisfaction of a modern mortal audience would take several hefty tomes of scholastic argument. Even then, without favourable reviews and a large marketing budget it would not be read. Life is short and art is long, as some pagan put it, though he wasn't thinking of my kind of life when he said it.

I'm also not about to ruin my prose by placing 'Guardian Angel' in inverted commas every time it appears. Suffice it to say that terms such as deva, household god, tree-spirit, fetish and even pooka or leprechaun convey some aspect of what I'm doing here. I am immaterial, powerful, and quite hands-on in my approach. At one point we were all hopeful that some human would manage to complete the project of a Synthesis of All Religions, which would have explained all this without me having to bother. There were some diligent Germans, but the chance of success fell off some time ago, and attempting it seems to have gone out of fashion since you lot finally invented computer games.

So, Guardian Angel it will have to be.

Obviously you have questions. Yes, there is a God. Yes, he passeth all understanding and no, he absolutely did not make man in his image. That was a piece of Hebraic vanity which has caused untold mischief through the ages. Take it from me as one of the Heavenly Host, God is far weirder than even the fastest-whirling dervish or most strung-out stylite has ever imagined. Yes, we angels do dance on pin-heads, and the usual number we fit on is one hundred and seventy-six for a standard gauge pin. This is not because of some restriction in size. As I say, we are entirely immaterial. It's just that for pin-head dancing, one-seven-six just feels like the right number. Call it tradition.

On the question of organised religion, as far as we're concerned church is entirely optional. We say yes to rituals, penances, fasting, sacrifice – go ahead. But none is more effective than any other. Sincerity is important. We appreciate that. But all these jihads and crusades, these isms and schisms, arguments over how many fingers to make the sign of the cross with, or whether to have images or smash them up, that's all way off the point. Basically, do what you like. Hang out. Take drugs. Sleep with each other. We want you to have fun, but for heaven's sake just try to be *nice*. You wouldn't think that was a lot to ask.

If you look in one of the wiggier books of medieval angelology, you'll find mention of me. Otto of Vaucluse, in his *Liber Argentum*, describes my particular host as 'somewhere below the archangels but still in the major dispensation league'. Athanasius Hermeticus, the sage of Dresden, was granted a vision of the whole lot of us while he lay prostrate one day in his cell. Sadly his description (*De Rerum Ignotum*) is a little colourless, since poor Athanasius was always better at meditation than writing. The anonymous thirteenth-century Magister of the Mendacia Lingua, author of the *Dictum Sapientiae*, gives my actual name, which I'm not currently at liberty to reveal. The Magister (whose own real name was, incidentally, Pablo) should have known better than to go bandying around that kind of privileged information. No surprise he ended badly, burnt at the stake after an ecclesiastical court found him guilty of holding heretical opinions concerning the sexual habits of the apostle Paul.

But all this is off the point. I am a Guardian Angel, and from the moment of her conception I have been looking after a young woman called Christina. Since the first proteins folded themselves into shape in the first cells of her embryo I have observed her with perfect, complete, angelic attention. As each filament of bone grew in her spine, each corpuscle of blood emerged in the miniature sac of her heart, I looked on, rapt and content, my Being fulfilled in the act of watching over her.

As is well known, God moves in mysterious ways. One of the most mysterious is His system of classification. To get technical for a moment, not everyone does have a Guardian Angel. Some people share. While not being entirely infinite, we angels do have extraordinary powers and capacities, so this is not such a bad deal for the sharers as first appears. Indeed there is a whole town in the southern United States who only have one angel between them. This is not some kind of heavenly snub. They get excellent service. And there is a logical method to the assignment of angels. However it is the Deity's method, and manifesting His filing system is something God is particularly averse to doing.

So I look after Christina. Just Christina. I find my purpose in the vast, almost luminous love I bear for her, a love which is, in its turn, just a reflection of the same implausibly humungous love which God bears for her as He bears for every living thing. Christina is twenty-eight years old. She has chestnut-brown curly hair that she wears long, in a kind of cloud which haloes her head as she walks. This causes other people to turn and watch her. She does not know this. Secretly she believes she is plain. This is partly because she has an unfashionable body, fuller and more womanly than is sanctioned by the style leaders of her particular place and period. But Christina is beautiful. Extraordinarily, achingly beautiful. The hollow of her navel, the line of her collar bone, the tiny pattern of whorls and grooves in her skin – I have observed all these come into being, and they are transcendent in their loveliness. She is sexy too. But then, I would say that.

Christina wants to be a poet. That is, she wants to be a published poet. She writes poems, has done since she was thirteen years old. They are very good, though that is not something she knows either. Christina doubts. She spends most of her day doubting, racking herself with worry over her talent, her looks, her future prospects. Recently she has been racking herself over her relationship with a man called Robert, who is worthless and has made her very unhappy. So unhappy in fact, that Christina is wondering whether she wants to die. Right now she is in the bathroom of her friend's London flat, holding a bottle of tranquillisers, examining its label in front of the mirrored bathroom cabinet.

The bottle holds a great fascination for her. The smudged printing on the label helps her make a decision, reminding her as it does of school reports and council tax forms and other things she associates with impersonal, bureaucratic fate. To imagine her death Christina always thinks of it as abstract and inevitable, perhaps even as happening to someone else. So the formal printing confirms her suspicion that her time has come. In a few moments she will unscrew the bottle top, pour out a handful of pills, fumble with full palm and tooth mug and tap, scattering pills like seed on to the hard porcelain basin, and finally swallow a gulp of tepid water and a gulp of bitter-tasting pills.

That's where I'll come in.

Christina looks at her face in the mirror. Her eye make-up has run and she thinks she looks like a panda, with her two dark circles and stained cheeks. Her image of pandas comes more from drawings in children's books than films or photos, and she has never seen one in real life, because the day her father took her to the zoo, the pandas didn't come out. In Christina's head, pandas always have the hint of a smile as they snack on a bamboo shoot, because that is the way the children's book illustrators drew them. Always a hint of human emotion. And so she smiles, to make herself look more like a panda, just for a moment in front of the bathroom mirror before she tries to commit suicide.

I know every inch of Christina's body and mind, each sensation, each mood. I know every one of her likes and dislikes, her favourite band, the place on her neck where she likes to be touched when a man is kissing her. I know the exact strength she likes her coffee and the words her grandmother whispered to her in the hospital just before she died. I also know the effect the handful of bitter pills will have on her physiology after she swallows them. I know every name of every chemical Christina will synthesise as each complex molecule of each pill starts to bond with receptors in her weary, stricken brain.

I certainly know far too much about Robert. Robert has a lot to answer for. At the book launch, he used a chat-up line on Christina which was old years before Boccaccio employed it in the *Decameron*. It is, in fact, a line which appears in variant forms in the literature of seventeen different cultures, including a version on a tenth-century runestone in Norway. And she bought it! Robert followed up his age-old approach with a series of pushy, sleazy moves in a taxi and, over the course of several subsequent weeks, a further series of outrages which Christina told herself were passionate and exciting. In fact, during the nine months and seventeen days which ended yesterday, when Christina caught him booking a Caribbean holiday for himself and his other girlfriend, she thought Robert was amazing.

Robert was mainly amazing to Christina because he was a published poet who had won an award. Christina thinks Robert is witty, soulful, tormented and brave – in short, a genius. I think Robert is a cheap, pompous, arrogant fool, who stole most of his best lines from a Manchester poet he tutored on a summer school ten years ago – a poet to whom, incidentally, Robert gave a 'B', telling him if he worked hard he might one day find something worth keeping. Robert is truly a sly, devious bastard. He is crap in bed too, though that is something Christina has been too lost in her fantasy of poetic love to notice, or at least to notice that she has noticed. I mean, it's not even as though he is good-looking.

I watch Christina swallow the pills. The face she makes is the same 'nasty taste' face she has made since she was four years old, a cascade of tiny tightening and relaxing muscles that is as familiar to me as the gesture she makes afterwards, a hand fluttering to her curly hair and brushing it with three fingertips. It was this gesture that made a young Frenchman called Hervé fall in love with her last year, in a café in Paris. Christina had gone to Paris on her own, to pick up the pieces after a disastrous affair with a worthless-but-published man called Richard. She was sitting in the café nursing a *citron pressé* and trying to remember the lyrics to her-and-Richard's song, which she didn't know had also done time as Richard-and-Wanda's song, and Richard-and-Gaby's song. Trying to remember, her hand fluttered up to her hair.

Hervé was also a poet, and hence stood a good chance of gaining Christina's attention, though by nature he was shy and unpublished. Still he took his courage in both hands and tried to talk to the beautiful foreign woman. Unfortunately his English was poor, and Christina was too full of thoughts of Richard to decipher what he was saying. She shooed him away, mistaking him for yet another of the legion of Parisian chancers who had tried to pick her up that afternoon. This was a shame, since she and Hervé would have been an inspirational couple. I have little doubt they could have shaped up as a Great Love. Instead Hervé dutifully pined away in his garret and Christina carried on floating around at poetry readings, ready to be picked up by creeps like Robert. Without the equanimity that comes from total prescience, knowing that sort of thing would make you sad.

Christina slumps down on the toilet seat, leans her head against the side of the basin, and shuts her eyes. Behind them, benzodiazepine molecules are nestling into her brain, shutting out all the worry and stress, chemical fingers smudging the delicate lattice of her thoughts, suggesting sleep, darkness, an ending. Against her cheek Christina can feel the contrasting sensations of cold porcelain and warm, fuzzy cloth, the collar of her favourite black sleeveless fleece. On the other side of the bathroom door, there is nobody. Just a sitting room with a coffee table on which sits a full ashtray, an empty bottle of vodka and a melted tub of ice-cream. Paulette is out. Everybody is out. There is no one here in this flat with Christina, who came here to cry last night away on Paulette's sofa, under the spare duvet which smelt of other people.

As Christina loses her grip on consciousness and slumps to the floor, there is, just audible, the note of a well-tuned car engine in the street outside the flat. That is as it should be. This evening, as Christina worked her way through her bottle of supermarket vodka, exploring a chain of vodka-based memories which start with an unfortunate experience in a cinema car park aged sixteen, I have been busy elsewhere, working behind the scenes to produce an alternative ending to the narrative my charge has created for herself. For the task, I have been using that greatest of labour-saving devices, the computer.

Computers are wonderful. Charles Babbage, Alan Turing, John von Neumann, even Bill Gates – all great favourites of mine. Since the marvellous machines penetrated every area of human society, my job has become considerably easier. You will of course find angels at work in all forms of technology, especially those which humans find complicated or hard to understand, like video recorders and fax machines. But the PC is the real centre of supernatural activity in the modern world. In an era when (owing to trends in celestial politics it would be otiose to discuss here), miracles and overt manifestations of superhuman power have been banned under a strict convention, the scope for angelic intervention is severely limited. We do very little carrying aloft on shoulders, appearing bathed in golden light or other flashy stuff these days. That is a shame, but every true artist can turn restrictions to positive use. There is a certain beauty in minimalism, and my own preferred aesthetic is semiconductor-based.

In this case, to alter fate I have restricted myself to moving nothing larger than electrons. Specifically, I altered the charge of half a dozen selected spots on a tiny sliver of treated silicon in the Central Processor Unit of a PC which sits on the desk of an estate agent called Suzie. In this way I changed some ones into zeros, and some zeros into ones, halfway through the operation of a tricky date-calculation algorithm. My little nudge set off, domino-like, a cascade of instructions that made a single minor alteration to Suzie's diary software. This morning, she arrived at work to find that an appointment she remembered as being for mid-afternoon was in fact scheduled for early evening. She found she would have to stay late at work and show Mr Harakami the flat at seven tonight, or in other words, about five minutes from now. Paulette Connolly is keen to sell, and thinks the place, though a little small, might suit Mr Harakami's needs.

Naturally, I have performed a similar operation on Harakami's personal digital organiser, which really is a superb piece of engineering. So light, so compact! Now both agent and client believe they must have misremembered, and have made arrangements to meet three hours later than expected.

The beauty of working with computers is their votive quality. As far as estate agents and cartoonists (for this is Harakami Yukio's profession) are concerned, the dull grey boxes which take up such a prominent place in their lives might as well function by animal magnetism, or focusing cosmic rays. They are profound and mystical objects, things of whim and prophecy which require complete deference. Suzie and Yukio propitiate their machines, asking for fault-tolerance, viral absence and continued bug-free living and working. When dealing with the divine, human fallibility is thrown into sharp relief, so neither of the two has thought to question whether their computer has 'got it right'. They just obeyed. This is why Angels find these machines so useful. They are the tools which replaced apparitions and holy relics.

Duly, Harakami Yukio and DeBrett Suzie are making small talk as they walk up the stairs towards an encounter with Christina's unconscious body, now picturesquely draped on the bathroom floor, the empty Halcyon bottle in the sink leaving no doubt as to the cause of her indisposition.

Paulette told Christina that she'd be back late because she was going out with Clive to talk things over. She told Christina that the estate agent was coming, and asked her to make sure the place was reasonably tidy. All this went in one grieving ear and out the other. Christina has spent her afternoon making a mess. There are sodden tissues, discarded jumpers, empty fag packets, the fall-out from several comfort snacks, and at least a dozen scribbled-on sheets of paper, relics of her attempt to tell Robert what she thought of him, in free verse.

Suzie's first thought, as she steps brightly into the living room and spies the detritus of Christina's day of depressed camping-out, is anger. Some people conspire to make her job particularly difficult. But there is no choice, she must tough it out, and so she smiles wanly at Yukio, who smiles wanly back. This is not because he is angry at the state of the flat. He is simply experiencing a sense of *déjà vu*. He has stood in this place before, breathing this very stale, smoky air with its undertone of something else, of a smell he wants to catch, to keep and savour. The smell of a person.

Just before Suzie steps trepidly over Christina's abandoned duvet and utters the fateful words, 'and this is the bathroom', Yukio has an impulse to stop her, to give himself time to prepare for what is on the other side of the door. He will never understand why this is. But he finds he is not surprised to hear the sound of screaming. Yes, at the sight of Christina's body Suzie screams, a response conditioned by thousands of hours of televised police procedural drama. Bodies in bathrooms say 'crime scene' to Suzie, and by the time Yukio pokes his head round the door to find out what has upset her, she is already half-plunged into a nightmare of masked axemen and running down corridors.

Christina is looking good, which certainly wasn't her intention. She has fallen into a pose reminiscent of several major works of Japanese and European art. An Ophelia. A swooning Hokusai courtesan. It also happens to be a pose in which Yukio sometimes draws his *manga* heroines, especially Lola Blue (of *Tokyo Blue Squad 2000*), who often acts as the

424

screen on which he projects his fantasies of ideal woman-hood. This is all very convenient – not my doing at all, I hasten to add, but nevertheless perfect. Of course, unlike Lola, Christina doesn't have eyes the size of dinnerplates or the figure of a pre-teen elf, but then Yukio is not very experienced with three-dimensional women.

So Yukio is struck first, not that there is a corpse in the bathroom, but that it is the corpse of a beautiful woman. Marvellous, if a little perverse, and very much in line with *manga* aesthetics. So much lies in that crucial first impression. By the time Suzie runs back into the living room, yelling extravagantly, Yukio has already inserted Christina's uncon-scious form into that mental list of 'things that make the heart quicken' which every human carries somewhere inside themselves. Most people's lists are unconscious, unexplicit, but every so often Yukio writes his down, in the manner of the tenth-century Japanese courtesan Sei Shonagon. 'The line of ink flowing from a fine-nib pen, the neon lights of the Ginza at night, a *Time Crisis* high score, the beautiful dead girl with the cloud of chestnut hair . . .'

Yukio crouches, and deftly takes Christina's pulse. It is so slow and faint that his inquiring fingertips almost miss the tiny ebb and flow. But she is alive. The realisation leaps in his chest like a bird.

'Call an ambulance,' he shouts to Suzie, unnecessarily. Still convinced that she has fallen into the plot of a slasher movie, Suzie is attacking the phone, calling everything from the police to an F-14 airstrike. Ten minutes away, a siren is already dopplering through the evening streets. Yukio experi-mentally slaps Christina's face a couple of times. She does not respond, and it makes him feel bad doing it, so he sits down next to her on the bathroom floor and pulls her head on to his lap.

This is how the ambulance crew find him. They take a look at the empty pill bottle, and inject Cristina with a stimulant, which gets things going again, heartwise, but doesn't quite bring her back to consciousness. Yukio decides to accompany her to the hospital. He gets into the ambulance, and spends the journey staring at the girl's face, which, now it has a plastic airway stuffed into it, is not looking as perfect as it was. Nevertheless, Yukio is entranced, and every so often gives her limp hand a meaningful squeeze. Back in the flat Suzie is chain-smoking Christina's cigarettes, waiting for Paulette to come back from telling tedious, boring Clive that he is now tedious, boring and single.

What else is there to say? My work is done for the day and, in purely artistic terms, everything has gone swimmingly. There was a purity of form and intent which I find particularly moving. Content with this as a statement, I can refrain from intervening again for some time. Once again I shall settle back to observe, my concentration absolute, my love for Christina undiminished. It will be interesting to see what happens. Yukio has his work cut out. *Manga* cartooning is not poetry. Japanese and English emotional registers are not always compatible. Christina is difficult, impetuous, far more articulate in her own language than he in his, and, these days at least, pretty screwed-up. But stranger couples have been made, some of them by me, and like Hervé, Yukio improves with acquaintance. I hope he realises he is a lucky man. He is being given an opportunity. His face will be the first thing Christina sees when she wakes up. To her, it will look like the face of an angel.

Esther Freud

THE WILD

Extract from a novel in progress

DEAR DAD,

We're living in a really brilliant house. It's got a garden with a badminton net and another one for vegetables and William says we can all have a garden of our own down by the garage. William is building it himself. (The garage) Also there's The Wild which is full of mud and trees and William says he will clear it out and build a chicken coop. He thinks that might be my job, feeding the chickens. I hope so. I'm very well. Jake sends his love. (He says he'll write when he's not in a bad mood.)

How are you? I'm very well.

Love, Tess

A week later for the first time in my life I had a letter back. Not just a card for me and Jake, but a whole letter with my name on it.

Dear Tess,

I'm glad to hear that you're so well. William sounds like quite a fellow. Maybe I should come and visit, see the garage for myself.

Love, Dad

We were having breakfast and William was making toast while Mum cleared away our muesli dishes. It was William's idea that we all eat the same thing, Jake and me and his three

427

daughters – all eat the same thing, at the same time, at every meal. Until last week we'd eaten when we felt like it, especially in the morning, and Jake in particular was having trouble adjusting to these rules. I glanced at William as he toasted bread on the hotplate of the Rayburn, wrapping each slice in a fold of tea-towel until he had a hot thick stack.

'Me first for toast,' Pandora said. Pandora was William's youngest daughter and still needed jam spreading for her with someone else's knife.

'She's spoilt.' Lolly kicked her under the table and they scowled at each other and stuck out their tongues.

'Mum,' I said, but she was running water into the sink. William handed the hot parcel of toast to Honour, who took a piece and handed it on to Jake.

'Thanks, Honour,' Jake said in a nasty high-up voice. Honour was in Jake's class at school and he couldn't see why suddenly they were expected to be friends. In fact Mum and William had met at a Parent–Teachers Evening when they'd talked about the problem of Jake being a bully. Picking on children like Honour who were new.

'Mum,' I called to her across the noise. 'Dad says he might come and visit.' Jake looked up, honey dripping from his knife.

'Really?' my mother smiled. She picked the letter up and still smiling, nodded over it. 'How nice.' But I could tell she didn't think for one minute it was true.

'Pass it here,' Jake ordered and my mother hovered between our outstretched hands. 'Me,' he demanded and Mum edged it his way. William took his seat at the other end of the table and Pandora climbed on to his knee. 'Daddy . . .'

'What?' He turned his good ear towards her. The other had been injured in an accident, something that involved a car explosion or a gun.

'Nothing.' She snuggled down. William used his long arms to butter toast around her.

'Today,' he said, his mouth full, 'we're going to cut down a tree.'

'Hurray!' Lolly and Pandora shouted. 'Hurray,' I joined in

428

a second too late. I wasn't used to such adventures. Honour sat up straighter as if in preparation for the most responsible of tasks and even Jake looked intrigued. 'I'm going to need help from Jake, and from all you girls.' He smiled around the table and crinkled his eyes to show that he meant Mum as well. 'We'll drive up on to the forest, and find the right kind of tree, and then . . .' His voice grew serious. 'You'll have to be very careful while I use the chainsaw.'

'Are you allowed to do that?' my mother asked. 'Just wander around cutting down trees?'

William put his head to one side, pointing to his deaf ear, so that she had to ask the question twice. 'Of course.' He thumped the table so that Pandora bounced into the air. 'Forestry rights come with the house.' He told us all to run along and get ready. 'We'll bring in enough firewood to see us through the winter,' he said, and he strode off to load the chainsaw into the van.

The Ashdown Forest was thick with bracken, fraying and unfurling red, but the wide soft lanes that ran up to the golf course were still green.

'There aren't many trees for a forest,' Honour said, sitting in the front between Mum and William while Jake was crouched as far away as he could get, keeping his balance by the rattling back doors.

'I know a place.' William drove the van as if it were a ship, rollicking over the humps and mounds as he steered us through a shiny copse of birch.

'Look, a little house.' Lolly craned to see. 'All hidden away.' And there it was, in a sudden valley, a crumbling old house that poked out of the earth.

William pulled on the brake and swung open the door.

'Who lives there?' We were out now and I was holding on to my mother's hand. It was the kind of house that should be haunted, with a front gate, crooked, and a garden fence all caving in. There were rows of Brussels sprouts and cabbages garlanded with thin white plastic bags. Bottle tops were strung in twittering lanes. There was even a broom scarecrow with a face like a Weetabix moustache.

'Mr Jenkinshaw?' William had one hand on the gate and he was straining forward. We waited and then the top half of the white front door fell open and an old man leaned out. 'Morning,' he said, and all five of us including Jake froze right where we were. We were so silent the air hummed high around us, but we still didn't hear a word of what was said.

'What happened to him?' We danced round William. 'What happened?' we hissed, and we shook our arms and legs and writhed against the grass, covering our faces and wondering what it would be like to live without a nose. 'What happened? Arrrggghhhh. Yuk.' Mr Jenkinshaw was safe behind his slatted door. 'Heebie geebie yikes.' The thought of him was like itching with the nits.

'Calm down, the lot of you.' William was scouting round for trees.

'Ssshh now.' And Mum wondered if Mr Jenkinshaw's nose was the result of syphilis, or an injury from the war.

'Blown off, you mean?' Jake gasped and we writhed and rolled some more, feeling strange electric tingles run up through our legs.

We drove the van up on to a shrubby plateau, and William carried the chainsaw towards a tall thin ash. There was ivy growing up into its branches and we were told that this was a sign that eventually the tree was going to die. 'Stand back, the lot of you.' William strained with one foot on the chainsaw, his face reddening a shade darker with each pull. I watched the sinews of his arm, dark veins against white skin as he stretched the string and tried to catch it as it ticked. Jake sniggered and I hoped and hoped that the next time William tried he'd kick it into life. 'Hurray!' Lolly and Pandora cheered when the machine finally caught and roared and William made them squeal away by threatening to brandish it against their long loose hair.

The noise it made was horrible, whining and screaming into wood, and then as if by magic, just at the point William had planned, the tree crashed down into the ferns. William switched off the chainsaw and shouted for us to gather round. 'It's all to do with angles,' he said, 'working out the exact direction in which a tree should fall.' 'He stopped for a moment to take his jacket off.

'How do you know these things?' Mum was flushed, her eyes hot, her lashes melting. William shrugged and flicked the hair back from his face. 'Just wait till you taste my ravioli,' he winked, flipping his tongue around the word and Jake turned in disgust and walked away. 'Jake.' I ran after him, but just then the chainsaw started up again and William began slicing the thin tree into logs.

Honour, Lolly and Pandora formed a queue. They waited, well trained, to carry each log as it came and heave it through the back doors of the van. William cut specially small ones for Pandora – kindling, they would have to be – and he formed Lolly and me into a team so that with our combined strength we could get one good log off the ground. Jake, Honour and Mum were the best workers and William stopped after a while to tell them so. He winked at Jake, man to man, and took the opportunity to take off his shirt. His back was white and long and his stomach when he bent down was ridged in a hard knot over his belt. There was a thin white scar curled over his left side and I wondered if it was caused by the same battle that had shot the sound out of his ear.

The next day I wrote back to my father. I imagined him in his tall white house where a bath stood alone in the middle of the floor. He lived there with Georgina, a woman as beautiful as pearls, and once when Jake and I went to visit he put his hand under her skirt. She was in the kitchen making us spaghetti hoops, and she didn't blush or struggle, but simply moved away to fetch two plates.

> *Dear Dad,*
>   *It would be really great if you did come and visit. I could show you the tallest tree in the Wild. I've been*

banging nails into it so that I can climb up to where the branches start. William might have made the chicken coop by then. I hope so, although we'll have to be careful about foxes.

Love from Tess

We were starting back at school next week and William was starting school as well. 'I'll be able to keep an eye on you,' he joked, looking at us seated round the table, but in fact he was teaching in the Upper School and none of us were old enough for his class. Jake and Honour were eleven, I was eight, and Lolly and Pandora were seven and four. Pandora was still in kindergarten. Upper School didn't start until you were fourteen but now that William was teaching in it, I couldn't wait till I was there.

Everything was going to be different for us this year. For one thing we'd drive to school with William in his van, and wouldn't have to wait out on the road for a lift. In the last place we'd lived, at Laurel Hill, a mile further away along the Oakfield Road, we'd been picked up by a family called Bigg who drove right past our house. We'd wait there every morning, betting on the cars, and every single morning we worried that we'd come out too late. At first Mum used to wait with us, but often she had cleaning jobs that started before nine, and she would take the bus that stopped especially for her just before the bend.

Sometimes Odin followed us out on to the road and I had to shoo him back when the Biggs' car eventually drew up. Odin was my cat. He was named after the most powerful of all the Norse Myth gods. Really he should have been called Thor, who was an angry god, but the name Odin carried better on the wind, and every night I had to stand by the back door and call and call him in for supper.

Odin was ferocious. He had claws like iron spikes and his eyes and ears were orange. I'd got him for my seventh birthday and from the moment I saw his pointy ears sticking out of a crêpe-paper box I fell in love with him. Arthur, I'd called him at first, but once his true character emerged his name had to be changed. It was partly because of Odin that we'd moved out of Laurel Hill. The Wilkses, whose two ground-floor rooms we rented, had had enough of him. He'd gashed Mrs Wilks's boyfriend and then one day, running at great speed along a corridor, he'd collided with Imelda. Imelda was Mrs Wilks's little girl, and instead of skirting round her, he'd run straight up her front and using her head as a propeller, he'd leapt from there on to the stairs. It made me laugh hard every time I thought of it, but I did feel bad when even a week later I saw Imelda still had red welts under her fringe.

William cooked porridge on the first morning of term.

'Porridge.' Jake was appalled, and even Honour dabbed at it half-heartedly with her spoon.

'It's delicious,' William insisted, and he sprinkled his with salt.

'Mum?' Jake looked to her for help, but she simply pushed a pot of honey in his direction, and as if to lure him on, swallowed down a thick white glutinous spoonful.

For special treats, Mum, Jake and I would have cheese on toast for breakfast. It was our favourite food and halfway through the toasting mum would pull out the grill and splash vinegar over the melting cheese. It gave it an extra delicious taste like the welsh rarebit served at Miriam's café, and we'd sit up, the three of us in bed, and eat it.

Jake stood up and moved towards the larder. He disappeared inside, re-emerging after a second with a jar of golden syrup, an old blackening jar that had made the move with us, and using the edge of his knife, he prised off the lid. He dipped a teaspoon into it and with the thick mass clinging, he wrote his name in gold across the porridge skin. 'That's better,' he said, and he looked hard-eyed in William's direction.

Jake had chosen his place at the far end of the table, as far away from William as he could get. William was the only one who had a chair. The rest of us squeezed on to benches, three on either side, and on that first evening of the day that we'd moved in, our places had been set. I'd marked out my place beside Pandora, my back towards the door, so that when inevitably she clambered on to her father's lap, it was me who was beside him. I could slide along the bench until I felt the heat of his white arm, and I would sit and snuggle close to his good ear.

William had his school bag packed and hanging from his hand.

'Time to go,' he shouted, and I noticed that his hair was newly cut in a slope around his head.

Jake clanked open the back door of the van. An old rug had been stretched across the floor, and the wood chips cleared away. He sat down on the raised metal of the hubcap and Honour, her pale glasses pressed tight against her face, climbed in and took the other. Lolly and Pandora slipped into the front, pinching and prodding each other across the foam tears of the black plastic seat. I tried my luck and squeezed in after them, pressing myself between Lolly and the door, so that I had to stand up sideways to slam it shut.

'Into the back now, Tess. Two's the limit.' William swung in, and sheepishly I climbed over the seat.

I sat down in the spare tyre, looking up occasionally at the wide windshield of sky, but even without a view I knew every turn, bump and slow that led towards the village of Twelve Ashes. I closed my eyes and felt the van swerve, take the bend beyond the church and trundle up the last hill towards our school.

Our school was different. I knew this because no one from Twelve Ashes really talked to us, and sometimes when we took the bus home, earlier or later than the other children, the bus driver snarled and made a fuss when we didn't have exactly the right change. Another strange thing about our school was the way that everything was sloped. The buildings, the signposts and the writing, everything was angled at a tilt. It was part of the philosophy, that no one should see corners, and so it meant the doors to the main building were curved over at the top and the window frames were cut up into eight. Letters of the alphabet were rounded, the backs of Fs and Es, for instance, bent and fat, so that they looked like ancient German writing, or some message on a scroll. There wasn't any uniform, apart from a ban on clogs, but between Michaelmas and Easter no girl was to be seen in ankle socks, no boy in shorts and it was often mentioned that the British habit of sending children out in winter with bare frozen legs was responsible for many of the ills of later life.

This year Jake's classroom was going to be blue. Blue was for Class Five, green for Four, yellow for Class Three and for Classes Two and One, a mottled wash of pink. I could see my Class Three yellow through the window as I passed, newly painted in a sea-sponge press of swirls, and there beside the blackboard was my own class teacher, Mr Paul. I raced over the main hall, past the carved stone sculpture of St George wrestling with a snake, and slid along the corridor. Mr Paul, Mr Paul, and in my mind's eye I flew into his arms.

'Mr Paul?' I said instead, and he half-turned to me and smiled. He was drawing a picture on the blackboard of a river flowing between reeds and there in a small basket I could make out the chubby elbow of a tiny arm. 'Hello,' I said, and I wanted to take hold of his square hand.

We stood there, smiling, shy after an endless summer break, and turning back he finished sketching the reeds around the stream. Now there was a baby's bonnet, peaking out in white, and I imagined Mr Paul standing there all holidays, chalking and shading to get the pastel colours smooth. Mr Paul had his own daughter, a pale girl in the class above, and when I saw her in the playground I wondered if she minded not being in his class. It was true she saw her father in the evenings and I supposed over the weekend, but we were with him every morning, heard the stories he made up out of everything he knew, and we'd had him to ourselves since we were six.

'Mum, I mean Mr Paul . . .' I said, sidling close, but just then, a stream of other children pressed in, and I rushed off to choose my desk.

'So?' William asked over supper. 'How was your first day?' He looked around the table at the five of us, the first strands of spaghetti slooped into our mouths. 'Honour?'

'Fine.' She kept her eyes on her plate and I saw Jake glance at the narrow line of her high shoulders pressed up against each ear.

'Jake?' William bent forward, waiting to hear the worst, but Jake looked clear into his eyes and said it had been good. 'We're doing woodwork. And I'm making a bowl.'

'That's great.'

'Yes, a pudding bowl,' he said, dipping his chin with mirth, and he glanced meaningfully at William's dark brown round of hair.

'At kindergarten,' Pandora piped up, 'we sang lots of songs.' And she started lisping one into her father's ear. 'And they played it on a ladle, a ladle, a ladle and they played it on a ladle and his name was Aikin Drum.'

'And how about you, Lolly?' William asked, serious, as if there might be a reason why she should need particularly to be asked, and Lolly told us all about her teacher Miss Bibeen, and how she'd been on holiday to Japan. 'She told us about it for the whole main lesson.' And Lolly launched into a detailed account.

I waited, sucking up spaghetti, slowing each mouthful for my turn, but William got up to fill the water jug and without seeming to see me, he began to tell us about a school play he wanted to direct.

'Just help yourself to fruit,' my mother called, as benches clattered and feet dropped to the floor and she started clearing dishes for the washing up.

'Mum . . .' I climbed on to her high bed, whistling for Odin to follow and curl against my knees.

'Yes,' she said, keeping both eyes on her book.

'It's not fair . . .'

'What's not?'

I hesitated. 'Jake's got the top bunk again.'

'I know.' She glanced towards the door where Jake was pasting a poster of a leopard, drooling and ferocious, over the magnolia of one wall. There were lions there already and an elephant and I'd made him promise to leave me an oblong empty square.

'What will you put up?' my mother asked.

'I don't know.'

I had my treasures laid out on the windowsill. There was Odin's first collar, matted with hair, one earring, and a half-eaten sugar pig. The pig had been my father's. He'd had it since he was a boy, and on a visit to London I'd come across it, abandoned and forgotten in the debris of his desk. I'd picked it up, stared at it, crooked and warmed it in my palm, until eventually he'd noticed and asked if I'd like to take it home.

'Thank you, yes, if you're sure . . .' And then that evening Jake had bitten off its head.

I'd been asleep, my ear against the window of the train, when I was woken by a horrible yowl. 'That's disgusting!' Jake snarled, pink splinters dribbling on his chin. 'I think I might be sick.' And through my sobs I explained the pig was an antique.

'No wonder it tastes so disgusting.' Jake threw the cracked remains into my lap.

Mum helped me sellotape it back together, a jagged strip around its neck and leg, and as soon as we were home I put it on my treasure shelf, propped between an eggcup and a three-legged silver box.

'How do you know Dad had it all those years?' Jake asked that night, leaning down towards me, draped like a bat over his bunk. 'How do you know?' But I refused to tell him, pretending stubbornly to be asleep, and eventually he gave up and swung back into his bed.

William wanted us to think what we should call the house. Before he'd found it and started building, it hadn't been a house at all but an old bakery. There was a great fireplace, big enough to sit inside where the ovens used to be, and above it was an enormous chimney. There was no upstairs, and the whole garden, even where the lawn was now, was wild.

'I wish I'd seen it then,' I said, and Pandora looked all pleased. 'I saw it,' she said. 'I saw it then.'

'Come on, girls,' William called. 'I want you all to think.'

'Honeysuckle Cottage.' Lolly's hand shot up.

William frowned. 'There isn't any honeysuckle.'

'We could plant some.' I agreed with Lolly. It was a perfect name.

'How about The Cake House,' Honour said.

'Very clever.' William approved.

'Or Cheery Bricks?' Jake smiled.

Mum laughed.

'Now Jake,' William said, 'let's be serious.'

'Cheery pricks,' he muttered just under his breath, and William swerved his eyes.

'How about . . .' He leant his arms on the table. 'How about The Wild?'

'That's brilliant,' all of his children clamoured. 'The Wild!'

'You don't think just The Bakery?' my mother said. It was the way our letters reached us now.

'Boring, boring.' William waved his hands. 'The Wild.' And suddenly we were whooping and hallooing, caught up in the excitement of the name.

William set out to make a sign. He chose one of the Ashdown Forest logs and cut a sideways slice. He planed it smooth and then with a tiny chisel he carved 'The Wild' into the wood.

He filled the grooves with dark brown paint and when it was dry he varnished it. The wood turned to a honey sheen and the bark was rough and frilled. When it was finished we went with him to the cattle-grid to hang it up.

The Gatehouse, The Coachhouse, Gamekeepers Cottage, The Lodge. The signs hung in a line, all smooth and plain with letters drawn in white. 'The Wild,' William said as he attached the sign and he stood back to admire it.

The estate of Bracken Hill was tranquil and maintained. There were rhododendron bushes and pine-green shaded trees and most of the inhabitants were off in London for their work.

'We love it,' we screamed and we ran back along the newly gravelled road.

'Odin!' William's voice was stern, stopping us short. 'Odin, bad cat!' And there by the half-built garage stood Odin with a bird, still twitching, in his mouth. As soon as he saw me, he ran over and dropped it at my feet. Lolly screamed and Pandora tried to clamber up her father's leg. Odin snarled and showed his teeth. 'Bad, bad cat,' William said again, and the bird gave one last quiver. Odin curled around my legs, back and forth, shimmying his tail, willing me to stoop down and run my fingers flat against his head.

'He's killed it, he's killed it,' Pandora shrieked, and Lolly looked as if she might be going to cry.

'Tess,' William said, 'you'd better bury that poor creature at the bottom of the garden.' He turned before going into the house and shouted, 'Be sure and do a good job now.'

Odin came with me to dig the grave. The bird was a starling with one broken, hanging wing, its eyes pale blue and newly clouded over. Odin did not look repentant. He kept his tail straight up and quivering, and while I dug he let his warm body fall against my back. 'You like it here, don't you?' We talked over my shoulder and he smiled with his orange eyes, his nose a velvet slope of pink. 'Naughty cat,' I muttered then, in case anyone could overhear, and I checked his neck to see his bell was working.

'When we get our chickens,' William said that night at supper, 'we'll have to watch out for your cat.' And in my defence Jake told him it was nature.

'Perhaps there's a pet that you'd like to have?' William asked, but the only animals Jake liked were wild. 'I wouldn't mind a llama,' he said, 'or a wolf.' Afterwards he sneered. 'That shut him up.'

Lolly and Pandora shared a huge bedroom with bookshelves right across one wall. They had a dressing-up box spilling out with glitter. Sequins, turbans and raw silk. And every night before they went to sleep William went in and sang to them. I could hear his voice drift through the floorboards, accompanied by the low hum of his guitar.

'You can go in,' my mother said, catching me perched, listening, at the bottom of the stairs.

'Are you sure?' I waited until, with my mother's prompting, William asked me in himself. I curled up on the end of Lolly's bed and let the warm songs seep into my skin.

> There was a fair maid who lived by the shore,
> May the wind blow high or low.
> No one could she find to comfort her mind
> She sang all alone on the shore.

Often the songs were tragic. Stories of mermaids, boats wrecked, or Red Indians revenging themselves on newly-settled whites.

> There was a sea captain who sailed the salt sea,
> May the wind blow high or low.
> 'I'll die, I'll die,' the captain did cry,
> 'If I can't have that maid on the shore.'

'More,' we begged, 'one more,' and William bent low over his guitar.

Bottle of wine, fruit of the vine,
when you goin to let me get over.
Leave me alone and let me go home.
Won't you gone let me start over.

'Bottle of wine, fruit of the vine . . .' I sang to Jake and he slapped his hand down over the top bunk and told me to shut up.

'Why don't you like him?' I asked, and he looked at me with his clear serious face and said, 'He's after Mum.'

After supper, as the evenings started to get cold, we all sat in the giant fireplace for bedtime songs. Whoever was closest to the flames would start to roast and every twenty minutes someone would have to swop. William sang a song about a woman. A woman with long black hair. But every time he sang it something in the words stumbled and tripped him up. 'She was fair, with long ge, bl . . . black hair.' Mum blushed and William's children laughed uncomfortably.

'What's ge, bl . . . black?' I asked Lolly, and she said that the real words of the song were 'golden'. 'She was fair with long golden hair.' And then she stopped and told me that he used to sing it for their mother. 'He didn't have to change the words for her,' she said, and when I didn't answer, she added, 'She's the prettiest woman in the world.' But she said it quietly because William didn't like to hear anyone mention her name. At first I thought it was because she'd died. But after a while I realised it was because she was evil. A sort of devil woman witch.

'He fought with all he had to get those girls,' my mother told a friend. 'After all, why should the woman get them automatically?' But as she talked she held tight on to my arm. 'He was just as involved as her. More so,' she said. 'And in the end she gave in and let them go.'

'He must have brought quite a case against her in the court.'

'Oh he did,' my mother said. 'He most certainly did.' And her voice drifted away.

Michael Hulse

THE POINTLESSNESS OF POETRY

for Peter Porter

Small comfort, thinking poetry
the furniture of heart and mind,
if Helen Schlegel's right and only
furniture endures while men and houses perish –

so in the end the world will be
a waste land of poetic chairs and sofas,
desolate through eternity
with not a soul to sit on them.

Paul Muldoon

ON

*Absalom was riding his mule and the mule passed under the
thick branches of a great oak. Absalom's head got caught in
the oak and he was left hanging between heaven and earth,
while the mule he was riding went on.*

II Samuel 18:9

I make my way alone through the hand-to-hand fighting
to J3 and J5. Red velvet. Brass and oak.
The special effects, it seems, will include strobe lighting
and artificial smoke.

A glance to J5. Patrons are reminded, *mar bheadh*,
that the management accepts no responsibility in the case of
    theft.
Even as the twenty-five piece orchestra
that's masked offstage left

strikes up there's still a chance, I suppose, that the gainsayers
may themselves be gainsaid
and you'll rush, breathless, into my field of vision.

Understudies and standbys never substitute for listed players,
however, unless a specific announcement is made.
There will be no intermission.

David Flusfeder

THE CASE OF SOLOMON HELLER

Extract from a novel, Morocco, *to be published
by Fourth Estate in January 2000*

THE PATIENT ARRIVED in the city four years before. He suffers
from vertigo and chronic, often acute digestive problems.
When he first came to town all he had with him, he once
uncharacteristically boasted, were the clothes on his back, a
blueprint for making money and a bag filled with anti-
dyspepsia pills. The blueprint has worked. The pills have not.

Solomon Heller is (*was?*) a slim blond balding man in his
mid to late thirties. His most prominent features are his blue
eyes, which protrude mildly in typical hypoglycaemic fashion,
and seem to convey gentleness and abstemiousness. One is
also immediately struck by the succession of noises produced
from his aberrant digestive system.

The tycoon runs his business empire from a grim office
building in a poor part of town. He has no close confidants,
no friends he thinks of as such – his social world is divided
into employees and rivals – and no contact with his family or
indeed anyone from his home town.

Clearly, he left his home town in something of a hurry.
Heller will not acknowledge this or even refer to it. Perhaps
he was driven out or, more likely, he needed or felt he needed
to get away from something or somebody. He does admit
that the dyspepsia began shortly before his departure, and
that is the extent of his reminiscences of adult life. When
pressed, he will talk about his early family memories but in a
way that resists interpretation or even interest. Put simply:
when I am with him I am bored. It is all too easy to say that

he is boring me deliberately, a form of resistance to analysis, to hide the causes of his neurosis. Certainly the boredom is a weapon he brings to sabotage our therapeutic alliance. But we mustn't forget that the boredom could have almost nothing to do with Heller and all to do with something as yet unnamed inside me that resists *him*. (Why?)

Consequently, the analysis has not so far been a success. Heller has yet to realise this. Two factors are on my side. First, he is still impressed by my manner at our first meeting. Our initial interview took place at his headquarters (initiated by my brother in fact, who works for him). *I have a problematical digestion*, said Heller the mild-mannered, the notorious, not looking me in the eyes, looking far past me at the window which gives out on to the courtyard below. *No doctor or dietitian has been able to help. It is bad for business, embarrassing for me*. That short time ago, I was absolutely confident of my own powers. I forced the tycoon's gaze to meet my own. I held it, and said, softly, certainly, *I can fix that*. Heller looked away from me again, lifted a hand to his mouth to stifle a burp, nodded, and waited for us to leave.

Second (and I write this modestly, this is nothing I am proud of, I merely want to offer the clinical picture, entire), I do have a gift for listening or at least appearing to. No matter how bored I am I can still give the impression that I hear everything secret and shameful and marvellous that lies behind my patients' unrevealing words – when actually of course I am often merely staving off sleep. So: twice a week Heller and I fail one another.

And then, things change. This is the magic and mystery of depth psychology. We are alone in my consulting room. Heller is stretched out on the couch. I am in my too-comfortable leather chair. We have our customary brief matching of selves. (What does he see? A young woman – too young – who gazes upon him eagerly – too eagerly – to stifle her ennui just as he stifles his belches and burps. Her hair is deep red, which unsettles him.) I ask him a question about his father. He hiccoughs. His eyes close. His right hand, as usual, enters his shirt to massage lightly his treacherous belly. *My father*, he says, *was a strong man who had been disappointed by things.*

And so it would go, nursery memories, nursery trials, the looming figure of the father, the soft aura of the mother, who was an invalid in exile in a dark forbidden room. And I nod every now and again even though Heller's eyes remain closed, and Heller's reminiscences are punctuated by burps and intestinal rumbles and the occasional fart.

Heller goes on talking and eructating and I battle against an overwhelming exhaustion that pulls my eyes shut; which can only be defeated by pinching myself hard, which I do on the thigh, professional bruises to examine later when I bathe. I fight to listen to what he is saying. That being impossible, I try to work out what inside me is making this analysis such a failure, and I reach the inevitable conclusion that I am just too young and inexperienced and too unalterably mediocre to cure the sickness in men's souls.

The tycoon's words stump meaninglessly by. What is he talking about now? A pet dog? An imaginary childhood companion? A trusted family friend who had cruelly molested the infant Heller? *Then*, he says, in his light, not unpleasant voice, *I didn't see him again until we went to the lake that summer.*

Revelation. Where does it come from? Partly intuitive and partly through the counter-transference – again, I try again to examine my own reactions to the tycoon: why, lurking behind the boredom, is there such an element of distaste? When have I felt such distaste before? That's an easy one to answer: when having pressed upon me the unwelcome attentions of inadequate men with dark circles under the eyes. (I offer no excuse for departing from the customary impersonality of case notes. There are two people in the consulting room. Every analysis is mutual.)

I make my intervention. Interrupting him I say, employing my most bland clinical manner:

Tell me, Mr Heller, how often do you masturbate?

The intervention startles us both. Heller's eyes open. His

hand pulls (guiltily?) away from his stomach. I think he realises as well as I that the insight, which had seemed to come almost from nowhere, is absolutely accurate and has attached to it, new-born and full-grown, a complete understanding of my patient's malady. This is where I should stop, let the silence spin out, wait for Heller to learn to reveal his own truth to himself. One of the skills I have yet to learn is how to withhold language from my patients.

Heller burps, hiccoughs, looks angry. I press on.

You have told me before how you would like to have a family of your own. Find a wife, sire some children?

He, perhaps fearfully, nods.

But instead you are too busy making money. Tell me now, I think the time is right, why did you leave your home town?

Silence. And on I go, for this moment at least (at last) no longer intimidated by my patient's wealth and power and reputation.

Tell me about the woman you left behind.

Heller manages to say, *No no, there was no woman.* I carry on, merciless. I get to my feet. I stand over my patient who sits up in response. We glare at one another. I am breaking all the rules, facing him like this, psychic adversaries.

The woman. You know the one I mean.

The dyspepsia is only (as it could only be, a child would know that) a symptom of Heller's neurosis. In the beginning was a blockage of the libido and that was caused (I am sure of this, some things we know) by the loss of a woman he had loved, to whom he had given himself or at least offered himself, fully, for probably the only time in his life; and maybe she had seemed at first to offer an equal love in return but then she had rejected him. Then came the libidinal blockage and because of the blockage there was the recourse to masturbation, which further dammed the blockage and strengthened the neurosis because on top of everything he now had the shame of a *disgraceful secret* to contend with (a secret that the master of the discipline has written about so often I suspect it might be the great man's own).

Your dyspepsia began shortly after she left you. And then

you returned to the habit of your youth and became again a chronic masturbator and your dyspepsia got worse. This is so, isn't it? Why did she leave you?

Heller gazes furiously away from his accuser.

My hands move to hold my patient's arms. I grasp him in a way that suggests comradely understanding, maybe even forgiveness.

There is no shame to this. Forget the woman. Forget shame. Move on. And your digestion will return to normal. I guarantee it.

The chronic masturbator pulls himself away from my consoling touch.

And before you can forget, first you must properly remember.

Solomon Heller shakes his head like a boxer who has taken too many blows. He looks me in the eyes. He speaks:

If you talk about this to anyone I'll have you killed.

I smile. The warm clear smile of the confessor-healer.

A gurgle and a rumble issue from Heller's bowels. He climbs unsteadily to his feet and struggles with his overcoat. I help him force his left arm through a difficult sleeve. We listen to the sound of feet trudging up the staircase. Heller's driver, the hooligan Bernard, one of his bought protections from the world, has come to collect his master.

I meant what I said, says Heller, *Nonetheless, I'd like to see you more often. Can we meet four times a week now?*

Truth always finds a way to slip through the narrowest of holes. In Heller's proposal, readily agreed to, we can hear the answer to my original question.

We drive at night. The tycoon's Buick cruises slowly through the rain along Marshal Street.

Heller has decided it is convenient to hold night-time psychological sessions in his car. I have given my consent to this unorthodox practice. Two reasons: 1) we have to move beyond our artificial boundaries: the psychologist's care must extend out of the consulting room; 2) I like to drive in Heller's car.

A thick sound-proofed window has been installed behind the driver's seat. This is to protect Heller's secrets and, therefore, the safety and future of his driver. Sometimes my eyes will meet the hooligan's watching us in the rear-view mirror. And sometimes I catch a glint of the steel razor that Bernard wears embedded in the front of his checked cloth cap. Why does Heller require this sort of physical protection? It's not my business. My job is to strip down his psychic defences.

The patient has been talking, fluently and mostly uninterrupted, for about twenty minutes in a kind of semi-hypnotic state. He refuses still to admit that there ever was a woman who had driven him from his home town, the woman he loved and lost and has dyspeptically mourned ever since, but he has consented to reminisce about his very first love. The psychologist listens and makes her old mistake of interrupting when she starts getting bored.

She was ten years older than me and to most people she was more or less invisible. She had three children. A husband who was neither cruel to her nor kind. He was a merchant. I worked for him and learned very quickly from his example how not to succeed in business. Once, I remember, he was buying a shipment of horse grain from, from, I don't remember where from, there was an intermediary in the west but the shipment came from somewhere in the east –

Excuse me, says the foolish psychologist. May we return to the matter of the woman herself?

And the moment is lost. I realise straight away that I should have waited to see where the story was leading, should have considered the meaning of my patient's forgetfulness. Heller usually forgets nothing. What is the significance of east versus west? Or is the meaningful thing horse grain? The horse is an obvious erotic symbol, and in this anecdote the merchant is being cast as the inadequate feeder of Eros. The patient was telling me, in symbolic code, about the cuckold, about himself.

449

But now Heller wipes condensation away from the window and looks out at the shops (he likes to see which products are selling) – a department store, a book shop, a milliner's, lingerie and ribbons, and cinemas, a mile of cinemas, the Elite, the Coliseum, Rialto, the Style, where *The Red Empress* is on, directed by my friend the 'Prince' and starring Sym's one-time protégé of the musical saw. Heller lifts his hand away from his stomach to catch a burp. Then the hand goes back inside his jacket.

My digestion is improving, he says. I tell him, That's only the start.

Heller turns towards me. Marquee lights refracted through rain glitter across his anxious mild face. Hard to imagine why this man is so feared. Maybe when I can imagine that, our analysis will move on to the next desired level. Could I be afraid of him? Physically, no. Psychically, only a little.

If the point is that I should have a woman then I'll get a woman.

No, I tell him, that isn't quite the point.

Then, Gloria, what is?

(Be careful, Gloria.)

Sexual desire, I tell him, is not just an itch to be scratched, a discharge into the momentary relief offered by a prostitute, a lover, or – excuse me – a hand. We must also consider object-relations in the world.

Too much jargon for a layman like me. What precisely are you talking about?

I am talking about, I suppose, the capacity for love.

Impossible to read Heller's response. Deadpan face, glinting hypoglycaemic eyes, the flash of some annoyance, but something else too, deeper, an animal baited.

Then, unfortunately, I had to ask Heller to stop the car so I could get out for a brief period to conduct a personal matter.

Excuse me, I say. We're approaching where I need to stop. Tell your man here. I won't be more than five minutes.

I'll come in with you.

Through the voice trumpet fixed into the glass screen

Heller instructs Bernard. The Buick pulls over. We are on Willow Street outside the Tip Top Club.

Gently, I say, I don't think this place would interest you much.

Gently, adamantly, he says, *I'm interested.*

We descend from the car into an empty street. I lead my patient – not just patient any more, what is he then: boss? prince? *friend*? – to the club. The rain has stopped. The city is silent. When, as slowly as I can, I pull open the door to the club, waves of noise and heat crash up at us.

A few words of explanation are perhaps required here. The personal matter I refer to involves my brother and in some way impinges upon the cases both of Heller and Sym. I had recently visited my mother and stepfather's apartment on Valour Street, the place which had once been the site of our most dreary family romances and dramas. I was looking for my childhood collection of cigarette cards, donated by my absent father.

The movie star series. Number 13: Igo Sym. Wearing a fedora Sym is almost full on to the camera but looking far past it – a passing girl has taken his fancy and he has been following her with his eyes while keeping his face still for the photographer and now she is about to disappear from view far off to the side. Sym's pale eyes watch her go with a mixture of admiration, anticipation and curious self-sufficient pleasure. Elfin ears. Fine nose. The sensuous mouth with just a hint of weakness about it. Sym's face, this card, had occupied a special place in my pubertal cosmology. For a start the cards came from Father, so there was already glamour attached. And number 13 in the series had been my own private symbol of modernity and passion, never spoken of, carried everywhere.

I walked quickly through the apartment on tiptoes, careful to disturb nothing, not even dust. No one was here, just the maid, our house Other, asleep in her kitchen cubby-hole, using her Bible for a pillow. I went into the smaller bedroom that once was shared with my brother. He still sleeps here, and keeps his law books and papers here, in the space allowed by the junk that Mother, with her more acute sense of taste, has forbidden her collector husband to display in the rest of the apartment. Somewhere here too, wrapped in oiled brown paper, was my old collection of movie star cigarette cards. I felt like a trespasser, opening stiff drawers of heavy ash furniture, peering into broken music boxes, moving aside rolls of paper tied with dark ribbon, searching for the cards in half-forgotten corners of times before.

What are you doing?

My brother, lawyer Daniel, standing by the doorway he'd silently entered through. I told him I was doing nothing.

Spying? What are you looking for?

His lower lip has always protruded, making him look permanently outraged and on the edge of tears. Now he added to the effect by jutting his chin forward. He brushed his wiry hair away from his brow. It sprang immediately back into its former position.

I couldn't resist teasing him a little. I asked him what he was worried that I might find.

Has He *sent you here?*

Lawyer Daniel was about to speak my old, forbidden name. I could see its initial letter take shape on his pouting lips. And then he thought better of it, the look of malice left his face, replaced by something sickly.

The situation had turned. He wanted something. Despite everything I've always liked my brother. I admire the transparency of his motives and the urgency of his drives. He, though, has never cared for me. On the day that I was born Daniel executed his favourite toy soldier and still blames me for its death. He holds me guilty of subsequent crimes nearly as bad as the original one of being born. Dangerous philosophies and loose morals and worst of all an ability to pass where he cannot. I may walk through Saxon Gardens or Dolphin Park, dawdle by the statues of misty characters from wars, throw crusts to the swans, sit by the bandstand unmolested except by the occasional man with a wolfish face who fancies himself a gigolo. Daniel would not dare. He can't enter these places either alone or in a group. At night he will cross over to walk a road's width away from the lilac bushes and chestnut trees and copses and formal gardens in which lurk dimly moonlit hooligans and thugs, the Others' youth militias, always on the look-out for examples of Us to punish for not knowing our place. Daniel will try always to keep to Our neighbourhoods. He has learned not to expose the crime of his difference to the Others' fists and boots and crowbars and razors and knives. His ambition has been taught to restrict itself to the aim of climbing the ranks of Solomon Heller's organisation. Heller may be an unscrupulous tycoon, but he's Our tycoon.

Perhaps you might do me a favour?

Of course.

I watched him struggle rather hopelessly and horribly with his face in an attempt to simulate fondness.

I don't see you often enough.

Nothing to say to that.

Zygelbojm asked me to put in a good word with you.

(Zygelbojm is the superfluous man, the very least of my suitors.)

Is that the favour?

Of course not. Hardly. I'm trying to get to see him. *But Mr Heller is always unavailable.*

We talked this way and that about Heller's busyness and business. Daniel has a most secret business scheme to put to him. It would make all the fortunes, he said. I let him talk, his dark eyes agleam as he devised scenarios for accidental meetings. He might be coming into my consulting room as Heller was leaving, or leaving it as Heller was coming in. He might be walking down the road as Heller's Buick suffered a prearranged flat tyre. Daniel would help, and in that moment could . . . Or perhaps I might take my patient for a walk, and Daniel, who could happen to be passing, might . . .

In my face he read his own absurdity; even he recognised the transparency of his schemes. Finally he was spent. I didn't permit myself more than a few seconds of silence. I have better things to do with my time than to make my brother suffer. I asked him if he still goes to the Tip Top Club. I knew the answer. Of course he does. He goes there with his friends to ogle the dancing girls, graduates of Madame Tatiana's cruel Academy of Theatrical Dance. I told him that my routine with Mr Heller was changing, that we were beginning to conduct some of the sessions in his car. (Daniel's eyes widened. Solomon Heller's Buick is an object of veneration to all his flunkies and acolytes and supplicants.) I could say, I said, that I needed to stop inside the Tip Top. He hates those sorts of places. He'd wait outside. I could be absent for five minutes. And you could easily be going in or going out . . .

We fixed our rendezvous. Daniel was delighted. I felt a twinge of something, regret perhaps – no, worse than that, guilt, raw guilt – for allowing bad faith schemes into the therapeutic alliance. He and I left the apartment arm in arm, just like brother and sister. I hadn't found the cigarette cards.

[Note to self: some of this may be extraneous.]

The Tip Top Club is the sort of place where everyone seems to be waiting for something. It's also always crowded. Heller had not been expecting this. He does not like a crowd; he experiences it as pain. We push through the foyer into the bar area. Heller is nervous, I am flustered, my brother is probably out there now, waiting by the car. Heller burps. I am seeking, somewhat desperately, an excuse for our presence in the club. A cavalry officer with the look of a man about to vomit lurches past, forcing our shoulders, mine and Heller's, to touch. When the officer is gone our shoulders are still touching. I realise that what Heller is feeling above all is the desire for me to hold him by the hand.

On the narrow stage a poet of sorts is proclaiming, in surprisingly euphonious verse, the imminent arrival of the end of everything, in flames, because *They* are coming . . . I've heard this sort of prophecy before and never been moved by it, just smoked and drank and talked over it as most of the crowd here tonight are doing, so why do I suddenly feel so chilled? Is it only the bridge of physical and psychical proximity to my patient that enables a small portion of the dread he always carries around with him to leak into me?

Heller, buffeted, crying above the crowd, reminds me that I am meant to be here for a purpose. I look around and try to find one. Florid faces, cocaine art, silver-ringed dancers' arms. A waitress with bad hair and bad skin. Bored band members sitting in a puddle of liquor. The house comics, Rappaport and Rappaport, bickering, waiting for the cue to go on. The manager, a spry lascivious little man who affects a monocle and a limp, is watching the singer who is also his wife conduct a whispery transaction with the pianist. Everyone else, it seems, is watching Heller and me. I am rather enjoying by now the looks we are getting. I've never felt so *noticed* before. Men and women gazing at us with respect, fear, distaste, or brazen invitation. This is the benefit of appearing in public beside the tycoon Solomon Heller.

The manager's attention swoops away from his wife on to us. He performs a bit of business with his monocle, then rubs his hands together as if he needs to raise the temperature of his skin before he can presume to approach such honoured customers. Heller farts. He is shrinking.

And there, sitting against the far wall, is Igo Sym, and beside him the astonishing woman. Her mouth is wide, full lips painted scarlet. The dress she wears shimmers like lightning. Her eyes are blue and her long hair blonde. She looks like a lioness. Her body is voluptuous. She is astonishing.

Gloria! Heller has taken up hissing. He has seen enough, endured enough respect, awe, distaste, noise, contact. I happen to have Sym's cigarette case in my coat pocket. I set off towards his table. Heller's left hand flails out. I reach back. I take it. He holds on.

We make our way to Sym's table. I recognise that this is potentially damaging material I am working with here, allowing patients to meet. The outcome could be awful. The star inclines his head to greet us. I realise I am staring too obviously at the astonishing woman. So I pretend briefly to be interested in the comics who are now on stage. Fast-talking Rappaport is explaining the mysteries of finance to his stooge Rappaport. I bring out the cigarette case, my alibi, and by so doing create a conspiracy between myself and my patient Sym, which is a risky manoeuvre at the best of times, of which this is not one. Somehow I manage to introduce the two men. Something passes between Sym and Heller but it is hard to say what; the beauty of Sym's mistress has scrambled all my powers.

Gloria the Astonishing favours Gloria the Astonished with her attention for the first time. The discovery of a flaw in her beauty perhaps might allow my legs to move, my tongue to unthicken. I discover no flaw. Heller tugs at my hand. Sym opens his cigarette case. The drummer executes a drum roll and we all look to the stage. Quick Rappaport is running off, hiding something precious in his hands. Slow Rappaport, abandoned, is looking for his wallet but failing to find it. Sudden clash of cymbals. The stooge falls over. The band strikes up. Gloria the Astonishing laughs. Her laughter enhances her beauty. I long to touch her hair with my fingertips. (Excuse me. But this is an exercise in laying bare.)

Lights glare on. We have the Tip Top Club.

Patient and psychologist, both a little unsteady, return to the car. Bernard in the Buick is reading a newspaper and smoking a cigarette and ignoring the rain-soaked lawyer standing beside the car. Heller pushes past him with a brief, unanswerable *How are you, Daniel?* and I follow after. We climb into the car. The door slams shut. (My coat tails get caught in the door but that is by the by.)

I release my coat. He chews on a bagel. (Heller is addicted to bagels.) We drive through night-time streets towards my apartment. I wait for him to say something about what went on in the club, to inquire about Sym, our relationship. Later in this session I will learn what I should have known – it is foolish ever to underestimate Solomon Heller.

We reach Sienna Street in silence. Just as I am gathering my coat and my thoughts Heller says, as if he is mentioning something of little interest, *I dreamt of my own death last night.*

I tell him that that is good. This is how our conversation then goes:

No. It was not good. It was fearsome. It still is. I haven't recovered from it since.

How did you die?

I threw myself out of a window. I was in my office and heard a noise at the window, then I was staring at the ground, which started pulling me towards it. I climbed over the window ledge and threw myself off and then I was falling. I hit the ground, my body broke, my head shattered. Shatters, keeps shattering, for ever. I woke up shouting.

Neurosis and pathology are very cunning. The closer you get to destroying disease the harder it fights to protect itself and destroy your will to change.

Heller says nothing but he obviously does not believe this to be an impressive line of interpretation.

You dreamed last night of transformation, which as you say is fearsome. The neurosis advises you that the danger is too great to be risked. Destroy me, it whispers, and you destroy yourself. Resist change, protect me, and you protect the best part of you.

It is most persuasive.

And a damaged life is guaranteed. And what do you have to fight with? A desire – perhaps as yet still weak – for change, a tiredness of familiar unhappy patterns, and a depth psychologist.

Who might not have the energy for the battle.

I am surprised by this. The light in the car is far too dim to make out the expression on his face but his voice is kindly.

You look exhausted, Gloria.

My days are long.

And your nights? Do you have lovers?

Something lies behind this also surprising question but I can't decide what it is. I have, to a certain degree, to be open with my patients. Every analysis, acknowledged or not, is a mutual analysis. If I demand disquieting secrets from my patient then I have to give him some of mine in return. Am I to tell him then about my suitors? Each one, honestly? Mr Mouse? The unreliable 'Prince'? Werner at the Institute who provides satisfactory libidinal services and, happily, nothing else? And what about the comic pursuit of me by a most superfluous man? My patients have to regard me as a loving woman who knows how to lead a psychically healthy life.

I have a lover.

You're happy with him?

Entirely.

Heller chuckles at a private joke or tragedy. His stomach rumbles.

I think you should stop working with the rest of your patients.

It is said so tentatively, as if Heller is timidly trying to share his thoughts with me so that together we might reach a decision. I am familiar enough with my patient to recognise an order when I hear one, regardless of tone.

All my patients?

All.

And if I said I wanted to keep just one?

(Is this my punishment for insisting on telling uncomfortable truths? Or for knowing more than he cares to have me know? Or for having Igo Sym as a patient?) Even in this dim light I can see – with my eyes closed I'd still be able to see – the knowledge in his mild blue eyes of who the chosen one would be.

I'd say no. You're wasting your time on egomaniacs. Think about it.

When Heller says *Think about it*, he means that only one answer is possible. What would happen if I disobeyed? Is it so unthinkable?

There'll be a banker's draft for you at my cashier's office on the first of every month. For personal expenses. I know your landlord. The rent on these rooms will be paid for directly. Now you can concentrate on your real work. It will be good for me to know you're not frittering away your atentions elsewhere.

The subject is closed. The session is over.

Edwin Morgan

A DAY OFF FOR THE DEMON

Dark shape on a white beach near Durrës,
Dark yet glistening too, spreadeagled,
Uncrumpling like a new-born dragonfly,
That's him, staring up, benevolent
As the blue above him, embracing
Whatever breeze there might be from the sea
And murmuring *falemnderit* to the sun for shining.
He does not look down at the fine zigzags
His sharp nails trace in the sand, any more
Than restless diodes in his mind preparing
Paths of dragons not dragonflies disturb
His somnolence, his vacancy, his pleasure.
Once in how many thousand years is it,
This heavenless hellless place, this peace, this pause?
He does not know; he does not think; he dreams.
The sunken wrecks don't rise, and Skanderbeg
Is motionless on his horse. There is nothing,
Not even weather, nothing at all.
He is lying there as blank as jetsam –
But you will not take that one home with you.

Alice Oswald

SISYPHUS

This man Sisyphus, he has to push
his dense unthinkable rock
through bogs woods crops glittering
optical rivers and hoof-sucked holes,
as high as starlight as low as granite,
and every inch of it he feels
the vertical stress of the sky
draw trees narrow, wear water round
and the lithe, cold-blooded grasses
weighed so down they have to hang their tips like cat's
    tails;
and it rains it blows but the mad delicate world
will not let will not let him out
and when he prays, he hears God passing with a
swish at this, a knock at that.

There is not a soft or feeling part,
the rock's heart is only another bone;
now he knows he will not get back home,
his whole outlook is a black rock;
like a foetus, undistractedly listening
to the clashing and whistling and tapping of another
    world,
he has to endure his object,
he has to oppose his patience to his perceptions . . .
and there is neither mouth
nor eye, there is not anything
so closed, so abstract as this rock
except innumerable other rocks
that lie down under the shady trees
or chafe slowly in the seas.

The secret is to walk evading nothing
through rain sleet darkness wind,
not to abandon the spirit of repetition:
there are the green and yellow trees, the dog,
the dark barrier of water,
there goes the thundercloud shaking its blue wolf's head;
and the real effort is to stare
unreconciled at how the same things are,
but he is half aware he is
lost or at any rate straining
out of the earth into a lifted sphere
(dust in his hair, a dark blood thread from his ear)
and jumps at shapes, like on a country road,
in heavy boots, heading uphill in silence.

Once his wide-armed shadow
came at him kicking,
his monkey counterpart pinioned to the rock;
the two grappled and the rock
stopped dead, pushed between them in suspension
and it was fear, quivering motion
holding them there, like in the centre of a flower
the small anxiety that sets it open
and for an hour, all he could think was
caught in a state of shadow – this persistent
breathing pushing sound, this fear of falling,
fear of lucidity, of flight, of something
bending towards him, but he pushed he pushed
until the sun sank and the shadow slunk away.

'I woke early when the grass was still a standing choir,
each green flower lifting a drop of water –
an hour of everything flashing out of darkness,
whole trees with their bones,
whole rivers with their bucks and backthrows,
there I walked lifting a drop of water;
I came to this cold field, the crowded
smoky-headed grasses singing of patience:

'Oh what does it matter?' they sang,
'longer and longer and all day
on one foot is the practice of grasses'
which raised in me a terrible cry of hope
and there I stood, waiting for the sun
to draw the water from my head . . .'

But Sisyphus is confused; he has to think
one pain at a time, like an insect
imprisoned in a drop of water;
he tries again, he distorts his body to the task
and a back-pain passes slowly
low down in the spine – a fine red thread
that winds his hands and feet in the struggle of movement;
and Sisyphus is a hump, Sisyphus is a stone
somewhere far away, feeling the sun
flitter to and fro with closed eyes,
unable to loiter, an unborn creature
seeking a womb, saying Sisyphus Sisyphus . . .
and he stares forward but there's nothing there
and backward but he can't perceive it.

Dorothy Nimmo

SEPTEMBER 1939

William Wilson is out in the garden
burning old copies of *Peace News*,
petitions, manifestos, resolutions and declarations.

Rosemary Wilson turns off the wireless
checks the blackout and looks out of the landing window
worried about William. They have been praying for
   months.

William served in the Ambulance Brigade last time
and he remembers. They thought the Lord
wouldn't let it happen again. Now it has happened

and the Lord is still Himself and lets things happen
as is His way, taking no notice of William who struggles
painfully with another box of pamphlets.

Burning, burning! The carton falls on his foot. He curses
   it
and God and the rain which is putting the fire out.
His face is all twisted and dirty. Rosemary Wilson

comes down the garden and takes him by the arm
to lead him back, she hopes, eventually, to a place of
   safety.

LIFECLASS

You suggest I start with charcoal. Get used
to working with the whole arm, moving
freely from the shoulder.

You tell me I am making decisions
with every black mark on the thick grey paper.
Notice the relationships.

Map the connections. My paper is covered
with black decisions. *Do you have
a putty rubber? It's not so much a question*

of learning to draw as of learning to see.
I am to think of the model
as an object in space. When you lean over

I can smell the soap in your wrist-hairs.
You say, *Do you mind if I make these marks
on your work?* I say, *Don't touch me.*

A. L. Kennedy

BACK

In all of the lost days I have spent
Going down on Chile,
New Zealand, Antarctica
And other Southern parts,
I know I would have found
The time for you.
I can imagine clearly our missed hours,
Ours and filled with rituals of us:
The split of the watch strap
From the wrist, the tongue
Loll of the belt, unbuckling,
That first hard slip.
And when I am tussled,
When I am punched in transit
By some high, night breeze –
One in a can full of bodies, clamped
And strapped together in orderly fright –
When my mind stumbles awake and
Rattles towards images of death,
I think first of my unforgiven
And my undiscovered sins
And then wish I had said
That I loved you.
Or, rather, that when I did
You had loved me back.

Barry Unsworth

MAHMUD'S TIP

AS THE BOAT approached the atoll, most of the people in the group left the covered space below decks and went up to get a first look at their holiday island. Gerald and Marjory Timmin went with the others and stood side by side in the stern, in similar white sun hats, glad for the protection of dark glasses in this strong light. It was late afternoon, but the sun was unwearied still – they felt the fierceness of it through the thin cotton of their clothes. Fierce too, it seemed to Gerald, the creaming of the sea ahead of them, where the water bucked against the underlying reef.

'Close to the surface in places,' he said. 'These fellows know the way through of course.' He glanced behind him at the dark-skinned, slender man in the sarong standing at the wheel. 'Nothing to worry about, they know these waters inside out.' But she never worried, he knew that. She was the one who had wanted to come here, to the Maldives. Somewhere new, somewhere different. He had wanted Tenerife again – he liked places he had been to before. He was an accountant with a firm that manufactured biscuits. His wife, Marjory, was an illustrator of children's books.

'Just think of it, Gerald,' she said now, rather loudly. 'Think of the millions of years it has taken to build up the coral from the seabed, all those billions of tiny creatures that have perished and left their skeletons to build it up.'

It was the tone she used when she wanted to stimulate his sense of wonder. She did not think he felt things enough, whereas he thought she felt them too much. The people

467

around must have heard her quite clearly and this was a source of uneasiness to Gerald, who was quiet-voiced and guarded.

'Well,' he said, 'so long as we don't add our skeletons to them.'

They could see the island now, a fretting of waves, a tangle of dark-green vegetation. As they entered the sheltered water inside the reef, quick shadows moved over the deck and Marjory glanced up to see long-tailed, graceful white birds wheeling above in a sky almost colourless. 'Tropic birds,' she said – she had seen a picture of some in a brochure they had got from the travel agency. She felt she knew what it would be like, loitering high up in that blank sky, looking down at these incredible colours within the ring of coral. 'Aren't they just absolutely beautiful?'

But Gerald had not looked up. He was busy aiming his camera here and there. He was a keen photographer and always took what he thought of as a complete pictorial record of their holidays.

On the wooden jetty there was some confusion with the luggage. Cases had to be unloaded, allotted to their proper owners, conveyed to the right bungalows – guests did not sleep in the hotel itself but in thatched bungalows strung out along the shore. These were cool and pleasant, with white walls and small open courtyards, equipped with wash-basin and shower. But the Timmins did not have much time to rest; they were required to return to the reception area of the hotel, where new arrivals were addressed by a representative of the tour-operators, a youngish man with a friendly smile and an impressive tan, who introduced himself as Mark.

He welcomed them to Kuredu, one of the most beautiful islands in the Maldives. This was a sun stronger than they would be used to, too much exposure could be dangerous. Blocking cream was absolutely essential, especially in the early days. If they had come without this they could buy it in the holiday shop. In case of sunstroke, illness or accident of any kind, there was a first-aid post situated at the rear of the building, with a qualified nurse in attendance. Visitors were not allowed to do any private fishing or to take pieces of coral away with them. At the end of their stay, to show appreciation, it was the usual practice to give the waiter a present – they would each have their own waiter throughout, depending on the allocation of tables in the dining room. Twenty dollars was the recommended sum. Optional of course, but the waiters had grown to expect it.

'I don't call that optional,' Gerald muttered in his wife's ear.

Daylight was fading now. Lights came on in the bar and along the path of duckboards that crossed the reception area and led off through groves of palm and frangipani towards the shore. The Timmins made their way to the dining room, where new arrivals were met at the door by their respective waiters, who shook hands and gave their names and led the way to the tables.

The Timmins' waiter was called Mahmud. He had a smile that came suddenly, very brilliant and captivating, but his features in repose were brooding and sad, as at the persistent memory of some wrong. He went before to show them to their table and as he did so they saw that he was lame: one leg kicked up in a jerky, spasmodic way with the heel turned awkwardly outwards.

He indicated their table with a half-bow. 'This one of the best table I give you,' he said. 'Very good view.' He gave them his sudden smile. 'See the lights down the seaside. What you like to drink?'

They asked for beer and Mahmud went to get it. 'How beautiful,' Marjory said, in a glow.

'What?'

'Those broken lines of light on the water.'

Along the jetty, suspended from wooden posts, there were globe lights in straw shades and the shades moved a little in the faint breeze, so that striations of milky light flexed over the water.

Gerald glanced around at the other tables, nearly all occupied now. The dining room was open-sided, thin poles held up the roof of palm mats overhead. Everybody in the place would have much the same view of the jetty and the lights as they had . . .

Mahmud came towards them with his jerky, somehow frantic gait, carrying two bottles of beer and two glasses on the tray. 'These the last bottle cold beer,' he said. 'I run to git them.'

'That was really nice of you.' Marjory was touched that he had hastened so in spite of his disability, and amused that he had drawn attention to it in such a way. 'Just like a child,' she said, when he had gone to get their order. She felt she understood children. 'He wanted to make sure we knew.'

'Do you think it was true?'

'Why not? The beer is cold enough, isn't it?'

'No, I was thinking . . . This business of the tipping, they really had no right to spring it on us like this, they should have told us beforehand. I mean, it amounts to an extra charge on the holiday, doesn't it?'

'Does it matter so much?'

'Well, it's the principle, you know. That fellow who gave us the introductory talk, Mark, he suggested twenty dollars, but that was a sort of basic minimum, there was more than a hint that people give more. They evidently do give more. Mahmud is wanting to let us know right from the start that in him we have found a star waiter.'

Marjory felt a knot of frustration tighten painfully within her. She always hated it when he talked about principles. We are on holiday, she wanted to say. Why are you so *measuring*? Why, when you talk about money, does your face always wear that wise little smile? That was what he did, he nibbled away at the edges of everything when what he should be doing was surrendering to experience. Here they were, in this exciting and exotic place, and they might as well have been at home going through the quarterly fuel bills. 'For goodness' sake, Gerald,' she said. 'It is only a few pounds more or less.' But she knew it would matter to her too from now on, because where there was doubt about how much to give there was always fear of hurting or offending. 'We'll have to see, won't we? Please don't go on about it any longer now.'

Warned by the tone, which was one he recognised, Gerald said nothing more. But the matter was still on his mind as they made their way back to their bungalow in the tropical night, with the straw-shaded lamps overhead, a faint breeze from the sea on their faces and the dry rustle of unfamiliar vegetation all around. He had counted the tables Mahmud was responsible for – there were twelve altogether. If each table gave him the basic twenty dollars once a fortnight . . .

Marjory had stopped and was gazing upwards. 'My God, Gerald, look at those stars,' she said.

It was a romantic moment. Gerald put his arm round her and looked up at the blaze and splendour of the sky. 'Wonderful,' he said. It would amount to one hundred and twenty dollars a week, more than the average wage here. Some would go to the people in the kitchens, some to the cleaners. It was a whole system. The staff wage-bill was being met out of tips.

They slept to the wash of the waves and faint clicking noises from the geckos on the walls and woke at first light to the querulous notes of some bird high up among the nearby palms. Breakfast was a simple affair, with the guests serving themselves. There was no sign of Mahmud. Gerald was eager to walk round the island. He was always restless until he knew where everything was. A reconnaissance trip, he called it, lending it thus a flavour of practicality and common sense. He thought of himself as a detached person – one of life's observers; but in this need to circle round things he was as instinctive as a cat.

The island, in fact, as they discovered, though small in extent – it took little more than an hour to walk completely round it – was composed of two quite different worlds, one that faced the wind, one that turned away from it, each with its own denizens, its own vegetation and climate. Gentle as it seemed, soft on their faces as they set out, the wind had called into being, on this narrow sandbank in the Indian Ocean, two orders of existence as diverse as if they had been a thousand miles apart instead of only one or two.

On the windward side there was continuous open beach of fine white sand, a constant fanning and fretting of small waves, sandpipers running along the wetline, dense vegetation reaching back from the shore, tall bushes with bright green, lobe-shaped leaves and white flowers like jasmin but scentless, palmetto trees with branches ending in tufts of saw-toothed fronds. The shore curved gradually, insensibly. Suddenly there was no whisper of wind; the heat intensified and began to seem dangerous. On this lee side the sea broke several hundred yards away against long, dark barriers of reef. They could see the surge and flash of the water across a waste of jagged coral, a tract alternately covered and disclosed as the tides moved. In these warm shallows fallen mangroves rotted and shoals of tiny fish flickered here and there; barnacles and clams abounded and hermit crabs dragged their houses along. They saw a moray eel questing for prey, sinuous and deadly.

Gerald took various pictures of this tidal waste, the leaning, dying mangrove trees, a dishevelled-looking grey heron standing motionless among the shallow, glinting pools. Then, as happened fairly frequently wherever they went, but more sharply now in these new surroundings, they began to get on each other's nerves. Marjory would always humanise everything. She made the creatures they saw into personages. The heron reminded her of someone she knew. She laughed at the absurd bluff of the tree-lizard when it froze into immobility at their passage under the impression that it then ceased to be visible. She said she could feel what it was like to be a small creature with no defence but stillness.

'For God's sake,' Gerald said. 'You can't possibly know what it's like to be a tree-lizard.' She was ruining the place for him, she was belittling the strangeness of things, belittling him too because in this strangeness lay the edge of his fear. If you didn't hold things apart from yourself, how could you ever truly see them? It was what he liked about photography, recording things in their otherness. 'You can know what it is like to be you and that's about it,' he said.

Hurt by this lack of sympathy, Marjory retaliated, as often before, by pitching things up. She pointed at a little group of hermit crabs that had drawn into a circle and rested nose to nose inside their borrowed homes. 'Look,' she said with false mirth, 'they have stopped for a gossip about the property-market.'

This was intended to annoy and it succeeded. 'Absolute twaddle,' Gerald snapped and he turned abruptly away from her into the grove of coconut palms that grew some way back from the shore. Possessed by hostility towards his wife, he pressed forward into the thickest part of the trees. Then he stopped and silence immediately settled around him.

Within these palms lay a different territory again, a sort of no man's land on the borders of the wind. The tides reached the outer fringe and this constant creeping eroded the roots of the trees and killed them in the end – dismembered trunks lay in the salt ooze and rotted there. In the midst of this, new palms were seeding and vivid green saplings grew here and there. Gerald recorded this contrast, then went farther in, camera at the ready, picking his way through a debris of dry palm fronds, fragments of coconut shell, driftwood wrought into strange shapes.

He was in the inner world of the grove now, quite out of sight of the sea. The trees grew close together and there was no breath of wind. Gerald felt the sweat run on his body. In the dark mixture of sand and humus at the foot of the trees, there were tunnels with large openings – as big as a man's head, some of them. He squatted down and looked into one. A reddish-coloured crab with a body that looked the size of a soup-bowl to Gerald and huge pincers was sitting just inside, regarding him fixedly at a distance of perhaps twelve inches.

He got up quickly and the sudden movement made him feel giddy for a moment. The sinister intensity of the place came to him, the strife of the trees and the creatures that lived in their shade. He began to go back, towards where he thought the lee shore should be, where he had left Marjory. But it was the wrong direction, the trees thickened round him. He turned at a wide angle, went forward again. Something scuttled away at his approach. Small black butterflies retreated from him into the darker shade. He stopped again, sweating heavily. On the edge of panic he heard voices and a series of sharp percussive sounds. He made his way towards them, blundered out into the open to find Marjory sitting on the sand with a family of islanders, man and woman and two smiling little girls. They were showing her how to open a coconut by beating the base against a projecting piece of rock. All of them, his wife included, looked up at his sudden appearance and regarded him with an identical expression of mild curiosity.

It was this identity of regard that Gerald was chiefly to remember. He had smiled and said hello and sat down beside his wife to watch the proceedings. He had seen how the casing of the coconut was broken at the base and peeled like a banana and how the nut itself was carefully cracked in the middle and broken into two cups. The islanders gave them one half each and they ate the moist fruit as they made their way back.

Something learnt then. Marjory was happy at having made this contact with the local people, she felt it had been an encounter full of grace and charm. But the image that remained in Gerald's mind was of himself as he must have looked when he came blundering out into the open, hasty and sweating as if pursued.

That evening Mahmud attempted to bring a couple about the same age as themselves, late arrivals, to share their table at dinner. Both the Timmins immediately objected to this and it was awkward, with the people standing there, already offering to shake hands, already uttering names. Marjory did her best not to hurt anybody's feelings. She and her husband saw so little of each other during most of the year, they were busy with their work, they looked forward to being together, being able to talk together, in the holidays . . . There was an immediate tact in this which Gerald knew to be beyond him. Moreover, it was true in a way: having survived twenty years of mutual irritation, they missed it now when they were apart.

The other couple, whose name was Slater, seemed rather offended, or perhaps it was embarrassment that made them stiff. A place was found for them at another table – not one of Mahmud's. Thereafter the Timmins seemed to detect some extra element of reproach in the sombreness of their waiter's regard.

'Of course,' Gerald said. 'He was hoping for two lots of tips from one table. The system is pernicious. How can there be any real understanding or friendliness of feeling when everything is put on such a mercenary footing? I am going to write to the Company about it when we get back.'

Settling into a congenial routine took longer than they had expected. Gerald got an ear infection almost at once and had to be treated at the first-aid post. Both of them had feverish nights after too much sun. But by the end of the first week these troubles were behind them. They sunbathed and explored the more accessible reefs and read the novels they had brought with them. Several times more they walked round the island, inspecting the zones of windward and lee and the different inhabitants of each – but Gerald never went back into the between-world of the palm groves.

The couple whom Mahmud had wanted to bring to their table appeared to have talked it over and decided to take offence. They ignored the Timmins in the dining room and cut them dead when they met on the path to the bungalows. Certain people began to stand out among the visitors for one reason or another. There was a man with a braying laugh and a girl who painted her toe-nails magenta; there was an elderly man who had suffered some kind of stroke, which had left him with strangely slurred speech, hardly human in sound at all; there was the man who had been bitten by a moray and spent the whole holiday with a bandaged ankle.

As the days passed Mahmud intensified his campaign. He lingered at their table, hinting how lucky they were to have him. He was older than the others, more experienced. He knew how to look after them well. He was popular in the kitchen and so they were served with the minimum of delay. He had friends everywhere – anything they wanted, they had only to ask. When he spoke of these matters he did not smile but glanced broodingly at them. His eyes were small and deep-set behind the heavy brows, so that they saw only the light in them, not the shape. His crippled walk as he approached, his way of kicking up his left leg with the heel turned outwards, came to seem like a signal to the Timmins, an announcement that fresh claims to merit were on the way.

Other people, they discovered, had been invited by their waiters to come and visit. All the staff and all the local people lived in a compound in the interior of the island, where strangers never went except by invitation. But Mahmud had not invited them and now their holiday was drawing to a close. 'I don't think he likes us, not really,' Marjory said. 'He probably thinks we are unfriendly. After all, we turned those people away.'

On the day before they were due to leave a trip had been arranged to a nearby island. It was not a holiday island but one where people lived and worked in a traditional way. No foreigners ever went there except on these trips organised by the Company and it was only the first year these trips had been running. Before that, almost nobody on the island had ever set eyes on a white person.

The Timmins learnt all this from Mark as they waited with the others to get on the boat that was to take them. Mark was to be their guide. The Maldive Islanders were people with an intense local attachment, Mark said. They were devoted to their islands and never wanted to leave. Hardly any of them ever did leave.

The trip took just under an hour over a sea that was empty and calm and glassy in the sunshine. While still at some distance they could see the brightly dressed people clustered around the little harbour.

'They have turned out to welcome us,' Marjory said. 'They are all in their best clothes. Touching, isn't it?'

However, nobody waved to them. And when they descended at the jetty the smiles they encountered seemed expectant rather than welcoming. Small, unsmiling children held out polished shells and clamoured for dollars. As, led by Mark, they proceeded towards the centre of the village over the soft warm sand which was all the roads had for surface, they were besieged by these voices of the children. 'Mister, hello Mister, one dollar, two dollar . . .'

People lined the streets, dressed as for a fiesta. And among them smiles and sometimes laughter and a ripple of words. The going was slow, what with pauses to look where Mark was pointing and negotiations with the grave-faced, diminutive vendors. Round these eddies and swirls in their progress laughter and comment intensified.

The village was built on the plan of a cross, with its two main streets intersecting at the centre. From this central point the sea was visible in all four directions. Within the angles of the cross there was a network of narrow lanes with low, dark-looking houses built of coral fragments cemented together. Hens scuffled in the warm sand and strings of washing ran from one side to the other. No street lamps, Gerald noted. Probably no electricity. Probably no mains services here at all . . .

At the centre, where the streets met, there was a huge breadfruit tree, its pale-green fruit like elongated plums. Here the party regrouped while Mark told them a few facts. The total population was two thousand, almost half of whom were children. Birth control was not much practised, families were large, the infant mortality rate very high. The average life-span was fifty-five. There was a high incidence of idiocy and deformity through centuries of inbreeding.

These statistics, delivered in Mark's rather high-pitched voice, while the people stood around in their Sunday best, made a painful impression on Marjory. They wouldn't understand, of course, but still . . . Such misery. She tried to feel what it would be like to be one of these people and live here, in this hot little place they never wanted to leave, nothing but a sandbank really, without a single notable building on it. 'But they don't seem unhappy, do they?' she said. They were full of smiles and chatter, but not friendly exactly. 'They are a laughter-loving people, of course,' she said uncertainly.

'They are laughing at *us*,' Gerald said. 'If you had looked at them, instead of trying to identify with them, you would have seen it by now. They don't want us here. This whole thing has been imposed on them by the government. Once a week groups of total strangers come and stare at them. They can't show their resentment openly so they simply stare back. And there are more of them, so their stare is stronger.' He paused a moment, then said, 'They've got more to laugh at, too.'

Marjory looked round at her fellow tourists in their T-shirts and shorts and variegated hats, at the girl with the startling toe-nails, the man with a patch over the bridge of his nose where the sun had caught him, the woman with thick legs and incongruously tiny feet, the moray victim with the bandage round his ankle. She looked at Gerald standing beside her with his narrow sun-reddened face and the camera slung across his body, bunching up his Hawaiian-style shirt. She thought of herself as she must look to them, her shorts that were rather too skimpy, her heavy thighs that shook a little, these days, with every step she took. To any unkind view they were a party of grotesques. So were all human groups probably, looked at like that. 'That's why they are dressed up,' she said unhappily. 'People dress up for the theatre, don't they?'

The man with impaired speech chose this moment to put a question to Mark, who did not at first understand and had to ask him to repeat it. With a sort of expanding horror Marjory heard the thick and oddly drawling speech mimicked here and there among the crowd of spectators. Splutters of laughter rose at each attempt.

The horror remained with her for the rest of the visit, underlying everything she saw; the little primary school, the boatyard, the fish-canning factory. Mockery of affliction, that was what the place would mean to her for ever.

She tried to express something of this to Gerald back in the bungalow, while they were packing. 'It was mutual,' she said. 'We did it to them, we looked at them in the same way.'

Quite unexpectedly, saying this, her eyes filled with tears. 'We were mocking them too,' she said. 'That is the terrible thing about it.'

'This is only the first year of the visits,' he said awkwardly, disturbed by this show of emotion. 'The people will get used to it, they'll start taking it for granted.'

'Yes,' she said, 'but we won't, will we? I mean, for us it is just the once. I'll never come back here.' Traces of tears were still on her cheeks. 'Gerald,' she said, 'I think we ought to give Mahmud forty dollars instead of twenty. After all, he'd have had forty if we'd agreed to share our table.'

Gerald paused a long moment. 'If you think so,' he said. 'I really do.'

'Forty dollars then.' He hesitated briefly. Then, jolted into recklessness by what he had already consented to, he said, 'It seems a bit mean just to give the basic minimum, don't you think? We could round it out to fifty. We won't have much cash left, just enough for a drink at Dubai airport on the way back.'

'That doesn't matter.'

The money was presented to Mahmud after dinner, as they rose to go. He looked down at the notes they had thrust into his hand, then up again. Over his face passed expressions different from any they had so far seen there, an astonishment so complete that it seemed like consternation, then a look of beaming pleasure. 'Thank you, thank you,' he said. 'Thank you, lady and gentleman. I come at the boat in the morning, say you goodbye.'

'But we leave so early,' Marjory said. 'Six in the morning, it will hardly be light. You work so hard, you should have your rest in the morning.'

Mahmud's eyes had a glisten in them that had not been there before. 'I come say you goodbye.'

He was there waiting when they arrived at the jetty in the dawn light, there to shake hands with them and help them with their luggage, there to wave as the boat pulled away.

'We gave him far more than he expected,' Gerald said.

'You saw how surprised he was.' He had the feeling he had somehow been conned.

But Marjory was smiling with superior wisdom. 'You never really see people, Gerald. You can't see people just by looking at them. Mahmud wasn't hinting for a tip at all. All that self-praise wasn't for money, it was so we should value him. He is a cripple, he has nobody, no wife, no children, no family – that's why he didn't invite us. All that talk of friends, don't you see?'

Marjory's voice had risen as she spoke. Gerald felt sure the people around could hear every word. As the boat drew away the shape of the island became indistinct. The last thing they saw, or thought they saw, was the figure of Mahmud making his way back along the jetty. In the uncertain light, the fling of his foot made it look as if he was dancing.

George Walden

LITTLE ENGLAND

JUST WHEN THERE seemed nothing else to go wrong with his life Billy woke up as a dwarf. At least, there was a dwarf in the mirror. The curtains were drawn tight to help him sleep and sometimes the morning light, more like dusk than dawn, played tricks in the glass. Billy ran an eye over the naked manikin that was himself, then fell back into bed with a rancid smile. All it needed was that. At least he would make the papers:

WILLIAM SWEETMAN

The death of Billy Sweetman, the 46-year-old MP so tragically dwarfed in his sleep, was announced yesterday. It is believed Mr Sweetman threw himself from his bedroom window on waking to discover that he had shrunk from five feet seven to something under four feet overnight. Colleagues say the news was not unexpected: in their estimation Billy had been shrinking for some time. His suicide following a final, massive contraction came as no surprise. Billy had been drinking heavily, and was easily depressed.

Billy grinned sourly at his jokes. The clock showed ten to eight. After a few minutes he got up. He thrust the curtains aside then stood back from the window, dizzied by the light. A noise like high tension power lines filled his head. The room was shrinking, expanding, till it finally settled, expanded. He was reaching to half close the curtains when he saw himself, sideways on, in the mirror. The smile returned, fleetingly. Then he threw himself on his bed, hugged his knees to his chest, and cried.

Man, they say, is a creature of habit. When the eight o'clock news came on automatically, Billy dried his eyes and listened. A three billion trade deficit, trouble in Bolivia, trouble over the Bill . . . Suddenly he sat up: *Why am I, a man who is sick, hallucinating – maybe mad – listening to this?* He reached an angry little arm to switch off the radio, then withdrew it. The announcer sounded excitable, like the commercial programmes. He checked the station – it was the BBC – and began mimicking his voice in derision, then stopped. There was no need for mimicry. He was speaking, naturally, in the same squeaky voice as the announcer.

He leapt to the window and stared down. A Volvo Estate was parking below. A man hopped from the car and, slamming the door with a swing like a forehand tennis drive, strode off on brisk, busy legs.

A manikin, no bigger than himself! He wasn't alone!

He reeled from the window, giddy with relief, and switched on the TV. An MP was squawking about the Bill. A dainty-looking fellow buried in a sofa, not camera shy, happy with his size. The interview ended, the presenter scrambled up to introduce his next guest, promising much as he marched about with his mike – a strutting homunculus!

Did no one know?

He dialled Anita's number, marvelling at his nimble finger. Anita was Billy's girlfriend. A journalist of the old sort, a person of informed opinion, Anita knew what went on.

'Billy? Bit bloody early, aren't you?'

Her voice was on the high side.

'*Billy?*'

But Billy was dumb. What could a man say? He was thinking, how would she look? Eventually he got out:

'I'm speaking in the debate on the Bill this afternoon.' He

paused, conjuring a dwarfed Parliament. Curious how easy it was to imagine the scene. Then said anxiously: 'You'll be there, won't you?'

'I'm always there when you speak. Bye now, sweetie. Good luck!'

She rang off. He went to the mirror and turned this way, the other. It could have been worse. The head wasn't overlarge, the legs weren't bowed, the thighs not stubby. He wasn't a dwarf, thank God. He was a midget. And it wasn't all loss. The buttocks were neater. The belly was down. The biceps stood out. As for *that*, well, on a second examination that was a nice surprise. Seen against the reduced length of leg things bulked larger. A question of perception . . .

He climbed back into bed and, smoking nervily, considered the position, but the position was simple. The country had shrunk by a third and no one knew.

Imagining a midget Parliament was one thing, the reality another. The place was a mockery. Wigs that gave dignity to normal-sized heads looked farcical on small ones, like children dressing up. And the members! These were not simply the same legislators in the diminutive. Shrinking had changed them, as every motion, every mannerism, seemed magnified by smallness. You could spot the Little Englanders easily now. They sat smugly, straight as planks, like miniature Buddhas. As for the smooth City types they looked smarmier than ever, insinuating slips of men so oily and small they could glide through the 'Aye' and 'Noe' lobby consecutively without anyone noticing.

He glanced at the public gallery. Pinhead faces craned down expressionlessly. Did they know, in their hearts, what had happened? Did they suspect? Were they registering, by their mute and impassive demeanour, their dismay at finding themselves represented by midgets like themselves?

The speech he had resolved to make contained nothing new, but there had been a lot of discussion and there was not much left to say. The debate on the Bill had gone on for months, which was unusual: the Little Englanders apart, no one opposed it. The most enlightened measure to come before Parliament in decades, everyone said. Here was a nation united as the press, the opinion polls, every thinking person in the country agreed that the reforms were essential, the sacrifices inevitable, the pressure for change irresistible.

In principle. When it came to voting it through, folks were cautious. What was the rush? Certainly things were in a poor state, with the economy on a razor, yob rule in the streets, the family a sepia memory. Yet even assuming that the country was in crisis, it was a rolling crisis with its highs and lows, soothing in its way, like the English countryside. So the discussion continued month after month, with pretty well everyone agreed about everything, and no resolution.

Like an afternoon showing of an old film the debate on the Bill played to a thin Chamber. Numbers thinned further as the midgets made their contributions, stayed to hear as little of the following speaker as they reasonably could, then scuttled off. Billy sat clutching his notes. He was a poor speaker at the best of times, and the idea of addressing his first dwarfed Parliament made his head zing in alarm. What if he began cracking incomprehensible jokes? Or what if, in a fit of hilarity, he were to blurt out the truth?

A woman came into the deserted press gallery and was filing along a bench, her back towards him. Billy glanced up. Nice lines. Dinky figure. She turned, sat down and gave Billy a wave. Anita! Miraculous! She'd shrunk to perfection, sloughed off pounds of flesh! She was wearing the sort of skirt and jumper combination that in a woman of her volume was normally a mistake – but not today! Billy gawked at her with such an imbecile smile that Anita frowned down, as if to say, what's up, sweetie?

'Mr William Sweetman!'

Billy groped for his notes. The Chamber waited, with no great sense of expectation, for Billy to start. The Speaker's buckled shoe, a foot from the ground, ticked time like a pendulum.

'Get on with it, Billy!'

'Tell us a joke, Billy!'

He glanced at the manikins lounging and laughing in their seats. How pathetic they looked! How witless their witticisms! Suddenly, his nervousness gone, in a gesture of magnificent disdain he tossed his notes to the floor and threw himself – heart, soul, the entire little personage – into his speech.

It turned out to be a long one, something in fact of an oration. Normally he was in two minds about the Bill, but not today. There were calls for radical change, much needling of the Little Englanders, and a fine peroration. Countries, Billy said, were like people: they lived, had their day, and faded into oblivion. Yet there was a difference. For countries it was never too late. So here was the question. Were the English a nation of pygmies? Or was there still in our breasts some remnant, some residue, some sputtering spark of the Great Men of History? He believed that there was. The Bill, he said, must go through, and sat down.

It was a passionate performance, nicely controlled. Fearing his voice might rise to the same peevish squawk as the midgets Billy kept it low. Sensing that his arms were too short to convey the full force of his gestures Billy made bigger gestures. As he spoke he drew himself to his full height, head back, chest out – a fine figurine of a man!

The effect was extraordinary. Midgets about to slip from the Chamber stayed to cock an ear. Anita, between incredulous glances, scribbled into her pad. Even the Speaker gave every appearance of listening. For once Billy had held an audience – and all done without jokes! As he sat there, his jaw still clamped and stern-looking from his peroration, a Whip swivelled on the front bench to nod commendation.

Billy's pygmy speech shook the nation, and no one was more shaken than Anita. Finally he was taking himself seriously as a politician. And how could Billy not? Living in a country cut down by a third, and him the only one knowing, entailed grave responsibilities. And so day by day he became a more responsible person in every way. When his smoking and drinking declined by a third, in simple proportion to his belly and lungs, delighted with his easier breathing and spruce figure, Billy cut back some more. Soon he was down from half a bottle of whisky to a glass or two of red wine per day, and from forty cigarettes to a five-pack of cigarillos.

He took to wearing nifty suits and stylish shoes, and as always new clothes were good for morale. Simply to run his eyes down the razor crease in his trousers to the gilt buckles of his Italian casuals made Billy feel good – so good that sometimes he gave himself sudden slaps on the backside, out of sheer exuberance with his little self, and for the feel of his neatened rump.

When friends complimented her on the astonishing change in her man ('one of politics' late developers', they said) Anita's face would take on a sardonic look, as though she were thinking: 'A late developer, eh? Well, you should see my Billy in bed!' Their love-life – in the big old days at once indolent and abrupt – had improved markedly. Finesse would be putting it high but at least Billy took his time, which was appreciated, Anita rewarding him with novel caresses that sent shivers down his tiny spine. With Billy in tip-top form, and with his new pride in his parts, few nights passed without some act of love between them, with Anita a willing partner, more or less. At times he sensed from the sluggish movements of her delectable limbs that, given a choice, she would have preferred to catch up on her sleep. In the past, at the first sign of reluctance, Billy would have let her alone. But the past, as they say, is another country.

It was a warm spring day, midgets were sunning themselves on the Embankment, and Billy was scurrying along Whitehall to see the Prime Minister. He looked up at Number Ten as he approached: a third taller now, the house seemed that much more impressive. It would have been risible to have some short-arse at the door but fortunately the constable on duty was a strapping fellow, getting on for five feet.

Inside a flunkey led him along a corridor, past a group of balding homunculi outside the Cabinet room – civil servants by the look of them – up the stairs and into the Prime Minister's office.

'Mr Sweetman, Prime Minister!'

The PM was squatting in an armchair, a red box at his feet, reading papers while swilling beer from the half-pint tankard the press said he loved to drink from.

'Have a seat, Billy.'

Billy chose the edge of a colossal sofa.

'Like a beer? I can offer you lager or bitter.'

'A lager would be nice.'

He would have much preferred whisky, this being something of an occasion, but what could you say?

As the PM went back to his papers Billy gazed round. Pitt, Wellington, Disraeli – to think of the Great Men who had worked in this room! He sat savouring the grand furniture, the pictures by Turner, the silence as the Prime Minister worked: relishing, in a word, the luxuriant stillness of power.

His drink came. The PM stopped working, said 'Cheers!', drank, then hugged his tankard to his chest.

'I've got a job of work for you, Billy. I want you to take on the Bill. Put steam behind it. Drive it through. We can't let the Little Englander lot hold it up for ever.'

'It can't go on,' Billy said warmly.

'It has to stop,' said the PM.

'Exactly!' said Billy.

'So you'll do it then?'

'I'm grateful to be asked,' said Billy, which was an understatement.

'Ah, but does that mean you'll do it?' The PM smiled, craftily.

'Of course it does.'

Insofar as you could be irritated with prime ministers Billy felt irritation. There was a pointless slyness amongst midgets in politics. He noticed it in himself.

'Excellent! I like a man who knows his mind. I'm going to China tomorrow.'

'It's a long trip.' Billy spoke quickly, not to be caught out. He was used to midgets flitting from one subject to another, like TV adverts. Again, he'd caught himself doing it.

'We have to compete.' The PM shook his raddled little head weightily. 'Otherwise they'll march over us like an army of ants.'

Billy nodded. 'Like so many ants.'

'You've been to China then?'

'No, I haven't. It's just that everyone says they're like ants.'

'That's because they *are*. A billion of them, all running about. So you'll push it through then?'

'The Bill?'

'That's what we're talking about.'

'Absolutely!' said Billy.

'That's the spirit,' said the PM, somewhat wearily it seemed to Billy.

Minister for the Bill! A giant step to – who knew where? For the first time Billy began thinking politically, which meant thinking small. The PM was exhausted. An election was in the offing. There was talk of a new leader. Putting points one, two and three together . . . Though it was not a question of personal ambition. His belief in the Bill was uncompromising, and to drive it through he would need to be Prime Minister. Which meant a deal with the Little Englanders. Which meant . . . compromising the Bill.

So it was that, to Anita's dismay, Billy began touring the country making speeches in which the Bill was scarcely mentioned, there were few calls for change, and none for sacrifice. The midgets loved it. At meeting after meeting throughout the land he saw their eyes widen and shine as he spoke of the big old days, entreated the midgets to stop running themselves down – and above all to stop seeing every foreigner as ten feet tall.

The tactic worked. Within weeks he was invited to a black-tie dinner given by the leader of the Little Englander faction. A well-born midget of commanding aspect, whose appearance was somewhat marred by a tic in his left eye, he was one of those big businessmanikins with interests so extensive that no one knew exactly what he did.

Billy arrived at his house, his DJ rather baggy on his sleeked-down figure, to be greeted by a dozen Little Englanders, beautifully turned out. Never since dwarfing day had he felt so ill at ease. Scarcely was the first course served – a *bisque à l'homard* – than the Little Englanders got down to their busy intrigues. Billy had his head low over his soup, trying to drink without slurping, and it was only after a glass or two of wine that, finally, he spoke.

In retrospect he said, holding his solid silver spoon at a philosophical angle, he profoundly regretted his pygmy speech. Our habit of selling ourselves short was inexcusable. As for the Bill, what was the rush? Changes that had waited for decades could wait a decade or two longer. His tongue oiled by the wine, Billy spoke well – so well that he began to convince himself of what he was saying, which in turn made him speak better and better.

The conversation turning to international affairs, foreigners came in for a good deal of stick. To begin with Billy was silent: he was engrossed in his *boeuf en croûte*, which was delicious. Asked for his opinion he passed a number of critical observations on foreigners, which went down well. Then, over dessert (bread and butter pudding, to which the Little Englander leader proclaimed a lifelong partiality but hardly touched), it was the turn of the Prime Minister. At first Billy preserved a loyal silence, though finally, his sense of humour getting the better of him, he joined in the lofty raillery. Pretending his glass was a pub tankard he gave a hilarious impersonation of the Prime Minister, at which the

Little Englanders abandoned their bread and butter pudding completely and laughed till they nearly fell off their chairs.

Suddenly their leader raised his glass and, his tic going so fast it looked like a succession of winks, proposed a toast:

'To Billy Sweetman! Patriot, man of the people – and a Great Englishman!'

'To a Great Englishman!' the manikins murmured, and drank.

Anita, appalled at his dealings with the Little Englanders, abandoned him in disgust. Billy was heartbroken for a week. With a politician on the up and up, how could it be longer? Otherwise everything was going Billy's way. As it stumbled on under an exhausted Prime Minister the country was falling apart in the most satisfactory manner. Then all at once the Party lost its head. Bypassing the usual procedures, an emergency meeting of backbenchers – described in the press as a raucous affair – was summoned. The midget press, not for the first time, was overstating things. In truth the meeting was over before it had begun, and for a simple reason: a deal had been struck between the supporters of the Bill and the Little Englanders to put Billy up against the Prime Minister. A vote was taken and counted, the Prime Minister lost handsomely, and Billy went to Number Ten Downing Street.

An audience with the Queen! Yet Billy felt strangely sad. The thought of Her greeting him, a mere speck of Royalty in those palatial rooms, affronted his sense of history. He need never have worried. From a glance at Her regal figure it was clear that Her Majesty had taken Her shrinkage with great dignity. She received him sitting on a sofa, her legs not dangling ungraciously but propped on a footstool. And to begin with, the audience went well.

Then things got stickier. Turning to politics She remarked somewhat severely that, for her taste, the Little Englanders were too inward-looking. Then, when Billy began describing his plans for the Bill with some enthusiasm, Her Majesty listened in chilled silence. It turned out She wasn't too keen on that either. For the life of Her, she said, grimacing delicately, She could never see the point of change for change's sake. Constantly rooting things up as if the country were a vegetable garden. The secret of good government, She concluded, was to take people as they were.

'Too true, Ma'am' Billy murmured, and stared at his shoes, captivated by the way the turn-ups fell, exactly right, just above the neatly tied laces. He looked up to find Her Majesty glancing from his shoes to his face. Something in Her expression – a kind of amused hauteur – made him colour violently.

She must know! Of course She knew! Monarchs have a sense of history – could tell a Great Man from a midget! The thought of Her Majesty seeing him as a dwarf Prime Minister, comically got up in a new suit and new shoes, made his head zing so loudly he was sure She would hear. Then She spoke:

'We were talking about the Bill. It would be interesting to know how you plan to handle the Little Englanders.'

Well, said Billy, with as authoritative an air as he could muster, in that regard his policy was – insofar as he was able and events allowed – to strike a balance. At which Her Majesty nodded frostily, signifying that the audience was concluded.

His first night at Number Ten (sleepless, naturally) was spent reading messages of congratulations. At the bottom was one from Vic Stuttaford, Chairman of the Over-Eighties Club in his constituency – a sort of Darby and Joan outfit, gone political.

Dear Prime Minister,
   It does my heart good to write those words and I've been having trouble with my heart it sort of skips every other beat so you'll have to excuse my punctuation. I

write this from hospital against my knees they should have proper facilities. Bring back the matrons I say though I suppose that would mean having some big black mama lording it so better not.

We don't need the Bill Mr Sweetman what we need are the following measures put through pronto without delay:

1. Cessation of foreign entanglements. *Now get us straight we don't mean withdrawal from the world we have to trade with them. We're not insular folk Mr Sweetman but now you're Prime Minister you'll see what's out there like we did in the war.*

2. Foreign aid. *This should be a priority in the sense of cutting it off. The point is the more we feed them the bigger they'll grow and have you seen one of them eating well I have here in hospital are mixed wards here to stay?*

3. Bigger pensions. *Where's the money to come from you'll say well think a little Prime Minister it follows from point two doesn't it?*

4. Immigration. *How many more can we take they're getting into the villages and I've said about the hospital.*

5. Crime, the reasons for. *See point 4.*

6. Sex. *Can nothing be done Mr Sweetman? No one can say I'm small-minded do you know the one about the difference between a pimp and a magician? The pimp has a cunning array of stunts whereas the magician well you've got it Mr Sweetman with your sense of humour. You can tell that one to your Cabinet they'll need a laugh but I'd advise you to wait till your female colleague excuses herself I take it you'll have just the one?*

Well I'm rambling a bit Mr Sweetman I suppose I'm getting old. So that's it for the moment because you'll have your hands full now you're Prime Minister. More power to your elbow I say,

Yours till the next election,
Vic Stuttaford

The appointment of his Cabinet was commented upon favourably. 'A wily tactician' and 'a consummate politician' they called him. Well, that was kind of them. The truth was that, fatigued by endless advice, he'd decided to allot one half of the places to the Little Englanders and the remainder to supporters of the Bill. And when an interviewer suggested that this might lead to clashes in Cabinet, and Billy riposted rather cleverly that if everyone agreed with him he wouldn't need a Cabinet at all, the observation was quoted widely, and with total approval, in the midget press.

The interviewer's question was more astute than it seemed. Sure enough, the Little Englanders were annoyed at not having a majority, as were the supporters of the Bill, for similar reasons. Holding the line between the fractious creatures was a wearying business. Their plots were of dizzying subtlety, yet utterly transparent. Watching their little eyes darting poison at one another over the Cabinet table made his head zing horribly.

Soon government began to seem a trivial business. Listening to his Chancellor, a clever-clever creature with stoat-like eyes, discuss changes in taxation so cunning that the manikin in the street would never know if he was better off or not, or to the details of a new dog warden scheme (the midgets were sentimental about animals, while allowing their children to run wild), he found his headaches growing steadily worse.

The constant pain depressed him. Being Prime Minister sealed him off from every joy in life. Tearing round the country in his big black Jaguar like a hearse in a hurry was no way to live. The police escort made him feel caged from the world – a prisoner being eternally transported from one place of detention to another. And why fool himself? The midgets didn't want their horizons lifting, they were content to be themselves. Her Majesty, a most sagacious Person, was right: people were what they were, and there could be no changing them. The Bill would never go through.

Gradually his self-discipline went to pieces. He began drinking again. He stopped doing his morning workout and began putting on weight. His ration of five cigarillos crept up in number till he was rarely seen without one: a clapped-out Churchill, the midget press called him, with his rotund body and steaming cheroot. More and more he longed to recline on Anita's consoling breasts and watch the world go by on TV, as they used to do, with a cigarette and a glass of malt whisky, instead of striving, heroically but fruitlessly, to change it.

The election was coming closer. Not that Billy cared. When his speechwriters pestered him with their little ruses he took a few slugs of whisky and did something different altogether. Casting aside his text he would ad lib in a folksy way, poking drunken fun at Cabinet colleagues, the Little Englanders, the midget press – anything except the Opposition he was supposed to be attacking. His opening gambit was always the same: 'Fellow pygmies!' The allusion to the speech that had made his name brought the house down.

They were not so much speeches as comedy turns. His frankness took their breath. He mocked them for driving round in cars ten times their size then holding their noses and complaining that the air stank, for their pinched hypocrisies about sex and the single midget, and their tendency to puff up their consciences fit to burst about international injustice, while asking ever more for themselves. As for the play he made on the *little* man, it was inexhaustible. It was Billy's contribution to modern politics that you could make as much fun as you liked of the *little* man, because to the midgets, it was never themselves.

The result? Billy was a star. Better, he got a note from Anita: 'You're a born leader, Billy! A twentieth-century Cromwell – with laughs!' If he enjoyed seeing the polls tick up it was not in the hope of a second term at Number Ten. On that score his mind was made up, and even Anita wouldn't change it. He had resolved to do something unprecedented in midget politics: win the election with as big a majority as he could, and throw in his hand.

*

'The Prime Minister!'

It was his last performance in Parliament before the election. Billy stood at the despatch box, peering at his notes. They were typed in capitals yet seemed absurdly small. There was a terrible pain behind his eyes.

'Get on with it, Billy!'

'Tell us a joke, Billy!'

A joke? Well, this time he might oblige – but not just yet. In politics, timing was all. He began speaking, off the cuff and in painful gasps. The midgets strained at their personal microphones, unable to make out what he was saying. Then came a word that was almost audible.

'Point of order!'

A member was on his feet, arm stabbing furiously at Billy.

'Is it in order for the Prime Minister to refer to Honourable members as midg –'

The stabbing arm fell to his side. There was nothing to stab at. After pulling himself erect, one hand clutched to his eyes, Billy had crumpled behind the despatch box.

Hospital flavours. Billy opened his eyes. Blackness. He raised a hand to his face, expecting a bandage. No bandage. The hand began feeling his body over the bedding, frantically, then stopped. How could he tell? To a small hand he would feel normal, to a big one – normal. He tried to touch the end of the bed with a foot.

'Lie still, Billy!'

It was his doctor. Billy lay still. What did it matter now, how big he was, or how small?

'Will I ever see?'

'There'll be an operation. There's a chance . . .'

'I don't want it!'

'Don't want it?'.

'*I'm* in charge of my body,' said Billy in prime ministerial tones, 'and I'll stay as I am!'

Happiness, it is said, comes from reduced expectations of life. That was Billy's experience. He got a generous pension, Anita took care of him, he learned Braille, and wanted for nothing. Theirs was a life without too much laughter, so when a letter arrived from Vic Stuttaford, Billy grinned in anticipation as Anita began to read.

> *Dear Mr Sweetman,*
>
> *I was sorry to hear of you being blinded in office. We saw you collapse in Parliament, someone got it on video, you went down with a hell of a whop. It's a shame you've gone I don't mind telling you. It made me feel better to know there was someone up there listening, and I'll say that for you Mr Sweetman, you always acknowledged.*
>
> *I saw in some gossip column that you had a good woman to look after you. I should have known you'd have someone up your sleeve, your sense of humour. They had a photo of her, her smile's a bit loopy, still she'll be useful to show you around, better than a dog.*
>
> *I had a second bypass operation which you'll be glad to hear was a success. They say I'm good for another ten years, which is more than you can say for the country, so you can expect to hear from me . . .*

As Anita read, Billy sat hugging his whisky and, between hacking laughter, gasping at his cigarette. Her smile at his pleasure vanished when she saw his blind man's pallor turn puce and the whisky slop on to his cardigan. She had almost finished the letter when she looked up to see Billy let go the glass and, tears rolling from beneath his dark glasses, with a look of pain indistinguishable from a grin, slump in his chair.

The funeral of Billy Sweetman was a great occasion. In the teeth of opposition from the Little Englanders, who claimed he was a man of insufficient stature, the cortège was allowed to process through Westminster Hall on its way to St Margaret's Church. It was a bright summer day yet the light in the Great Hall was as crepuscular as ever, and owing to the hastiness of the arrangements, the TV coverage was a mess. The pictures were dim, and eerily out of perspective. Against the vastness of the Hall, Billy's English oak coffin looked pitiably small, like some ten-year-old child's.

The matter of Billy's funeral dominated the correspondence columns for days. In the end no less a person than the Director-General of the BBC brought it to a close. Given sufficent notice, he wrote, and by the use of the necessary angles and lenses, his cameramen could have adjusted things to give a better picture: enhanced Billy's coffin, or shrunk the Hall. Though whatever they had done (the Director-General concluded wearily) there would have been complaints. In the last analysis it was a subjective matter, on which there were as many opinions as viewers. A question of perception, in a word.

Louis de Bernières

A DAY OUT FOR MEHMET ERBIL

MEHMET ERBIL SLUNG his tattered but faithful white plastic sack over his shoulder, and stepped off the ferry at Kilitbahir. It was a short and easy crossing from Çanakkale, and he always enjoyed it. He would contemplate the choppy waves, keep an eye open for good-looking girls, and take in the spectacle of Sultan Mehmet II's castle as it grew nearer and more distinct. It always made him think of harder and wilder times in centuries past, when sultans took titles such as 'Shedder of Blood', 'The Grim', or 'The Merciless', and mighty cannon roared across the Dardanelles in order to deter impudent Russians, pirates and invaders. The only trouble with the crossing was that it took up money, eating into his tiny profits, and increasing the despair that gnawed away at his hope. 'One day I will have money,' he thought, 'one day I won't have to live like a dog. One day I won't have to do this work. Or perhaps it will always be like this, perhaps I will die as I have lived, in hardship and ignominy.' Mehmet's sole concern was that, in the conduct of his daily life, he should earn just slightly more than he was obliged to spend. It was a question not merely of survival, but of personal pride.

Mehmet evidenced his pride by taking care of his appearance. His light blue trousers were carefully pressed, his shoes, worn down at the heel and scuffed though they might be, were thoroughly polished. His shirt was clean, and the collar had been removed and then sewn back on the other way so that the frayed side was invisible. His woollen waistcoat was neatly darned in wool that was almost of the same hue as the original, and the brass buckle of his belt was well-rubbed in order to bring out its shine. He carried his shoulders well back and square, as he had learned during the years of his national service, and his black hair was clean, neatly trimmed, and lightly greased into place. One would not have known that Mehmet Erbil was desperate, unless one looked into his pained and evasive dark brown eyes, and noted how he smoked successive cigarettes with the air of someone who compulsively resorts to remedies that time and experience have proved to be inefficacious. Mehmet also smelled faintly of beer, which was the one medicine for world-weariness that he could actually afford. He was forty-one years old, he was thin but reasonably fit, and his skin was darker than most on account of his wanderings with the white sack. His other career had imbued him with the habit of glancing frequently at his cheap but functional black plastic watch.

It was May 19th, and Mehmet was taking full advantage of National Youth and Sports Day. He had gone dutifully to his local school and had stood in the sun, since the canny women had got to the shaded places earlier than the men, and had watched the youngsters being put through their paces. When he was young he had been a good runner, and it filled him with wistfulness to see the boys, their arms pumping as they sped around the track. It was more amusing to watch the girls' races, because you could tell that their hearts were not in it. He cheered ironically, along with all the others, when, in the five hundred metres, two of the girls ran out of breath with one hundred metres to go, and peeled off sheepishly, to disappear into the crowd.

Mehmet listened to the numerous speeches, in which there was not one sentence that did not somehow manage to mention Mustafa Kemal, and he stood through the formation manoeuvres. About a hundred boys in white shirts and black trousers did a kind of choric callisthenic display of such length that he marvelled at their memory rather than prowess, and then the girls did something equally long and elaborate, each of them clutching a huge red fan, boldly emblazoned with the white crescent moon and star. The best display by far was performed by a small group of girls in scarlet robes, their foreheads adorned with gold coins, who gracefully danced, clutching large silver trays in their hands, stepping and swaying together to a long and ululating melody rendered by a small band that consisted of clarinet, violin and drum. Having done his duty to the school and to National Youth and Sports Day, Mehmet slipped away, and took the ferry across to Kilitbahir.

Mehmet had been correct in supposing that patriotic coachloads of school parties would be converging on the sites and monuments of the Gallipoli peninisula, and it was with satisfaction that he noted the swarms of teenagers clambering over the remains of the gun batteries, prodding the wild tortoises, posing on the battlements of the castle, and scattering Coca-Cola cans in the wake of their thirst. It was only May 19th, and the onset of summer's implacable heat was yet a few days off, but it was hot enough nonetheless for the schoolchildren to be buying plenty of soft drinks. Mehmet set about his work.

At about midday he felt that there was not much more to be done for the time being, and he decided that he would try to cadge a lift to the great monument at Mount Hisarliktepe. Accordingly he set off along the sinuous coastal road, in the secure knowledge that before long someone would give him a lift. In a country where most people had no car, but everyone could still be trusted, it was accepted that one gave lifts as a matter of course. Before long, a white car passed him, and he signalled frantically for it to stop. When it did, he picked up his white sack and sprinted.

When he arrived at the passenger door, he bent down to look at the driver, and knew immediately that he had flagged down a foreigner. The fellow was wearing shorts, white socks and a straw hat. His face, forearms and legs were burned a painful brick red by the sun, and he had the strength and bulk of someone who had flourished in a land of plenty. Like many foreigners, he looked somewhat ridiculous, and Mehmet wondered whether he would be safe to drive with. Also, foreigners were usually quite rich, and this often seemed to bring with it some unpleasant and offensive attitudes.

'*Günaydın*,' said the foreigner, and Mehmet thought 'At least he speaks Turkish.'

The driver was in fact a phrase-book foreigner. He had conscientiously learned all the phrases he needed to know for telling people that he did not understand and did not speak Turkish. He had been hoping that in this way he might avoid the embarrassment of having to listen intelligently and nod at appropriate moments whenever Turks engaged him in conversation. He had discovered, however, that Turks were like the English; they thought that if they talked loudly enough in their own language, and paraphrased and re-paraphrased themselves often enough, then sooner or later a foreigner would grasp their point. This particular foreigner had also come up against the usual difficulty of the phrase-book user; it was all very well being able to ask things in Turkish, but one never understood what one's interlocutor said in reply. He asked, '*Nerede?*', and immediately knew that he was not going to comprehend Mehmet's response.

'Well,' said Mehmet, 'I'm just going round and about, sort of following all of these school parties, so I'm not really fussy. If you're going by any of the monuments, perhaps you could just drop me off.'

The foreigner looked at him blankly, and said, '*Anlamam. Turkçe bilmiyorum.*'

Mehmet furrowed his brow and looked at him through the window. 'Well, that's very odd, that you tell me in Turkish that you don't understand Turkish and you don't speak it. You must admit it's a little peculiar.'

The foreigner shrugged and raised his hands in a gesture of helplessness. '*Anlamam*,' he repeated, and again asked '*Nerede?*'

'I've already told you where I'm going,' said Mehmet. He was beginning to wonder whether the foreigner might not be a little mad, and whether it might not be better to wait for

another car. He waved his hand in the direction of Seddülbahir. 'Look,' he said, 'there's only one road and only one
direction, so that's where I'm going.'

'*Anlamam. Türkçe bilmiyorum,*' repeated the foreigner,
with the same dumb expression upon his face. Mehmet
sighed, realising that he had let himself in for a difficult lift,
but he opened the door anyway, dumped his plastic sack on
the floor, and climbed in. If he was going to get this foreigner
to understand anything, then he was going to have to repeat
himself an awful lot.

'No problem,' said the foreigner, and Mehmet's eyes lit up.
This was universal language. 'No problem,' he repeated,
nodding his head as the car pulled away.

On their left the Marmara Sea glowed in the sun, lapping
on the tiny beaches, and above them on their right rose the
slopes of dense Mediterranean scrub. Mehmet began to relax;
the foreigner might be strange, but he was a careful driver. He
reached into his shirt pocket and extracted a crushed pack of
cigarettes. He had already lit one when he remembered that
some of the more outlandish foreigners go crazy if you smoke
anywhere near them. He indicated the cigarette and raised
anxious eyebrows. 'OK?' he asked.

'No problem,' said the foreigner, and Mehmet repeated the
phrase happily. He offered his packet of cigarettes to the
driver, who indicated 'no' by a small wave of his hand.
Mehmet considerately held his cigarette out of the window so
that its smoke would not offend. The foreigner noticed, and,
having once been a smoker, became anxious that in the
slipstream the cigarette would burn out too quickly. He
pulled out the ashtray in the dashboard, and gestured
towards it. 'OK, no problem,' he said.

Mehmet smiled. He too had been anxious about the
cigarette being largely wasted. 'I suppose you're a tourist,'
observed Mehmet, 'I suppose you're going around taking
photos of everything. We get a lot of tourists here. Austral-
ians, New Zealanders, Germans. Where do you come from?'

'*Evet,*' replied the foreigner, who was tired of saying 'I
don't understand. I don't speak Turkish' and thought that he

might be able to get away with simply saying 'Yes.' Mehmet
looked at him askance; the foreigner's brain must be a little
disconnected. They passed an old peasant woman whose
donkey was laden with firewood. '*Fotograf?*' he suggested,
assuming that the foreigner would like to take snaps of the
peninsula's more picturesque sights. He felt mildly insulted
when the foreigner shook his head. 'Well, I suppose you just
want to take pictures of the monuments,' said Mehmet.
'Perhaps your grandfather is buried in one of the cemeteries.'

The foreigner thought it safe to continue to reply in the
affirmative, even though he did not understand at all. '*Evet,*'
he said, unwittingly assenting to the proposition that his
grandfather lay thereabouts in a hero's grave.

'Well,' said Mehmet, 'my grandfather fought in that
campaign as well. Obviously it was on the Turkish side. You
should have heard his stories. They were amazing. He got
shot three times on the same day, and then he was bitten by a
snake. He lived through all that, and the war of national
liberation (the one against the Greeks), and then he lived until
he was ninety-seven years old.' Mehmet grew serious. 'You
know, it's true what Atatürk said, that the war we fought
made us respect each other. The effect of all that blood was to
make us brothers. English, Anzac, French, Turkish, all
brothers.' He looked very intently into the foreigner's face,
and asked, 'Don't you agree?'

The foreigner resorted once again to '*Anlamam. Turkçe
bilmiyorum,*' and Mehmet shook his head. This foreigner was
undoubtedly a bit strange, agreeing with you part of the time,
and then saying that he didn't understand. Perhaps there was
some interesting psychological or intellectual condition
whereby you momentarily forgot your foreign languages, and
then remembered them again a few minutes later.

Mehmet made the foreigner drive to the huge monument
and war cemetery at Hisarliktepe. It was forty-two metres
high and was visible for miles around. Mehmet naturally
assumed that the foreigner would want to photograph it, as
well as all the heroic statues that surrounded it, and he elected
himself to be the guide. In fact it was really a stroke of luck

that he had been given a lift by a tourist, since this would take him to all the sites where the parties of schoolchildren were.

Mehmet left his white sack in the car, and the foreigner reluctantly took pictures of the monument, and the cemetery, and of Mehmet smiling in front of the statues. He had come to Turkey with only a limited amount of film, and did not know how to explain to Mehmet that he was a botanist who had come to the peninsula to study the wildflowers, which at this time of year bloomed prolifically in all the fields and grassy banks. The Turkish farmers did not use herbicides, and the wheatfields were swathed in scarlet poppies. The botanist found it depressing to think that once upon a time his own country had been as lovely as this, and he also found it frustrating that he was unable to explain to Mehmet that he was interested not in Turkey's valiant past, but in its flowers. All the same, he was moved when he saw the tears in the corners of Mehmet's eyes as he read the names of the soldiers on the gravestones. Two beautiful teenage girls were walking together, arm in arm, reverently placing bunches of marguerites on the graves. He found himself wishing that he was able to love his own country as much as the Turks loved theirs.

Mehmet picked up an abandoned Coca-Cola can, and the botanist thought, 'Ah, what a good man, he cares enough about this place to pick up other people's rubbish.' The botanist was very strong on the idea that each of us is responsible for the environment. In his own country he had often got into trouble with groups of youths, on account of confronting them and demanding that they pick up their sweetpapers and cigarette packets. Mehmet crushed the tin can in his hands, and held on to it. The botanist was surprised that he did not put it in the bins that they passed. He was even more surprised when Mehmet signalled him to continue walking, and then rummaged in one of the bins.

Mehmet was ashamed of having been reduced to this, and he did not want the foreigner to see what he was doing. The foreigner, however, was perplexed; his immediate thought was that Mehmet must be an oddity, perhaps someone who was obsessed with rubbish. However, he saw Mehmet's hurried shame very clearly, and pretended, when Mehmet caught him up, not to notice that he was carrying three or four cans behind his back. The foreigner let Mehmet back into the car, and affected not to notice that he was hurriedly stuffing them into his white sack.

The foreigner spotted a can on his side of the car, thought about it, picked it up, and, when he got in, handed it to his passenger. Mehmet looked at him, took the can eagerly, and then felt the blood rush to his face and ears. His expression became miserable; he had been detected so soon in his humiliating occupation. He tried to explain.

'I do it for money,' he said. 'I've got a proper job, but it's the inflation. They say it's ninety per cent, but I think it's more like three hundred. Everything's getting more and more expensive, and life is harder and harder every day. I can't afford anything any more. The prices go up and up, and my salary doesn't.' He reached into his back pocket and drew out his wallet. He showed the foreigner his small wad of lira. 'Turkish lira,' he said disgustedly, 'they're not worth anything. I don't know whose fault it is, but they ought to be shot. How am I supposed to manage? Unlike some, I've got nobody sending me Deutschmarks. It's a shitty life.'

The foreigner nodded; he needed no Turkish to understand the gist of these gestures and complaints; there were so many zeros on a Turkish banknote that even a dog was a multimillionaire.

Mehmet reached into his sack and showed the foreigner the bottom of a tin can. 'I look at the serial numbers,' he said, 'and that way I know which ones I ought to collect. Some of them are made of good metal that's worth recycling, and some of them aren't. I only take the best.'

The foreigner thought for a moment. He had two days left, which was probably enough time for the fieldwork that he had to do. It looked as though he would just have to give up the idea of spending the last day lounging on a beach. It was frustrating that Mehmet had somehow taken over his day, but on the other hand he was in a splendid position to help him, since he had the car and plenty of time. He criticised himself inwardly for being tempted to let Mehmet wander off somewhere, and then speed away in the car. He would have despised himself for doing it, and besides, how often does one get the chance to help someone else earn an honest living? He felt obscurely that his comfortable life on a comfortable income placed a special obligation upon him, and anyway, a few hours collecting cans was surely pleasant enough on a day as lovely and springlike as this. '*Seddülbahir*?' he suggested, and Mehmet nodded. There would be lots of schoolchildren at the First Martyrs Memorial, and at the Sergeant Yahya Memorial, all swigging soft drinks, and throwing away the cans.

As they drove around the coast the foreigner marvelled all over again that this idyllic place had been the scene of so many months of bloody battles. Mehmet waved a hand towards the fields and their swathes of flowers. 'I love this place,' he said. 'I used to know it very intimately. I did my degree in agronomy, at the university in Istanbul, and I came out here to do my fieldwork. I know the names and habits of all these flowers, but unfortunately no one in the real world is interested in such things. Nobody pays for it, anyway. I'm like most of my friends; I've got qualifications I can't use, and I scrape through life like a stray dog in the street. If you've got the time I'd like to go for a short stroll and have a look at the flowers, for old time's sake. Some of them are very interesting. I was working on the use of selective herbicides to get rid of them, but you can't get peasants to spend money on herbicides anyway, and now I'm quite glad that nothing came of my work.' He turned and looked at the stranger. 'I like the flowers now, even though they used to be the enemy.'

'*Anlamam*,' said the foreign botanist hopelessly, frustrated and irritated that Mehmet kept on talking without seeming to realise that no communication was occurring.

Mehmet was also wearied by the lack of communication, however. 'Oh well,' he said, 'I suppose we'll just have to go on looking at these monuments. I don't really see the attraction of it myself, but there you are. At least there'll be a lot of kids throwing away cans.'

At the Cape Helles monument Mehmet became excited by the thought that perhaps the dead grandfather of the stranger was mentioned on the walls or the obelisk, but the latter did not seem to want to go and look. In fact, he had already set about picking up tin cans. Mehmet approached the owner of the refreshments stall, stood with as much dignity as he could, and said to its proprietor, 'I am recycling cans as a sideline, and I am wondering if you might give me your permission to sift through your rubbish bins. I will leave no mess, I promise.'

The proprietor considered him, and nodded his head with resignation. It was hard to have to maintain oneself in any profession these days. 'Who's the foreigner?' he asked.

'I've no idea,' said Mehmet. 'He's a mystery. He picked me up when I was hitching, and now he's just driving me about whilst I pick up cans. I don't know what he's up to or where he's really going.'

'Not all foreigners are shits,' observed the proprietor, a middle-aged man with a comfortable paunch. 'Maybe you've struck it lucky.'

'All the same,' said Mehmet, 'it's a bit strange, driving me about and collecting cans when he doesn't have to.'

'Don't question God's plans,' said the proprietor, pleased with his little flash of pious wisdom, 'maybe he's your angel for the day.'

'That's a pretty thought,' said Mehmet, and the stallholder nodded knowingly, saying 'God's the boss.'

'Perhaps you could lend me a plastic bag?' suggested Mehmet. 'My sack is getting heavy.'

Mehmet rifled through the rubbish bins, and then he and the foreigner trailed in the wake of the schoolchildren, who were photographing each other in the gun emplacements, and by the Sergeant Yahya memorial. The foreigner was a little disappointed when he saw that Mehmet was simply discarding cans that he did not deem worth recycling; he had still not quite disabused himself of his first faulty notion that Mehmet was an environmentalist. 'All the same,' he thought, 'this fellow is certainly a good rather than a bad thing. At least half of the cans get collected, that wouldn't otherwise.'

Mehmet had not eaten since breakfast, and had not really eaten properly for several days. His stomach was starting to rumble, and he was feeling somewhat weak and dizzy. It was by now late afternoon, the heat of the late spring was beginning to oppress the brain, and he was longing for a beer. The trouble was, that if he invited the stranger to a *pastahane*, then it would be up to him to pay for the drinks and a snack. The thought made him panic a little; he was a generous and honourable man, but money was the one thing with which he could not possibly afford to be generous. Nonetheless, he asked, 'Hungry?' in a tentative and non-committal tone of voice.

The word '*acıkmak*' was one that the foreigner knew from his phrase-book, and he shook his head. He had been trying to lose weight, and had deliberately been missing out lunch, which in general was quite easy to do when you were tramping about in the wilderness, looking for flowers. Additionally, the equable climate made him feel less greedy than usual, and it was actually quite nice just to drink a litre of water at midday. He was puzzled by Mehmet's response to his denial of hunger, however; he seemed both relieved and disappointed. It occurred to him that perhaps the Turk was angling for a free meal, and this thought at once annoyed him and made him feel sorry.

Mehmet glanced at his watch, and realised that before long he would have to return to the ferryport in order to catch the boat, reluctant as he was to leave behind so many collectable cans, and therefore he suggested, 'Kilitbahir?'

'OK,' said the foreigner, both amused and bemused by the manner in which he had lost a complete day going in a big circle with a perfect stranger.

On the way through the dense pine forest that had been the site of the second battle of Kritia, they both simultaneously spotted a heap of rubbish that had been jettisoned by the roadside. They exchanged glances, and the foreigner stopped the car and reversed. 'At least we now understand each other a little,' they both thought. They found seven cans. 'Seven,' said Mehmet, pleased, and '*yedi*' repeated the foreigner, also pleased.

The foreign botanist stopped the car at an open-air café on the side of the road by the Havuslar cemetery, intending to buy Mehmet food and drink, but was beaten to it by Mehmet, who ordered a beer for himself and an orange juice for the driver. 'Would you permit me to take away your used tin cans?' Mehmet asked the patron. 'I recycle them, you see. It's a little extra money for the family. I promise I won't make a mess.'

The patron weighed this proposition, and gave his assent with a shrug; everyone had to struggle and improvise these days. The government changes, and the problems stay the same. 'Who's the foreigner?' he asked, puzzled that a tin collector should be chauffeured about in a nice new car.

'I don't know who he is,' said Mehmet. 'He's been driving me around all day, helping me collect cans. Someone suggested earlier that he might be my angel.' Mehmet giggled, 'Anyway, I don't know anything about him except that he speaks Turkish, but doesn't understand when I speak it back. It's very strange.'

'Maybe he's deaf,' proposed the patron.

'No, I'm sure he's not,' replied Mehmet. 'But anyway, we've collected hundreds of cans today.'

'I'll tell you what,' said the patron, 'since he's been so good to a Turk, I'm not going to charge you for his drink, OK? I'll give you some of your money back.'

'You're a saint,' exclaimed Mehmet. 'May the blessings of God be upon you.'

'It's nothing,' shrugged the patron. 'If a foreigner can be kind to you, then I can too.'

Later, back at Kilitbahir, Mehmet found that he still had twenty minutes to collect cans before the ferry departed, and that renewed coachloads of patriotic schoolchildren had liberally strewn the grounds of the old castle with drinks cans. He became quite agitated about this bonus, and his natural generosity got the better of him. At the café he ordered a cheese-toast for the stranger, as if he could assuage his own hunger by offering food to another. The waiter was somewhat reluctant to take a food order, since the kitchens were not yet opened, but Mehmet waxed eloquent about the duty of hospitality to foreigners, and stated firmly that the stranger had not eaten for ages. The waiter eyed the plump foreigner sceptically, but ultimately could not refuse this appeal to his honour. He went and got the cheese-toast ready.

Mehmet signalled to the stranger that he was going to go and look for cans whilst they waited for the food. He was thinking that it would be so painful to watch the other eating when he was so hungry himself, that it would be better to be out and about. Accordingly he stayed away from the restaurant as long as he possibly could.

The foreigner began to be uneasy and suspicious about Mehmet's long absence. What if he had gone back to the car? His passport was in there. Where the hell was Mehmet? The foreigner had cut the cheese-toast in half, and had eaten it reluctantly, out of politeness rather than because he wanted it. In deference to Mehmet's obvious hunger, he had left the second half, and now it was going cold on the table. He was annoyed because he had wanted Mehmet to enjoy it at its best.

The stranger paid the bill, and was just thinking that he would never see Mehmet again, when the latter reappeared, all triumphant smiles. 'Thirty-two,' he exclaimed.

'*Otuziki*,' repeated the foreigner, impressed. Mehmet was about to sit down, when he noticed that his hands had become very grubby indeed. He looked at them, showed them to the foreigner with a disgusted expression on his face, tutted, and disappeared into the men's room. He washed first his hands, and then his face. He sprinkled water on to his hair, and stood in front of the mirror to comb it carefully into place. When he reappeared he was neat and respectable, and his shoulders were squared.

Mehmet sat down at the table, and the foreigner indicated the cheese-toast, pointed at him, and said, '*Yemek*.'

'I'm not hungry,' said Mehmet. 'I bought it for you. You eat it.'

The stranger saw the longing in Mehmet's eyes, and understood the delicacy of the situation. He linked the fingers of his hands, and made a rotund gesture above his stomach, indicating that he was completely full. He wrapped the cheese-toast in a paper napkin, and pointed at Mehmet, and then at his own watch, showing a later hour. Mehmet was initially puzzled, and then realised that the stranger was telling him to eat it later. It was an excellent compromise. With every show of reluctance and indifference, Mehmet accepted the cheese-toast. He put it carefully into his shirt pocket, and then eagerly knocked back the beer that had been waiting for him. When they got up to go, he very deliberately left the can on the table.

He was vexed and consternated to discover that the foreigner had already paid the bill, his vexation being exacerbated by the realisation that he was also quite relieved. He turned angrily on the stranger, but was completely disarmed by the big smile on the latter's face. Mehmet threw up his arm in mock exasperation. 'You are a very bad man,' he said, 'you tricked me.'

Mehmet inquired of the waiter as to whether any of the staff spoke the foreigner's language, and was pleased to discover that there was one. For a short while he talked to the waiter, who then approached the foreigner: 'Mr Mehmet says that he likes you very much, and he wants to know if you like him very much, because you have spent the whole day with him.'

The foreigner was slightly embarrassed. 'Tell him that he is a very good man, and that I like him very much.' He put his hand on his friend's upper arm, and patted it in a brotherly manner.

When Mehmet heard this translated, he found it hard to master his emotions. He embraced the foreigner, squeezing his shoulders in his suprisingly strong hands, and looking away so that no one would notice the sentimental tears that were threatening to well up in his eyes. Apart from a decent

511

living, all that Mehmet Erbil really wanted in life was a little honest respect, and it was not often that he received any.

The foreigner presented Mehmet with a business card, upon which he had added his country's code. He knew that if Mehmet telephoned, they would not understand each other one little bit, but it was the gesture that mattered, after all. Mehmet found a scrap of paper in his wallet, and wrote his own address and telephone number. As an afterthought, he added his profession, '*öğretmen*.'

Mehmet walked with the foreigner back to the car, and for a moment the latter wondered whether Mehmet was thinking of coming to Eçeabat; but Mehmet just wanted to see the foreigner off. He shook his hand repeatedly, saying, 'It would be nice if you came over with your car to Çanakkale. You've got my address. It would be wonderful to see you. It's a shame to go back whilst there's still light' (he grinned), 'and plenty of cans to collect, but I've got four classes tomorrow. I've got to prepare the lessons for the kids, you know how it is, and I've got a mountain of exercise books to mark. What a job, what a life.'

The foreigner was as nonplussed by this speech as he had been by all of Mehmet's remarks. He had given up saying '*Anlamam*' and '*Turkçe bilmiyorum*' and had even given up saying '*Evet*'. Mehmet talked anyway. He saw the foreigner's perplexity, and continued, 'I suppose you're wondering why I came over on the ferry to collect cans when I could have collected them at home in Çanakkale.' Mehmet scratched the back of his neck, and then stroked his chin. 'Well, I wouldn't want any of my own pupils to see me doing this.' He raised the bulging white sack. 'It's not just a question of my self-esteem. No, it's not that. It's that I want my pupils to value education. I want them growing up to think that a school-teacher is a fine thing to be. It would not be good for them to know that we are reduced to collecting cans.'

The foreigner did not understand, but he knew that Mehmet had been speaking of grave matters. He nodded, and Mehmet nodded too, glad that something had been cleared up.

Mehmet and the foreigner kissed on both cheeks. In the foreigner's country men never did this, but here in Turkey it seemed completely natural and unremarkable, although the scrape of another man's stubble on his cheek did feel distinctly novel and disconcerting.

With a clatter, Mehmet hoisted the white sack on to his shoulder and began to walk away. Over his shoulder he called, 'Remain well.'

'*Güle güle*,' returned the foreigner, remembering the correct formula from his phrase-book. He got into the car and drove away without looking back, knowing that Mehmet would not eat the cheese-toast until he was out of sight, and wanting to give him the chance to eat it as soon as he could.

Back at the hotel the foreigner transferred Mehmet's details to his address book, and then looked up '*öğretmen*' in his Turkish dictionary. He was deeply puzzled to find that it meant 'schoolmaster', and it dawned on him only very slowly that Mehmet must already have had a proper job, and was only collecting cans out of desperation. He shook his head; sometimes it was humbling to comprehend so intimately the hardship in other people's lives. When he telephoned his wife that evening he told her, 'I've just had a really strange day. It was bizarre, but sort of heartening.'

'Oh, do tell me,' she said.

In Çanakkale, Mehmet dumped his haul of cans by the front door of his apartment, and went into the kitchen to greet his wife. 'I've just had a really strange day,' he told her. 'It was bizarre, but in its way it was quite heartening.'

His wife stirred the wooden spoon in the pot, wiped her hands on a cloth, and said, 'Tell me.'

David Mitchell

MONGOLIA

THE GRASSLANDS ROSE and fell, years upon years of them.

Sometimes the train passed settlements of the round tents that Caspar's guidebook called *gers*. Horses grazed, old men squatted on their haunches, smoking pipes. Vicious-looking dogs barked at us, and children watched as we passed. They never returned Caspar's wave, they just looked on, like their grandfathers. Telegraph poles lined the track, forking off to vanish over the restless horizon. The large sky made Caspar think of the land where he had grown up, somewhere called Zetland. Caspar was feeling lonely and homesick. I felt no anticipation, just endlessness.

The Great Wall was many hours behind us now.

A far-flung, trackless country in which to hunt myself.

Sharing our compartment were a pair of giant belchers from Austria who drank vodka by the pint, told flatulent jokes to one another in German, a language I had learned from Caspar. They were betting sheaves of *togrugs* on a card game called cribbage one of them had learnt from a Welshman in Shanghai, and swearing in multicoloured oaths. In the corner of the top bunk sat an Australian girl called Sherry, immersed in *War and Peace*. Caspar had been an agronomist at university before dropping out and had never read any Tolstoy. I caught him wishing he had, though not for literary reasons. A Swede from the next compartment invited himself in from time to time to regale Caspar with stories of being ripped off in China. He bored us both, and even Caspar's sympathies were with the Chinese. Also in the Swede's compartment was a silent middle-aged Irish woman who either gazed out of the window or wrote numbers in a black notebook.

Night stole over the land again, dissolving it in shadows and blue. Every ten or twenty miles tongues of campfire licked the darkness.

Caspar's mental clock was several hours out, so he decided to turn in. I could have adjusted it for him, but I decided to let him sleep. He went to the toilet, splashed water over his face, and cleaned his teeth with water he disinfected in a bottle with iodine. Sherry was outside our compartment when he came back, her face pressed against the glass. Caspar thought, How beautiful. 'Hello,' he said.

'Hello.' Sherry's eyes turned towards my host.

'How's the *War and Peace*? I have to admit, I've never read any Russians.'

'Long.'

'What's it about?'

'Why things happen the way they do.'

'And why do things happen the way they do?'

'I don't know, yet. It's *very* long.' She watched her breath mist up the window. 'Look at it. All this space, and almost no people in it. It almost reminds me of home.'

Caspar joined her at the window. After a mile had passed, 'Why are you here?'

She thought for a while. 'It's the last place, y'know? Lost in the middle of Asia, not in the east, not in the west. *Lost as Mongolia*, it could be an expression. How about you?'

Some drunken Russians along the corridor groaned with laughter.

'I don't really know. I was on my way to Laos, when this impulse came over me. I told myself there was nothing here, but I couldn't fight it. Mongolia! I've never even thought about the place. Maybe I smoked too much pot at Lake Dal.'

A half-naked Chinese toddler ran up the corridor, making

a *zun-zun* noise which may have been a helicopter, or maybe a horse.

Sherry's face turned into a huge yawn. 'Sorry, I'm bushed. Being cooped up doing nothing is exhausting work. Do you think our Austrian friends have shut up the casino for the night?'

'I only hope they have shut up the joke factory. You don't know how lucky you are, not speaking German.'

Back in their compartment, the Austrians were snoring in stereo. Sherry bolted the door. The gentle sway of the train lulled Caspar towards sleep, thinking about Sherry.

Sherry peered over the bunk above him. 'Do you know a good bedtime story?'

Caspar was not a natural storyteller, so I stepped in. 'I know one story. It's a Mongolian story. Well, not so much a story as a sort of legend.'

'I'd love to hear it.' Sherry smiled, and Caspar's heart missed a gear.

There are three who think about the fate of the world.

First there is the crane. See how lightly he treads, picking his way between the rocks in the river? Tossing, and tilting back his head. The crane believes that if he takes just one heavy step, the mountains will collapse and the ground will quiver and trees that have stood for a thousand years will tumble.

Second, the locust. All day the locust sits on a pebble, thinking that one day the flood will come and deluge the world, and all living things will be lost in the churn and the froth and black waves. That is why the locust keeps such a watchful eye on the high peaks, and the rainclouds that might be gathering there.

Third, the bat. The bat believes that the sky may fall and shatter, and all living things die. Thus the bat dangles from a high place, fluttering up to the sky, and down to the ground, and up to the sky again, checking that all is well.

That was the story. That was the story that started it all.

Sherry had fallen asleep and Caspar wondered for a moment where this story had come from. I closed his mind and nudged it towards sleep. I watched his dreams come and go for a little while. Asia, raining things, flowerbeds in Copenhagen, childhood.

My own infancy was spent at the foot of the Holy Mountain. There was a dimness, which I later learned lasted many years. It took me that long to learn how to remember. It would be the same for a sentient bird who begins as an 'I'. Slowly, the bird understands that it is a thing different from the 'It' of its shell, and perceives containment, and as its sensory organs begin to function, it becomes aware of light and dark, cold and heat. As sensation sharpens, it seeks to break out. Then one day, it starts to struggle against the gluey gel and the brittle walls, and cannot stop until it is out and alone in the vertiginous world, made of wonder, and fear, and colours, made of unknown things.

But even back then, I was wondering: *Why am I alone?*

The sun woke Caspar. He had dried tears in his eyes and his mouth tasted of watch-straps. He badly wished he had some fresh fruit to eat. And the Austrians had already beaten him to the bathroom. He slid out of bed, and we saw Sherry was meditating. Caspar pulled on his jeans and tried to slip out of the compartment without disturbing her.

'Good morning, and welcome to Sunny Mongolia,' Sherry murmured. 'We get there in three hours.'

'Sorry I disturbed you,' said Caspar.

'You didn't. And if you look in that plastic bag hanging off the coat hook, you should find some pears. Have one for breakfast.'

'So,' said Sherry, four hours later, 'Grand Central Station, Ulan Bator.'

'Strange,' said Caspar, wanting to express himself in Danish.

The whitewash was bright in the pristine sun. The wind came from over the plains, and went to the vanishing point where the rails led. The signs were in the Cyrillic alphabet, which neither Caspar nor any of my previous hosts knew. Chinese hawkers barged off the train, heaving bags of goods to sell, shouting to one another in familiar Mandarin. A couple of listless young Mongolians on military service fingered their rifles. A group of steely old women were waiting to get on the Irkutsk-bound train. Their families had come to see them off. Two figures hovered in the wings, in black suits and sunglasses. Some youths sat on a wall.

'I feel like I've climbed out of a dark box into a carnival of aliens,' said Sherry.

'Sherry, I know, erm, as a young lady, you have to be careful who you trust when you're travelling, but I was wondering –'

'Stop sounding like a Pom. Yes, sure. I won't jump you if you don't jump me. Now. Your *Lonely Planet* says there's a half-way decent hotel in the Sansar district, at the eastern end of Sambuu Street . . . Follow me . . .'

I let Sherry take care of my host. One less thing for me to worry about. The Austrians said goodbye and headed off to the Kublai Khan Holiday Inn, no longer laughing.

Backpackers are strange. I have a lot in common with them. We live nowhere, and we are strangers everywhere. We drift, searching for something to search for. We are both parasites: I live through my hosts' minds, sifting through their memories to understand the world. Caspar's breed live in a host country that is never their own, and use its culture and landscape to learn, or to stave off boredom. To the world at large we are both immaterial and invisible. We chew the secretions of solitude. My incredulous Chinese hosts who saw the first backpackers regarded them as quite alien entities. Which is exactly how humans would regard me.

'Did I blink?' remarked Sherry. 'Where's the city? Beijing was a city, Shanghai was a city. This is a ghost town.'

'It's like East Germany in the Iron Curtain days.'

Ranks and files of faceless apartment blocks, with cracks in the walls and boards for windows. A large pipeline mounted on concrete stilts. Cratered roads, with only a few dilapidated cars trundling up and down. Goats eating weeds in a city square. Silent factories. Statues of horses and little toy tanks. A woman with a basket of eggs stepping carefully between the broken flagstones and bottles and wobbling drunks. Streetlights, ready to topple. A once-mighty power station spewing out a black cloud over the city. On the far side of the city was a gigantic fairground wheel that Caspar doubted would ever turn again.

Ulan Bator was much bigger than the village at the foot of the Holy Mountain, but the people we saw here lacked any sense of purpose. They just seemed to be waiting. Waiting for something to open, for the end of the day, for their city to be switched on, or just waiting to be fed.

Caspar readjusted the straps on his backpack. 'My *Secret History of Genghis Khan* did not prepare me for this.'

That night Caspar dug into his mutton and onion stew with relish. He and Sherry were the only diners in the hotel, which was actually the sixth and seventh floor of a crumbling apartment building.

The woman who had brought it through from the kitchen looked at him blankly. Caspar pointed at it, gave her a thumbs up sign, smiled and grunted approvingly.

The woman looked at Caspar as though he were a madman, and left.

Sherry snorted. 'Well, she's about as welcoming as the customs woman at the border.'

'One of the things that my years of wandering has taught me is, the more impotent the country, the more dangerous its customs officials.'

'When she showed us the room she gave me a look like I'd run over her baby with a bulldozer.'

Caspar picked out a bit of fleece from a meatball. 'Service sector communism. It's quite a legacy. She's stuck here, remember. We can get out whenever we want.'

He had some instant lemon tea from Beijing. There was a flask of hot water on the sideboard, so he made a cup for himself and Sherry, and they watched the waxy moon rise over the suburb of gers and campfires. 'So,' began Caspar. 'Tell me more about that Hong Kong pub you worked in. What was the name? *Mad Dogs*?'

'I'd rather hear more stories of the weirdos you met during your jewellery-selling days in Okinawa. Go on, Vikingman, it's your turn.'

So many times in a lifetime do my hosts feel the beginnings of friendship. All I can do is watch.

As my infancy progressed, I became aware of another presence in 'my' body. Stringy mists of colour and emotion condensed into droplets of understanding. I saw, and slowly came to recognise, gardens, paths, barking dogs, rice fields, sunlit washing drying in warm town breezes. I had no idea what these plotless images were. I walked down the path trodden by all humans, from the mythic to the prosaic. Unlike humans, I remember the path.

Something was happening on my side of this screen of perception, too. Like a radio slowly being turned up, so slowly that at first you cannot be sure of it being there. I sensed an entity that was not me generating sensations, which only later could I label loyalty, love, anger, ill-will. I watched this other clarify, and pull into focus. I feared it. I thought *it* was the intruder! I thought the mind of my first host was the cuckoo's egg that would hatch and drive me away. So one night, while my host was asleep, I tried to penetrate this other presence.

My host tried to scream but I would not let him wake. Instinctively, his mind made itself rigid. I prised through clumsily, not knowing how strong I had become, ripping my way through memories and neural control, gouging out great chunks. Fear of losing the fight made me more violent than I ever intended. I had sought only to subdue, not to lay waste.

When the morning brought the doctor he found my first host unresponsive to any form of stimulus. Naturally, the doctor could find no injury on the patient's body, but he knew a coma when he saw one. In south-west China in the 1950s there were no facilities for people with comas. My host died a few weeks later, taking any buried clues of my origin with him. They were hellish weeks. I discovered my mistake – *I* was the intruder. I tried to undo the damage, and piece back together the vital functions and memories, but it is so much easier to destroy than it is to re-create, and back then I knew nothing. I learned that my victim had fought as a brigand and a soldier in northern China. I found fragments of spoken languages which I would later know as Mongolian and Korean. That was all. I couldn't ascertain how long I had been embryonic.

I assumed that if my host died, I would share his death. I turned all my energies to learning how to perform what I now call transmigration. Two days before he died, I succeeded. My second host was the doctor of my first. I looked back at the soldier. A middle-aged man lay on his soiled bed, stretched out on his frame of bones. I felt guilt, relief and power.

I stayed in the doctor learning about humans and inhumanity. I learned how to read my hosts' memories, to erase them and replace them. I learned how to play with my toys. But I also learned caution. One day I announced to my host that a disembodied entity had been living in his mind for the last two years, and would he like to ask me anything?

The poor man went quite mad, and I had to transmigrate again. The human mind is so fragile! So puny!

Three nights later the waitress slammed a bowl of mutton

down in front of Caspar. She had turned and gone before he had a chance to groan.

'Mutton fat for dinner,' beamed Sherry. 'There's a surprise.'

The waitress cleared the other tables. Caspar was experimenting using mind control to make his mutton taste like turkey. I resisted the temptation to help him succeed. Sherry was reading. 'Get this for Soviet doublespeak. From the 1940s, during Choibalsan's presidency. It says, "In the final analysis, life demonstrated the expediency of using the Russian alphabet." What the author says this means, is that if you used Mongolian they shot you. Oath, how did people *live* under a master race like that, and why –'

The next moment all the lights in the building died.

Dim light came from the window of smoked stars, and a glowing red sign in Cyrillic beyond the wasteland. We had wondered what the sign meant, and we did again now.

Sherry chuckled and lit a cigarette. Her eyes reflected little flames. 'I suppose you paid the power station ten dollars to stage this black-out, just to get me alone in a dark room with the manly smell of mutton.'

Caspar smiled in the darkness and I recognised love. It forms like a weather pattern. 'Sherry, let's hire the jeep from tomorrow. We've seen the temple, seen the old palace. I'm feeling like a moody tourist. I hate feeling like a moody tourist. The Fräulein at the German Embassy reckoned there would be a delivery of gas in the morning.'

'Why the rush?'

'The place is going backwards in time. I feel the end of the world is waiting in those mountains, somewhere . . . We should get out before the nineteenth century comes around again.'

'That's a part of UB's charm. Its ramshackleness.'

'I don't know what *ramshackleness* means, but there is nothing charming here. Ulan Bator proves that Mongolians cannot do cities. You could set a movie about a doomed colony of germ warfare survivors here. I don't even know why I'm here. I don't think a lot of the people who live here know either.'

The waitress walked in, and put a candle on our table. Caspar thanked her in Mongolian. She walked out. 'Come the Revolution . . .' thought Caspar.

Sherry started shuffling a pack of cards. 'You mean Mongolians are designed for arduous lifetimes of flock-tending, frostbite, illiteracy, *guardia lamblia*, and ger-dwelling?'

'I don't want to argue. I want to drive to the Khangai mountains, climb mountains, ride horses, bathe naked in lakes and discover what it is I am doing on Earth.'

'OK, Vikingman, we'll move on tomorrow. Let's play cribbage. I believe I'm winning, thirty-seven games to nine.'

I would need to move on soon, too. Hosted by a Mongolian, my quest in this country was formidable. Hosted by a foreigner, my quest was plainly impossible.

I was here to find the source of the story that was already there, right at the beginning of 'I', sixty years ago. The story began, *There are three animals who think about the fate of the world* . . .

Once or twice I've tried to describe transmigration to my more imaginative human hosts. It's impossible.

When another human touches my host, I can transmigrate. The ease of the transfer depends on the mind I am transmigrating into, and whether negative emotions are blocking me. That touch is a requisite provides a clue that I exist on some physical plane, however sub-cellular or bio-electrical. There are limits. I cannot transmigrate into animals, even primates; if I try, the animal dies. But how it feels, this transmigration, how to describe that? Imagine a trapeze artist in a circus, spinning in emptiness. Or a snooker ball lurching around the table. Arriving in a strange town after a journey through turbid weather.

Impossible.

The morning wind blew cold from the mountains. Gunga stooped through the door of her ger, slapping the chilly morning air into her neck and face. The hillside of gers was slowly coming to life. In the city an ambulance siren rose and fell. The River Tuul glowed pewter. The big red neon sign flicked off: *Let's Make Our City A Great Socialist Community.*

'Camelshit,' thought Gunga. 'When are they going to dismantle that?'

Gunga wondered where her daughter had got to. She had her suspicions.

A neighbour nodded to her, wishing her good morning. Gunga nodded back. Her eyes were becoming weaker, rheumatism had begun to gnaw at her hips, and a poorly set broken femur from three winters ago ached. Gunga's dog padded over to be scratched behind the ears. Something else was wrong, too, today.

She ducked back into the warmth of the ger.

'Shut the bloody door!' bawled her husband.

It was good to transmigrate out of a westernised head. However much I learn from the non-stop highways of minds like Caspar's, they make me giddy. It would be the krone's exchange rate one minute, a film he'd once seen about art thieves in Petersburg the next, a memory of fishing with his uncle between islcts the next, some pop song or a friend's Internet home page the next. No stopping.

Gunga's mind patrols a more intimate neighbourhood. She constantly thinks about getting enough food and money. She worries about her daughter, and ailing relatives. Most of the days of her life are very much alike. The assured dreariness of the Soviet days, the struggle for survival since independence. Gunga's mind is a lot harder for me to hide in than Caspar's, however. It's like trying to make yourself invisible in a prying village as opposed to a sprawling conurbation. Some hosts can perceive movements in their mental landscapes, and Gunga was very perceptive indeed. While she had been sleeping I acquired her language, but her dreams kept trying to smoke me out.

Gunga set about lighting the stove. 'Something's wrong,' she said, looking around the ger, looking for a missing something. The beds, the table, the cabinet, the family tableware, the rugs, the silver teapot that she had refused to sell, even when times were at their hardest.

'Not your mysterious sixth sense again?' Buyant stirred under his pile of blankets. Gunga's cataracts and the gloom of the ger's interior made it difficult to see. Buyant coughed a smoker's cough. 'What is it this time? A message from your bladder, we're going to inherit a camel? Your earwax telling you a giant leech is going to come and molest your innocence?'

'A giant leech did that years ago. It was called Buyant.'

'Very funny. What's for breakfast?'

I may as well start somewhere. 'Husband, do you know anything about the three animals who think about the fate of the world?'

A long pause in which I thought he hadn't heard me. 'What the devil are you talking about now?'

At that moment Oyuun, Gunga's daughter, came in. Her cheeks were flushed. 'The shop had some bread! And I found some onions, too.'

'Good girl!' Gunga embraced her. 'You were gone early. You didn't wake me.'

'Shut the bloody door!' bawled Buyant.

'I knew you had to work late, so I was extra quiet.' Oyuun wasn't telling the whole truth. 'Was the hotel busy last night, Mum?' Oyuun was an adept subject-changer.

'No. Just the two blondies.'

'I found Australia in the atlas at school. I couldn't find – what was it? Danemark?'

'Who cares?' Buyant rolled out of bed, wearing a blanket as a shawl. He would have been handsome once, and he still thought he was. 'It's not as if *you'll* ever be going there.'

Gunga bit her tongue, and Oyuun didn't look up.

'The blondies are checking out today, and I'll be glad to see the back of them. I just can't understand it, a mother letting her daughter wander off like that. I'm sure they're not married, but they're in the same bed! No ring, or anything. And there's something weird about him, too.' Gunga was looking at Oyuun, but Oyuun was looking away.

''Course there is, they're foreigners.' Buyant burped and slurped his tea.

'What do you mean, Mum?' Oyuun started chopping the onions.

'Well, for one thing, he smells of yoghurt. But there's something else too . . . it's in his eyes . . . it's like they're not his own.'

'They can't be as weird as those Hungarian trade unionists that used to come. The ones they flew in the orchids from Vietnam for.'

Gunga knew how to blot out her husband's presence. 'That Danemark man, he tips all the time, and he keeps smiling like he's touched in the head. But last night, he touched my hand.'

Buyant spat. 'If he touches you again I'll twist his head off and jam it up his arse. You tell him that from me.'

Gunga shook her head. 'No, it was like a kid playing tag. He just touched my hand with his thumb, and was gone, out of the kitchen. Or like he was casting a spell. And please don't spit inside the ger.'

Buyant ripped off a gobbet of bread. 'A *spell*, ah yes, that must be it! He was probably trying to bewitch you. Sometimes I feel it was your grandmother I married, not you!'

The women carried on preparing food in silence.

Buyant scratched his groin. 'Speaking of marriage, Old Gombo's eldest boy came round asking for Oyuun last night.'

Oyuun stared steadily into the noodles she was stirring. 'Oh?'

'Yep. Brought me a bottle of vodka. Good stuff. Old Gombo's a buffoon horseman who can't hold his drink, but his brother-in-law has a good government job, and the younger son is turning into quite a wrestler, they say. He was the champion two years running at school. That's not to be sniffed at.'

Gunga chopped, and the onions made her nostrils sting. Oyuun said nothing.

'It's a thought, isn't it? The older son's obviously quite taken with Oyuun . . . if she gets Old Gombo's grandson in the oven it'll show she can deliver the goods *and* force Old Gombo's hand . . . I can think of worse matches.'

'I can think of better ones,' said Gunga, stirring some noodles into the mutton soup. A memory passed through of Buyant visiting her in her parents' ger, through a flap in the roof, just a few feet away from where her parents were sleeping. 'Someone she loves, for example. Anyway, we've already agreed. Oyuun will finish school and, fate willing, get into the university. We want Oyuun to do well in the world. Maybe she'll get a car. Or at least a motorbike, from China.'

'I don't see the point. It's not like there are any jobs waiting afterwards, especially not for girls. The Russians took all the jobs with them when they left. And the ones they left, the Chinese grabbed. Another way foreigners rip us Mongolians off.'

'Camelshit! The vodka took all the jobs. The vodka rips us off.'

Buyant glared. 'Women don't understand politics.'

Gunga glared back. 'And I suppose men do? The economy would die of a common cold if it were healthy enough to catch one.'

'I tell you, it's the Russians –'

'Nothing's ever going to get better until we start blaming ourselves! The Chinese are able to make money here. Why can't we?' Some fat in a pan began to hiss. Gunga caught a glimpse of her reflection in her cup of milk, frowning. Her hand trembled minutely, and the image rippled away. 'Today is all wrong. I'm going to see the shaman.'

Buyant thumped the table. 'I'm not having you throwing away our *togrogs* on –'

Gunga snapped back at him. 'I'll throw *my togrogs* anywhere I please, you *soak*!'

Buyant backed down from this fight he couldn't win. He didn't want the neighbours overhearing, and saying he couldn't control his woman.

Why am I the way I am? I have no genetic blueprint. I have had no parents to teach me right from wrong. I have had no teachers. I had no nurture, and I possess no nature. But I am discreet and conscientious, a non-human humanist.

I wasn't always this way. After the doctor went mad, I transmigrated around the villagers, I was their lord. I knew their secrets, the bends of the village's streams and the names of its dogs. I knew the rare pleasures that burned out as quickly as they flared up, and of the memories that kept them from freezing. I studied extremes. I would drive my hosts almost to destruction in pursuit of the pleasure which fizzed their neural connections. I inflicted pain on those unlucky enough to cross my path, just to understand pain. I amused myself by implanting memories from one host into another, or by incessantly singing to them. I'd compel monks to rob, devoted lovers to be unfaithful, misers to spend. I stopped short of killing, though not from a love of humanity. I had, and have, only one fear: to be inhabiting a human at the moment of death. I still don't know what would happen.

There was no blinding conversion to humanism. During the Cultural Revolution, and when I transmigrated into hosts in Tibet, Vietnam, in Korea, in El Salvador, I experienced humans fighting, usually from the safety of the general's office. In the Falkland Islands I watched them fight over rocks. 'Two blind men fighting over a comb,' a host commented. In Rio I saw a tourist killed for a watch. Humans live in a pit of cheating, exploiting, hurting, incarcerating. Every time, the species wastes some part of what it could be. This waste is poisonous. That is why I no longer harm my hosts. There's already too much of this poison.

Gunga spent the morning at the hotel, sweeping and boiling water to wash sheets. Seeing Caspar again from the outside was like revisiting an old house with a new tenant. They paid and waited until their rented jeep turned up. I bade Caspar goodbye in Danish as he slung his backpack in, but he just assumed Gunga was saying something in Mongolian.

As Gunga made the beds, she imagined Caspar and Sherry lying here, and then thought about Oyuun, and Gombo's youngest son. She thought about the rumours of child prostitution spreading through the city, and how the police were being paid off in foreign money. Mrs Enchbat, the widow who owned the hotel, stopped by to do some bookkeeping. Mrs Enchbat was in a good mood – Caspar had paid in dollars, and Mrs Enchbat needed to raise a dowry. While Gunga was boiling some water for washing they sat down and shared some salty tea.

'Now Gunga, you *know* that I'm not a one for gossip,' began Mrs Enchbat, a little woman with a mouth taut as a lizard's, 'but our Sonjoodoi saw your Oyuun walking out with Old Gombo's youngest again yesterday evening. People's tongues will start wagging. They were seen at the Naadam festival togther. Sonjoodoi also said Gombo's eldest has got a crush on her.'

Gunga chose counter-attack. 'Is it true your Sonjoodoi has become a Christian?'

Mrs Enchbat considered her reply coolly. 'He's been seen going to the American missionary's apartment once or twice.'

'What does his grandmother have to say about that?'

'Only that it proves what suckers Americans are. They think they're making converts to their weird cult when they're just making converts to powdered milk – whatever's the matter, Gunga?'

A riot of doubt had broken out in my host. Gunga knew I was here. Quickly, I tried to calm her. 'No. Something's wrong. I'm going to see the shaman.'

The bus was crowded and stuck in first gear. At the end of the line was a derelict factory. Gunga had already forgotten what it had once manufactured. I had to look in her unconscious: bullets. Wildflowers were capitalising on the brief summer, and wild dogs picked at the body of something. The afternoon was weak and thin. People from the bus trudged their way past where the road ran out to a hillside of gers. Gunga walked with them. The giant pipe ran along on its stilts. It had been part of a public heating system, but the boilers needed Russian coal. Mongolian coal burned at temperatures too cool to make it work. Most of the locals had gone back to burning dung.

Gunga's cousin had gone to this shaman when she couldn't get pregnant. Nine months later she gave birth to boy twins, born with cauls, an omen of great fortune. The shaman was an adviser to the president, and he had a reputation as a horse-healer. It was said he had lived for twenty years as a hermit on the slopes of Tavanbogd in the far west province of Bayan Olgii. During the Soviet occupation, the local officials had tried to arrest him for vagrancy, but anyone who went to get him returned, empty-handed and empty-headed. He was two centuries old.

I was looking forward to meeting the shaman.

I am gifted: I am immune to age and forgetfulness. I possess freedom beyond any human understanding of the word. But my cage is all my own too. I am trapped in one waking state of consciousness. And the knowledge I most desire eludes me: I have never found the source of the story I was born with, and I have never discovered whether others of my kind exist.

When I finally left the village at the foot of the Holy Mountain, I travelled in south-east Asia, searching the attics and cellars of humanity for other minds without bodies. I found legends of beings who might be my kindred, but of tangible knowledge I found not one footprint. I crossed the Pacific in the 1960s.

Remembering my insane doctor, I mostly maintained a vow of silence. I had no wish to leave behind me a trail of mystics, lunatics and writers. On the other hand, if I came across a mystic, lunatic or writer I would sometimes talk with them. One writer in Buenos Aires even suggested a name for my kind: *noncorpi*. *Noncorpo*, for male, *noncorpa*, for female. I spent a pleasant few months debating metaphysics with him, and we wrote some stories together. But the I never became a We. During the 1970s I placed an advertisement in the *National Enquirer*. The USA is even crazier than the rest of humanity. I followed up each of the nineteen replies I received: mystics, lunatics, or writers, every one. I even looked for clues in the Pentagon. I found a lot of things that surprised even me, but nothing related to noncorpi. I never went to Europe. It seemed a dead place, cold in the shadows of nuclear missiles.

I returned to my Holy Mountain, possessing knowledge from over a hundred hosts, but still knowing nothing about my origins. The Holy Mountain was the only place on Earth I felt any tie to. For a decade I inhabited the monks who lived on its mountainsides, leading a tranquil enough life. I found companionship with an old woman who lived in a tea shack and believed I was a speaking tree. That was the last time I spoke with a human.

'Come in, daughter,' said the shaman's voice from inside the ger.

Sun-bleached jawbones hung over the door. Gunga looked over her shoulder, suddenly afraid. A boy was playing with a red ball. He threw it high into the hazy blue, and caught it when it fell. There was an *ovoo*, a holy pile of stones and bones. Gunga asked for its blessing and entered the smoky darkness.

'Come in, daughter.' The shaman was meditating on a mat. A lamp hung from the roof frame. A tallow candle spluttered in a copper dish. The rear of the ger was walled off by hanging animal skins. The air was grainy with incense.

There was a carved box by the entrance. Gunga opened it, and put in most of the *togrogs* that Caspar had tipped her the day before. She slipped off her shoes, and knelt in front of the shaman, on the right hand side of the ger, the female half. A wrinkled face, impossible to guess the age of. Grey, matted hair, and closed eyes that suddenly opened wide. He indicated a cracked teapot on a low table.

Gunga poured the dark odourless liquid into a cup of bone.

'Drink, Gunga,' said the shaman.

My host drank, and began to speak – the shaman halted her with his hand.

'You have come because a spirit is living within you.'

'Yes,' both Gunga and I answered. Gunga felt me again, and dropped the cup. The stain of the undrunk liquid spread through the rug.

'Then we must find out what it wants,' said the shaman.

Gunga's heart flapped like a boxed bat. Gently, I dimmed her consciousness.

The shaman saw the change. He picked up a feather and drew a symbol in the air.

'To whom am I speaking?' asked the shaman. 'An ancestor of this woman?'

'I don't know who I am.' My words, Gunga's voice, dry and croaky. 'This, I wish to discover.' Strange, to be uttering the word 'I' once again.

The shaman was calm. 'What is your name, spirit?'

'I've never needed a name.'

The shaman struck a bone against another bone, muttering words in a language I didn't know. He sprang to his feet and flexed his fingers like claws.

'In the name of Khukdei Mergen Khan art thou cast hence from the body of this woman!'

Human males. 'And then what do you suggest?'

The shaman shouted. 'Be gone! In the name of Erkhii Mergen who divided night from day, I command it!' The shaman shook a rattling sack over Gunga. He blew some incense smoke over my host, and sprinkled some water in her face.

The shaman gazed at my host, waiting for a reaction. 'Shaman, I'd hoped for something more intelligent. And you'd be doing Gunga more good if you used that water to wash her. She believes that the Mongolian body doesn't sweat, so she doesn't wash and she has lice.'

The shaman frowned, and looked into Gunga's eyes, searching for something that wasn't Gunga. 'Your words are perplexing, spirit, and your magic is strong. Do you wish this woman ill? Are you an evil one?'

'Well, I've had my moments, but I wouldn't describe myself as evil. Would you?'

'What do you want of this woman? What is it that ails you?'

'One memory. And the absence of others.'

The shaman sat down and resumed his initial repose. 'Who were your people when you walked as a living body?'

'Why do you think I was once human?'

'What else would you have been?'

'That's a fair question.'

The shaman frowned. 'You are a strange one, even for one of your kind. You speak like a child, not one waiting to pass over.'

'What do you mean, "my kind"?'

'I am a shaman, like my master, and his master before him. It is our calling to communicate with spirits.'

'Let me explore your mind. I need to see what you have seen.'

'The spirits do not commune with one another?'

'Not with me, they don't. Please let me in. It's safer for you if you don't resist.'

'If I allow you to possess me for a short time, you will leave this woman?'

'Shaman, we have a deal. If you touch Gunga, I will leave her now.'

I experience memories like a network of tunnels. Some guarded, some serviced and brightly lit; others are catacombs, yet others are bricked up. Tunnels lead to tunnels, deeper down. So it is with memories.

But access to memories does not guarantee access to truth. Many minds redirect memories along revised maps. In the tunnels of the shaman's memory I met what may have been spirits of the dead, or delusions on the part of either the shaman or his customers or both. Or *noncorpi*! Maybe there were many footprints, or maybe there were none. Or maybe evidence was there in forms I couldn't recognise. I deepened my search.

I found this story, told twenty summers earlier on a firelit desert night.

Many years ago, the red plague stalked the land. Thousands died. The healthy fled, leaving behind the infected, saying simply, 'Fate will sift the living from the dead.' Among the abandoned in the land of birds was Tarvaa, a fifteen-year-old boy. His spirit left his body and walked south between the dunes of the dead.

When he appeared in the ger of the Khan of Hell, the Khan was surprised. 'Why have you left your body behind while it is still breathing?'

Tarvaa replied, 'My lord, the living considered my body gone. I came here without delay to pledge my allegiance.'

The Khan of Hell was impressed with Tarvaa's obedience. 'I decree that your time has not yet come. You may take my fastest horse and return to your master in the land of birds. But before you go you may choose one thing from my ger to take with you. Behold! Here you may find wealth, good fortune, comeliness, ecstasy, fame, wisdom ... come now, what will you have?'

'My lord,' spoke Tarvaa, 'I choose the stories.'

Tarvaa put the stories in his leather pouch, mounted the fastest horse of the Khan of Hell, and returned to the land of birds in the south. When he got there, a crow had already pecked out Tarvaa's body's eyes. But Tarvaa dared not return to the dunes of the dead, fearing that to do so would be ungracious to the Khan. So Tarvaa took possession of his body, and rose up, and though he was blind he lived for a hundred years, travelling Mongolia on the Khan of Hell's horse, from the Altai Mountains in the far west, to the Gobi desert in the south, to the rivers of Hentii Nuruu, telling

*stories and foreseeing the future, and teaching the tribesmen
the legends of the making of their land. And from that time,
the Mongols have told each other tales.*

I decided to go south like Tarvaa. If I lacked clues in reality, I
would have to find them in legends.

Jargal Chinzoreg is as strong as a camel. He trusts only his
family and his truck. As a boy, Jargal yearned to be a pilot in
the Mongolian Air Force, but his family lacked the bribes to
get him into the Party school in the capital, so he became a
truck driver. This was probably lucky, in the long run:
nobody knows what would happen if the handful of rusting
aeroplanes that constitutes the Mongolian Air Force were
started up again. Parliament is talking of scrapping the air
force altogether, given Mongolia's glaring inability to defend
itself against any of its neighbours, even lowly Kazakhstan.
Since the economy died, Jargal has worked for anyone who
has access to fuel: the black marketeers, the iron works,
timber companies, meat merchants. Jargal will do anything to
make his wife laugh, even put socks up his nose and chase her
around the ger making a noise like a horny yak.

The road we are travelling, from Ulan Bator to Dalandzadgad, is the least worst in the country. It's usually passable,
even in rainy weather. The road is 293 kilometres long, and
Jargal knows its every pothole, bend, checkpoint, and every
checkpoint guard. He knows which petrol pumps are likely to
be working, how much life is left in various parts of his
thirty-year-old Russian truck, and possible sources for spares.

The horizon widens, the mountains toss and turn and then
begin to lie down where the grasslands begin. There's a lonely
tree. A dusty café, boarded up since 1990. A barracks where
the Soviet army once did manoeuvres, desolate now with the
plumbing and wiring ripped out.

The sun changes position. A cloud shaped like a marmot.
Jargal wipes the sweat from his eyes, and lights a Chinese

cigarette. He remembers a Marlboro a Canadian hitch-hiker gave him last year. There's a settlement beyond those rocks, where the chestnut horse stands on the ridge. The cloud-marmot has become a cylinder valve. There's a rock shaped like a giant's head seventy kilometres outside of Daland-zadgad. Many years ago a wrestler used it to crush the head of a monstrous serpent. The sky turns clear jade in the evening cold. Jargal lights another cigarette. Five years ago, just off this incline, a truck rolled over with its cargo of propane gas. You can still see the burning driver running towards the road screaming for help that will forever be too late. Jargal knows him. They used to drink together at the truckers' hotels.

Jargal sees the town lights in the distance, and he thinks of his wife's body. He thinks about the toy goat that his aunt Mrs Enchbat made for his baby daughter out of old scraps of cloth and string. She is still too young to talk well, but already she rides as if she were born in the saddle.

I have never felt pride.

'You've never been interested in the old stories before.' The wizened man in an army jacket frowned. 'The Russians prohibited them. All we had was goat-shit about the heroes of the Revolution. I was a teacher then. Did I ever tell you about the time Horloyn Choibalsan came to our school? The President himself?'

'About fifteen minutes ago, you senile fart,' muttered a drunk. A radio in the bar was playing Chinese and English pop songs. Three or four men were playing chess, but had become too drunk to remember the rules.

'If I told any of the old stories in the classroom,' the old man continued, 'I'd have been "re-educated". Even Gingghis Khan, the Russians said he was a feudal class enemy. Now every bunch of gers with a covered cesspit is rushing to prove Gingghis was born by *their* bend in the river . . .'

'That's very interesting,' I said. Jargal was bored. It was uphill work for me to keep him here, polite. 'Do you know one about the three animals who think about the fate of the world?

'I could tell you a few stories of my own, though. Like the time Horloyn Choibalsan came to my school? In a big black car. A black Zil. I want another dumpling. How come you're so interested in the old stories all of a sudden?'

'I'll get you another dumpling. Look, a nice big one . . . lots of lard. It's my son. He complains if I tell the same story twice. You know what kids are like . . . I remember when I was young, about three animals who think about the fate of the world . . .'

The wizened man burped. 'There's no future in stories . . . Stories are things of the past, for museums. No place for stories in these market democracy days.'

Suddenly a shouting-match broke out. Chessmen whistled past. A window cracked. 'He came in a big black car. There were bodyguards and KGB men. Trained in Moscow.' The drunk was standing on a table, shouting down into the foray. A man with a birthmark like a mask was smashing the board down on his rival's head. I gave up and let Jargal get us out of there.

The man in the museum looked at us in astonishment. '*Stories*? About Mongolia?' He started laughing, and I had to stop Jargal taking a swipe at him. 'Why would anyone be interested in stories about Mongolia?'

'Because they are our culture,' I suggested. 'And it's the origin of the stories that I want information about.'

There was a silence. I noticed the wall-clock had stopped.

'Jargal Chinzoreg,' says the curator, 'you are spending too long in your truck, or with your family. You're sounding like a crazy old man, or a tourist . . .'

A man wearing the smartest suit in Mongolia walked out of an office. The director was chuckling like a man of no importance. The suit was carrying a briefcase, and chewing gum.

'We've got our stuffed birds,' continued the curator. 'Our

Mongolian-Russian eternal friendship display. Our dinosaur bones, our scrolls and any Zanabazar bronzes we could hide from the Russians. But if it's stories you want, you've got no business here. I ask you!'

The suit drew level. It was a dull day, but he had already slipped on a pair of sunglasses. 'You know,' he says, suddenly addressing us, 'what's-his-face down in Dalandzadgad is putting together an anthology of Mongolian folk stories. It's a quaint idea. He's hoping to get it translated into English and flog them to tourists. He put a proposal to the state printing press last year. It was turned down – no paper. But he's been doing some lobbying, and at the next meeting he might pull it off.'

The suit went. I thanked him.

'Now, Jargal Chinzoreg,' said the curator, 'will you please get lost? It's lunch-time.'

The manager shut his office door with a loud sigh of relief.

Jargal looked at the curator's watch. 'But it's only ten-thirty.'

'Exactly. We'll re-open at about three.'

The moon was a globe of cobweb. 'Sir!' Jargal ran across the empty road in front of the museum. The suit was getting into a Japanese-made four-wheel drive. Jargal was nervous: the owner of such a car must be a powerful man. 'Sir!'

The suit turned, his hand twitching inside his jacket. 'What?'

'I'm sorry to bother you, sir, but would you try to remember the name of the gentleman you just mentioned? The folklorist? It might be very important to me.'

The suit touched his forehead, and dropped his keys. Jargal picked them up and handed them to him. I make sure their hands touch, and I transmigrate. Like Gunga's, it was a difficult mind to penetrate. Viscous, like jumping through a wall of cold butter.

I searched my new host. 'The folklorist's name is Bodoo. Now, I have business that won't wait.'

Yes it will. Here's a picture. Bodoo is a short, balding man with glasses, and a tufty moustache. We are going to meet, Bodoo. You are going to direct me to my birthright.

I watched Jargal walk away, a man awakening from a strange dream.

Punsalmaagiyn Suhbataar is a senior agent of the Mongolian KGB with a disdain of vulnerable things. We sped south, his jeep spewing up clouds of dust. He chewed gum. The grass grew sparser, the camels scraggier, the air drier. The road to Dalandzadgad wasn't signposted, but there was no other road. The checkpoint guards saluted.

I feel guilty when I use my hosts so selfishly, but as I read Suhbataar's past I feel vindicated. During his career he has killed over twenty times, and supervised the mutilation or torture of ten times that number of prisoners. He has accrued a medium-sized fortune in a vault in Geneva at the expense of his old overlords in Moscow, and his new ones in Petersburg. Even I can't see into the hole where his conscience should be. Outside this hole, his mind is cold, clear and cruel.

As night fell I let Suhbataar stop to stretch his legs and drink some coffee. It was good to see the stars again, the whole deep lake of them. Humans thicken the skies above their cities into a broth. But Suhbataar is not a man given to astral contemplation. For the fiftieth time that day he wondered what he was doing there, and I had to snuff out the thought. We spent the night at a trucker's boarding house, scarcely bothering to talk to the owner whom Suhbataar didn't intend to pay. I made inquiries about Bodoo the Dalandzadgad curator, but nobody knew him. While my host slept I broadened the Russian I had acquired from Gunga.

The following day the hills flattened to a gravel plain, and the Gobi desert began. Another day of horses and clouds and mountains nobody names. My weariness was exacerbated by Suhbataar. Most human minds are constantly busy, editing conversations and mixing images and telling themselves jokes or replaying music. It's something to watch. But not Suhbataar. I might as well have transmigrated into a cyborg.

Suhbataar drove over the body of a dog and into the dusty regional capital of Dalanzadgad. An unpainted place that had dropped from nowhere on to a flat plot of dust-devils. Doomed strips of turfless park where women in headscarves sold eggs and dried goods. A few three- or four-floor buildings, with suburbs spilling around the edges. A dirt-strip runway, a fly-blown hospital, a corrupt post office, a derelict department store that sold nothing. Beyond stories of black-market dinosaur eggs fetching $500 and snow leopard pelts from the Gov'-Altai Mountains to the south fetching up to $20,000, Suhbataar knew less about the southernmost province of Mongolia than he cared about it.

There was a police office he could go and scare, but I took Suhbataar straight to the museum to inquire after Bodoo. The door was locked, but Suhbataar can open any door in Mongolia. Inside was similar to the last museum, booming with silence. Suhbataar found the curator's office empty. A stuffed buzzard incorrectly labelled as a condor hung from the ceiling. One of its glass eyes had dropped out and rolled away somewhere.

There was a middle-aged woman knitting in the empty bookshop. She didn't seem surprised to see a visitor in the locked-up museum. I doubted she had been surprised by anything for years.

'I'm looking for a "Bodoo",' Suhbataar announced.

She didn't bother looking up. 'He didn't come in yesterday. He didn't come in today. I don't know if he'll come in tomorrow.'

Suhbataar's voice fell to a whisper. 'May I ask where the esteemed curator is vacationing?'

'You can ask, but I dunno if I'll remember.'

For the first time since I transmigrated into Suhbataar, he felt pleasure. He slipped his gun on to the counter, and clicked off the safety catch. He aimed at the hook suspending the buzzard.

BANG!

The thing crashed to the floor, disintegrating on impact into a cloud of plaster, powder and feathers on impact. The noise of the gunshot chased its own tail through all the empty rooms.

The woman threw her knitting high into the air. With her mouth hanging open I could see how bad her teeth were.

Suhbataar whispered, 'Look, you tapeworm-infested dung-puddle peasant bitch – with bad teeth – here is how our interview works. I ask the questions: and then you answer them. If I feel you are being even the least bit evasive, you will spend the next ten years in shit-smeared prison, in a distant part of our glorious motherland. Do you understand?'

The woman blanched and tried to swallow.

Suhbataar admired his gun. 'I don't believe I heard you.'

She whimpered, 'Yes.'

'Good. Where is Bodoo?'

'He heard that the KGB man was coming. He did a runner. I swear, he didn't say where. Sir, I didn't know you were the KGB man. I swear, I didn't.'

'And where does Bodoo reside in your fine township?'

The woman hesitated.

Suhbataar sighed, and from his jacket pocket pulled out a gold lighter. He set fire to the cardboard No Smoking sign on the counter. The quivering woman, Suhbataar and I watch it shrivel and burn up into a flapping black flap. 'Maybe you want to be locked up and maimed in prison? Maybe you want me to castrate your husband? Maybe you want your children to be taken into care by a Muslim-run orphanage in Bayan Olgii with a nasty reputation for child abuse?'

Beads of sweat sprang up through her mascara. Idly, Suhbataar considered ramming her head through the glass counter, but I interceded. She scribbled an address on the margin of her newspaper, and handed it over. 'He lives there with his daughter, sir.'

'Thank you.' Suhbataar yanked the phone line out of the wall. 'Have a nice day.'

Suhbataar circled the house. A prefabricated little place on the edge of town with only one door. There was a barrel for rainwater, which falls ten times in a good year, and an optimistic herb garden. Suhbataar ground some lavender between his thumb and forefinger. The wind was loud and dusty. My host pulled out his gun and knocked. I clicked the safety catch on without Suhbataar noticing.

The door was opened by Bodoo's daughter. A boyish-looking girl in her late teens. We note that my host is expected. Suhbataar guessed that she was alone in the house.

'Let's keep this painless,' said Suhbataar. 'You know who I am and what I want. Where is your father?'

This girl had attitude. 'You don't really expect me just to turn in my own father? Without even knowing the charge?'

Suhbataar smiled. Something in the dark hole was humming. His eyes ran over the girl's body and imagined slashing it. He stepped forward, gripping her forearm.

But for once Suhbataar was not going to get what he wants.

I implanted an overwhelming desire to drive to Copenhagen via Baghdad into Suhbataar's mind, and made him throw his wallet containing several hundred dollars at Bodoo's daughter's feet. I transmigrated through the young woman's forearm. It was difficult – the girl's defences were high and thick, and she was about to scream.

I was in. I clamped the scream shut. We watched the dreaded KGB agent throw money at her feet, spring into his Toyota and drive west at breakneck speed. My order might not get Suhbataar quite as far as Caspar's flowerbeds, but it should take him clear of Dalanzadgad, and into a displeased border patrol in a volatile country where nobody spoke Russian or Mongolian.

My new host watched Suhbataar's car disappear. Dust hung in the desert air, and blew away.

I saw her name, Baljin. A dead mother. There! *The three animals who think about the fate of the world.* A different version, but the same story. Her mother is weaving by firelight, on the far side of the room. Baljin is safe and warm. The loom clanks.

Now all I had to do was find out where the story is from. I overrode Baljin's relief and took us into her father's study, which was also his bedroom and the dining room. Baljin was her father's amanuensis, and accompanied him on fieldwork. The notes for his book were in the drawer. No good! Bodoo had taken them with him when he fled.

I laid Baljin down on the bed and closed down her consciousness while I searched her memory for the origin of the tale. In what town is it still known and told? I spent half the afternoon searching, but Baljin's only certainty is that her father knows.

So where was Bodoo? Yesterday he had left for his brother's ger, two hours' ride west of Dalandzadgad. Unless he received an all-clear message from Baljin by noon today he would depart for Bayanhongor, five hundred kilometres north-west across the desert. I woke Baljin, and looked at her watch. It was already three. I assured her the danger had passed, that the KGB do not want to question her father about anything, and that he can be contacted safely and told to come home. I waited for Baljin to choose the next logical step.

We needed to borrow a horse, or maybe a motorbike.

Two hours later we were thirty kilometres west of Dalandzadgad in a sketchy village known only in the local dialect as 'The bend in the river'. Baljin found her uncle, Bodoo's brother, repairing his jeep. I had missed Bodoo by five hours. He had left before noon, believing that the KGB must have reopened the file on his part in the democracy demonstrations. Baljin told her uncle about the wallet thrown at her feet. Bodoo's brother, a tough herder who can wrestle rams to the ground and slit their throats in ten seconds, laughed. He stopped laughing when Baljin gave him half the money. This would feed his family for a year.

We could go after Bodoo in the jeep, if we can get it working. I transmigrated, and, with Jargal Chinzoreg's

543

automative knowledge, started re-assembling the engine.

Evening came before I got the engine working, so we decided to wait until dawn of the following day. Baljin brought her uncle a cup of *airag*. In the cold river children were swimming and women were washing clothes. The river flowed from springs at the feet of the Gov'-Altai Mountains, born of winter snow. The sunset smelt of cooking. Baljin's niece was practising the *shudraga*, a long-necked lute. An old man was summoning goats. How I envy these humans their sense of belonging.

Some Men arrived on horseback from the town, hungry for news. They had learned of Suhbataar's visit the day before on the truck drivers' grapevine. They sat around the fire as Baljin told the story yet again, and an impromptu party got going. The younger men showed off their horsemanship to Baljin. Baljin was respected as one of the finest archers in all Dalandzadgad, male or female, and she was unbetrothed, and the daughter of a government employee. Baljin's aunt made some fresh *airag*, stirring mare's milk into fermented milk. The mares were grazed on the previous autumn's *taana* grass, which makes the best *airag*. It grew dark, and fires were lit.

'Tell us a story, Aunt Baljin,' says my host's eight-year-old. 'You know the best ones.'

'How come?' says a little snotty boy.

'Because of grandpa Bodoo's book, stupid. My Aunt Baljin helped him write it, didn't you, Aunt Baljin?'

'What book?' says Snotty.

'The book of stories, stupid.'

'What stories?'

'You are so *facile*!' The girl exhibits her recent acquisition. 'Aunt Baljin, tell us *The Camel and the Deer*.'

Baljin smiles. She has a lovely smile.

Now; long, long ago, the camel had antlers. Beautiful twelve-pronged antlers. And not only antlers! The camel also had a long, thick tail, lustrous as your hair, my darling.

'What's "lustous"?' asks Snotty.

'Shut up, stupid, or Aunt Baljin will stop, won't you Aunt Baljin?'

At that time the deer had no antlers. It was bald, and to be truthful rather ugly. And as for the horse, the horse had no lovely tail, either. Just a short little stumpy thing.

One day the camel went to drink at the lake. He was charmed by the beauty of his reflection. 'How magnificent!' thought the camel. 'What a gorgeous beast am I!'

Just then, who should come wandering out of the forest, but the deer? The deer was sighing.

'What's the matter with you?' asked the camel. 'You've got a face like a wet sun.'

'I was invited to the animals' feast, as the guest of honour.'

'You can't beat a free nosh-up,' said the camel.

'How can I go with a forehead as bare and ugly as mine? The tiger will be there, with her beautiful coat. And the eagle, with her swanky feathers. Please, camel, just for two or three hours, lend me your antlers. I promise I'll give them back. First thing tomorrow morning.'

'Well,' said the camel, magnanimously. 'You do look pretty dreadful the way you are, I agree. I'll take pity on you. Here you are.' And the camel took off the antlers, and gave them to the deer, who pranced off. 'And mind you don't spill any, er, berry juice on them or whatever it is you forest animals drink at these do's.'

The deer met the horse.

'Hey,' said the horse. 'Nice antlers.'

'Yes, they are, aren't they?' replied the deer. 'The camel gave them to me.'

'Mmmm,' mused the horse. 'Maybe the camel will give me something, too, if I ask nicely.'

The camel was still at the lake, drinking, and looking at the desert moon.

'Good evening, my dear camel. I was wondering, would you swap your beautiful tail with me for the evening? I'm going to see this finely built young filly I know, and she's long

been an admirer of yours. I know she'd simply melt if I turned up in her paddock wearing your tail.'

The camel was flattered. 'Really? An admirer? Very well, let's swap tails. But be sure to bring it back first thing tomorrow morning. And be sure you don't spill any erm, never mind, just look after it, all right? It's the most beautiful tail in creation.'

Since then many days and years have passed, but the deer still hasn't given back the camel's antlers, and you can see for yourself that the horse still gallops over the plains with the camel's tail streaming in the wind. And some people say, when the camel comes to drink at the lake he sees his bare, ugly reflection, and snorts, and forgets his thirst. And have you noticed how the camel stretches his neck and gazes into the distance, to a far-off sand dune or a distant mountain top? That's when he's thinking, 'When is the horse going to give me back his tail? And how about my antlers?' And that is why he is always so sad.

Dust-devils bounced off the shell of the jeep like kangaroos. Nothing amongst these rocks but scorpions and mirages, for the length and breadth of the morning.

Bodoo's brother stopped in an isolated ger. A camel was tethered outside, but nobody was around. As Gobi etiquette permits, my host entered, prepared some food, and drank some water. The owner's camel snorted like a human. A warning flared up from my host's unconscious, but it went before I could locate its source. The wind was strong but the world was silent. There was little to blow against, or in, or through.

We got back into the jeep. Gazelles darted through the distance, flocks of them turning like minnows in a river. Bodoo's brother drove down the Valley of the Vulture's Mouth, where we stopped at a store for enough provisions and petrol to get us to Bayanhungoor. Bodoo had passed through early that morning. We were catching him up.

Hawks circled high. One of the last Gobi bears shambled along the fringe of forest. There are less than a hundred left.

Bodoo's brother slept in the jeep, under several blankets. It gets cold at night, even in summer. Dreams came, of bones and stones with holes.

The next day, the dunes: the longest running for eight miles, swelling and rolling, grain by grain. Bodoo's brother sang songs that lasted for miles, with no beginning and no end. The dunes of the dead. There were bones, and stones with holes.

There was a stationary jeep in the shimmering distance. Bodoo's brother pulled up to it, and cut his engine. A figure was asleep under a makeshift canopy slung over the back.

'Are you all right, stranger? Are you in need of any help? Any water?'

'Yes,' says the figure, suddenly sitting up and showing his face, chewing gum. 'I need your jeep. Mine seems to have broken down.' At point-blank range Punsalmaagiyn Suhbataar fires his handgun twice, a bullet for each of my host's eyes.

Nobody replies. Firelight without colour. Outside must be night, if there is an outside. I am hostless and naked. The faces all stare in the same direction, all of them all of their ages. One of them coughs. It is Bodoo's brother, his eye wounds already healed. I try to transmigrate into him, but I cannot inhabit a shadow. I've never known silence. By being what I am, I thought I understood almost everything. But I understand almost nothing.

A figure rises and leaves the ger through a curtain. So simple? I follow the figure. 'I'm sorry, I'm afraid you can't come through here.' A girl I hadn't noticed, no older than eight, delicate and tiny as an ancient woman.

'Will you stop me?'

'No. If there is a door for you, you are free to pass through.' Wrens flutter.

I touch the wall. There is no door. 'Where is it?'

She shrugs, biting her lip. 'Then what shall I do?' A swan inspects the ground. She shrugs.

*

547

Tallow candles spit and hiss. These few guests are many multitudes. Thousands of angels swim in a thimble. From time to time one of the guests stands up, and walks through the not-there way out. The wall of the ger yields, and re-seals behind them, like a wall of water. I try to leave with them, but for me it never even bends.

The monk in a saffron robe sighs. He wears a yellow hat that arcs forward. 'I'm having some problems with my teeth.'

'I'm sorry to hear that,' I say. The little girl mutters to her twitchy marmot.

Horses galloping by, or thunder? The swan spreads its wings and flies up through the roof. Bodoo's brother has gone through the door.

'But why can't I pass through? The others have.'

The little girl is playing cat's cradle with a length of twine, knitting her brow. 'You chose not to.'

'I chose nothing.'

'All your tribe leave your body while it still breathes.'

'What do you mean, my *tribe*?'

The monk with the yellow hat is here, humming through his broken mouth. He whispers in her ear, she stares at me distrustfully. 'Very well,' she concurs. 'The circumstances are uncommon, but what can I do?'

The monk turns to me. 'I'm sorry – my teeth.' A prophet's nod. 'Time has gone around, the years are cold and far away . . . I kept my promise,' and he, too, passes through the wall of the ger.

Last to leave is the little girl, carrying her marmot. She feels sorry for me, and I don't want her to go. I'm all alone.

I was in a human host again, and the walls of the ger were living, pulsing with viscera and worry and nearby voices. I explored the higher rooms, but found nothing! No memories, no experiences. Not even a name. Barely an 'I'. Where were those voices coming from? I looked deeper. There were whispers, and a suffusion of purposeful well-being. I tried to open my host's eyes to see where I was, but the eyes would not open. I checked that there were eyes – yes, but my host had never learned to open them, and couldn't respond to my action. I was in a place unlike any other, yet my host didn't know where. Or rather, my host didn't know anywhere else. A blind mute? The mind was pure. So very pure, I was afraid for it.

The well-being transformed into palpitating fear. Had I been detected? The knot of pain was being pulled tight. Panic, such panic I had never known since I butchered the mind of my first host. The curtain was ripped, and my host emerged into the world between her mother's legs, screaming with indignation. The cold air! The light, even through my eyelids, made my host's tender brain chime.

I transferred into my host's mother along the umbilical cord, and the depth of emotion is sheer and giddy. I forgot to insulate and I was swept away by joy, and relief, and loss, and gain, and emptiness, and fulfilment, a memory of swimming, and the claw-sharp, bloodied love, and the conviction that she would never again put herself through this agony.

But I have work to do.

Another ger. Firelight, warmth, and the shadows of antlers. I searched for our location. Well. Good news and bad. My new host was a Mongolian in Mongolia. But I was far to the north of where Bodoo was last heading, not far from the Russian border. I was in the province of Renchinhumbe, near the lake of Tsagaan Nuur, and the town of Zoolon. It was September now and the snows would be coming soon. The midwife was the grandmother of the baby I just left, she was smiling down at her daughter, anaesthetising the umbilical cord with a lump of ice. Her hair cobwebby, her face moon-like. An aunt bustled about in the background with pans of warm water and squares of cloth and fur, chanting. This flat and quiet song is the only sound.

It is the early hours of the morning. The mother's labour had been long and hard. I dulled her pain, put her into a deep sleep, and set about helping her unstitched body repair itself.

As my host slept I had time to wonder where I had been since Suhbataar. Had I hallucinated the strange ger? But how could I have? I *am* my mind – do I have a mind I don't know about within my mind, like humans? And how was I reborn in Mongolia? Why, and by whom? Who was the monk in the yellow hat?

How do I know that there aren't *noncorpi* living within *me*, controlling *my* actions? Like a virus within a bacteria? Surely I would know.

But that's exactly what humans think.

The door opened and an autumn sunrise came in, with the baby's father, grandparents, cousins and friends and aunts and uncles. They had slept in a neighbouring ger and now crowd back into their home, excited and eager to welcome their newest relative. When they speak I have great difficulty understanding – I have a new dialect of Mongolian to learn. The mother is glowing with tired happiness. The baby bawls, and the elders look on.

I left the mother, and transmigrated into her husband, as they kissed. His tribe was known to Baljin as the reindeer people. Reindeer are their food, currency and clothing. They are semi-nomadic. A few of the men visit Zoolon several times a year to exchange meat and hides for supplies, and to sell powdered reindeer antler to Chinese merchants who market it in their country as an aphrodisiac: other than this there is little contact with the rest of the world. When the Russians were creating a proletariat in this feudal country, the reindeer people had proved impossible even to find, much less conduct a census among. Later, when the local Buddhist clergy was being liquidated, the reindeer people just vanished into the forest and snow and one of the harshest climates on Earth.

My host is only twenty, and his heart is brimming over with pride. I'm rarely envious of humans, but I am now. I am, and always shall be, wholly sterile. I have no genes to pass on. For my new host, his offspring is the last bridge into manhood, and will increase his status with his peers and his ancestors. A son would have been preferable, but there will be other births.

I notice his name, Beebee. He lights a cigarette, and leaves the ger. I envy the simplicity of his expectations. He knows how to ride reindeers, and how to skin them, and which of their organs, eaten raw, assist which aspect of human physiology. Beebee knows many legends, but not one about three animals who think about the fate of the world.

The night ebbed away, the dawn dripped into a pool of light, and the shadows in the pine trees around the village murmured. An early riser's footfalls crunched in the heavy frost. His head was hooded, and his teeth shone. A late shooting star crossed the sky.

Well, what now?

Nothing about my quest had changed. Bodoo was still the only lead I had. I had to get back south, to the town of Bayanhongor. If I can access the museum network, it should be fairly easy to track him down. Three months had passed since he had fled Suhbataar. This setback would cost me time, but immortals don't lack time.

I told Beebee's grandmother-midwife that Beebee had some business in town that day. I hated to separate the young father from his baby daughter, but the grandmother gladly shooed us away. Men get in the way.

Beebee and his eldest brother rode through forests, between hewn mountains, along narrow lakes. Fishing boats, willows, and wild geese flying up and down the morning. An ibex stands on a hill-crest. I learn from Beebee about the moose, elk, lynx, argali sheep, wolves and wild boars living there, and how they can be trapped. We see a bear fishing in a river thrashing with salmon. Sharp rainbows, misty sunshine. There are no roads, but the freezing night firmed the mud and so the going is easy.

Beebee and his brother discuss the new baby, and her name. I wonder about kinship. For my Mongolian hosts, the family is the ger, to be protected in, to be healed in, to be born in, to make love in, and to die in. A parasite, I could experience all of these, second-hand, but I could never be *of* these.

Unless, perhaps . . . This hope keeps me going.

Zoolon was another decrepit town of wooden shacks, concrete blocks, and dead lorries rusting in shallow pools where dogs drank. A power station churned smoke into the perfect sky. Another ghost factory with saplings growing from the chimney stack. A few squat apartment blocks. A crowd had gathered around the small corrugated shack that served as the town's only restaurant. Beebee usually drank there after trading with the tannery owner.

'Some foreigners in town,' a bearded hunter told Beebee. 'Roundeyes.'

'Russians from over the border? Anything new to trade?'

'Nah. Others.'

Beebee walked into the restaurant, and I saw Caspar poking at something on his plate with a fork, and Sherry poring over a map with a compass.

'It's good to see you!' I speak before I think. Townsmen in the restaurant stare amazed. Nobody knew this nomad could speak any language other than a reindeer-flavoured dialect of Mongolian.

'G'day,' replies Sherry, looking up. Caspar's eyes are more guarded.

'How are you enjoying the country?' This is very indulgent. I have to dampen and then erase Beebee's shock at hearing himself speak in a language he's never learned.

'It's beautiful,' Caspar and Sherry say at exactly the same time.

'Full of surprises. Anyway. Enjoy the rest of your stay. I'd advise you to get somewhere warmer before winter sets in . . . Somewhere nearer the ocean. Vietnam can be beautiful in November, up in the hill country, at least it was . . .'

Beebee sat down, and ordered a plate of food while waiting for his brother. His tribe exchanges reindeer meat for credit with the restaurant owner. I picked up the three-week-old newspaper from Ulan Bator. Beebee himself was illiterate: his dialect has no written form, and his tribe has no schools. No news. Whitewashing, whitehousing, a belated report on the national day festival: none of it meant much to Beebee. He rarely left his tribe, had never left the province, and had no wish to. I was turning past the obituary page when an article caught my eye: *Double Tragedy for Mongolian Culture.*

Bodoo was dead.

I rarely feel despair, I forget how it gouges.

Both brothers had died in the same week of a heart attack, which I knew from Suhbataar was one of the Mongolian KGB's favourite ways to dispose of political liabilities. *This tragedy was made more poignant by the imminent publication of the professor's life-work, an anthology of Mongolian folk stories. Out of deference to our national father of anthropology, we include one story below, retold by the professor.*

I should have sent Suhbataar over a cliff. Damn him. And damn me.

A hand slapped down on Beebee's shoulder. My host's hand slid to the hilt of his hunting knife. The drunk man swayed. His breath made Beebee flinch. 'What are you pretending to read the newspaper for, Reindeer Man? Where were you when *I* was fighting for democracy? That's what I want to know.' His pupils were huge, and his eyelids red. 'You can't read Cyrillic. You can't read Mongolian. And it sure ain't written in reindeer. Where were you when I was fighting for communism? That's what I want to know. Go on, read for me, then, antler-head.' Then he bellowed. 'Oy! Vodka! It's story-time . . .'

I was back to where I had started. I was frustrated enough to transmigrate into this wino and hurl him through the wall, but what would be the point? I read the story. I owed it to Bodoo.

A long time ago, in the days of the Buriat nation, Khori

553

Tumed was walking along the south shore of Lake Baikal. Winter was melting from the birch trees, and Khori Tumed gazed at the distant mountains, snowcapped and turquoise over the lake.

Presently, nine swans came flying in a circle from the north-east. Khori Tumed hid behind a willow, for fear of enchantment. And sure enough, when the swans alighted on the lakeside, they turned into nine girls. Each one was beautiful, with pale skin and slender limbs and long dark hair. They undressed, and draped their white gowns in the very willow tree that concealed Khori Tumed. Khori Tumed fell in love with all of them, and he stole one of the gowns. After the girls had finished bathing they returned to the willow tree. Eight put on their garments, became swans, and rose in a circle, flying further and further away. The ninth was left running around, looking desperately for her gown.

At length she found Khori Tumed huddled amongst the roots of the willow, clutching her dress. 'Please give me back my dress.'

'I can't do that, I am in love with you,' said the young man. 'Please, marry me. When summer comes I will give you gowns of finest silk from China, and skin of bears will keep you warm when the snows return.'

The swan girl saw that she had to accept, or freeze to death that very night. 'I will go with you, mortal, but be warned. If sons are born to us, I will never tell you their names, and thus they will never cross the threshold into manhood.' So she returned to Khori Tumed's ger and his tribe, and became his wife. And in time, she came to love the precocious young hunter, and they lived in happiness together. Eleven sons were born to them, but the swan girl was bound by her promise, and never blessed Khori Tumed's sons with names. And sometimes, especially at evening, she would gaze towards the north-east, and at these times Khori Tumed knew she was thinking of her sisters, and her homeland beyond the winter sunrise.

One day at the end of autumn, when the forests were dancing and dying, Khori Tumed was gutting a young ewe, while his wife sat embroidering a quilt. Their eleven fine, but nameless sons were out hunting.

'Husband, do you remember my swan's robe?' asked the girl.

'Yes,' replied Khori Tumed, stirring the stew.

'Would you let me try it on again? I want to see if it still fits.'

'And see you fly off again? What do you take me for? A marmot-brain?'

'No, my love . . . I just want to see if it still fits. If I wanted to leave now, I could do so by merely walking out of the ger.'

She was smiling, and Khori Tumed's resolve melted. 'Very well,' but as a precaution he bolted the door. He unlocked the chest, and gave the swan's robe to his wife, who slipped into it as she sat on the bed.

There was a frantic beating of wild wings, and the mighty swan flew around the ger, and up through the flap in the ger's roof, which Khori Tumed had left open for the cooking smoke, and which he had forgotten to seal. With a sooty pot holder, Khori Tumed just managed to catch hold of one of the swan's feet. 'No, my love, come back to me! Please!'

'My husband, my time with you is over. My sisters are calling for me from our country, where dawn spills from the north-east . . . I must leave now, my mortal beloved.'

'Tell me the names of our sons, so that they may in time become men!'

And so the swan girl named the sons: Khovduud, Galzut, Khuaitsai, Khalbin, Batnai, Khudai, Gushid, Tsagaan, Sharaid, Bodonguud and Caragana. And the swan circled above the tribe's gers three times to bless all who lived there, they say.

Thus, the Khori Tumeds were such people, and the eleven sons became eleven fathers.

The drunk's eyes had closed and his face had drooped into his plate of lukewarm meatballs. Three young children sat on the other side of the table, entranced by the story. Beebee remembered his new daughter. I looked at Bodoo's picture in the newspaper, and wondered who he really had been, this man I had only known through the memories of others.

The restaurant was emptying, and the conversation reverted to recent wrestling matches. The sight of two round-eyes eating was only gossipworthy for so long. I watched the way Sherry whispered something to Caspar, and I watched the smile spread over Caspar's face, and I knew they were lovers.

This venture was futile. To look for the source of a story is to look for a needle in a sea. I should transmigrate into Sherry or Caspar, and resume my search for *noncorpi*.

The bearded hunter walked in with his gun. The memory of being shot flashed back, but the hunter leant the rifle against the wall, and sat down next to Beebee. He started dismantling it, and cleaning the parts one by one with an oily rag.

'Beebee, right? Of the Reindeer Tribe of Lake Tsagaan Nuur?'

'Yes.'

'With a new baby daughter?'

'Arrived last night.'

'Your ger needs you,' said the hunter. 'I met your sister at the market just now. She's looking for you, with your brother. Your wife's hysterical and your daughter's dying.'

Beebee cursed himself for coming to town. I wanted to beg his forgiveness. I thought about transmigrating into the hunter, and from him back into Caspar or Sherry, but my guilt made me stay. Maybe I could help with his baby's illness if we got back in time.

I've often thought about that moment. Had I transmigrated, everything would have been different. But I stayed, and Beebee ran back to the market-place.

Dusk was sluggish with cold when we reached Beebee's encampment. The breath of the yaks hung white in the twilight. From far up the valley we heard the wind. It sounded to me like a wolf, but all reindeer people know the difference.

Beebee's ger was full of dark shapes, lamps, steam and worry. A bitter oil was burning in a silver dish. The grandmother was preparing a ritual. Beebee's wife was pale in her bed, cradling the baby, both with wide unblinking eyes. She looked at Beebee, 'Our baby hasn't spoken.'

The grandmother spoke in hushed tones. 'Your daughter's soul was born loose. Unless I can summon it back she will be dead by midnight.'

'At the hospital back in Zoolon, there's a doctor there, trained in East Germany in the old days –'

'Don't be a fool, Beebee! I've seen it happen too often before. You and that mumbo-jumbo foreign medicine. It's not a matter of medicine! Her soul's been untethered. It's a matter of magic!'

He looked at his limp daughter, and began to despair. 'What do you intend to do?'

'I shall perform the rites. Hold this dish. I need your blood.'

The grandmother pulled out a curved hunting knife. Beebee was not afraid of knives or blood. As the grandmother washed his palm I transmigrated into the old woman, intending to transfer into the baby to see the problem for myself.

I got no further.

I found something I had never seen in any human mind: a canyon of another's memories, running across her mind. I saw it straight away, like a satellite passing over. I entered it, and as I did so I entered my own past.

There are three animals, says the monk in the yellow hat, *who think about the fate of the world*. I am a boy aged eight. I have my own body! We are in a prison cell, smaller than a wardrobe, lit by light from a tiny grille in one corner, the size of a hand. Even though my height is not yet four feet, I cannot stand up. I've been in here a week and I haven't eaten for two days. Our excrement stinks from its corner. A man in a nearby box has lost his mind and wails through a broken throat. The only thing I can see through the grille is another grille in a neighbouring coffin.

It is 1937. Comrade Choibalsan's social engineering policies, a carbon copy of Josef Stalin's in distant Moscow, are in full swing. There are show trials staged everyweek in Ulan Bator. Several thousand agents of the impending Japanese invasion from Manchuria have been executed. The Minister for Transport has been sentenced to death for conspiring to cause traffic accidents. The dismantling of the monasteries is almost complete. First the taxes were sent skywards, and then began 're-education'. I and my master have been found guilty of Feudal Indoctrination. We were told this by the hand that brings us water, some days ago. We, also, are to be re-educated.

'I'm afraid, master,' I say.

'Then I shall tell you a story,' says the monk.

'Will they shoot us?'

'Yes.' It hurts my master to speak. His teeth were rifle-butted into spiky fragments.

'I don't want to die.' I think of my mother and father. My mother and father! Lowly herders, who worked their knuckles to the bone to bribe their son's way into a monastery. Five years later their ambition signed his death warrant.

'You won't die. I promised your father you wouldn't die, and you won't.'

'But they killed the others.'

'Listen. They won't kill *you*. Now listen! There are three animals who think about the fate of the world . . .'

The sky is thick with crows. Their noise is deafening. Stones are being broken. I, my master, and about forty other monks and their novices are taken over a field littered with naked corpses. The ground is blotched with coagulating crimson. Those who cannot walk are dragged. Beside a copse of trees the firing squad is waiting. The soldiers are a roughshod band: this is not the regular Red Army. Many of them are brigands from the Chinese border, who become soldiers when times are lean. There are some children, brought here to dig mass graves, and to watch the executions of us counter-revolutionaries as part of their socialist education. My own brothers and sisters have already been dispersed all over Mongolia.

Wild dogs look on from a pile of rocks.

We wait while the Soviet officer strolls over to the mercenaries who will do the killing. They discuss the logistics of the execution as though they are talking about planting a field. They actually laugh.

The master is intoning a mantra. I wish he would stop. I am numb with fear.

There is a girl standing in the mouth of a ger, making tea. Domesticity, here and now, is dreamlike. My master abruptly breaks off his mantra and summons her. She hesitates, but she comes. Her eyes are big, and her face is round. My master touches me with his left hand, and touches her with his right hand and I feel my memories drawn away on the current.

My master knew how to transmigrate me. My mind is untethered and begins to follow my memories – but at that moment a soldier slams my master's arm away from the girl, and the connection is broken, and the girl is kicked away.

This girl's own memories piece together my last minute of life. We watch the boy – myself – we watch the master chanting. Even as the barrels of the guns are levelled –

Everything moves so slowly. The air thickens, and sets, hard. Every gleam is polished. An order is given in Russian. The rifles go off like firecrackers. The row of men and boys folds and topples.

There is one thing more. This the girl cannot see, but I know how to look. The boy's body is in the mud, too, its small cranium shattered, but with an unmoored mind. I can see it! Adrift, pulsing. One of the mercenaries strolls over to the pile of bodies, lifting the bodies on top with his foot to ensure the ones underneath are dead. He touches the boy, and in that instant my anima pulses into its new home.

Many years later it would stir, unable to identify itself, long after its host, this hapless mercenary, had returned to his native corner of China, at the foot of the Holy Mountain.

That is the end.

The present. The grandmother is motionless. I would have liked to have read her life, how she was sent away to a far corner of Mongolia, how she was married into a tribe of strangers. But there was no time.

'I am here.'

'Well, I didn't think it was Leonid Brezhnev poking around in there,' says the grandmother. 'It's about time! I saw the comet.'

'You know about me?'

'Of course I know about you! I've been carrying your early memories around with me for all these decades! Rumours of the Sect of the Yellow Hat were common currency in my tribe. When your master linked us on your execution day, I knew what he was doing . . . I've been waiting.'

'It was a long journey. The only clues were in my memories, and you had those.'

'My body should have ground to a halt winters ago. I've tried to die several times, but I was never allowed through . . .'

I looked down at the baby, 'Is she going to die?'

'That depends on you.'

'I don't understand.'

'My granddaughter's body is *your* body. She was born with *you* as her soul and mind. She is a shell. Her body will stop within three hours if you don't return to her. If you want her to survive, you have to choose to be shackled by flesh once more.'

I considered my future as a *noncorpo*. Nowhere in the world would be closed to me. I could seek out other *noncorpi*, the company of immortals. I could transmigrate into presidents, astronauts, messiahs. I could plant a garden on a mountainside under camphor trees. I would never grow old, get sick, fear death, die.

I looked down at the feeble day-old body in front of me, her metabolism dimming, minute by minute. Life expectancy in Central Asia is forty-three, and falling.

'Touch her.'

Outside, bats dangle from the high places, fluttering up to the sky, and down to the ground, and up to the sky again, checking that all was well. Inside, my wail, screamed from the hollows of my eighteen-hour-old lungs, fills the ger.

Biographical Notes

Jeffrey Archer was educated at Brasenose College, Oxford, and has published ten novels (of which the most recent, *The Eleventh Commandment*, appeared in May 1998), four collections of short stories and two plays. His work is published in sixty-four countries and twenty-one languages. He was elected MP for Louth at the age of twenty-nine, was Deputy Chairman of the Conservative Party 1985–86, and was made a Life Peer in 1992.

Simon Armitage was born in 1963 and lives in Huddersfield, West Yorkshire. His latest publications are *The Dead Sea Poems* (1995), *Moon Country* (1996), and *Cloud Cuckooland* (1997). He has written extensively for radio and TV and his prose memoir *All Points North* was published by Penguin in 1998.

Julian Barnes was born in Leicester in 1946. He is the author of seven novels, among them *Metroland*, *Flaubert's Parrot* and *A History of the World in Ten and a Half Chapters*, and a collection of essays, *Letters from London*. His latest novel, *England, England*, appeared last September. He is the first Englishman to have won both the Prix Médicis and the Prix Fémina, and in 1988 he was made a Chevalier de l'Ordre des Arts et des Lettres. His work has been translated into more than thirty languages.

Elizabeth Berridge has published nine novels and two short story collections. *Across the Common* was serialised twice on radio, won the Yorkshire Post Literary Prize and is read by Sian Phillips on audio-cassette, as is her latest novel, *Touch and Go*. She edited Elizabeth Barrett Browning's early and only Diary for publication by John Murray and is a Fellow of the Royal Society of Literature. She is currently preparing a collection of short stories, which she prefers to novels.

William Boyd was born in Accra, Ghana, in 1952. He is the author of two collections of short stories and seven novels, the latest of which is *Armadillo* (1998). His stories and novels have been published round the world and have been translated into over two dozen languages. He divides his time between London and south-west France.

A. S. Byatt's first novel, *The Shadow of the Sun*, appeared in 1964, followed by *The Game* (1967), *The Virgin in the Garden* (1978), *Still Life* (1985), *Possession* (1990, winner of the Booker Prize for Fiction), *Angels and Insects* (1992) and *Babel Tower* (1996). She has published four collections of stories, *Sugar and Other Stories* (1987), *The Matisse Stories* (1994), *The Djinn in the Nightingale's Eye* (1994) and *Elementals: Tales of Fire and Ice* (1998). A volume of critical essays, *Passions of the Mind*, appeared in 1991.

Billy Childish left school at sixteen, an undiagnosed dyslexic. He is a prolific painter, poet and song-writer and over twenty years has published over thirty collections of poetry, recorded seventy full-length LPs and produced over 1,000 paintings. His second novel, *Notebooks of a Naked Youth*, was published in November 1997. The poem published in this volume received a commendation in the 1997 National Poetry Competition.

Lana Citron is a history graduate of Trinity College, Dublin now living and working in London. Recent publications include *Sucker*, her first novel, and short stories *The Kiss Hoarder* printed in Waterstone's *Book of Light* and *The*

Craic Run appearing in the anthology *Shananigans*. She is currently working on her second novel.

Rachel Cusk was born in 1967 and has written three novels: *Saving Agnes* (1993), *The Temporary* (1995) and *The Country Life* (1997). She won the Whitbread First Novel Award in 1993 and a Somerset Maugham Award in 1998.

Louis de Bernières was born in 1954, and is now a full-time writer. He is the author of *The War of Don Emmanuel's Nether Parts*, *Señor Vivo and the Coca Lord* (Commonwealth Writers Prize, Eurasia Region, 1992), *The Troublesome Offspring of Cardinal Guzman* and *Captain Corelli's Mandolin* (Commonwealth Writers Prize, 1995).

Isobel Dixon was born in 1969 in South Africa and studied English and Xhosa language and literature at Stellenbosch University, then went to explore her Scottish roots, completing Masters' degrees in modernist literature and applied linguistics at Edinburgh. She now lives in Cambridge and works in London as a literary agent.

Patricia Duncker teaches writing at the University of Wales, Aberystwyth. Her first novel, *Hallucinating Foucault* (1996), won the Dillons First Fiction Award and the McKitterick Prize and has been translated into seven languages. Her most recent publication is a collection of short fiction, *Monsieur Shoushana's Lemon Trees* (1997). Her novel about the nineteenth-century transvestite colonial doctor, *James Miranda Barry*, will be published in 1999. 'Stalker' is one of a series of Gothic tales dealing with violence and sexuality.

Christopher Emery was born in 1963 and studied painting and printmaking at Leeds. His poems have appeared in numerous magazines, including the *Honest Ulsterman*, *Oxford Poetry*, *PN Review*, *Poetry Wales* and *The Rialto*. He is currently working on two collections, *Scally* and *Perfect*

Dust. He is Production Manager of Cambridge University Press.

David Flusfeder was born in 1960. He is the author of *Man Kills Woman* (1993) and *Like Plastic* (1996) which won the Encore Award. 'The Case of Solomon Heller' is an extract from a new novel, *Morocco*, to be published in January 2000. He lives in London.

Michael Foley was born in Northern Ireland in 1947. He has published three collections of poetry (*True Life Love Stories*, *The GO Situation* and *Insomnia in the Afternoon*) and two novels (*The Passion of Jamesie Coyle* and *The Road to Notown*). His most recent novel, *Getting Used to not Being Remarkable*, was published last September.

Esther Freud was born in 1963. She trained as an actress and has worked in theatre and television as both an actress and a writer. She has written three novels, *Hideous Kinky* (recently made into a feature film starring Kate Winslet), *Peerless Flats* (of which an extract appeared in *New Writing 2*) and *Gaglow*. She lives in London.

Lavinia Greenlaw was born in 1962 in London, where she still lives. She has published two collections, *Night Photograph* (1993) and *A World Where News Travelled Slowly* (1997), the title poem of which won a 1997 Forward Prize. These poems are from a sequence she has written about the architecture of London Zoo.

Philip Hensher was born in 1965. His novels are *Other Lulus*, *Kitchen Venom* (which won the Somerset Maugham Award) and *Pleasured*. A selection of his short stories will be published later this year as *The Bedroom of the Mister's Wife*. He wrote the libretto to Thomas Ades's opera, *Powder Her Face*, which has been performed across the world and is now available on EMI. He lives in South London and East Berlin.

Michael Hofmann was born in Freiburg in 1957 and lives in London and Gainesville, Florida. He has published three books of poems; a fourth, *Approximately Nowhere*, is due later this year, along with a book of essays. Among his numerous translations are novels by Franz Kafka, Wolfgang Koeppen and Joseph Roth.

Michael Hulse grew up in Stoke-on-Trent and Germany and works in publishing and TV in Cologne. His poetry collections include *Knowing and Forgetting* (1981), *Propaganda* (1985), *Eating Strawberries in the Necropolis* (1991) and *Mother of Battles* (1991). He co-edited *The New Poetry* (1993) and has won the National Poetry Competition and Eric Gregory and Cholmondeley Awards.

Liz Jensen was born in Oxfordshire in 1959, and has worked as a journalist in the Far East, as a sculptor in France and as a radio producer in Britain. Her short stories have appeared in various anthologies, and been broadcast on radio. Her first novel, *Egg Dancing*, was published in 1995 and her second, *Ark Baby*, was shortlisted for the 1998 *Guardian* Fiction Award.

Emma Kay (born 1961) is an artist who lives and works in London. She studied at Goldsmiths' College and her first solo exhibition, 'Shakespeare from Memory', was held at the Approach Gallery, London, in 1998. She has exhibited in USA, Canada, Belgium, Netherlands and Britain and has published two artists' books: *Paperback* (Toronto, 1997) and an edition of *Bookworks' New Writing* (1999).

A. L. Kennedy has published three collections of short stories, *Night Geometry and the Garscadden Trains*, *Now That You're Back* and *Original Bliss*, and two novels, *Looking for the Possible Dance* and *So I Am Glad*, and has won numerous literary awards. She was listed among the *Granta/ Sunday Times* Twenty Best of Young British Novelists. Her first full-length film, *Stella Does Tricks*, was released in 1998.

Her most recent book, *Everything You Need*, will be published in 1999.

Hari Kunzru lives in London. He writes journalism for publications including the *London Review of Books*, the *Daily Telegraph*, *Wired*, and the *Guardian*. His short fiction has previously been published by Serpents Tail, *Mute* magazine and *Telepolis*. He has just completed *Weekender*, a novel.

Hanif Kureishi was born and brought up in Kent. He read philosophy at King's College, London, where he started to write plays. His films include *My Beautiful Launderette*, *Sammy and Rosie Get Laid*, *London Kills Me* and *My Son the Fanatic*. His first novel, *The Buddha of Suburbia*, won the Whitbread First Novel Award. His other books include *The Black Album*, a collection of short stories, *Love in a Blue Time*, and *Intimacy*. His play, *Sleep With Me*, opens at the National Theatre in April. He lives in west London.

Linda Leatherbarrow is three times 1st Prize winner of the London Writers Competition. Her stories have been published in magazines including *Ambit*, *Cosmopolitan* and *Writing Women*, and in the anthologies *Sleeping Rough* and *The Nerve*. They have also been broadcast on BBC Radio 4. In 1995 she set up the Haringey Literature Festival and co-ordinated it for three years. She teaches at the Mary Ward Centre and the City University and is Reader in Residence for Enfield in the National Year of Reading 1998–9.

Tim Liardet is a poet, critic and tutor originally from London, now living in Shropshire. His work has appeared in many leading literary periodicals, including *London Review of Books*, *New Statesman*, the *Independent*, *Poetry Review*, *Ambit*, *Stand Magazine* and *The Rialto*. His poetry has been broadcast on BBC Radio and anthologised in *The Forward Book of Poetry* and *The Poetry Book Society Anthology*. He has published three collections of poetry: *Clay Hill* (1988),

Fellini Beach (1994) and *Competing with the Piano Tuner* (1998) which is a Poetry Book Society Special Commendation.

Toby Litt was born in 1968. He grew up in Ampthill, Bedfordshire. He has published a book of short stories, *Adventures in Capitalism* (1996), and a novel, *Beatniks* (1997), which he has also adapted as a film script.

Ian McIntyre studied French and Russian at Cambridge and he spent a post-graduate year at the College of Europe in Bruges. After National Service in the Intelligence Corps, he joined the BBC as a talks producer and subsequently presented current affairs programmes. From 1976 to 1978 he was Controller of BBC Radio 4 and, from 1978 to 1987, of Radio 3. His previous biographies were of Robert Burns and John Reith, the BBC's first Director-General. He has also written about the English language, the State of Israel and the civil aircraft industry.

David Malouf is internationally recognised as one of Australia's finest writers. His novels include *Johnno*, *An Imaginary Life*, *Harland's Half Acre*, *The Great World* (which won the Commonwealth Writers Prize and the Prix Fémina Étranger, 1991), *Remembering Babylon*, which was shortlisted for the 1993 Booker Prize and won the first IMPAC Prize, 1996, and *Conversations at Curlow Creek*. He has also written five collections of poetry and three opera libretti. He lives in Sydney.

Pauline Melville's first book of short stories, *Shape-Shifters*, won the *Guardian* Fiction Prize, the Macmillan Silver Pen Award and the Commonwealth Writers Prize for the best first book. *The Ventriloquist's Tale*, her first novel, was published in 1997 and won the Whitbread First Novel Award for 1997. Her second collection of stories, *The Migration of Ghosts*, appeared in 1998.

Claire Messud was born in 1966. Her first novel, *When the World was Steady*, was published in 1994 and was a finalist for the 1996 PEN/Faulkner Award. She reviews for numerous British and American publications, including *The Times*, *The Times Literary Supplement*, *The New York Times* and *The Washington Post*. 'Leaving Algiers' is a chapter from her new novel, *The Last Life*, which will be published by Picador later this year.

David Mitchell was born in Lancashire in 1969, grew up in Worcestershire, studied Comparative Literature at Kent, lived in Sicily, scrubbed about in London and moved to Hiroshima in 1994 where he still lives. *Ghostwritten*, the novel from which 'Mongolia' is taken, will be published by Sceptre in 1999.

Edwin Morgan was born in Glasgow in 1920 and served in the war in Egypt, Palestine and Lebanon. He taught English Literature at Glasgow University, resigning as titular Professor in 1980. His books include *Collected Poems* (1990), *Collected Translations* (1996), *Sweeping Out the Dark* (1994), *Virtual and Other Realities* (1997), a Scots translation of Rostand's *Cyrano de Bergerac* (1992). He has recently collaborated with the jazz musician Tommy Smith on *Beasts of Scotland* (1996), *Planet Wave* (1997) and *Monte Cristo* (1998).

Alex Moseley is twenty-five years old and lives in Sussex. He is currently writing his first novel as well as writing short stories. After that he intends to return to the sherry capital, Jerez de la Frontera, where he can watch bulls in the fields and lizards on the walls. His ambition is to write, listen to flamenco music and keep Irish wolfhounds and a well-stocked cellar.

Paul Muldoon's most recent collection of poems was *Hay* (1998). A book for children, *The Noctuary of Narcissus Batt*, was published in 1997, when he also edited the *Faber Book of Beasts*.

Naeem Murr was born in London to an Irish mother and Lebanese father. He has won fellowships and awards for his fiction and poetry in the United States where he has lived on and off for the past eight years. His first novel, *The Boy*, was published in a number of countries including Britain and America in 1998; he has been working for some years on a novel, *Companions of Fire*, from which 'Sidney's Story' is excerpted.

Clare Naylor was born in 1971 in Yorkshire and studied at London University. She worked as an editorial assistant in publishing until she became a full-time writer two years ago. She is the author of two novels, *Love: A User's Guide*, and *Catching Alice*. She is working on an original screenplay and her third novel. She lives in Hampshire.

Courttia Newland was born in 1973 and brought up in west London. After four years of unemployment he published his first novel, *The Scholar*, in 1997; a book of interlinked short stories set on the Greenside Estate in west London, *Society Within*, will appear in June 1999. He has written numerous short stories and is currently involved in community film making.

Dorothy Nimmo was born in 1932, has been an actress, a wife-and-mother, a gardener, a goatherd and a cook, and is now Warden of the Friends Meeting House in Settle. She started to write in 1980 and has published four books of poems; the most recent, *The Children's Game*, was a Poetry Book Society Recommendation in 1989. She won a Cholmondeley Award in 1987.

Jeff Noon was born in 1957 and studied painting and drama at Manchester University. A few months after leaving university, he won a playwriting competition organised by the Royal Exchange Theatre in Manchester with *Woundings*. *Vurt*, which was published in 1993, won the Arthur C. Clarke Award, and was followed by *Pollen* (1995) *Automated Alice* (1996), *Nymphomation* (1997) and *Pixel Juice* (1998).

Alice Oswald was born in 1966 and educated at Kendrick Grammar School and New College, Oxford, where she read classics. She trained as a gardener at the Royal Horticultural Society, Wisley, then worked for seven years in various gardens, including Cliveden, Eythrope Gardens near Aylesbury, Clovelly Court Gardens in Devon and the Chelsea Physic Garden. In 1994 she was given an Eric Gregory Award for poetry and in 1996 published her first collection, *The Thing in the Gap-Stone Stile*. This was a Poetry Book Society Choice and was shortlisted for the T. S. Eliot and Whitbread Awards. She lives in Devon.

Don Paterson was born in Dundee in 1963. *Nil Nil* (1993) won the Forward Prize for the best first collection, and *God's Gift to Women* (1997) the T. S. Eliot Prize and the Geoffrey Faber Award. He works as a musician and is poetry editor for Picador Books. He lives in Edinburgh.

Emily Perkins was born in New Zealand and has lived in London since 1994. Her collection of short stories, *Not Her Real Name*, won the Geoffrey Faber Memorial Prize and she has published stories in various anthologies. *Leave Before You Go*, her first novel, was published in 1998. 'The Third Girl' is an extract from a novel in progress.

Dan Rhodes was born in 1972.

Mordecai Richler is the author of nine novels, including *Cocksure, Solomon Gursky Was Here* and *Barney's Version*. He travels widely and his commentaries on exotic places and literary phenomena from Marrakesh to Hollywood have enlivened leading American and British magazines and have been collected in volumes such as *Keeping Tracks*. He was born and raised in Montreal where he now lives.

Derek Robinson was born and lives in Bristol. He served in the RAF and read history at Cambridge where he learnt to write badly. Eleven years with top advertising agencies in London and New York put that right. He has written eight novels, most of them about the RAF or the Royal Flying Corps. *Goshawk Squadron* was shortlisted for the Booker Prize in 1971. *Piece of Cake* became a TV mini-series. His current novel is set in Kentucky around the civil war.

Nick Rogers was born in Gloucestershire and brought up in Wandsworth and Suffolk. His fiction has been published in *Random Factor* (1997) and *The Agony and the Ecstasy* (1998). 'Destination Earth; or, Polishing the Rocket' is an extract from *Unputdownable*, his first, unpublished novel. He lives in south London.

Neil Rollinson was born in Yorkshire in 1960 and studied fine art at Newcastle. His first collection of poetry, *A Spillage of Mercury*, was published in 1996 and was a Poetry Book Society Recommendation. He lives in London and is currently finishing his second collection of poems.

Salman Rushdie is the author of six novels, including *Midnight's Children* (winner of the Booker Prize) and *The Moor's Last Sigh* (winner of the European Aristeion Prize for Literature). He has also published a collection of short stories, *East, West*, a book of reportage, *The Jaguar Smile: A Nicaraguan Journey*, a volume of essays, *Imaginary Home-lands*, and a work of film criticism, *The Wizard of Oz*. His next novel, *The Ground Beneath Her Feet*, will be published in spring 1999. His books have been published in more than two dozen languages.

Lindsey Sill lives in Winchester. She read literature at Essex University in the seventies and has been a journalist and broadcaster. Her poetry has been published in magazines in England and South Africa.

Iain Sinclair lives in London and has worked as a bookdealer and filmmaker. His novel, *Downriver*, won the James Tait Black Memorial Prize and the Encore Award. He has written two other novels, *White Chappell, Scarlet Tracings* and *Radon Daughters*, as well as a book of London journeys, *Lights Out for the Territory*. *Lud Heat*, a collection of poems and speculative essays, originally published in 1975, has recently been reissued. *The Falconer*, made with Chris Petit for Channel 4, is the second film in a proposed trilogy.

Christopher Sinclair-Stevenson was born in 1939 and educated at Eton and Cambridge, where he read modern languages. He went into publishing in 1961 and remained with Hamish Hamilton as editor, editorial director and finally managing director until 1989, when he left to set up his own eponymous company. He left publishing in 1995 to become a literary agent. His own books include *Inglorious Rebellion*, a history of the Jacobite risings, *Blood Royal*, about the first four Georges, and *That Sweet Enemy*, a survey of French character and history.

Harry Smart was born and raised in Yorkshire but has spent most of his life in Scotland. His first book was *Criticism and Public Rationality* (long since pulped). He has published three collections of poetry with Faber and Faber, most recently *Fool's Pardon* (1995). His most recent book is a novel, *Zaire* (1997). He gardens, breeds rabbits, likes good whisky and spends too much time online for his own good.

Matthew Sweeney was born in Donegal, Ireland, in 1952 and moved to London in 1973. His poetry collections include *Blue Shoes*, *Cacti* and, most recently, *The Bridal Suite* (1997) and a selection of his work is in *Penguin Modern Poets 12* (1997). He has written for children *The Flying Spring Onion* and *Fatso in the Red Suit*, and co-edited with Jo Shapcott the anthology *Emergency Kit: Poems for Strange Times* (1996) and with Ken Smith, *Beyond Bedlam: Poems Written out of Mental Distress* (1997). With John Hartley-Williams he co-wrote *Writing Poetry* (1997). He was Writer-in-Residence at London's South Bank Centre in 1994/5 and, in 1997/8, on the Internet for the electronic publisher, Chadwyck-Healey.

George Szirtes' *Selected Poems 1976–1996* are a selection from his last seven books. His most recent individual collections are *Metro* (1988), *Bridge Passages* (1991) and *Blind Field* (1994) and *Portrait of My Father in an English Landscape* (1998). He is also a translator of poetry and fiction, and has translated the selected poems of Zsuzsa Rakovszky (1994) and *The Colonnade of Teeth*, an anthology of twentieth-century Hungarian poetry, co-edited with George Gömöri (1996). He has won the Faber Prize, the Cholmondeley Award and the Dery Prize and is a Fellow of the Royal Society of Literature.

Jonathan Treitel was born in London in 1959 and trained as a physicist and philosopher. His stories have been broadcast by the BBC and have appeared in the *New Yorker*, in *New Writing 4* and in a number of other magazines and anthologies. He received a Literature Award from the Arts Council of England. He is working on a novel about Einstein in America.

Barry Unsworth was born in 1930 in a mining village in Durham County, England. He studied English at Manchester University and has taught English in Athens and Istanbul and held literary residencies at the Universities of Durham, Newcastle and Liverpool in Britain and Lund in Sweden. He has written twelve novels, including *Pascali's Island*, which was made into a feature film, and *Sacred Hunger*, which won the 1992 Booker Prize. He is a Fellow of the Royal Society of Literature. He currently lives in Italy.

George Walden was a Member of Parliament from 1983 until 1997. A former diplomat specialising in Russia and China, he has been Minister for Higher Education, a columnist for *The Times*, the *Daily Telegraph* and the *Evening Standard* and Chairman of the 1995 Booker Prize panel. His book on education, *We Should Know Better*, appeared in 1996. An "anti-memoir" is to be published this spring, 'Little England' is the nucleus of a novel.